# FALLEN TO FURY

# Fallen to Fury

## Spear of the Gods
### Book Three

## Gregory Amato

SED FERRO PRESS

Published by Sed Ferro Press
Copyright © 2025



Cover design by James T. Egan of Bookfly Design
Illustrations by Blane Bellerud
Edited by Sydney Taylor

Paperback ISBN: 979-8-9880613-5-9
Hardcover ISBN: 979-8-9880613-6-6

Published by Sed Ferro Press
3439 NE Sandy Blvd, #484
Portland, OR 97232

*This series is for Emlyn Amato. You didn't read this story, mom, but you were first and foremost in believing.*

# ALSO BY GREGORY AMATO

### THE SPEAR OF THE GODS SAGA

*Burden to Bear*

*Rune to Ruin*

*Fallen to Fury*

### PREQUEL SPEAR OF THE GODS STORIES

*Trollsbane*

*The Skald*

*The Sorcerer's Reward*

### STANDALONE STORIES

*The Once and Future Sword*

# Contents

# Author's Note

*Hávamál*, the poem from the Poetic Edda in which Odin gives advice about living a good life, runs through the Spear of the Gods Saga like a vein of silver. Some references are obvious, some subtle, but in *Fallen to Fury*, the poem becomes an explicit part of the plot.

I've read *Hávamál* more times than I can remember. The poem isn't all advice, and not all the advice is straightforward. It requires the reader to think and apply general ideas to specific situations in our own lives. I usually come away noticing something new or thinking about something differently.

Like many books of wisdom, *Hávamál* is cited as a source for a "way to be" by lots of people who have obviously never read it. There's no shortage of Internet gurus claiming to represent "Viking Age philosophy" who are actually cynical revisionists trying to wrest *Hávamál* away from its own words.

In the space of Nordic stories, languages, history, etc. ("That Northern Thing"), it's important to identify the good influencers from the bad. I can tell a lot about someone talking about "That Northern Thing" within a few seconds. But what about 16-year-old me? If he were inundated by shady information from folkish influencers rather than guided by a competent teacher, how would he tell up from down?

Well, *Hávamál* helps with that, too. Good influencers tend to act in accordance with most of the poem's advice. That advice, over and over again, is to be generous, sociable, courageous, and yet moderate. Wide travel and listening to others help make a person wise. Money and alcohol are likely to make a person less wise. Wisdom is good, but difficult, and not a thing to show off or browbeat others with. Self-reliance is important, but not as important as socializing well and being a good friend.

Encouragement. Inspiration. Hospitality. Some wariness, but not fearfulness.

Instead of those qualities, does the influencer focus on imagined heritage, hierarchy, and a sense of romantic nationalism? Are "threats" a constant subject? Rather than expressing curiosity, is the influencer likely to contradict someone else's experience? These tells, especially denialism, are inconsistent with the advice from *Hávamál*.

The line between living *Hávamál*'s principles and ignoring or distorting them is also the line that separates heroes from villains in my books. *Hávamál*, therefore, has always been this story's North Star, and mine. And that North Star has rarely been as important as right now.

-Gregory Amato, 6 July 2025

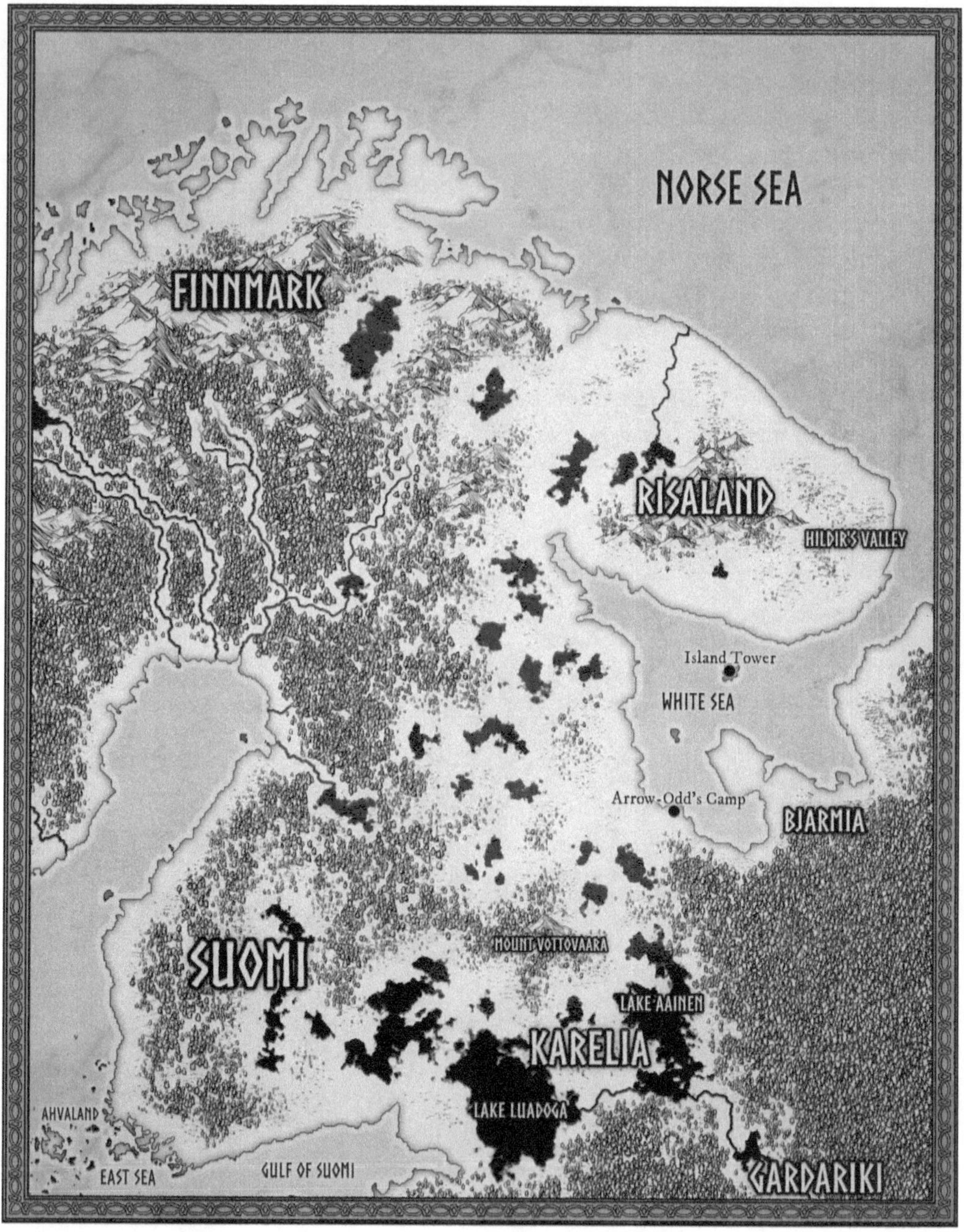

NORSE SEA
FINNMARK
RISALAND
HILDIR'S VALLEY
Island Tower
WHITE SEA
Arrow-Odd's Camp
BJARMIA
MOUNT VOTTOVAARA
SUOMI
LAKE AAINEN
KARELIA
AHVALAND
LAKE LUADOGA
EAST SEA
GULF OF SUOMI
GARDARIKI

SWEDES
AHVALAND
Uppsala
EAST SEA
GEATS
GOTLAND
Asmund's
Mead Hall
Monastery
DANES
SCANIA
Roskilde
Lejre
SJAELLAND
MØN
BORGHUND
FALSTER
LOLLAND

# RUNES - THE ELDER FUTHARK
## (PRE-VIKING AGE ALPHABET)

| Rune | Name | Ideographic Meaning |
| --- | --- | --- |
| ᚠ | fehu | wealth; cattle |
| ᚢ | uruz | aurochs; strength |
| ᚦ | þurisaz | þurs, jǫtunn |
| ᚨ | ansuz | god |
| ᚱ | raiðo | ride, journey |
| ᚲ | kaunan | ulcer, blister, boil |
| ᚷ | gebo | gift |
| ᚹ | wunjo | joy |
| ᚺ | hagalaz | hail |
| ᚾ | nauðiz | need |
| ᛁ | isaz | ice |
| ᛃ | jera | harvest; good year |
| ᛈ | perðo | pear tree or game piece |
| ᛇ | eihaz | yew tree |
| ᛉ | algiz | moose or elk |
| ᛊ | sowilo | sun |
| ᛏ | tiwaz | the god Tyr |
| ᛒ | berkana | birch tree |
| ᛖ | ehwaz | horse |
| ᛗ | mannaz | human |
| ᛚ | laguz | water |
| ᛜ | ingwaz | the god Frey |
| ᛞ | dagaz | day |
| ᛟ | oþala | inheritance |

# The Story from Book Two

Ansgar Styrgrimsson—actually, it turns out he's not the son of Styrgrim after all—is farther from home than he's ever been. And worse, things have gotten awfully serious lately.

He hadn't even wanted to join Haldor Skullsplitter (leader on land) and Kraki Bentleg (captain of the *Sea Squirrel*) in the first place. He just wanted to prove his worth—to Styrgrim, and to himself. Joining up led to meeting his the first love of his life, Fanya, and to uncovering a mystery in Lejre involving the sorceress, Alfhild. Also constant self-doubt, many head injuries, and the pain of Fanya's death.

Alfhild escaped the Battle of Lejre, but the crew of the *Sea Squirrel* was not about to give up on revenge against her. It's just that they had to travel to realms Down-Below and then sail halfway around the world in pursuit. Ansgar's invisible follower (a *fylgja*) and a shapeshifting sword (Need) aided him a great deal, but knowledge of Alfhild's location came with a price. That price was Ansgar's need to visit Jarl Varg Tiorfi on Gotland to make a delivery of steel through his heart.

(Actually, stabbing Varg Tiorfi through the heart would have been a great kindness compared to the way he died. Good riddance.)

Ansgar befriended Joni the Karelian, one of Varg's former thralls, who guided the crew through the land of a thousand lakes. Joni then set off to find his people—hopefully, a warrior riding a moose—while Ansgar and crew sought out the legendary Arrow-Odd and his army.

Arrow-Odd was up against his old enemy, Ogmund. That was good luck, because it turned out Alfhild was allied with Ogmund, whose position was not looking good at all.

Or that's what our heroes thought when they sailed to Alfhild's island fortress on the White Sea. They found more than they had bargained for, there, including Ogmund's huge troll of a mother, and Alfhild's prize possession, the mythical torc, the Brisingamen. Worse than the troll, Ulf had already turned traitor and had convinced Svein and Hemming to join him.

Ulf found Ansgar sneaking around with the Brisingamen. They had a slight disagreement about who would keep it. The disagreement involved some of Ansgar's ear being bitten off. Ansgar held onto the torc, though.

Meanwhile, the crew freed Alfhild's prisoners. Not just any prisoners—these were mostly the sons and daughters of gods. The few who hadn't been turned to do Alfhild's bidding.

Alfhild sprang her trap on the crew. Haldor killed the troll, Grimhild, but was slain right after. Styrgrim led the effort to fight their way to the exit, but it was the sacrifice of the 'Steins that secured everyone's escape.

We never saw those two die, though. And that was some poem Ansgar gave them, as soon as he had the chance.

Returning to Arrow-Odd's war camp, it became clear that things had not gone well for them, either. Attacked by the Rus on one side, nearly attacked by the Bjarmian navy on the other side, and attacked by a winged dragon all at once. The army held, but just barely.

A few familial revelations came after that, and that's why Ansgar knows Styrgrim isn't his real father. At least he knows his mother now—it's been his *fylgja* the whole time. His father is one of the gods, but which one?

*Please, not Odin* is what Ansgar is thinking, since Odin is the one who set so many awful events in motion. *The Spear of the Gods* is what he called it, a plan to seed many god-children throughout Midgard, get them to do famous (or infamous) things, and make more stories the gods could be remembered by.

But Ansgar has spoken to several of the gods at this point, and if he had to guess, not all of them were of quite the same mind as Odin . . .

# Fallen to Fury

# Chapter 1

# Blood Oath

Lightning flashed, revealing island-sized jaws emerging from the dark sea. White breakers glowed for a moment, contrasting with the massive yellow teeth slowly breaking the surface. A froth of freezing salt foam poured over our ship's starboard side, soaking half the crew. The wind could not whip the sail anymore—that had already torn free.

Chaos reigned on the deck of the *Sea Squirrel*. No one was at the rudder. Men and women ran up and down the deck, their faces indistinct, their voices conveying confusion and uncertainty.

I looked to the fore of the ship, where Haldor Skullsplitter stood. He would know what to do. He always did. As long as Haldor led us, we would find a way to victory.

A vague memory pulled at my mind. How was Haldor with us? There had been a big fight, and victory had come at an awful price.

"And aren't you dead?" I shouted.

He crossed his arms and nodded.

"Can you get us out of here?"

He shook his head and pointed at me.

I didn't get a chance to ask what he meant. One of the crew slammed into my side, sending me a step to my right, where there was no room to step. My thigh collided with the gunwale at the same time as a wave rocked our ship. The combination was just enough to send me face-first over the side.

Freezing saltwater hit my lungs like a giant's fist. I tried to swim, but couldn't tell which way was up. My consciousness went black as the bottomless sea for a time.

The tug of a current pulled at me, and soon I saw light above. I swam to the surface and let waves wash me into water shallow enough to stand in. I walked up the rocky beach on a warm and bright day. Very warm, in fact, as if a fire were close by.

A dragon screeched overhead. Its target became clear soon after: A small hut at the base of a hill. Small for the two adults and two children standing outside it, at least. They looked up to see the monster and scrambled indoors.

The dragon tipped its wings down to descend lower. Hooded ears splayed out from the sides of its face and shook as it vomited flames over the hut. It flapped those mighty wings a few times and kept itself airborne. Eventually, the fire stopped. The dragon flew away, leaving only charred remains.

I walked toward the hill, not really knowing why. The house at its base was nothing but ash. Up the hill, however, sat a grand longhouse.

Not squat and strong like I'd seen before. This longhouse was narrow and tall. Outside, a woman in silk robes of bright red and yellow stood before a throng. Alfhild's hair shone bright as the sun. Her skin was pale as milk, and she wore an intricate gold necklace. Her only blemish was a long scar down her cheek. That, and her rotten personality.

Alfhild congratulated a group of farmers who looked much like the ones just roasted. They were clad in browns and tans spun of rough wool. Most of them had mud or soot on their faces.

"You are a king!" Alfhild as she used her thumb to smear blood across the forehead of one man. "And you are a king! And you are a king!"

Thus congratulated that they were all royalty, the newly blessed pranced down the hill with giddy expressions. They ignored me, but Alfhild caught my eye. She nodded, as if meaning to convey a curt thanks.

"You going up there?" asked one of the anointed. He stared at me as he walked downhill and tripped over a body with a loud "Oof!"

The corpse had been a man of trollish size and aspect. Here lay Alfhild's half-god son, Olgram. That was one ugly face even before his head had been cracked open. I had done the cracking, but out of mercy rather than spite.

Two other corpses lay beside Olgram, both women. One had been decapitated, and I had known her as Valborg. I'd rescued her reanimated head, but she, too, had asked me to end her life. The other was ghastly white, her insides spilling out of her. I didn't need to see her fire-red hair or the many freckles down her face and chest to know that was Fanya, briefly the love of my life, slain at Lejre.

"Alfhild will use you up," I replied. "Just as she used them."

The man stood and shouted at me for being ungrateful. Soon, many others coming down the hill joined him, pointing their fingers at me.

There seemed no point in going up that hill, so I turned from them all. I walked in the other direction, toward a small town splayed over a grassy flatland. The smoke from its many cookfires seemed to invite guests to come right in.

Near the center of the town, a small market of carts sat tantalizingly full. Apples of many colors nudged up against rutabagas, leeks, and mushrooms. Smoked salmon and pig carcasses hung, ready to be sold, but no one was selling. Everyone was in the middle of the muddy square, entranced by a storyteller's narrative.

As I got closer, I realized it was two men, and that I knew them.

"No, no, Haldor was no easy troll to slay," said Ulf. "It really did take the both of us! I outwitted him with a verse, you see, and in doing so, I robbed him of his immunity to steel. Then Svein fought him in single combat. Cut his head clean off with this very axe!"

Svein grinned stupidly, a big ball of a man with moppy blond hair wagging in front of his eyes. He hefted the great axe from his hip to show the crowd. Not just any axe. Haldor's axe, Silence.

"I dispatched the redhead myself," Ulf continued. He drew his long seax with a dainty grip, as if holding a flower, and examined it. The blade was wet with fresh blood, as was his hand.

Rage coursed through me like it would burst from my eyes and ears. As if I might change into a bear again, only without the control. And without control, or forethought, I grabbed the nearest weapon within reach and charged Ulf.

The nearest weapon being a rutabaga.

Ulf stepped out of the way at the last moment. My ill-advised attack found only air and sent me face-first into the mud.

The people listening to Ulf and Svein laughed. They were not just laughing at me. They laughed at Ulf's lie and how he stole not only Haldor's life but his history.

The mud stuck like tar around me. I could not fight, could not even get up. I tried to say something, but the words rolled out of my mouth at random rather than in verse. My wrath became so intense that my attempt at words turned into a wordless scream.

All I had left was one impulse: To stand up as Ulf's negation. To undo him. To unmake him. To tear down his memory, shred it with claws, and burn the remains. To end everything, human and *vættir*, showing any hint of his rotten influence.

The more I raged, the less volume I could manage, until all I had was a quiet moan.

Someone kicked me. I heard my name. And eventually, I woke.

***

"WILL YOU STOP SHOUTING?" demanded Magnus. "It's hard enough to sleep. As if this tent hadn't got smaller already!"

I sat bolt upright, soaked in sweat. I was not in some strange town with Ulf and Svein. I was in my tent, near our crew, still among Arrow-Odd's army. Almost no light showing through the tent's seams told me it was still hours from what we would consider dawn. A relative thing, since that far north, the late summer sun never fully sets.

Lucky for me, Magnus was the kind of friend who knew when I needed a few soft kicks to the ribs. And he was right, the tent was smaller than usual.

On the other side of Magnus, Vilgrip Tyrsson shifted. A third person made for a tight fit, even though we all lay head to toe. All of our crew now shared tents with the prisoners we'd freed from Alfhild's island. Including Vilgrip, a reasonably quiet tent-mate. Unlike me.

"Was I shouting? I didn't mean to. Or I did, but I meant to shout in the dream."

Magnus sighed. "What was it about this time?"

The close quarters appeared to be the worst of what I had woken to. Dragons were not actually flying around, burning people up.

Oh, wait, there was a dragon flying around, burning people up. It had attacked the army just days ago, and Arrow-Odd had driven it off. Presumably, the dragon was not in the camp at that moment, but you never know.

"A confusing dream, but I'm clear on one thing: If it is the last thing I ever do, I will kill that *níðingr* Ulf and wipe his influence from Midgard."

"Ulf, not Alfhild? She was behind Ulf's plans. And what about Ogmund? He was the one who set Alfhild in motion. Then there is Svein, who . . ."

"Hel's dragon, man! Ulf!"

Vilgrip sat up. No doubt he was tired, but say the word "vengeance" or anything related, and he was interested. "He did bite your ear off."

I shook my head as I recalled my nightmare. "Don't underestimate his power or how bad it is. We tell stories to preserve wisdom; he tells them to get what he wants. If he gets his way, it will be a rot festering in the minds of Midgard. I won't let that sort of corruption take hold."

"Fair enough," said Vilgrip. "But we also need to destroy the Brisingamen. It's often difficult to balance two goals at once."

By all rights, the Brisingamen shouldn't even be in Midgard. A dwarf-forged torc of purest gold, it should be in Asgard, the most prized possession of the goddess, Freya. But according to Odin, Freya didn't want it anymore.

It was Freya who taught Odin *seiðr* and split the battle-slain with him. I didn't trust Odin's word, but if Freya wanted the torc back, I had no doubt she could have taken it.

I still had no idea what to do with the torc. Which was why it sat in my beaver skin pouch, its voice sealed away as much as possible.

"Three goals," croaked a very tired Magnus. "We need to kill Alfhild, remember? I am not certain the order of killings matters much, though."

I drew Need from its sheath, closing my eyes for a moment, and my shape-shifting sword took the form of a short seax. Having already sworn my oath about killing Ulf, I cut the palm of my left hand and squeezed until the blood flowed through my fingers.

"That's a serious thing," said Vilgrip.

"And not because he bit half my ear off. He is a traitor."

Magnus turned over to see what I'd done. "The betrayal of a friend is worse than an enemy's."

That oath took something out of me. Better to swear blood oaths well-rested and on a full belly. I added that to my mental list of mistakes and fell back on the straw, hoping the fatigue would let me sleep.

The sound of boots tromping outside was faint at first. Then it was distinctly nearby. Moments later, a mailed figure, burgundy hair held back with a headband, stuck her head in. "Ansgar, get dressed." Then, glancing at my bloodied hand and seax, "Those work better if you grab them by the handle."

Much as I was glad to see Steinvor, a terrible thought occurred. Could "the redhead" Ulf referred to in my dream mean her? Or for that matter, Magnus?

"Ansgar is busy," mumbled Magnus. "Why don't you skalds . . . have a council . . . or something . . ."

Steinvor the Slim One ducked into the tent, her mail shirt clinking softly. A shield was strapped to her back and a long seax sat at her hip, just the longest of many blades she kept at the ready. Scars on her head and hands competed for chances to tell their stories. A fresher cut ran down her face from above her right eye to her cheek.

She was one of the most beautiful women I'd ever known, and the only one I'd had feelings for other than Fanya. She'd taken me back to her tent the night before we sailed against Alfhild, one of the best nights of my life.

The next night had been one of the worst of my life. The night when Haldor Skullsplitter died laughing, and everything changed for our crew.

"Two skalds are having a council at this very moment," she replied. "Ansgar, Huld needs you."

"Huld the Healer?" asked Vilgrip.

I'd never heard her called Huld the Healer, but it was a fair description. Huld, the mysterious *vǫlva* whose motivations I still did not understand, had taken charge of the injury tents for Arrow-Odd's army and saved many lives.

Magnus bolted upright, his eyes wide. "Is she brewing with the crazy mushrooms? I haven't eaten those in a long time. Maybe it is a good time to—"

"No, and stop," said Steinvor, putting a hand up. "She said nothing about fetching you, Magnus the Red, or your friend—"

"Vilgrip. Does she need another hand?" He held up his left hand and the stump of his right wrist and played at looking surprised. "I offer the one to help where it's needed. I'm also in the market to buy, in case you have an extra."

"I'm not in the hand-trading business. As for the offer, there is work for the willing at the injury tents. Huld needs Ansgar the Skald, however, as he can speak many languages."

"A translator?" I asked. "Now?"

"If you are not too injured. I could report you as bedridden, unable to leave your tent. That will sound better than 'he was too sleepy.'"

I closed my bloody fist tight. "I am fine."

"Then see Huld immediately. She has healed one of the enemy enough for him to answer questions, but he speaks in a foreign tongue. Better to question him early." She ducked back out from our tent and was gone before I could respond.

Magnus rubbed his eyes. "Awkward? Complicated? I had better go with you." He did not have a skald's subtlety, but he could sense when things were off.

Steinvor's last statement, and what she *didn't* say, was clear as pristine water to me. *Better to question him early* meant there might not be another chance. The war camp's politics had gotten tricky, and this was an opportunity to question a man while most of the political players in camp were still asleep.

"Should I go with you as well?" offered Vilgrip.

I shook my head as I got my things together. I cinched the beaver skin bag tighter, the better to keep the temptation of the Brisingamen at bay. "Steinvor mentioned they need help with the injured. Maybe relieve her so she can get some sleep. Magnus will be with me, just in case."

Magnus yawned and checked his weapons. "Just in case of what?"

"I don't know, but Huld thinks we need to move quickly. Without Odd's presence, it's not clear who leads. Which is why the army hasn't sailed back to Alfhild's island to attack her in force. Gardar and Sirnir are self-important jarls and surly about command."

"Why is that, again?"

"Were you listening when I told everyone what I'd heard at the Circle of Skalds the other night?"

"I listened at first, but perhaps I did not listen to all of it." Magnus shrugged, as if I had tried to lecture our crew on the idiosyncrasies of barnacle scraping.

"Odd has been inconsolable since Vignir was killed. You remember Vignir? Almost as tall as you?"

"Very amusing, Ansgar the Jester. We all remember Vignir, and I think he was twice my height. You really think Ogmund ripped his throat out with his teeth?"

"So you remember that part!"

"Everyone remembers that part because it was exciting and gruesome! The politics part was boring."

"Then I will keep it short: No one is sure of Odd's state. He has not left his tent since the end of that battle. "

"So who leads the army?"

"Gardar and Sirnir tell everyone to follow their orders only, but Styrgrim says he acts in Odd's stead. He is by far more competent, but he's not a jarl. Not many ship captains are willing to go against Gardar and Sirnir outright, but no one is stupid enough to challenge Styrgrim."

"Whose orders do *we* follow, if it comes down to it?" asked Vilgrip. "We followed Styrgrim to get off that island, but later you said he did not lead."

"He's not part of our crew, so he can't continue to lead us on land," said Magnus. "The *Sea Squirrel* is not sworn to Arrow-Odd's army. New leader on land to be decided soon."

Magnus was looking down, tying his shoes, as I caught Vilgrip's gaze. I tipped my head toward Magnus in the hope Vilgrip would understand: *Magnus will be our next leader on land.*

Vilgrip nodded. "The crew of an independent ship can choose its own course."

I thought that was his way of agreeing with me. The statement reminded me of a difficult fact to accept, though: That to destroy the torc and kill Alfhild and Ulf, we could not just choose our own course.

We needed Arrow-Odd's army, and that meant we would need to play some politics ourselves.

## CHAPTER 2

# MEANWHILE, IN ASGARD

INNSTEIN WOKE UP HAVING SLEPT LIKE THE DEAD, AND SOON wondered if dying was exactly what he'd done. As he blinked away the blurriness, he noticed he and his brother were on a ship. Sort of. A longhouse laid out like a ship, he realized. Benches replaced sea chests, and it was much wider than any transport ship he and his brother had ever seen, but then again, it stretched down so long, he couldn't see the end of it. Massive double doors stood to their left, the handles of which looked like rudders. They were in the aft, then, if it was a ship-hall.

"Brother," he said, looking to his right to see Utstein on his own bed of straw. "Hey!"

"Mrmph." Utstein appeared less eager to shake off the grogginess.

"Are we in Hel?"

Utstein shifted and pulled his blanket up, exposing his bare feet. "Curse whoever took our shoes if we are."

"I thought you two would be happy to wake up on a ship."

A lady of unsurpassed beauty stood before them. That sonorous voice was gentle and sweet, yet clear and commanding all at once. Her dress shone like gold as it hugged her body's curves—fine clothing that showed off the wearer and not the other way around. Her skin was unblemished, her hair falling in gentle waves past broad shoulders. Her eyes, though—those were not the eyes of the soft and privileged.

Had she just appeared? It was all very suspicious.

"I think it depends on the ship," said Innstein.

"And whether they serve mead on that ship," continued Utstein.

"This is a poem," replied the lady.

So that was cryptic. If she thought it was going to make them look surprised, she was in for a surprise herself.

"Poems are more comfortable than expected," said Utstein.

"A bit lacking in mead, though," added Innstein.

The lady smiled softly and left them. Hopefully, to find some food to go with any mead she would bring back.

Utstein rubbed his eyes as he sat up, as if that would clear up the confusion. Brightly lit and finely adorned, this was more than some stylized longhouse. Trees provided a thick canopy of green and a fresh forest scent. The 'Steins rested on beds of straw with soft woolen blankets.

Innstein lifted his blanket to check for pants. As did Utstein, as they were usually of like mind.

"She may be pretty," said Utstein, "but we must be in Hel."

Definitely dead. They never went anywhere without pants.

"What do you remember?" asked Innstein.

Utstein propped himself on one elbow and pulled at his beard in thought. "Heather and salt."

"I'm not sure about that."

"Well, what do you remember?"

"I remember fighting."

"No shortage of that." Utstein was silent for a long time. "I think they got out of there, don't you?"

Flashes of memory came back to Innstein. He ground his teeth at recalling Haldor's death. He'd wanted to kill every shitling on Alfhild's wretched island, but that was not his fate. He and his brother had chosen to play *hnefatafl* for real, but instead of getting a king to safety, it was their Brothers and some prisoners. Better that way, in his view. The 'Steins never had much use for lords.

Brothers were different. The 'Steins rarely had much besides each other, sometimes not much more than pants. The Brotherhood had been a very different thing for them—friends who had become family. So they made sure their family could get away safely.

Innstein remembered his mother and Utstein's. Long ago, the 'Steins had been too small to fight, and their mothers fought while they escaped. It seemed only right that the 'Steins would protect their people the same way.

Innstein told his brother what he remembered. It went something like this:

Alfhild wanted the skald, or the torc he had skillfully and rightfully stolen. The 'Steins were at the front of the line protecting the Brotherhood's retreat. Meanwhile, the skald fumbled with his spear, yelling things in that high-pitched voice of his that came out like the angriest mouse to ever squeak. Innstein couldn't quite make it all out. He had been focused on driving his shaft into deserving recipients at the time.

Alfhild had plenty of sorcery to make her voice heard over the din. She also had a lack of sense, loudly announcing her tactical intent. What a dumb witch! It had been an easy decision to draw her warriors away from the exit, where their Brothers were headed.

Innstein grabbed a couple of discs out of the skald's pouch while Utstein screened him doing it, and they made like they had the torc when they didn't. They announced their plan as loudly as possible, stating they would send that torc down the poop chute, well away from the exit.

Alfhild bought it. Sent all her shitmen to chase the two of them instead of their Brothers, just as planned. Alfhild's *seiðr* was powerful, but all the *seiðr* in the world can't fix stupid. Some of those god-children had grown in size and strength from whatever spell she had cast, but they were still dumb as Svein.

"Alfhild was so impressed with herself," said Innstein. "She collected all those children of gods like they were stronger and tougher just because of their accidents of birth."

"Stronger and tougher is what comes of fighting for your life," said Utstein, echoing one of the sayings they had between them.

Innstein nodded. Their Brothers were tough the one way you can get tough: Through pain. That was why the 'Steins took a liking to that crew so quickly. The god-children didn't know much about that sort of wisdom.

"We gave them a good lesson in it," said Utstein.

"We did."

The god-children eventually got a more coordinated attack ready. Innstein remembered thinking that was likely the final push.

Then the floor was frozen with a good few inches of ice, and that coordinated attack was full of idiots skidding and slipping and smashing their stupid faces onto the frozen floor. They saw the skald disappear down that exit corridor, finally. He had cast a spell that would do them little harm but would hinder their enemies quite a bit. The 'Steins were still wearing crampons from the climb up that cursed mountain, and Alfhild's smooth-footed softhearts were not prepared for fighting on ice.

The 'Steins loved fighting on ice. So that's what they did.

"How they howled!" said Utstein.

"Many a shitman died complaining that day," added Innstein. "Complaining and cold."

"I wonder if they came back as *draugar*."

"Could be."

That ice spell had bought them an advantage, and one they used to stab, slash, and bludgeon every comer they could find. In a few minutes, it was clear their friends had plenty of time to get gone. The 'Steins were dead men, but they had already won. Just like their Brother, Haldor.

So they made a few good taunts to rub it in the faces of their foes a bit. Innstein swung his spear sideways and crushed knees; Utstein hooked his axe and pulled down shields, knocking over the owners of those shields when they slipped. All interspersed with the dirtiest insults they could think of.

Alfhild was so angry!

It couldn't last forever, though. Eventually, Utstein took a spear in the side, and Innstein, an arrow in the back. Innstein had thought it really was their time, but wanted to add a final insult because that was his nature. He shouldered Utstein back to near the cells, intending to go down that poop chute themselves and deny Alfhild even knowing there had been a deception. Innstein took another arrow, this one to the leg, but was still doing better than his brother.

The poop chute is not a conventional way to exit a battle. Certainly not going into any sagas as a glorious end. But as a means to frustrate hated enemies, it was perfect.

Innstein pressed his brother onto a shield and shoved him through. Around that time, he took a third arrow, this time in the back. Moving his left arm was a lot harder after that. Harder to breathe, too.

A good thing for the 'Steins to die in the sea, since that had been the source of their best times.

Innstein stuck his ass out, gave Alfhild their final regards, and dove in on his own shield, murmuring a further thanks to the skald on the way down.

That could have been one stinky trip, but it was all coated in a thick layer of ice.

The water was cold when they hit. Even summer on the White Sea doesn't make for good swimming. That was fine. They had both taken our last injuries, and the cold would be a blessing.

"But then the heather!" said Utstein.

"What?"

"You don't remember?"

"I remember floating on a shield. And then falling off the shield and into the water."

"And then Heather-Back rose up!"

"The sea monster?" Innstein shook his head. "Nearly swallowed the *Sea Squirrel* whole when we first met him. I thought the wine we dumped into his mouth was enough to make him forget that idea. Did he eat us?"

"I think he took us away from there on his back."

The lady returned and handed them a horn of mead each. "That would be the gist of it."

Innstein received the horn with much gratitude. "Any smoked pork?"

She looked at him like he was being rude, for some reason.

"Seems unconventional hospitality to offer a drink with no food," added Utstein. Because that's absolutely correct.

"It seems the only meat present is our own," said Innstein.

Both brothers had a laugh at that and drank deep.

"You are in an unconventional situation," said the lady. "You have other visitors interested in your story. They should arrive shortly. I suggest you take them seriously."

"Are they bringing smoked pork?" asked Utstein.

"More like fruit."

Innstein watched this lady with a careful eye. She didn't move like most women he'd known. She had the lithe grace of a cat. Her eyes and bearing gave the impression of intensity, controlled but ready to spring at any moment. Contours of her shoulders and neck indicated she was as comfortable in armor as in a dress. She had said they were in a poem, which didn't make any sense. But then again, the poor hospitality of waking up with no pants didn't match up with the good hospitality of being served mead.

It turned out that mead from Hel was quite good. Sweet but not cloying.

Hints of many wildflowers going into the honey—buttercup, for one, but not too much. Catmint. Clover. Whoever made this knew their craft.

Innstein swirled his horn and sniffed the aroma. "What's your name?"

"Freya."

He looked at his brother to see if he had the same I-can't-believe-it-but-I-believe-it feeling. He did.

Freya, The Lady, Asgard's chief sorceress. The one who'd taught *seiðr* to Odin. Promiscuous and not to be trusted, if you were intimidated by women; loving and tantalizing, willing to take chances, wise and strong, if you were a grown-ass man. Either way, there was one other quality about Freya they both knew was her most important aspect at the time.

"We're dead," said Innstein. "You get half the battle-slain."

"I choose half when I ride to battle," she clarified, her friendly smile and penetrating gaze both unbroken. "But as I said, we are in a poem."

"Not much alliteration for it being a poem," said Utstein.

"This is more the result than the composition. Your friend, the skald, cast a powerful spell. It took almost everything out of him."

"The ice thing?" asked Innstein.

"He ran down the corridor after that," said Utstein. "Seemed fine to me."

"That was a good trick, but not the spell I mean. I mean the one he cast once he was back on the ship. You asked for a good verse. We heard it, even in Asgard."

Just as Innstein thought things were getting weirder by the moment, something even more strange happened. The doors of the hall flung wide, and through them strode a man almost too big for the entrance. Beard redder than Magnus', neck thicker than Haldor's, he bulged a bit at the middle, but it was easy to see there was much more muscle on him than fat. A huge, ornate girdle sat at his waist. One iron-gloved hand scratched at his chest where a tiny hammer necklace hung.

The 'Steins knew that symbol well. It was a design carved into many a rock and tree, molded into many a silver amulet. That was no smith's hammer. That was Mjolnir, and the wearer of it had to be Thor.

Behind Thor walked a man with hair and beard so bright, they lit the hall as much as the hearth fires did. He wore a hardened leather cuirass embossed with the likeness of a ram's head. Those deep blue eyes seemed to pierce whatever they saw. Innstein was ready to bet that, when this man spoke, they would see the golden teeth of Heimdall the Watchman.

What was the Watchman doing carrying two apples?

"And my brother?" asked Freya.

"Still wooing Idunn," said Heimdall, confirming the golden teeth.

"I thought she was with us in this plan."

"Have no doubt about that," replied the Watchman. "But better that she is not outwardly on our side, in case Odin is watching. Better to make it as if Frey distracted her with a seduction while I stole the apples."

"Is that just a distraction then," asked Freya, "or does he really want to seduce her?"

"It's Horse-Dick Frey," rumbled Thor. "What do you think?"

Freya sighed. "I think he may find himself frustrated on that count."

The 'Steins both mouthed *What is going on?* silently to each other.

"All this sneaking about is tiresome." Thor waved in the direction of the 'Steins. "What do you want me to do with these two? Take them into my hall before Odin sends a valkyrie and steals them out from under you?"

"They are in a between-state, and not yet choosable either way," said Freya. "They're close, though, so we must make a decision. We don't want them taken into a hall here at all. We want them back in Midgard."

Thor threw his hands up. "What does that have to do with me? I have no idea how that would happen."

"It could happen if you fostered them."

Thor's jaw dropped to the floor. Expressing surprise was generally considered unmanly, but for men sufficiently confident of themselves, or a god, in this case, social conventions didn't apply much.

"Foster them? Whose are they?" The floors shook when the Thunderer spoke, and he hadn't even gone from surprised to angry yet.

"No one's," said Heimdall. "That is why we think you will like them."

"This is not what we talked about," boomed Thor. "I've already expressed regret for sleeping with that witch, but none could have known how the son would turn out. It was not my doing that turned him into a troll—that was Alfhild's rotten mothering. I am not responsible for—"

Utstein interrupted. "You abandoned your son in Lejre?"

"Ballsy," added Innstein. "In a not-ballsy-at-all sort of way."

Thor ground his teeth and pulled the necklace from his neck. As he did, the hammer grew to its full size—short handle, massive head. A spark crackled across Mjolnir's face.

The 'Steins might be facing the fury of the thunder god, but as Innstein saw it, there was little to lose. They were already dead.

Sort of/probably.

"Gods do not stay for mortals," growled Thor.

Innstein shrugged. "Why should mortals tell stories of gods, then?"

"We've made our way without you, without even a real father," added Utstein. "What does your fostering even offer?"

"I'll show you what Thor offers!" Thor raised his hammer, and his face went from pale to pink to red. Lightning flashed between the hammer and his beard.

Freya put her hands on her hips. "Are these the enemies Thor chooses, two men recovering from injuries?" It was a chiding, matronly posture. Only her tone was neither chiding nor matronly, but hard as steel. A purposeful discordance, and a powerful one.

Hammer raised, Thor took a few deep breaths that could have powered a small longship all the way to Ireland. Slowly, he let the hammer down.

"A new idea," said Heimdall. "A different idea. Not like Odin's, where we would all sire as many children as we could. Look at what has resulted from that—an army of brats that cannot wait to tell of their heritage. No great deeds from them. No *drengskapr*. Only an obsession with stealing our names to add to their own."

"Odin says it is the battle that counts," growled Thor. "Whatever the outcome."

"Odin seeks a higher place in Asgard than he has right now, and more battle will certainly bring him closer to that," said Freya. "Do you recall when it was often Tyr's good judgment their rulers called on? Now they care less for judgment, only success in battle. Odin has crept in, and would change things yet more."

"What is this new idea, then?" demanded Thor.

"To choose," said Heimdall. "Look at their lives and their choices, and choose the ones best suited to you. Here are two such choices, we think. I've watched them take their tragedy and make Midgard better for their presence. They started with nothing—and with plenty against them. Still, they grew strong and wise, brave and bold. Better friends would be hard to find. You heard the skald's verse—*second lives as legends*. I say take them as your foster children—chosen sons, not accidents of birth."

"Hmph," said Thor, pulling at his beard. "Why don't you?"

"I've already chosen a champion," said Heimdall. "And it's not my nature to bestow blessings or great power. I move unseen and unheard, you know this. These two are more of your nature. Might and Wrath, if you recall from the skald's verse."

Thor sat down on a bench opposite the 'Steins and eyed them a while.

Innstein waved an empty horn. "Is there more mead?"

"And why are we the only ones drinking?" asked Utstein.

"That is the best question yet asked," said Thor, glaring at Freya.

Freya collected the horns. She refilled them and gave them back to the 'Steins before serving the gods. Thor's face turned even redder than it had before.

Thor accepted a large horn and drained it in one gulp. Then he belched so loud that it rattled the floors. When he spoke again, he was far calmer. Thoughtful, even.

"I want to know something: Freya took you into a place where few can ever leave, but didn't bind you. Frey and Idunn dissembled on your behalf to get you apples of immortality. All of which was orchestrated by Wide-Eyes, here." He jabbed a thumb in Heimdall's direction. "Now I'm asked to foster you. Let's say that happens. That's a lot of gifts from a lot of sources, and you know about gifts and repayment. I want to know, then: Who are you loyal to after all those gifts?"

Innstein looked at his brother and let Utstein speak first.

"We're Haldor Skullsplitter's men."

"We're Kraki Bentleg's men."

"Is that all you have to say about that?" demanded Thor.

"We've seen gifts change loyalties in others," said Utstein. "We've no desire for that."

"A man is loyal to his friends, or not at all," finished Innstein.

Thor rose slowly and with a growling sigh. Still, the 'Steins were not about to bind themselves to the will of any god. Gods had not fed them when they starved, protected them when they were in danger, or clothed them when they were freezing. People had done that, generous people, and some-times to their detriment. The Brotherhood and *Sea Squirrel* crew had been their family, if just briefly. A blessing from a god with his own ends in mind was nothing comparable.

"Give me the apples." Thor reached out with one huge, gloved hand. Heimdall handed them over.

Innstein expected Thor would crush the apples in that iron glove and laugh in their faces. Then he would send them to cross the Gjoll in the Down-Below, where they would enter Hel proper, and not have any more mead.

Instead, Thor stepped closer and raised Mjolnir between the brothers, making the Sign of the Hammer.

"You're men of Haldor Skullsplitter, of Kraki Bentleg. Might and Wrath, if I've ever seen them. With that in mind, I name you my sons: Magni and Modi. Might and Wrath. Here are your gifts to seal your names."

He tossed them each an apple.

"Now get your lazy asses out of this hall. I didn't give you such names so you could lay in bed all gods-damned day."

# CHAPTER 3

## THE INTERVIEW

THE WEE HOURS OF THE MORNING WERE NOT ENTIRELY DARK ON the White Sea. Most of the camp was still asleep, though, and would be until well after sunrise. Assuming the prisoner didn't wake everyone up with his shouting. Huld was right that we had to move quickly.

Magnus and I ran the rest of the way after I heard the first shouts. We found our *berserkr* captain and leader at sea, Kraki Bentleg, standing sentinel by a prisoner bound to a post just a stone's throw away from the injury tents. The old captain was pale and gaunt as ever, his body giving no indication of how dangerous he was. He looked bored out of his mind.

The prisoner, on the other hand, appeared to be having a grand old time. He wore what I assumed was his own torn tunic and a lot of bandages covering his left eye, right shoulder, and right leg. Blond hair cut about shoulder-length framed a stocky, grinning face. The man displayed a strange sort of bravado. Most hardened warriors staring down death would have stood silently, denying the enemy any satisfaction. This one was a talker, albeit what he shouted wasn't all that interesting.

"*You will see the power of King Valdar!*" over and over again.

He spoke Greek, which was not the language of his people, the Rus. Maybe he thought he was being cryptic and clever. Fine with me, as I knew Greek very well, but Rus hardly at all.

Huld made her way down from the injury tents after leaving her blood-soaked apron and picking up her distaff. I wanted to wait for a full explanation, but I wanted to shut this man up first.

*"Good morning, have you had anything to eat yet?"* I asked in Greek.

He went quiet, and that answered at least one question: The man was sane. Probably not happy about his bindings or future prospects, but he was not the raving madman he'd been playing at.

Huld looked tired and unkempt as she approached us. She had taken off the apron, but some blood had spattered her gray hair. Eyes bloodshot, breath short, the old *vǫlva* had probably worked all night tending to the wounded.

"What am I doing here?" I asked. "Other than quieting this man down so he doesn't wake up the entire camp?"

Huld pointed to my bloody hand. "Needing a bandage, apparently. Were you attacked in your tent?"

"I had a dream, swore a blood oath."

"In your sleep? Impressive. The cut needs cleaning, though. Come see me after you've finished here. For now, we need whatever answers we can get from this man."

"Odd's people will want more than answers," Magnus cut in. "Half will want to drown him, and the other half will want to cut off his thumbs. And then drown him."

I also wanted blood. Blood for my fallen Brothers. Blood for who knew how many prisoners tortured and murdered on that awful island in the White Sea.

Huld nodded at me. "And so you are here before any such stupidity takes place. Perhaps you can find out the enemy's plans. Why haven't we been attacked again? That would be a useful thing to know." She shuffled off, as if that was plenty to go on.

"How do I entice him to answer such questions?"

"Do as you think is best," she replied over her shoulder.

"No sacrifices," Kraki growled.

The Rus warrior writhed against the ropes with a newfound energy. Wild eyes fixed on nothing and no one in particular. It seemed to me he was redoubling his act. Maybe he had understood us.

*"Do you speak Norse?"* I asked in Greek. He gave me a toothy growl. Fine, Greek it was. *"What is your name?"*

A dry tongue lolled out of his mouth as he smiled. *"Borisu, you dog."*

*"Borisu Youdog! A fine name. We will tell your king of your bravery."*

He shook his head. "*You will never even get close to him, such is his power. Greater than Perun. Greater than the Nailed God. I have seen it! I was one to look deep. Hand over that pirate, Arrow-Odd, and beg the king's forgiveness. He might let some of you live.*"

He still hadn't mentioned Ogmund Tussock, and that was unexpected. Asking directly was not likely to get me anywhere, so I thought of a way to make him react.

"*I want to hear more about this Valdar. He must be very impressive. Not at all like those who ran from the battle a few days ago. You know Ogmund Tussock?*" I pulled some of my hair at my forehead forward and let it hang in front of my face. "*Ogmund the Runner, we call him now. Or Ogmund the Swimmer. Or Ogmund the Scared Little—*"

"*Our king will devour you from the inside!*"

I try not to be too judgmental of other cultures, but that seemed a bit strange. I could use it, though.

"*Oh, is your king the dragon? You know, the dragon that was so scared it flew away. Arrow-Odd only shot two arrows at the thing, and it had enough.*"

"*Fool!*"

Granted, those two arrows had been Gusir's Gifts, the gold-fletched arrows that could pierce anything. But I wasn't going to tell him that.

"*Flew away and didn't come back to free those we took prisoner.*" I leaned in to provide a little unsolicited analysis. "*I think you have been abandoned.*"

"*My death was guaranteed when I was captured. Do not deny it.*"

"*How were you captured, anyway?*" I pulled at my beard in mock confusion. "*I know: You took the shoulder injury and retreated, but you tripped and took the leg injury. Then, someone who was better at retreating than you stomped on your head on the way out.*"

That was too insulting not to respond to, which is exactly what I'd hoped for.

He spat, his face red with rage. "*Those fool Bjarmians! They were the ones—*" He stopped and spat at me again, apparently realizing he was about to say more than he'd intended.

"*Did you hire them? If you did, maybe you want your money back.*"

Not a fair criticism, seeing as how we had a powerful *vǫlva* call the wind that pushed those ships back out to sea. But he didn't know that. All he knew was that the Rus army had attacked, and the Bjarmian navy had failed to attack Arrow-Odd's army from the other side. And so, given his understanding . . .

"*Borisu,*" I said, "*I'm going to offer you your life. All you have to do is answer my questions, and we'll set you free.*"

Borisu spat. "*You foreigners all lie.*"

"*I offer you your life,*" I reiterated. "*Here is a witness who knows my honor will be stained if I don't let you go.*" I repeated myself in Norse, so Magnus could understand.

Magnus clenched his jaw slightly, which was his way of expressing extreme shock.

Borisu shook his head and looked away. A little like he'd understood enough Norse to keep me honest, and a little like he was interested in keeping his life.

Magnus motioned for me to step away and council for a moment. I followed, and we whispered a bit in private.

"What by Surt's flaming ballsack are you doing offering him his life?" demanded Magnus, in the quietest voice possible. "He is a dead man, no doubt about that. People want revenge, and there's nowhere else to get it at the moment. And to put the army at risk by letting him go?"

"What risk to the army?" I asked. "The Rus know where we are, if their main host is even close enough to care. All this man goes back with is a good accounting of Odd's healers. And—"

"But—"

"*And,*" I put a hand up for him to stop, "he will have other stories to tell. Stories about Ogmund running away and the Bjarmians failing to attack. Thor's hairy balls, man, even their *dragon* ran rather than fight it out! That man will carry bitter stories back to his people and end up spreading them like a disease." I paused. "Assuming he doesn't run into a Karelian warrior riding a moose, first."

Magnus nodded the sort of nod to indicate he didn't agree at all. "He's still not talking."

"We have offered one thing, but not the consequences of refusing it," I said. "Follow my lead." I turned and walked back within spitting distance of Borisu Youdog.

"Kraki," I said, "it seems to me the prisoner is cold."

"Should I boil him?" There was no hesitation in his response. Kraki was well past joking when it came to violence.

Borisu jerked. So, maybe he couldn't speak Norse, or maybe just not well. But he could understand it well enough.

"There's an idea . . ." said Magnus, now grinning widely.

"I think boiling is a bit much," I said. "Perhaps just a torch for now."

"Hmph," said Kraki. I think it meant *That's stupid, but I'm bored, so I will go find one.*

"I'll help," said Magnus, following my lead.

I let the silence hang for a few awkward moments before addressing Borisu again. *"Not much use, a dead man. Not much use to his family or his friends. Not much likelihood of him doing any more deeds of note."* Another awkward pause. *"A man can lose much of himself and still talk, however. And then he's still of use to me."*

I squeezed my cut hand and watched the blood drip from my fist despite the pain. He got a good look, but said nothing. Neither did I until Kraki and Magnus returned with a torch. By then, Borisu Youdog had taken back to struggling and howling.

*"Just a few questions, Borisu Youdog,"* I reiterated. *"Where did the Bjarmians sail off to? Where is your main host now?"*

Borisu rolled his eyes back into his head and moaned.

"Will you talk if we warm you up a little?" Magnus asked.

No response.

"I think we have our answer," continued Magnus. "What do we do, given our friend's reticence?"

"Maybe he needs to be a lot warmer," I said. "Maybe he will talk if he is so warm, his hair is on fire."

"Right!" said Kraki. "Magnus, get his pants down."

I suspect my face may have betrayed my surprise. A bad look to show surprise, almost as bad as showing emotion. But try as I might, I could not make the connection between *set his hair on fire* and *get his pants down.*

Until I did. And then my face definitely betrayed my surprise.

"Goat's breath and cat piss, Kraki! His hair!" I put a hand on my head for emphasis. "His *regular* hair!"

Kraki looked back in confusion, then disappointment.

"Starting slow, are we?" said Magnus. He sounded like I had just contradicted the best idea since smoked pork.

Borisu Youdog, perhaps realizing what kind of nuts Kraki had intended to roast, went very pale.

Extremism can look a lot like madness, but it is not the same thing. Getting answers out of Borisu was much easier after that. In fact, he was happy to offer all manner of information, inferences, and hearsay that was almost certainly made up. All delivered as if his life depended on it. Which it did.

Unfortunately, some of the man's answers were too complicated, too fast, for me to think they were lies. I got more details out of him, plenty to share with the other skalds, but the bottom line was: King Valdar was just another name for Ogmund, and his son Svart had secured an alliance with King Harek of Bjarmia.

Arrow-Odd's army wasn't chasing one sorcerer and a few adherents. It was at war with all of Gardariki, and then some.

# Chapter 4

## Fallen

I saw Huld at the injury tents right after questioning Borisu. I told her what I'd learned while she cleaned and bandaged my hand. She didn't react much, except to work more quickly.

"The camp begins to wake," she said after finishing. Meaning, I think, *people will soon talk about what they saw, so you had better share this information right away.*

That meant calling the skalds to the Circle. They might not all come at my request, but they would all answer the call of Odd's skald, Hallfred, who some called Horsefly. I made off for Arrow-Odd's tent, thinking that was the most likely place to find Hallfred. As I walked, I noticed how different the camp seemed from the day we arrived.

Whatever brave faces and cheery words I encountered, nobody could deny that Arrow-Odd's war camp reeked. Blood and vomit had seeped into every path. We tried to keep bowel movements to the beach, but the men had given up on a dedicated place to urinate days ago and went where they felt like it. People didn't speak their thoughts out loud, but the lack of discipline had plenty to say about what they were thinking.

While Arrow-Odd stayed in his tent, his army was on the verge of breaking up. If that happened, I had no idea how we would pursue Ulf and Alfhild with any success.

Hallfred had done much to conceal his thoughts in the last few days. His ever-present smirk melted when he thought no one was looking. The bright green of his tunic had faded with the hard washing necessary to get bloodstains out. Deep bags had formed under his eyes.

Was Hallfred consoling Odd? Advising him? I had gotten more details of the battle and its aftermath, and my guess was some of both.

Ogmund had finally come out of the cliffs and made a challenge: He and his eight followers against Odd and Vignir. Vignir was still angry about a comment his father had made that questioned his courage. Vignir, therefore, demanded to fight Ogmund himself while Odd fought the eight followers. That way, there would be no mistake that he had no fear of such a fight.

It had been a fight unlike any other. Vignir and Ogmund leaped among the cliffs and slopes as they fought, the sorcerer and the half-giant moving unlike any mere men could.

Odd expected Ogmund's eight followers to be hard against steel, so he used a club to deal with them. At first, it looked like they might have him, but Odd had let himself be surrounded to draw them in.

Styrgrim had explained Odd's intentions. "Give them a chance to think they can win, and the wolves will snarl," he'd told us.

Ogmund's followers did snarl as they encircled Odd. They weren't ready to fight a man moving that fast, though. Soon, one had a crushed skull, and another, a broken arm. When the rest were panting from the intense fight, Odd did not look tired at all.

Meanwhile, Ogmund was such a slippery foe that even Vignir's enormous hands had trouble getting a grip on him. He settled for punches and throwing a few big rocks at the beginning of the fight. Some said Vignir was a more dangerous fighter than Odd, even. Vignir finally got Ogmund in a bear hug, but Ogmund slipped Vignir's grasp and headed out among the highest cliffs, out of the sight of the onlooking army, whose attention was transfixed on the two fights.

Ogmund's eight followers fared poorly in the meantime. One by one, they all fell dead to Odd's club. Odd then went to see how his son's fight was going.

That was when Vignir crashed back down onto the near cliffside. The latter part of the fight had not gone his way, and Ogmund was on him immediately. Though both were bruised and bloodied, Ogmund took the last advantage. He drew up Vignir's head and bit out his throat. Odd saw it happen but was too far away to help.

So ended Vignir Oddsson, maybe the most promising young hero of his time, the most popular man in Odd's army, and the only son Arrow-Odd ever had.

But that was just the beginning of bad news that night. Ogmund had a bit to say after that, in a voice that carried unnaturally on the air for the entire army to hear.

"If I had been merely a man, then this one here would have had me. He broke every bone in my body! But I am as much spirit as man now, and you set a man against me. So it goes when you try to chase me down, Odd. You'll always find something other than what you were looking for!"

Ogmund ran for the sea, dove in, and was not seen again.

That was when the army heard the first sounds of the attack. A small army of Rus had come from the south, unnoticed because everyone's attention had been on the cliffs. Captains tried to organize their crews, but everyone had spread out all over the camp to see the fight. Then came the warning cries about Bjarmian ships approaching from the north.

Hard to imagine being scattered in that army at that time and being attacked on two fronts, but harder still to imagine the roar of the dragon. It flew low over the southern edge of the camp, a winged horror screeching through the dusky light. Long and lean, it spread its wings like the sails of two warships. Noxious clouds of black smoke trailed from its mouth and nostrils. It spewed fire over a dozen warriors on its first pass.

That opened up a hole in what scattered defenses the army was able to muster. Some of the Rus found their way through. Accounts varied about what happened at that point and in what order, but I believed two things to be true: Huld called for aid from the skalds and got it. They guarded her as she sat *seiðr* and turned the wind against the Bjarmian navy, preventing their ships from landing.

The other was that Styrgrim's second in command, Helgi Pike-Tooth, mustered who he could and conscripted every warrior at hand, regardless of their chain of command. It turned out the Pike-Tooth did indeed have a lot more to him than just sharpened teeth. His counter-charge into the Rus flank stopped their advance.

It had been a desperate fight, though, and very close.

Meanwhile, there was still the threat of the winged dragon. Odd had only three arrows special enough to threaten a beast like that. Gusir's Gifts, they were called, gold-fletched arrows from an ancient Sami sorcerer-king that always returned after being loosed. He shot two at the dragon and missed, though the second nicked a wing.

Odd lost those two arrows, but drove the dragon away with that second shot. With no naval support, no dragon, and their noses bloodied from Pike-Tooth's near-suicidal charge, the Rus withdrew. It left Arrow-Odd's army victorious, and feeling anything but.

Huld had added a detail that no one else told me: That Odd had despaired after seeing Ogmund get away, and his army attacked on two fronts. He'd collapsed and given up. Hallfred Horsefly, fighting his way through the camp's chaos, was the one who'd brought Odd his longbow and arrow bag. Hallfred Horsefly had roused the army's leader, screaming into his face to fight again, before Odd got his mind back enough to loose Gusir's Gifts at that dragon.

Some had said Odd looked very old as he entered his tent after the battle. Difficult to imagine Arrow-Odd despairing, but he also hadn't come back out of the tent.

So when I stood outside Arrow-Odd's tent and announced myself, I was quite uncertain what I might find inside.

I announced myself again as I stepped in, feeling a bit like I was crossing a threshold to more than just a tent. The size of a house, parts of it were walled off with roughly weaved drapes for separation and perhaps a measure of privacy. A dozen steps ahead of me sat a long table and chairs. The table was clear, and I wondered what Odd used it for. Laying out a map to visualize the surrounding area? Private conversations with the rest of the War Council?

I took a few tentative steps forward. "Hallfred, I need you to gather the remaining skalds." There had been thirteen of us skalds before. Now there were eight. "I have information from a prisoner, and it needs to be shared among the skalds so it can be told to their lords. Are you here?"

I heard a loud sigh and took a few more steps. I turned the corner of a makeshift wall that looked like it had been made out of rejected sailcloth.

Around the corner was a small room with a straw floor. A longbow, unstrung, was propped against a wall. Beside it was an arrow bag made from the entirety of a goat skin, hooves and all. An old man sat on a wooden bench made for sleeping upright. He kept his scarlet cloak drawn up to his chin like a blanket.

'Old' did not describe him sufficiently. He was shriveled, like a dried-out husk somehow still moving and breathing. Gray skin threatened to crack with every movement. Wisps of white hair hung on like stubborn oak leaves refusing to fall despite the cold. If Odd removed his golden headband, I wondered if his skin would come right off with it.

No wonder Horsefly had done so much to conceal his thoughts.

Odd snorted and blinked and seemed to notice me for the first time. "Come to gawk?" His voice sounded as dry and broken as his body looked.

I shook my head. I had thought I wanted to see, but this is why they say it's better to remain middle-wise than to know too much. I wished I had settled for middle-wise in this case, but once I saw, I could not look away. To look away from terrible things is to give them power.

"I came for Hallfred. I questioned a prisoner, and the information should be told to the other skalds."

"You do not wish to linger." Odd coughed before continuing. "I must disgust you." Whatever half-assed negation I was preparing stopped cold when he raised a hand to silence me. "Perhaps you should tell your father he was right. I did not sacrifice to Odin, thinking myself my own man. That is advice in *Hávamál*, is it not? But I ignored gods as well as men. Redbeard told me not to pursue Ogmund, but I went against his advice. Never sacrificed to Odin. Now, Odin has cursed me."

Something turned the wrong way in my guts. Here was a man with an injury of the mind, not one for Huld's tent full of gashes, bone breaks, and wounds going sour. This was an illness of ideas, all causing Odd to tear himself down.

"Odin was right here," I said. "If there was a failing, it was his. Ask Styrgrim about that, and he'll say the same."

Half-dead eyes stared back at me, and I knew I'd gone down the wrong path. I was reminding him he'd been fooled by the god's guise. I'd attempted to provide comfort by saying what I thought I might want to hear. I chose wrong.

Arrow-Odd and I were not similar people. He was a warrior, through and through. I had come to find some acceptance in that world, but I was no champion. What words would make a difference to this man? Did any even exist?

My bag of rune carving discs pulsed against my leg. The Brisingamen meant to get out, to be used. The bag quieted the torc's voice, but could not silence it. The torc offered to help me. To find the right words and prevent the army from falling apart.

"And what would Vignir say?" countered Odd. "All of my gold I would give in tribute, if only it meant I could have him at my side right now."

But he could not give gold to get his son back, and pining after Odin would do him no good. It would only keep him old and infirm, waiting on the dispensation of a higher power. That was no way to live.

A high-pitched noise rose from the bag like the chiming of many crystals. Gentle but sharp. Fragile but powerful. This was unlike Need's hum. This was enticing, ingratiating, the ring of a silver coin promising a hoard beneath it.

I could not help Odd break his mental torpor without the torc, it seemed. I reached for the bag, thinking the power of influence was exactly what I needed now. If Alfhild could use the thing to convince, surely I would use it even better—

Stinging heat ran through the double axehead design of Haldor's armring as I was in mid-thought. Anger at Alfhild and all her works flared in me, and I realized the Brisingamen's power was exactly the trap. Shocked out of the spell the Brisingamen was luring me to, I withdrew my hand. The torc hissed something that felt like *I'll get you* as the bag closed.

*No*, I thought, as an idea came to me. *I'll get you.*

"I never thought I would find that at his core, Arrow-Odd was a gold-hound. If that's what you want, you might as well die fast instead of slow. But if it's word-fame you've always been after, then you had better get to living sooner rather than later. I stole a thing from Alfhild, a thing she wants back very much. The Brisingamen, a beauty that hides an ill influence. It calls to me right now to use it on you. Is that what you want—to be ensorcelled?"

Cracks formed at the corners of his mouth. His eyebrows twitched. Blood ran from one nostril.

"*No*," he said, hate in his voice.

"I will destroy this thing," I said. "Who helps me is sure to win lasting word-fame for it. Is *that* what Arrow-Odd craves?"

He sneered and tossed his cloak aside. His knees creaked as he stood up. "How?"

The man didn't want to be consoled, didn't desire pity or even goodwill. He needed a quest.

"I also have advice from Odin," I said. "He spoke to me in a dream, told me to seek out the sword, Tyrfing—that no other blade could destroy a thing like this."

Odd's eyes went wide. He looked up as if into a memory. "Of course!" he rasped. "How did I not see it?" Which was a bit of a strange response, and I wanted to add a caveat to that idea, anyway.

"But wait, Odin's advice is best for him, not for us. We can find another way, I think. First, I need your help. Alfhild's island is within striking distance, but one ship isn't enough."

"You . . . need—"

"I need an army."

Arrow-Odd sank back down to his chair and looked around, his expression blank. Had I gotten close? Had I lost him for good? I couldn't tell.

A hand fell on my shoulder, and I barely stopped myself from whirling around.

"I heard you were looking for me," said Hallfred Horsefly. "Now you've found me, so let's allow Odd to rest for the moment."

As we left, I glanced back at the leader of the army, the man who had gone from living legend to very near a living corpse. What was that last expression? A grin, maybe? But even if I was right, I had no idea what it meant.

# Chapter 5

# Circularity of Skalds

I waited until Hallfred Horsefly and I were well beyond earshot of the tent to ask "What in Hel was that?"

Horsefly shrugged. "You must know some of Arrow-Odd's lore. He's sailed and raided for hundreds of years, written a legend of his name in the blood of champions and kings. Some heroes are fated with such long lives."

"How does that answer the question? He looked like a man last time I saw him. Now he looks like a desiccated corpse!"

Horsefly grabbed me by the back of my neck with a stronger hand than expected and hissed into my ear. "Keep your voice down! He is despairing, giving up. For all I have counseled, I am not sure he can see his way past Vignir's death. But until that is certain, I will have no one know of it."

I swallowed hard. "He has an army to lead," I whispered back.

Horsefly let me go and patted me on the back, quickly returning to a show of normalcy. He led us at an unhurried pace toward Styrgrim's crew.

"We'll find Bjorn first. The morning is young, so he's probably still oiling his blade." He fixed me with an obvious fake smile, and I realized he knew all the implications of a leadership failure here. It was his burden to make sure this leader did not fail and that the army did not panic while Odd recovered.

I had many concerns, all of which would have their time. At the moment, everyone was waiting to find out one thing and base their next decisions on it: What was Arrow-Odd going to do?

Now I wondered if the answer was *Arrow-Odd is going to shrivel up and die of sadness.*

"Can he . . ." I was uncertain how to ask my question. *Can he be less dead?* was the general direction, though I did not want to express it that way.

"You want to know if he can recover his prolonged youth as his outlook turns, if it turns?"

"Yes, that."

He nodded. "I think so. He once told me he aged a great deal when his friend Hjalmar the Brave died and that it took him a while to recover. I have no more details than that. I think this aging is what he meant."

That was Hallfred Horsefly: Casually relaying lore so esoteric that no one else in Midgard knew it, grinning as he stared down his army's dissolution. That was some good skald.

"I heard you were a troublesome poet. Yet it seems to me the lone rope keeping the ship moored to the dock is not a troublesome thing."

He laughed. "I *am* a troublesome poet. Why else call me Horsefly? But the trouble I make is not because I enjoy trouble or chaos. It's a needful thing, whether Odd recognizes it as such or not."

After meeting Arrow-Odd, I had considered his legend overrated. A blowhard, a glory hound, a man who dared much whenever it came to the lives of others. But he kept no sycophants nearby. His poet was not known for elaborate praise, but for pointing out flaws and voicing unpopular views.

No blowhard would willingly keep a man like that close at hand. No blowhard would even tolerate Horsefly's presence. Maybe Odd was more of a *drengr* than I'd given him credit for.

We found Bjorn, Styrgrim's madman of a skald, and he was eager to hear what I had to say. He also chided me for going around with my face unwashed and my hair uncombed, and suggested I get myself together a bit while he and Hallfred went to find the others.

Bjorn handed me his wash bowl. "Things will go better for you if you arrive at the Council washed and fed." He nodded at a steaming cauldron of porridge nearby, and then he and Hallfred left

I looked down at the thick beard hairs and spit swimming in that wash bowl and sighed. Bjorn was not one to give advice if it wasn't important, though, so I took his advice and washed up.

I hadn't realized how hungry I was until one of Bjorn's crewmates offered me a bowl of hot porridge, and I took my time eating rather than wolfing it down. When that had gone on long enough, I headed for the Circle of Skalds.

The circle had been undamaged in the attack by the Rus. Not a huge enclave, only thirty paces across, but it was for skalds alone. Low piles of rowan branches did not keep anyone out physically, but the boundary was respected by people and ravens. Here we could gather, exchange information, and then bring it to our respective leaders.

The other skalds had already arrived. Bjorn and Hallfred, of course. Then there were Kormak and Gizur, the fattest and hardest to miss. I knew Einar least of the skalds. Most of my attention was focused on the two women sitting together, Jorun and Steinvor.

Okay, mostly on Steinvor.

I had visited her tent once. Uncertainty gnawed at me about whether I would be welcome there again. In the days since our crew had returned to find Odd's army victorious yet demoralized, I'd had little time to myself. None that had allowed me to slip away, in any case, or to have much more than a few words with her.

But did Steinvor know that? Did she know how much I wanted to shed my responsibilities every night and curl up in her warm embrace?

No, because I couldn't tell her that. It would be unmanly, and being considered manly was more important than anything.

I did the "manly" thing and avoided eye contact with her.

"Styrgrim is disappointed he was not invited to torture the prisoner," said Bjorn, never lacking for a good opening line.

Bjorn had been a bit terse when we found him, and now I knew why. Word had spread of the interview, and Styrgrim must have already voiced his displeasure. Bjorn wasn't going to say any of that until we were in the circle, though.

"I did not torture the prisoner." I took a seat at one of the empty logs arranged around the fire pit, and Hallfred sat next to me. The others sat down as well. "I questioned him."

Bjorn shrugged. "I make no dispute and don't question your story at all. I also ferry my lord's words as he has asked me to." Translation: Styrgrim was furious and yelled a lot, but his skald had a much more even temper. And wasn't quite as interested in dismembering people.

You wouldn't need much sense to pick out Bjorn as the best fighter among us. Broad shoulders and thick arms were clues. The clearest indication, though, was that he was Styrgrim's skald. Styrgrim didn't accept warriors on his crew unless they were a cut above most others.

Hard as iron, that was Styrgrim the Bear. The man I had called my father up until just a few days ago. He had been little more than a stranger to me, even when I'd thought he *was* my father. Now that I knew he wasn't, he was a stranger entire.

Styrgrim also had the weight of the army on his shoulders. As clear as I saw Hallfred bearing that burden with a false smile for appearances, Styrgrim was spending every minute of his day organizing, inspecting, and leading skirmishing parties.

I doubt that finding out I was really the son of some unknown god, maybe even the fickle and feckless Odin, helped improve his mood. It showed.

"Tell Styrgrim he was not invited to the conversation because his name is not Styrgrim of the Honeyed Words. We will invite him first thing to any events that involve killing or maiming as the desired outcome."

"Well spoken," said Bjorn. "Now, as to the honeyed words, what new knowledge did they result in?"

"The only way I could get the prisoner to talk was to promise his release," I said, deciding to lead with the least popular thing. "And I won't see my word turned dishonorable about it."

The other skalds made a lot of frustrated sounds as I said this.

Hallfred held a hand up. "My friends, if you keep shouting over the man, you won't be able to convey his words to your lords, which are to be told exact and not in an exaggerated way."

"I more anticipate an exaggerated reaction when I convey the words as spoken," grumbled Bjorn.

"A thing you are well-practiced at," said Hallfred. "Ansgar, what did the prisoner say in exchange for his life?"

"First, I want to say that I offered him his life only after hearing him curse the Bjarmians. He thinks they are not good allies. And I reminded him that both Ogmund and his dragon fled the battle. The stories he returns to his people with won't be good for our enemies."

Bjorn nodded. He was practically admitting I had done a good job. Now, for the bad news.

"As for what I found out: Ogmund doesn't go by that name with the Rus. To them, he is King Valdar of Gardariki and is worshipped by some as a god. He has an alliance with the Bjarmians, brokered by this Grim Aegir we'd heard of. Grim Aegir is really Ogmund's son, Svart, a powerful sorcerer in his own style."

Sighs, looks, and shaking heads answered that statement. A few began to speak but stopped, perhaps uncertain of the best thing to say next.

A sense of unease crept into the circle. This was the safest place in the entire camp for discussion, a place full of ideas and wisdom. Even a drop of despair or panic was anathema to the Circle of Skalds, and yet that tone carried on the air like an off-tune note from a lyre. Arrow-Odd's army had been recruited to go after one powerful sorcerer and his followers, not three sorcerers aided by the armies of two nations and children of the gods.

"Shit," said Bjorn. He was always quickest to get to the heart of things.

"The Rus intended to move south after the battle here," I continued. "That's probably why they didn't try another attack."

"South, where?" demanded Einar. "For what?"

"The prisoner didn't know that. But so what? We can attack Alfhild's island right now, fight Alfhild without the Rus hitting us from the other side."

"Assuming we attacked Alfhild's supposed children of gods *and* the Bjarmians, who are probably together now, who would lead that attack?" Einar asked.

"If Odd cannot, why not his right hand?" I replied.

There was no one in the camp who didn't fear or respect Styrgrim the Bear, or both. No storm cloud followed the man—he was the storm. Warriors came to attention when he walked by, and with good reason. Coiled wrath threatened to strike at any moment in response to perceived laziness or insubordination. It was not for Styrgrim's ego. He knew the army was holding together by a thread and did not tolerate anyone pulling at that thread.

Einar shook his head. "I won't pretend there aren't some who would like to see that, but there are many others who would not like to see it. It must be Odd, or leadership of the army must be ceded."

"Let Sirnir lead the attack," said Bjorn. "Or jointly with Gardar, if that makes them feel better."

Einar shrugged. "If they have full leadership of the army, maybe they will."

Styrgrim had only one ship. However, many more warriors than his own would follow him on instinct. For men with higher titles, I imagine that was an irksome quality. The hardheadedness grated on me. It sounded like Gardar and Sirnir agreed on the best course of action, but having our most competent commander remain part of the War Council wasn't acceptable. They had to be the *only* commanders.

"I suppose there is another tactic," I cut in. "We could sit here and wait to be attacked."

"Styrgrim—" Einar was quick with a response, but Hallfred cut him off.

"Hold! This is not the time to poke at each other; otherwise, we will have lords poking at each other. We can already count a great number of people who would happily kill us in this part of the world. We will not add to that number from among our own ranks."

Einar guffawed at that and started to say something, but Hallfred interrupted again.

"Or leave this circle."

Einar put up his hands and stayed where he was. "Sirnir provides the most ships, and he expects to be represented here. He thinks we must know, one way or another, whether Arrow-Odd will lead again, before committing to any further course of action."

"The three of us have spoken on our own time," said Gizur. Somehow, all of Gardar's skalds—Gizur, Kormak, and Steinvor—had survived the battle. "Spoken and listened to our people. Many of them say much the same as what Einar described."

"Not all," added Steinvor.

"No, not all," admitted Gizur. "But most, yes, I think you agreed. There was a question of why not attack, and that's a reason why. I offer no judgment about it being a good or bad reason, only that it is."

Kormak nodded. "I'll add only that this is what we hear, and we mean to share what we hear rather than gossip in secret. If it's advice our lords want—"

"Then we attack," finished Steinvor. Kormak and Gizur both nodded.

Gods, I was in love with that woman.

"The War Council is for advice," said Hallfred. "We are for stating what is, as Gizur described so well."

"The War Council has two empty seats," said Jorun. "And I don't think I am poking when I say so, but neither Gardar nor Sirnir has shown much interest in sitting at that table when Styrgrim is there. Nor have we heard of them attempting to fill Vignir's seat. So: What War Council?"

"Again, advice." Horsefly looked like he had a very bad headache.

"I don't think it's advice to state that two seats out of five being filled is hurting morale," I said. "Nor that morale is low."

Einar nodded. "I won't disagree on either point, but I see no morale boost without a decision from Odd." He looked at Hallfred. "Or the admitted inability to make one."

It was like half the ship was rowing one way and the other half was rowing the other. The results were predictable even by the dimmest halfwit. Here were our leaders, leading by waiting for change. As long as it wasn't them changing.

Einar turned to me. "Speaking of decisions: The *Sea Squirrel* crew is still not a sworn part of this army. And further, your crew still has to choose a new leader. Not your captain, apparently. Have you done this thing yet? And if so, do you intend to join our army, or not?"

"That's a complicated thing," I said, trying to buy myself some time. "And yes, Kraki Bentleg decides where the ship sails, but he does not lead on land. That was Haldor Skullsplitter, and he fell killing Ogmund's troll of a mother. We lost many good people that day and took on a few new ones. It's not yet clear who will continue to sail with us, or who will lead everyone on land."

"Your leadership situation is murky," replied Einar. "But it seems to me that you're with us, whether you declare it or not."

And we were, unless we could find another army to help us fight Alfhild. We had thought our one ship of heroes was plenty to put her down, and we had been wrong. Now I was caught between two stubborn lords and one stubborn captain.

It occurred to me that I had to speak to Kraki about another matter, anyway. And Ketill. If anyone could think of an alternative to finding Tyrfing, it would be the old wizard. Still, I didn't want to give a too-earnest response. Einar had rubbed me the wrong way.

"Right now, we have more enemies than I can count. I'll tell Kraki that. I think he'll agree it's time to be done with talking, that it's time to act."

Einar gave me a nasty look. Horsefly sighed. But Steinvor smirked, and that was enough for now.

## Chapter 6

# Meanwhile, on the White Sea

Utstein woke with the taste of sour apple in his mouth. The taste faded as he opened his eyes to see a pretty, but dirty and smelly, young woman staring down from behind him.

The iron collar around her neck marked her as a thrall. A loose-fitting dress did a poor job of holding her breasts in, but perhaps that was the idea. She held a baby in one arm as it cooed and played with her dark, stringy hair. With her other hand, she tapped gently on Utstein's forehead, as if that would tell her what this strange being was. Meanwhile, she worked a hard crust of bread over in her mouth loud enough to wake the dead.

"An open-mouth chewer," grumbled Utstein. "Good thing the skald isn't here, or he'd be out of his mind."

The woman sat back and ceased examining Utstein's face. "Skoooooooliii-iii," she called, followed by a string of nonsensical words. She stood up and walked past Utstein, who lay next to his brother. Over her shoulder, the baby took one look at Innstein and started screaming.

The 'Steins lay half-covered near the aft of a ship, not quite as far back as the rudder. The vessel was longer and sleeker than the *Sea Squirrel*. It held position for the time being, but would clearly cut the water at speed given a decent wind. The brothers shared that space alongside a few other invalids, all covered with thin, blood-stained blankets.

Utstein rose to an elbow, still a bit groggy. The smell of the salt spray refreshed him, though, and he looked around. The man at the rudder was also a thrall. The strange woman stood a few paces down the deck, talking to another thrall. The crew sat beyond them, fiddling with clothes or tying shoes. They looked bored.

He glanced at Innstein, who looked angry. But Innstein always looked a little angry, so Utstein figured he was fine.

The brothers both checked and found that they were indeed wearing pants.

"It's good to be alive," said Innstein, uncharacteristically positive.

"Confusing, though," added Utstein. He recalled a little of what they'd just woken up from and flexed his hands.

"Think your name is appropriate, Magni?"

Utstein nodded. He felt like he could put his fist straight through the bottom of that ship if he wanted to. "And you, Modi?"

Innstein nodded. "I've got patience enough to find out what language she was speaking and not much more than that."

"A strange one. Didn't sound like Joni."

"No, I don't think it's Karelian. What, then?"

The brothers went quiet as a man with an iron collar approached them. His hair and beard were unkempt, but his clothes were in better shape than that woman's filthy dress. He even had a decent leather belt, a bit strange for a thrall. "I don't know Karelian," he said, his accent marking him as a Norseman. "But I do know some Irish. Bec has been watching over you."

The young woman with the baby reappeared from behind him, her eyes wide with interest. She cradled the baby, which had reduced its screaming to whimpering. She muttered another unintelligible sentence or two, her eyes never leaving the brothers.

"It's a surprise to see you awake," said the Norseman. "Men who sleep for days at a time are generally considered to be dying. But here you are, not dead at all!"

Utstein reached for his side. His shirt was rent and stained with blood, but there was no scar where he'd been speared. "Perhaps a little bit, not too much."

"Better to take such things in moderation," said Innstein. "Do you have any mead?"

The Norseman grinned and said something to Bec. She let out a single, high-pitched laugh, and the baby screamed. She sat down to nurse, and that quieted the kid down.

It seemed like a fair question to Utstein, but he kept his mouth shut, silently marveling at how loud that child was.

"Halfdan will be pleased," said the Norseman, his tone beginning joyous and ending not. "He will return you to your ship. Where did you come from?"

"Most recently?" asked Innstein. "A place with good mead."

Utstein could hear in his brother's voice what he wasn't saying. They were both suspicious of their circumstances. It was not time to answer questions, but to ask them.

"I must have been hit in the head," said Utstein. "Can you tell us what happened and where we are?" He glanced sideways. "And why there is an Irishwoman nursing a baby on a warship?"

"Ah," the man nodded. He came closer and sat with them, lowering his voice. "I am Skuli, although I'm of little account." He tapped the thrall collar on his neck. "You're on the *Worm's Tongue*, and over there is its captain, Halfdan the Toothless."

Utstein's eyes shot up to the sail to see red teeth set on a white field. It was Halfdan, alright, the same *níðingr* who had killed a bunch of sleeping men after accepting their hospitality. The King of Fretborg, if you could call it kingship to lord over that cold, stinking hall.

"Never mind the mead," said Utstein. "I've been to his hall. Worst ale I've ever had in my life."

Innstein grinned. "Where are his *berserkir*?"

"I don't know about that," said Skuli. "We were underway a few days ago when someone spotted a strange island full of heather. When we got there, the island disappeared, and we found you two in the water."

"Bad luck to leave men stranded in the sea," said Utstein.

"Very," agreed Skuli. "And Halfdan will no doubt look for a reward when he finds out what ship to return you to."

Utstein wondered if Halfdan would remember them. He seemed like the type to remember every slight, and the 'Steins had won a lot of money off his men. Still, maybe Halfdan only remembered Magnus, since he had killed all those *berserkir*.

"Did Halfdan pull us up himself?" asked Innstein.

Skuli shook his head. "He's been in a mood and doesn't move much from his seat while we're out on the water. I pulled you out with some help from the Irish. I couldn't figure out where you'd come from, though, so we weren't sure if we should head to the island and bring you to Alfhild or if you went overboard from one of the Bjarmian ships. You weren't dressed as Bjarmians, though. Halfdan said to just wait for you to wake up. Or not."

"What other ships," asked Utstein, "and why is there a baby on board this one?"

"Vikings from here and there, and some Bjarmians sent by their king. All waiting on orders about where to sail next. I don't think Alfhild thinks much of Halfdan after his attempts to give us to her as thralls." Skuli suppressed a laugh and went to a whisper. "She's got us babysitting, and that's the crux of it. The baby is her child, Sigurd. It sounds like an important task, but I think it was Alfhild's way of getting rid of the screaming. Sigurd was loud before, but he seems to like the sea even less than land."

Innstein shook his head. "Those are answers that make more questions. Maybe start from the beginning. Halfdan is the Lord of Fretborg. Are you from there?"

"I'm a Rogalander, joined Halfdan as he came around looking to fill out crews. We headed for Ireland to take thralls. Halfdan said he'd heard they were paying good money for thralls up in the north. He didn't mention 'they' meant Ogmund Tussock, though." Skuli shook his head and then straightened up. "I mean, not that there's anything wrong with Ogmund. I only mean—"

"We know what you mean," Innstein interrupted. "And it's the reason you're still alive right now."

"That, and he speaks Irish," added Utstein.

Skuli stared back wide-eyed.

"Don't worry so much," continued Utstein. "We're not who you think we are. Whoever you think we are."

"Who are you, then?"

"We'll get to that later," said Innstein. "Keep telling your story. I want to know how you went from crewman to thrall."

Skuli looked to Bec and then farther down the deck. No one was rowing. Crewmen talked or stretched or busied themselves with whatever tasks to distract themselves.

Sigurd started wailing again. Some of the crewmen from farther up the ship shouted for Bec to shut him up. Bec caressed Sigurd's head and made gentle shushing sounds. When that effort failed to suppress the wailing, she held Sigurd in front of her and made faces at him. Crying mixed with laughter, and he quieted. A bit.

"We raided in Ireland, mostly looking for people about twenty winters old and younger. That was what Halfdan said would fetch the best prices up north. Bec was one of them.

"We sailed back east and up the Northway coast, but it was hard going along Halogaland. Some of the thralls died of disease or infection. Too many. So when we got to Lofoten, Halfdan figured too many had died to do good business. So we raided a Norse village or two for thralls. But it was still a long way past Halogaland to get to the White Sea.

"A lot of thralls died, and Halfdan got angry. He blamed some of us for not taking care of them, which wasn't true. I learned some of the Irish language and tried to keep them healthy. Didn't make me popular with Halfdan's regulars, though. I tried my best to save Bec's baby, but I couldn't, and that was the last straw.

"Halfdan blamed the least popular of us for bad luck. And as a result, I went from crewman to thrall. Then we got to the island where he'd heard was the place to bring us thralls for payment. It turned out that Alfhild was not interested in the Irish at all, and not much in the Norse we'd taken. Our saving grace was that she couldn't stand to be around little Sigurd, and we had a woman who could nurse.

"I don't know what she's paying Halfdan. Less than he wants, but enough to make it worth his while to stay? Not as much as the ships she sent for the big attack on Arrow-Odd's army."

Utstein ground his teeth when he heard that.

"How'd that go?" asked Innstein, his voice giving away a bit of what was building inside him.

Skuli gulped. "Strange stories. I heard they couldn't land, but that Odd's army was mostly destroyed, anyway."

Utstein grunted. He wasn't sure what that meant, or how much they should believe the story. If Odd's army had fallen, it was not clear where they'd go. Where would the *Sea Squirrel* be, in that case? Already on its way back to Lejre, he hoped.

"Who is Sigurd's father?" asked Innstein.

Skuli shook his head. "No one knows."

Utstein didn't think it was terribly important for them to know that. But sometimes, one of the brothers picked up on irrelevancies that were not irrelevant. Utstein played along. "When was he born?"

"Late spring last year."

"That would put conception . . ." said Utstein, reversing time in his head. "Wait."

"That was before the battle at Lejre," said Innstein.

The brothers looked at each other, knowing the dates were right but not comprehending.

"That bodyguard of hers with the stupid haircut?" guessed Utstein.

"Or Ragnvald?" offered Innstein. "Or Ulf!"

"Ulf wouldn't let his son near Halfdan, swine as he is," said Utstein, shaking his head. "But you can make odds for the others."

"Fifty to one on the bodyguard," said Innstein. "And a hundred to one on Ragnvald."

"Which one of those do you want to take?"

Innstein considered this. "Neither. I'd better make the odds longer on both counts."

"Who else could it be, though?"

Utstein imagined little Sigurd raised by that ice witch, Alfhild, and being turned into a troll like her son, Olgram. Well, according to the skald, Olgram was not so trollish; he only looked that way. Either way, the brothers would not want Sigurd returned to Alfhild. For one thing, they already hated Alfhild and intended to kill her. But for another thing, Alfhild, the mother, had sent her son away when he was inconvenient and put him in the hands of Halfdan the Toothless: A pirate, and not even a good one.

Their mothers never sent them away. That had been their father, who tried to have them both killed. And eventually, their mothers had given up their lives so the 'Steins could live.

Sigurd looked as happy as he could be with Bec, both of them seeking solace from the terror all around them. The 'Steins had instincts for people at that point, and Utstein's instinct, doubtless shared with his brother, was that Bec would put Sigurd's life ahead of hers. The identity of Sigurd's father mattered little. Bec would be his mother. Already was, it looked like.

Innstein spoke with that voice he uses when there is his way or the axe-way. "Sigurd wants to go home with Bec."

Utstein nodded. Bec's home was Ireland, as it was for some of the other thralls. That would be a long trip.

"So, who are you two?" Skuli asked again.

The 'Steins tossed their blankets aside and stood up.

"Get behind us," said Utstein. "And we will make it plain."

"Halfdan!" roared Innstein. "King of shitty ale! Your mead hall smelled of farts when we left it, and your men smelled worse than that! We challenge you to step forward."

They stepped past Skuli and Bec to a lot of confused looks and chuckles from Halfdan's crew. Between the blood stains and their salt-crusted beards and hair, the 'Steins must have looked like feral madmen.

Skuli spoke something in Irish and waved. The thralls still between the brothers and the crew ran to the aft. Eventually, two of Halfdan's men stood up and drew their seaxes. The 'Steins let them make the first attacks.

The larger one went for Utstein. The feeling that he could put his fist through the bottom of the ship redoubled. He was Might, after all, but what did that mean? He waited for the thrust and grabbed the man's wrist.

It was light and easy, like grabbing a small twig. Utstein bent it upward. Like a small twig, the wrist snapped.

Innstein turned the thrust aimed at him away, extended the man's arm, and brought his knee up. The elbow cracked, and he bent the man's arm all the way down. The 'Steins threw those two warriors overboard but kept their weapons.

"Now we have seaxes," said Utstein.

Halfdan stomped toward the 'Steins from his seat at the fore and pushed past the crowd in the middle of the ship. "You two!"

"You one-half!" retorted Innstein.

*"Half a Dane, half a drengr,"* quoted Utstein. "Remember that?"

Halfdan snarled. It might've looked dangerous, but he was busy pointing out men to fight for him. "Kill them."

One after another, Halfdan's warriors came at the 'Steins. Thor's names were well-chosen. Innstein was faster and more brutal. Utstein was bigger and stronger. After half a dozen had fallen, Halfdan disappeared into the crowd of warriors behind him.

"Where is Halfdan?" shouted Innstein as he held a man's neck down on the gunwale. "I'll let this shitrag go if you give me the Toothless one in his stead!"

The crowd amidships showed a distinct uncertainty. Two men should have been easy to put down. But the crew did not produce Halfdan, so

Innstein drove a hand into the midsection of the man he'd offered in trade. Not a knife, just his hand. It came out holding a ribbon of intestines. He shoved the gaping man overboard and let the ribbon extend as the man sank into the sea.

"Who knew a man's guts were so long?"

Halfdan called for his champions. Apparently, he had got more *berserkir* since Magnus and Kari had killed those other twelve, but he hadn't found as many as he had before. Three behemoths came at the 'Steins, all armed with big, unwieldy axes.

"It's good you found replacements," said Innstein.

"Otherwise, this would have been boring," added Utstein.

The first of these would-be *berserkir* swung his axe sideways at Innstein like it would cleave him in half at the waist. But Innstein was inside his range quicker than thought itself, grabbed the axe, and completed the swing right into the knee of the man beside him.

Then he raked that axeblade right up the disarmed man's leg and severed the main artery there. Blood spouted, men cried out, and the third supposed *berserkir* held up mid-charge.

"We want Halfdan!" Utstein shouted. "Who among you is still loyal to him, the one who starves you and sends you to die in his stead?"

"Halfdan, you coward," yelled Innstein. "Come out now to fight your own fight!"

Halfdan announced his presence with his sword through the back of his own man, the *berserkr* who had held back. The man dropped his axe, probably out of surprise, and tried to turn around. Difficult to do that while stuck on a sword, especially as Halfdan twisted the blade.

"That's the price of disloyalty," roared Halfdan. He withdrew the sword and let the man fall. "Anyone else want to pay it?"

Halfdan had donned a fine mail shirt and steel helmet while his people died for him. He held a shield rimmed with iron in addition to that sharp sword. He probably thought he was ready for anything—certainly ready to make his crew more afraid of him than of the 'Steins.

"Maybe they're considering the price of loyalty," said Innstein.

"I doubt they can afford it, given what you pay them," Utstein continued. "Now you'll earn the title of *niðingr* if you can't face us yourself."

"Well, that's a bit unfair, brother," said Innstein. "After all, there are two of us, and that's difficult to face for half a man."

"You're right. Let him face me, then, fully armed and armored, and I'll forego any weapons." Utstein tossed his seax at Halfdan's feet and stepped forward. Innstein stepped back.

Halfdan came at Utstein with an overhead slash. Utstein dodged and laughed when the viking's sword struck the deck and stuck fast.

"Terrible disrespect for a ship," said Innstein, shaking his head.

Utstein waited with crossed arms, letting Halfdan free his sword and come at him again.

This time, Halfdan led with his shield, trying to push Utstein off balance before slashing. Utstein punched straight into the boss. Halfdan's wrist buckled under the sudden assault and twisted upward. The top of the shield's rim snapped back into Halfdan's mouth, breaking at least one tooth.

"You're really earning your name, now," said Innstein.

Utstein briefly reconsidered his next move. After all, good chain shirts, steel helmets, and swords were not easy to come by. But these had Halfdan's stink on them, and he didn't want them. So when he grabbed Halfdan, he just tossed him up and over the gunwale. The flight was graceless, but the splash at the end of it was satisfying.

Some people, like the 'Steins, can swim just fine weighted down in armor. But Halfdan was not such a one, and his body sank after a bit of thrashing and gasping.

Some nameless, faceless lieutenant spoke up and pointed at the 'Steins. "Those men were dead!"

"Maybe we were," responded Utstein.

"Who is dead now?" asked Innstein.

A raven croaked above them. It stood on the yard, probably saw the whole thing. Who knows how long it had been there before the fight? Utstein was surprised when it croaked and flew off without a word. Usually, they have something to say or fresh eyeballs to request. This one moved off like it had places to be, a bit impulsive for a raven.

That same pointing fool pointed up at the raven as it took flight. Said it was a sign. He started leading a chant of *Odin! Odin! Odin!* that was quickly adopted by much of Halfdan's remaining crew.

"Those are Odin's men," he proclaimed. "We should follow them!"

Utstein wasn't going to tolerate that sort of nonsense. He strode through the half-cowering crowd and punched the chanter in the face so hard it nearly took off his lower jaw.

"I didn't see Odin anywhere," Utstein bellowed. "We're Haldor Skull-splitter's men."

"We're Kraki Bentleg's men," added Innstein, lower in volume, just as dangerous in tone.

Utstein pointed to the vague outline of land visible across the water. "If you don't like it, you can swim. For anyone staying on this ship, there are rules."

# CHAPTER 7

# A SONG OF STEEL

I LEFT THE CIRCLE OF SKALDS LESS CERTAIN THAN EVER. THE *SEA Squirrel* could sail, if Kraki chose, but sail where? There was a big difference between being *independent* and being *on our own.*

Independent or on our own, I was still uncertain about how to deal with the Brisingamen. Maybe we could bring it somewhere. Where, though? I needed advice.

Ketill hadn't been my teacher for very long, but he had taught me everything I knew about runic magic. A *galdramaðr*, we called that sort of wizard. His art was a bit different from Huld's *seiðr*. Ketill wasn't an expert healer, but he often helped Huld in the injury tents, which is where I found him. Huld was still there, so I ended up talking to them both at the same time.

Could we give the torc back to Freya? Huld shook her head. If it was in Midgard, that meant Freya wanted it out of Asgard. That much, at least, Odin must have been truthful about. I suggested dumping it in the sea, but Ketill warned me off that idea. A sea monster could retrieve it, or it might wash up on an unfriendly shore. Like Bjarmaland.

Odin's advice had been to find the cursed sword, Tyrfing, and use it to destroy the torc. But was that really help for us or just another one of his games? I told them how Odin had described this *Spear of the Gods* plan as a game of *hnefatafl* on a board too big for me to see. Huld laughed and said that was just Odin trying to sound intimidating. Odin never played *hnefatafl* because he never played games he couldn't cheat at.

Ketill pointed out that my name, ANS-GAR, was composed of two elements that added up to *God-Spear*. Or, *Spear of the Gods*. Which left me feeling about as bright as the bottom of the sea, since I had never put that together.

"Odin says you can't see the board," said Ketill, "yet he is awfully interested in you as a player. It's up to you what to do with that."

Odin wanted me to find that evil sword, and I didn't see an alternative. Was it even capable of destroying the Brisingamen, though? Both Huld and Ketill thought so, but they couldn't be sure.

I left the injury tents to find Kraki Bentleg, the expert I needed to ask. I went back through the camp and all the way down near the beach, to where some of the ships had been pulled up onto the berm. The *Sea Squirrel* sat on low risers there. Kraki was scraping barnacles from the hull.

Kraki had been raised by dwarves and fought for them for years. He'd made his bone club in the Down-Below after killing a deep *jotunn*. His friend, Finnr, was an expert weapon smith, even among the dwarves. If anyone could guess whether Tyrfing would destroy the Brisingamen, it was Kraki.

"Of course it can!" In addition to his words, his tone told me: *That was a stupid question.*

Well, at least I had a straight answer.

Not so long ago, it would have been Innstein and Utstein cleaning the ship before anyone else could even think it needed doing, but they were gone. Maybe this was work that needed doing right now, or maybe Kraki was doing it to remember those brothers. Either way, he continued working without looking up, as if the task was too important to put off.

I drew Need, and it came out as an appropriately generic tool. I started scraping the other side of the hull.

"You want to destroy it because Alfhild wants it?" Kraki asked.

"Yes, but also because it's an ill-natured thing that will corrupt whoever uses it."

Kraki grunted. I took it as a vague agreement without needing to know the details.

"We left Hrolf Kraki with a dwarf-made sword last year, and it has the advantage of not being curs—"

"No, no, no." He started as soon as I mentioned the Danish king's name.

"Why not?" A frustrated sigh was my only response, so I continued. "Right, it's obvious to everyone but me."

"That much, you see clearly."

"You've skipped the part where I don't know what you know, because I wasn't raised by dwarves."

"Mmm. Well. Smithing is . . ." he trailed off, and I heard only scraping for a long time. "It's a song of steel. That's what Finnr told me, once."

I nodded to myself before realizing I didn't understand what he meant at all. "A song has a point. You sing it to make others happy, or sad, or tell a story. How is that like making weapons?"

"Finnr's smithing was the same," said Kraki. "He had an intent every time. Had to be inspired by a theme, or he couldn't make anything."

I scraped a few more barnacles. "So if he was confident he had to forge a sword, but wasn't clear on what he needed it for . . ."

"Ah!" said Kraki. "There, that's it. That's your blade. With a bit of the unexpected thrown in from tempering it in dragon's blood."

"So I could just try using Need—"

"Do you understand nothing?" I could feel him shaking his head even though I couldn't see it. "You can't have all themes at once! It muddles the song."

Need hummed low in my hand. It agreed with Kraki.

I thought I understood. "My weapon's theme is adaptability. But it won't cut through just anything. Not like Hrolf Kraki's sword, Skofnung. That can cut through solid rock."

"If he needs it to. That's a sharp sword, but willful. Restraint is hammered into it, just like the king who carries it. You can't use restraint to cleave something as powerful as the Brisingamen."

"What is Tyrfing's theme?"

He stopped scraping and walked around the hull, looking confused. "Do you know the story, or not?"

"Well, yes, I mean, there are a few different versions—"

"It's not my story to tell." He shook his head and went back to scraping. "Hate. That thing is full of grief and hate, and its purpose is to cut. As long as it destroys, it doesn't care what."

"Have you seen this sword?" It sounded like he had.

"No." There was more there, but his tone told me not to ask about it.

"All right," I said, responding to what he hadn't said. "I think we should talk about a new leader on land tonight."

"Talk?" That was a criticism, and for some reason, it touched a raw nerve.

"Yes, Kraki, *talk!*" I shouted. "That's what people do before voting! I don't even know who gets to vote! Is it everyone sailing with us? Is it only Brothers? Do we give armrings to the new people who fought with us, even though we hardly know them?"

These were serious questions, maybe the exact sort of questions nobody wanted to ask out loud.

Kraki stopped scraping again. "If you didn't know, why didn't you just ask? See who wants an armring. If all Brothers agree, and the new person swears to our rules, then they get the armring. Only Brothers get to speak for a new leader on land, and they must all agree."

Or maybe they had been questions *I* had not wanted to ask out loud.

As Kraki described it, the whole process seemed obvious. And I couldn't think of anyone who would object to Magnus being our new leader. This was progress! There was just one more question to answer.

"I don't suppose you know where to find Tyrfing?"

"Not at all."

Nobody knew that. If they did, every warrior in the North would have been after it. Everyone wanted a dwarf-made sword, and they probably didn't believe it was quite as cursed as it was. But if it was as ill-natured as Kraki described, then there was a rarely told story I'd heard that might lead me in the right direction.

I'd heard the story from a drunk. A sloppy performance, both in narrative and due to the spitting and drooling of the teller. I had no doubt the story had been changed too many times over the years to tell me anything exact. It was self-contradictory, badly told hearsay.

But that might be enough. Ravens are experts on hearsay.

# Chapter 8

## A Rare Unkindness

The Saga of Hervor and Heidrek isn't really about Hervor or Heidrek. The sword, Tyrfing, is the most important character in the story. Strangely, the saga's end does not mention what happened to this most important of characters.

Not the most widely-told versions, at least. All of these followed the same general storyline, though some described huge differences in how the events played out. One time I heard a version that was a bit off, to say the least. It was badly told and easily dismissed. But who could tell if it had some forgotten truth the other versions had lost?

The ravens were ideal to try this out on.

An unkindness of ravens is an expression like a flock of sheep or a herd of goats. But an unkindness is a bit different, because ravens tend to be solitary animals. They may pair up or even form loose groups and winter together for survival, but my experience indicated they preferred to be on their own. Some said they were more spirits than birds—specifically, the spirits of dead skalds. I wasn't sure I believed that.

Ravens love two things more than anything else in the world: One is the fresh eyeballs of the dead, and the other is new and interesting stories. Especially if those stories include humans coming to violent ends. It didn't take much wisdom for a raven to know that Arrow-Odd's army was a likely place to find stories written in blood or fresh eyeballs.

Not ours, of course. The Rus were fair game, though.

Many ravens had gathered near our camp, a bigger group than I'd ever seen. They stayed on the sea cliffs near the camp and occasionally swooped in to talk. The skalds had made a deal with them that there would be a free exchange of news and stories, not tit-for-tat trading. Again, ideal for my purposes, and probably not an opportunity I would see again.

I headed up a gentle slope towards the sea cliffs. The fine granules beneath my feet soon gave way to stones, and then larger rocks, and then boulders. I passed the areas some of us would go to for privacy or solitude, where we could sit on a rock and look at the sea and wonder how we had come to this place so far away.

I climbed up one of the boulders to where the area plateaued ahead of the cliffs. That was when I saw my first bird. Or more like, when he saw me.

"The skald!" croaked Humor, the bird I was so familiar with from his days with Ketill. Ravens were *usually* solitary. And this one would shit on your head if you referred to him as 'Ketill's raven,' but he had attached himself to the wizard for years.

"You do realize there are many skalds in the camp?"

"*The skald is here!*" he called out even louder.

Heads popped up and looked quizzically at each other, croaking in bird-speak rather than any human tongue. A flurry of blue-black wings lifted from a dozen points or more along the rocks. Some beat a path upward and stared down from on high, while most headed straight toward me.

I knew some of these ravens. Their size, the way they cocked their heads or not, and the amount of blue sheen visible through the black of their feathers were a few ways to tell. I knew others from their voices, having traded stories with them before. Humor, of course. I'd met Judgment while traveling east of my home in the fjordlands. Subtlety, I'd met in Fretborg; no surprise she would leave that stinking place.

Those and many more made up the unkindness.

"I think he has a story for us!" shouted Humor.

Coarse cries of approval rose, and wings beat like a round of applause. I wasn't sure if Humor was trying to help or hinder, or just play a joke on me.

A moment passed, and I realized: Of course he's trying to play a joke on me. "Settle down, now. I haven't even stated my purpose in coming here, let alone what I might tell you."

"I bet what he has to tell us is grand!" continued Humor.

"It has been before," added Judgment.

"Oh, you know him?" asked Subtlety.

A quick conversation in ravenspeak erupted among the unkindness, which included a lot of gesturing and hopping. Doubtless, Judgment was telling the stories I had traded to him a few years ago. I wasn't sure what path to take in a forest and got his reluctant help. Then I sort of went my own way, was saved from a witch, won a challenge of wits, and nearly died at the hands of a *draugr*.

A pretty good story!

"Judgment, how is that forest lately? Find any more strangers with good mead?"

"No, I left there soon after you did and flew east. You westerners all talk funny."

I shook my head. "And Subtlety, what did you do after the *Sea Squirrel* left Fretborg?"

"There was plenty to listen to after that," said Subtlety, as if that was the whole story. And of course, that's how she said it. She was Subtlety.

"Maybe you could be more explicit."

"Ah!" said the raven, realizing many eyes were on her. "Halfdan the Toothless sat on the high seat for a while. He was angry he had lost his dwarf, so his new wife, Gulldis, tried to make him feel better. She brought out the things the dwarf had made to show him how much treasure they had. A lot of jewelry. Many small trinkets. Halfdan hated all of them."

"Why was that?"

Subtlety considered this for a moment. "Something was wrong with them. Made of gold and silver and jewels, but the designs made them look sad."

I recalled Finnr telling me about those treasures. *You would not want them. Ill luck went into those pieces, and ill luck will come of them.*

"Perhaps Halfdan had a sense those things were no good," I said.

"Gulldis liked them a lot, but Halfdan didn't seem to like much of what he had in Fretborg." Subtlety was being subtle again, and I took her side-eye after that statement to mean *Halfdan didn't like Gulldis very much.* "He told his crews there were better prospects by joining Ogmund, so he set sail again."

"Halfdan was no *drengr*, but he was crafty," I said. "I suppose he knew a bad deal when he saw one. So, Gulldis is back to calling herself queen?"

"She was looking a bit green when I left to fly north." Subtlety was leaving something out again, but I didn't have the time or patience to figure this one out.

Gulldis would be as happy, or happier, to remain in Fretborg without her new husband. Perhaps she had enough treasures that she would not need new ones to amuse her. Or maybe, just maybe, she would stop sucking all the wealth from the sparse population there, and life in Fretborg would improve. That was a possibility.

A stronger possibility was that her servants would stab her to death, divide up the treasures, and go their own ways. Maybe I would stop by Fretborg one day and see for myself.

"So, lucky skald, what do you have for us?" asked Humor. "I am certain it is very interesting!"

Expectations were high. I didn't want to fall short and then ask for information, so first, a little misdirection. "Nothing so grand as what you've already shared, Humor, of that I have no doubt."

The ravens all looked to him.

"You knew that wizard for how many decades?" I continued. "He must have told you stories. It might be difficult for me to compete with that."

Flapping and croaking needed no translation. As expected, Humor had not shared much on this count.

"Oh, maybe you haven't. Well, there is always tomorrow for that. But let me tell you why I am here before we get too distracted: I want to share the story of Tyrfing for any who don't know it."

"We all know that!" shouted Judgment. "I mean, come on, who doesn't know about the cursed sword, Tyrfing?"

"Do you know how it ends?" I asked.

"Everyone knows that," said Judgment. Dozens of black beaks turned their way toward him. He had said the dumb thing, the thing you never say. It was insulting, at a minimum, to claim *everyone knows* a thing, and probably foolish. Whatever story you claimed *everyone knew* probably had ten different variants. "I mean to say, I expect the version you know would be widely recognized by many of us."

No loss in telling what I knew, but I did not have time to tell the full version. It would need to be a summary. "Tyrfing's story begins with two dwarves forging a sword. A golden hilt and a blade that shone bright as the sun. But in rode a greedy king who caught up the dwarves and bound them, forcing them to give him the sword. If you believe the legends, that king was

Svafrlami, the first King of Gardariki. I'm not sure Gardariki has history that far back, but ignore that. Myths and legends aren't often subject to the requirements of consistency or logic."

Many knowing nods of agreement.

"Svafrlami got his sword, but the dwarves cursed it as he rode away. The sword would kill its owner, for sure, however many times it changed hands. Once drawn, it could not be re-sheathed without the blood of a new victim on the blade. Anyone taking even the slightest cut from it would die of the wound. And just in case the sword's owner was very, very careful, three evil deeds by this sword were guaranteed.

"The king didn't think much of these evil deeds, it seemed. And he thought very much of the sword's power to kill with the slightest cut. That sword could cleave armor or even solid rock like it was butter, too. So for a time, Svafrlami used this weapon to great effect.

"Eventually, he lost a duel in splendid fashion. He fought the *berserkr*, Arngrim, and the sword cut right through the man's shield. Unfortunately for Svafrlami, it cut through part of the shield that Arngrim didn't need all that much, and then continued down into the earth. And there it stuck firm for just a moment.

"In that moment, Arngrim cut off Svaframi's arm. That was the first of the sword's betrayals. But not its first evil deed. Svafrlami wasn't exactly deserving of any better than he got, after all."

"What about the other version?" demanded Judgment.

I sighed. "I should mention that there's a version of the story where Arngrim makes friends with Svafrlami instead, and even marries his daughter. Later, Svafrlami gives Arngrim the sword as a gift. That seems a lot less believable to me, but you can tell the story how you like. Anyway . . .

"Arngrim took the sword and raided all over the world. He had twelve sons, all *berserkir* like him, and the story shortcuts to the eldest of these sons having the sword. His name was Angantyr, the first in his family to have that name. He and his eleven brothers were feared throughout the North.

"That reputation earned them attention from some heroes of the North. Their last fight was with Arrow-Odd and his friend, Hjalmar the Brave.

"Arrow-Odd said he should fight Angantyr because his shirt would protect him against the blade. Hjalmar wouldn't have it, though, as he wanted to be the one to kill Angantyr. He did kill Angantyr, but not before taking just a nick from the sword. Odd finished off Angantyr's eleven brothers by himself, and they won the day, but Hjalmar lay dying from the wound.

"Nobody survives a cut from Tyrfing."

A chorus of "Nobody!" from ravens throughout the unkindness punctuated the statement.

"Odd buried the bodies as per the funeral rites requested before the duel. That meant Tyrfing got buried with Angantyr.

"But that was a long time ago, and not at all Tyrfing's last resting place. Angantyr's daughter, Hervor, came for the sword years later. She even confronted Angantyr's ghost for it. He did not want to give her the sword, but he eventually relented. She took it and raided for years before settling down. Didn't even do any evil deeds with it.

"She handed it down to her son, Heidrek, who some called Heidrek the Wise. He built on his family's reputation and became King of the Goths.

"Heidrek eventually died. Two of his children, Angantyr the Third and Hlod, went to war over how to split up his kingdom. Angantyr led the Goths, and also the Geats, who had fostered him. Hlod led the Huns, who had fostered him.

"Where exactly that all happened, nobody is sure. But if you believe the story, it was a bloody mess. In the final battle, Angantyr met the whole host of Huns in the middle of a river and just hacked them down with Tyrfing. Nothing could withstand him while he wielded that blade. He left so many Huns and their horses dead, the bodies clogged up the river. Then, he slew his half-brother Hlod in single combat.

"Or at least, that's the short version of it."

Knowing nods all around, with low chatter. I waited a few moments and cleared my throat.

"What I want to know is, what happened to the sword?"

"Ohhhhh."

"Ahhhhh."

"Hmmmm."

"Anyone hear anything more than that?" I cleared my throat, but the ravens had nothing to add. Time to offer the addition, then. "I did, one time. See if this is familiar to you.

"Some, and I mean very few, tell about the sad story of what happened after the Battle of the Goths and the Huns. The short of it being that there is no more Gothic kingdom in the south, or not one that I know of. What I have heard might not be knowledge of the events; it could be a mix of lots of different battles over the years. But, anyway, one time I heard about Angantyr's reaction after he killed Hlod.

"Angantyr fell stricken with grief after his victory, too bitter that he'd slain his own brother to continue. He came back to his senses, but he was full of bloodlust all the time after that. The Gothic court ended up scattering, with Angantyr and those still loyal to him traveling north. They headed to Gotland. The storyteller I heard this from said that's why it's called Gotland—because of those Goths that went north. But he also said it was called Gotland because that was where the Goths were from in olden times. I can't say either way. But supposedly, some of them made it to Gotland, Angantyr died there or on the way there, and he didn't leave Tyrfing to anyone."

"That story needs work," said Humor. "Maybe color it up a bit and fill in the unknown parts. Just make some decisions!"

"Maybe fold in a more recent battle and blend in those events?"

"Exactly!"

I shook my head. That was probably why this saga was so full of contradictions. "Anyone hear other details than those?" I paused and waited. The ravens looked at one another, shuffled their feet. "It sounds to me like none of you have anything to add to the end of this story. Maybe Tyrfing is lost forever."

"Riddle!" shouted one raven with a cocked head. His voice had the round softness of a simpleton. When not shouting at me, his tongue lolled outside his beak.

The other ravens began to leave, the prospect of a good story dampened even further by the outburst. Humor stayed put, watching and listening.

"Yes, I know about the contest of riddles in that saga," I said. "But that was between Heidrek and Odin, and I don't think it indicates anything about Tyrfing's whereabouts."

"Riddle!" he shouted again, frantic this time.

Another raven hopped close to him and nuzzled against his neck. He calmed down right away. Then she spoke in his stead.

"He's not himself these last few years," she said with a thick eastern accent.

"You're his mate, then?"

She nodded. "I am Attention. This is—was—Intellect. Now they call him Forgetting."

I winced. "Why would they do that?"

"He can't remember much past the previous minute or so," she said. "Not since the injury. Someone threw a rock and hit him in the head. Most of what he'd learned before, he still remembers," she sighed. "It just comes through in drips and drabs. I try to help him sort through it."

"Who would do that to a raven?"

"Do you know King Athils of Uppsala? It was one of his *berserkir*. I'm not sure which one, though they all laughed about it. We don't go near there anymore. But you had a question!" she brightened all of a sudden, as if helping me would help her mate. "I think he has the story for you. Or part of a story. Try speaking just the barest outline of what you told, but speak slowly."

I nodded and found a rock to sit on. No other ravens had remained besides Humor, so it was just the four of us.

"The dwarves curse the sword," I began. "A family of *berserkir* takes it. Heidrek gets it from Hervor. Then, there's the great Battle of the Goths and Huns. Then, maybe—"

"Wrong way!" shouted Forgetting.

Something in the back of my brain buzzed. "The Goths did not go north?"

Forgetting shook his head.

"No, that's not what he means," said Attention. "He means you have the story the wrong way around."

"I'm confused. How is that?"

"Well," said Attention, "from what I remember Intellect telling me, he had a distant ancestor who went mostly for the roots of stories. That was Curiosity! Nobody much likes the story sources. People prefer the stories that have been told over and over again until they're so familiar, they can't be questioned. Even if they're really bits of a lot of different stories."

"Are you telling me that this Curiosity found the ultimate source of Tyrfing's story?"

"More like found a part that was wrong." She turned to her mate. "'Wrong way' doesn't mean direction, does it?"

Forgetting shook his head, his tongue slipping from one side of his beak to the other.

I scratched at my beard. "You mean it's the story's order that's reversed."

Forgetting switched to an aggressive nod for a few seconds before stopping and fixing me with a blank stare.

"Who are you?" he asked.

If I ever found the *berserkr* responsible for turning Intellect into Forgetting, it would be time to have Kraki boil a man after all.

"It's okay, he's a friend," said Attention. "He's asking about the Battle of the Goths and Huns."

"Ohhhhhhhhh," said Forgetting.

Forgetting pulled in his tongue and met my gaze. A wall in his eyes came down for just that brief moment, and I knew he was as lucid as he might ever be these days.

"Goths and Huns was before everything, not after."

Goat's breath and cat piss, how could I have not seen that? The wrong history with the King of Gardariki, the timeline that never made sense with the Goths. Geats showing up half a world away. "That makes much more sense, but *how* did Curiosity determine that?"

"Told a big lie!"

"Who told a big lie?" I asked, desperate to keep the desperation out of my voice.

"Wise! Not wise!" The raven sounded as desperate as I did. As he spoke, the wall in his eyes came down again, and he struggled to say even those words. His head lolled to the side, and his tongue fell out of his beak once more.

Attention nuzzled her mate to calm him. "Understand, please, this was never a story to be traded. It was told in confidence, and then handed down in Intellect's family to preserve it."

"Told in confidence—to Curiosity? Who did the telling?"

"A champion at Uppsala," said Attention. "That's what he's trying to tell you. King Athils' grandfather was quite good at finding the best champions to keep at court. One of those champions, the one who told this story, was a man named Heidrek, who some called Wise."

Ymir's bones!

"But this man was no Gothic king," she continued. "He was not a lord at all."

"This Heidrek," I said, "where did he come from? Did he have Tyrfing?"

"South!" shouted Forgetting.

"That's as many details as I recall about that," added Attention. "This man did not discuss his origins. And he never spoke about Tyrfing."

"But he confided in Curiosity that the saga, as most people know it, is wrong?"

Attention nodded. "This one thing, apparently, he felt the need to tell. Only that the story was reversed, though, and not a full or true version of it."

"But not a king? Maybe he was made a jarl later?"

"No," said Attention. "Athils' family would . . . not have allowed that."

Of course the legends didn't add up, because they had been mosaics with ancient names attached to them while trying to depict events across centuries, all held together with half-truths as glue.

"Arrow-Odd buried that sword with Angantyr," I said. "That much seems to be true. Now I hear of Heidrek the Wise. Does that mean Hervor taking the sword from Angantyr's grave is true as well?"

"I don't know," said Attention. "It could be this Heidrek the Wise got his name as a reference to the saga rather than because he is the same Heidrek."

"Riddle!" Forgetting shouted again.

And then I understood Forgetting's initial outburst. He didn't mean the contest of riddles. What was left of Intellect was trying to tell me the whole saga was a giant riddle. One that even he didn't have the answer to.

I had heard of Athils: Crafty as Halfdan the Toothless, though much more powerful. A sorcerer, some said. And a keeper of *berserkir* who had injured a raven.

That was where I needed to go? I would need to be as lucky as my reputation indicated to deal with a king like that. Giving the ravens another glance, I hoped for something more. Some piece of insight or wisdom I could keep tucked away that might prove useful in a difficult situation.

"Who are you?" asked Forgetting.

# CHAPTER 9

# GRINS OF THE FATHER

I'D GOTTEN MORE FROM THE RAVENS THAN I'D EXPECTED, WHICH was good. And in doing so, I'd added another sorcerer for us to deal with in King Athils.

I made my way over the rocky ground back to the war camp proper. Out there, on the incline toward the sea cliffs, things seemed peaceful and simple. I wanted to linger and enjoy the light smell of salt and the sound of waves lapping at the shore, but there was no time to delay.

A few men and women starting a late cook fire nodded as I passed by. Josur the Daring's people, I knew. Josur being a young jarl and sworn directly to Arrow-Odd rather than Gardar or Sirnir. I nodded back, and some even smiled when they saw me. Perhaps I would have stopped to talk on another day, but I had to get back to my crew. We had decisions to make.

I guessed Kraki would be willing to sail to Uppsala. But the rest of the crew? They might want revenge on Alfhild more than the destruction of her jewelry. I could argue the two goals were one and the same. If Magnus agreed with me, and I knew he would, the others would follow. But would that make sense, or would it make more sense to attack Alfhild while we still had the army with us?

The situation was as clear as the muddy thoroughfare I trudged through, and it was about to get muddier. Lucky for me, I had friends. One of them yanked hard on my arm while I was lost in thought.

I whirled around, expecting to see one of the bigger men from the crew. Maybe Moose-Frothi or Vilgrip. Bjorn, if it was a skald. Instead, it was Nanthild. Still a head and some shorter than I was, still with the slight frame and delicate features of a young woman. Still silent, ever since her brother Ulfberht was killed at Lejre.

I stumbled after the pull, and she let up. "Are you ever going to explain this uncanny strength of yours?"

She shrugged. I've still never seen a sweeter face wearing a chain shirt and sword.

"Right, hard to explain when you can't talk," I continued. "Well, you have my attention."

She made a motion around her neck and then pointed in the direction of Sirnir's tents. Then toward Gardar's tents. Then, she opened her hand and closed it over a phantom necklace.

"Sirnir and Gardar," I said, "and the Brisingamen. They want to use it, no doubt." It dawned on me that possessing a powerful artifact from the gods might change the dynamics of the camp. I had been foolish not to consider that.

Nanthild shook her head. She opened her hand and closed it over my neck instead of her own, yanking it away.

"They mean to take it? Where did you hear this?"

Languages change and mores change, but there are a few hand gestures that are unmistakable through time and culture. Nanthild made a circle with her left hand and then stuck one finger of her right hand into the circle. Then she pulled it out and put it back in a few times. There was no mistaking what she meant. But referencing Steinvor that way, how did she know we had . . .

My face turned beet red. I think I managed a nod.

Nanthild shrugged as if sorry to embarrass me so, but she really had no choice.

"Shit!" I said it in reference to Nanthild knowing I'd slept with Steinvor. "Shit!" I repeated, realizing that, if those two jarls decided to take the Brisingamen from me, I could do very little about it.

Nanthild nodded, seeming to agree that my situation was, indeed, shit. We hurried through the camp with my heart in my throat.

My heart stayed right there as we came near the injury tents. We were close to the open area in front of the tents, where Borisu Youdog had been staked for questioning, when I heard Gardar and Sirnir. They were arguing with

Magnus, something about Borisu and the torc. Magnus stood by Borisu, who was still tied to the same pole.

I hissed at Nanthild to stay with me as I turned off the path and hid behind a tent to peek around. Both jarls had brought three warriors each. Not just men with weapons, but their big champions in good armor.

Nanthild's hand went to the hilt of her sword. I put a hand on her wrist before she could fully draw.

"Not an attempt to take the Brisingamen," I whispered. "Not with so few men." So few men that either Nanthild or Magnus, alone, would probably kill them all. And tear the army apart in the process. I had to fix this, somehow. "It will sound cowardly if people say I was avoiding them, so I will confront them here in the open. Better if the whole thing is heard and seen by more people, though, especially ours. Go find who you can of the crew, and tell them to come armed."

She blinked at me.

"I don't know, use hand gestures!"

Nanthild sprinted off toward our little section of camp. No doubt she would find some help, but I needed an armed presence big enough to prevent a melee. Hopefully, Magnus was enough presence to deter them from any immediate stupidity.

Gardar and Sirnir's people were between me and Magnus, so I didn't reveal myself right away. I walked back up the path a bit and came into the open area at an angle so I could head for Magnus. He saw me coming and interrupted the conversation.

"Be reasonable, Sirnir! Promises were made. Oaths were sworn! And if I recall, the skins of all you fine gentlemen were saved by one of our 'hangers-on,' as you put it."

"You must be reasonable yourself," said Sirnir. "You went treasure-hunting while our army fought back an onslaught. We lost many good men and have little compensation for that fighting. Now, here is a powerful artifact, but your skald speaks not of using it for our benefit, only of destroying it."

"He talks about more than that," countered Magnus. "He also talks about poetry, stories, and who has the best ale in Midgard. If you took more interest in such things, Sirnir, it's likely you'd be a cheerier person."

My friend was delaying and distracting, giving me a chance to go somewhere else. But no, better to have the confrontation now than later.

Gardar sighed. "Magnus, this is not a time for jokes."

"Who is joking? I know you've had bad ale before, Gardar, and I don't imagine you'd care to have it again. Too much sour ale, and your asshole will clench up forever, and then you won't be able to—"

"Silfast has the best ale," I interrupted. "The best I've had, at least. Perhaps he is just the most generous host and willing to share his best with all his guests rather than a select few." I made it to Magnus' side, and stared back at the many stares aimed at me.

"An apt comparison," said Sirnir. "To share generously rather than hoard is why we're here. This treasure you've found may be of some help, especially with Arrow-Odd still ill in his tent."

"Is that your intent as well, Gardar?" I asked. "You think the Brisingamen could benefit the camp if we used it for . . . 'some help'?"

"It was a thing our enemies did not wish to part with," said Gardar. "It would hearten the men if we could put the thing to use."

I gestured at Borisu. "Your timing is excellent, then. We can demonstrate the thing's power for you." For the second time that day, I was glad I had prevented Kraki from setting a man's balls on fire. "Borisu Youdog! You have visitors."

The prisoner had taken little interest in the argument up to that point. He lifted his head just enough to show his sneer, and then dropped his head again.

"I will give the man some ale," said Magnus, who tossed a nearby bucket of water into Borisu's face. "The ale was very young, unfortunately. Not even really ale yet, I suppose, but I'm sure he understands the good intent behind the gesture."

"Thank you, Magnus," I said. "Here is an example of the Brisingamen's power."

"I see a man," said Gardar. "Not one of any particular note."

"Not a great specimen, in fact," added Sirnir.

Borisu spat in their direction.

"You jarls are often quick to judge such things," I said. "Even quicker to seize anything with power attached to it. If all you see is a man, then you definitely should not get anywhere near that torc."

"We will be the judge of that," said Sirnir.

"Hard to judge without knowing his story. Let me tell you a little of it. How do you think Ogmund Tussock became 'King Valdar' in Gardariki?

Borisu has seen what Ogmund offers, even seen him wearing the torc before he must have given it to Alfhild. But to Borisu, Valdar is more than a king. I think he understands enough Norse to follow. Is all that right, Borisu? Is Ogmund a god?"

"*There is nothing more clear in the world. And he offers the greatest of gifts.*"

I translated from Greek for the benefit of the others.

"*What does Ogmund offer his servants?*" I asked.

"*Power. Transcendence. A boon to open the eyes and see the world as it is.*"

I explained all that in Norse before continuing, "Here is the power of the Brisingamen, the power you think to wield with ease. The torc has poisoned Borisu's thoughts against *anything* but loyalty to Ogmund. If I told Borisu that Ogmund was ugly, he would say that was a lie, that Ogmund was—"

Borisu spat on my pants. Rhetoric: Excellent. Timing and positioning: Not ideal. I stepped away.

"If it is with ease, so much the better," said Gardar.

I balked, looking from Sirnir to Gardar. Then, from champion to champion. The lords were impatient, and their warriors were getting restless. I looked around and still did not see Nanthild or the others. That worried me.

What worried me more was the lone figure coming to join the impromptu meeting. Worried me, and made my blood boil at the same time. Styrgrim the Bear was known to all as my wayward father. Both of us knew he was no such relation. Whoever my father was had fair hair and was likely a god. Styrgrim's hair was black, marked with the gray of age. Thick, wavy strands of it heaved with the fast pace of his approach.

I had made a little peace with the man, but not much. If he joined in this rabble, it would tip the scales against me. I would not forgive him for throwing his support behind this abortive plan of Gardar and Sirnir.

To win fame with prowess in battle is an honorable thing, even if it was not my way. To court influence by convincing people was another, and that was my way. But to gain it by trickery of wearing magic jewelry? The idea of winning an audience by dumbing people down rather than lifting them up disgusted me. Doing a thing like that would be a tacit admission of weakness. And one thing I had thought of Styrgrim was that he was no weak man.

"I agree, we could use something easy," said Sirnir. "Now, let us see the torc. We have heard enough from inconsequential men."

"Ooooh!" cooed Svipul from behind me. My *fylgja* had come out of nowhere, which was standard for her. She was also my long-dead mother, and only I could hear or see her. "I suspect Styrgrim the Bear would like to hear more on that subject, don't you?"

She backed away as if the whole situation had been resolved with that sideways comment. Was she getting more vague? It was difficult to tell. Maybe she only spoke at length when there was time for speaking, and now was not such a time. Or maybe she knew I would understand the intended line of attack. Which I did.

"Inconsequential men." I spoke those words through my teeth, eyeing Styrgrim as I did, and continued in a louder voice. "It seems to me, Sirnir, that you consider all those who aren't jarls to be inconsequential."

"It seems to me," said Sirnir, "that by definition, they are."

Stygrim's predatory grin told me he had not come to join them. The black of his leathers was so dark, it seemed to suck the light away from his mail shirt. In black and silver, he sidled up behind the biggest of the champions. One of Sirnir's men, based on his position.

"And yet, I heard no tales of your consequence when the Rus attacked," I said. "In Alfhild's fortress, your brother, Haldor, was in the front line. Then, forward of the line, he took the biggest risks himself. He slew a monster that would have taken your head in seconds. Meanwhile, I heard you hid in a tent at the sound of the dragon's first fart." Sirnir's eyes went wide enough for me to see the whites all around them while his face went red. "I should add that my father always told me it was inappropriate for children to handle weapons they did not understand."

I never said the intended line of attack was a subtle one. Styrgrim grinned at the further insult to Sirnir, the white of his teeth showing strong approval.

"You stupid shitling!" roared that biggest of champions. "I'll—"

Styrgrim got his attention just enough to have him turn around. The Bear grinned as he unloaded a punch as hard as I've ever seen up under the man's ribs. A liver shot, and not by chance. Had the man not been wearing a chain shirt, I'm confident that blow would have killed him. Instead, it just made him wish he'd died.

The champion closest to the downed man turned, but not fast enough to prevent Styrgrim from kicking his knee in sideways. He stumbled and took a mailed elbow to the head on the way down to the mud.

The next closest man had time to draw the axe in his belt but not enough time to square up. Styrgrim grinned as he charged him, shouldering into the champion low, and lifted him up by his ass. He pitched the champion backwards over his head, landing him face-first.

Three remaining champions surrounded Styrgrim, their weapons drawn. They circled him and tested distance and reaction as they feinted forward or to the side. Styrgrim looked around, but did not react. Not even to draw his sword.

Relief coursed through me when I saw Nanthild round one of the tents. Vilgrip shot past her, a spear in his one hand. Moose-Frothi and his brother, Thorir Houndsfoot, padded close behind. Kraki followed, his limping gait making for a slower charge than the others. Any one of them might take those three remainders.

Styrgrim saw them coming and put a hand up to hold them back.

One champion moved in to strike, his shield held high. Styrgrim made a hint of a move rather than committing, taking a step that was not a step. In that short time and space, the hint manipulated where the man's axe fell. For a moment, it looked as though it would find its target, but missed by a hair's breadth.

Both his hands free, Styrgrim grabbed the man's wrist with his right hand and stretched it out. He grinned as he smashed his left forearm into the man's locked elbow. The arm bent in the wrong direction with a wet crunch.

To that champion's credit, he took the injury and was still in the fight until Styrgrim's right fist careened into his face, heedless of the steel helmet protecting it. The champion stumbled backwards and fell to the ground, visibly dazed.

Blood dripped from Styrgrim's knuckles as he grinned at the remaining champions.

"Enough!" shouted Gardar. "This was to be a conversation, not some back-hills brawl."

"You didn't bring enough men for a brawl," grinned Styrgrim. "If what you brought can be called men."

One of the two remainders growled, apparently unwilling to stand for that insult. Styrgrim grinned as he shot forward at the growling man. Grabbing the rim of the man's shield with both hands, he twisted it one way and then the other in a sharp motion.

The champion had kept a tight grip. He grimaced as his wrist twisted at an awkward angle. With full control of the shield, Styrgrim shoved the rim into the man's weapon arm, preventing an attack. The champion let go of the shield, perhaps with good reason, but took a knuckle strike to the throat immediately after.

As the man fell, gasping for air, the lone standing champion was behind Styrgrim. He readied to throw his axe. I wanted to shout, to warn Styrgrim of the unseen danger, but I knew my words would take too long, and I felt my tongue tied in a knot as the throwing arm arced up . . .

. . . and released almost straight up into the air. An arrow had shot through the man's forearm.

About thirty yards away, a tall, broad figure wearing a garish red cloak and a golden headband eyed the result of his shot. He pulled another arrow from his goatskin quiver without looking away from his target. Arrow-Odd looked his old self, with none of the signs of old age I had seen earlier.

Styrgrim turned to see what work had been done on his behalf, and he grinned again as he addressed Gardar and Sirnir.

"I heard you might challenge my son for his jewelry," he roared. "But he stole that torc fair and square, and I prefer him as its owner to either of you. Now, take heed of that preference, and take better care of your champions. If I smell another such challenge brewing, I might draw my sword."

Wordless, the jarls picked up their champions and guided them back to their camps.

Ogmund said he was as much spirit as man, and that was why Arrow-Odd couldn't kill him. That was the day I realized many whispered a similar thing about Styrgrim the Bear. With Arrow-Odd absent, fear had held the army against breaking up. Fear of Styrgrim the Bear, that he was as much demon as man. He was Odd's demon, one that nobody wanted coming for them, even with an army at their command. And while I still could not bring myself to like the man, I decided this might be an important thing to remember in the months to come.

## Chapter 10

# The Will of the Crazy People

It didn't take Arrow-Odd long to decide: At the next dawn, he would lead an assault on Alfhild's island fortress and any ships nearby.

What was undecided was who led the crew of the *Sea Squirrel* on land. That left us in an unfamiliar situation, and I was grateful that Kraki knew how we would decide.

The crew gathered round a central fire after the evening meal. We didn't need the fire to see, as it would be daylight and then twilight-like long into the night, but it seemed appropriate for the occasion. People sat on logs or benches or whatever they could find, except for Moose-Frothi, who stood.

So many missing faces. I would have given much to hear Haldor's booming voice again, or the snide banter of the 'Steins as they played *hnefatafl*. Three of our best, gone. Also Ulf, Svein, and Hemming, but they had turned on us. Hemming had tried to warn me at the last moment, at least, but that was little comfort.

There were new faces to replace the old, and more. Many of those who'd signed up to travel with Haldor Skullsplitter, but were not sworn Brothers, had left us. Haldor's loss lessened the draw of the *Sea Squirrel*, and plenty of captains were eager to pay for new recruits. But some of the freed prisoners had seen Haldor die for their freedom, and they joined our crew, Frothi and his brother, Thorir Houndsfoot, among them. I hadn't seen Thorir's feet, but

Moose-Frothi was named quite literally, having the hips and legs of a moose. They were in for revenge: Revenge for their folk who'd been killed, revenge for their kidnappings, revenge for Haldor.

Vilgrip joined us as well. The one-handed son of Tyr had resisted Alfhild's allure even as she wore the Brisingamen to influence him. He cared little about Alfhild, however. Svart had cut off his right hand in a capricious attempt to see if it gave the man any god-like powers. It had done no such thing. Luckily enough for Vilgrip, he was a natural left-hander.

We offered those three their armrings if they wanted to be part of the Brotherhood. They did, and there were no objections.

Not all our new recruits were those we'd set free. A few came from the camp, willing to sail with us but not yet ready to swear loyalty on a permanent basis. No fame-seekers here, no one enamored of Haldor Skullsplitter's name. They came for Huld, having defended her while she turned the sea against the Bjarmian navy. I knew few of these. They were welcome to listen, but only those with armrings could speak.

The crew of the *Sea Squirrel* was still made of mighty folk, but who would command them while not at sea? I'd already played out the possibilities in my head. Ingolf was too quiet and sullen. A reliable man, but not an inspiration. Huld kept her motives to herself. Even those she inspired were more in awe of her power than confident in her leadership. Ketill was too frustrated even by teaching archery skills to those in the army and showed no inclination to lead. Nanthild was a reasonable choice, but for that rather significant drawback of being unable to speak.

It still seemed clear enough to me: Magnus must lead on land.

He'd worn the armring for years as a man of Haldor's Brotherhood. He'd crewed with Styrgrim before that. He was cheery, implacable—a man we could all follow through good times and bad.

Low conversation came and went, and we all looked to the fire, or to the sky, or to each other for some sort of sign. Everyone knew what was to be decided, but not how to begin. This sort of thing had been Ulf's job before he betrayed us, and it wasn't something I had a talent for. I stood up, anyway, and pitched my voice for all to hear.

"So, we sail tomorrow morning." Lame. Also, it sounded like overstepping until I added, "That is Kraki's decision."

Kraki nodded. I hoped he might say something. Soon, it was clear the nod was as much as I could expect. No help there.

"But Kraki does not lead on land," I continued as Kraki shook his head. "Haldor led us on land. It was his Brotherhood, Haldor's Heroes, who wore his armring. Now, there is still the Brotherhood because our bond is not easily broken. But who leads on land is what we must decide, and we must decide tonight, as tomorrow we sail into battle."

Nods, murmurs of agreement. Things were going well. I decided it was time to make my play for Magnus to lead us.

Magnus was not just my closest friend, but a man I knew everyone could trust. A bit brash and cavalier, sure. And not the choicest warrior for the head of a charging swine array. But it had turned out that our best shield wall fighters were dead or gone, and those taking their places were almost all free-fighters, like Magnus.

"It seems to me that not one of us is a good choice to replace Haldor Skullsplitter," I continued. "No one can match him for holding the shield wall. No one can match his voice for command. So we should not pretend we can choose a person quite like him. He was unique. Now we need another unique leader, and I think there is only one reasonable choice."

I cleared my throat, buying more time to gauge the crowd. No reactions yet either way. Maybe they knew where I was going and were just waiting.

Magnus stood up. "There is one thing I think is important to say before you go any further."

I nodded and sat down, but I was confused. Why interrupt when he was about to accept the burden of leadership?

"You all know me," said Magnus. "Maybe just for a few days, but you know me. I trained with Haldor, and I knew his mind on many things. He would not have been satisfied with revenge on Ulf and Alfhild and letting the Brisingamen loose in the hands of others. He would say we had to destroy it. Who will tell me I'm wrong about that?" Murmurs and shaken heads. Nobody could deny this. "It will be a tricky thing, though. We will need more than one ship, yet we don't swear oaths except to one another. We will need the next leader on land to be tricky, too."

"And that is why we need—" I tried to say, but was cut off.

"That is why Ansgar the Skald must lead," bellowed Magnus.

No murmurs. No nods or head shakes. Just stunned silence, especially from me. I stood there, frozen, afraid to ask what was going on, afraid to show surprise. Even more afraid to agree.

"This skinny thing?" Moose-Frothi asked, an outstretched thumb pointing in my direction. "He was the weakest part of the shield wall, other than the dying men."

"You mean those prisoners not so hardy as you and your brother?" asked Magnus. "It's fair to say he is no Haldor. But you made no disagreement about needing someone quite different from Haldor."

"I don't like it," said Frothi. "It's *too* different."

"Did you like weapons and shields brought to the prisoners?" demanded Vilgrip. "It was Ansgar who made that happen. And it was Ansgar who stole Alfhild's torc, which confounded her and helped us escape that place."

"Hmph!"

"Let's give credit where it's due, brother," growled Thorir. "But let's also be clear: It was you, Vilgrip, who knew where Alfhild's chambers were. That's credit to you, however involved the skald might have been."

"Who do you think got me out of the pit in the first place? He saved my life, stole the witch's torc, and doubled back for his people when he realized there was a trap. And he's the only one who's drawn blood on their old mate, Ulf."

Moose-Frothi grunted in approval at that. He had respect for the drawing and shedding of blood, if little else.

"Ingolf!" shouted Magnus. "You were with us in Lejre's burning hall when we were trapped inside. Who got us out of there?"

"That was Ansgar," said Ingolf with no hesitation. "Turned into a giant bear and broke through a wall. He tore Alfhild's biggest champions apart after that."

"Huld!" shouted Magnus. "How did that leave Ansgar? Was it easy for him?"

"It nearly killed him twice over," said Huld. "But for my help, he would be dead. That sort of skin change is no easy thing, even without the many injuries he endured."

Nods and murmurs. Many of the newer people had not been with us at the time. It had not occurred to me to tell my own story to them. Hearing it for myself, it was an impressive thing. If you don't count the fact that I had no idea why it was happening at the time.

"Nanthild!" shouted Magnus. "Last winter, you were lost in a blizzard with an injured friend. And that was no regular snowstorm. It was *seiðr* so strong, you couldn't find your way out of it. Who saw you and chased you down despite the danger? Who spoke a verse to cut through the spell and save you both?"

Nanthild stood and stepped forward. With one raised finger, she pointed at me as she locked eyes with each crewmate in turn.

Nods became vigorous. Murmurs turned into shouts of approval.

"Kraki!" shouted Magnus. "When you went to the Down-Below and sent Ansgar to parley, what did he return with?"

"He stole a book of Roman lore from those shits," said Kraki. "And freed a captive. No one we much cared for, it's true. But it would have been worse to leave her to the trolls there, so he was right to do it."

"We learned much from her," said Magnus. "Even some things we did not intend on learning. If I recall, Ansgar was ready to leave the crew unless you sailed where he thought we ought to go. Tell us, Ketill, why was that?"

"There's little to tell about that," said the wizard. "He sought the deep lore, where few can travel to and return with their minds intact. From what he learned, he swore revenge on Varg the Charmer."

"And took it," added Kraki. "We sought out that sorcerer and his demon cow. We ate the cow, and sent Varg to Hel without his manhood."

'Little to tell about that,' my ass. And the crew knew it, even those who had not been there. There was little love for Varg the Charmer. That we'd overcome his magic battle cow was worth celebrating by itself.

We had not, strictly speaking, eaten that cursed thing, but I was not about to make a correction. Not that I could have. Now there was no holding back the reactions of the crew.

All were on their feet. Fists pumped the air and banged chests. Whoops and howls echoed through the camp, turning the heads of our neighbors. Even Moose-Frothi nodded, having heard of enough violence that he approved of me after all.

I looked at Magnus. "This was not according to my plan."

"You didn't mention a plan. But I got the distinct feeling you had one, and that it involved a foolish idea."

"And your idea is full of wisdom?" I asked, shaking my head. "A rare source, if I've ever seen one."

"You're a skald," he replied with a grin. "Shouldn't you welcome wisdom, wherever it comes from?"

# CHAPTER 11

# HOLLOW MOUNTAIN

Part of Arrow-Odd's legend was that he could call the wind when any sail was ready to take it, and that part of the legend was true. So what would have been a long journey to Alfhild's island fortress was much shorter the second time around. We took a small attack force, intending to hit hard and fade away. Five ships ferried the best warriors we had.

Odd's ship, the *Whaleslayer*, led the way as the sleekest of warships. Not far behind him and to one side was the *Long Claw*, under Styrgrim's command. Sirnir and Gardar kept close in their main ships, *Ran's Favorite* and *Aegir's Favorite*, respectively.

Some of our crew complained that the *Sea Squirrel* lagged behind in the rear, as if we were, ironically, the least important part of the attack on Alfhild's tower. Our ship was built for more than war—it could bring warriors to battle as well as haul supplies or deliver trading goods. The wider hull meant greater versatility, but less speed.

Kraki asked, loudly, whether the complainers thought a narrower ship would be better. Nobody answered, and that was the end of the complaining.

I did not mind being at the rear of that formation, as I was in no rush to arrive. I wasn't sure what we would find other than battle, and I wasn't sure how to command in a battle whatsoever. So I thought of everything I might do in advance, including asking Ketill to make a triangle with his hands as we approached Alfhild's tower.

You could see much if you looked through a sorcerer's hands—maybe something as it more truly was, or as it was to be. Ketill just shook his head, though. "The sky is gray and lifeless. The sea is opaque, even in the shallows. And that . . ." he trailed off, pointing at the island, "that is no good place."

You didn't need to be a wizard to know that much.

Most of the island was a solid mountain, with Alfhild's fortress carved out of its insides. A narrow beach with a small dock was the only place five ships could land. We knew from our previous trip that the other sides barely had enough room for a single ship to beach, and anyone disembarking from there would face a steep climb up the mountainside. Our only way into that mountain was onto the beach and up a long set of broad stone steps that led to the front door.

Odd's rudder man, Hjalti, signaled that we should moor at the dock behind the other ships. I relayed the command to Kraki, and halfway through, realized it couldn't be a command. I rephrased it as a suggestion, but the awkwardness remained. He pulled in as suggested.

No ships were moored there besides the ones we'd brought, and we hadn't seen any at sea. That didn't mean no people inside, of course. We were still mooring the ship when Arrow-Odd led his people off the dock and onto land, forming a skirmish line ahead of everyone else.

Our people had been well-outfitted for war. Those few who could not afford chain shirts and steel helmets had been gifted them by Odd. And by "gifted," I mean "redistributed from people he liked a bit less." So, despite them owning little more than the shirts on their backs, Thorir Houndsfoot and Moose-Frothi were outfitted as well as jarls. Well, almost. Hard to find a full chain shirt for Frothi's proportions, so he had sewn spare bits of chain into a patchwork on his tunic.

I hate wearing armor. But I led the crew on land now, and there were expectations. I got away with a lighter chain shirt rather than a heavier one, at least. The steel helmet was good protection, but was uncomfortable and made it difficult to hear.

I heard Odd call for the captains despite the helmet. When I looked over my shoulder at Kraki, he was quick to remind me. "That means you, skald." As we had just reached land, of course it was me.

I hopped over the gunwale and onto the dock, stumbling as the weight of the armor threw off my balance. Could I even run in this getup? I hurried up the dock to meet with the other captains and tested that idea. Yes, though not nearly as fast as without it.

"No resistance," said Odd. Then, looking at Styrgrim, he continued, "A trap, as it was for you the first time?"

Styrgrim shrugged. "We're their equal in numbers or more this time. If they surround us, so much the better."

"What do you say, skald?" asked Sirnir.

I thought about it for a long moment. I had a bad feeling about what we'd find inside. Past experience predicts the future, after all. But my suspicion was that Sirnir only asked my opinion to see if it would clash with Styrgrim's, so I imagine it surprised him when I had something more interesting to say.

"Send our people in first."

Odd grinned, fixing me with a quizzical look. Sirnir raised an eyebrow the breadth of a fly's wing. Styrgrim shook his head.

"My crew wants Alfhild's head, and most of them are poor shield wall fighters. Send us through first, and we'll charge the witch if she's there. Squaring up and establishing a shield wall first, that might make sense against a conventional army, but not here. Not if it gives her time to conjure a spell."

"And when you're surrounded in your charge?" growled Styrgrim.

"Then you advance your shield wall against an enemy that doesn't know which way to face."

Styrgrim's head stopped shaking. "They won't expect that." After a moment, I thought I even detected a slight nod.

"Very well," agreed Odd. "The *Sea Squirrel* crew is first through. We'll come through behind you. Go tell your people."

I nodded and headed back to the crew. All were ready, or as ready as they might be. Ketill had strung his longbow and already nocked an arrow. I was not sure how to deploy him. Then there was Huld, who had come with us this time, and I was even less certain what to do with her.

I gathered our crew and explained the idea, adding, "Stay together." Moose-Frothi and Thorir Houndsfoot smirked as I spoke, and I knew they would easily outrun the others.

"It seems to me that the faster we get to the witch, the better," growled Frothi.

"Alfhild isn't for you two, or the rest of you fools, either," said Huld. "But I'll do what I can to keep you alive."

"It's unlikely to be that simple," said Ketill.

And then half the crew was talking, adding their thoughts to the mix. I said something that nobody heard, then repeated myself to have only Nanthild hear. She eyed me, drew her sword, and banged the flat of the blade loudly on her shield boss twice. The voices quieted.

"As I was saying," I continued, grateful for the interruption, "charge through and go for Alfhild if she's there, but do it together."

"That's clear enough," said Magnus. "What if she's not there?"

*I have no idea.* "No plan survives the first arrow's flight," I said, hoping that was sufficiently vague to mask my uncertainty.

"Are you ready?" called Arrow-Odd.

I turned around and told my crew to fall in line, intending to keep a formation of two abreast all the way up those steps and into the corridor. Who should be at the front of the formation?

Oh. Me.

Magnus shouldered his way past me. "Are *you* ready?" he shouted back at Odd. "We've got two sorcerers to deploy."

"So?"

"So *you're welcome,* as we all know *you don't have any!*"

If there was ever a better second in command than Magnus, I don't know who that could have been. In one moment, he reduced the pressure on me and reminded me I had forgotten something. All without me losing face.

Huld stepped in close to me and whispered. "Alfhild is mine as much as Ulf is yours." I'd never heard Huld speak much of Alfhild other than to warn me to watch out for her early on. This sounded like something more.

"If you engage her, you will need protection," I said. "Ketill: Stay close to Huld and shoot anything that even vaguely threatens her."

"Enough of this!" Odd shouted through grinding teeth. The *vǫlva*'s mere presence was enough to set him on edge.

"Enough after you provide a few warriors dedicated to guarding her," I said. "We're at the front. She needs to be near the rear. If Alfhild readies a spell, Huld is the counter."

If that happened and the charge failed, though, I would be dead. Which reminded me that I didn't fight well in a shield wall, and I was even worse outside a shield wall.

Magnus waved us forward. I hoped nobody saw me swallow hard.

We headed up those long stairs, two abreast, and up to the passageway leading into the fortress. Our exit from that place was now the entrance again, a dark tunnel I had no desire to revisit. Planning and recommending an attack was one thing. Now that I heard mail clink and weapons butt against linden shields, I wondered if I had really gotten what I wanted. As I stepped into the tunnel, my hands were numb.

*Breathe, remember to breathe.* I breathed, and my breath echoed through that blasted steel helmet and was soon the only thing I could hear. The moss and salt brine smell brought back exactly where I was: Grimhild, Ogmund's troll of a mother, had been even more ghastly than the stories let on here. Haldor Skullsplitter had his last laugh here after slaying her. Ulf and Svein took their traitorous masks off here. The 'Steins stood their ground for chosen family at the cost of their own lives here.

And I had stolen a piece of jewelry. My head hung with the inadequacy of that as I remembered how much more others had given.

The butt of an axe knocked into the side of my helmet. Hard.

I looked to my right, and Magnus glared back. For just a moment, I swore I saw his eyes glow orange as fire, as if torchlight ahead glinted off them, only there was no torchlight ahead. He knocked axe and seax together twice. *Bang bang. Might and main.* The same as Haldor had at the Battle of Lejre. I nodded. It was not an understanding either one of us could speak, only one we could feel. Magnus had said it more eloquently than I could have done in any verse.

We emerged from the tunnel into the cavernous chamber we'd fought so hard to escape. I held my shield high against whatever we might find there, and charged forward with Need humming in my hand. Echoes of feet slapping the wet stone and armor clinking were the only sounds I could make out. My eyes adjusted to the darkness well enough to see no enemy host on the ground floor.

I checked the most likely places for enemies. Ambush from the staircases to either side of the tunnel? Nothing. Archers on the higher floors? I didn't see anyone there, either.

I can see well in the dark, and my hearing is acute. But even I couldn't make out any sounds other than from my sides and behind me. A few dozen strides in, I slowed down. Something was wrong, but it was a different sort of wrong than the last time.

"Hold!" I shouted, gesturing for everyone to stop.

Moose-Frothi growled at my side, his brother, Thorir, on Magnus' opposite side.

Thorir sniffed loudly, making even less happy sounds than Frothi, and that was saying something. Iron and bile swirled together in a state of humid rot. The smell was far worse than the camp, and not just because it was under a roof.

"He'll go crazy if you make him stand still for a smell that strong," Frothi said of his brother.

I looked at Thorir's twitching face and believed he really was part dog. The smell was clearly worse for him than for any of us. But I didn't know what to do with him or how to direct my free-fighters since there was no fight. Magnus must have read it on my face.

"You two," he gestured with his axe at Frothi and Thorir, "and Vilgrip," he continued, pointing with his seax. "You three spent some time here. Check the next level."

"And if we find the enemy?" asked Vilgrip.

"If the enemy is few, kill them. If numerous, draw them back here."

Right. Scouts. Good idea.

My eyes fixated on something ahead of us. It was still a long way across that floor to the contained area where Alfhild had kept her prisoners. A gap just wide enough for a few abreast led to the cells. Something hung above that gap now, something I couldn't quite recognize in the dimness. As I approached it, the smell got stronger.

Time slowed down as I got close enough to make out the severed arm hanging above the prison's entryway. A big one. Just an arm could not account for that smell, though.

I passed through the gap feeling like I had crossed the bridge to Hel. Piles of bodies littered the cells. I say bodies, but few were left whole. Those that still had all their limbs had muscles and organs stripped away. Intestines and bile pooled in one of the cells. Bones lay in another.

My shield already forgotten, I took off my helmet to see one corpse more clearly. I did not want to see, but I had to. I owed that much, at least.

Ketill rushed to my side. The others from the *Sea Squirrel* came with me, too. I did not look back, but I knew they were there. Magnus and Nanthild. Ingolf and Kraki. The wizard said something to me. I'm not sure what. I fixed on the hollowed out ribcage of that one large body, one arm butchered, the other having been severed.

Few men were as big as Haldor Skullsplitter, and few had that recogniz-able chestnut beard. He was smaller now, with the larger muscles cut from his body. His midsection had been hollowed out, exposing his ribcage. That had to be his arm hanging outside the cells like a trophy.

The awful lightness inside me threatened to make me puke. But I was a leader now, and I couldn't do that. The nightmare of our ship being swallowed whole came back to me. So did the sense of overwhelming chaos. What could I do? Did any of my choices matter?

My heart raced as I broke out in a sweat. I bit my tongue, fighting the urge to vomit. Lightheaded, I gripped my sword harder than ever, willing myself to keep standing. Need hummed in my hand, its rune blazing blue on the fuller. Soon, I realized I wasn't breathing, so I started doing that again. After long minutes of standing still, I regained some measure of control.

When my senses came back around, it was Ketill's voice I heard. "They ate them. They ate the dead."

"What for?" asked Ingolf. Even his voice cracked in disbelief. "They were well-supplied. Why eat people?"

"This was ritual, not sustenance," said Ketill. "They're Eaters now. Eaters of the dead. If the torc was there to charm them initially, this act will bind them far more. Ogmund has convinced them this is the way. The trolling process has begun."

## CHAPTER 12

# THOSE ONCE LOYAL

I WAS STILL IN THE MIDDLE OF THE PRISON AREA WHEN OUR three scouts returned. The crew of the *Sea Squirrel* was still with me, in the center of all that carnage Alfhild had left behind. It had been difficult to look away, but what our scouts brought with them was yet another surprise.

"We found this sorry thing hiding in a pile of straw," said Moose-Frothi.

"Vilgrip said we should bring him to you." Thorir Houndsfoot nodded toward Vilgrip, sounding even less enthused than his brother.

The moose-man carried a small, gaunt figure. Bits of straw stuck to his clothes and hair, and that straw was the cleanest thing about him. Dried blood and filth matted his clothes. He yelped as Frothi threw him at my feet.

"I said he shouldn't be killed," said Vilgrip. He shrugged. "I tried to explain that we might kill him, anyway, but not before you saw him alive."

Me, specifically, since who they'd found was Hemming. I could hear what hadn't been spoken, that Thorir and Frothi had argued with Vilgrip. "Argument" among those men might mean "fighting" any other time, but they had all taken our oaths. No fighting amongst Brothers.

Hemming had been in poor shape when they found him, they said. Now he panted, looking from one Brother to the next, and I'm certain he saw no hint of mercy. The man went into a convulsive panic as he saw the contents of the cells. He curled into a ball and covered his head.

"Vilgrip was right to spare him," I said.

"For now," added Magnus. "Was this all you found in the levels above?"

The scouts had not encountered any resistance and had gone through the upper levels quickly. We were, indeed, alone in the place. Consistent with that aloneness, not a single spear or helmet was left in the armory, nor any hint of treasure. All they had found was Hemming.

Magnus shook his head. "I thought you said Ulf killed him."

"Ulf stabbed him," I said. "I don't know how he could have survived."

I thought I'd seen Ulf's seax go all the way through Hemming's body. By blood loss or infection, Hemming should be dead. He clutched at the mass of dried blood around his belly. The wound seemed to still bother him, but he was recovered enough that he could move.

"So, is he a troll now?" asked Magnus.

"Maybe he was a troll before," suggested Ingolf. "Maybe he just showed it differently."

"I'm not a troll!" shrieked the hapless tracker. He uncurled and looked up at me. "I crawled away, made a poultice, found a place to hide." I'd seen Hemming help Magnus recover from an injury faster than expected in just that way. It still seemed implausible, but it made sense.

"He begged for food," said Vilgrip. "I mean, after begging for his life. I gave him some water." Again, I heard what Vilgrip wasn't saying: Hemming was not part of the trolling process. He could have eaten the dead like the others, but instead, he was starving.

I'd heard of "trolling" or "being trolled" in a general sense. Nobody would agree on the specific timing or amounts, but everyone would agree that eating human flesh turned a person into a troll. Which Hemming, apparently, was not.

So what?

"I helped you, remember?"

"I remember you separated from the rest of the crew," I said. "And I remember a warning when it was too late to do much good. How long did you know Ulf was a traitor?"

"It wasn't like that!" he squeaked.

I resisted the urge to kick him in the guts, settling for a hard stare.

"It wasn't! Ulf had a way about him, you know he did! He told me how I was mistreated and how the others didn't consider me one of them. If only someone wiser led us, he said it would go better for me!"

"And you believed him? You heard that and thought Haldor to be a poor leader despite everything you'd seen with your own eyes?"

"You . . . they . . . made fun of me!" Hemming panted as he looked to the others. "He said I could be a lord, and then . . . it seemed right at the time . . ."

"It seems right to me that we should gut this coward," said Magnus, stepping forward with his long seax. "He was with Ulf, not with us."

I raised a hand to stop him. "I have more questions for him."

Magnus stepped back and huffed. "Questions for a dead man are getting tedious."

Out of the corner of my eye, I saw Ingolf nod. I could feel my need to know things scraping against the hull of others' need for vengeance. Not that I didn't want vengeance, but Hemming might still be of some use.

"We will share that tedium with the others." I grabbed Hemming by his filthy hair and wrenched him upright. Then I dragged him out of the prison area and out into the cavernous chamber.

Magnus and Ingolf ran ahead and cleared a path to the center of the space. "This is a former crewmate!" Magnus' voice echoed through the place. "He's ours to deal with, but you can hear him questioned."

Social convention soon took over, with the captains coming forward. Nearly every warrior in the place tried to crowd in close behind them. The skalds brought some order to the area.

"Move your asses back!" shouted Hallfred Horsefly. "If we let every person have a say here, we'll grow old on this island before we're done. And there's not one of us who wants that!"

"Captains and skalds only," echoed Steinvor. She gestured at two warriors to take more than half a step back. These two looked less than pleased to take orders from a woman, but Gardar had two skalds with him.

"Make room," shouted Gizur, "or see it made!" The portly skald threw his considerable girth into the pair of warriors, knocking them back. "And keep quiet!"

I pushed Hemming to his knees and cut away his shirtsleeve, exposing the armring that had marked him as a Brother. I let Magnus take it off him. We would decide what to do with it later.

"You'll answer my questions in front of everyone," I said. "You warned me that Svein had turned. Why did you only do that at the last moment?"

"You brought me the stew," whined the tracker, his eyes tearing. "Ulf had me convinced you hated me, spoke ill of me behind my back. But you brought me the stew on your own. I thought maybe you were playing a trick at first, but I saw no trick. That was when I first suspected something was wrong."

"Something *was* wrong, you cowardly little shitling!" shouted Magnus. "You helped Ulf lead us into a trap, and you didn't even have the courage to die in the fight!"

Hemming winced. "I didn't know what would happen!"

"You knew what Ulf said about Haldor, and that it was behind his back," I said. "Did you know he had recruited Svein long before that?"

A pause, and then he nodded.

"What about the longhouse in Lejre?" I asked. "Ulf could have died in the fire with the rest of us. Why did he get trapped in there, if he was with Alfhild?"

"He wasn't, I mean, I don't think he was with her then," said Hemming. "It was after the battle when he started talking that way. Started going out in the night."

"Going out in the night? You mean Alfhild was still hiding near Lejre, and he met her?"

"I only followed him once, and the forest seemed wrong. I just know he went out and talked. It seemed like someone was there, but no one was. I didn't know he knew *seiðr* at the time."

"Ulf knows *seiðr*?"

"A little bit. Not much, he said, and he only said so after I said I'd followed him."

Traditionally, *seiðr* was women's magic, though not exclusively. Ulf was probably embarrassed to admit practicing it.

Huld stepped forward to speak. "Alfhild wouldn't need to be nearby to speak to Ulf. She could have cast her *hugr* out and spoken to him from far away." Murmuring erupted at the *vǫlva*'s willingness to involve herself.

"Not a lord—"

"What is she—"

"Shut your sheep-seducing mouths!" bellowed Magnus. "Ansgar leads us on land *and* is our skald. If he chooses to have the *vǫlva* speak, the *vǫlva* speaks!" It helps to be holding two razor-sharp weapons when delivering such commands. Magnus' reputation for using such weapons reinforced the silence.

Arrow-Odd hated *vǫlur*, and the shock of a *vǫlva* speaking like an equal was lost on no one. I cared not a bit.

"From *this far* away?" I asked.

The *vǫlva* nodded. "From this place, especially. It offers a high place to sit, and it is surrounded by water, which she is strong with."

"That may be how they spoke, but how did she recruit him?"

Hemming shook his head. He was not the lord of his own hall as Ulf had promised. He was just a pawn made to feel important. Feeling important, he had gulped down everything Ulf told him. But Ulf had no need to tell him any secrets.

"Do you know anything of any use at all?" I demanded.

"Where they're going!" croaked Hemming. "I know their strategy."

"How would you know anything like that?"

"I hid," he said. I bit my tongue while many of those listening commented, guffawed, or spat. "In an old barrel, at first. I heard those sons and daughters of the gods bickering about who would get what, and when. Alfhild has a special ship, or something. She's taking the god-children north around Finnmark, toward the North-Way mead halls. The children said they hoped the jarls there resisted swearing fealty to Ogmund. That way, they could take their lands. Svart is returning to Gardariki, and then moving west."

"And what of this place?"

"A gift to King Harek once his army has done enough of Ogmund's bidding."

"Won't Alfhild be losing her nice rooms upstairs?" asked Magnus.

Hemming turned to Magnus with wild eyes. "She wants the Danish throne. And the torc! She wants that back like nothing else."

"And where is Ogmund in all this?" I demanded.

"I don't know where he's going! Nobody said. Not with Alfhild or with Svart."

Sirnir sniffed as if disbelieving. "Probably back to Gardariki."

"If Ogmund were merely a man," said Odd, "then perhaps that would be true. But he's as much spirit as man, at this point."

"In either case, we should forget about Ogmund and focus on his vassals," said Gardar. "At least we know how to fight them."

"Or turn them," added Sirnir. "If only we had something that could convince them to turn." He didn't look my way, but everyone present knew what he meant.

"You might as well try to keep a lindworm as your guard dog, with that kind of thinking," I said. "That Ogmund has found this much support means Midgard is too full of foul influence already. The more of it we destroy, the better."

"Influence is like a spirit," said Sirnir. "It's an idea. It's not a body."

"You're wrong about that," said Arrow-Odd. "Even a spirit can be destroyed, and it's destruction Ogmund will get. No matter the cost."

Something in the tone of those last four words brought my mind back around to a previous conversation with Odd. The one we'd had in his tent when he was old and desiccated. I'd mentioned Tyrfing to him as an idea for a quest, because I thought a quest was what the man needed. A quest to destroy the Brisingamen with me.

He'd said, *"Of course!"* I'd thought my idea had worked.

But Arrow-Odd wasn't interested in finding Tyrfing to destroy the Brisingamen. What had breathed the youth back into him was a different quest. He wanted to find Tyrfing, just for a wholly different reason: That weapon could finally end Ogmund Tussock, and Odd didn't care what wielding that sword cost him. Or us.

I could almost hear Odin laughing in the background.

Soon, every warrior we had brought had a definite idea about what was next, given what we had found and heard. Two sides emerged, and the argument went about like this:

*What did our friends die for if not to finish this business with Ogmund?* cried one side, principally Styrgrim.

*What is there left to do but return to our homes and defend them?* cried the other, principally Gardar and Sirnir.

Odd had the good sense to cut off the argument, saying we had friends and allies who shouldn't remain in this rotten place, and neither should we. Nobody disagreed with that.

It was to great disappointment that I told the others Hemming was not to be killed. Not because I thought he deserved to live. For one, I wanted to punish him by forcing him to drag some of the bodies out of there. Let him get a good look at the results of his cowardice. That was not my only reason, though.

"You could kill him and seem to have managed a measure of vengeance," I said, "but it would be a false feeling. I don't like the idea of feeling we've accomplished a thing when we haven't."

This was not a popular decision. So unpopular, in fact, that Kraki asserted himself. "We'll leave him here, then," said the old man. "He will not set foot on my ship again."

I didn't care much that Hemming would wither away alone on that island. But something nagged me about it. Like he might still know something I had failed to ask.

Having heard this all play out, Odd approached me out of earshot of the others. "I think you wish this man to stay alive," he whispered. "Is that so?"

I hesitated, hoping no one was listening. Did I want him to live? And what for? I think I nodded inadvertently. Or maybe Odd just decided I had nodded and went on from there.

"You, skinny-rat!" Odd shouted at Hemming. "Few men have a second chance at life, and fewer still, a second chance at honor. You must be luckier than lucky to still be alive, and I could use some luck right now. I offer you service under my command. It will be a hard thing, that service. Do you accept?"

Wide-eyed, Hemming nodded.

Odd turned back to me. "You helped me through a hard time. Now I've repaid the favor." He clapped me on the shoulder.

Not exactly an even trade. I'd helped bring Odd out of a pit of despair and back to his former youth. What I got in return was Hemming's life. But Odd was canny, and he would not carry a debt longer than he had to. In his eyes, we were even. And as we were even, he left my company to organize his crew.

Magnus and I carried Haldor's body to the *Sea Squirrel* ourselves. I don't wish to describe that any further.

# Chapter 13

## Raise Your Horns

We had a lot to explain upon returning to the war camp. News about eating the dead would travel fast and create a lot of speculation. I wasn't sure what to do about that, if anything, but Arrow-Odd did. Without declaring why, he ordered that every crew be set to work on something. Those who couldn't find work were tasked with digging even more defensive fortifications than we already had.

We didn't need more fortifications. And I was confident we wouldn't even be in that camp much longer. Hard work won't cure fear or uncertainty, but it will often prevent them from festering.

Odd also reassigned the crew of one of his ships, the *Sea Worm*, to fill out other ship crews. The *Sea Worm* was to be used as a pyre for all the remains we took with us. I asked that the preparation of the *Sea Worm* be done only by those who had fought through that mountain fortress. The crew of the *Sea Squirrel*, those freed prisoners who'd elected to join other crews, and Styrgrim and Bjorn worked without break. We hacked that ship's insides to bits and provided more kindling and pitch in the hollowed-out hull. We built platforms for the bodies, making sure even the smallest parts were laid on top and not forgotten about.

Kraki laid a hand on the *Sea Worm*'s hull and whispered something at one point. It sounded like an apology, or maybe a few words of honor for its final voyage. That ship would burn, but it would bear many memories.

We lit the *Sea Worm* and pushed it out to sea. Arrow-Odd called the wind to fill its sail; otherwise, the waves would have kept it on the shore. The ship burned hot and bright in the dusky midnight of late summer on the White Sea.

Then, in very short order, most of us were drunk.

It's important to get sufficiently drunk during funeral rites. Not because alcohol is a mental salve, but because it lowers boundaries. Mental boundaries, spiritual boundaries. And with those boundaries lower, or maybe thinner is a better word, you might have a final chance to speak to the dead. That's my spiritual explanation.

My cultural explanation is that alcohol heightens a sense of grim, brooding misery, and that being miserable was most appropriate. The more miserable, the better, at least as a shared experience among those still living. Also, sufficiently drunk people can't remember much, so a man might cry out of sadness, but it's safe to do so because nobody will recall it the next morning.

Hemming looked pretty miserable, but I suspect that was a reflection of his own sorry life. Magnus' jokes got even grimmer than usual. The more awful they became, the more praise he got for them. Styrgrim said he kept trying to die, but was so worthless that he kept failing at it. Odd suggested he try again that night. Styrgrim replied that was a fine idea.

I had plenty of experience with getting drunk. Too much, in fact. Therefore, I would get appropriately drunk like everyone other than Ketill. Only this time, I would be circumspect rather than stupid. Quiet rather than brash. I would use that drunkenness and lean into its effects rather than let it lean into me, pushing me to do foolish things.

That really was my intent before I made such an ass of myself in front of at least three people.

There was one main bonfire on the beach, but lots of little campfires, lots of smaller conversations. Steinvor shared a small fire with Huld and Jorun, all of them well into their horns. That was good, them being more drunk than me. Not that they were, but I definitely thought they were at the time.

"I want to talk to you," I said, breaking into the conversation and probably slurring a bit.

"Talk then," said Steinvor. "Now is a good time to speak things otherwise left unsaid."

I realized I had little clear idea of what I wanted to say to Steinvor. I wanted her to take me back to her tent again. And I had more feelings for her than just sex, but I didn't understand those feelings very well, even when sober. And I didn't want to talk about any of that in front of Jorun or (gasp) Huld.

"I just," I said, taking another sip to stall. "You helped me!"

Steinvor raised an eyebrow.

"With the people. The champions! Sirnir and Gardar wanted to take . . . the thing. But you warned Nanthild."

Steinvor's expression tightened. "I did that, as I'm sure Gardar suspects. He told me tonight that two skalds were enough for him. As I was the third to be taken on, well . . ." She raised her horn and drank to her dismissal.

I was surprised and dismayed. Also excited, because I knew what to say next. "You can join our crew!" I looked around for our captain, but didn't see him. No matter. "I don't care what Kraki says, I'll *make him* take you on."

Jorun rolled her eyes. Huld cackled loudly, holding her side as she spilled some of her ale.

"Thank you for your generous offer." Steinvor sure did blink a lot when she said that. "But I have already found another ship to crew on." Then, instead of inviting me back to her tent, she just got up and walked away!

Huld laughed some more.

"You're a cat," I said, unable to think of anything else.

Jorun shook her lolling head. "What? Ansgar, how drunks are you?" Okay, Jorun was hammered.

"Drunks enough!" No idea what that meant, but I was confident it was the right thing to say.

"Oh, it's all right," said Huld, wiping away tears. "*That* statement makes sense."

I turned around at hearing a few shouts by the main bonfire. Nothing like a good bonfire to go with drinking. The flames had to be twice my height. Styrgrim had the remaining six prisoners brought out and began a speech directed at them.

If they loved "freedom" as much as Borisu had, they must be willing to fight for it. Borisu had been released already. The rest of them would need to earn their freedom in a different way. "They say they love freedom!" shouted Styrgrim. "Love freedom in a way we can't even understand. Is that right? 'Freedom,' it turns out, means 'eating people.'" Styrgrim turned to a chorus of hisses and insults directed at the Rus. "Which does seem like freedom, but only for one of the two people involved."

Our people drank and laughed and drank some more.

I turned back to Huld. "*You* don't make sense."

"From your limited perspective, perhaps."

"Why should we crew with someone who's a . . . a sneaky sneak! I don't want any more surprises."

"Ansgar!" Jorun was just about falling off the log. "Huld saved us. The whole army!"

"Mmm-hmm. And Odin grants victory. Until he *doesn't*."

Huld patted Jorun on the knee. Jorun mumbled something about going to find Steinvor and stumbled off.

"If you think I'm like unto Odin, boy," said Huld, "then you've got less sense than—"

"You're a secret schemer. You keep to yourself and disappear. Sure, you saved me from Alfhild, but—"

"And Svein."

I nodded, trying not to recall the pummeling he'd given me. "And Svein. But the *why* is more important than the *what*, and you won't say *why*. Not why about *anything*." I shook my finger at her. "You think I don't know your name is sneaky, too? *Huld*, eh? Just means *hidden*. Like Grim Aegir was a false name. What's your *real name*, I wonder?"

The *vǫlva* fixed me with a stare hard enough to bore into solid rock. "You should talk, *Ans-gar*."

"Oh yeah? I know what that means, but what does it *mean?*" I leaned in close to whisper. "I don't know! You're such a wise woman, you tell *me* what it means! Oh, you can't? Let's ask the thing!"

At the apex of my stupidity that night, I opened my beaver skin bag and reached for the Brisingamen. It seemed so obvious to use the thing. Why hadn't I done that before?

Huld put her hand over my wrist, and her touch stopped me cold. I wasn't frozen, it was just that her hand felt familiar and . . . gentle? Comforting? The urge to grab the Brisingamen left me, and I pulled away from it.

Huld patted the spot vacated by Steinvor. I remember thinking I didn't want to sit down, but I sat anyway. It was just an open space on a log in front of a fire, but as I described, this was a funeral night, and the boundaries are thin at those times. Consistent with those thin boundaries, Svipul stepped out from behind the firelight.

Styrgrim continued his speech, saying he would cut the bonds of these prisoners. The Rus were well enough to fight. He offered to face them unarmed and unarmored. Someone suggested giving them to Odin. Stygrim countered that Odin was too busy avoiding fights to get involved, drawing "oooooh"s and "aaaaaah"s from the audience.

One of the Rus started drooling. I think he was trying to foam at the mouth, playing that *I'm in a frenzy* bit. Funeral rites, too much alcohol, and frenzy all went together, even if the last one was pretend. And badly timed.

Styrgrim pointed at the drooler. "What a sad case: He shot his load before he had a chance to thrust his spear!" A chorus of laughter followed.

Svipul walked over to the side of Huld opposite me. "You can trust her." She took Jorun's seat.

The fight brewing distracted me. "Styrgrim is going to get himself killed!"

"You've seen Styrgrim fight," said Huld. "You think he is in danger?"

Part of me hoped he was. But not too much. Just a little. Not that it would kill him. "He's not even wearing armor. Does he *want* to die?"

"Fury doesn't plan for the future," said Huld. "It doesn't worry about odds or likely outcomes. Fury decides in spite of those things, not because of them, and fury is how Styrgrim knows himself."

That single-mindedness sounded awfully desirable. My mind was constantly turning over every possibility, every potential problem and mistake. When I was very young, there had been times I actually stopped moving and had to be shaken out of whatever thought spiral I'd gotten myself into. "I couldn't be less like him."

"Couldn't you?" Huld grabbed my left wrist and twisted my palm up, tracing one finger over the bandage. "Is this the mark of one who *doesn't* know fury?"

Onlookers tossed their axes and shields at the feet of the Rus. They may not have been fully healed, but it was six against one, and the one had no weapon. They exchanged a few words and armed themselves, and the fight was on.

The drooler yelled a war cry as he charged. His friends didn't join him, though, and he stopped short. Styrgrim used the hesitation to crouch and grabbed two handfuls of sand. He charged that first warrior with a big, obvious punch.

The prisoner bought the feint and raised his shield higher. The real attack was a kick to the side of the knee. He fell. Styrgrim stomped on his throat.

I wrenched my hand away from Huld. "So, what, I am Odin's son? Maybe a special case among the children of gods, given my name means *god-spear*?"

"Did Odin name you such?"

"Of course not!"

Huld shrugged. "How did the name come about?"

The warrior closest to Styrgrim's back came at him but got an eye full of sand for his efforts. Styrgrim closed in and laid him out with a massive uppercut with the hand still holding sand.

"My parents named me such."

Svipul shook her head.

"How easy it is to assume," said Huld. "So easy, you don't even know you're assuming!"

"How, then?" I looked at Svipul, but she just stared back. "I suppose my mother was dead as soon as I was born, so she wouldn't know."

Styrgrim threw the man he'd just punched into the remaining four, but to little effect. They circled him and attacked all at once. In the chaos, Styrgrim turned one warrior into the path of another's axe, punched the throat of one, and lifted a third off the ground and broke the man's back over his knee.

Huld nodded. "But Styrgrim was there."

"So I should ask him about my name?" I shook my head. Even drunk, that sounded like a bad idea. Or if not bad, a thing I didn't want to do.

"It is your choice to look or to turn away."

I looked over at Svipul, who stared at the end of the fight. One Rus warrior was left. He stood with his back to the bonfire. Not a bad idea, I supposed, using the fire to blind his foe.

Styrgrim charged. The axe came down and bit into his forearm as he batted it away. The Rus kept his footing and his shield in front of him, but staggered when Styrgrim's shoulder bowled into him. Stygrim had kept his balance and followed up with a hard push kick. The last prisoner fell into the giant bonfire.

"I've never been what he wanted," I said. "It was hard to accept that, but I did. Now I should revisit the subject?"

"Remember that everyone else still thinks he's your father, and that bond makes certain demands of him. Whether he looks or turns away, that's a choice he has, too."

"Pfah. He's been turning away ever since I was born. I took his wife from him. That's always been who I am to him, and always who I'll be."

A great cheer rose for Styrgrim. Someone brought him a horn full of ale. He drained it all at once, looking appropriately unhappy. Frustrated, even. As he was my not-father, I thought that meant we would have little to ask of one another. And that thought had given me some small measure of relief.

"There might be a great difference between what people are born into the world for and what they become known for," said Huld. "Names often follow the differences."

# CHAPTER 14

# A Problem of Giant Proportions

I entered Arrow-Odd's tent alone the next morning. My head throbbed. My limbs felt wobbly. I was hungry, but the smell of food put me off. So much for controlling the alcohol rather than letting the alcohol control me. But Hallfred Horsefly had delivered a message first thing: Odd wanted to talk to me, and sooner rather than later.

Sunlight glowed through the top canvas as the flap closed behind me. To my left and right were small areas walled off as rooms. The big table sat ahead of me, which is where I thought I would find Odd. I stepped toward the table, where Odd's longbow and arrow bag lay.

"Hello?" I shook my head. Why summon me when—

I felt the point of a seax pinch my lower back just behind one of my kidneys.

"I heard a man needs to move quiet like nothing else to remain unheard around you," said Arrow-Odd. He let the seax drop away and walked to the other side of the table.

Sneaking up on me was no easy thing given my sharp hearing. Only Fanya had ever snuck up on me that way. Until today. I was hungover, but still. "I may not have Heimdall's hearing, but I don't miss much. How did you do that?"

Odd shrugged. "I move the wind, I move with the wind. You should know. I think there is something of that in you."

For a moment, I blanched. Was he saying something about my heritage? "I've never been able to call the wind into a sail. Or anywhere else."

"I don't mean that specifically. We all have different skills, if we choose to develop them."

I had been taken off guard physically and then mentally. What did Odd know about me, and how could I find out without giving anything away? I wasn't sure. "You wanted to speak to me, or was I just for practicing your sneaking skills?"

"The sneaking was extra. I summoned you here because it's not clear where to go next."

The funeral rites could only put off that decision temporarily. "Right."

"Well, where?"

I was dumbfounded. The leader of Arrow-Odd's army was asking *me* where to go?

"Perhaps you don't know the precise location," Odd continued.

*Oh shit, you think I know where Tyrfing is.*

"I don't know, exactly—"

Odd held a hand up. "Let's be clear: You said you intended to destroy the Brisingamen. You said you intended to do this with the cursed sword, Tyrfing. Gardar and Sirnir want nothing to do with this quest, but I do, so out with it: Are you after the sword or not?"

"I wanted to consider other ideas for destroying the Brisingamen." Which was true, but more true was the fact that I was on the spot and playing for time to think. "One idea is to drop it into the deepest sea. Another is to bait the Midgard Serpent into swallowing it." *Let's see how he reacts to those.*

Odd shook his head. "I have heard two ideas now, and neither one is good. Between Alfhild and Ogmund, I'm sure one of them could have a sea monster retrieve the torc from the sea, however deep. As for the Midgard Serpent, I'll ignore the obvious issue of 'baiting' it, because the outcome is still bad. What happens when that monster shits the necklace out? It could wash up in some realm of *jǫtnar*. Or even worse, Bjarmaland. Or even worse than that, Ireland!" Arrow-Odd hadn't lived so long without being a canny sort.

I shook my head, deciding there was no point in being coy. "Tyrfing might be the only way to get rid of it."

"Hmmm."

Whatever that meant.

"You think the sword cannot destroy the necklace?" I asked.

"I think there is *nothing* that sword cannot destroy. The barest scratch of it slew my friend, Hjalmar. I buried the sword with his killer, that stinking *berserkr*, Angantyr, as I'd promised to do. But that was long ago, and the stories say his daughter retrieved the thing, and that it was handed down at least two more generations after that. Do you know where to find it?"

"No," I said, too quickly and with too high a pitch. Something about Odd getting that sword felt very, very wrong.

Arrow-Odd approached and stood too close to me for comfort. He wracked my nerves, turned whatever cleverness I thought I had to a blank. I couldn't think of anything but a direct answer, so I said nothing more.

"A difficult place to start from," said Odd. "I could continue with my army, such as it is. Probably convince Gardar and Sirnir to hunt down the Bjarmian fleet rather than wait for it. But I've heard enough of their rumblings now, and they failed to act while I was out of sorts. This army would be harder to lead than before. And I know, now, that this army can't kill Ogmund. Vignir broke every bone in his body, but that wasn't enough. So I need to keep whatever of this army is still loyal, I need time for more of our wounded to heal and be ready to fight again, but most of all, *I need that sword.*"

Perhaps if Odd had spoken about the need to stop Ogmund's plan or the terror of trolling a bunch of children of gods, I might have shared my information freely. But Odd was not talking about a threat to Midgard. He was talking about his personal vengeance.

The thought of a demon sword in the hands of an abnormally long-lived, abnormally egotistical saga hero hadn't sat well with me before. After hearing Odd's voice when he spoke those last words, it sat even less well with me now.

"What about Gusir's Gifts?" I asked. "They're said to—"

"Ogmund has dodged them. Every time." Perhaps sensing my unease, he backed away a bit and adopted a more charming tone. "I know your crew has an independent streak, so I won't demand you swear loyalty the same as others in my army. And I'll swear to use the sword to destroy that torc once I have it. But only if you help me find it, and that includes telling me what you know."

"That's reasonable. I will just go talk to—"

"Now."

I cleared my throat. Something seemed off. Not terribly wrong, as if our lives were in danger, but off. It would be a while before I understood that politics was a kind of sorcery, and longer still before I had any skill with it. I only knew I was losing, and that made me want to break his rhythm.

"How will you pay for the army's needs?"

He looked at me like a wolf that had trapped a squirrel.

"Kraki doesn't like you in the first place," I continued. "You don't take women against their will, but you've still taken thralls. If you think to raid for that sort of plunder to raise your money, I can tell you right now, we will sail in different directions. Kraki won't be moved on that subject."

"Rules." Odd nodded and withdrew to a more comfortable distance on the other side of the table. "Hjalmar had rules. That is how we came to not rob women or take them against their will, among other things. I think your rule against thrall-taking is fine. I had no intent to make money that way. I retrieved a pile of my old treasure last summer and still have plenty of it. But we won't need to pay for hospitality where I intend to winter us."

"Where could that be?" I had thought we were far from any mead halls other than those belonging to King Harek of Bjarmaland.

"Risaland."

He could not be serious. The land of giants? And I mean giant-sized giants. *Jǫtnar* might be huge or the size of humans. Either way, they are quite dangerous. Those living in Risaland, however, were all *literal giants*. Odd seemed to read my thoughts.

"Of the many realms of Jotunheim, Risaland is the most friendly to humans. Vignir's mother was a *risi*."

An image of how things must have worked between Odd and a giantess occurred to me, as did the difficulties involved. I shook the thoughts out of my head.

"The King of Risaland is a friend. I helped him become king, in fact. We can get there before storm season and spend the winter there. Or," he continued, drawing out the word, "you could travel on your own. A single ship, a slow one, traveling north around frozen Finnmark. Or south through the lakes, where I'm certain there are no Rus waiting to ambush stray ships coming out of the White Sea."

We were already farther north than most people would even think of going. Very little around us was friendly. A single ship traveling by itself was practically an invitation for raiders to attack. Fighting our way out of a mountain was one thing. Fighting our way through hundreds of miles of unfamiliar territory would be quite another.

"You said you did not know where Tyrfing was. You know something, though, or I think your voice would not have cracked that way."

"I have to ask Kraki—"

"I'll put the situation another way. When Gardar and Sirnir leave, they will go north, then west, around Finnmark. Then they can come south along the North-Way. If you want to get to Trondelag, that makes sense. A long way, though. If you want to get somewhere else, you might prefer to go south. That way is tricky. You would need a guide to get you through all those lakes and rivers. Do you have one?"

My mouth was dry, so I shook my head.

"I spoke to your old friend, Hemming. He remembers you coming up through those lakes and rivers very well. Maybe I need him to guide us south. Or maybe I don't. Maybe I like him less than I thought I would, so I give him to your crew. They will kill him, and then nobody is going south. Oh, you could step in and stop that, but that would be an unpopular decision. And is it even possible that Kraki would take back his words from before to never let Hemming on his ship again? I don't know. Maybe he is more flexible than I think."

I swallowed hard. "I don't know where the sword is, but I would start looking for it in Uppsala."

Odd grinned. "That's progress! I will keep Hemming with me. Now, go consult with your captain. Just understand that, as your ship is not part of my army, it's important we remain friends as well as allies. It's only my friends, after all, who will receive hospitality in Risaland."

CHAPTER 15

# FRIENDS IN COLD PLACES

KRAKI WAS NOT INTIMIDATED BY THE PROSPECT OF GOING TO Risaland, but he had fought and killed *jǫtnar* before. "It's a *jǫtunn*, one way or another. Some might not be so bad, same as humans." The comment did little to improve our crew's outlook. But when he served the hated *hákarl* that day, the sheer promise of food other than that was encouragement enough.

A chill air blew over the camp as we prepared for the departures. The final meeting of the Council of Skalds was short and lacking in side comments and quips. I noticed how much warmth there had been between the other skalds only after it had disappeared. Those remaining loyal to Odd did not speak much with Gardar's or Sirnir's people. The ravens began to disperse. I told Magnus about my name, but the whole business seemed self-obsessed in the context of our imminent departure.

Arrow-Odd waited for Gardar and Sirnir and anyone who would follow them to leave before loading his ships. He spoke little in the few days leading up to the departure from the camp, and when he did speak, it was with regard to preparations. Moving that many ships and people is a hard thing, especially with so many of the people injured.

Some, we knew, would not survive the voyage. Others would not survive the winter. But for those still injured or barely recovered, this was a far better prospect than huddling together in the camp. Storm season on the White

Sea started in early autumn, which we were on the cusp of, and autumn dropped into winter quickly. It was time to go, no matter where we were going.

Five ships sailed with Arrow-Odd, the *Sea Squirrel* and the *Long Claw* among them. Josur the Daring had chosen to stay with Odd rather than return home, but he'd lost so many warriors he could only outfit his main ship, the *Wave Climber*. Birki the Obstinate captained the *Sea Goat*, while Odd remained on the *Whaleslayer*.

Jorun had decided to leave Sirnir's command for Josur's, so that was something. And it turned out that the ship Steinvor had taken up with was the *Sea Goat*, under Birki's command. Plenty of good people had stayed, people we would have welcomed on the *Sea Squirrel*. Styrgrim's rudder man, Hjalti, for one. And the woman who went by a man's name, Hrafn. She was tougher than nails and had left Gardar's service to join Odd.

With five ships and a man who could raise the wind to push them, we made quick time to Risaland.

No one announced when we had entered the land of those giants, and no one needed to. The White Sea was just about to open up to that great expanse, the Norse Sea, whose boundaries no one knew. The water got darker, as if the bottom had dropped far lower. Soon after, we came in sight of high cliffs. They took longer than expected to approach because we were farther away. As we got closer, it became clear that the scale of everything had changed. The mountains were taller. The boulders were bigger. What appeared to be smaller breakers sloshed water into the ship.

That was nothing compared to seeing our first giant.

He spotted our ships from the shore and took off running, his salt-crusted beard swaying back and forth. He wore tattered brown leathers that looked like they had seen a hundred winters, and he didn't bother with shoes or boots. Each stride had to be about three times the length of mine.

"Tell Hildir that Arrow-Odd comes!" shouted Odd from the prow of the *Whaleslayer*.

We landed on a mercifully sandy beach. A gravelly beach to these giants would have been so rocky as to scrape our hulls raw. Nearby were other ships, all strangely colored in whites to dark grays—stone ships, just like the stories told.

Odd's announcement must have been heard, because two giants met us on the beach. They were better dressed than the first one we saw, and wore heavy chain shirts and steel helmets. But ready for war as they might've been, they greeted Odd with deep bows as he walked up the shore.

"Arrow-Odd is most welcome in this land," said one of them.

"But as we've never met him," said the other, his tone still polite even as his low voice boomed through the air, "we're instructed to ask: What did King Hildir leave you on the Wolf Islands?"

"That was a sword, a chain shirt, and a helmet," said Odd. "All of fine quality. And he left gold and silver as well, but that was beneath a stone slab. Now, are you satisfied?"

"Most satisfied," said the first.

"Please, go right to the hall," said the other. "We will pull your ships inland and cover them from the weather."

We had landed on the shore of Risaland like so many sea-going ants, scurrying up the beach with our sea chests rather than tiny bits of food.

A wide path made itself visible once we were well up from the water. Flattish stones that must have been placed as rough steps led us upward until we crested the top of a ridge. The vantage point provided us a picturesque view of the forested valley below.

As tall as the forest's trees were, we could see the great hall beyond them. Again, it looked like it was close, but it only looked that way because it was so big. It took us over an hour to get there.

It was at least two levels in height, and that height had been measured for giants. What was more, it was made of stone—an impossible structure, or so it seemed at the time. Then again, the giants here made everything from stone, including their ships.

The doors were open wide for us. A guard bowed to Arrow-Odd as he approached.

"I take it the king knows to expect us," said Odd.

"Whether that's true, I couldn't say," replied the giant. "He is away at the moment. But Hildigunn awaits you inside, and she is expecting you for certain."

"Who is Hildigunn?" I whispered, realizing I hadn't really directed it at anyone, and just hoped someone knew.

Hallfred gave me a disapproving side-eye. I took it this was a question I wasn't supposed to ask.

Long tables hosting great trenchers of food stood at just over eye height for most of us. A dozen giants put down their spoons to look at the humans walking in. They pushed back bowls of savory stew, the aroma of which was a great relief. One of the older giants squinted, as if we were too small to see normally.

How puny we must have seemed to them! Had Odd not led us here and received a respectful bow at every turn, we would never have come near such a place.

At the far end of the hall, a giantess sat on the high seat. She was beautiful, if sad-looking. Bright hair framed sea-blue eyes that regarded us with wary interest. A white linen underdress and a shorter, brown overdress were loose enough not to reveal much about her physique. Her posture and bearing, though, indicated strength. Two golden brooches, intricately designed, fastened the straps of her overdress. Those and a necklace of colored stones were the only concessions to her high station.

An axe danced on the arm of her chair as she played with it. She laid the axe down and put her hands in her lap.

Five ships worth of warriors was a lot. Even in a massive hall like that one, it was still a lot. I stood near the front of what remained of Odd's army with Josur, Styrgrim, and Birki, the four of us close behind Odd himself.

Odd motioned us to remain where we were and approached the high seat alone. "Greetings, Hildigunn. I'm told your father is away at the moment."

Hildigunn shifted in her high seat, craning her neck forward. "He is."

"I hope he is well, then!"

"He is still King of Risaland, if that's what you mean. He has business elsewhere at the moment." Hildigunn's voice took on a chillier tone then. "I am certain he would receive you warmly if he were here, though. Have your people pull up to the tables. I will have food and ale brought for you."

"For that, I thank you. And it's fitting that Hildir would leave a wise one in charge while he was away. Given that wisdom, I want to ask something else. I won't be two ways about it: I ask for hospitality for the winter. For myself and for my friends."

"A large asking for such a tiny man," said Hildigunn.

"There was a time when you found me not so tiny after all."

Hildigunn gave a half smile at that. I wondered if it was safe to laugh, or if that would earn me a death sentence. That banter was too familiar for anyone but lovers. And it was getting a bit awkward.

"There is little need to ask," said Hildigunn. "We both know Hildir owes his kingdom to your good advice. And if you need tiny people fed and sheltered for the winter, even many of them, then the answer is yes."

Nods and murmurs all around. A few claps on the back. A wave of relief washed over the remnant of Odd's army as the awkwardness of that conversation dissipated. Almost every face had a smile, ready to climb onto those giant benches and eat from those giant trenchers.

Huld did not smile. Her lips were pressed thin, her eyes narrowed. I didn't know much about that woman, but I knew she saw or heard something I couldn't. I was so relieved that it made me slower to size things up. But warm words spoken in a cold tone should be disquieting to anyone paying attention.

"My thanks to you," said Odd. "We'll make ourselves useful, I promise that much. But I do have one piece of ill news that I should relate. Our son, Vignir, he is—"

"Dead," interrupted Hildigunn, her voice steady. "I knew he was dead the moment you walked through my doors. If he were still alive, he would have charged in straightaway to greet me, and a dozen guests here would have slapped their tables in excitement. Instead, it was your tentative steps that first crossed my threshold, quiet and shuffling. And still you wagged a cunning tongue to secure hospitality before giving me bad news. You're safe here for the winter, of course, though your return is not what I would call very honorable."

Odd had didn't say much after that.

We ate in near silence that day. The giants of Risaland had little to say to those who'd spent Vignir's life so easily. I didn't blame them.

It would be a long winter.

## CHAPTER 16

# A SMALL COUNCIL

EVEN THE WIND WAS BIGGER IN RISALAND. GUSTS THREATENED to knock us down on the worst days while we were out exploring or trying to make ourselves useful. Which we had to do, because we couldn't just scurry among the giants in that big hall all day. Hospitable as they were, it was clear from their conversations not involving us that we were less significant in Risaland than elsewhere.

If that was not reminder enough, Arrow-Odd's War Council was visibly diminished. Until recently, it had included one of the North's most feared warriors, two powerful lords, a gregarious half-giant, and Odin going under a false name. Now, a couple of brash young lords, a skinny skald, and an old man who grunted more than he spoke took the places of all but one of those.

Only the presence of Styrgrim the Bear was unchanged. Imposing as the silver-and-black-clad warrior still was, the overall lessening of Odd's War Council was something you could feel as much as see. The *Sea Squirrel* wasn't even under Odd's command.

It was a small council any way you looked at it. Especially if you were one of the giants who occasionally spared us a glance.

If there hadn't been a hot spring near that stone longhouse, I think some of us would have gone insane during that winter in Risaland. It also helped that the ale they brewed was among the best anyone had tasted. A healthy addition of rye to the barley mash resulted in a sharper, earthier ale. On days they brewed, the aroma of grainy sweetness carried on the air like a spell to put everyone at ease.

Small council or not, captains and skalds met weekly to discuss what was happening. Or what might happen next. Or just to remind Odd that he could call us over to a corner of the great hall and sit us down. Tables were of no use. Sitting on the benches left us looking at one another under the table. Standing on the benches was better, but the tables were so broad, we had to shout at one another to be heard. So, corner it was.

The skalds all thought the pursuit of Tyrfing was a bad idea. The sword was known as evil for more than one reason, and might begin to wield itself. I didn't like to hear that idea, but I had assured everyone that this was exactly the danger of the Brisingamen. It was hard to then argue that Odd would be fine to use the sword.

Especially since I suspected Odd would not be fine if he got hold of that sword.

I would not cross that bridge any sooner than I had to—a philosophy that Magnus strongly approved of. He, at least, remained cheery and reliable.

With only skalds and captains at the War Council, my only shipmate in attendance was Kraki. Reliable, yes. Not cheerful.

Despite hot springs and rye ale, general cheeriness spiraled downward quickly in the weeks following our arrival. There was finally one meeting where Odd brought up, again, the idea of the *Sea Squirrel* swearing allegiance and joining his army, and that meeting was more interesting than most.

Not because we had found a table of suitable size. We were still sitting in a corner and trying to act like this was just fine.

"You only want the sword for one thing," said Odd. "Destroy the torc, and then you've no more need of it. But you have need of an army if you want to get to Alfhild. And even with the sword, I will need every ship I can find. Better that we act as one than act apart."

"Would that Gardar and Sirnir had thought the same," said Birki the Obstinate. Which helped the mood not at all.

"Sometimes a job is better done by fewer people," added Josur the Daring. Because of course he would.

Jorun was Josur's skald now, and she sat behind him. She said nothing and made no gestures or expressions. This was unlike the Council of Skalds, where we spoke freely. Jorun chose her words and reactions carefully.

Hallfred Horsefly was quiet, letting Odd do the talking and keeping

Steinvor from speaking in the process. As Odd's newer skald, Steinvor was not about to take a political risk she didn't know how to calculate. Hallfred had long experience with Odd the Legend. Choosing to say little meant the new skald should say even less. Especially with the captain of her ship already known as "the Obstinate."

As the *Sea Squirrel*'s skald, I was canny enough to recognize political precariousness, but not canny enough by half to know the best way forward. Not that Kraki cared one whit for political precariousness, but I was trying not to make a bad situation worse.

And then there was Bjorn. If Styrgrim's skald knew the calculus behind stepping lightly around the politics, his brash manner did not show it. "There is no point in reflecting on past disappointments. We're best off finding new allies drawn to a famous archer with a famous arrow."

"Gusir's Gifts aren't likely to kill Ogmund, if that's what you mean," said Hallfred, speaking only in response to another skald. "Ogmund avoids every shot. Odd would have to take him entirely unaware, which seems unlikely. And now, only one of those arrows is left."

Bjorn pulled at his beard. "And we'll improve our luck with a cursed sword?" He turned to Odd. "You ran into it once before. It slew your friend Hjalmar the Brave and also turned on its wielder. I counsel against piling one tragedy on top of another. Leave Tyrfing buried, wherever it may be."

Odd was undeterred. "It was on Samso Island last I saw it, but that was generations ago. Stories about its retrieval have since sprung up, been half-forgotten, and then revived with half-truths and speculation. If its history can be so convoluted, why not the specifics of its curse as well? I think the sword is not so dangerous to wield as some say."

"If that's true," replied Bjorn, "it may also mean it is not nearly so powerful as to be a thing that can kill Ogmund. If he's as much spirit as man, you would be better off consulting a *vǫlva* on his defeat than seeking out the most cursed sword in Midgard."

"You have not seen the thing," countered Odd. "No one here has seen it wielded but me. I have no doubt that sword would cut him down, spirit or man. Bright as the sun in high summer, sharp enough to cleave solid rock. I could smell the malice on it, so heavy as to quench the life of anything it touched. That blade is a thing to behold, and I never should have buried it with that scum, Angantyr, but I kept my word. Now, I will have it, and that is that." He turned toward me again. "So much the better you should ally yourself with a larger force rather than remain hangers-on."

If that is politics, Kraki's response was whatever the opposite of politics is. "My ship. Not your ship." If Odd had made a veiled threat, Kraki's response was a bald-faced dare.

I was generally going to let Odd go on as he would, but the repetition was tiresome, and he had used that same term, 'hangers-on,' that Sirnir had described us with. I wasn't going to sit down for any more of that. I mean, I continued sitting in the literal sense. But I also knew how to make that vein in Odd's forehead throb.

"Odd, I'll make you an offer instead: Why don't you swear loyalty to the *Sea Squirrel*? Our crew saved you from Ogmund's biggest monster, and our *vǫlva* saved your army from annihilation. We're sworn to kill Alfhild, and I've personally sworn to kill Ulf. You want Ogmund's head, and Bjorn thinks a *vǫlva* might give you good advice about getting it. Well, we have one. Joining us seems to be all benefit for you."

Odd's forehead vein pulsed so hard it could have beat a drum.

"I think it's wiser to keep Huld out of this council," said Hallfred.

"I don't know about that," said Birki, who seemed to want this pot to boil right over. "They say 'a wise man's heart is seldom glad,' but as I see it, we're already quite un-glad. Might as well face what she has to say rather than shrink from it."

In the space of no more than one second, I got dirty looks from Jorun and Steinvor and confused looks from Bjorn and Hallfred (the *why are you like this?* sort of confused). Kraki nodded with approval.

"I'm not afraid of staff-bearers or their advice," barked Odd. "Prophecy I won't stand for, as that's been made clear in the past. But if she's got something practical to tell us, bring her over! Maybe I can hear something useful for a change."

"I'll fetch her," said Styrgrim, to my surprise.

"I will go," I said, suspicious of why Styrgrim would suddenly volunteer. "She is our crewmate. I should be the one to ask her advice."

Styrgrim was already up and headed toward the door. "No one is stopping you."

I matched his stride and glanced over at the man, getting no reaction. He moved with purpose beyond the immediate need. My guess was that he just wanted to get away from the discussion. We paused only to let the giant guarding the door open it for us, saving us the awkwardness of pushing it slowly open ourselves.

As soon as we were outside and the massive door closed behind us, I got the impression that maybe Stygrim had just wanted to get away from me.

"I wonder how far your luck stretches before it breaks," he said. "Speak out of turn to Odd again, and I think they will hear your luck snap in half throughout the whole of Risaland."

"Odd spoke out of turn himself. 'Hangers-on?' He hasn't exactly been a ring-slinger when it comes to thanking those around him, even if just with words."

"So it is with such men, and it's foolish to poke at them. You chose to take up with him knowing this. I suppose if you were a duck, you would then complain about all the water."

A bit more indirect than expected. Actually, that barb was a bit more poetic than expected. Maybe there was more beneath Styrgrim's waters than I knew. I took a deep breath, considering. We were alone. The man was sometimes freer with his speech when under stress. Was now the time to ask about my name?

No.

We found Huld sitting in the shade of a tree wider than my arm span. Her distaff sat tucked up into one forearm. She was seated with her back against a giant tree root, her head tucked into her knees. None of which was the strangest part of the scene.

"Why have you wrapped a blanket full of plants around your head?" I asked.

Grain stalks stuck up from the top of the wrapping. Some of the seeds had come loose, but that was not the only plant wrapped into the bindings. How she had managed to handle that much stinging nettle was a mystery to me, with stingers all over the stems and leaves. The plant had its uses, but I didn't think they matched the pain of handling it.

Styrgrim waved me off. "I don't care what she's wrapped around her head." He reached to unwrap it.

"Wait!"

Styrgrim fixed me with a look of disappointment. "Afraid the witch will curse you? Come on now, witch. Arrow-Odd wants an audience."

"That's not why—"

But I was too late or too quiet or both. Styrgrim grabbed the side of Huld's head, recoiling and shouting in an instant.

*"Sons of Muspell!"*

It was the tone a man might use if suddenly stung on the hand by four or five wasps. I'd ignored my foster mother's advice about handling stinging nettle carefully once, and that memory was seared into my mind. Now, a similar memory was seared into Styrgrim's. Tough as he was, those were Risaland nettle stingers. Much bigger than the ones I'd encountered. And, I assumed, much more painful.

"It's not just rye in there; she's wrapped a bunch of stinging nettle into the folds. The spines will get you, and there is poison in them."

Styrgrim examined the rapidly reddening spots on his hand. "What a shit way to die."

I shook my head, uncertain if he was serious. "Not that kind of poisonous. They're just painful, and you'll have a rash on your hand."

"Hmph." He shook his hand out as if to flick the poison off it. Which, if not obvious already, did not help. "What possible reason could she have for all this?"

"You can use the plant to treat pain," I said. Judging from the look I got in response, the information was not well-received. I turned to the *volva*. "Huld! I know you can hear me. Why is your head all wrapped up like this?"

"To kee the siris avay." She spoke through the wrappings, and as if moving her mouth as little as possible.

"What?"

"You her vee!"

"Enough of this." Styrgrim bent low and slung Huld over one shoulder. Huld protested, not that I could understand what she said. She whacked him with her distaff while upside down. It mattered not at all. Styrgrim headed back to the longhouse, and I followed.

The same giant at the door opened it again. He gave us a quizzical look, but said nothing. Which was probably what we all should have done that day.

Styrgrim carried Huld to our council corner. "I've done as you wanted," he said, lowering her slowly. Eyeing the swelling lumps on his hand, he continued, "Though I won't speak to the wisdom of that request."

"That request was to *get* wisdom," replied Odd. "Woman! Unwrap that ridiculous thing and regale us with your high-minded lore. Tell us what you can of the cursed sword, Tyrfing!"

Huld's still-wrapped head shook side to side.

"This is what Ansgar the Lucky calls wisdom?" asked Odd. "It seems to me, there might be a very thin line between wisdom and insanity, then."

And of course there is, but it was not the time for philosophizing.

Odd might have left it at that and had Huld led back out to where we'd found her. Might have, but couldn't. He had said he wasn't afraid to hear her wisdom, and now he was bound to do just that. Anything else would cast doubt on his previous statement, making everyone wonder if Odd was secretly glad Huld had not spoken.

Nobody, including me, had considered this scene from Huld's point of view. Having not considered it, I added my voice to Odd's.

"Come on, Huld, we are not here for games."

She shook her head again. She tried to rise, but Stygrim's paw was firm on her shoulder, and she stayed put.

This was getting us nowhere, so I decided to intervene. The head wrap was not a complicated thing. One end of the fabric was simply stuffed into the folds. I knew how to avoid the nettle well enough and, carefully, I pinched a bit of fabric and pulled.

Styrgrim pinned Huld's arms to prevent her from swatting at me while I did this. Meanwhile, the *vǫlva* mumbled incoherent curses at us until I pulled the last fabric away from her mouth. She fell silent as her face was exposed, her eyes shut hard.

"Huld!" I shouted. "Stop playing around. And remember to breathe."

But she wouldn't breathe. At first, I couldn't understand why. Understanding dawned on me when she sniffed and jerked back all of a sudden, as if she'd snorted a thumbnail of salt. In that instant, it was too late.

Spirits can be called. They also might get inside you if they're motivated to do so, and if there's an opening. I recalled a night when Huld had me chant for her while she sat *seiðr*. With spirits being called nearby, she had advised me to plug up my ears and clench my asshole tight. It had not been a joke.

*They have ways of getting in.*

Her eyes opened red. Not reddened from lack of sleep, I mean solid blood-red. Her mouth opened so wide I had to take a step back or fear falling into it.

Styrgrim let her go, his right hand going to the hilt of his sword. The council members rose and stood back.

"*Hear me,*" said a voice that was not Huld's. A bony finger trained on

Arrow-Odd. *"I see a future for you, young-but-old. You killed your horse to avoid the last one."* Maniacal laughter followed. Not the crazed battle glee I'd heard among some of the men. At least that was familiar. This sound was so unfamiliar as to be not of this realm. *"What will you do, knowing this one?"*

The Hel-voice spoke a verse:

> "A brother slain by
>     the sword already—
> grasp at it again
>     and grind the others.
> That bright cleaver
>     will carve you hollow,
> hastening victory
>     for villains and trolls.
>
> What lessons learned
>     from long ago
> of leading hosts
>     only to hasten their doom?
> The arrow's flight
>     ends in ruin—
> A constant tragedy
>     of the Traveler's character."

A moment after speaking, the faintest mist rose from Huld's body, coalescing with a faint upward gust. Huld fell sideways. I caught her, or caught enough of her that she didn't smack her head on the hard floor, and eased her down.

Muffled shouting from just outside the hall broke the stunned silence that followed the prophecy. Soon, it was unmuffled shouting as Ketill squeezed through the heavy double doors without waiting for the giant's help. The wizard's face was aghast as he raced toward us.

"What did you do?!"

Obviously, something stupid.

"She just—I mean, we wanted to hear her wisdom, so we brought her in, but she was playing this game—"

*"Game?!"* The wizard's voice thundered through the hall as he pointed to

the wrapping on the floor. Two giants eating at a table nearby moved farther away. "She has been holding back against a prophecy since we arrived! Doing her best not to speak it, and at great pains. And for what? For you idiots!" He said *idiots*, plural, but pointed at Arrow-Odd.

Odd shrugged. "It appears she failed."

"When a spirit has decided to make a *vǫlva* speak a prophecy, do you think it's easy to stop it?" He picked up the wrapping. "You stripped all her protections away while I was gone." Somehow, he knew to look at me as he said it.

"What's done is done," said Styrgrim. "The only question is what Odd intends to do about this prophecy."

"It seems a waste to ask the woman her wisdom and then ignore it," said Hallfred Horsefly, doubtless interested in Odd *not* pursuing the sword further if it meant the death of them all. Or, us all.

Huld coughed and ripped an arm away from my supportive embrace and stumbled over to Ketill. "Stop badgering him, you fools! It's bad enough what you've let loose. Now you paint him into the corner you expect him to walk out of!" The *vǫlva* staggered out of the place while Ketill helped her remain upright.

The council left, one by one. Hallfred Horsefly started to speak to Odd, who waved him off. Odd would be alone with his thoughts for a while.

I shook my head at my own stupid self. I didn't understand the nettle, but I knew grain was strong against sorcery. The evidence was right in front of me, I just hadn't bothered to put it together at the time. Such is the way of the biggest mistakes.

I found myself a giant-sized cup of ale and a quiet spot on the other side of the longhouse to brood in. This was bad, as if things hadn't already been bad enough.

Then again, was the warning really new? Tyrfing was well known for killing those who wielded it and those close to them. The prophecy was a surprise, but should not have been. With that fate laid bare, though, what would Arrow-Odd do? And how long would the rest of us follow him as he did it?

My thoughts were interrupted by Styrgrim's heavy footfalls. He, too, had sought a large serving of ale after that debacle. Soon, my quiet spot was not so quiet after all.

"Congratulations," he said.

"I am aware of my error. There is no need to remind me of it."

"You mistake my meaning." He raised his cup to mine. "It is a hard thing to grow from follower to leader. And in growing from follower to leader, boy to man, whatever to whatever, one commits at least one gods-worthy cock-up. Here we have cocked it up, the both of us."

The sentiment was more shocking to me than a *vǫlva* with blood-red eyes. Eventually, I raised my cup back. We both drank deep.

I came up for air first and burped. "Just one gods-worthy cock-up?"

"If the first one doesn't kill you, then it's more than one." He took another deep drink and came up from it with a grim expression. "I have managed more cock-ups than anyone I've ever known. They never seem to kill me, and so they keep coming." His voice was bitter, almost as if he'd rather have died than make another big mistake. Then he looked at his swollen hand, now almost twice its normal size, and laughed.

"If the prophecy is right," I said, "then helping Odd to get Tyrfing is likely to be our last big mistake."

"And he knows it, but he won't be swayed. And we know it, but we won't change our course." He shrugged. "Maybe the Norns don't really carve our fates. Maybe we're just predictable."

I continued after a long pause. "Since we're on such a grim course, it should be no great burden for you to tell me my real name."

He stopped cold and silent, sniffing the air as if to detect something unseen. Suspicious, but unable to pin down the suspicion. Eventually, he drained the rest of his cup and set it down. Then he left me with a thing he had never offered before, a challenge.

"Earn it."

# CHAPTER 17

## NARRATIVE GRADIENT

KING HILDIR RETURNED A WEEK AFTER HULD'S PROPHECY. WE all sat awkwardly at the giant tables as the King of Risaland took his high seat and held court. He had many matters to hear about, and appeared to enjoy hearing about them in detail. Most of these matters were told by his daughter, Hildigunn, since she had acted in his stead. The last item was the issue of hospitality for Arrow-Odd's army.

"I'm glad you saw fit to accept that request," said Hildir. "And I've already heard some news related to that, so there's no need to repeat it here. I've known Odd for a long time, but it's also been a long time since we last saw one another, and I want to hear everything he's been up to. Now, that could take a while! And it's no reason to delay everyone's next meal any longer. Bring out the food! I will catch up with Odd on my own time."

Hildigunn, then, didn't need to recount the death of Vignir in front of the entire court. And Odd didn't have to explain his ill-fated prophecy in front of everyone. I liked King Hildir right away.

I'm sure Odd told his friend Hildir of Huld's prophecy in private, but he never addressed the army about it. Whether Odd confided something in Hallfred Horsefly, I don't know. No public statement made meant Odd's plan had not changed.

Despite the warm friendship between Odd and Hildir, the army's mood continued to darken. Everyone had heard of the prophecy by then, and it wasn't ambiguous that Odd was leading the army toward destruction. Fear of Styrgrim's wrath did not prevent talk of abandoning Odd. I heard only whispers, as people were not about to speak openly in front of a War Council member.

My hearing had always been most acute, though. And it didn't take a wise man to understand that warriors may remain loyal to a legend despite great risk, but remaining loyal with certain doom hanging over one's head was a different thing. Some questioned Odd's sanity.

The mood became gloomier as the days grew shorter. At its darkest, we had maybe two hours of full daylight a day. There was some twilight, but night was most of the day. The White Sea would have frozen by then, not that we would have considered sailing even to alleviate the sense of being shut in. We didn't even venture far out in the dark.

During such times, people need leaders less and skalds more. The battles are against boredom, rumination, hopelessness. Weapons are useless against such things, but a good storyteller with a fair hand on the lyre can dispel the kind of thoughts that make people sick.

We had five good skalds, and all of us were needed to get the army through that winter.

Steinvor was the best poet. I will always remember the imagery of her kennings and heiti, and the resonance of her voice as she told of ancient heroes and monsters. Jorun was even better with the lyre than I was, and that was saying something. Bjorn kept his music simple, but he knew how to weave it into his own style of telling stories. He often paused his playing to make humorous asides, speaking directly to the audience. Hallfred Horsefly was my favorite. Where Steinvor and Jorun told the big myths and legends and Bjorn of epic battles, Hallfred related the smaller happenings of stories—the events that aren't often told. The humor, the foolishness, the humanness of gods and rulers.

Also, Hallfred did the most hilarious voices I'd ever heard. Puffed-up Thor. Drunken Odin. Oversexed Frey. A story of King Skjold of the Danes became a new favorite of mine. The legendary king was tragically overwhelmed, not by the spears of his enemies, but by bureaucrats who interrupted his sleep and harassed him to death while he tried to take a shit.

Those stories did more than lighten the mood. They made us seem less small, the world less remote and more relatable. The gods sitting high up in

Asgard had many of the same insecurities we did. Perhaps they were not as far off as they seemed.

That's the power of good stories, and why the giants started to pay us more attention. Including Hildigunn, who issued a challenge early one evening, when it seemed like the days couldn't get any shorter. With humans and giants all gathered in the hall, she stood by the high seat and pointed in the general direction of us shorter folk.

"These five have made the nights cheerier for some time now. Who among the *risar* can match them? You're not afraid to try, are you?"

We were smaller but far more numerous, taking up one entire side of the longhouse. Those of us on the War Council sat closest to the high seat. Sat or stood, as it was still a bit awkward either way. Though not on the War Council himself, Magnus stood next to me.

On the other side of the longhouse, none of the giants volunteered to play skald for a night. A tricky thing for them, I supposed. Taking a bold chance would be considered manly, but failing to measure up against such tiny people left one open to insults nobody wanted to endure. It seemed the Norse Code of Manliness applied to giants as much as humans.

King Hildir took that bold chance, anyway. "I won't claim to be a great teller of stories, but neither am I afraid to fail. I would rather fall flat on my face trying than cringe away from a difficult thing! In fact, I will tell a story about just that, where I risked all to become king." The giants cheered, and so did we. The king wasn't done yet, though. "Let's make it interesting, then! I will tell a story tonight, but we will have one of you five each subsequent night. Bring your best, with the winner to be judged at the end!"

"Tomorrow is not far off," said Hildigunn. "The first skald to perform will have the least preparation. Who is bold enough for that?"

Bjorn spoke up faster and louder than anyone else. "I won't pretend to be the boldest, but I am the brashest. I think that honor should fall to me."

Hildir nodded. "We giants don't mind a bit of brashness now and then, although it can be a tricky thing. In any case, I think some reward to the winner is appropriate, but I'll have to think of something. Now, listen, because what I lack in skill of narrative, I make up for with truth."

Hildir was the least among three brothers, he said. Least in size and strength, in age, and in future prospects. He never had much hope of becoming king. A chance meeting changed that, so he would begin there.

He was rowing his stone boat one day when he heard a tiny voice call out. The tiny voice was Arrow-Odd's. He was stuck high on a high cliff.

Odd said he'd been captured by a giant vulture. Hildir replied that he hated the vulture, but he was no good at climbing, and couldn't get up there to help. Odd said he had a way to deal with the bird, but only if Hildir could throw him some rope. That much, he could do, and that was enough for Odd. Odd set fire to the nest the next time the vulture came by, and then escaped on Hildir's rope.

"It flew off from there, but fell dead not long after. I keep the beak and claws up there." Hildir pointed upward from his high seat. The beak and claws were mounted on the wall behind it. That beak was nearly as long as a man, even bigger than the giant eagle I had run into.

Hildir said that despite his small stature, Odd was no less wise than giants. More so, in many ways. In fact, Odd had an idea of how Hildir could become king.

Kingship was decided by a dogfight, and the dogs of Hildir's brothers were big and fierce. Odd said he knew of a bigger, fiercer dog by far, and showed Hildir where to find it.

Odd scouted out the dog's lair and took Hildir to it. He told Hildir, since he was a giant, to reach in and pull it out of its den despite its protestations. Odd told him this dog was called a 'grizzly bear,' and that it was just starting to get really hungry and mean.

Hildir took a chance with this dog and won. Thus, he became King of Risaland.

He gave more details, but that was essentially all of it. It was not a bad story but was a bit disappointing. He'd said he 'risked all' to become king, but then had not told us about the risk involved. He focused more on his friendship with Arrow-Odd.

As with all the stories and performances, humans and giants then discussed what we'd heard for the rest of the night. To that end, the story was not so bad. There was a great deal of interest in Hildir's past with Odd. Interest, but not excitement.

"It seemed like the story was missing something," said Magnus.

I kept my voice low when I replied, "There was no tension." I had a lot more thoughts about what a good story should include but thought it best to keep my reply concise. Even concise and spoken in a whisper, I looked up to notice King Hildir's eyes flick my way. He couldn't have heard me, could he?

Nothing came of it, so I put it out of my mind.

On the next night, Bjorn told the story of the theft of Thor's hammer, Mjolnir. You might think that story is a tense thing, with the gods losing the most powerful weapon in Asgard. Instead, it is full of absurd humor, all delivered in Bjorn's characteristic deadpan.

The *jǫtunn* lord, Thrym, steals Mjolnir in that story, though it's never explained how. The way this tale is told varies greatly by the teller, and Bjorn folded the inconsistencies into the performance. How does Thrym steal the hammer? Doesn't matter. The teller finds the premise just as implausible as the audience and laughs along with them.

Loki is entrusted to find out who stole it. When there is chaos in Asgard, it is usually because of Loki. But not this time! Loki finds Thrym, who admits he's got the hammer. Thrym wants to trade: Mjolnir for the beautiful Freya as a wife.

Loki takes that offer back to Asgard. Thor thinks it's a fine trade and asks Freya if she'll marry Thrym to get the hammer back. She gets so angry, the hall shakes. Shakes so much that her treasured torc, the Brisingamen, falls off her neck to the floor. Needless to say, Freya refuses.

Heimdall proposes a plan so stupid it just might work: Thor should go to Thrym's hall dressed in Freya's finery, right down to the Brisingamen. Thrym won't know who is under the veil. Loki speaks up for the idea, the only time he and his nemesis, Heimdall, agree on anything, and says he'll go with Thor in the disguise of a bride's maid.

Thor hates this idea, but he is out of options.

"Sometimes you just need to shut up and wear the dress," Bjorn quipped, to a lot of table-slapping and laughter. Except from Arrow-Odd.

Thor drives to Jotunheim in his chariot in a foul mood, but Loki is with him to smooth out any misunderstandings. Thrym welcomes them and offers food and drink. Thor eats an ox and eight salmon, washing it down with three casks of mead. That gets Thrym's attention, and he asks why Freya has such a great appetite.

Loki replies that they'd traveled eight nights and that Freya had eaten nothing during their trip, so eager was she to be married. Thrym finds this completely believable.

Well into his horns, Thrym leans in to steal an early kiss. He recoils at what he sees behind the bridal veil, though, because Freya's eyes are bloodshot and terrifying.

Loki replies that they'd traveled eight nights and that Freya had slept not at all during their trip, so eager was she to be married. Thrym finds this completely believable.

"The Brisingamen may have been working its magic to hide Thor's giant red beard, but who knows?" Bjorn shrugged. "The extent of men's idiocy, when it comes to women, is epic in its own right. And too much drink does not improve judgment."

My ignorance regarding women was indeed epic, and I knew too well what alcohol did to one's mind. Bjorn was telling us a big joke, all the while conveying truths that were completely serious. I cast my gaze about and found Steinvor looking at me. I wasn't sure what to do about that.

Then she winked and looked away, and I was even less sure what to do about that.

Thrym is satisfied with Loki's answers, but impatient to be married. Loki says they need Mjolnir, both to consecrate the marriage and to pay the bride's price. Thrym agrees, brings out the hammer, and lays it right on not-Freya's lap.

The thunder god rises, tearing the veil from his head. Lightning shoots through the hall while steel splits *jǫtunn* heads. Thor makes such a slaughter of those *jǫtnar* that it's heard for miles around. A manly thing for the most manly god!

Then, Thor returns to Asgard in a dress because he had not thought of bringing a change of clothes. In a manly fashion, he blames Loki for the lack of forethought.

"And that is how Thor got his hammer back," Bjorn concluded.

That was a great story, but Bjorn was certainly the brashest of us. I wasn't sure quite what the relationship was between *risar* and other *jǫtnar*, but I knew that sometimes, the terms were interchangeable. Which meant that Bjorn had told a story that ended in the mass killing of people who were probably related to the giants in the audience.

Most of the applause came from humans.

Hildir sighed. "That's about how I heard it. Though I can't say there were many of Thrym's relatives around to tell it a different way."

After an awkward pause (not awkward for Bjorn, by the look on his face), I had an idea to change the subject a bit. "How did the Brisingamen come to Midgard? Freya let Thor use it, but then the story just ends. Was it left among the carnage? Did Loki steal it?"

A few chuckles while Bjorn sated his parched throat. "I don't rightly know, but that would be my first thought!"

"Make up a story about it!" shouted Magnus.

"But we don't know how it happened," said Josur.

"How do we really know what happens among the gods?" Birki shrugged. "It's all their word, anyway."

"The gods can make whatever claims they like," said Arrow-Odd. "But never forget that they live by the stories we choose to tell, and the way we choose to tell them."

Arrow-Odd reclaimed a great deal of my respect by saying that. I only hoped he wouldn't lose it again. Odd was a complicated man. I was never wholly in awe of him or against him, and perhaps that was the quality that made him so compelling.

Jorun played the lyre to accompany her story the next night. I won't recount it fully because I've already told the story about the bet between Odin and Frigg. Frigg sends her handmaiden, Fulla, to set Odin up for failure. Odin runs afoul of the trap and gets bad hospitality. That story, about the bet, bookends Odin's long and poetic description of many things in the world. Which is really just Odin showing off. After the long description, he kills the king who refused to serve him mead and leaves in a big huff.

That's a prose story with a poem in the middle of it, and it's a testament to the skill of the skald how well the verses describe the different names for things. Jorun was pitch-perfect in her phrasing and matched the mood by playing the lyre as few others could do.

The giants liked Jorun's story a lot better than Bjorn's.

Steinvor went on the next night, and she told about Loki's battle of insults against the gods. Not content to orchestrate Baldr's death, Loki comes to Aegir's hall, where the gods are drinking, and begins the night by killing one of Aegir's well-liked servants. The meat of the story is the choice of what gods are present and the quality of insults that are levied back and forth. The insults can't just be cutting; they need to rely on quality kennings and heiti and have multiple meanings. The more esoteric the references, the better.

I heard a few lines familiar to me, but the best insults were original, including a vicious one from Loki about pissing into Njord's mouth. I've rarely heard alliteration so perfectly phrased, or from as sonorous a voice. Based on their reactions, neither had the giants of Risaland, who cheered for more.

On the fifth night, it was Hallfred Horsefly's turn. He had a tale I'd never heard, one he'd picked up from a Karelian, though he didn't say when or where. It was a tale about Vainamoinen, the Eternal Skald.

"That name sounds familiar," said Magnus.

I nodded. "Remember Joni? He guided us through Karelia and told a story about Vainamoinen on the way."

"Ah!"

I wasn't convinced Magnus really remembered. But I didn't think that would dampen Hallfred's telling.

"This is a story about some of the heroes of Kalevala," Hallfred began, "and about the power of skalds and their songs."

This story vexed me quite a bit, so I'll recount it in full:

"It is a time of sadness and loss in Kalevala. Vainamoinen tries to console his brother, Ilmarinen, the Eternal Smith. Ilmarinen is sad about his wife's recent death. She'd mistreated a thrall, and that thrall had arranged for her to be mauled to death by bears."

"This is the best story already!" shouted Kraki. Hallfred ignored him.

"Vainamoinen knows his brother needs a quest, or he will just keep brooding. They decide to sail north, to the land of Pohjola, ruled by the evil witch, Louhi."

"She wasn't so bad," Hildir interrupted.

Hildigunn gave her father an aggressive shushing. He shrugged, but didn't say anything more.

"They find other heroes of Kalevala to go with them. Their goal: Ask Louhi if she will share in the bounty of her machine, the Sampo. This machine produced endless salt, flour, and gold, so she could easily share with Kalevala. Besides, it had been Ilmarinen who built the thing. It was only Louhi's because he'd traded the Sampo for his wife. Who turned out to not be so good!

"It is a long way to Pohjola. And you know what happens during long journeys over unfamiliar waters: Sea monsters. The heroes encounter the Great Pike of the North, big as their ship or more so, and find him a difficult fish to deal with.

"Vainamoinen draws his sword and sings a song of power into it. Lightning flashes as he drives the sword down into the spine of the pike, slaying the creature. He cuts up the giant fish for a feast and fashions a kantele out of the lower jawbone.

"The heroes of Kalevala are in awe of the beautiful instrument and of Vainamoinen's songs with it. When they all arrive in Pohjola, even Louhi is impressed with the music. Pohjola's best—wizards, heroes, maidens, even Louhi—try to play the thing. They get nothing but the most discordant music. Only Vainamoinen can coax harmony from this kantele."

Magnus and I exchanged a look. I had played this kantele, the one Hallfred was talking about, in a dream. Other than Ketill, Magnus had been the only one I had trusted with my dream of Njord and Skadi. They'd had a strange stringed instrument fashioned out of a fish's lower jaw, and neither of them could play it. I'd worked out how to get music out of the thing, faded into wakefulness, and from then on, I was able to speak Karelian with Joni.

"The heroes of Kalevala ask Louhi to share in the profit of the Sampo. Ilmarinen had created it, after all, and Vainamoinen had recruited him to do it. Besides, was there not more than enough to share?

"Louhi refuses angrily. She gets even angrier when one of the brasher heroes announces they will take the Sampo by force. Vainamoinen sees that Louhi is about to order her warriors to fall on them, so he starts playing.

"Powerful as Louhi is, she and her warriors fall under the spell of Vainamoinen's kantele. The skald plays a song to put all of Pohjola to sleep. Thus free to steal—ahem, liberate—the Sampo, the heroes of Kalevala find it bolted to a mountain. The Eternal Smith undoes the bolts, and the heroes take the Sampo to their ship.

"The crew from Kalevala is so overjoyed, they all want to sing a song of victory. Wise old Vainamoinen forbids it, however. They are far from home and still far from success.

"They sail for a few days until one hero can no longer control his enthusiasm. He breaks into song, a poor one, and wakes a bird. The crane is so upset at this horrible noise that it cries out, waking up the rest of Pohjola.

"Louhi casts three spells to aid her in taking back the Sampo. The first spell is a dense fog that slows the fleeing ship to a crawl. The second spell summons a monster from the depths to devour the heroes and return the Sampo to Pohjola. The third spell sends the winds to raise the very ocean against her enemies.

"In her fastest ship, Louhi and a thousand warriors set out in pursuit.

"The mist delays the heroes of Kalevala. It resists their every turn until Vainamoinen cleaves it with his sword. Finally able to see, the heroes hoist the sail.

"Soon, a sea monster rises, and Vainamoinen meets it face to face. He speaks to it before battle begins, asking why the creature pursues them. It replies that it is bound by sorcery to Louhi's will. So the Eternal Skald speaks a verse to release the creature from its binding, leaving it free to choose. The sea monster utters its thanks and vanishes into the depths."

Hallfred craned forward and cupped his mouth in an aside, saying, "Nobody likes being told what to do."

Hairs on the back of my neck had been standing throughout the story. A witch in pursuit of heroes? Three spells, one of them a summoned monster? Some of this story paralleled the Battle of Lejre, and I could work out what that might mean.

"The sea rises against the heroes of Kalevala. Soon, the strakes are cracking and water is getting into their ship. The spell seems too powerful to overcome. As a last idea, Vainamoinen sings a verse of offering and tosses his kantele into the ocean. This great treasure from the sea, now returned, stops the sea's roiling, and the heroes of Kalevala sail on.

"Louhi's ship closes in on them. Vainamoinen tosses a flint down into the sea and sings a song. The flint sprouts into a mountain beneath Louhi's ship.

"Try as she might, Louhi cannot dislodge the ship and get it back into the sea. But the Queen of Pohjola is as resourceful as the Eternal Skald. She breaks the ship apart and uses the pieces to fashion a wooden eagle that will carry her army through the air.

"As the eagle approaches, Vainamoinen shouts a last chance offer: Share the Sampo and divide its spoils. Louhi laughs in his face.

"The crew of Kalevala raises shields in defense. The wooden eagle swoops in to attack, its spearmen trading thrusts with the sailors, its archers sending a hail of arrows. Over and over, the crews clash with losses on both sides.

"Seeing no way to fight every warrior Louhi has, Vainamoinen raises the ship's rudder and strikes the eagle with it. The massive hit shakes the eagle, knocking Louhi's spearmen and archers into the sea. The eagle grabs the Sampo with one talon and lifts it high into the air.

"But it is only one talon, and the Sampo is large. The eagle loses its grip, and the Sampo falls into the sea, breaking the machine into pieces. Fragments wash away among the great billows. The Sampo is no more.

"Louhi takes the lid with her back to Pohjola, but it is a hollow thing, and she knows it. She speaks powerful curses against Kalevala and all its people. To steal the sun and moon, to send nine diseases, to bring famine and destruction to its children, and more.

"Vainamoinen gives thanks for a safe return home. He finds remnants of the Sampo on the shores of Kalevala and gathers them to see what use they might be to his people, if any.

"That ends the story of the Sampo, but not of Louhi and Vainamoinen. Those curses would be dealt with, but that is another story."

Cheers met the end of Hallfred's tale. Every skald in that room was a legend for the ages. The kind of skald the world, if it still has any sense, would pay a great price to have more of. But among them was Hallfred Horsefly, and I looked up to him in the greatest awe. I would never forget his stories, or the way he brought them to life.

"Well told, well told!" cheered Hildir.

"A story familiar to you?" asked Arrow-Odd.

"Quite, though I haven't heard it told in some time. And as I said, I don't think Louhi was quite so bad as those heroes of Kalevala described her."

"Difficult to tell what might be left out of old stories," replied Odd.

"We should think of our own version of that one," said Josur. "The Karelians have a skald for a god, but what skald is there in Asgard?" Nods all around. The *Æsir* had no main teller of stories, singer, or player of music. It seemed like a glaring omission.

Odd clasped hands with Hallfred and congratulated him. That was some good story. Exciting, inspiring. It even had the rest of us wishing for something more from our more familiar myths. Now everyone wanted to discuss it, especially me.

Magnus had a different idea. "We need to work on your story for tomorrow night."

"I have a story in mind. What work do you think it needs, not yet knowing what it is?"

Magnus looked over both shoulders, then lowered himself off the bench and to the floor. I followed as he edged us away from the din of dense conversation near the center of the hall. Even with nobody close by, he still spoke low, for my ears only.

"You need to win."

I laughed. "We don't even know what Hildir's reward is!"

He stared at me wide-eyed—a little drunk, but honest in his surprise. "Hildir's reward doesn't matter! You aren't just a skald, you're a leader. And

Arrow-Odd isn't just a leader, he is *the* leader. If his skald tells the best story of all, he secures more confidence in his leadership. You need more confidence in *your* leadership so that if you need to speak against him, people want to listen. That doesn't mean just a good story."

I sighed, knowing he was right. "It means *the best* story. But Hallfred's story was grand. And new, too. I'm good, but I don't know if I'm that good."

Magnus nodded. "You're plenty good, and you speak the meanings of stories better than he does. Remember the night we met? Come on! You told a story, it failed, and then you told *the same story* in a different way. You added *why* it was a good story, and it succeeded! Now, tell me what you were thinking, and let's make sure it is one for the gods to remember."

# CHAPTER 18

## ILLUSIONAL DEFEAT

THE SCENTS OF GOAT STEW AND FRESH ALE FILLED THE longhouse. Even more giants had crowded in than the previous night, and Hildir had more food and drink readied as a result. As for the goat stew, that had been my request: An accompaniment for the story.

My stomach rumbled at the smell of the food. I had eaten a bit, because it was folly to entertain on an empty stomach. But I had eaten sparingly, because it is also folly to perform while overfull.

I held a drinking horn almost too big for one hand. It was good for effect, but was filled with water from the fresh snow. Too many nights, I had gotten too drunk, and I was done with that childishness. I would need all my wits to tell my story and make it memorable to humans and giants alike.

The humans stuck to our familiar side of the hall but bunched together on the floor rather than down a long set of tables and benches. Tonight, it was just a single row of tables stretching down the middle of the hall, and that's where I was. Not sitting, but standing on the table.

A bit dramatic? Maybe, but also effective. I like to move around when I tell a story, like to gesture and make eye contact. And I wanted everyone to hear me well enough. That's where I began after Hildir announced it was the final night of the skaldic competition, standing on that central table. Magnus and I had prepared a telling, not just a story.

"I've owed Magnus a story about Thor since the night we met," I began, to low growls of approval. "Or at least Magnus thinks I owe him a story about Thor. And tonight is a good night for one!"

Hands slapped legs in applause. Little hands, at least. Stories about Thor were almost always exciting. Bjorn's story about Thor was a good one, if a bit short. Odd's people were excited to hear another, perhaps a longer and more involved adventure. The giants were less enthused at this idea.

Hildir crossed his arms. "Thor is not exactly a hero in Risaland." Translation: *Don't embarrass me in front of my people.*

"I think you would not deny Thor's importance, Hildir," I replied. "And some say this is not a nice story to tell, because it shows Thor as a loser. I say it shows no such thing, but I'll leave that until later. Nice or not, let me be judged by the story and not whether its hero is well-liked in Risaland." Translation: *Trust me.*

Hildir did not look very trusting when he gestured for me to begin.

"This is a story of Thor's travels through Jotunheim. He and Loki were out there, far to the east. Or maybe not so far from here, as we are already far east—and north—of our homes. But I think he was farther out, in a wilder place where the land is unknown."

"That's east of here, for certain," rumbled Hildir. "Where it's unlikely men of Midgard would be given good hospitality."

"Then let's drink to hospitality before we go too far!" I raised my horn. "Here's to Hildir! Here's to Hildigunn!" Humans and giants raised cups and horns and thanked their hosts. Hildir nodded in return. He may have been a magnanimous king, but I've never met anyone who didn't appreciate just a little thanks for their efforts.

"Thor and Loki rode out to the border of Midgard. This was in Thor's chariot, pulled by two goats. They stopped at a small farmhouse there and asked for hospitality for the night before they pressed on to Jotunheim.

"The family was willing to share what they had, but they didn't have much. Thor offered his goats for the meal. He slaughtered them and set the couple's children—the boy, Thjalfi, and his sister, Roskva—to cooking the meat. Thor asked for them to follow a single rule: Keep the bones whole, and pile them onto the skins intact.

"The family hadn't had such a rich meal in ages, and they thanked Thor over and over. But they hadn't seen much of the world yet or taken in the wisdom of experience. Thjalfi wanted to split one of the bones to suck the marrow out and have an even richer dinner. Roskva shook her head.

"'Why not?' he demanded. But before she could say anything, Thjalfi cracked the bone open.

"The next morning, Thor piled up the bones into their respective skins and consecrated them with his hammer, Mjolnir. As he'd done many times, the ritual restored his goats to life, whole and ready to pull the chariot again. Except that one of them was not ready to pull the chariot due to a broken leg.

"The thunder god saw this, and his knuckles went white as he gripped his hammer. His brows arched down so much, you couldn't even see his eyes anymore.

"'Couldn't you all follow one simple rule?' chided Loki. He enjoyed being on this side of a wagging finger, for once.

"Thor raised his hammer. Lightning flashed across the hearth and tables, destroying cups and bowls. The parents offered all they had if only Thor would forgive them. When he saw them quaking on the ground, though, his wrath uncoiled as quickly as it had gathered.

"What need did he have of smiting fearful farmers? He was Thor, whose hammer sought out the strongest of Asgard's enemies. He was not the slayer of frightened weaklings. He had to demand some compensation for the damages, though. He accepted that Thjalfi and Roskva would join him as bond servants while the goat healed.

"Brother and sister both thought this was a great thing at first.

"'Where are we going?' asked Thjalfi.

"Thor said they were headed to Jotunheim. He added that since one of the goats was lame, the four of them would go on foot.

"Thjalfi rather regretted snapping that bone after hearing this.

"The four traveled a long way into a vast forest in Jotunheim. One day, Thor kept them going into nightfall, and they had to seek shelter in a cave. They were grateful for the shelter, but earthquakes throughout the night made it impossible to sleep.

"The next morning, the weary group found that it was not a cave at all but was the inside of a huge mitten, and the owner of that mitten was still sleeping. The huge *jǫtunn* snored so loudly, they realized this was the source of the 'earthquakes' they had experienced throughout the night.

"Thor strapped on his girdle of might and readied his hammer, Mjolnir. Then, he struck the sleeping giant on the head as hard as he could.

"The giant opened his bleary eyes. 'Oh, hello, little people. It seems I've slept in. Good thing that leaf fell on my head just now. Who are you, wandering out so far in the forest?' Thor gaped at the giant. It had been a square blow. Or so he thought. 'Oh, I know! You are Thor of the *Æsir*. Who are your companions?'

"The *jǫtunn* was friendly enough. His name was Skrymir, and he offered to travel with the four of them so they would be safe. They accepted and somehow managed to keep up despite his long strides.

"Skrymir's snoring only got worse. After two nights with no sleep, red-eyed Thor had enough. He pulled out Mjolnir brought it down on the sleeping giant's head, burying the entire front of the hammer in his skull.

"'Oh, hello Thor,'" said Skrymir. 'I think a fly just landed on my head. Did you shoo it away?'

"Thor grumbled something about sleep and walked off, shaking his head in disbelief.

"The next night, Skrymir offered to share food with them. 'But I am tired, so I am going to sleep. You can have whatever you like in my pack.'

"Thor was hungry, so he went after the pack. It was tied shut, though, and no matter how hard he pulled, the knot would not come undone. He could see the way to undo it, so he set his feet and pulled with all his strength. Still, the knot refused to give even a nail's width.

"In a fit of sleep-deprived, hunger-induced frustration, Thor summoned every bit of might and wrath in him and channeled it through Mjolnir for a final strike on Skrymir's forehead. The hammer struck true, and the blow was so powerful that he buried the weapon down to its haft. Now, at least, he would be able to sleep.

"'What are you still doing up, Thor?' asked Skrymir. 'Did an acorn just fall on your head as well?'"

I had the giants laughing along with the story. Thor unmanned by dressing as a woman had its own sort of humor. But Thor unmanned by vexing his strength, the most important thing about him, was a different sort of joke.

"Thor fell asleep much later on that night, muttering to himself and wondering about his sanity. In the morning, he was not much better. Skrymir bade them all a very good morning, but said he had to turn north from there and head into the mountains.

"'I suggest you go farther east if you want some good hospitality,' he said. 'If you keep on that way, you'll come to Utgard. Just keep in mind that they are even bigger than me, and they don't take well to poor manners. If that doesn't sound good, I think your best course would be to turn back now.'

"He left them without waiting for an answer. Thor did not hope to see him again.

"The four continued east until they came to a great fortress at about midday. They squeezed through the bars of the gate in the front and walked right into the longhouse at the center of the place. Many eyes followed them, but no one challenged their presence. Thor decided that walking in and announcing himself straightaway would be best.

"These people were bigger than Skrymir, just as he'd described, with a big longhouse to match. At the end was a *jǫtunn* dressed in bright colors sitting in the high seat. He smiled at their presence and waited until they were a respectable distance to address them.

"'Is that Cart-Thor?' asked the *jǫtunn*. 'It must be—look at his girdle and hammer! But no cart? Tell us, Cart-Thor, do you stop here because your chariot is broken?'

"'I often walk when I'm not in a hurry,' huffed Thor. 'I left my chariot a long way back. We stopped because we heard the lord here was generous with hospitality.'

"'That's a true enough statement. I am Utgard-Loki, lord of this hall.'

"Thor and Loki exchanged confused looks at this name.

"Utgard-Loki continued before they could say anything. 'But not just any passers-by are welcome here. You may stay as long as there is some feat one of you can perform.'

"Loki tugged on Thor's shoulder. 'There's one feat I'm quite prepared to have a go at.' He strode forward and announced, 'I think there is no one among you who can eat food faster than I can.'

"'That will be a good feat if you can perform it,' said Utgard-Loki, though he sounded doubtful this would happen. He called down his man, Logi, and seated the contestants at opposite ends of a long table. Then, he ordered trenchers full of meat brought to the table in equal amounts on both sides.

"'I think there is something you should know,' said Roskva.

"Quiet, girl!' said Loki. 'Can you not see a man at a serious task here?'

"Roskva crossed her arms and blushed at the chiding, but said nothing more as the eating contest began.

"Loki devoured the meat with no care for table manners. He smacked and chewed with his mouth open, sometimes hardly chewing at all before swallowing. Thjalfi and Roskva marveled at the change from silver-tongued guest to manhandler of meats. Spittle, grease, and bones flew as Loki worked his way down the table until he ran into Logi.

"Loki stood as tall as he could and turned around to see how far he'd come. Seeing they'd met in the middle, he took it to be a tie. Then, he looked at Logi's half of the table and saw he had lost. While Loki had eaten the meat all along his length of the table, Logi had eaten the meat and also consumed the bones.

"'That was a good try,' said Utgard-Loki. 'Most would not have gotten that far. But as you can see, we have a faster eater among us.'

"Loki waddled down from the table feeling like his stomach would burst open. 'That's the fastest I've ever eaten!' he hissed at Thor. He burped and had to hold his hand to his mouth to keep anything more than a burp from coming up.

"Thjalfi tugged on Thor's shoulder next, eager to win the thunder god's favor. 'I can run faster than they will expect. Let me try.'

"Thor looked down at the boy. Maybe closer to man than boy. If he could do it, then perhaps taking him as a servant would prove a wise decision after all. Thor nodded.

"'Brother, I think—'

"But Thjalfi interrupted his sister. 'I will perform a feat! No one has ever been able to outrun me in a fair contest.'

"'That would be a good feat,' said Utgard-Loki. 'And we'll certainly have a fair contest. Let's go outside where there is a long stretch of flat ground.'

"Utgard-Loki called his man, Hugi, down to compete in the footrace. When they started, Thor and Loki were both impressed by Thjalfi's speed. Hugi, however, overtook him and turned around to watch as Thjalfi crossed the finish line second. They ran two more races, but Hugi won by a wider margin each time. Utgard-Loki pronounced that the competition was decided.

"'I will say this, though,' he added. 'We have never seen a guest run as fast as that, even if it was not fast enough to win.'

"'That's enough of these games,' boomed Thor. 'I will perform the feat, as I should have in the first place. There's not one among your people who can out-drink me, so let's get on with it.'

"'That would be an acceptable feat,' said Utgard-Loki. 'And I don't want to be accused of bad hospitality, so I hope you can do it. We have a rather large horn to drink from. The best drinkers can drain it in one draught, though most will do it in two. There is no one incapable of finishing it in three. If you match our best by finishing it in one, I will consider that sufficiently impressive.'

"They brought a huge horn filled to the brim with ale. Thor took it in both hands and grinned at the prospect of a good, long drink.

"'Thor,' said Roskva, 'that horn is awfully long . . .'

"'All the better, woman,' said Thor, and tipped it back. He was thirsty, and that was saying something. On and on, he poured the ale down his throat until he wondered if he would run out of breath. On he went anyway, forcing it down until he could breathe no more and had to set the horn down.

"Looking inside, it seemed to Thor the level of ale had not gone down much at all.

"'As you're so much smaller, I think draining it in two gulps would be satisfactory,' said Utgard-Loki. 'Perhaps you will give it another try.'

"Thor tipped the horn back a second time, taking the ale in huge gulps until he could drink no more. Out of breath a second time, Thor cursed when he saw the level of ale seemed to have gone down even less than before.

"It seems to me you've a sense for moderation,' said Utgard-Loki. 'That's a fine thing, just not worthy of a feat, in this case.'

"Thor snarled at that comment and threw back the horn a third time, ale splashing into his mouth and all over his great red beard. Though he drank and drank and drank, the ale kept coming. Eventually, Thor could drink no more and had to stop.

"'It seems we're getting nowhere with this contest,' said Utgard-Loki. 'Do you want to try your hand at something else?'

"Thor handed back the horn with a hall-reverberating belch. 'What game do you offer next?' he demanded.

"'It seems you are not as mighty as I've heard, so I think I will lower my expectations. We do have a contest for the very young among us. That contest is to lift my cat off the ground. The cat is a big one, and you are so small that I think it would be a suitable feat in this case.'

"A gray cat walked out from behind the high seat and licked its paw. It was much bigger than a normal cat, but Thor had no doubt he could lift it. He scooped it up in the middle with one hand and lifted. The cat arched its back and meowed, so that when Thor had lifted it as high as he could, the cat would raise one paw and its opposite paw would come down. Thor tried with two hands, but the cat arched its back more and seemed to flow around him so that he could never get a good grip on it.

"'I feel bad that the cat does not comply,' said Utgard-Loki. 'Perhaps we should try something smaller.'

"'Small, am I?' bellowed the thunder god. 'Come fight me, and then see how small I am!'

"'I think there is no one here willing to do that. It would be demeaning to fight a person so much smaller. But, wait one moment—I think I have one more idea.' Utgard-Loki called for his old nurse, Elli. 'She can still pick up children when they misbehave, and most of those are of similar size to you, so it should be a fair wrestling match.'

"The match began, and Thor locked hands with Elli. At first, he didn't use all his strength because he didn't want to cause a frail old woman undue injury, but soon, he was straining against her. The more Thor pushed, the firmer Elli seemed to stand. She grinned at him, and Thor was unable to make any headway. In a few moments, Elli pushed back, and Thor was forced down to one knee. With all his strength and rage, he pushed back again. However, he could not press back enough to gain the advantage.

"'That's enough of that,' said Utgard-Loki. 'As you've failed to perform a feat, I would not normally accept you as guests. However, the night has grown late, and I can see that, despite being very small people, you were quite earnest in your attempts to do more than you could. Therefore, I extend my hospitality to you for the night.'"

The giants of Risaland laughed openly. Here was a lord of giants who was generous and fair and yet could not have his hall spoiled by Thor the giant-killer. It served him right after so much wanton destruction he had brought with him in times before.

In the faces of the men and women of Arrow-Odd's army, I saw confusion. This was the reason some said the story was not nice to tell. Thor was Midgard's champion, the one people spoke to for protection. They did not want to hear a story of that hero laid low.

No matter. This story had a few twists, and I would add one of my own at the end.

"Nobody wanted to argue with being fed and having a roof over their heads. And Thor at least got to sleep without Skrymir's terrible snoring nearby.

"The next morning, Utgard-Loki fed the four travelers again and escorted them out of the fortress. At their parting, he asked Thor how his travels in Jotunheim had gone so far.

"Thor said it was obvious he had lost a lot of face during his time there. 'I think you and your folk will say I am a person of little account, which will dog me the rest of my days.'

"'Ha!' laughed Utgard-Loki. 'I think it is time to tell you the truth, now that we're well outside my fortress. Which, by the way, I will have you nowhere near a second time, should you come exploring again. I would never have brought you in, even to deceive you, had I known the real measure of your strength or how close it would bring me to disaster.'

"'We are deceived!' said Loki. 'How is that possible?'

"Roskva crossed her arms and sighed.

"'That part was not difficult,' said Utgard-Loki. I met you in the forest to see what you were up to. When I gave you my knapsack, the knot was tied to look like the ways of tying it and untying it were reversed. That was easy. But Thor, those times you struck at my head—those required quite a bit more effort at illusion on my part. So much effort, I had to conceal the very real effects of those hammer blows, each one of which created a new, square-shaped valley.

"'I left you and took the Stone Road to Utgard faster than you could walk and had my illusions well in place before you arrived. When Loki said he could eat faster than anyone, I pitted him against fire. Even then, the contest was close. When Thjalfi offered a race, I pitted him against my own thoughts. No one can run that fast, and yet Thjalfi was so fast, I really had to concentrate.'

"'But Thor, I had to deceive you three times. First, when you drank, the tip of that horn was settled into the ocean. None of us expected you would lower the sea with your drinking, and yet you did that three times. When I set you to lift my cat, that was actually the Midgard Serpent. People were shocked when you lifted that thing into the sky and almost entirely off the ground. Then, I pitted you in a wrestling match with old age. There has never been anyone, nor will there be, who is not laid low by old age if they live long enough. Yet somehow, this most undeniable of powers forced you down only to one knee, and you continued to fight from there.'

"'I have to admit that I greatly misjudged your power, though I am comforted that I did give you good hospitality. Now, let that be the end of things between us. You go your way, and I will thank you never to revisit me in Utgard!'

"Thor replied with a wordless roar. He swung his hammer at the *jǫtunn*, but Utgard-Loki vanished in a whirlwind of dust. When the dust cleared, Utgard itself was also gone, disappeared from the landscape as if it had never existed. The thunder god was left staring at an empty field with no one to take out his frustration on.

"He rounded on Loki, who stepped back. Thor had that look in his eye, the look that preceded something or someone being smashed to bits.

"'And what do you have to say for yourself? A master trickster would have been quite welcome just now, if he could have seen through any of those glamours! Are you going to tell me that for all your skills, you were completely taken in?'

"Loki made a lot of placating sounds and gestures. He was innocent. He was blameless. Nobody could have seen through such sorcery.

"'That may be,' said Thor, 'but you are a *jǫtunn* who keeps company in Asgard, and I think you should see such deceptions sooner than anyone. These two are mere humans, so nothing much can be expected of them.'

"'It appears nothing much should be expected of the great Thor, either,' said Roskva.

"Now Thor was really angry, and he turned to the girl. Not quite a girl, yet not quite a woman. Either way, it would be dishonorable to deal with her with his hammer. Thor locked eyes with her and spoke through grinding teeth. 'I don't need such reminding from you, unless you want to walk home alone.'

"'It's clear you don't need reminding from me, or you would have listened to me the three times I tried to warn you all in that fortress.'

"'What's this?' demanded Thor, grabbing Loki by the throat. 'What is she talking about?'

"'Don't blame him any more than you blame yourself! I tried to warn him before his feat, and Thjalfi's before his, and you before you started drinking the ocean!'

"'I don't recall any of that,' Loki croaked.

"'Oh!' Thjalfi slapped his forehead. 'I was thinking about moving so fast, I missed what you were trying to tell us.'

"Thor's grip on Loki loosened.

"'There, you see?' said Loki. 'The boy could have told us to listen to his sister!'

"'It's not the first thing you've missed, and won't be the last.' Roskva sighed and hugged her brother. 'You were always the fast mover.'

"Thor's wrath left him in one giant breath. 'I remember now. I was so intent on winning. And I wanted that drink!'

"The four traveled out of Jotunheim the way they had come, and they had no adventures on the way out. When they returned to the farmhouse, Thor told Thjalfi he had done well for himself and asked if he wanted to go back to his family or come live in Asgard. Thjalfi was set on adventure, so he chose Asgard.

"When Thor asked the same question of Roskva, he piled on the praise. 'I think it would be a good thing if I had a seeress such as you to rely on.'

"'That sounds better for you than for me. You want wisdom, yet you don't listen when it's spoken. What good is hearing it, then? I want to travel on my own terms and find good listeners.'

"Thor said that was fair, and he wished her well.

"'I'll offer you one other thing I saw as a parting gift, though,' said Roskva. 'Are you still humiliated by your defeat at Utgard?'

"'I'm angrier than ever about it. I don't know how I'll live it down.'

"'But you were not defeated.'"

Here I stopped and took stock of my audience at that surprising statement, which was not part of this story as I had ever heard it. Thor had been soundly bested, even if sorcery had been used. Some people told the story as if Thor was dumb or easily duped. I knew better than that.

The humans looked up with hope and curiosity in their eyes. The giants listened closer, a little confusion on their faces. Nobody knew what was coming next, which was exactly how we'd planned it to heighten the tension.

"'Did you not hear what Utgard-Loki said?' Roskva continued. 'He never would have tested you had he known how close to ruin you would bring him. He set you tasks that were impossible, and yet you did impossible things with them, making those *jǫtnar* fear for their lives. They expected you to lose easily, but to win or lose was not the point. What you did in the face of certain defeat was the point. Finally, he set old age on you, just a step away from death, and still, you fought back in a way that shocked them to their core.

"'I have no doubt his name was something other than Utgard-Loki, and I equally have no doubt that he knows he lost that encounter. That is why he fled the field, and you did not.'

"And that was wisdom Thor listened to."

If any of my audience had heard this story before, they'd heard a different version. Not nice to tell indeed. Most other versions portrayed Thor's visit to Utgard exactly as he took it in the story: A major loss of face.

In those versions, Roskva was hardly present. I was up much of the night talking with Magnus about this story, and he had asked why Roskva is even mentioned if she doesn't attempt any feats. I had no good answer, but it sparked a thought: I could give life to her character and show why this story was so important.

It was important because it laid bare an unspoken thing from our culture, a thing maybe some had forgotten: That victory did not matter as much as the refusal to accept defeat. Even, maybe especially, when defeat was certain. In those cases, the struggle couldn't be for wealth or fame or power. It could only be for defiance. That was the thread weaved into so many ancient myths and sagas. It was subtler than a god calling down thunder or casting powerful spells, but it was that particular subtlety that had always driven my love for our stories.

And I knew the story had rekindled a common love, because our people were screaming their heads off as they charged the table I stood on.

Ale sloshed, and the tables, despite their massive size, rattled with the pounding of fists. Cheers went up randomly at first but quickly coalesced into chants of "ANS-GAR! ANS-GAR! ANS-GAR!" I bowed as someone handed me a horn of actual ale. I took my long-awaited drink to shouts of "Make sure it's not really the sea!"

Magnus grinned and gave the slightest nod. We had stayed up all night planning. I'd had trouble choosing the right story, and Magnus had given me the answer.

"You can't just tell a story about victory," he had said. "If you want to lift their spirits, you need to tell a story about what looks like a defeat, first." That, and a subtle dig at Arrow-Odd's need to listen to a woman's wisdom, had gotten me what I needed.

When things calmed down just a bit, Hildir held up a hand for quiet.

"Your story ends with Thor listening to wisdom, but I think you have told it so that the story would convey wisdom to those hearing it."

"You praise me a great deal with that comment."

Silence. Had he meant to praise me, or was he leading to a criticism? What victory I'd handed to the people of Midgard, I had taken from those who felt closer to Jotunheim. Hildir's face was inscrutable.

"I've heard the same story, told a little differently," said Hildir. "I want to know one thing about it, from your perspective. Who do you think Utgard-Loki was?"

The easy answer was that Utgard-Loki's real name was unknown, as many among the *jǫtnar* lords were strong with sorcery. Others suggested it was really Loki, playing an incredibly elaborate trick on Thor. Or at least the story had maybe started that way and changed over time to include Loki as Thor's travel companion, confusing his role.

"It seems to me there are common enough explanations," I said. "And who can say how the story began? But I think the way I've told it, Utgard-Loki is not so unknowable at all. I think he is Odin in disguise."

Styrgrim raised an eyebrow a quarter of an inch at that, which for him was like jumping up and shouting.

"The story contrives to frustrate Thor, but also to test him," I continued. "I think Odin has an interest in doing both. And we all know Odin is not to be trusted. Especially if he wanted to be considered highest among the *Æsir*, he might want to test Thor first."

Hildir leaned forward. "What an interesting interpretation! I have had five nights now where I was certain I would pronounce someone different as having the best story. Well, four, maybe," he said, eyeing Bjorn for telling a story that was all about killing giants. "Here at the last, I am confident in awarding the prize to you, Lucky Ansgar."

Pause.

"You will have the honor of marrying my daughter, Hildigunn!"

It's not easy to stumble when you're standing still, but the surprise caught me so unprepared, it was like a fist hitting the back of one of my heels. I spilled some of my ale, recovered my balance, and looked up with wide eyes.

"But—I would—the size difference . . ."

"Haha! I am only joking. The reward will be something else, as I can't marry my daughter to such a tiny man. I just wanted you to understand: You are not the only one who knows how to create tension."

# CHAPTER 19

## MEANWHILE, ON THE NORSE SEA (OR THEREABOUTS)

THE 'STEINS RENAMED THEIR NEW SHIP *HALFDAN'S GIFT*. Innstein swore it cut the water just a bit faster with its new name. Which was good, because Alfhild had a lot more viking crews milling around the White Sea than just Halfdan's, and the 'Steins had no desire to meet them. They sailed north and east as fast as the wind would take them.

*Halfdan's Gift* soon left the White Sea behind and entered the vast Norse Sea. Which some assumed was the Encircling Sea of legend, the sea that ringed Midgard. They kept within sight of the coast, where everything looked much bigger. No time to stop and look around, though, as autumn would soon bring storm season.

There was one day when the ship was under sail and cruising fast, and the chaos of organizing the crew was at a low. The sun shone bright in the sky, and the salt of the sea had that fresh tinge to it, like a mackerel might jump out of the water and straight into your mouth at any moment. The 'Steins decided it was a good time to explain to their crew what would happen next. They addressed those who spoke Norse and had Skuli translate for the Irish as well as he could, with some help from Bec.

They said keeping people on board and calling them free did not make them free. And since nobody else could take the former thralls back to their homes, the 'Steins would do that. But anyone could choose to stay on if they really wanted to join crazy people on a crazy quest. Most of the former thralls on board wanted to go home.

For Halfdan's surviving crew, it was a little different. The 'Steins made it clear that this contingent could choose, too, but the choice was between swimming and rowing. Or, if no rowing was required at the time, between swimming and keeping their mouths shut.

Rowing service would end when this contingent undid as much of what they'd done as possible. Or when the natives of Lofoten or Ireland murdered them, which the 'Steins said they would try to prevent, but nobody is perfect.

"For those wanting to stay, we should be clear about our eventual intentions," said Innstein. "We have specific designs for this ship. We will need some large pieces of iron to work with and a good forge. And then we will be looking for Alfhild's people, regardless of the numbers involved."

"Including all those children of gods," added Utstein. That last detail required some explanation.

They let the crew discuss things without being bothered any further, expecting nobody to stay with them. And the crew did sound skeptical of the brothers' sanity at first. Soon, though, the crew recounted what the 'Steins had done to Halfdan and his champions.

"We'll just have to see how it goes," Innstein said to his brother.

Utstein pulled at his beard. "Another issue, though: What if we end up with Norse and Irish on the crew? They don't usually get along together."

"This crew has rules and will always get along together," replied Innstein, in what his brother had termed "the tone."

Skuli heard them and said something to the Irish. He reported back, saying the Irish understood "the tone" as well as the words.

"What about you, Skuli?" asked Utstein.

"It looks to us like you're more attached to Bec and little Sigurd than a man who just translates," added Innstein.

Skuli winced a little. He was a man apart from himself in some ways, and it was easy to see why. "I think I can't stay with Bec where she's going. I was no less a part in taking her as a thrall than Halfdan was. Besides," he perked up, "you two will need a translator if any Irish stay with you."

Innstein thought that sounded right on the face of it, but his instinct told him it was not right. He looked at his brother and read the same thing in his face. They would just have to see how it went.

Little Sigurd was rarely quiet while at sea, which was another good reason to get where they were going as quickly as possible. Sigurd seemed to get louder by the day. Whether out of good manners or fear of reprisal, nobody complained. Skuli did a lot more than not complain, though.

There were times when Bec needed food, or rest, or just to not have the kid screaming in her face for a few minutes. She would hand little Sigurd off to Skuli. Whether he had been up early in the morning or had been rowing for hours, he would take Sigurd without hesitation, speaking soft assurances.

Sigurd would give Skuli a big hug, screaming right into his ear. Skuli would smile back despite it all.

Innstein noticed that happen more than once as they rounded Finnmark and got his brother's attention. "I think we are seeing how it goes right now."

"Think Kraki would forgive him?" Utstein asked.

"Kraki didn't know the meaning of the word."

"Do we?"

The 'Steins looked at each other and realized the answer was no.

"Kraki knew what it meant to shoulder a burden without complaint," said Innstein.

Utstein nodded. "And he knew what family meant."

The 'Steins had been cast off without the thing that Skuli offered to Sigurd. Maybe Skuli didn't deserve forgiving friends, but they wouldn't deny Sigurd a father due to Skuli's previous failings. Or let anyone else do that, either.

Sigurd was mostly quiet when they made landfall at Lofoten. They moored *Halfdan's Gift* in the town of Vagar and sent out word to the other islands nearby that many people had returned. Most of the Norse opted to leave the ship and go home, a few more than expected. It's one thing to conjure an idea of sailing for revenge, but for reasonable people, home and family are more important.

On the first day, the town was all celebration and warmth. By the second day, most people had heard the 'Steins tell the story of taking the ship, and that people taken as thralls were returning. Some people heard the story with great cheer, only to find they had no family returning after all.

The 'Steins stayed a week in Vagar, working on the ship. They had plans based on a codex that a monk had read to them once. Plans they remembered perfectly. Plans so good, they had inspired the brothers to new ideas not even contained in that codex.

The 'Steins would need iron, but not yet. First, they needed wood. One of the white-bearded men of Vagar offered his help. His name was Fjornir, and he asked if they were taking on new crew members.

The 'Steins said they were but warned that joining their crew was not a prospect for wealth or fame. And that they were about to sail to Ireland in the middle of winter, which sane people did not do. Fjornir just nodded and got to work.

Fjornir was a practiced woodworker and could use an axe equally well in either hand. He kept two axes on his belt, both sharp enough to shave with. It looked like he was not inclined to shave, though. His beard grew out in all directions, a white, scraggly mess.

If the man hadn't been so obviously competent, the 'Steins might have taken him as simple. He spoke only when absolutely necessary, did not groom his beard, and wore a comically pointy wool hat with a puff ball at the end of it. It was too long to stay straight up, so it fell down at the side. It had not been dyed, had obviously been made from the wool of very different sheep, and the yarn frayed too much to have been spun by a skillful hand. Fjornir never went anywhere without it.

Innstein couldn't help but think this hat looked like it had been woven by a child. He also couldn't help but remember that when they had landed, Fjornir looked at the returning thralls with a lot of interest, but no one came up to him.

He mentioned that thought to his brother, who said he'd noticed the same thing. However, it was inappropriate to ask about that. Instead, they focused on the help Fjornir was giving them.

The 'Steins had never been able to reinforce a sail against luffing, that frustrating state when you have all the wind behind you but the sail is pushed so far forward it's practically flattened out, parallel to the sea. Weight at the bottom of the sail doesn't prevent luffing and makes it more dangerous for the crew. So, how to keep the sail firm against the wind and catch more of it?

Their idea was to attach the forward corner of the sail to a stretching pole. With some appropriately strong post holes inside the ship, that pole could hold the sail steadier in high wind coming from more directions. Which corner was forward would change, of course, so they had to figure out how to handle that and make the parts they needed. They called that stretching pole a *beitass* and hoped it would get them to Ireland all the faster.

A sane crew would have wintered in Vagar, but they were not a sane crew. They had things that needed doing, and they would not be delayed. So they pushed on to Ireland right away, to much uninterrupted screaming by Sigurd.

"What's he saying?" asked one of the Norsemen who'd opted to stay with them.

"He says, 'I hate the sea!'" Skuli shouted back.

"Who doesn't?" quipped a third.

The rare times Fjornir spoke, it was to ask about the Irish language. It was a long trip, and he learned a bit from Skuli along the way. The 'Steins joked that in a month or two, Fjornir would be speaking more Irish than Norse.

Those were good ways to help pass the time. The 'Steins loved turbulence at sea, but even they hated the non-stop screaming. How did Sigurd manage that volume? How could he go on so long without becoming hoarse? They never answered those questions. Luckily for them, the *beitass* worked even better than anticipated.

The moment they reached the Irish coast, Sigurd finally shut up.

Innstein didn't blame him. "Ymir's bones, it's green."

"You sure this is still Midgard?" asked Utstein.

It was not just vaguely green, but *so* green. Much of the northeast coast was rocky or offered only shallow beaches for landing, but everything was covered in impossible greenery. Not just green moss, but fields of green foliage everywhere. And it was winter.

They found a sandy shoreline to land on and hopped off into the swash. It wasn't green, of course, but the undergrowth just over the first berm was. Beyond the berm, copses of trees dotted the fields, while thicker forest flanked them on both sides.

Weird things started happening almost immediately. The 'Steins had hardly pulled *Halfdan's Gift* up past the shoreline when a murder of crows gathered to sit on the ship's yard. Bec spoke to the crows like they were a coast guard sent to assess a potential threat. They cawed and croaked and sometimes honked, and Bec would talk right back to them, pointing at Sigurd and Skuli. Skuli asked a few questions, but Bec waved him off. Whatever the conversation was, it started getting heated on her side.

Soon, the 'Steins saw riders approaching from the other side of the field. They always knew that would be a thing, and let Bec do the talking. She addressed the warrior at the front of the group. He had pretty good armor and weapons, as far as the 'Steins could tell. His mustache was a little overly groomed, but to each his own.

"Think this is going well?" asked Utstein.

"No," replied Innstein. "Mustache just pointed at Skuli. I think he recognizes him."

"That will mean a lot of explaining, or none at all."

Bec's explaining appeared to be sufficient when the riders departed. She approached the 'Steins, waving Skuli over. Skuli translated for Bec and explained what was going on.

"We're granted safe passage. For now."

"Sounds like that might change," said Innstein.

"That sort of change would be ill-advised," added Utstein.

"They're leaving that decision to the witch," said Skuli. "She's deep in the forest. Bec says not to worry, though."

"Witch?" asked Innstein. "You sure about that?"

"The witch is the island's protector. We're on land controlled by Aed Roin, King of Ulaid, but he takes his orders from her."

"Are all their kings so unpronounceable?" asked Utstein.

Skuli checked with Bec. "His full name is Aed Roin mac Becce Bairrche."

"This is a silly place," said Innstein.

Through Skuli, Bec assured the 'Steins there was no silliness. She knew the way, but they should still take utmost care as they traveled.

"I don't fully understand her," said Skuli. "And I don't want to assume too much, but the way she's talking, it sounds like the *landvættir* of this place are watching. Only . . . more so? Not just watching."

"Protecting?" asked Utstein.

Skuli nodded. The 'Steins searched the sky for those crows, but they'd gone.

Bec led the group to a rough path that meandered through the forest. Soon, there was no more path, and they were headed up the gentle slope of a small mountain. It was easy going and just as green everywhere. The grass grew thick but low. Moss covered rocks and trees. It was easy to breathe, but just as easy to feel all the unseen eyes on them.

Not like they were visitors. Foreigners, more like. Or invaders.

Bec had a definite idea of where they were going. Or a feeling. Or maybe she just made up the route as she went. The 'Steins never did ask.

They did ask about the strange old woman clad in black. She sat at the base of a tree, watching the group. Bec froze at the sight of her at first, then turned to Skuli. He relayed instructions to pass by quietly and not look this woman in the eye.

"Why not?" asked Innstein. He could feel the threat, he just wasn't about to put his head down and shuffle on.

Utstein clapped his brother on the shoulder. "Better she should take our measure."

The 'Steins walked right up to the old woman. Three crows cawed in the branches above.

She looked into their eyes, expression blank as death. Innstein looked back and felt more than he could see, but he didn't think this was some land spirit. He didn't know what she was, but she could have caused them trouble if she wanted to.

"Some people were taken from this place," said Innstein. "Now some are back."

"We haven't come for a reward," added Utstein. "But we'd be grateful for hospitality."

"We won't tolerate any violence, though," Innstein finished in "the tone."

The old woman gave them a lingering look, especially Innstein. Appraising. Sizing them up. Yes, she could have caused them trouble. She seemed canny enough to know the 'Steins could make trouble of their own, if they decided to.

She gave a half grin and nodded.

The group moved past. And just like that, the 'Steins felt the land spirits of that place weren't quite as hostile.

After a few more miles of trekking inland, they came to a grove loosely encircled by hawthorn trees. Bec pointed to the trees and to the mistletoe that grew on them. They were the only hawthorn trees within sight.

"Bec says we five go into the grove," said Skuli. When the 'Steins both counted four, the Norseman responded that Sigurd counted as much as any of them, the only time they ever heard the man sound snappish.

The grove was not a physical boundary that would stop anyone or make them go around or over. The 'Steins had seen similar thresholds before, though. They took off their weapons and laid them down before entering the grove. Not a common thing for a Norseman to do, especially if he finds himself in Ireland.

The 'Steins told the others to wait where they were, and not to worry. It looked like only one of those directions would be followed.

"You know this could go quite badly," Innstein said to his brother. "She might turn us all into pigs."

Utstein nodded. "Fjornir! If we get turned into pigs, you're in charge."

Fjornir didn't say anything in response, just licked his lips.

The 'Steins stepped across the boundary without acquiring any pig-like features at all and approached the woman standing in the middle of the grove. Tall and thin, with a strong chin and a handsome face, "the witch" looked to them like a *vǫlva*. Silver brooches fastened her long dress. Thin hair, even more silver than her brooches, fell straight down to her waist.

"Welcome," she said in Norse. Which was not expected.

"Who are you?" asked Utstein.

"Olvor."

"Maybe you could introduce yourself a bit more," suggested Innstein. "As we don't recognize the name 'Olvor.'"

"I rule this land, though not in title. Ask the king and he'll tell you the same. And if I ask you your names, you who don't belong in this land, what would you say?"

"I think our names matter very little compared to our actions," said Utstein.

"And I think we've laid our actions plain already," Innstein added. "We've brought people back here who were taken."

"You also brought the takers." She didn't bother looking at Skuli.

He tried to say something, but Innstein waved him off. "Bec will speak about Skuli if you ask her."

"As for the rest," Utstein added, "they don't get the choice to die in battle. Yet. They get the choice to row or to swim. It's not advisable for anyone to try to get ahead of that."

Olvor spoke to Bec in their language, Bec making a lot of respectful gestures and doing almost all the talking. Eventually, she turned little Sigurd toward Olvor to show him off.

That was one inscrutable witch, her face revealing absolutely nothing, except for looking at that child just a little too long for it to be mere interest in a baby. She turned to Skuli and switched back to Norse. "Bec says you are the child's father, but I know that can't—"

"I am, now." A great Norse answer, where fewer words convey more.

Olvor shook her head. Not a denial, more like how the 'Steins' mothers would shake their heads at them when they got into trouble. "You two! Noble intentions, but you've no idea what troublemakers you are, do you?"

Utstein laughed out loud at that. "Woman, we were born to trouble."

"Twice."

# Chapter 20

# Phantom Limb

For telling the best story, King Hildir rewarded me with a barrel of whale oil. He said I could use the oil to brighten the long nights we weren't used to. Or I could drink it, seeing how I was so skinny; my overall skinniness being the primary quality that prevented him from marrying me to his daughter. I think he was joking. Hard to tell, though.

As barrels in Risaland were giant-sized, we had to make a few smaller barrels to be able to take the oil with us. We did that and still had some left over, so we fashioned some crude oil lamps and set them up for use in the cave with the hot springs. The story had gained me credibility, and the shared reward made me more popular with the army.

Arrow-Odd piled on the praise, though it was all for the part of my story that described the enemy fleeing. He told his army they had not lost, but endured the impossible while the enemy had fled. Not an exact allegory for my story, but I didn't want it to be too on the nose anyway. He never mentioned the part about listening to a woman's advice.

My newfound credibility gave me enough confidence to finally talk to Steinvor, where success was more mixed. She had enjoyed our time together, but she had no interest in being so attached as to become any man's wife. She was a great skald and wanted adventure and word-fame, not protection.

In talking about what she wanted, I realized I had hopes as well, but my hopes were entirely incompatible. I'd been acting like I might find a woman so amazing, I would marry her. It was an old assumption from when my life was more predictable, an old hope from when I'd known Fanya. My life had changed, I had changed, and my blood oath clashed with my desire to settle down.

I had stumbled into my life of adventure after drinking too much mead and swearing an ill-advised oath. But what had been ill-advised at one time had become the best decision I'd ever made. I was still adjusting, though, still making mistakes. And it hurt to know Steinvor did not return my feelings.

I think I kept my composure during that conversation, letting none of those feelings on. A very Norse thing to do—which I might often make fun of, but not in this case. So I leaned on gritting my teeth and enduring, and had to admit that in this case, refusing to show emotion made sense. Lashing out would be childish. Steinvor wasn't responsible for my feelings, only I was. And taking responsibility for myself, I felt more like a man. No less sad, though.

However, a man can confide in a good friend. The next day, I asked Magnus to walk with me around Risaland for as long as we had daylight and give me counsel. The cold was more bearable without the heavy winds. Frozen snow crunched underfoot as we made our way down the main path we'd followed to get to the longhouse. Even the underbrush was tall there, and the trees were giant-sized. I opted to take us down a smaller path, almost human-sized, before I explained what had happened with Steinvor.

"This is such a ridiculous thing," I said, frustrated with myself. "The truth is, I hardly know Steinvor."

"But your feelings for her are strong."

I nodded. "That's not the ridiculous part, though. I must have known she did not return my feelings, yet hearing her say so felt like a loss all over again."

"This is why they say no man should mock another for being in love. What do you mean, 'all over again,' though?"

"It's like thinking about Fanya dying." I swallowed hard. "She was in part of that last dream I had in the camp. She was dead, with Olgram and Valborg. They all lay at the foot of a hill where Alfhild was doling out boons to idiots. I told the idiots not to buy what Alfhild was selling, but they didn't like hearing that."

"Ah, a logical dream!" Magnus slapped me on the back with excitement. "Finally, something that makes sense! Fanya, Olgram, and Valborg were people Alfhild used before. Those other idiots will be the ones dead at

Alfhild's feet, soon, but they wouldn't accept that even if one of the Norns came by to tell them their fates." He nodded to himself. "It seems I'm our resident expert on dreams, now. Have you had any others?"

"What do you mean, 'resident expert'?"

"Well, Kraki came to me the other day to ask about his dream. He said skalds are shit at dreams, so he wasn't going to ask you again. Not after he told you about the wolf dream and you didn't know what it meant."

"The masturbating wolf dream?" I shook my head. "Did he mention that *he* didn't know what it meant, either?"

"Not at all. But he told me his most recent dream. In fact, there's no harm in sharing it if you'd like to hear."

"Please tell me it's not a masturbating lindworm this time."

"I'm not sure how that would work with their stubby appendages, but maybe you can work that out in a new story! Now, listen: Kraki dreamt that the *Sea Squirrel* sailed over the land rather than the sea. The ship was on fire, with flames so big they rose to the sky!"

"That's an ill omen, if I've ever heard one."

"No, no, that's just it. I thought this meant maybe we should leave that whale oil of yours behind, but Kraki said I had it all wrong. He said the fire was on our side, like it was fire brought to the realm of the ice giants."

No more details appeared to be forthcoming. "And then?"

"And then he said I was shit at dreams, too, and left."

I stopped and rubbed my temples. "Kraki had a prophetic dream once before. We just couldn't understand it at the time. I hope this one doesn't mean 'death in fire' for us all."

Magnus was a few steps ahead of me when he stopped, too. He held a hand up for me to be quiet, then beckoned me to come forward a few paces to the edge of a massive, multi-trunked birch. I peeked out from the side of the tree and looked farther into the forest where someone was gesturing.

It was easy enough to move to the next tree closer and get a better look. From there, I could not only see, but hear what was going on.

Hildigunn spoke in hushed tones. As she was so much taller than Arrow-Odd, she looked down as she spoke. Her face and gestures made it clear she was pleading with him. Odd, keeping his arms crossed and his face stony, was having none of it. My heart just about broke to hear her say she still loved him and wished he would stay in Risaland.

"If you don't wish to see our son avenged," retorted Odd, "then I think we have little to say to one another."

"Ogmund will have many enemies by now, any of whom might avenge Vignir," countered Hildigunn. "And you have defied one prophecy already!"

Odd snarled at that and looked away. "That stupid *vǫlva*! I should never have told you about her."

"I think it's only a problem if you make it one. *You killed your horse.* Killed it because that *vǫlva* from your youth foretold the horse would be the death of you!"

"Yes, and what of it? I took action to avoid a prophecy once, so you think I should live my life running in fear every time a seeress wags her finger in my direction? You want to see me diminished, as small in reputation as I am in height compared to you?"

"That is nothing like what I want. What is more important: Ogmund's death, or your role in it?"

Odd growled something about immortal word-fame. Then he looked up and, seeming to realize he had very much changed his reasoning for Ogmund's pursuit, continued. "Vignir's memory will not live on with others if I let Ogmund go."

Giant tears streamed down Hildigunn's cheeks. "I remember Vignir, and that will never change. You always set yourself on a course to find a few temporary victories, but you move from tragedy to tragedy, the same as Ogmund."

"You think I'm like Ogmund?!"

"No! You are better than Ogmund, because you can choose to live happily!"

Odd spat and stormed off. He disappeared farther into the forest.

Magnus and I shrank back from there and back to the path we'd come down. Once we were nearly back to Hildir's longhouse, Magnus asked me what I thought. I had no idea what to tell him until I remembered something my not-father had told me.

"Styrgrim said that maybe the Norns don't carve our fates beforehand. Maybe we're just that predictable."

Magnus shrugged. "That's easy, then." When I looked at him in confusion, he explained, "It means all we need to do to win is something completely unpredictable, and then the Norns have got nothing on us!"

I believed he was right. I just wasn't sure any of us were capable of it.

# CHAPTER 21

## A WOLF AGE

WE LEFT RISALAND AT THE EARLIEST HINT OF SPRING. ROUGHER water than in the summer, but it's easy to sail when you have a man who can call the wind.

With the vast depths of the Norse Sea behind us, we sailed southwest along the edge of Risaland. We hugged that coast until turning south, retracing the way we'd come. I caught sight of Alfhild's island in the distance at one point, but I didn't point it out. No one would want to go back there, or even be reminded of what we'd found there.

We weren't returning to the site of Odd's war camp, though. With Hemming as a guide, we found the same river the *Sea Squirrel* had sailed down to get to the White Sea. From the prow of the *Whaleslayer*, Hemming set our route back through the series of lakes and rivers of Karelia. He seemed to have no less skill navigating through the waterways than he had on land. It bothered me when he was congratulated for this, but I reminded myself that this was better than going the long way around.

The rivers were hard work. Calling the wind is excellent for the open water, but the narrow waterways required rowing. We had some brief rests when we could get under sail in those two huge lakes, but it was never very long before the oars went out again.

I thought I'd hated rowing before, but going upstream for that long made me hate it even more. The first night after hard rowing, my arms felt like they would fall out of their sockets. After the second night of rowing, my arms felt like they had fallen out of their sockets and been put back in by one of Hildir's folk.

Magnus told me it would get better. I asked when. He shrugged.

One day, my arms seemed lighter and easier, ready for anything. That was the day the *Sea Squirrel* and the rest of our fleet burst forth from the Karelian rivers and into the Gulf of Suomi. Then, Odd called the wind again, and there was no rowing at all.

We headed west, and I thought we would be in Uppsala in almost no time. We were nearly there when we stopped. Not by necessity, but because I stopped us. Not long after the waters of the Gulf of Suomi mixed with other seas, dark clouds of smoke hung over the islands to our north.

"What's that over there?" I asked whoever might be able to answer. "Something strange is going on."

"Ahvaland," Kraki answered from his position at the rudder.

"Who rules there?"

Kraki shrugged. "If someone lays claim, I don't know who. Swedes, maybe. We're not far from Uppsala."

If it was King Athils, he might reward news of what was going on in his realm. "Should we take a look?" I asked Kraki.

The old captain nodded and turned the *Sea Squirrel* sharply north. The other ships were ahead of us, but not so far that they didn't see us diverge. They followed, to the great annoyance of Arrow-Odd. He had the *Whaleslayer* pull up alongside our ship and demanded to know what we were doing.

"Investigating what's going on," I shouted, pointing to the smoke that hung low over one of the islands.

"What about Uppsala?" he shouted back.

"Uppsala can wait." I would let him complain if he wanted. It would look bad for him, especially since I had a longer answer ready for when I wouldn't need to shout.

Kraki took us straight toward the smoke and landed the ship on a broad, sandy beach. Odd summoned the two of us over immediately when the *Whaleslayer* landed, before we were even done helping pull the *Sea Squirrel* farther up the shoreline. With the crews still working to secure the ships, all captains and skalds met in the middle of the beach.

"That smoke is still a good way away, and there's no reason I can think of to be interested in it," said Odd.

I'd expected something like that. "Hemming navigated us through weeks of travel, and we were not attacked once. Yet here we see what might be signs of battle."

"It's not battle we're seeking right now, but something in Uppsala."

"And we'll arrive in Uppsala soon. I think King Athils will want to know what's going on so close to his doorstep. If we have something interesting to tell him, so much the better when we ask him to tell us something in return."

"Assuming we make it there," said Styrgrim. "The longer we keep the ships beached, the longer we need to protect them. We should leave. Or if not leave immediately, make this foray a brief one."

That was true. We couldn't leave the ships by themselves, or even with just a token force to protect them. Though we'd encountered almost no one on our way, it was possible we'd happen upon an unfriendly fleet at any time. And then we might need every person available.

Nevertheless, my need to explore was a strong one, and this cloud of smoke was the first sign we'd had of something to investigate.

Arrow-Odd nodded. "Choose who you will take from your crew, then," meaning me. "Assume they will have to fight, and assume those left behind will have to fight while we're away. And assume you will have to fight, as this is your expedition."

He made it sound like a bad idea, but it was his army, and I noticed he didn't order everyone out to sea again. I think Odd knew I was right, but realized that this way, any failure out here would be attributed to me rather than him.

That changed nothing for me or my crew. I told Ingolf to come with us, but most of the crew made their own choices. Kraki wouldn't leave defending the *Sea Squirrel* to anyone else, despite my desire to have him go inland. Moose-Frothi and Thorir Houndsfoot wouldn't stay on the ship a moment longer than they had to. Magnus would come with me, of course.

Ketill and Huld held a silent conversation as to who would go and who would stay. Ketill strung his bow and nocked an arrow soon after. The wizard drew up alongside Arrow-Odd and seemed to size the man up.

Odd also had his longbow strung, goatskin arrow bag tapping at his side. He had plenty of arrows, but only one more of Gusir's Gifts. The one was enough, if it kept returning to his bow, and it was proof against any enemy but Ogmund.

Odd and Ketill took one another's measure with silent stares.

Vilgrip and Nanthild wanted to accompany us, but I had to tell them to stay.

"I need you here for now," I told both of them. "If there is an attack, and it's by anyone with a pinch of sense, they will head straight for Huld. I need reliable people who understand this to stay and protect her." *And Kraki is a madman,* was the unspoken part of that.

As long as Huld could sit *seiðr*, I was confident any attacking force would have little success.

Ahvaland was much more than just the island we had landed on. It was a series of densely forested islands, so we could not see what was ahead other than to know what general direction we should travel in to find the source of the smoke. Odd had Hemming lead the way, scouting far ahead of the main group, three or four dozen of us in total. Styrgrim came, leaving Helgi Pike-Tooth in charge in his stead. Birki and Josur stayed, probably arguing about who was in overall command.

It was slow-going. That many warriors creeping through that many trees would never be a fast thing. Snow decorated the pines even though it was late in the season for snowfall. The forest was quiet but for feet crunching over fallen branches. We had not gone too far into the island's interior when Hemming returned to tell us what was ahead.

"The smoke is from a burned village ahead."

"How many burners?" demanded Odd.

"It was too recent for me to want to investigate closely. Some of the attackers might still be nearby, but I didn't see any openly walking around. Wherever they went, it was not back toward the water. More likely into the hills beyond the forest."

"Perhaps, with sufficient protection, Hemming will take a closer look," suggested Magnus, who could not keep the venom out of his voice.

Odd looked to me again. I decided we would all have a closer look.

Blood painted the ground, bright on the late-season snowfall. Every building had been torched, melting the areas around them and blackening the ground beneath. Though partly covered by tall pines overhead, one end of the village opened up to a field beyond. There sat the beginnings of cordoned-off gardens, now broken down and dug up. The only untouched area was on the far end of the village, where piles of dead leaves met with a shallow latrine.

"Where'd they go?" asked Frothi.

Thorir sniffed the air like a hunting dog as he wandered the ruined area. "Something," he said once, and then shook his head as if he'd lost it.

"Nothing to salvage," said Odd. "There's little value here, I think."

Magnus shook his head. "Where are the dead? Did they get up and walk away?"

"Doesn't matter," said Styrgrim. "If they got up and walked away, then we should still leave, but even faster."

Thorir started sniffing again, and this time he appeared to have a trail. He headed for the piles of leaves.

Magnus, willing to poke at a bear even in the best of times, was clearly in a mood. "Is that why we came inland?" he said smoothly. "To *not* see questions answered?"

"We do not have time to search the whole of this island," said Odd.

I stayed out of the argument and watched Thorir. The dog-footed man seemed to be onto something again, but what could he possibly find except a place to take a shit?

At first, that was what I thought he might do. Instead, he leaned over the edge of the trench and reached down. I ran over to see what he'd found. After more squishing sounds than I wanted to hear, Thorir pulled a man out of the latrine and dragged him onto the dirty snow.

"Please!" he pleaded, "Please don't hurt me!"

Shit and mud and dead leaves covered the man from head to toe. He wore a long, heavy robe, which I assumed would never really be clean again. Around his neck was a large wooden cross of the White Christ. This man's head was not shaved on top like the monks on Gotland, however.

"We aren't the people who did this," I said. "We saw the smoke and came to investigate. What happened here?"

It took a few moments for him to catch his breath and recognize that we didn't intend to kill him. Or probably didn't intend to kill him.

His answer came in a lot of fragments and gasps for a bit. It took some more reassuring and a few drinks of water, but eventually he gave us some answers.

"They were monsters," he said, shaking his head. "They came on like demons, hacking people down, taking them. I hid in the latrine and covered myself with leaves."

"When was this, and who were these 'monsters'?" demanded Styrgrim.

"Two days ago, maybe? Some people ran and got away, but they came back, and then these . . . these *trolls* returned and took them, too, and burned what was left."

"So you've been hiding in shit for two days?" asked Odd.

"God showed me the way! He protects his faithful."

I shook my head. If some god told him to hide in a pile of shit, it was probably Odin, and probably just to have a laugh.

"It seems to me you might have helped defend them if you cared so much for their eventual faith," said Odd, a bit louder than necessary. "I also demand faith in my leadership, but that rope pulls two ways. They can expect me at the forefront of any danger, and I don't plan to fail them."

He was grandstanding, but he wasn't wrong. That rope pulled two ways, or not at all.

Orm repeated something about faith that I didn't care much to hear about.

We were about done with the priest when Hemming reported back again. Now that he'd had a closer look and had explored all around the place, he knew which direction the attackers had gone. He pointed past the forest and the clearing where a few gardens had been set up. About half a mile beyond was a hill fort. All tracks led in that direction.

"And the size of that force?" demanded Odd.

"About as many as we have."

"And how many might that fort hold?" demanded Styrgrim. "How many could be up there who you didn't see tracks for?"

"A lot . . . more than our number?"

Magnus gave an unsatisfied grunt and shook his head. "Sounds conveniently lacking in details. I tell you, don't trust him."

Odd held up a hand for silence. "I'll trust who I might. Don't forget, he led us through all those riverways faithfully."

Styrgrim shook his head. "A full crew from a single warship will be far more than our number. And we are out of position to call on the others as a reserve force."

"This is the lucky skald's expedition," Odd reiterated. "Well, skald, what do you say? Are we going to that fort or back to the ships?"

If we met with King Athils and he was disappointed at having only partial information, the blame would be mine. And it was still a risk that the foray would go badly, which he would also blame on me. It seemed like things going badly could work out well for Odd.

"We've found one survivor already," I said. "The priest says there might be others. I think it would make for a poor accounting if we fled the field without even looking for them."

Odd grinned and sent Hemming up to scout the best way for the rest of us.

It's not easy to move two dozen warriors or so without being spotted. I had plenty of confidence in our fighting force to overcome a similar number —even double our number—but a dozen archers would be able to hit us hard as we scrambled uphill, and that would change things fast.

The snow was just deep enough to crunch and slow us down a bit, not nearly deep or soft enough for snowshoes. Footprints and ski tracks confirmed the raiders had gone up to the hill fort. Hemming found a natural rise in the land a few hundred yards from the fort's main earthworks. It was a major defensive oversight, this being a blind spot to the hill fort. But I suppose a real attack on the fort would consist of a lot more people than we had with us, too many to hide. We advanced as far as the rise Hemming identified and spotted no movement in response.

I peeked out to watch the fort for a while. No lookouts were high up, and there was still no movement. But nothing the rest of the way up could hide two dozen warriors. It's also not easy to keep that many people stationary when they're impatient to fight, and soon Odd and Styrgrim wanted to know my next steps.

"You're the lucky one," Odd reminded us all.

Every pair of eyes was on me. It had been my idea to come here, and we could not put the entire group at risk. Someone had to get up there, spy on our enemies, and report back. Not the job for a tracker. A job for a lucky man.

"Maybe his luck rubs off," said Styrgrim, stepping forward. "He should have one other with him, at least."

Ketill stepped forward right away. Odd nodded, but I shook my head.

"If there is nothing up there, fighting ability is not needed. If there is something up there, and we don't like it, even a great fighter and an archer won't make a difference when we're swarmed. No, I am the best choice, but that's because I can run. If there's a problem up there, I can get out of trouble fast."

"I may be old, but I can still run," said Ketill. Which I doubt anyone believed.

"I don't want you to run, I want you to shoot anyone running after me if I come back in a hurry!"

Odd nocked an arrow. "That's easily arranged."

"Better to take another who runs fast, then," said Thorir, stepping forward.

His brother, Frothi, snarled at that and thumped a fist against his chest. "There's no one faster than the two of us. We will go with the skald."

Hallfred Horsefly grinned and winked at me, as if to say *you are a lucky one after all.*

The snow made us stand out even more, but the hill was mercifully uneven, allowing the three of us plenty of opportunities to scramble from one area of partial cover to another. I moved first each time, and then watched for movement, listening for warnings or horn blasts before signaling Frothi and Thorir to move up.

There was nothing other than the wind and the smell of smoke. And maybe a few other smells I couldn't make out. I expected we would find the fort empty, the attackers having looted it and moved on.

As we got closer, there was less cover, and every movement was riskier. My heart beat faster just from the anticipation. With no other way up the slope, I abandoned crouching and ran as fast as I could to the outermost wall while keeping an eye out for anyone on guard duty.

Still no one.

The giant opening near where I stood was not part of the design. The gate had fallen forward, pulled down from the outside. I peered around the corner to the inside, but still saw no one. The brothers moved up with me, our backs flat against the wall. Thorir sniffed the air.

"Roast pork?" he whispered. "Lot more than that, too."

"They're in there," snarled Frothi, a seax in each fist.

"We're not here to fight," I whispered back. "Stay hidden. Watch and listen."

The second wall stood about twenty feet inside the outermost wall. They were both simply constructed, made of logs driven into the ground. The second gate had been torn inward just like the first, allowing us to see through to what I imagined was the third and final wall of the structure.

The areas between walls were spattered with blood. Defenders had fought here, and no doubt been driven back behind the final wall. This last defensive perimeter had a solid stone base supporting an elevated wooden wall above it. One short tower rose from the innermost area of the fort. No movement in it, though. Perhaps they thought there was nothing to watch for. Apparently not, since nobody had bothered watching the entrance.

We crept ahead, hunched down beneath the stone base. Stone steps led up to the main level of the fort on two sides. I didn't want to go up either one of them. I would be too obvious and too exposed.

Not all the wooden posts above the stone wall were in good repair. Some had been knocked over or hacked at. I had the brothers give me a lift up at one of these points to get over the stone wall. There, I would pass through some of the broken remains.

Peeking first, all I could determine was that I was looking out from under a lean-to on the other side of the wall. There were supplies under the over-hang. Sacks, baskets, and chests would all give me some cover after squeezing through. Some, not much, and I couldn't see far beyond the shack standing a few paces beyond the lean-to.

Smoke wafted from the other side of the shack, the back of which looked like an angry boar had charged through it. I could kind of, sort of, almost see through the structure to the other side.

I turned back and tried to communicate with improvised hand gestures that I could pull one of them up if the other lifted from below. This was the easy part of the silent conversation. The more difficult part was when the two brothers argued, entirely without words, about who would lift and who would go up.

For a moment, it was like Innstein and Utstein again.

However they decided it, Frothi lifted and Thorir went up with me. I pointed for him to creep further along the wall and look inside from cover while I went in through this opening. I meant to convey that we would both look in from different angles and then come back, as that should give us a good idea what was going on here. Then we could leave, hopefully with as little attention as we'd entered.

I heard guttural, incoherent mumbling as I squeezed through the open-ing. Still seeing no one, I crept up to the rear corner of the shack and confirmed no one was inside. Someone was close, but on the other side of the shack, as was the pork. Now I could see through to the other side, where the shed's door was. Or used to be.

A cookfire was flanked on both sides by piles of bodies. A cauldron hung between the piles, its contents steaming while it tugged down on an iron spit inserted into bodies on both sides for support.

In one pile, the spit had been thrust deep into a man's abdomen. Fluids seeped out from the hole down the pile of bodies. It looked like a combination of blood and bile dripping while fat rendered from the heat of the spit. The liquid that did not drip straight down sizzled on the hot bar in a sickening display that threatened to empty my stomach.

Stuck into the ground around the fire were half-limbs. Metal skewers held arms below the elbow and legs beneath the knee upright against the sides of the fire. Skin crackled as the meat beneath it roasted. Where the digits had not already fallen off, nails were burned black.

I'd had no idea human meat smelled so much like pork.

The source of the grumbling stepped forward past the bodies and adjusted the limbs, turning the outsides toward the flame for even cooking. His brow was broader than a man's, and his lower jaw jutted forward unnaturally. He worked his mouth over and over, as if chewing something or perhaps feeling out the unfamiliar shape of his face. Dark blotches ringed his eyes like disease.

A *jǫtunn* or witch could be a troll. But there was something about the corruption of this man that to me was the very essence of the word *troll*. I held my breath, my heart hammering like three dwarves trying to pound out a new sword in record time.

The troll shuffled off, and I breathed out. I counted to ten and crouch-walked into the rear of the shack. Moving to the front of the structure allowed me a better view of the fort's interior.

There were a few small buildings, some broken down. Tents with other cookfires. Maybe a dozen warriors that I could see engaged in all the most boring activities of a war camp. One other, at least, was also a troll and was much bigger than the one doing the cooking.

All their shields were crudely painted with a single symbol, the winged *othala* rune. Alfhild was supposed to have taken her god-children north. Had Hemming lied to us?

I had to get back to the others and tell them. Was this enough information, though? Styrgrim would ask how many were up here, and I still didn't know. Was I lucky enough to continue, or wise enough to know when to stop?

My right hand dropped to Need's hilt. The grip pulsed in my fist, the weapon humming in its single, hungry monotone. The tone comforted me, even if Need was as eager for a fight as I was to avoid one.

I would be in an exposed position if any of those trolls walked toward the shack. This was as far as I could go without exposing myself, which might expose Thorir and Frothi. So I stepped back, intending to retreat to the cover under the lean-to and crawl back out. Perhaps the brothers had a good idea of the number of warriors here, anyway.

A dog barked somewhere in the camp. I wheeled around to see if I'd been discovered.

"O-ho! Another one to add to the pots," said the limb-cooking troll.

He hadn't walked away. He had walked just a few steps aside into what was a blind spot for me. And when I had started backing away, he had come from the other side of the shack.

I started to draw Need, but the troll already had his weapon deployed. His weapon being a big wooden spoon, he brought it down on top of my right wrist and held it firm. A moment later, a sidelong punch from his left fist found my right side, just under my ribcage.

I gasped. My legs went out from under me. The world went dark.

When I opened my eyes a moment later, I was curled up on the ground. I knew I had to run, to get out of there, but my body would not obey. I could hardly even breathe. This was a physical pain I had never experienced.

I finally knew what being punched in the liver felt like.

"Ha!" said the troll. "Kind of scrawny, but you'll do."

# CHAPTER 22

# THE IMPORTANCE OF NAMES

I TRIED TO RISE TO ALL FOURS AND FAILED.

A dog barked again, closer this time. Footsteps told me at least some of the others in the fort had taken notice that something strange was going on. Grunts and shuffling gaits indicated they were in no hurry. The troll tossed his spoon away and drew his seax.

All I had to do was crawl backwards, but I didn't have even that much control. That's the thing about being hit hard in the liver: It is instantly incapacitating. The troll grabbed my head with one hand and turned my face to the left. All I could do was gasp as he wiped the blade on his filthy sleeve.

The dog barked again, so close, it had to be inside the shack with us. The troll turned as if more surprised than I was and stood up.

I didn't see Thorir Houndsfoot bury his axe in that troll's skull, but I did see the results after he helped me up.

"Run," I croaked.

"Pull your trollshot-self together," growled Thorir, "and we'll do just that."

"Can't . . . move . . ."

Trolls in the fort were no longer taking their time. Instead they were shouting, running, or grabbing weapons. We would be swarmed in a matter of seconds.

I tried to stand on my own, but still could not.

"Shit," said Thorir. He growled and dragged me back to the lean-to I'd squeezed through. "Come on," he said with growing frustration. "Come on!"

But I couldn't do much on my own, and he finally worked out that he would need to go through first and pull me. The dog man snarled as he squeezed through, and by that time, I knew we'd been seen.

The big troll I'd seen from afar towered over the shack as he approached. He growled and took an angry swipe at the structure when he saw we were almost away, and the whole thing crashed down. "Get around the sides, you good-for-nothings! They're sneaking through the back."

Laughter rose behind him as he looked back, but that wasn't the only thing to hear. In the middle of that central area, a sound between a man's shout and a moose's roar rang out. I could see the side entry, where one of the sets of steps led. Three warriors were ready to go down them and follow us. The last thing I saw as Thorir pulled me through was Moose-Frothi charging up those steps, a seax in each hand, and running straight through those three.

Horns blasted and every troll in the camp shouted in alarm. Most of them were headed for Frothi.

Before I could tell Thorir I couldn't climb down the rock wall on my own, he threw me over one shoulder and leaped down. The impact did not improve my disposition.

"Ah, you're fine," said Thorir, despite the total lack of evidence this was true.

After the first few strides, his gait smoothed out, and the jostling was at a minimum given the circumstances. Out past the outer walls in seconds, Thorir was panting, and, I thought, already winded.

Soon, I realized he was not winded. He was panting like a dog, and running just as fast as one.

Moose-Frothi laughed and bayed like a madman. Those moose legs powered through the broken wood, crashing through the damaged barriers to join us. He still had his blades and had also stolen a spear. I've seen others just as good at creating chaos, but none who enjoyed it more.

"Want a hand, little brother?"

"Just keep moving," barked Thorir, his aim fixed straight ahead. "There's a lot of them."

"A few less, now!" He bayed in what sounded like a moose version of a taunt.

I was probably functional, but could definitely not run as fast as Thorir could carry me. Over his shoulder, I watched a small army of trolls pour out of the hill fort. Definitely more people than we had brought. Most ran, while others pushed off on skis. The big troll came out last. He moved slower, but his great, loping strides almost made up for it.

As fast as Thorir ran, he could not outpace that thing or the skiers. Only our head start gave us a chance at getting far enough for help.

An arrow whistled over our heads. One of the skiers had already closed the distance and was shooting on the move. A graceful, practiced attack: Taking a wide cut out to her left, she turned to come back to her right as she drew, loosing while her momentum carried her smoothly in one direction.

"Watch out," I croaked, pointing her out to Frothi and still limited in what I could say at any one time.

Frothi looked back, then looked forward. Then he looked at me and grinned. "You worry too much."

An arrow took that skier in the throat just as she was drawing back for another shot. I gaped. We were hundreds of yards from the safety of a shield wall. Had the group moved up the slope? Even if they did, that shot was *uphill*. Frothi seemed to read my disbelief and answered what I hadn't asked.

"Think they call him Arrow-Odd for nothing?"

Thorir taunted our pursuers with a howl, and Frothi followed with a bellow.

The skiers among them seemed to gain speed as they came closer. Another arrow found its mark in a troll's chest, and he fell in a tumbling mess. Those on foot leaped over or around him, no worse for wear.

"Fast trolls," I choked out.

"And tough," said Frothi. "I had to stab them more than usual." He sounded thankful for the plentiful stabbing opportunities.

"Not far now," panted Thorir.

I turned my head to look in the direction we were going. Our people were still a long way off, arrayed in a shield wall with a gap that Thorir was headed toward. On one flank, I saw the red cloak and golden headband of Arrow-Odd as he loosed yet another arrow, flying impossibly far and with impossible accuracy.

We had to be over three hundred yards out.

"Don't need to get much farther," panted Thorir. Which seemed not true at all.

Frothi pivoted to throw his spear at the closest skier and just missed. It was a good dodge, but took the troll so far off-course that he fell over and lost one of his skis. The skiers behind him slid to the sides.

"Three skiers left," I warned Thorir.

Frothi barreled into one of the remaining skiers, who went down hard. The other two, armed with spears, breezed by him in wide arcs. They were set on another target, namely us. Meanwhile, the footsteps of the big troll seemed to shake the very hill. He was getting closer despite Thorir not slowing down.

"Two on skis getting close," I warned.

"We're just about there," said Thorir.

"They're about to be on us!"

"He has an angle."

"Who? What angle?"

"The *wizard!*" shouted Thorir.

An arrow, heavier than one would expect an arrow to be, shot over my head like a bird of prey. It took one of the skiers down hard, nailing him to the hill.

"Ha!" laughed Thorir. "They will have a bad time of it, now."

The last of the skiers came bearing down at Thorir, spear outstretched. I reacted without thinking and drew Need, pushing it down across Thorir's back and hoping to all hope that my will was in sync with the weapon.

Need changed into a shield. The spearpoint glanced off the boss and caught the wood. There was no time to get the point unstuck. The skier crashed into Thorir, sending all three of us tumbling.

Moose-Frothi charged over and stomped that last skier's head in with a hoof. Thorir was up easily, but I struggled to find my footing. Struggled so badly that the moose man gave a frustrated growl, yanked me up, and pushed me past him. "Come on!"

An arrow struck him in the back.

It was one of those scenes where time slowed down for me, just for a moment. The same thing happened when Kari reached his shield out to block a javelin and ended up taking it through his arm. And when Haldor made his last stand against Grimhild, one severed arm and one arm whole, bringing his axe down on her head. This time, it was Frothi who grunted and continued pushing me forward despite the wound.

Thorir was somewhere nearby. He had to be. I was dimly aware of shouting. Not Thorir's, though. Time came back to normal, but the sounds were chaos as Frothi stumbled. He grabbed at the arrow but couldn't reach it. Then it was my turn trying to drag him forward, though not very effectively.

I looked up to see Thorir stand fast against the charge coming down the hill. No formation, no order. Just a lot of trolls. One of them much, much bigger than any of us. We had a few moments before they were on us. Not enough time to carve a spell, even if I had one in mind.

"Pull it," growled Frothi.

"You'll bleed out!"

"Pull it!"

The rage tinted my world gray and muted its sounds with Need's hum. I forgot my injury, forgot everything other than the moment. I shouted back in his face as I dragged him by the collar. "Frothi, you troll-cursed, Norn-cursed, elf-cursed fool! Find your legs and move!"

Either the force of it or the surprise, or both, shocked him out of his single-mindedness. He looked over my shoulder, then back at Thorir.

"Brother, let's go!"

Reluctantly, Thorir stepped back to us.

Frothi was not the only one shouting, however. A din had risen behind me as I dragged Frothi back. Our people had moved up faster than I thought they could have. Bjorn and Magnus at their head, they formed a shield wall in front of the three of us. All of them but two.

Arrow-Odd had abandoned his bow and drawn his sword. Styrgrim ran a few paces to his side, and together, they were going up that hill.

I shook my head. "Are they insane? There are dozens of those . . . things!"

Ketill as he loosed another arrow. "Dozens minus one."

Bjorn did not look worried. "I've seen much crazier than this." He nodded at Ingolf, who helped set Frothi down and examined his wound. "Orders to protect the injured."

"What about the big one?" I asked.

Bjorn waved me off without looking up. "See for yourself."

The fastest trolls swarmed Odd and Styrgrim, no doubt smelling easy blood. And it looked like they soon would be as the two disappeared into the crowd of foemen.

Weapons flashed bright in the daylight, and those foemen soon gave the two maniacs a much wider berth. Three were down in a matter of seconds, and none wanted to be next.

Ketill loosed again. "Dozens minus two."

Styrgrim stood firm on lower ground, parrying and counterattacking as if cowed, until it was time to strike. Then, he would rush two or three trolls at a time and cut them down, drawing the enemy formation around him. He did this while Odd distracted the big troll, leaping away from every earth-shaking swing of his massive axe.

At every opportunity, Odd disengaged from his opponent for just a moment, attacking the rear of those focused on Styrgrim. Blades and points connected with Odd, but his shirt had been woven by a witch and was made to shrug off steel of any kind. When the trolls piled on, no doubt thinking they finally had Odd, Styrgrim waded in and cut them down from behind.

Ketill's voice was regular as a drum. "Dozens minus three."

"This can't be serious," I said.

"What in the coldest reaches of Hel is happening?" demanded Frothi.

"The enemy is slowly realizing they are outclassed," said Magnus. "They're afraid to attack Odd now, but they haven't had any luck going at 'Grim, either."

"Dozens minus four."

"Also, the wizard is a keen shot."

The giant troll thudded his axe down into the earth and missed Odd by a hand's width. Attacks from the other trolls became tentative. Two had pulled back, ready to run. Styrgrim laughed at them, then passed on an opportunity with his sword to break the teeth of one with his shield. He shoved that troll back towards his giant friend.

The man-sized troll collided with his much larger, much angrier ally, to the latter's great annoyance. With another massive swing, the big troll took off the head of his former comrade in arms.

If that wasn't the thing that broke the rest of them, it was Styrgrim's evil laughter that followed. The remaining trolls moved away from the big troll and away from the rest of our group. Then, they ran.

The giant troll roared and turned from Odd to charge the laughing Styrgim. I think Styrgrim would have handled this one as he had so many others. We never got an answer, however, because Ketill's next arrow had, shall we say, an extra dose of malice behind it. That arrow struck lower than the others and pierced the troll's heavy chain shirt.

A collective groan went up from our front line, including me. Not that I felt bad for our enemy, but nobody really wants to see that.

"Ha!" laughed Ketill. "Dozens minus four and a half."

The big troll roared as he went down. Surprise and pain in his voice rattled the air as he tried to rise and failed.

"Someone explain to me how the wizard has shot half a man," demanded Frothi.

Thorir sighed. "Through the balls, brother. He shot him through the balls."

# CHAPTER 23

# A HOLLOW TRUCE

ODD AND STYRGRIM HAD KILLED OR ROUTED EVERY FOEMAN FROM the hill fort, whether human or troll, except the big one. And that one was in bad shape. A man whose blood is already up can have his balls kicked and continue fighting like nothing has happened, but an arrow through the balls is a bit too shocking to endure. That last troll lay on the ground, his comrades having fled, and he asked Styrgrim to run him through and end his suffering.

I was a bit surprised when Styrgrim didn't respond with a look of disgust or dismissal. Perhaps he had a bit of empathy for that sort of injury. Empathy or not, though, he demanded the troll answer his questions first.

Meanwhile, Bjorn turned to me. "What was up there?"

The liver shot I'd taken had faded to a dull ache. I looked away from the troll being questioned and started to answer, to describe the human meat being roasted, when I caught sight of Hemming.

I charged the tracker, but Bjorn grabbed me and held me back. "The winged *othala* rune," I spat, "that's Alfhild's symbol! He said she was going north, but here it is!"

"You hearing this?" Bjorn called to Styrgrim. Which he probably did, but I was too busy flailing in Bjorn's vice-like grip to take notice.

Panic came over Hemming's expression. He looked from me to some of the others, and I'm sure he considered running. Ketill nocked an arrow, and Hemming fell to his knees, pleading ignorance.

Arrow-Odd put himself between Hemming and the larger group. "This man sails on my ship. If there is something to do about him, then no one will do it but me."

Bjorn let go of me at that point. Even with my blood up, I was not so foolish as to challenge Odd to a fight. "Now perhaps you can tell us what you found up there?"

It took me a moment to collect myself. "No one still alive." I described the scene of butchered human parts roasting by a fire. Thorir confirmed the story. And with a great deal of growling involved, Frothi also confirmed what he'd seen, though he was smarting from that arrow in the back.

"Ingolf," I said, "how is he?"

"Just pull it out!" Frothi shouted, not for the first, or fifth, time.

"Do not pull the arrow out," responded Ingolf. "I've cut down on the shaft and cleaned it as well as I can, but *do not pull it out*. That is a thing for Huld to do, and only once she's prepared something to stop the bleeding that will follow." Ingolf looked up and must have seen in my face what I wanted to know, but couldn't ask. "I think Frothi will be fine. The arrow found an open spot above his armor, but his hide—"

"*Watch it,*" rumbled the moose-man.

"Ah, his skin is . . . thicker than most."

Thorir's laugh sounded like a few quick barks. "You should see how thick his skin is below the waist."

The joke made even Frothi laugh. It almost distracted me from wanting to kill Hemming for lying to us again. The only killing was of that big, miserable, testicle-shot troll, however. Styrgrim ran his sword through the thing's heart, and we all waited for him to come tell us what he'd learned.

"I think the tracker told the truth," he began, to my great disappointment. "That was a viking crew hired by 'Grim Aegir.' And that," he pointed at the big corpse, "was their captain. He didn't seem to know this 'Grim Aegir' was Ogmund's son, Svart. He did have a few things to say about what Svart offered him. Said others were elevated by their blood, but that he and his could find their own elevation, assert their rightful dominance. Predators rather than prey. And the symbol for that elevation, he said, was the winged *othala*."

"'Elevation,' meaning 'eating people and turning into trolls,'" said Ketill.

"His words, not the ones I would choose." Stygrim wiped his sword on a piece of fabric. A quick glance told me it had been cut away from the troll's pants. "There are no children of gods here. Just crudely painted shields."

Odd clapped Hemming on the back. "Did he know anything about Ogmund?" he asked of Styrgrim.

"Not at all. Nor where Svart and his Rus were headed."

"What was this crew doing here, then?" I asked.

"Svart brought this captain into his trollish fold with a ritual of consumption. The captain did the same for his crew, but that was a mistake, because then they needed more meat to sustain themselves. So they raided the nearest village. And did not have any plan for what might come after that."

"They lose something of their intellect when they go this way," added Ketill. "They won't be getting it back, either."

"Gained some in size, though," said Styrgrim.

Ketill nodded. "Some will be like that and grow large. Some will shrink in size, but become quicker. Most will find more comfort underground, given enough time."

I shook my head. "All those years hearing stories about 'being trolled,' whatever that meant, and now I see it."

The wizard chuckled. "All those years? You mean three? The last time I saw something like this was an age ago."

"What stopped it?"

"People were starving at the time, so it was not the same cause. I couldn't say what stopped it, but it wasn't me. For all my efforts, I despaired and wandered into a barrel of ale. But it wasn't the gods, as they were too busy hiding to help."

"Perhaps I might be of service to you," said Orm.

What the priest had done during the battle, I had no idea, but it made sense that he had stayed with our group. Now he piped up, surprising everyone, especially with his claim of usefulness.

"Do we need someone who smells worse than Hemming?" asked Magnus.

Hemming made no reaction to the insult. Still standing at the edge of our war party, perhaps he meant to play it off as if he hadn't heard.

Odd brought the conversation back to the priest's suggestion. "Of what service could you be?"

"As a father of the church, I could baptize you and bring you into the fold! Any one of you willing to bathe in the glory of G—"

"A man who smells as you do should not speak of washing others," snapped Styrgrim. "Your name is not Father. Your name is Asshole-Orm. And you won't bring your stink on my ship." I think he was not just referring to Orm's physical smell.

"Nor mine," added Odd.

The priest's mouth moved soundlessly. He looked from one man to the next, hoping to find a mote of compassion. It was the wrong group to do that with, and the wrong group to be a priest among. I didn't want Asshole-Orm on the *Sea Squirrel* at all, but I knew he needed to come with us.

That didn't mean I had to relieve his anxiety right away, though.

"I can . . . be of use! It might do you some good to deliver me to . . . where are you going?"

"To King Athils' court in Uppsala," I said. "Are you sure you want passage there? Athils is not exactly friendly to Christians."

The priest crossed himself. "You will need my protection! Athils is a warlock. He conjures demons to do his bidding. Nothing can stand against such dreadful power except the light of our Lord Jesus Christ."

"We didn't do too badly standing against that power with our own sorcery," said Magnus. "And Cow-Killer, that one time."

"What's Cow-Killer?" asked Thorir.

"A long story," I said. "I'll tell it once we're underway. For now, priest, you can walk with us, and you can entreat our vessel's captain for passage."

"Are you not the captain? You seemed to be the leader of this bunch."

I wished I could've seen Odd's face when he heard that comment. "I am not the captain. I lead the crew of my ship on land. The captain is Kraki Bentleg." Based on his reaction, he clearly knew something of the name, just as he knew the reputation of King Athils. It would be interesting to see how he asked the savage Kraki Bentleg for a favor.

With Frothi well enough to walk, we headed back the way we'd come. Hemming remained ahead of the group, but this time, Arrow-Odd stayed with him. Far ahead of the rest of us, I saw them talking but couldn't hear their conversation.

Asshole-Orm sidled up to me on the way back. "They know me at the monastery in Uppsala. They can pay! What should I offer your captain?"

I told him to jump in the sea as soon as we got to the ships and to scrub himself raw before offering anything. Orm took my meaning and gave us some distance for the rest of the walk. And he did wade into the sea, cold as it was, at the first opportunity.

The shoreline was filled with a lot of bored crewmates. They had seen nothing of any trolls or even other ships. All were glad of our return and eager to hear what had happened. Most did not react much to the story other than to cheer at the cheerable parts. When I explained the priest's story, I noticed Vilgrip's jaw clench. If he did not like Christians, I thought, he would still need to live with Kraki's decision.

Orm returned while I was still telling what had happened. He was soaking wet and shivering, and went to the nearest campfire to warm up. Soon after, I addressed the issue of the priest directly.

"Kraki, I know it's your ship and your decision to take that man on, but I want to say a thing first. I think we might need Orm to speak as a witness in Uppsala. Athils is a suspicious one and may not take our word."

Kraki walked over to the shivering priest and circled him, looking him up and down. "So?"

"Soooo . . . yes?" asked the hopeful priest.

"Hmm," said Kraki, an uncertain sound. "You know the rules?"

"Rules?"

"Rules!"

"He's saying you must agree to no fighting amongst the crew," I said. "And also that there are no thralls aboard the vessel. Therefore, anyone on the ship is not a thrall, no matter who declares that they are."

"Of course!"

The priest clasped arms with Kraki, and it was done. I looked for Vilgrip to see if this had any effect on him. It seemed to me he was even less pleased than before, but he said nothing.

Uppsala was not far, as the raven flies. But we were not ravens, and so we took the circuitous sea route along the coast, then west and north through the series of islands and inlets leading to the city.

We docked under a bright sun with few clouds in the sky. Uppsala was even bigger than Lejre, promising all manner of secrets, rumors, and commerce. The docks themselves stretched so far that I could not even count the number of ships there.

The *Whaleslayer* pulled in first, with Odd standing up at the prow. He beamed with pride as his golden headband gleamed in the sunlight. It would have been difficult to mistake him for anyone but Arrow-Odd, so when a heavily armored guardsman shouted a generic greeting and asked his name before letting Odd disembark, it was a bit surprising.

"Who do you serve?" shouted the guardsman, even more surprising.

"I am Arrow-Odd," he roared back. "I serve no man and sacrifice to no gods. Who are you, who does not know my name or reputation, and why do you delay me?"

If the guardsman was impressed or surprised, he did not show it. His chain shirt was fitted well to a svelte but muscular form. Impenetrable eyes stared out from the sockets of a battle-scarred helmet. Arms folded across his chest held a two-handed axe so casually, it might have been a big spoon.

"My name is Svipdag, and I am between you and the king because I am between everyone and the king. Of course, I've heard of you, Arrow-Odd. But I don't know who you are with or why you are here. There is no one allowed into King Athils' presence if I don't like it, regardless of their name. And when I see a flotilla of ships prepared for war, especially during turbulent times, I begin to not like it."

Hallfred shouted his answer before Odd could. "You would like it less if we were not here. We were just in Ahvaland, to the detriment of a trollish host that destroyed a village there. It's important we speak to King Athils about that right away."

"You found trolls in Ahvaland? That is the second most interesting thing I have heard today. Come down from there and let's talk without needing to shout."

Captains and skalds disembarked. I gestured for Orm to join us as well. We met for a closer conversation with Svipdag on the dock.

"Describe these trolls and your interaction with them," said Svipdag. "I'll decide whether you should speak to the king after I hear what you have to say."

I was about to respond and tell about my experience with these trolls and their dinner preparations when Orm surged forward. "They were demons! Demons from Hell! Of all the things I have seen on this earth, I never thought the Lord would allow such to walk among us. Yet they did more than walk. They killed everyone in my village! Every man, woman, and child. Razed the huts to the ground, then broke through the gates of the hill fort and slaughtered what defenders remained. God's favor brought these fine men to lay them low, and so I pray you grant them audience with your king!"

Svipdag laid the long handle of his axe on his shoulders and stretched a little. "Killed everyone, you say?"

"Everyone!"

"And how is it you know such a thing? If you are part of everyone who was there, you must have been killed. Is it a dead man who speaks to me?"

"I—I—"

"He hid in a pile of shit," I said.

Svipdag sniffed at the priest and curled his lip. "Good enough evidence for now. For five ships, I'll take five of you to the hall. You'll need to leave your weapons outside, and swear oaths against fighting in Uppsala."

"Ha!" laughed Odd.

"And you can do those things, or you can stay here. Staying here still carries a prohibition against fighting, I should add. King Athils has told me to make certain there is no misunderstanding about that."

I successfully argued for five plus Orm. We didn't like the conditions but agreed anyway. Odd wasn't keen on taking all the captains, however. He chose to keep Styrgrim and Hallfred close by. Kraki had refused to leave the *Sea Squirrel* and to give up his weapon, anyway, so I chose to take Magnus in his place.

Ketill would not be left behind entirely. He grabbed my shoulder as I turned to go and whispered into my ear, "If Athils is as I've heard, do not expect him to negotiate like a lord you have encountered before. He is crafty, and whatever he wants, he will not say it outright. You will need to find it out before you can offer it."

I nodded and headed off, though I didn't understand why a king would hold back saying what he wanted. That's a mistake I came to call the Poets' Folly, the idea that purpose lay in true expression, or the closest we could get to it. But in politics, or in any hostile place, true expression is just a vulnerability.

Uppsala was huge, well-fortified with two tiers of palisades, and filled to the brim with people trading, crafting, and cooking. Three men worked at a forge, rows of completed axe and spear heads lining the shelves on one wall. A butcher directed two assistants as they took down one of four pig carcasses. Bakers pulled rough loaves of bread out of ovens by the dozen. The amount of commerce was unmatched in my experience.

Conversations were in all manner of languages. Some I could not understand but could at least identify, like Rus. Others were completely unfamiliar.

If I'd had my way, I would have spent hours just walking the streets and listening.

Hopefully not to too many more Rus, though. I tried to look sly as we passed by a group of them. An ill feeling crept up from my feet and settled in my stomach, but I dismissed it, actually waving it away with a hand. Of course there were some Rus in Uppsala! We were not so far from the city of Holmgard in Gardariki, and Uppsala was a great center of trade. Still, I wished I'd had time to sneak around and see who they were trading with.

Svipdag led us to King Athils' great hall, and 'great' hardly began to describe it. It was not just big, it was so big I screwed up my eyes and wondered how it had even been built. Ornate double doors at its head were twice as tall as a man and opened up to admit as many as six abreast. And open they did, though only after giving over our weapons to Svipdag's guardsmen.

With one exception.

"What sword?" I asked, focusing my intellect on *not a weapon* and my will on Need itself.

"Hey, didn't you have—" The guardsman caught himself and pointed at what he swore had just been the hilt of a sword at my hip.

I looked down to see a wooden comb. "It is best to be well-groomed when meeting a king."

The guard shook his head and moved off as I put the comb away. I had no intention to use a weapon in the hall, I just didn't want to hand Need over to anyone else. And maybe I wanted to flaunt the king's rules a bit.

"I saw that," Magnus whispered.

I grinned. Maybe more than a bit.

A crush of people bulged outward from the high seat at one side of the hall. Svipdag continued right into the thick of the group and motioned for us to follow. I thought it might take a while before we had our audience. That turned out not to be the case when Svipdag roared his command, "Clear away or be cleared away!"

Other than Athils himself, I could hardly imagine who would command the immediate reaction Svipdag got. The audience parted in the middle, and Svipdag, great axe still held casually across his shoulders, swaggered forward amidst a quieting crowd.

"It has got loud in this place," said Svipdag. "It must be that many important things are being said, that we have so many voices all at once."

We followed the man forward and soon saw the figure sitting on the high seat. Long-bearded, chisel-faced, slightly hunched as if more from disposition than from age—this had to be King Athils.

"A good king listens more than talks," said Athils. "As I listen, is it your voice that carries the most importance?" His voice was higher-pitched than I expected. Like a bird of prey's screech, only with the slow cadence of a man who has all the time in Midgard.

"I am but a humble champion, of little consequence myself. However, I've run into a few fine fellows with a bit of word-fame. That alone, I would not bother you about. However, they told me something of their recent adventures, and I thought you would wish to hear them straightaway."

"Fascinating. Do they vouch for our most recent guests?"

"It seems to me," said Svipdag, turning and gesturing toward us, "that Arrow-Odd and company can speak for themselves on that count."

Every voice in the hall seemed to say *whisper whisper whisper* in the loudest possible manner at that, filling it with noise even if not saying anything in particular. Odd's name still carried its reputation.

The king nodded. "It is well to consider all possible arguments, even if the guests do not agree. Perhaps my current guests see now why I insist on a prohibition against weapons inside my hall."

"Should it come to a question of weapons, I think that would clarify many things." The voice was cool and calm, yet shot through the remaining clamor in the hall like an arrow wrapped in silk.

I did not know the voice, but my hand went to Need out of pure instinct. Identifying the owner was easy enough. He stood tall even among tall men, with a broad chest and shoulders to hang a bright yellow cloak off of. A simple gold chain hung from his neck, while the intricate weaving and embroidering of his tunic were anything but simple. His manner and dress indicated wealth and power, and his smirk spoke of eagerness to use it. A smirk somewhat obscured by a shock of black hair hanging in front of his face.

"Shit," Magnus whispered out of the side of his mouth as he took a half step ahead of me.

"Is that who I think it is?" I whispered.

"Seems likely."

"There was a question of weapons, Svart," said Arrow-Odd, his voice growing from growl to roar. "Not long ago, it was my army that answered such questions, and another army that fled the field."

"What army is that?" Svart turned one way and then the other with open hands, as if confused. "An army you brought with you? The ravens all say Arrow-Odd's army is no more. The bulk of it sailed away. Perhaps this is a group of deserters? But then that would mean Odd deserted his own army!"

Odd's stare never moved from the tall man's eyes. He gave the impression of a volcano not just about to erupt but to explode, but he made no move forward. Only the barest twitch of his lips curled up one side, baring his teeth, and that vein in his forehead throbbed.

"What a wonderful happenstance," squeaked Athils, to no one's amusement but his own. "It is so fortuitous to have both sides of an argument. And here are the arguers, both receiving hospitality at my hall, both agreeing to keep their peace, as my city requires.

"Welcome, Odd Grimsson! And welcome to your men. And know that just as welcome here is Svart Ogmundsson. Oh, I have misspoken! He goes by his mother's name—Svart Geirridarson. Or do you prefer to use a byname instead? I would hate to insult one of my guests by misnaming him."

Svart bowed, his forelock dipping low. "One thing I would never do is deny my heritage. Even if it has become fashionable for others."

The bastard looked right at me while he said it, and I knew without declaration that it would come to a battle of wits between us. The only question was, what would the stakes be?

# CHAPTER 24

# POET'S FOLLY

KING ATHILS LOOKED QUITE PLEASED TO HAVE SVART AND ODD in his hall at the same time. Most people would not want to be anywhere near those two. Even with their retinues disarmed and limited in number, Odd having four of us, Svart's group looking like twelve or fifteen, someone was likely to cause a problem.

The big longhouse was packed full of lords, merchants, freemen, and others, and they all went very quiet after Svart spoke about heritage. Now it was a question of what Arrow-Odd would do, and I had a pretty clear idea of what should come next. We would tell King Athils what we had learned in Ahvaland, he would throw Svart and his people out, and then we could get back to our real business: Finding Tyrfing.

"We're not here for argument, but to tell of things that happened," I shouted. "We were just in Ahvaland and found a village that had been attacked. Here is Orm, a priest of the White Christ and the only survivor."

"I heard the White Christ was not so white, actually," quipped Athils. "I heard he was brown."

"Lies!" shouted Orm.

Athils hmmphed. I couldn't tell if this king really was another sorcerer or just off-putting. He certainly looked like he was having a fun time with all the chaos in his court.

"We met your man, Svipdag, at the docks," I continued. "He determined Orm's story was fit for your ears."

"He should tell his story at once!" Athils cried. Then lower and more menacing, "And for all to hear."

I motioned Orm forward past a still-glaring Arrow-Odd. The priest strode forward with a confidence I had not yet seen. He told the same story he had told us, more or less. His Yahweh appeared and told Orm where to hide and wait. Then Yahweh sent a wind to bring us to avenge the villagers, which, of course, required Orm to have stayed alive to tell us all what had happened.

I wished I had spoken to the priest before putting him up to give this impromptu testimony. He reverted to Latin terms over and over again to describe these trolls as devils and us as avenging angels. Athils seemed to follow, but doubtless thought less of the account for its foreignness.

I added to Orm's account, mentioning the cannibalism and winged *othala* runes. The islands of Ahvaland could be filled with others Svart had recruited and turned. Other people living on those islands likely needed help.

"What is this about my men?" Svart cut in, playing amused and hurt at the same time. "I have only brought a few ships to trade and talk a bit of politics, and you'll see no runes on my sails, only my dragon sigil. My men are all in Uppsala. Take a look! Some are in this hall, though most are with our ships, or milling about the city. I left strict instructions with them to be good guests by supporting the ale-and-whores economy."

His tone, timing, and gestures were perfect. Others in the hall laughed, as if they did not hear the horrific details I'd just given, only Svart's glib response. The king remained unmoving as he listened.

"Is the son of Ogmund afraid to admit his own deeds?" I demanded. "The island you frequented for torturing prisoners on the White Sea, for example. We found the remnants of what was left there—men butchered and left like hung meat. Now we find vikings you hired, trolled from the eating of human flesh, eating the locals of Ahvaland,"

"Island?" he exclaimed. "Was I on this island?"

"No, it was Alfhild, your father's—"

"He is a persistent one—persistently foolish! Really, who is this one with the tiny beard?"

"Ansgar Styrgrimsson," said Styrgrim, his voice like the bear of his byname. "The Bear of Lejre. The Sorcerer's Bane. The Skald of Risaland." That got some attention.

"Impressive titles," said Svart, nodding along with many others. "But did you question these eaters of the dead? Did they mention my name?"

"Yes and yes," growled Styrgrim. "As Grim Aegir."

"Who's this now? Not a name to be confused with Svart, that's for certain. Perhaps it was impossible to tell, as they spoke Rus? No? Perhaps they also suffered from very bad hair." He grabbed a handful of his thick forelock to the amusement of those in the hall. "But I don't think that would make them mine."

My blood was up, and I was going to win this war of words, whatever it took. "I know some of your prisoners. I will produce witnesses to the kidnappings and torture at that island on the White Sea. They are with our ships now, but they will be most interested to say their piece if summoned."

"What are their names?" asked Athils. Snapping his fingers, he beckoned Svipdag over. "I'll have them fetched."

"Vilgrip Tyrsson. Moose-Frothi. Thorir Houndsfoot."

Svart grinned at this. I had no idea why at the time. But grin he did, wide and wolf-like. Off went Svipdag, and I wasn't prepared to fill the time between him leaving and returning. That was a mistake, and Svart took advantage of it.

"It seems a pity to me to waste a king's time with idleness. While we wait for proof of misunderstanding, allow me to continue where I had been before the interruption."

Athils gave a perfunctory nod and hand gesture.

"As I was saying: It is good blood my father offers! He is a wise one, and wise enough to know that it is blood that runs through new generations to retain the power, the stability, the safety of a ruler's people. The proud House of Ynglings knows this well, or are you not descended from Yngvi-Frey, the very builder of Uppsala's temple? We come in friendship, not to cut the old lines, but to revive and extend them!"

He spoke with a fervor I had not seen before and did not like. When he continued, it was with a somber tone. "Meanwhile, there are many who can't see past their own personal issues, ignoring the greater ideas at play."

Svart didn't bother training his gaze on Arrow-Odd as he said this. There would be few in the hall who did not know what he referred to.

"Why come at all?" asked Athils. "If your plans are so secure for these supposed children of gods, you don't need my help."

"Power can be a delicate thing. But what if power were predetermined?

Every man and woman knowing his or her place, every rulership decided by blood rather than by battle? Would this not benefit the Swedes, keep them clear of conquest? The gods have given us a great gift! We have simply collected those gifts and determined who among them is fittest to rule."

"Perhaps one of them might be fit to rule the Swedes," crooned Athils.

"Not at all! But consider, my king, how many minor territories and outlying islands are in need of strong jarls to govern them. You don't intend to find a raven every time there is a question that needs answering in the whole of your realm, do you? You will need competent underlings, and hopefully enough to stretch throughout an empire of Swedes. If Ahvaland had such a competent overseer, it seems to me your most recent guests would have nothing to report."

"And you offer such leaders?"

"Who can offer better leadership for others to look up to than the sons and daughters of the gods?"

"What an interesting question!" squeaked Athils. "A question for me, among many questions I have myself. You must admit, Svart, that this is all quite new. It will take me some time to consider your approach, and that assumes the details are borne out by your description."

"Of course, of course. I have not come to harry the King of Swedes, but to help." He bowed low in deference.

I'd heard twisted words before, but this was a new champion of their twisting. I wondered if he'd learned from Ulf.

That bloviated back and forth took a while longer than I've related. I've summarized the major points, as I do not intend to torture the reader. I mention this only because by the time it was over, Svipdag had returned with Vilgrip, Frothi, and Thorir. To my mind, Svart had no way out.

"These are your witnesses?" asked Athils.

"Two half-monsters and a cripple," said Svart. "Rich testimony, indeed! I think I'll need another drink for this."

Low laughter began in the hall. It lingered too long for my comfort, and I felt the rhetorical ground beneath my feet shifting. The Brisingamen pulsed against my leg, calling me to use it.

*If I just stick my hand into the pouch and touch it, maybe I can use just a little of its power.*

Need's hum grew to a roar. One that only I could hear, but so loud that I had to shake it off. I moved my hand away from the bag of runes, and the roar quieted. The thought of using the torc returned, but this time I recognized the voice as not my own thoughts at all. The voice became easier to ignore.

"These are men of the *Sea Squirrel*," boomed Arrow-Odd. "I saw them go up against those trolls, and it was not to the benefit of the latter."

Strong words spoken from the voice that needed to speak them. But I feared Svart's comment had already done its damage. That description of them—Frothi and Thorir as half-monsters and Vilgrip as a cripple—would remain.

"Frothi and Thorir," I said, "tell the king, and the rest of this rabble, where you were when the crew of the *Sea Squirrel* found you."

"That *niðingr* had us locked up," said Thorir, pointing at Svart. "Asked a lot of questions about where we were from and who we were born to. Tried a lot of weird and absurd things, like feeding me raw meat and my brother a bunch of leaves."

Thorir would have continued, but too much chuckling broke his train of thought. He looked around in disbelief, unused to speaking in front of crowds. Especially in front of a crowd primed to believe Svart.

"I'll admit we were low on food during the winter," responded Svart. "The dog man and the moose man? That's what I thought they ate!"

Laughter increased. Men with money are apt to believe other men with money over those who've worked their way through hardship.

Frothi growled, and in growling so loud, his moose-voice overtook his man's voice. The impressive volume silenced the crowd for a moment but brought them back to even more raucous laughter. Frothi snarled, but there were too many faces to focus on to leave his stare on one.

"Vilgrip," I called out over the din, "tell the king of the experiment Svart tried on you."

Vilgrip stepped forward, more composed than the semi-feral brothers. He held up the stump of his right wrist for all to see.

"Svart said I was a son of Tyr. He tried to convince me to join his army. Said I might have latent powers. Tyr lost his right hand, so Svart cut mine off to see if that awakened such powers."

"Did it?" asked Athils.

Vilgrip turned to the king. "Divine heritage is not so impressive as some would have you believe."

Which was a strong and well-crafted statement. If only it hadn't been directed at a king of the house of Ynglings, whose family justified its rule by such heritage. That blade cut both ways in this case, and Vilgrip hadn't realized that before speaking.

Athils grinned.

"There is a great deal left unsaid from those stories," Svart responded. "I remember these men. I tried to help them reach their potential, yes, though I think their accounts are rather exaggerated. But, King Athils, if I may ask one question, did any of this crew of the *Sea Squirrel* challenge me when they reached this place in Ahvaland?"

"You were not there for me to throttle," said Vilgrip. "But now that you've nowhere to hide, I challenge you to a duel."

"That's a challenge I'll accept!"

King Athils waved the potential combatants off. "That's all very good for the next time you are both outside my city! In Uppsala, you're prohibited from fighting."

Svart bowed. "Until that time, then. But in any case, I fail to see how we, who were not on Ahvaland, could be associated with these supposed eaters of the dead. And as you can see, it's an entourage of Rus I travel with, only those most loyal to my father's court. I can't very well be associated with any of this eating. Unless . . . unless this one-handed man accuses me of eating his hand!"

All eyes went to Vilgrip, but I knew his answer before he spoke. "No," he said. "You fed it to your bird."

"Ah!" said Svart, wearing a wide grin. "Men will come to disagreement, no doubt, but I think we have established that me and mine have nothing to do with this business in Ahvaland."

He had contradicted himself by admitting he had been at that prison after all, but no one seemed to notice or care. To Svart, they were just words, frivolous things to be used as distraction. Meanwhile, he obliged his adversaries to be responsible in their accounts rather than frivolous, and his audience to laugh at supposed horrors rather than be horrified.

Acting in bad faith delights such people. When caught in the act, you'll most likely hear them accuse others of being "naive." Press them hard enough, and they will fall back on some broad but irrelevant idea, and lament that the time for argument is past. Unfortunately, Svart had an impatient audience willing to do that for him.

"Have you any better evidence than this?" asked the king. "I am little interested in arbitrating such grievances as I've heard. Doubtless, you will want them redressed, but it will not be in my hall or in my city. As for the business in Ahvaland, I will look into it."

"But Svart—" I got out before Athils cut me off.

"I understand Arrow-Odd and his people do not like Svart or his people. It is understandable you would attribute anything terrible you've seen to them. However, I've yet to hear a connection, unless this priest is willing to change his testimony. And I am busy with important matters. So, please! Eat and drink in my hall." Athils showed a toothy smile. "And mind your manners!"

Svipdag thumbed the blade of his axe. I got the message. But received or not, I was not ready to heed it. One of the powers of verse is to illuminate the truth more powerfully than common speech, so I tried one on Athils:

> "Kings come and
>     kings go,
> but one thing
>     wants to stay:
> The king's way,
>     if he's a wise one,
> or the doom coming
>     from craftier men."

Good verse is like a sharp blade and can be used for ill as easily as good. Svart stepped forward and spoke one in response:

> "What manner of beast
>     browbeats a king
> in his own happy
>     longhouse?
> Knowing when to stop
>     seems still unlearned:
> Even the cows know
>     when to come home."

And that's how I had my ass handed to me.

# CHAPTER 25

# ALL WARFARE IS DECEPTION

IT HADN'T BEEN A FORMAL POETRY COMPETITION AGAINST SVART,
but it had still been a battle of wits. And I had lost badly. Magnus dragged me
back to a bench with the others and sat me down. Arrow-Odd, Styrgrim, and
Hallfred sat with us, their faces unreadable. Vilgrip, Frothi, and Thorir
remained in Athils' hall, but looked confused and defeated.

I sat there in a daze. For a while, I was alone with my thoughts despite
being surrounded by chatter. It took a while for me to come back to my senses
well enough to hear. Magnus put a cup of ale into my hands.

"Want to try again?" asked Arrow-Odd.

I downed my ale and said nothing. The correct Norse answer was *yes, I
want to try again,* demonstrating a spirit that could not be extinguished, even
in defeat. I did not feel in possession of such a spirit. I checked my cup to see
if the spirit was hiding in the bottom, but no, it wasn't there, either. Svart had
crushed me in a straight contest of verse, in front of an audience, with high
stakes involved, without any part of the truth being on his side. That had
never happened to me before.

"He's never been much of a fighter," said Styrgrim. His tone was as heavy
with disappointment as it ever had been.

Magnus stared hard at Styrgrim. "If our friends speak so of us, I can't
imagine what our enemies are saying."

The verbal poke at the bear brought me fully back to my senses. "We were losing. I had to try—what did he say again? Was it that good?"

"His verse was sloppy, but that didn't matter," said Hallfred Horsefly. "He got here first, got to know Athils and his retainers, got to tell his story. He disrupted our attempt to tell what we'd seen because we relied on the truth, and he did not. He made jokes, made quips. Small waves lapping at the shores of small minds, just big enough to keep their attention off the bigger issues. Then you used a verse to speak of things far off in time, while Svart insinuated you were insulting the king the more you spoke. Kings will always react more to the here and now than anything that might happen later."

"Bad timing," said Odd. I wasn't sure if that was a criticism of my timing or a recognition that we had been fighting uphill since we arrived. "Now we need to wait until Athils is willing to talk to us again."

"It sounds like Athils doesn't care what we have to say," I said, waving for a thrall to bring more ale. "It sounds like he's about to take Svart up on his offer."

"You had better offer another idea then," said Odd. "One that does not involve refilling your cup as a primary tactic."

The thrall came with a pitcher and refilled my cup. I thought about taking a drink in open defiance of Odd's not-so-subtle remark, but leadership and contrarianism do not mix well. Seeing Magnus and Styrgrim still locked in a staring contest, I laid my now-full cup down. Then I grabbed Magnus by the shirt and dragged him off the bench with me.

"Where are you going?" demanded Odd and Styrgrim at the same time.

"To try again." Dragging Magnus was not easy. His need to continue the staring contest with Styrgrim was stronger than expected.

Ten or twenty strides from the table, Magnus pulled his attention back to the present. "You have a plan?"

"Svipdag seems to be in charge here. He doesn't want chaos in the city, much less the longhouse. The longer we stay, the more awkward things become. Maybe Svipdag will talk to us if he thinks it will get us to leave."

Athils had disappeared into the back rooms of his hall. Svipdag stood a few paces outside the entrance to those rooms, holding his axe across his shoulders.

The big champion nodded as we approached, giving an impression of neither favor nor disfavor. He listened without making any reaction until I was completely done requesting information about Heidrek the Wise.

"Well, that's easy," he answered. "I don't know anything about him."

"But others in the city might," I said. "King Athils might, if you advise him to tell us. And why hold back? We came to inform the king in good faith and were treated like halfwits. It seems to me that was not your intention. Or was it?"

Svipdag took a deep breath and fingered the cutting edge of his axe. "It seemed to me you had something important to say, or I would not have brought you here. What happened after that was not my doing."

"Well, now we have questions for the king rather than information. Perhaps he'd do us the courtesy of answering them, as he's been generous with his hospitality."

Svipdag shook his head. "I can tell you are not familiar with the Swedish court, but I'll put your case forward. Expect nothing. What is your question, again?"

"What does he know of Heidrek the Wise? We heard he came to Uppsala some generations ago and hoped his wisdom had been passed on through Athils' forefathers."

"I can ask him that. And what knowledge would you trade for his answer?"

"Trade?" I asked. "Is he a raven?"

"I know my king, and I know what his response will be. So instead of me running back and forth between you like some errand boy, I ask what you offer now to save myself a few trips."

"What about the knowledge we just brought him?" asked Magnus. "You know, the kind we risked our lives for?"

"Oh, that," said Svipdag. "Definitely expect nothing."

The big champion disappeared into the back while Magnus and I milled awkwardly around the tables set near the high seat. Here, at Athils' literal right hand, is where Svipdag sat. And though the hall was filled with visitors, the benches closest to the high seat—the ones usually reserved for champions —were only half-filled. I marked six other warriors as likely champions. They were neither interesting nor interested in us.

"Where are the *berserkir*?" asked Magnus.

I looked at the tables and empty benches. There were seats enough for another dozen men, sure. But *berserkir* usually sat together as one rowdy, smelly group and did not let anyone else use those seats while they were away. There were not twelve empty seats together anywhere.

"Maybe they're away?" I said. "And maybe he has fewer than twelve, despite the stories?"

Svipdag returned shortly. "The king says you're trying to trade a rumor for deep lore, and he's beginning to think you're bad guests."

Magnus turned and whispered into my ear, "Maybe we should cut his throat and tell him the seax was just a rumor."

That had a certain appeal, but I shook my head. "We won't get any deep lore that way for certain." Turning back to Svipdag, I could tell there was no point in pleading with the man. He did not make the decisions, and arguing with him would only waste time. So I tried something else and asked, "Where are the *berserkir*?"

"Those shitmen? They failed to comport themselves to the king's standards, and he outlawed them. The ones that were still alive, at least."

"Still alive after what?" I asked.

"After I killed six of them."

"Oh, killing six *berserkir* by yourself is very impressive," said Magnus. "I mean, I killed eleven myself—"

"Magnus!" I hissed. "Not the time for measuring broadswords." Magnus muttered something about it always being time for measuring broadswords before trailing off into silence. "How did it happen that you killed six, and the others are outlawed? Was it because they injured a raven?"

Svipdag shook his head. "I heard about the injured raven, and that was bad. But no, not because of that. Those twelve *berserkir* were particular about forcing men to bow and scrape before them, and when I came to the court, I refused. So we agreed to fight, but the king stopped us after I felled four of them. He made me his champion and gave those *berserkir* a proper dressing down, saying I was more valuable than all of them."

"That's only four," said Magnus.

Svipdag gave the nod of a man breathing out a limited amount of patience. "I reasoned they were likely to attack if they thought I was vulnerable, so I made sure they saw me leave the hall alone one night. I only managed to cut down one more before the king separated us. He was so disgraced that they had all attacked me at once, he outlawed the survivors right there."

"That's only five," said Magnus.

Svipdag nodded, his teeth grinding a bit. "They left quite unhappy and started raising their own little army to raid towns and villages. I led an army against them and pushed them back, which is where the sixth was killed. There are six more, and they've still got a few hundred followers."

"Hmm!" said Magnus. "Well, I suppose you might get them eventually."

"So King Athils must want them dealt with . . ." I trailed off in words and thought, and Ketill's advice came back to me. We had offered information that we'd thought Athils would want, but he didn't seem to care. Coming back to the conversation, I asked Svipdag point-blank: "What is it Athils wants that he won't say he wants? Is it that he requires an alliance with Svart's people to help him solve this problem?"

Svipdag sighed. He took a long look at me, then Magnus, then me again. "Walk with me."

He strode out of the longhouse, switching that big axe to a readier position over just one shoulder. Magnus picked up his weapons. Lucky for me, Svipdag was looking at where we were going rather than noticing I had no weapon to pick up. We followed the champion as he walked away from the longhouse and toward a row of merchants.

Svipdag spoke again once we were surrounded by the noises of commerce, and we talked as we walked down the row. "The king wants you in his service, and so do I."

"I thought we were bad guests," said Magnus.

"The king is not a straightforward man," replied Svipdag. "If he puts you in a position where you are indebted to him, maybe you fight alongside us in what's coming. And then he also has the carrot to offer you: That knowledge you seek about Heidrek the Wise. Athils is the King of the Swedes because he is a tricky one, and being tricky, he is dangerous."

We turned a corner around a fishmonger and headed down another pathway, this one quieter than most of the others. There was less commerce on this street and still less on the next.

"I believed your story," Svipdag continued. "I still believe it. And I believe Svart offers a smile with a snarl behind it. The real choice he's offering is that we can swear fealty or be conquered. King Athils buys time for a mustering."

We passed a squat structure, simply but efficiently made. Plain as the look of it was, the look of its inhabitants was even plainer, wearing long, brown robes with ropes tied around the midsection. That had to be the monastery Orm had mentioned, but I didn't see Orm. I nodded at a monk as we passed by, and he nodded back. A few houses beyond the monastery, we turned onto another path loud with the sound of hammering.

On this street, three forges were busy with three smiths each. They each took it in turns to heat their blades, pull them out, and hammer them before returning the blades to the fire. Spearheads, axeheads, and seax blades sat in huge piles. This was not production for general sale. This was preparation to outfit an army.

"We trade plenty with the Rus, and some of them have loose tongues. Based on what I've heard, Svart's army is bigger than ours at the moment. We also heard Svart is a sorcerer of some power. We don't yet know how powerful he is or what he can do. And even if we broke hospitality to kill the few ships' worth of warriors he has here, which we wouldn't do, I'm confident he has the great bulk of his army readied somewhere just south of the city, on Lake Malaren. They may just move on, but if they sail up the river and attack right now, we will lose the city."

"And your lives," added Magnus. "What? He's making sense to me."

Svipdag nodded. "I hear some other things as well. I hear you have your own sorcerers. I don't know what *seiðr* Svart might conjure from his ship, but I know I would feel better if it were opposed by some of the same. Is it true you have such people with you?"

"Two such people!" said Magnus.

"You might put it to them that Svart's ship, the *Wingfarer*, is moored in the northeastern-most part of the inlet. You won't miss it. It's the longest warship moored there."

I leaned in, incredulous. "You want us to set it on fire?"

"Haha, no!" laughed Svipdag. "Maybe?" He thought for a longer moment. "Not right now, because that would be bad hospitality, and I won't break my word. I meant that those sorcerous types—maybe they can do something, knowing which ship is Svart's. Assuming, say, he was to attack us after being thrown out of the king's hall." He shrugged. "Sorcerers know these things. I am just a simple man with a simple axe."

He sounded a lot like a bigger, younger version of Gudbrand the Staller. Neither man was just a simple anything. And they both held back a great deal about how dangerous they were.

No doubt the Swedes wanted our help. And here we had another army to work with. I wondered what mischief Ketill and Huld might get up to if I told them about that ship.

"So the only way to get the information we need," I said, as much to myself as to Svipdag, "is to play along for now, and then fight on Athils' side when Svart's army attacks him?"

Svipdag shrugged. "It seems to me this might be rather agreeable to an army led by Arrow-Odd."

I looked up into Svipdag's bright blue eyes. If there was any falsehood to him, I failed to see it. The champion seemed to be exactly who he was: Honest but competent. He was also a large man. Just a bit taller than I was, but with the thick neck and shoulders of one very fond of swinging a two-handed axe.

The man seemed true. The offer made sense. It was even to our benefit—both fighting Svart now with allies and getting information later. So why did something in the back of my brain soak me to the pores with suspicion? Maybe one of the fate-carving Norns was watching a little too closely, and I caught her scent. Or maybe I just didn't believe anything in my life could be easy.

"We wouldn't have it any other way!" said Magnus.

# CHAPTER 26

## CREWED BY THE DAMNED

SABOTAGE IS A GREAT DEAL MORE ENJOYABLE THAN BATTLE. After we sabotaged Svart's ship, the *Wingfarer*, I resolved to do more of it in the future.

Ketill had nearly giggled when I asked him to carve a stave with a spell that would tamp down Svart's sorcery. Huld, wearing the cat's shape, had taken the stave onto *Wingfarer* and secured it under one of the ship's ribs. According to Ketill, the carving would prevent Svart from casting any sort of spell while on the ship, or from changing his shape, so long as the sun was out.

Athils claimed he didn't like strife in his hall, and so he told both Svart and Odd to leave. Separately, though, as he didn't want to be the cause of a fight. Svart and his retinue had to leave first. Then we finalized plans with Svipdag to leave the next day. It was a good plan, with our four ships intended as bait, and the eight Swedish ships under Svipdag's command intended as the counterattack once Svart engaged us. King Athils would follow with a reserve force of four ships.

It was a bright day with fair wind when we unmoored and headed south to Lake Malaren. Everything was going according to plan. And then, right after sailing from the city, Svipdag, most famous of the Swedish champions, most trusted advisor of King Athils, and a most respected leader of the Swedish army, jumped ship.

Not jumped ship and fled. I mean literally jumped off his ship, the *Sea Valkyrie*, and onto the *Whaleslayer*. I couldn't tell if I was madder that he'd done something unexpected or that he had jumped onto a ship that wasn't the *Sea Squirrel*, preventing me from finding out what in Hel was going on.

"What in Hel is going on?" demanded several voices in succession, as if I knew all about it.

It had been an awkward delivery, requiring the *Sea Valkyrie* to first race past the *Sea Squirrel* and our other ships. Then the crews of both ships had to pull their oars in to get side by side. The *Sea Valkyrie* fell back and rejoined the main fleet of the Swedes after that. As it fell behind the *Sea Squirrel*, a portly warrior—who must have paid a big premium for extra wide armor—stalked the deck of the ship, giving commands. It appeared Svipdag planned to remain on the *Whaleslayer*.

On the deck of the *Whaleslayer*, Odd and Svipdag exchanged words. Svipdag did most of the talking.

There wasn't much to do other than row and speculate for a while. Once the river opened up into Lake Malaren, we were at least done with rowing. Arrow-Odd called a wind up into our sails, and we headed toward our planned destination on the island of Adelso.

The *Sea Valkyrie* and the other Swedish ships did not follow us after a certain point. They would station themselves northwest of us, hidden from anyone approaching from Malaren's east coast. Which, Svipdag guessed, was where Svart had set up.

We beached our four ships on the rocky northwestern shore of Adelso and pulled them up to secure them. As soon as that was done, dozens of people converged on Svipdag to ask him why he had left the *Sea Valkyrie*.

He raised one hand for quiet while he talked.

"But why—" a chorus of voices came up and was cut off.

"Arms and armor!" shouted Odd. "You can have explanations when you're dead. Be ready for battle in five minutes, or you'll answer to Styrgrim."

The black-clad figure was already armored as he looked out from the fore of the *Long Claw*. He echoed the command, but amended the allowed minutes to three. Whether for fear of what Odd prepared for or fear of Styrgrim himself, there was little hesitation in obeying.

I ran back to the *Sea Squirrel* and donned my own armor, much as I hated to do it. Styrgrim took to form-fitting chain shirts and a heavy steel helm like a seal to water. I took to armor like a cat to water, making unhappy sounds while in it and looking to get out of it at the first opportunity. At least my chain shirt was a relatively light one. My helmet offered some protection and fit well, but the jangling of mail links that hung down to protect my neck itched. Worst of all was the shield. Shit, if I never had to carry one of those again! I even grabbed a spear, my first line weapon before I went to Need.

"Shit," I said under my breath. "There's going to be a shield wall."

"Cheer up," said Magnus, donning his own chain shirt, which was heavier than mine. It fit him without a single loose part as if it had been made for him and merely waited until it had found the right owner. "There will probably be plenty of free-fighting."

I shook my head and donned my helmet. Hopefully, the enemy would be engaged elsewhere, or if engaging me, would only hit the thickest parts of steel I wore.

After three minutes, Odd summoned captains and skalds to a spot on the beach by the prow of the *Whaleslayer*. Svipdag stood with him, wearing a chain shirt so heavy, I wasn't sure a horse could have carried him.

Svipdag addressed the commanders, and it turned out that, indeed, nothing in my life could possibly be simple. "The king intends to use you up."

Josur the Daring spoke over the chorus of confused murmurs that followed. "We are to draw out Svart's forces as bait. They think they surprise us, we hold them back, and your forces counterattack. Athils cuts off their retreat with his ships in reserve. If you intend to retreat when Svart's fleet shows up instead, you have a strange way of showing it, now that you're on the front line with us."

Svipdag nodded. "There will be no retreating today. And such were not my orders. My final orders were to delay the counterattack."

"Delay how long?" demanded Birki, incredulous.

"Until most of us were dead," said Bjorn. "Is that right?"

Svipdag nodded. "King Athils did not say that explicitly. He only told me to delay. The rest is my supposition."

Murmurs turned to angry shouts about betrayal. Styrgrim stepped forward and bellowed over the noise. "Shut your holes, you squeaky lot! The man is here instead of safely away, so be quiet until he can tell us why." He paused and let the command take effect. Then, he roared, "And then shut up some more!"

Arrow-Odd looked to Svipdag and indicated he should continue. "I am the king's man and sworn to uphold his word or else break my oath. I am no oathbreaker, so I can't go against his command. But I am no *níðingr*, either. I am no longer in a position to command the fleet. I will fight with you, if you'll have me."

"That's a welcome thing," said Josur,

"It doesn't solve the problem of having no force for a counterattack until we're dead," added Birki.

"I did not leave command of those ships to some wet-assed lackey. It's Thick Alrek I left in charge."

"The fat one?" I asked.

"No. Well, yes. He was Thick Alrek before he got fat. He's a stubborn man and won't leave allies to do his fighting for him. And the king did not give him a direct command, nor did I feel the need to tell him about that last-moment order. Alrek will bring his ships to bear when Svart engages us, as planned. If we rout the enemy, Athils' best option will be to attack them as they retreat, and it will play out as planned."

This sounded like quite a good way of working things out after all. So it was a bit surprising that Arrow-Odd suddenly decided he had to string his massive longbow right then and there, with no sign of Svart's ships bearing down on us.

I looked back out to where we'd beached the ships and most of the army still stood. Everyone was moving faster now, a sense of urgency as plain on their faces as in their legs. No ships were visible to the west, and the coastline to the north and south was empty.

Then, I looked behind me. Beyond the beach, to the southeast, the land was clear as far as two long bow shots, except for the remains of many tree stumps. The rest was dense forest as far as I could see, the problem being that an army was now stepping out of the forest and into the light.

Six very large, very ugly men led the way. If looks could kill, their mothers had surely died young. These were not the well-muscled giants Magnus had faced in Fretborg. They were just as big, but their physiques were monstrous. Shoulders that sat one higher than the other. Grimy hands that ended in claw-like fingers held massive, two-handed axes. Athils' old *berserkir* wore no armor, and looked like they didn't need any.

Each of the six led a small contingent, all haphazardly dressed men and women in disorderly formations. Most of them had long spears, though, and running into a lot of dumb people holding long spears was, as far as I could tell, exactly as lethal as running into a lot of smarter people holding long spears.

Hrafn, the woman with the man's name, stepped forward from the rest of Odd's crew and addressed Svipdag directly. "Were you expecting this bunch?"

"Not at all," said Svipdag, cradling his huge axe. "Though it's good to see my old friends again. I think we can finally finish our conversation."

Today seemed a day we were destined to fight *someone*, even if not the people we'd intended to fight. Only there was one great, glaring problem. It wasn't glaring for most of us, as it was just barely visible to me given my keen eyesight.

A ways out at sea to the northeast, a large number of ships sailed west. Not on a course toward Uppsala or toward us. The bottom dropped out of my stomach, and I pointed with one hand and tried to get Odd's attention with the other. "Svart's fleet! They're not taking the bait, they're headed for Alrek!"

Surely Athils would be nearby to reinforce his people? I didn't see the reserve ships anywhere, though. Perhaps Athils intended to wait until Svart's forces were nearly beaten and cut off their retreat. Or to let whatever ships still remained sail away, tails between their legs, and call it a victory he'd been on the field for. Whatever his intention, it seemed to me that Alrek's ships were about to be overwhelmed, and then what?

Athils' scheming was about to get the better of us after all, just not the way he had planned.

# Chapter 27

## Disorder of Battle

Svipdag said he would kill those *berserkir* if it was the last thing he did. I wished he hadn't phrased it quite that way, because it seemed very likely to get the attention of a bored god who might help *make* it go that way.

I said so, but he didn't much care. "If such is my fate, speaking of it that way will change nothing."

Hallfred Horsefly was less resigned to fate. "Alrek's forces will be overrun if we don't support them." A simple statement, shouted directly into Odd's face. Sometimes the role of advisor is less about sagely spoken advice and more about screaming the need for things.

"We cannot run from a fight," Odd shouted back.

"We can sail to aid Alrek after dealing with this lot," added Styrgrim.

"Svart has twice as many ships as Alrek does," Hallfred said.

"He will need to fight hard, then," replied Styrgrim.

Odd ordered a wide semicircle formation to prevent the enemy from flanking us or getting to our ships. The crews spread out and locked shields, ready to fight back a charge. With the enemy so close, those *berserkir* could come at a full run and be on top of us any minute.

They weren't moving that fast, though. They kept a slow pace, which was much better for them given the broken ground. And they kept a loose formation, with the six *berserkir* all in front. One of them pointed at Svipdag as he walked.

We outnumbered the *berserkir* and their feral followers, but no way could we finish things on Adelso and still have time to aid Alrek. His ships were about to be taken by surprise. If he had perfect information, he might sail towards us or even around Adelso. If he could force Svart to chase him, that would give us time to finish the fight on Adelso. Then the numbers would not be nearly so overwhelming.

But information and battle are like lava and glaciers. Both definitely exist, but one retreats as the other grows.

I looked to Svipdag to see his reaction and found none. He knew what would likely happen to the fleet he'd left behind. But he was here now, and he would not run from a fight any more than Odd would. It would not be manly. It would not be Norse.

In that moment, I *hated* manliness and Norse-ness. Leaving allies to be crushed because it might be considered embarrassing was not manliness. It was just a more complicated form of cowardice.

The bone club tapping on my shoulder cleared my head.

"If these cunts won't warn Alrek, I will," growled Kraki.

One ship, the ship with the fewest warriors, would not make much differ-ence. But he was right, we might prevent the surprise and give them a better chance. I told Odd what we were doing, ordered the crew back to the *Sea Squirrel*, and helped push the ship back into the water.

While we pushed, Odd said something about fleeing the field that stuck in my craw. I turned from the ship, channeling all the anger I had at seeing friends die and all the venom I had for Odd's manly logic. I called him out, locked eyes with him, and spoke a verse:

> "One wonders
>     what the wall of
> shields is meant
>     more to guard:
> Is it the warrior's heart,
>     heaving in his breast,
> or just proof against
>     the pricking of his pride?"

Arrow-Odd snarled back at me from the front line. He was about to say something when Hallfred Horsefly interrupted him. I don't know what the skald said, but the result was not what I expected when Odd spoke again.

"The *Wave Climber* goes as the fastest ship, but the *Long Claw* commands. Styrgrim the Bear, now's your chance! The rest of us fight here."

That would leave us outnumbered in both battles, but would give Alrek and his crews a fighting chance.

Styrgrim and Josur ordered their people out of the shield wall and set off soon after the *Sea Squirrel*. Wind filled our sail, and I chanced a look back at those still on Adelso, wondering how many friends on that island I would see again. Hallfred. Steinvor. And more than just the skalds: Hrafn, who used a man's name, and Svipdag, who defied a king's order for us.

I would have to live through the fight I was sailing into to see any of them, and that was far from guaranteed. I was not much of a fighter on land, but I'd never even been in a sea battle before. Kraki led at sea, so at least the decisions were not mine to make. Hopefully, none of his decisions would end up setting the ship on fire, like he'd seen in his dream.

The *Wave Climber* passed us. The *Long Claw* was not far behind. Whatever our fate was, we were headed straight for it.

Kraki demanded updates on what was happening ahead, so he sent me to the fore. I shouted back to him at the rudder. "Svart's people are lashing their ships together. I think they mean to surround Alrek and prevent an escape."

"Good," Kraki replied.

"How is that good?"

"It slows them down and makes them vulnerable."

I didn't follow how a strong line of ships lashed together was a vulnerability. It seemed like they were doing that because it was a good idea. "What now?"

Somewhere between "bleed them dry" and "grind their bones into paste," Kraki did have some semblance of a plan. "Hit their flank. Clear the end ship's deck, and draw attention away from the middle. Attack. Always be attacking. Tell the others!"

Tell Styrgrim the Bear what to do. Right.

The *Long Claw* was still within shouting distance. I got the attention of Styrgrim's rudder man, Hjalti, and told him what Kraki intended. I think he had the same feeling about telling Styrgrim what to do as I did. He must have found the right words, because the Bear nodded. He said something to Hjalti, who shouted back to me.

"You hit their flank, but we need to support Alrek first! There is no time to wait for you," *and your slow ship*, he seemed to imply. He was out of shouting distance soon after. I relayed all that to Kraki.

The *Wave Climber* cut the water true to its name and made fast progress toward Alrek's fleet. We had no agreed-upon signals to use, but allied ships leaving Adelso and heading for the Swedes must have been enough of a sign. Thick Alrek started readying his people for battle.

Then, the waiting began. There is a dreadful time before battle when anticipation gnaws at your mind like harts gnaw at the roots of the world tree. Nothing can make it go any faster, and we had nothing to distract us until Magnus asked a question I wished I had thought of.

"Hey, wizard! What should we expect, attacking this sorcerer at sea? Sea goblins? Lightning? Sharks?"

Ketill looked up with an amused sneer, an arrow already nocked on his longbow. "The sun is out, so I think you can expect very little of Svart's sorcery, unless he's discovered the stave hidden on his ship. It is a confounding spell, and the harder he works at anything, the more disoriented he'll become."

Which didn't address the question *What happens if he finds the stave and chucks it?* But I was not about to ask that question out loud.

With speed on his side and with one of the best archers I would ever know, Josur the Daring first ordered a risky maneuver toward the same flank we were about to attack. Jorun and a few other archers peppered the enemy with arrows. It was a good skirmishing maneuver, diverting Svart's attention away from swarming the Swedes. It gave the *Long Claw* just enough time to join Alrek's ships.

Svart's ships closed in, and the fighting began in earnest. We were still headed for that same flank, just much slower than our allies.

The chop of the waves was enough to be inconvenient and unsteady as the *Sea Squirrel* closed in. The sound of water sloshing against our vessel soon mingled with shouts and the ring of steel on steel. I had no idea what to expect next, other than *no shield wall, after all*. Did I even want my armor anymore, or would it better suit me to take it off in case I fell overboard?

"Keep your wits," Kraki shouted to the entire crew. And as if hearing my thoughts, "And keep your armor. If you fall into the sea, swim. Only the hopeless flail and sink. Some of you have not fought at sea before. Well, it's just like fighting on land, only more wet!"

Which is not true, whatsoever.

We took in our sail, the front line locked shields, and the crew shouted a collective war cry as our ship banged into the Rus dragon ship on Svart's southeastern flank.

I stood behind our front line and thrust with my spear. Unsteady on my feet in the chop and chaos, I stumbled once before Nanthild caught my shoulder and helped me right myself. I nodded at her. She nodded back and held her shield against me, as if telling me to stay back for now.

The *Sea Squirrel* turned after the initial encounter so that it was facing the opposite direction of the enemy ship. Without oars or sails, Kraki worked furiously at the rudder to position us directly alongside them. As some of our people traded spear thrusts with the enemy, others from the *Sea Squirrel* boarded them. Most of our warriors had left the ship by the time we drifted just outside of leaping distance. With only a few of us left on the *Sea Squirrel*, the current pushed us behind the enemy line.

There was no reversing our momentum with oars now, and no way to board the nearest ship. Kraki worked the rudder hard to turn the *Sea Squirrel* and creep around the rear of the enemy line. Which is when the crew of the next ship over took notice of us. Grappling hooks landed in the *Sea Squirrel* and began to pull us in. Soon, it would be just a few of us against the entirety of that ship's crew.

A grappling hook took hold of the gunwale near me. Kraki's footsteps thudded up the deck of the *Sea Squirrel*. "Hel's dragon, boy, *cut the lines!*"

My limbs seemed to move slower as my mind tried to take everything in. I managed to drop my spear, draw Need, and finally cut the lines near me, still in a mental torpor.

Cutting those lines only delayed our being pulled in. Nanthild looked at me, forward, then back at me with surprise as she lifted my shield. I looked up just in time to see the arrow headed toward me. The shock of that arrowhead clanging off the steel of my shield boss brought me back around. There's nothing quite like almost dying to prevent overthinking and focus on the here and now.

We were about to be set upon by too many attackers to fight, even for us. I took a step back and crouched into a defensive stance, readying for the assault. Nanthild charged forward and met the first boarder with her blade.

She leaned forward and cut him through as he leaped from his ship to ours. It was a good attempt, and his upper half had enough momentum to fly right onto our deck while his lower half fell into the sea.

One of Ketill's arrows flew past me, hit a man in the throat, and continued through to hit the next man behind him. Another arrow followed soon after and brought down a heavily-armored warrior when it pierced his mail.

"Board them!" shouted Kraki. Meaning, the three of us with one archer for support.

Over the gunwale I went. It was an awkward thing made even more awkward by my uncertainty as to how to do that. Lead with my shield? It's hard to see past a shield unless you lower it, and lowering a shield drastically increases the chance of taking a spear to the face. Then there was the swaying of the ship to deal with. Fighting at sea is nothing like fighting on solid ground.

I ran and jumped, hoping for the best. And like a lot of people who survive such battles, I survived mostly due to the ferocity of my friends. Strikes from Kraki's club rang like thunderclaps against armor and bone. A spearman thrust into his side, but the point turned on Kraki's stone-like skin. Kraki grabbed the spear with his left hand and stove in the warrior's helmet with the other. That gave some of the others pause.

One of the Rus grinned at Nanthild. She cleaved his shield right down to the boss. The warrior grimaced at the shock of the blow, and Nanthild push-kicked the shield to disengage her sword. She followed up with a low slash that took his leg out below the knee. The Rus warrior fell, blood geysering from the stump.

Three Rus with axes and shields charged Nanthild while a spearman sat behind, looking for an opportunity to strike through the holes in the melee.

I won't pretend I was a brave or even competent warrior, but I at least had the presence of mind to lend my shield to that fight. I crashed into the closest warrior to me, shield held close to my body. It did not knock him back as I'd intended, but rather sent me backwards. I had intended a follow-up stroke, but ended up reaching out to catch my balance.

Nanthild danced sideways to avoid being swarmed. There is only so much room on a ship, and she kept the side of the ship at her back to prevent anyone from getting behind her. For a time, we could swing however we wanted without endangering one another. These Rus we were fighting had an advantage in numbers, but each swing of an axe might hit an ally. We used that, and the shock of a slight woman and an elderly man hewing down warriors, and it bought us some time.

That warrior I had collided with was more than a match for me in this space. We took turns banging our weapons on one another's shields. Each of his strikes came down harder than the last. I couldn't match his ferocity despite my dwarf-made sword. Need seemed to cry out that I should hit harder or more cleanly.

If only I had trained for that sort of thing.

This would not end well if it kept going as it had. I might be cut down, or a spearman might stick me in the side when I wasn't looking. But all warfare is deception, as I'd remembered Styrgrim saying once in my youth, and all fighting is warfare. So I took what he had inadvertently taught me, and what I knew my opponent knew about me, and realized I could subvert his expectation.

I took the next axe blow on the rim of my shield, where it was already cracked. The blade bit through the leather rim and into the cracking linden as I intended, trapping the axehead. I twisted my wrist outward and turned his weapon hand to an awkward position. Before I could see the opening, before I even believed I would really create one, I slashed down with Need into the space I expected his weapon arm to be.

I'm not sure if he was more surprised when I cut through his wrist, or if I was.

More of the Rus on that ship turned their attention to us. One raised his axe against me, let out a war cry, and got one of Ketill's arrows through an eye. The wizard was still on the *Sea Squirrel*, which was drifting far out on the current at that point. I raised my shield in thanks.

I realized that was a stupid mistake when a spear struck me in the stomach. It was a good throw, and it hurt, but my chain shirt stopped the point from piercing me. I grunted from the force of being hit and turned to face my attacker. There were three.

I kept my back to the side of the ship. The Rus pressed in, leaving me nowhere to dodge or retreat. Ketill could not shoot fast enough to get me out of the immediate danger. I would have to fight. Let them come at me and counter them? Always be attacking? I decided the former was a better idea, as some ideas are only good if you've got the stone-like skin of Kraki Bentleg.

And who knew if Need would come up with something unexpected at the last moment?

There was something unexpected in that moment, but it was not Need.

Arrows. Not the long, heavy arrows of Ketill's longbow. Lighter and faster arrows, loosed with uncanny speed. My attackers raised their shields and ducked away, and I followed their gaze to the source.

The *Wave Climber* had come around the enemy's rear to support us. Jorun stood near the prow, her Hunnish hornbow singing a one-note song. As she moved down the deck for a better position, an arrow took her in the left side of the chest, and she fell to the deck.

Something fell away inside me, too, but I knew I could not think about it at the moment. I lashed out at a foeman with an arrow in his shield, cutting low at his leg. I think I cut him, but I didn't linger when he leaped back. I was on to the next, and then the next. Maybe I looked like a fool and failed to injure anyone with my flailing, trying to make up for my lack of fighting intellect with more will. I may have drawn more blood on myself than anyone else during that foray, Need's pommel cutting into my wrist as I struck about.

A Rus warrior, better armed than most, came at me with sword and shield. I thought I had him, his overhead slash telling me to raise my shield high and step back. I saw his blade raised straight up, and then it was gone, and then I felt a sudden shock in the left side of my ribs. He'd changed direction during the swing to come in where I was vulnerable, hitting my chain shirt.

Unless you have a dwarf-made sword, you're not going to cut through armor. Nevertheless, the solid blow knocked the wind out of me. He continued with slash after slash, going for my unprotected legs, and I somehow managed to avoid or parry the attacks.

Desperate for some sort of counter, I stabbed upward at his face. The attack failed to connect, but it forced him to hop back. I got a second breath as he eyed something at the ship's fore. He disengaged completely and sounded his horn. Rus shouting turned frantic as many of them retreated from the first ship to the one I was on, and then took defensive positions on the starboard side. With good reason.

The *Long Claw* shot forward from the prow side, inserting itself between the boarded enemy ships. Styrgrim the Bear took a running start and leaped onto the ship's fore.

Maybe some of those Rus didn't know what was coming. I think some of them did. The figure he cut could hardly have been a greater contrast to me, his heavy mail and helmet looking like they had grown out of his own skin. The raven symbol on his shield may have been a clue if they knew the reputation behind it. And the sword, its wavy lines telling of the finest war-make, at least by human hands. All good clues.

Styrgrim did not move with Nanthild's speed or Kraki's barbaric ferocity. Instead, he moved with the utter certainty, not of what he wanted to happen, but what he *knew* would happen. When he moved, it was just enough for a blade to nick his mail or helmet. Just enough for a weapon to glance off his shield and unbalance his foe. Just enough to cut what he wanted to cut.

Styrgrim's movements were slow, even lazy, until he struck like lightning. He took hands and limbs, cut throats and faces. Shield-butts, pommel strikes, and kicks gave him the timing and openings for lethal slashes. Step by step, he cleared the deck.

On the port side, Magnus bounded over from the first ship, his face and beard stained red. Thorir Houndsfoot leaped onto the deck with spear and shield. Moose-Frothi followed his brother, a bloodied seax in each hand, and he was so heavy that he rocked the ship when he landed. The rest of our crew, small as it was, followed them.

The Rus warrior who had nearly killed me organized a fighting retreat to the next ship. The last few over the gunwale cut the lines lashing the two ships we had taken. We could board the third ship, but we would need to pull it in first.

As Svart's line of ships drifted slowly away, we looked to our own. Plenty of our people were wounded. Ingolf had taken a nasty cut to his leg, and some of the newer crewmates fared much worse. Ketill raised the *Sea Squirrel*'s sail and navigated it back in. I looked for Athils' reserve force, but saw no help coming.

"We can continue just this way," Styrgrim shouted to us. "Send one ship to board their side, the other ships to attack from fore and aft in support. Three against one, all the way down!"

He sounded awfully happy at this prospect, but I wasn't so sure.

Maybe if Alrek had managed to maneuver his ships to attack Svart's other flank, we could have worn them down. But one look told me he either hadn't seen that opportunity or couldn't deploy his ships fast enough for it.

In what I considered a brilliant defensive move, he had emptied two of his ships and lashed them ahead of all the others. They stuck out from his formation and forced Svart's superior numbers into two tight spots.

It would buy him time. And Svart's people would pay in blood. But they would eventually cut those lashings and envelop him. Svart would win if it came down to attrition.

"Alrek doesn't have that much time," I shouted back.

We needed a decisive element that would force a retreat. And there was only one thing I could think of that would force such a decision, barring our own fire-breathing dragon.

Styrgrim's gaze fell on the unfolding scene and took it in. "Nothing else we can do."

"We have two extra ships," I said. "And we're already in position to get behind their line."

"You want to attack him with unmanned ships?" Styrgrim demanded, his tone even shorter.

"No," I said. I had decided on my own interpretation of Kraki's hopefully-not-prophetic dream, only it didn't involve the *Sea Squirrel*. "I want to attack him with fire."

# CHAPTER 28

# FRONT TOWARD ENEMY

"Got to have a lot of kindling for a good fire ship," said Kraki, doubtless from direct experience. He leaned against the mast of the Rus warship and scowled. "Not much for kindling here."

"How about turning the other ship into kindling and adding some Risaland whale oil?" I asked.

The old cook grinned wider than I'd ever seen and immediately ordered the crew of the *Sea Squirrel* to cannibalize the first of the enemy warships. Its mast, benches, oars, and even its rudder got hacked to bits. Meanwhile, Kraki lifted a barrel of whale oil out of the *Sea Squirrel*'s hold, and then a second for good measure.

Kraki took commands from no one while at sea, but Styrgrim still had command of two ships. "There is wind at their backs, but the current is pushing away from their rear. We can't set the ship ablaze and leave it. It will just drift off."

Magnus joined me and Styrgrim by the mast. "Send it at their flank?"

I shook my head. "Too likely they can cut more ships away from the flank and forget them. This has to bring total chaos into their fleet, make them want to retreat. We have to hit them from behind, as close to their middle as possible." I turned to shout toward the fore. "Kraki! Will they be able to push it away before it catches other ships on fire?"

He placed one of the barrels down at the very front of the ship. "We'll build a pyre around this one," he said, indicating the barrel. "A big one! Use oil from the second barrel to make that pyre burn hot. Get it hot enough, and the sealed barrel will burst, and it will catch everything on fire for . . ." He trailed off as he gestured, then shrugged. "It will work!"

"And the wind against the sail will keep the ship from being pushed back out to sea." Styrgrim suddenly sounded most interested in making the plan work. "It could be done, but it's a bad deal for whoever guides this fire ship in. It should be one of the injured, unlikely to survive. I say—"

"I will do it," I said. If that sounds like I was volunteering for the riskiest part of the battle, just remember how bad I was with sword and shield. By comparison, it was far safer. Or seemed like it at the time.

"And then what?" asked Magnus. "We need a ship in position to get you after, and we can't afford to keep anyone out of the fight."

"No, I can swim!" I threw off my helmet and wriggled out of my chain shirt. Maybe I could swim while wearing them, but it would be easier without, and I might need to swim fast. Also, it felt good to get out of that armor, much as it had just served me. "The sea is pushing outward from their rear, as Styrgrim said. I will guide the ship in close, light the fire, and jump off the rear. The current will help me swim to one of the small islands nearby. Just find me after the battle."

So I found myself at the rudder of a captured warship full of whale oil. The wind was favorable enough to offset the current. We set a torch burning in an iron sconce near the rudder. I even had a plan to survive the whole thing. We cut the lashings from the other captured ship, and our crews returned to their respective ships to reinforce Alrek. The last preparation before the *Sea Squirrel* pulled away was Ketill coming to me with advice.

"Do not use this." The wizard pressed a disc into my hand. "This is my carving. But you can learn from it and carve the same yourself if you need to."

"What will it do?"

"Do you remember when I told you of my friend who blew himself up from carving the wrong runes?"

"Yes?"

"And do you remember you asked what those runes were, and I told you I did not know, because he was not around to tell me?"

"Yes?"

"I lied." My eyes widened at the implication, but Ketill shook his head. "I also exaggerated the story. He did not blow himself up but was burned quite badly. The effect came on faster than expected, and he collapsed from what the spell took out of him. You may have need of this spell if your torch goes out. But do not use it except as a last resort, and only near the last moment."

"Okay . . ."

He paused. "It will burn fast, make you very tired."

"I understand!"

The crew gave my dragon ship a good push. Wind took the sail, and I pulled away from both the *Sea Squirrel* and the fighting, taking a wide arc that would come back at the enemy formation's center.

There was a lull of quiet while the ship was at its farthest point from the battle. It occurred to me that despite all the bouncing around the water and all the nearly dying, I had not been seasick. The sky was blue. A few clouds in the sky were just enough for contrast. Sailing seemed like a wonderful thing, if just for that brief moment.

I turned the ship around and headed for my target. The wind was behind me, but not too directly behind me. I thought I should be outside the range of any of their bows for at least another minute. That's what I was thinking when the first arrow embedded itself in the pyre.

Could the retreating commander have guessed what we intended next? If he had, he would have every archer available trying to stop me. I hadn't kept a shield for myself, which now seemed the biggest cock-up I'd ever made.

Other arrows came down but did not reach even mid-ship. I spotted a mostly intact shield up by the mast and decided to take care of two things at once. I grabbed the torch from its sconce on the stern, ran forward as far as the shield, and threw the torch at the pyre. Aha! The fire would make it harder for archers to see me, and now I even had three-quarters of a shield.

I returned to the rudder and righted the ship's direction. The fire had started, but wasn't catching very quickly. I thought that was fine, I had time.

An arrow came farther on than the rest and stuck fast in the heavy sail. The fire remained little more than the torch. Had I thrown it onto a spot with no whale oil?

Arrows rained onto the deck, with many hitting the sail. One nicked the forestay, and that rope began to fray. Would it hold long enough? Would the mast fall backwards without it? The 'Steins knew that sort of thing. I did not. So, I focused on what I did know and the carving Ketill had given me to get that fire going faster.

Which was up by the mast. Where I had *thoughtlessly put it down to grab this shitty, broken shield!*

I dropped the shield and pulled out a disc to carve, holding the steering oar steady under my right arm. Could I even remember the spell? It was only two runes. Was one of them *kauna* for torch? No, that wasn't the source of the fire . . . the fire rune was inverted. What would be fire if it were inverted?

*Laguz.* Water, but inverted. That was the source of the fire. What was the other rune? *Shit shit shit!* Maybe *gebo* for *gift of fire* or *ansuz* for *fire from the gods* or *dagaz* for *fire, all gods-damned day* or something?

No, it was *fehu:* Lots of fire!

Ha! *I mean, it's not how I would have chosen to cast such a spell, but beggars can't always be—*

An arrow thunked into the stern of the ship about a spear's length from my foot. I carved those two runes as fast as I'd carved anything in my life. I had to be in position to go farther, though. I had thrown the torch, and it landed badly. I would need to place the disc right in the pyre to guarantee it would catch, and that meant running to the fore of the ship and back.

*Should've kept the armor on.*

Arrows whizzed over my head or hit the side of the ship. Most of the arrows came from my starboard side, so I ran down the port side of the ship with my disc and shield and dove into the crook behind the prow.

I had to remember being as close to fire as I had ever been for a spell like this. I recalled King Ragnvald's burning longhouse, the rising heat, the smoke, being trapped. Panicking. Failing. Refusing. And then the change. Flaming wood splintering as I exploded out of that place in bear form.

I sliced open my hand and let my will flow through my blood into the runes. Then it was not flowing so much as draining, and my limbs felt weak. I dropped the disc on the center of the pyre and stumbled back down the deck, barely keeping myself up.

White flames burst from the foredeck, igniting the whale oil and kindling in a massive conflagration. They must have chewed through the forestay in seconds, but there was nothing to do about that now. In fact, I could hardly keep my legs under me.

Then I couldn't keep my legs under me, and I fell to the deck near the mast. I could hear the shouts of the Rus, hear the loud cracking of the fire. I needed to get back to the aft, but crawling was too slow. Either the heat or the enemy would soon get to me.

I grabbed the gunwale and pulled myself over the edge. In my weakened state, that leap into the water I'd intended was more of a flop. I turned upward under the water and pawed at the hull of the fire ship until I came to the aft. The ship crunched into the Rus line, and I grabbed the steering oar as I rounded the back. Gasping, I held onto it to keep my head above the water and get my breath back.

The barrel went boom. I grinned, took a deep breath, and kicked off from the rear of the ship toward a small island.

Lake Malaren was not the coldest water I had swum in, which led to a miscalculation. I soon realized my exhaustion from that spell, which my mentor had specifically warned me about, meant the cold was taking a toll on my body much faster than usual. My arms and legs could barely move. Soon, I was fighting to keep my head above the water with every stroke.

A breaker washed over me as I inhaled, filling my nose with water. I gagged and turned myself face up. I could breathe as long as no more breakers washed over me. And I could float as long as I breathed, but I couldn't float forever. I had to move with the current to get to that island and out of the water.

My arms and legs barely moved. Fear rose with every breath that failed to bring them back to life. Another breaker washed over my face, and I panicked, unable to get back to the air.

Something grabbed my collar and lifted my head just above the surface.

It might be difficult to imagine a cat, even a big one, dragging a man through the water. Collar in her teeth, Huld started all four limbs pumping like both our lives depended on it. She hissed with the exertion. Those hisses grew louder and faster quickly.

We were not moving fast. It would not work. I wasn't sure I had the courage to tell her to leave me and save herself. That seemed like more than I could manage to say between breaths, anyway. So I spoke a last wish, the thing I knew needed doing if I wasn't going to do it.

"Kill Ulf."

Waves buoyed us up and down. Breathing got more difficult each time. The cat sputtered and coughed. Fatigue must have been setting in, I thought, or at least the knowledge that this was an impossible task. I closed my eyes and resolved not to die complaining.

She let go, and I sank.

# CHAPTER 29

# MORALE OF THE STORY

I TRIED TO MOVE AGAIN, BUT MY LIMBS FELT LIKE THEY WERE filled with frozen sludge. I thought I would drown under a bright sky as my face sank just beneath the surface. And though I'd had a few moments to get used to the idea, I can tell you: I was not at all used to that idea and was screaming on the inside.

A moment later, my butt touched sand.

A moment after that, Huld—the old woman rather than the cat— dragged me onto a beach. I coughed and spat, trying to catch my breath. Huld pulled me up next to a campfire.

Someone else was on the island, standing on the other side of the fire. He said something to Huld, and she responded, but I was too groggy to understand what was happening. I shivered by the fire and focused on breathing for a long time.

Day turned into twilight. Whoever else was on the island kept feeding the fire, but didn't bother me. I rubbed my arms and moved my legs just to see if I could. My limbs were still stiff, and I ached all over, but I felt more like myself the more I moved.

"Give yourself time." I knew that voice. Steady. Amused, even.

My teeth had stopped chattering, but speaking was still an effort. "Th— that was Frey's advice. Y—you said—"

"'Go where the others will not'?" I could hear Heimdall grinning even if I couldn't see him do it. "You certainly haven't ignored that advice."

I pushed myself upright. The island couldn't be much more than a hundred feet long and half that wide. A sparse copse of trees indicated the place wasn't of any note, probably didn't even have a name. Just one lonely campfire and the Watchman of Asgard. He sat rigid on the other side of the fire. If I had not known him from his voice, I would have known him from his eyes. Those blue glowing coals watched me with an intensity humankind rarely matched.

"Heimdall," I acknowledged.

"Ansgar the Skald," he responded.

"Where is Huld?"

"Where she works best, healing who she can heal."

I looked out across the water, which had calmed. There was no sign of ships with torches. Difficult to sail at night even in calm water, though. "Did she swim all the way back to Uppsala?"

"I loaned her a falcon skin."

I nodded. "I had not pieced together that she works for you."

The Watchman flashed a smile bright with golden teeth. "'Works for me'? Don't let her hear you say that."

I sat silent for a few breaths. "Is that all you have to tell me? You appear, create for me another question, as if I didn't already have too many, and then laugh about it?"

"Huld's story is not mine to tell. If you have other questions, however—"

"Who is my father?" I blurted out. "What is your interest in me?"

He nodded. "I don't know for certain who your father is. But I know more about it than you do, and it's related to my interest. Your birthright, however, is not what I find most interesting."

"What, then? My skill with poetry?"

"You say that in irony, but it's close to the truth. Your poetry speaks to who you are." He pointed at my left hand. "And what you're against."

I opened my left palm and examined the scar. Cuts from casting spells had scarred a permanent X into that hand. The cut from casting that last spell on the fire ship still bled a little, but he didn't mean that. "You mean the cut from swearing my blood oath to kill Ulf. What does that have to do with you?"

"What to do with me?" A spark of disappointment lit a fire in his tone.

"Everything! Who do you think speaks to Ulf in his dreams, who tells him how to be and not be?"

His voice pierced me in a way I could hardly stand upright for. Was it a rhetorical question? No, he wanted an answer. I shook my head. "Ulf lives for Ulf. Even if he's taken instruction from Alfhild or Ogmund, he's out for himself only. And he is not a worshiper of gods, to give sacrifices or other offerings."

Heimdall shook his head. "Ulf worships in the only way that matters, by modeling his life on his master's example."

I screwed my face up. Ulf would have no master, so what did he mean? I thought about how Ulf and I both used language, but how his use was so far removed from mine. He had been a good diplomat and negotiator. He had used words for what the end result would be. He was no storyteller. Stories are meant to convey truths through lies. Ulf lied with the truth—or just lied, if he found it convenient.

"He's one of Loki's," I said before I even realized I was thinking it. "Your nemesis."

Heimdall threw another stick on the fire. "Your purpose and mine are the same."

"Fine purpose!" I laughed at that idea, which made me cough. Still not quite myself. "So, you all got one child, me, who tells stories. How many other skalds? And why do the entitled brats all seem to know their parentage, but I don't? Close to your purpose? You leave me less in the know than anyone!"

"Think you should have been raised in Asgard to know more of our business?"

In a second, I went from angry to miserable. "I think I should have been raised by my mother."

"There was meddling with your life before you had one, that's certainly true. But how are you to know if you'd be better off one way or another? Think being told you are special from the beginning is a good way to raise a child?"

"I think it would be better than my mother dying in childbirth, yes."

"Yet you were raised as not-special-at-all, and you have more to offer Midgard than your cousins."

I was getting tired of the conversation. The constant telling me I saw everything the wrong way. The holding back of knowledge 'for my own good.' The assurance that I was wrong even about wishing I had known my mother as she lived and not as a here-again, gone-again spirit.

"Tell me what I want is not what I want again, and . . ." And what? Was I about to threaten the Watchman of Asgard?

He just grinned at me, flashing those golden teeth. "You can cling to the past and wish it had been different, or you can appreciate the good of where that past led you. I'll tell you a story about that, and that will tell you as much as I know about your father."

"Get on with it, then," I sighed, expecting more mysterious commentary.

The Watchman took a deep breath as if to summon more patience, but he did get on with it. "There was a valkyrie. One of Odin's women, a chooser of the slain. You think you know what a valkyrie is, but you do not. Spirits of fury are no less real than the spirits that might guide you in a forest. It's Odin they flock to. They are often simple, but not always.

"One such valkyrie was not simple at all. What she was born of is lost to time. Not even she knows where she came from. No, don't worry, I don't think she held out on you when she told her story. Neither do I think she can remember it all. She was one of Odin's, and she was a complicated one. One who did not want the same thing over and over like the others. So, Odin named her Svipul—*Changeable*.

"Many generations later, Svipul fell in love with a man. She wanted to choose, but not for Odin's *einherjar*. She chose him for herself and put it to Odin that this choice would benefit him. After all, Styrgrim was one of his devotees in the first place, and their offspring would be mighty indeed.

"Styrgrim chose her as well. Not for a straw-bed wife, but for a spear-wife. They loved one another because they understood one another.

"But in choosing the man, Svipul became mortal, and as a mortal, Odin barred her from battle. She would need to stay home and take a new name, he said, claiming this was to ensure she lived to become a mother. I think that decision had more to do with being able to strip a valkyrie of her power, but no one truly knows Odin's mind.

"So Svipul took the mortal name Bodda. She stayed home while her husband sailed away. A final campaign, he said, and that would be enough for him before settling down.

"It was an epic war, I think you know. The last war between Arrow-Odd and Ogmund Tussock. Many sailed to that war, and very few sailed back. Styrgrim was one of them, only he returned without his seed. The arrow through his balls ended the possibility of children. I wonder what Odin thought after that arrow found its target. But none truly know Odin's mind.

"So Styrgrim returned home. And here is the difficult part of the story."

"He returned on the third night," I interrupted. "But the first two nights, someone wearing his skin came home and lay with her. Someone very convincing. Someone with fair hair."

"It was two nights and two impostors," he corrected. I swallowed hard as I stared at the god. "Finally, the real Styrgrim the Bear returned home to embrace his wife. He had a sad story to tell, but he would not dishonor his wife by lying to her. I think she carried the greater pain, though, as she had a sad story to tell him as well. But what was done was done.

"That was no easy thing for either of them. Bodda, unable to go to battle, now unable to be a mother. Styrgrim, now supposed to stay home, but unable to get an heir. Think your past makes you sad? Think about *that*. Bodda could have asked to go back to Odin. Styrgrim could have sailed away to battle again. Instead, they reiterated their vows and chose that life as it had turned out.

"And then, surprise, Bodda was pregnant. That required another choice. Styrgrim the Bear could have taken that badly, a responsibility for a child not his own. But he swore the child *would* be his own, as family he *chose*. Ill-tempered as that man was, he learned to be happy about that choice.

"Bodda's birth was difficult, and Styrgrim fetched a *vǫlva* to help her through it. The *vǫlva* said she would make sure she got the best possible result, which Styrgrim thought was an odd way to phrase it. Then came the result, and he realized what she'd meant.

"The *vǫlva* said she was able to save the child, but that Bodda was bleeding very badly and would not live to see the next day. Bodda died, and Styrgrim had a son. The *vǫlva* was so sad, she refused any payment.

"Then you were called Ansgar, and Odin got very interested in you. After all, he already knew your family well, and here was your name conjuring the name of his very plan, the Spear of the Gods."

The hairs on the back of my neck stood up. Had Odin set up my life to play out as it was? Was I really just a piece on his giant *hnefatafl* board?

"I'll tell you a thing that few could hear: Bodda spoke boldly with her last words. Spoke of having no regrets, despite all her plans turning upside-down. Spoke only of the joy she'd found. That's how she left life—like a *drengr*.

"Now that's the end of the story, which of course is just the beginning of another story. Beginnings and ends are just arbitrary decisions. But you know much of what happened from there. I'll add only one other detail, a thing that you won't hear anywhere else: On the second night, when Bodda greeted who she thought was her husband, I was the one wearing his skin."

Blood rushed to my face. Many emotions welled up, some contradictory, all unwelcome. "Why did you visit her?" I asked, failing to keep the panic out of my voice. "Was it because you were watching Loki, and you were balancing it out?"

"I saw *someone* go, and I knew it was not Styrgrim, and that is all I knew. Loki has gone to Midgard in many guises. So have others."

"It doesn't answer why I'm called after your grand plan, or what my real name is. At least one question is answered: You are my father. Must be. For one thing, my hair is fair, like yours. Bodda's and Styrgrim's are black."

Heimdall shrugged. "As to your name, that's something for Styrgrim to tell. As for the hair, Odin and his brothers, Vili and Ve, have fair hair. So do Loki and many other *jǫtnar*. So do Frey, Baldr, and Forseti. And others, depending on how fair you think fair is."

"What about my early rising? And that I see and hear better than anyone else? You need less sleep than a bird, you can see a hundred leagues at night as if it were day, and you can hear the grass grow. I have these . . . abilities? But less so."

"You assume a lot about what's inherited. You still need sleep. Your sight is good, but no better than many others. You hear well because your ear was trained with poetry and music and languages. Don't be so eager to ascribe your qualities to an accident of birth, or you will lose the things you earned with hard work."

My head fell. Naming Heimdall as my father had filled me with hope. Hope that I would not need to worry about being the spawn of Loki. Or of Odin. Hope that I might finally have answers instead of just new questions. "You lot don't make things very easy for us. It seems like every time you intervene, it's for your own ends, and it makes our lives more difficult."

Heimdall shrugged. "I am the Guardian of the Bridge, the Watchman of the Gods. When I act, it is no small thing. Mistakes, when I make them, have no small consequences. Despite my intention to not make mistakes, there have been many. Among those mistakes: Now some of us in Asgard wonder if this plan of Odin's may have masked his ambitions."

"Because none can truly know Odin's mind?"

The Watchman nodded and rose, as if to leave on some unseen ferry. "Not the first time I have missed seeing a thing far into the future. One day, I might tell you how the Brisingamen came to Midgard. The short version is: It was my doing. Even with my long view of things, I did not see far enough ahead."

"Do you know where to find Tyrfing?"

He shook his head. "I can't help you with that. And most of what I can tell you will only make more questions than answers. But consider the question-inducing story I've just told you and think about who you are now before you look on your history with regret. Make what use of it you can."

# CHAPTER 30

# HONOR

THE *SEA SQUIRREL* APPROACHED MY LITTLE ISLAND. WHO ELSE could it be, sailing around Lake Malaren when it was impossible to see anything? I knew my Brothers, and the impossibility of accomplishing a thing was nothing that would dissuade them from trying it.

By the time the ship pulled up, Heimdall was long gone, having disappeared when I looked away for a brief moment.

"There he is, sound the horn!" Magnus shouted from the prow. "Is this a holiday? Look at him on his own island with that cozy fire! Maybe we should leave him be." No voice in the world could have made me feel better.

Someone sounded a horn three times. I waded right out to the ship and pulled myself up. Every crewmate was there to greet me with clasped arms. Frothi and Thorir had visible wounds bandaged all over, but both gave me snarling smiles at seeing I was still alive. Nanthild gave me a giant bear hug that lifted me off the ground. Kraki asked if I wanted some *hákarl*, and I was so hungry, I said yes.

We got underway and headed back to Uppsala. I wanted to know everything, all at once, but I noticed one thing I had to ask about first. "Where is Ingolf?"

"Fell in the final push," said Magnus. "Caught in a grapple with two of Svart's men, he took them both over the side. None came back up."

Any delight I felt dropped out of my stomach, through the ship's deck, and down to the bottom of that lake where our steadfast Brother, Ingolf, lay. A warrior's death was what we were supposed to hope for, to celebrate. Instead, I fought back a bitterness that wanted me to hang my head. Haldor had never hung his head, though. As our leader on land, as the one we all looked to, he could not do that.

"I should have brought the fire ship in sooner," I said. "Maybe then—"

"There is no point in that," interrupted Magnus. "Nothing to be learned, nothing to be gained. Ingolf had a good death."

"A good death." I nodded, not nearly as content as I looked. "That's one bit of news, and I expect there is a lot more to tell. What did I miss?"

Magnus did most of the talking on the way back to Uppsala. The short of it was that the fire ship had caused just as much chaos among Svart's fleet as I'd hoped. Flames had spread out from the line of Rus ships, dividing their forces. Styrgrim led a counterattack against one of the halves, and soon the decks were cleared. Svart had been on the other half and retreated before that was even done.

Everyone had their own tale about something that had happened: A close call with an arrow, or fighting shoulder to shoulder with the Swedes, all excitedly relayed. The best was Thorir's story of missing a jump and falling into the water, only to climb up the enemy ship's rudder and surprise them. But the one that made me happiest was when Ketill told how he and Jorun had stopped one ship by taking turns shooting whoever took up the rudder.

"I saw her take an arrow to the chest, though," I said.

The wizard nodded. "I saw that. Her armor must have stopped the arrow, because her aim is still as good as ever."

Magnus estimated that Svart had four ships left, with three crews' worth of warriors at the most.

Josur and Styrgrim had pursued Svart at first, but eventually turned back to join the *Sea Squirrel* in looking for me. The Swedes had helped, too, but had turned back to Uppsala at twilight. Those three horn blasts were meant to signal to our people that I'd been found.

That still left a lot of questions about who had survived. The *Whaleslayer* and *Sea Goat* had hurried back to Uppsala while it was still daylight. Magnus speculated that meant a lot of injured people.

Huld tending to the injured was on my mind as the *Sea Squirrel* pulled into the docks of Uppsala. We passed a score of other wounded ships on the way, all hacked by weapons, stained with blood, the marks of grappling hooks dug into their insides and prows. No ships survived unscathed, and neither had we.

I expected a sleepy city once we disembarked, but Uppsala was just as active that night as it had been during the day. Makers were making, sellers were selling. The sound of hacksilver clinking sang the same song of commerce as the day we'd arrived. There was no less smoked fish, cheese, or pork on display. It turned out King Athils was holding a feast and was buying up more food and drink for his guests than ever.

Athils' mead hall was packed when we arrived, with the doors left open and the guests spilling out of it with hands full of food and drink. Hundreds of raucous conversations weaved together in a celebratory hum, but one was close enough to be distinct.

Svipdag had a small audience just outside the hall. "Then they charged, and it was just the two of us against all six!" He looked up mid-story and strode right up to us, clasping hands with me straightaway.

"Now here's a welcome crew to see!" he bellowed. The champion wore a long, white bandage around his head, and a bloodstain bloomed over his right eye. A big enough stain to indicate the eye was gone. No good way to address that, or to admit I was sad for him. So, I did what I thought Haldor might do and made a joke.

"Glad you saw your way to victory."

Svipdag clasped me harder and laughed again. "Come inside, all of you!" The crowd was elbow-to-elbow, but he shouted, pushed, and cajoled a way through. He took us to a table near the hearth but away from the high seat. It had plenty of people sitting down already, but Svipdag told them to make way for the Brotherhood, and two dozen warriors immediately stood up. Many of them shook hands with the crew as they did.

One of those standing was Thick Alrek. Fairly called Alrek Greasy Beard, now that I saw him in action. He gave up his seat while halfway through a pork rib. He took the rib with him, though.

I sat down with Magnus and Svipdag closest, but something felt off. "You don't need to sit closer to the king?"

Svipdag made a more-assertive-than-necessary call for ale before turning back toward me. "The king is angry with me for disobeying, so I won't be sitting next to him at the moment. But I have no regrets, as I've finally ended my conversation with those *berserkir*. You and your people are not used up, which is also good."

The champion had put himself in the greatest danger for people he hardly knew. He'd done it on principle and knowing it would bring him bad consequences. Now he'd lost some favor and an eye, with nothing to show for it but his own honor. I suppose that is the only way one has honor, and why the dishonorable are so quick to rationalize their actions.

The warriors who had just given us their seats returned with food and drink, not even waiting for Athils' thralls to bring them. I grabbed a hunk of fatty pork and stuffed it into my face. Ymir's bones, it was good. A little pang of guilt about making fun of Swedish accents nagged at me. I decided I would stop doing that.

Well, I would do it a bit less.

I asked Svipdag about how things went on Adelso and got plenty of updates. Not many had been killed, but plenty had been wounded. All the skalds had survived, which was a great weight off my shoulders. Birki the Obstinate had fallen, the results of which I wasn't sure about.

"We lost Ingolf. A good man. Steady, reliable. Took two foemen with him."

Svipdag nodded. "That's how it goes for us all, so we can only hope to die well. One of Odd's men—a woman, actually—she fought well, too. Took a gut wound." He shrugged. "Hope the onion soup says her fate is to fight again."

I swallowed hard. Onion soup was not a delicious thing to eat in this context; it was the harbinger of life or death. The idea was to let the person injured with a gut wound eat the soup and then wait a few hours. If the wound smelled of onion, that was the sign of too much internal damage to recover from. Death would come in slow, agonizing waves.

"This woman," I asked, "did she go by a man's name?"

He nodded. "That's right! Hrafn." He shrugged. "If you fight that well, I say you choose your own name."

Hrafn was not part of our crew, though I would have welcomed her on board. I'd met her after the attack on Arrow-Odd's camp. She'd taken an axe through her foot, and her foot had to be further opened to clean out the wound. While I had winced just to watch, she had smiled through the entire process.

I had to see how she was. I didn't understand why at the time. In retrospect, I think one fish out of water trying to prove his worth recognizes another. Recognizes and respects. I asked Svipdag where the injured were being seen to. He told me injury tents had been set up on the other side of the longhouse.

Magnus looked like he was about to come with me. "Magnus is in charge," I shouted. Some of our crew's rowdier personalities balked at that, mostly Moose-Frothi. Magnus nodded and let me go.

I pushed my way out of the hall and found myself back in the night air. I turned the corner of the longhouse and saw the torches and oil lamps that had to be for the injury tents. Simple canvas overhangs with no walls protected them from in case of rain, but left everything open to see.

The smells hit me as I got close: Pus and blood, vomit and spilled bowels. Then it was the sounds. Some growled at the pain, knowing no other sound to make. Others were sweat-soaked and breathing as if they had just run up a mountainside, cool cloths on their foreheads more for comfort than anything else. Some spoke softly as if in delirium.

The worst were the sucking noises among those with chest wounds. Huld worked furiously at one of these. A big man like Svipdag, he pushed her away until he had no more strength to do so. Then Huld stabbed his chest with a conical knife and inserted a sharpened copper tube. She tapped the tube gently with a wooden mallet.

On the third tap, blood geysered out of the tube, spraying Huld's apron. In a few moments, the man started to breathe again. He looked down at the tube in confusion.

"Next time," I heard Huld chiding the man, "try not to kill yourself by stopping me."

I exchanged a brief look with the man. I think he still wasn't convinced this was "healing." I gave him a brief nod, as if nothing particularly strange was going on, and let him decide whether to trust her.

Hallfred Horsefly sat with Hrafn, the latter being in good spirits, other than the occasional silence-inducing waves of pain. I sat down opposite the skald and congratulated both on winning against a bigger force.

"They were shit," coughed Hrafn.

Hallfred clasped her hand and spoke in her stead. "Svipdag strode out first and foremost. He challenged the *berserkir* himself and said the rest of their people could go. They agreed to come one at a time and met him in the middle. Only Hrafn went with him, saying Svipdag needed a second to carry extra axes, if nothing else. The first fight started, and then all six rushed him." He looked down at Hrafn.

"You met the charge with Svipdag," I said.

Hrafn nodded. "Just ... one of them ... got me ... just wish I'd ... fallen on the field ..."

"We need that onion soup," said Hallfred.

Hrafn swallowed hard and sighed, sounding like the wave of pain had passed. "It is not time for onion soup. It is time for me to fall in combat. Find Arrow-Odd! If he would honor my service, he won't let me die slowly."

"I'll find him." I was relieved I'd kept my voice steady.

I headed back to the longhouse, assuming Arrow-Odd would be in there, as close to Athils' high seat as possible. It was not easy to move or see in there, though, so I asked around before going back in. I ran into some of his crew who were milling around outside, and they directed me to another street down.

I found Arrow-Odd drinking from an oversized horn and talking to Orm, the priest, of all people. Orm had improved his wardrobe significantly over his previous shit-smelling robes. Now he had a long tunic and cloak of bright yellow. To his side and a bit behind stood a monk marked by that silly shaved head, wearing what looked like a brown rutabaga sack. Darting eyes and fidgeting hands told me he did not want to be there, even if Orm did.

Why Odd was talking to these two, I had no idea, but he sounded amused. "So, you're saying I could become a Christian, and I wouldn't have to change a single thing I was doing?"

Orm nodded vigorously. Converting such a famous pagan hero would doubtless earn him some fame. "You wouldn't be able to sacrifice to your old gods, of course."

"I've refused to do that my entire life."

"Excellent! You are practically a Christian already."

I would have laughed openly at that statement if I had been in the mood, which I was very much not. "Tell him about forgiving his enemies."

Odd shot the priest a quizzical look. "What's this now? I won't renounce vengeance against my son's killer."

"Well, um ..."

"You're supposed to forgive all your other enemies, too," I continued.

"It's their way: Forgive forgive forgive. They forgive so hard, it's practically a weapon."

Odd looked back and forth from his horn to the priest a few times. He looked at the monk, who nodded. Then he poured his ale over Orm's head. "So, you need to forgive me for this?"

The priest managed to smile. "I already have."

Odd let out a throaty laugh and turned away from the soaking priest.

"Hrafn is dying," I said.

"Many are dying. It is a given of battle."

"Hrafn left Gardar's service to join yours when most were doing the opposite. She is dying slowly now because she took a gut wound while standing with Svipdag."

"Ah," said Odd, shaking his head. "She has had the onion soup? That's too bad. It was a hard fight. I told Svipdag I should be the one to challenge those *berserkir*, but he insisted, and Hrafn stood with him. She reminds me of my old friend, Hjalmar. Her death is a good one."

"Hrafn isn't dead yet, but she is certain it's coming even without the soup. She wants you to end her. Give her a death in combat so she doesn't need to wait for it pointlessly."

Odd sighed. "I can understand that. A woman with a man's name, though? That, I never understood."

"I don't know that understanding matters. In any case, she is not the first. Skadi is Njord's wife, and she has a man's name. As far as I know, all Hrafn wants is to be called Hrafn, to be treated like a warrior, and to end her life in combat. Combat with you, as that would honor her service."

"It is not—"

"It is little to ask for what service you've received," I said, fully meaning to interrupt and be rude about it. It was not just impertinence, it was a threat that I would call Odd a poor leader if he did not do this thing.

Odd sized me up, surely not wishing to be told what to do. Especially by a poor warrior. By the same logic, though, it would be dishonorable for him to fight me unless I had truly insulted his honor. And I didn't intend to go quite that far. I just wanted to poke it a little.

"Hmmm," said Odd, which sounded a lot like *don't poke me again*. "I won't execute a friend who has lost hope only. Get Hrafn the onion soup and make certain. If it is certain, then we will have combat. In Athils' hall, no less. That bloated bag of air can clean up the mess himself after it's done."

So it was spoken, and so it was done.

Hrafn took a bit of soup but waved it off well before finishing. It was too much for her, and she said she could feel the stuff leaking out of her insides. By the time Hallfred and I could verify the smell from her wound and help her into the hall, Odd had already spoken to King Athils.

I wish I could have seen that interaction, Arrow-Odd telling the king what was going to happen in Athils' own hall. There weren't many who could act with that much arrogance in the face of that much power and get away with it, but Odd was one of them.

When we did get Hrafn into the hall, many of the revelers had been cleared out. There was a big enough space for a fight. A small fight, at least. Holding onto Hallfred for support, Hrafn refused a shield, asking instead for a two-handed axe. Using the long axe for support, she stood by herself, and Hallfred stepped back.

"When you said you needed space to honor one of your warriors," Athils began, almost absent-minded in his tone, "it did not seem to me that I was agreeing to a fight in my hall."

"I offer no fighting," replied Odd. "I will reward a warrior in here, where it's proper, rather than outside under the tents. Hrafn stood fast against our enemy rather than keeping behind the lines where it was safe. She's not asked for any gold as a reward, though. She prefers her thanks in steel. I presume the king here does not deny rewards to those who've shown loyalty and courage."

That was two barbs thrown at the king. Even one might be enough for a very bad result. But he was Arrow-Odd, and he didn't care about the approval of kings any more than Kraki did.

Orm stepped forward into the fighting area. "King Athils, I have heard this Hrefna fought bravely for the rest of us. I would offer prayers for her, with your leave, before and after."

"Why are you asking me?" demanded Athils. Whatever he thought of the idea, Athils knew how to read a room. "Say whatever prayers you wish in your own privacy."

"My . . . name . . . is . . . Hrafn." The words choked out slowly, each one a mountain to climb.

"But that is a man's name!" said the priest. "Hrefna is the female of your name. Surely you would not confuse St. Peter, I mean one of Odin's valkyries, by giving them the wrong name. It could go badly for you!"

There is a shared feeling between those with shared experiences. When you've fought with people side by side, you often feel with them in joy and sadness. Hrafn's labored breathing was something I didn't just see and hear. I felt an echo of it, and it made my own breathing harder. Likewise, I could feel Hrafn's acceptance of fate, feel that relief was within an arm's reach. And I could feel her rage at this priest who would rename her and replace her magic with his own against her will.

If silent, angry stares around the hall were not enough to tell me I was not the only one, it soon became clear enough. Kraki shoved his way forward, turned Orm around, and kicked him in the balls.

Not letting him fall to the floor, Kraki lifted the man by the throat. "If that's how your Saint Peter offers hospitality, he can have it twice that way. And then more, if he complains."

He let the priest drop to a wave of silent nods through the crowd. The monk who had been talking to Odd just minutes ago shuffled through the crowd to pull Orm back. He had a hard time getting through a forest of stiff elbows and shoulders.

Vilgrip pushed his way forward. With the monk's help, he pulled Orm out of the way. They got him to a bench and sat him up, where, I can only assume, Orm offered those prayers he'd mentioned.

Odd and Hrafn swore oaths over their weapons. They would both attack as best they could and give the other no quarter. Hrafn could hardly stand, but that was no surprise. Odd could give her a quick death, but she had to make what effort she could to fight. Otherwise, it would not have the same meaning.

So, it was a fight. Unless it was King Athils asking about it. In that case, it was a reward.

Hrafn hefted the axe in two hands, panting with the exertion of standing without leaning on the handle. Sweat poured down her face. Her posture slouched and righted, doubtless from waves of pain.

Odd drew his fine ring sword. They both took two steps back.

"Call the beginning," said Odd, though it wasn't clear to me who would do that calling.

Athils sighed. "Begin, then."

Hrafn's bearing changed in an instant. Her eyes went wide, her posture straightened, her shoulders broadened. She drew the axe back over her shoulder and charged with a roar, all signs of fatigue vanished.

Arrow-Odd stepped aside as the blow came down and thrust his sword through her heart. It stopped her cold even before he withdrew his blade, but he didn't turn away from her like an enemy. He caught her rather than let her fall.

Hrafn died in Odd's arms. He bore her gently to the floor, a smile permanently on her face.

# Chapter 31

# The Last Tantrum of Kings

King Athils retired to his bed after Hrafn's death. Something about the sight of all that blood on his floors putting him off. I hoped that blood would never come out.

Arrow-Odd had regained my respect for the way he'd treated Hrafn. Not that I had forgotten his politicking ability or his callous response to Hildigun. Odd was a complicated man. I'd now seen enough to know that honor was as much part of his complication as the parts I disliked.

The morning after the feast, most of the wounded were either much better or much worse. We had lost a few from the crew of the *Sea Squirrel*, as every ship had. Many such characters flow through this story like phantoms—always present, though I don't remember all their names.

By mid-morning, King Athils still hadn't shown himself. Our ship captains and skalds sat close at one table in the longhouse, eagerly awaiting the king's presence. Space was not nearly so tight as the previous evening, and nobody had the bad manners to talk too loud with that many hungover people present. Svipdag and some other Swedes sat a bit farther down the same table. No Thick Alrek, though. Maybe Athils wasn't the only one sleeping in.

I asked for Ketill to join us. He'd known what to expect from Athils without even meeting him, and our next step was to get the king to honor his word. If Athils could tell us anything about Heidrek the Wise, we might be able to find Tyrfing after all.

"I don't trust that king," Odd whispered through his teeth.

"Nor should any of us after the deception he tried," Styrgrim growled. "I've killed lords over less."

Bjorn shook his head. "Complicated to do that here. Being both completely outnumbered and also needing his information."

Styrgrim shot his skald a look of disapproval. Bjorn returned it with a dare to contradict him. Eventually, Styrgrim sighed and nodded.

"It's Odd who approached Athils initially," I said, "but last night, he antagonized the king in his hall. Perhaps someone else should address Athils when he appears."

Hallfred tapped the table. "I speak for Odd often enough, and I am not the source of the antagonism." That seemed like a good idea to everyone.

King Athils took his time in appearing. He marched up to the high seat, making shooing motions with his hand at anyone who approached him who wasn't carrying food or drink.

"I've rarely disliked a place more than this one," Kraki said. "We leave soon."

"We'll get his information first," I said.

"We leave soon." Kraki's tone had a finality few could match.

Hallfred got up to address the king, who waved him away.

"It is too early for entertainment!" Athils sucked the meat off a bone and held his head up as he chewed. "If there's something of importance, I'll hear it from a leader rather than a lackey."

Hallfred bowed and excused himself, because what else could he do? Some people hurl insults only at those unable to hurl back.

Hallfred's dismissal left Odd doing the talking, unless we chose a different captain. Josur? Perhaps, but he wasn't a great speaker. Styrgrim mostly spoke with shouted commands. Gazes went to me, and before I could say anything, Odd nodded.

A scent, subtle but bitter, wafted over me as I approached the high seat. How to begin? Just by acknowledging things, I supposed. I had the strange feeling that my next words were important. "Well, King Athils, it seems to me you've had very good luck these past few days. When we arrived, a hostile force was in your hall trying to worm its way into your court and your lands. Now that force is broken and running, and your former *berserkir* who raided your lands are dead. We've fought for you faithfully in agreement for some information you had. Now that you've had some time to savor your victories, we'd like to hear what you know of Heidrek the Wise."

Athils ignored me at first, continuing to gnaw on his bone. The smacking sounds made me wince. Open-mouth chewers: Trolls, every one of them.

The bitter odor increased, and I looked around for a source. Had the wrong thing fallen into a hearth fire? I didn't know it at the time, but politicking can have a scent just as *seiðr* can.

The king began without looking up from his food, cheery-toned and high-pitched. "I don't desire any misunderstandings, especially with such fine folk as yourselves!" He wiped the grease from his fingers and worked some loose bits out of his teeth with a fingernail. "Of course I will tell you what I know of this man, Heidrek! But let's be clear about a few things, first. You recounted how lucky I have been for your presence, and how good things have turned out for me. Doubtless, you would like this to be true, as it puts me all the more in your debt. I understand that. But I don't agree."

If there was any time I wished we still had someone on the crew with Ulf's diplomatic skills, it was that moment. I gulped and braced myself for what was coming, knowing that I had been weak against this art before.

"For one thing, that 'hostile force,' as you describe it, was not necessarily hostile to me. Would I have preferred they just move on? Certainly. Which they were likely to do, had their sworn enemies not shown up. That makes me wonder how lucky your arrival really was. I think you can't disagree that your presence here forced a confrontation I had otherwise been able to avoid. Svart had more interest in fighting smaller battles he could control. It was only a matter of time before I lulled him into a false sense of confidence, cornering him when he least expected it.

"For another thing, Svart is not soundly defeated, as you described. He retained enough of his ships to raid my coasts and much more. Now I still need to muster my forces, only to track a faster-moving enemy, one who is now more motivated to attack my lands, and likely to do a great deal of damage on his way.

"I consider myself most unlucky for another thing entirely. My best champion let ill influence fall over him and turned into a completely unreliable man. That is bad enough, and he doesn't even have both eyes anymore!

"Now, those *berserkir* . . . it is good they are dead. That much, I cannot disagree with."

I had never wanted to choke a king to death so much in my life. Athils' brazen dishonesty playing as truth struck me as if I'd been kicked in the balls. It left me just as angry, and it put me off my focus. "They were allied with Svart!" I shouted. "There is no separating the two."

"Again, an assumption." He held one finger as he sipped his ale. "There were no Rus with those *berserkir* that I heard of. A wholly separate force."

"They attacked *at the same time Svart's ships did!*" I was about to throw the king's previous words, "We have won a great victory," back at him. That would get him, this wizened old fool! Except, of course, it wouldn't. There is a near-universal shame in hypocrisy, but people like Athils don't share it. Instead, they delight in the outrage over their contradictions.

A firm hand fell on my shoulder. "To be a king is to consider much," Ketill interjected, his tone warm and ingratiating. "All decisions have consequences, and all consequences require new decisions. It is only right that the King of the Swedes is able to see many interpretations." He bowed low.

No doubt: The wizard had heard all this aurochs-shit before.

Athils thanked him for conveying such wisdom. Not everyone understood the complexities of being king, Athils told us, and it was good that at least some appreciated his skills.

The sycophants who had taken no part in the battle cheered and clapped, bowed, and banged their cups together. What a great king!

"He has ensorcelled you," Ketill whispered to me. "You cannot see the forest for the trees right now. Look further than the immediate reaction."

I took a deep breath. The anger did not recede. But I trusted Ketill's wisdom, so I kept my mouth shut and let him continue.

"Let us not dwell on too many assumptions," continued the wizard. "As you described, there are many! None can know the fates the Norns have carved for us, so let us dwell longest on what we do know: Arrow-Odd's army fought alongside yours on a red day, on land and sea, and together, we won."

Steinvor shot up from the table to raise her drink and cheer. Our other skalds joined her, all banging their cups on the table and repeating the cheer. By the third cheer, she had the entire hall behind her.

"Odd's army, if small, is still powerful," Ketill continued. "We are proud to call the Swedes our friends."

Again, Steinvor led the cheering between the wizard's oration.

"Now we enjoy good hospitality with friends, but we do not intend to raid our host's pantry until it empties!" Some laughter, as this was absolutely true. Feeding a few hundred people at a time required an absurd amount of food and drink. "It is near time for us to take our leave. Only, where to go? Now we need your wisdom, King Athils, and what lore you have of this man, Heidrek the Wise. That will, we hope, give a hint at our next destination."

There was no trace of the crotchety old wizard, annoyed at everything he saw. If I had ever wondered whether Ketill had been a skald in his younger days, I was convinced. He had all my skills and all of Ulf's, but none of my narrow-mindedness. With those skills, he weaved a counterspell to Athils' rancid rhetoric.

"That is all well-spoken," said Athils. "It is good to part on the best of terms, as you say. And now, let me tell you all I know of this Heidrek. This lore was handed down to me directly from my father, and he from his father, and I do not share it lightly.

"Heidrek was not always so wise. My grandfather met him while he was off raiding in the south. He was impressed by Heidrek's fighting prowess, and befriended the man. He even invited Heidrek to Uppsala to be one of his champions.

"My grandfather was pleased at having Heidrek as a champion at first. Once he saw how Heidrek was when not fighting, however, he wasn't so sure. Heidrek did not sleep much and prowled the hall at night, muttering to himself. He was prone to fits of anger for no good reason. It became clear to my grandfather that this young man was quite disturbed. Some started calling him Heidrek the Wise as an ironic name.

"I suppose Heidrek was the first *berserkr* brought to my family's court. There has not been another quite like him. I thought I had found some to keep order myself, but you know how that turned out.

"After Heidrek thrashed another champion in one of his fits, he sat in the back of the hall for a week. My grandfather was unhappy at waiting for one champion to recover in body and another to recover in mind at the same time, and made that unhappiness known.

"What my grandfather said to Heidrek was not passed down to me, but sometime soon after that incident, Heidrek took baptism and converted." Athils shrugged and took a drink. "Most people still gave him a wide berth. Others, like my grandfather, made to placate him by asking for his opinions on things. He seemed to recover some of his sanity during that time. My grandfather and his counselors gradually found that he could offer a perspective they did not have.

"Heidrek had the wisdom of one who has seen much and suffered from his own actions. He often counseled men to be forthright about their regrets. They did not need to convert as he had, he said, but they could act in ways that might undo some of their regret, and that was better than drinking too much. Other champions found it soothing to speak in confidence with Heidrek. He spoke wisdom without lecturing and listened without judgment. He became known as Heidrek the Wise, but without irony.

"Years later, Heidrek left the city. He did not say where he intended to go, only that he was leaving. He thanked my grandfather for all he'd given him, and when my grandfather offered rich parting gifts, Heidrek said he had already received more than his share. He said treasure wasn't needed where he was going, anyway, and insisted on leaving everything he had earned to be distributed as my grandfather saw fit. Then he boarded a trading ship headed south. Where he went from there, none can say."

Athils finished his story with a drink of ale and a smug expression.

"What did your grandfather do with his belongings?" I asked. *And did that include Tyrfing?*

Athils shrugged. "Distributed them among the other champions, I presume."

*Those belongings could not have included Tyrfing. That sword would have made a new story.*

"You said he was from the south, but also that he left and went south," I continued. "Do you know where he was from, and if he returned there?"

"If those details were known before, they weren't passed on." Athils scratched his beard in thought. "Now you know all I know, and I have a question myself: Why do you wish to know of this Heidrek the Wise and where he was from?"

A shiver went down my spine as I considered what might be behind that question. Had Athils already puzzled out part of the mystery? How could I answer without giving away any more than we had already?

Arrow-Odd saved us when he stood up and spoke. "I heard there was a man who had suffered much and put it behind him. I heard he had wisdom to share about such things, and that he came to Uppsala. I'll be blunt: I am old. Older than anyone here, and I feel older than ever since my son, Vignir, was slain by Ogmund. If this Heidrek had wisdom he'd found in his suffering, I would learn it. As long as it isn't the advice of that priest—that I should forgive my enemies. Can you imagine that? Forgive them?" He laughed, half-humor and half-madness.

The rest of the hall laughed with him, if briefly, and probably out of fear. I laughed along with them, in awe of his quick thinking and willingness to aggrandize himself to keep our intent secret.

"I can't speak to what that wisdom was, or if it was wisdom," said Athils. "Such conversations are lost to time. I fear I repay your fighting skills poorly with such a story, since it does not give you the thing you were looking for. Let me make another offer then, especially since I am short a champion."

What I thought Athils had meant by that last statement was that he'd lost a good man in the fighting. Alrek had taken losses, and I looked to the Swedes sitting next to our people. When Svipdag grimaced, a new thought occurred to me, and it seemed I had been oblivious to it before. Before Athils could continue on, I wanted to confirm something.

"It's a pity when good men die in battle," I said. "Which champion fell, and shall I compose a verse for his memory?"

"You can compose all the verses you want, but I have no use for men who can't or won't follow orders." Athils' voice retained its high pitch but was stonier, more gravelly. If he hadn't said it outright, it was clear now: Svipdag was no longer one of the king's champions. The tone in the hall shifted, as if something deep beneath us had warped.

The king continued in a sweeter tone, regaining his courtly tongue. "In fact, compose later, if you would. It is time to consider a generous offer. I'll employ any person who fought Svart. Good fighting men are not easy to find sometimes, and you will see that Athils is a generous lord. There are better benefits, too, for the best of those I hire: I could use a few more champions to sit at my table."

The warping increased. This was not just tension you could cut with a proverbial knife. This was an attempt to buy Arrow-Odd's army out from under him. Which, as one might imagine, was not a thing Odd would take sitting down.

"Sit at your table until they show some honor or take an injury?" demanded Odd, as the diplomatic course of the conversation came crashing down like an avalanche. "It's poor treatment you've shown one champion here, and only a fool would take his place!"

"Shut up, Odd!" spat Athils, dropping any semblance of respect. "There's no one in this hall who doesn't know you're destined to fail! I reward loyalty, but what do your people have to show for following you? Where are your closest friends, Asmund, Thord, and Hjalmar, other than ground to dust beneath your arrogance? You murdered for a wife in Ireland, only to leave her and get a son with another. Then you left her and let your son's life be wasted on nothing!" He shook his head and tapped one arm of his chair, switching to a slower and more controlled tone. "The famous Arrow-Odd. These fine folk think they want to be your friends, you, a shiny thing they can cling to. But you are shiny like the cursed hoard of the Volsungs: Gleaming bright to entice new fools to seek it, only so that it can destroy every one of them!"

Odd stood stone-like, refusing to show how deep the comment had cut him. "It seems hospitality here is at an end. If it could have been called hospitality in the first place. We will take our friends, the living and the dead, and see off last rites on Adelso."

"A fine idea," hissed Athils.

I don't know if Ketill lost his temper with that shitheel king, or if he knew it was time to let me loose. When his hand fell from my shoulder, I was done holding back.

> "Little to be gained
>    in the greedy house
> of a Volsung serpent
>    sitting high.
> All visitors vanish
>    eventually,
> Though it's few
>    who find the exit."

Athils, his face beet-red, rose to his feet and flung a verse back with a force I'd rarely felt. The shock of it rolled over us like a wave, though its barbs were not intended for me.

> "Fell luck
>    fletches the Arrow,
> felling allies
>    as often as enemies.
> The hapless Traveler
>    hews them down,

> His ego tears them like
>   an eagle's talons."

Our people rose to leave. When it was clear that none were staying, it enraged the king even further. "Take that lamed champion with you, then, for all the good he'll do!"

Svipdag may have thought he could regain the king's favor, but not after hearing that. A champion fallen out of favor might regain his place at the king's table, but a man labeled as lame could not be a champion.

Kraki snarled at the king, and I seriously wondered if he was about to find the nearest blunt object and start swinging. Instead, he turned away from Athils and toward Svipdag. "If you want to join us, you should know: There are rules."

# CHAPTER 32

# A MAN WITH A PLAN

SVIPDAG WOULD BE MOST WELCOME ON OUR CREW. NO DOUBT Arrow-Odd would make a case for joining his command. Either way, the champion was a small consolation. We'd traded the lives of good people for what King Athils knew, and what he knew wasn't much. I left that hall with a bitter feeling.

Odd advised the captains to send their people into the city one last time. It was worth buying better weapons or armor, colorful clothing, and food that was not disgusting while we still had the chance. We would gather on the docks at midday.

Merchants waved at the crowd leaving the longhouse. I was thinking about what I might buy when I heard Orm offering to baptize anyone who wanted to convert before leaving. I walked away from the priest, not wanting to hear any more of his blather. Odd's hand fell on my shoulder and gripped it hard, steering me back in Orm's direction.

"It is good that we beat Svart so badly," Odd said, louder than necessary. "But now what? Even if this Heidrek was the key, we don't know where he went."

I set my jaw, suspicious that Odd was dressing me down in front of the others. "We have a story passed down two from generations ago. Not one that has been remade a hundred times. There is something to it, I think." *I hope.*

He leaned in and whispered. "You are determined to find the sword, then?" His tone was strangely warm. It sounded more like encouragement or approval.

"To destroy the Brisingamen? Of course."

"I think you will need the sword for more than that." He backed away, no longer whispering. "You swore a blood oath to kill that traitor of yours, and you will fight Alfhild as well."

"You don't need to remind me of our need for you and your army." I locked eyes with him, unable to parse the contrast in his tone and words. "I'm no less determined to do all that than you are to kill Ogmund."

He nodded, seeming to approve of whatever it was he saw or heard. He pointed toward Orm, who was shouting something about salvation. "It seems one bit of lore has led to a place where other lore may reside," said Odd, his tone distant.

"What?"

Odd looked at me like I was slow. "Where else would you look for an addition to your story, other than with the people who converted this Heidrek?"

*Goat's breath and cat piss!* Who knew what Heidrek had told those who baptized him? Who knew what they had written down? I left Odd and practically charged at Orm.

Seeing me do this, Vilgrip ran over. "You're not going to kick that priest in the balls, are you?"

A bit confused, I shook my head. "I need him."

Orm saw us coming and crossed himself. Maybe he thought he'd won two converts. Or maybe he didn't really believe anyone would convert, and we were going to kick him in the balls again. I suppose the idea behind that gesture worked either way.

"My sons," he said, which was a particularly poor start, "have you decided to accept our savior?"

"I think we are your saviors," I replied. "Or we were on that island. Now we have a thing to ask of you: Do you know anything about Heidrek the Wise?"

He shook his head.

"What about the monks here?"

"I would need to ask." He sounded like he hoped the answer was "No."

Vilgrip interjected before I could continue. "May I ask them? I met one of them last night. Albrech was his name. I would say hello again, in any case."

Orm considered the request. I can't be certain, but I think 'considered' in this case meant 'looked for a reason to deny it.' He clutched his wooden cross and smiled as he came to a decision. "It *was* good of you to help me last night," he told Vilgrip.

The warrior shrugged. "I did not want to see you come to further harm, being unable to defend yourself."

The priest shuffled off and waved for us to follow him. I was about to say that Orm should have kept his stupid mouth shut rather than insult our friend, Hrafn, but Vilgrip stopped me with a look. I kept my own mouth shut as we made our way down the streets of Uppsala, making no replies to Orm's many claims about why we should convert.

Albrech welcomed Orm when we reached the monastery. The simple structure was a bit longer than most houses, but by no means the size of a mead hall. Strangers were not permitted inside. Orm went in and spoke with Albrech in Latin, doubtless thinking I could not understand.

I didn't catch the entire conversation, but it sounded like Orm wanted Albrech to exchange pleasantries with Vilgrip, but nothing more. Orm was quite displeased about having been kicked in the testicles. Albrech reminded Orm that he only had testicles for kicking because we had saved him. The conversation went on for a few minutes until both men came out to speak to us.

Orm held a bucket of water and wore a giant grin. Albrech stood beside him.

"It appears they have some record of this man, Heidrek," said Orm. "However, I think this is not something that can be shared with pagan men. If the two of you were willing to take baptism, however—"

"One should be enough," Albrech interrupted. Bare-headed and still wearing that dull rutabaga sack with a rope for a belt, he was among the least imposing figures I had ever come across. A thin man with a voice that did not carry well. And clearly, Orm was his superior. Despite all that, he spoke with confidence and finality.

Orm nodded. "One, then."

Vilgrip stepped forward. "I accept." When Orm responded with a displeased look, as if he'd really wanted one of the leaders to convert, Vilgrip held up the stump of his right arm. "Not satisfied with a son of Tyr? I even look the part."

Orm nearly threw the bucket right at him, pausing only when Albrech put a hand on the priest's arm to stop him.

"I should add," said Albrech, "that there are rules. The history we have of this man is a written testimony. I must accompany you in the reading. We take good care in preserving our writings, so they must be handled a certain way. You must follow my directions at all times."

"That's fine," I said, thinking about how it might not be. "As long as you don't speak of what we find out." In case Athils asked after us, that should secure his silence.

"Agreed." Albrech nodded and gestured for Orm to continue.

Orm wasted no time in splashing Tyr's son with water. Then he spoke some sorcery in Latin. I suppose they didn't like to call it sorcery, even though it is. Either way, Vilgrip bore it without difficulty. Orm left us soon after, no doubt to brag about his new convert.

Albrech led us inside. Straw mats dotted the floor. This had to be their main quarters, but not where they did their work. Not a lot of room for work, it looked like, just a few places to sleep, a central hearth for warmth and cooking, and a few household tools hanging on the walls. I thought the monks on Gotland had it much better.

Vilgrip didn't have a way to dry off, so he just dripped while the monk fetched the manuscript and some candles.

"Why did you consent so readily?" I asked.

"I was already a Christian, so it seemed silly to have you convert when you did not want to."

I tried not to look surprised and probably failed. "I didn't realize that. You didn't do or say anything very different than the others."

He shrugged. "It's not as if I disbelieve in our gods. I mean, I am Tyr's son. He never acted as a father to me, though. I just don't like those gods, any of them. I like the White Christ story." He paused and looked at me for recognition. "The main story, you know?"

"I know they talk a lot about forgiveness," I said. I thought of Tafi's comment on Gotland. *A man cannot seek both forgiveness and revenge.*

"I won't claim to know any deep Christian lore. But I'll tell you this: Their god gave himself up for torture and death on my behalf. Odin hung for nine nights, spear-pierced, but for his own gain. Imagine: Gods willing to suffer for people rather than just for themselves!"

I nodded. "I can't deny the many flaws of the gods, especially Odin. To me, they are stories. Inspiring. Instructive. Whispers that carry wisdom over time." *And sometimes they give me cryptic advice?*

"Of how to be?"

"And sometimes, of how *not* to be."

"That makes more sense to me than sacrificing to them," he continued. "I thought about that a lot in Svart's cell. And I thought, well, if this Jesus can endure all that torture and still deny his captors any satisfaction like a *drengr*, I can endure this temptation of the Brisingamen."

I wasn't about to follow the man in baptism, but his explanation made sense to me. And I was glad he'd had that story to help him through a hard time. What else are stories for, anyway?

Albrech returned with two candles and a rolled-up scroll of parchment. He placed the scroll on the table and stretched a string from it to the left. He marked where the string went to with one thumb, then turned a candle and its holder over sideways so that the wick touched his thumb. He marked where the bottom of the candleholder was and measured its length a second time before placing the candleholder upright. He repeated the process on the other side and then lit both candles.

"Two lengths away, should a candle fall over," Albrech said. "Do not move them closer, even if you struggle to see."

I nodded and stretched out the parchment with a gentle hand. I might not have been a scribe, but I understood the rare value these things had. An exciting time! Almost like stealing a codex from the Down-Below. And a bit like that codex, I found I could not read the scroll.

I knew the letters of Latin. But letters might be drawn by very different hands, and I had seen few examples. I could hardly read a single word with so many extra tails and loops, and everything so tightly bunched together. I explained all that to Albrech, and he sat down in my place.

He read the first part slowly in Latin. Soon, the characters became more recognizable. Satisfied I could follow the writing, I asked him to translate into Norse for Vilgrip's benefit. The testimony went like this:

*I remember those days on Gotland as never being good enough for me. Now, I only wish I could return to them.*

*My brother, Angantyr, was better liked among our peers. But with our mother, Hervor, it was always me first. She spoke often of our Gothic heritage and how I, pinched at the waist but with broad hips and shoulders, was an exemplar of our people. I felt this favoritism was a fair thing. If Angantyr, the firstborn, should have more attention outside our home, why should I not have more inside? I thought I did not begrudge him at the time, that I only looked for balance.*

*It was balance I always sought because I admired Angantyr. He had an easy way about him that I did not. I caused trouble even without intending to. Some things just tried my patience. Too many things. When I lost patience, I could hardly remember what occurred after. Often, it was violence.*

*One day, our mother pulled me aside, and I knew it must be important. She handed me a sword. Her old sword, she said, the sword of my grandfather, the first Angantyr. A powerful weapon that could cut through steel as easily as cloth. Any cut from it would be lethal. When drawn, it could only be resheathed with warm blood still on the blade.*

*"You will take this sword and become famous," she told me.*

*I knew this sword. Knew it from stories that had become legends. Yet I had never seen it, nor even heard my mother speak of it. The stories of her fell wielding of it were from decades past, and I never heard them from her. Whispers of her exploits reached me from other mouths. I was not even certain the sword existed. Yet here it was, Tyrfing, bequeathed to me. Not to Angantyr, but to me!*

*That I had been entrusted with this heirloom gave me the most special feeling. I wished to share that specialness, to show it around. Perhaps I wished to brag a bit to my brother. But I also wanted him to see that I, too, would carry our family name further. In my great excitement, I had to show him the sword, show him how I would be his peer despite my flaws. And to express a magnanimity that, even being favored, I would always remain his brother and would always share my great wealth with him.*

*I do so swear, upon my savior Jesus Christ, that I showed him the sword with no ill intent.*

*That sword could not be unsheathed without taking a life, and there was no one else around. I remembered the warning only when that gleaming blade came free of the scabbard. It shone like the sun, and Hervor's words rang in my ears, but it was too late to matter.*

*I remember resisting at first. And then I remember the worst of it. It was not like one of my episodes. I knew what I did when I cut my brother down. The act seemed right, seemed as necessary as a starving man eating, and then as soon as I had done it, before he even fell, the feeling fled.*

*He asked me why. I had no words.*

*I could not undo my crime, so I ran from that place. In my wake, my father had me outlawed. Perhaps he thought that would prevent my return. But the memory of that evil deed would never allow me to return, not with that shame. I cursed my mother, cursed her favoritism, cursed her for handing the sword to such a fool as me. I cursed myself for failing to heed her warning.*

*I curse myself still for using it. Not just then, but many times since.*

*I do not know what else to do with it. Taking a hammer to the sword, after I have sated its bloodlust with another's life, has only destroyed the hammer. I still hear my brother's voice when I sleep. He tells me to keep the sword out of the hands of others. But how to prevent another Hervor from finding it? I know of no way but to keep it within my reach.*

*I have contrived a new story for the sword, so that anyone looking for it will look for a king of the past rather than an outlaw of the present. I do this as misdirection, yet I wonder at the sword's fate after I die. I ask my brother what else to do, but he never answers.*

*I will hold back this blight and suffer it as long as the Lord deems it necessary. I only hope that one day, my brother can look on my service. Look on and tell me how it might end.*

There were multiple difficulties with the text, one of which was that it seemed unlikely to have been dictated in Latin. Heidrek would have spoken Norse, and the scribe writing his statements down would have been translating into Latin. Hard to tell if an important detail was "corrected" into something incorrect or dismissed as irrelevant.

I thought Albrech had done a fine job of translating, although some things are too subjective to be exact. 'Become famous' was somewhat inexact, not in meaning but in tone. That was likely Heidrek talking about the immortality of word-fame. His mother had intended him to go out and create word-fame like those stupid gods had tried to do by siring so many mortal children.

"There is more," said Albrech, pointing to further text separated from the main writing. "You can see these letters are different. This part must have been added later. The text here is . . . difficult. I think he had learned some writing but was not fully trained."

"He wrote it, not a scribe?" I asked.

Albrech shook his head. "This is not the hand of one of my order. It is quite sloppy, and I can barely read it. It seems his brother answered him after some years? The meaning is hard to discern. Something about 'returning harm to its dwelling.'"

Vilgrip's eyes widened a bit. "That sounds like he intended to run himself through."

"That seems one interpretation," said Albrech. "Among a dozen others."

"I don't think he would have written such a thing if he intended to do it," I added. "That would mean going against what he'd written before, about protecting the sword even after he died."

My mind kept returning to those final lines. "Harm" was not the only translation possible. If those last lines were scrawled by Heidrek himself, was he trying to convey the same idea as the original scribe had translated as 'blight'? A sickness or corruption? Did it matter?

"Perhaps he sought to atone by slaying a monster?" offered Vilgrip. "Were there any stories like that around the time?"

Albrech shook his head. "If there were such stories then, I do not know them."

"He went south," I said. "At least according to what was passed down to Athils. And he was from the south."

Albrech nodded. "He mentions Gotland, which is south of here."

"But he said he would not return there because of the shame of killing his brother," I said. "Why would he go b—" The realization dawned on me as I spoke. "I think I know what he meant in Norse. I think he meant 'return the disease to its lair.' He did return to Gotland."

"To what?" asked Albrech, fear sneaking into his voice. "What would that accomplish?"

"Revenge on his mother?" suggested Vilgrip. "But that also seems at odds with his earlier intent."

"Not for revenge. Hervor would likely have died by then. The bit about not knowing what to do after he died, these lines are him realizing what to do with it. He had already spread the false narrative to throw people off. But people might still look for Heidrek—any Heidrek. He knew that, and disappeared, to bring the sword to a place no one would think to look for it: His mother's grave mound."

"That would explain why he did not say where he was going," said Vilgrip. "And no one would think to look for it in the mound of the previous owner. But even if it is on Gotland, where exactly?"

Albrech shivered. "Your purpose then . . . it is easy enough to guess now."

I had been too caught up in trying to puzzle out the mystery to realize we did not want our intentions announced. I looked at Vilgrip and he at me, both of us considering what to do.

"You have been good for your word," I told Albrech. "And your word included to repeat this to no one."

"I swore to reveal none of the testimony!" The monk's voice was high and thin, and he was near tears. "I swore no secrecy to keep silent about your ill intent. This man," he panted, tapping the scroll, "this man held sin captive in his heart, though it was heavy on him. And then he secreted away an evil thing, not for his own ends, but to prevent it from troubling others. If he did not find forgiveness in life, I am certain the Lord raised him up after. You would undo his efforts and return this demon sword to the world?"

Vilgrip put a gentle hand on the monk's shoulder. "Brother, I understand your fear. You are right to feel it. But if you protect this secret, know that it is in service of a worthy cause. It is not for word-fame we seek that sword. It is the only thing we know that might destroy another object. A thing that has no place in Midgard. A torc of power that belongs to the gods, the Brisinga-men. I know this thing first-hand, what it did to me and those around me. It must be destroyed. We have no other way to destroy it but to find the sword, Tyrfing."

Albrech wiped tears from his face and looked up as if to get an answer from his god. "Is this a Christian life?" he asked Vilgrip. Pointing to his stump of a hand, he asked, "You say you must do this terrible thing, but what has that got you before?"

"This old thing?" asked Vilgrip. "I wasn't using it much, anyway."

"Wait," I said. "Tell the monk the story behind losing your hand. He thinks it's because you wanted to be famous."

Vilgrip dropped his right arm onto the table, jarring the candle holders. The stump where his right hand would have been pointed at Albrech. "It is not a pleasant story."

The monk turned to me, but I shook my head. "Don't look at me. He jokes about his hand, but this story is part of his faith. It's a matter of whether you're willing to hear it."

Albrech considered the man for some time before furrowing his brow. "Faith? I thought you were just baptized!"

Vilgrip shrugged. "I never said I was accepting my first baptism! Besides, I'm glad Orm is not the only one to have sprinkled water on me."

I was afraid that wouldn't go over very well. To my surprise, Albrech let out a burst of laughter and then covered his mouth.

Vilgrip was shorter in telling his story than he might have been, but he left out no significant parts that I knew of. From his capture to his imprisonment, then his torture at the behest of Svart, and later, Alfhild's attempts to use the Brisingamen on him. He spoke about how he had resisted the torc and how the story of Jesus helped him through that time. He spent the longest time on Haldor's end and fighting our way out of that island prison, only to return to find it a more evil place than we'd seen before.

"I know their intent, the people who did this," said Vilgrip. "They will succeed if they get that torc back. It will be a close thing, even if we find the sword."

"But what is this torc's power?" asked Albrech. "That it has much power seems clear, but what does it do?"

"Influence," I said. "I can feel its pull. Especially when I am failing, I feel it try to tempt me."

"It is more than that," added Vilgrip. "I saw people as they came under its spell. It does not destroy will. It twists, instead. It shows people what they want to see rather than what is there. And it twists whoever uses it as well." He shrugged. "A small consolation, but Alfhild craves it without having it, and that must make her miserable."

We discussed it for a longer time, but I could tell Albrech believed us. He still advised us to abandon the quest and find some other way, but assured us he would not share what we were doing.

"It is a burden you ask of me, and I will ask a thing of you in return," he added, to my surprise. "Will you take Father Orm with you to Gotland? There is a scriptorium there, and he wishes to oversee it. You might use his influence to learn about Hervor's grave mound from the monks there."

"Where Tafi is the Abbot?" I asked. "We know them already. I don't think you—"

"Doing this will also give you another advantage," continued Albrech. "An important one, because you will be taking Father Orm away from Uppsala right away!"

"You don't like Orm very much, do you?" I asked.

"He . . ." the monk trailed off and sighed before continuing. "My feelings are of no consequence, nor should they convey judgment. Judgment is for the Lord. But that was not what I meant. I meant getting Father Orm away from Uppsala would keep him from reading what we have just read. Which, as you must know, he is not sworn to secrecy about."

"Shit!" said Vilgrip.

Albrech was right. Orm wanted to curry favor, and he would get it quickly if he found out what we had just read and told King Athils about it.

"All right," I said. "Perhaps don't leave this scroll out to be read in the meantime."

The monk nodded vigorously as he blew out the candles and began to put everything away. Vilgrip and I left him to it, stepping out of the monastery and into the warm light of midday.

We had fought, we had charmed, we had puzzled our way through. Now we knew where we were going, and I could hardly hold back my elation. Vilgrip could not keep from grinning, too.

As we made our way down the streets and into the busier parts of Uppsala, I spied Jorun. It looked like she was in search of something. When she saw us, she ran right over. Her face told me she had urgent news, and not the good kind.

"What's happened?" I asked.

"A lot has happened in a short time, and Styrgrim is ordering an immediate departure before we lose anyone else."

"Lose?" I demanded. "Did Athils attack us?"

She shook her head. "The crew of the *Sea Goat* has taken Athils' offer," she said. She kept her breath steady, but we both knew how bad that was for us. "But that is not the worst of it. Come back to the ships with me, we need to leave!"

We set off at a brisk pace. "What do you mean that is not the worst of it?" I asked on the way.

Jorun did not seem to want to answer.

"I don't wish to walk into a trap—" I stopped myself mid-word, thinking of another detail that concerned me. "Is Steinvor with Athils now?"

Jorun laughed. "No, she left before they made that decision." She leaned in and whispered, as if the act of doing so would bring more ill luck on us than we'd just seen. "She went with Arrow-Odd. He has left us."

# CHAPTER 33

# FATE'S WARNING

STYRGRIM WAS TRYING TO MAKE SOME ORDER OUT OF THE CHAOS when we reached the docks. He shouted from the prow of the *Long Claw*, telling people to board their ships and succeeding only halfway. A lot of them had questions, and they weren't shy about asking. "Where is Arrow-Odd?" was the principal question, regardless of what crew anyone belonged to.

"Get on board now if you don't want your tongues pulled out through your assholes!" was Styrgrim's general response.

I had the same question as everyone else, but I had the sense not to ask for an answer yet.

Orm exacerbated the situation despite being part of no crew at all. He paced back and forth along the docks, making up terrible stories in the form of questions and then answering them. "Has Arrow-Odd been carried off by demons?" he mused. "It would not be impossible, as only the light of—"

I grabbed Orm by the ear and pulled his head in close. "I heard you wanted to go to Gotland. Well, I am taking you to Gotland!"

"I just need to get—*owww!*"

I twisted his ear hard until I was confident he was listening. "I said I would take you to Gotland. I did not say you would sail all the way there. Get on our ship and shut your mouth, or halfway to Gotland, I will throw you overboard and pull you the rest of the way on a rope!"

I had my own crew wanting answers by then, but of course, I had none to give. Even what I had just learned needed to wait. Magnus took the hint and ushered Orm on board the *Sea Squirrel* himself.

It was around that time that Styrgrim's shallow well of patience ran bone-dry. He hopped off the *Long Claw*, walked to the back of the crowd that wanted answers before they boarded, and drew his sword. He didn't make any more threats, just let people get a good look. Everyone got on board.

Except for the crew of the *Sea Goat*. Birki the Obstinate had fallen in battle like a good warrior. His ship remained empty and moored as we pushed off.

I had thought Birki's crew would remain loyal to Arrow-Odd. But Odd had left, so who was there for them to swear loyalty to? Styrgrim, it seemed. A hard man offering a hard, and probably short, life. Or King Athils, who had made his offer sound far more comfortable.

Styrgrim had been right to get us all out of that place as soon as possible. And I assumed he now had control of the army, especially when I noticed Helgi Pike-Tooth, his right-hand man, take the helm of the *Whaleslayer*.

I hadn't had the chance to tell anyone what Vilgrip and I had learned yet. And maybe I wouldn't, depending on the news we got. I was not about to announce Tyrfing's likely location just to hear our crew was competing for it rather than working with the army.

I waved at Kraki to get his attention. "Where are we going?"

"Adelso!" he shouted back.

We rowed our way south down the river. The chatter was constant, but amounted to only one additional detail I hadn't heard: Many of the *Sea Goat*'s crew did not want to sign on with Athils and had been seen scrambling aboard the ships we still had. How many, though?

Kraki shook his head at all the banter, chuckling a few times.

The *Sea Squirrel*, *Long Claw*, *Wave Climber*, and *Whaleslayer* fanned out into Lake Malaren after what seemed like hours. The oars came in as soon as we could go under sail in Lake Malaren. With the oars up, I approached Kraki at the rudder and found that he had seen more than anyone else since he'd been on the *Sea Squirrel* the whole time.

"Odd left on a ship," he said.

"Did he say why or where he was going?"

"No."

I shook my head. Sometimes getting the old man to talk was harder than a conversation with a spirit in a rock.

"Steinvor—what about her? I heard she went with him."

He nodded. "Made a leap from dock to stern as the ship pulled away. I thought it was impossible, but she cleared it. Then she looked back and winked at me." The old man grinned.

"Did she say why Odd was leaving?"

"No."

"Kraki, can you tell me *everything* you know about what happened?"

He shrugged. "It seems to me it's mostly good news. We lost an unreliable leader. Well, this Steinvor, I wish she had stayed. But that rat-dick, Hemming, he went with them, and that's no loss."

The why is always more important than the what, and I wasn't getting any why. I could only think of one more question he might answer. "What ship did they leave on?"

"Ah," said Kraki. "The *Sea Valkyrie*. I suppose it could be better news—I liked that Svipdag fellow and would have been glad to have him on board. But at least he's not with Athils anymore. Thick Alrek took the ship, and Svipdag joined him. So did a lot of the other Swedes—the good ones, I say. Odd and Hemming asked to get on after that."

"So, King Athils has bought one of our crews, or part of a crew, but he lost some of his best people and the *Sea Valkyrie*?" That made me feel a bit better. "Where was Alrek headed?"

Kraki shrugged again. "'For a better court,' was all he said."

I thought the sky had a stormy look to it. No weather came up on us as we sailed to Adelso, though. The *Sea Squirrel* landed on the island last, as our ship was the slowest. Same spot as we had landed before, only much of the sand was stained dark red this time. Soon after we beached the ship, Bjorn came by and told me that Styrgrim had called for captains and skalds to meet and hear what he knew.

Kraki and I left the crew under Magnus' direction. We joined the other captains and skalds in front of the *Whaleslayer*. No seats, no fire, just a bunch of confused and angry-looking people standing around. I expected to hear a bit of explanation, mostly Styrgrim's intentions, possibly some new rules.

Styrgrim's first statement caught me off guard. "You have some explaining to do."

I looked to see if some phantom was hiding behind me. Seeing nothing, I still didn't believe I had understood him correctly. "You mean me?"

"Yes, you!"

"I have no idea what's going on!"

Styrgrim took a giant breath as Bjorn's hand grasped his shoulder. The skald stepped forward. "Let's not get ahead of things." Bjorn eyed everyone in turn before he continued. "Ansgar, I saw you speak to Odd after we left that longhouse. What did he say?"

I rubbed my beard, trying to remember. "He asked me some strange questions. 'Do you intend to see this through?' or something like that. And of course, I said I did, and he added that I would need the sword for more than the Brisingamen. I didn't understand why he would say those things at such a time, especially if he intended to leave us."

"Of course that's what he asked as he intended to leave!" roared Styrgrim. It was the most aggressive posturing he'd given me since I called him a liar for not telling me how my mother had died.

Kraki stepped forward with an equally aggressive posture. He didn't speak up and didn't have to, with that sort of bearing. *Back off from our leader on land, or we fight* was clear enough.

"This will be our last meeting if things continue as they are," said Jorun. "Both of you, take a step back if you want to hear what I know."

Neither Styrgrim nor Kraki moved.

Josur the Daring broke the stalemate. "Jorun can just as easily speak for my ears alone. Is that what you want?"

A few moments later, Styrgrim and Kraki both stepped back.

"Listen, then!" said Jorun. "Steinvor knew what was about to happen. She was Birki's skald, but Birki was slain, and some of the crew were grumbling. She looked for Arrow-Odd to ask who he would have captain the ship. He told her outright that he was no longer in command because he was going off on his own. Well, except he took the tracker with him. We were spread out all over the city, but Steinvor found me and said she was going with him. I tried to find out more, but she was already hurrying to the docks. She barely made it on board."

Kraki nodded. I realized I should translate the nod. "Kraki was at the docks and witnessed it. He also saw Steinvor hop onto the ship as it was leaving."

"And she winked at me."

*Don't make a joke right now. Don't make a joke right now. Don't make a joke right now.* "I think Kraki also saw that this ship was the *Sea Valkyrie*, and that Thick Alrek was taking it and a lot of good Swedes."

"That's right," said Styrgrim. "And with Odd gone, the crew of the *Sea Goat* took Athils' offer and left us. And that's not all. What I want to know is why Odd fled."

"I can't say for certain, but I can guess better than most," offered Hallfred Horsefly. "Odd came to speak with me last night. He asked if I thought fate was fixed. So, I told him true: I don't."

Which was a bit of a shock. Fate was carved by the Norns—inescapable. Everyone knew that. Or rather, everyone said that, over and over, until the assumption was so deeply embedded that questioning it seemed laughable. Josur laughed out loud, in fact.

Hallfred ignored him. "Maybe there are Norns carving our fates. More often than not, I think it's a failure to choose. Not because we're unwilling to choose, but because we think we can't, or because the choices seem so uneven. We call it fate and say it's already carved, make it easier to accept. I think fate is carved only once a thing has happened."

"Uneven choices can make one predictable," growled Styrgrim. "That explains nothing. Odd was already acting as though his fate was not fully carved, or that he didn't care about the prophecy. Something changed, and that was not it."

Horsefly nodded. "Odd has taken steps to avoid prophecy in the past. He resisted making any reaction to Huld's prophecy, but I suspect Athils tipped the scale. He described Odd as a gleaming trap to entice new victims, getting those closest to him killed. The king didn't know we were after Tyrfing, and yet he conjured the same sort of imagery."

"So Athils convinced him not to 'grasp at the sword and grind us down,' or whatever the prophecy said," said Helgi. "He thinks we're only destined to lose if he leads the army, so he's stepped away."

"That's a curious thing, but understandable," said Styrgrim, still looking like he was about to breathe flames out of his nostrils. "But curioser, and not understandable at all, is why he left leadership of the army to Ansgar."

A bad look to express surprise, so I shook my head in disbelief. "I think it's not the time for jokes—"

*"Sons of Muspell! It is no joke!"*

Everyone was staring at me, and I had no idea what to say or do. After a few silent moments, Bjorn spoke up. "I heard Odd say this. So did Styrgrim and Hallfred. Odd wanted no misunderstandings."

The bottom of my stomach dropped. "But . . . it doesn't make any sense . . ." It seemed like an unreal thing, like I was about to wake up from a disorganized dream to a world that made sense again.

Styrgrim crossed his arms. "That, at least, we can agree on."

# CHAPTER 34

# LIBER ABSURDUM

THE ARMY HEARD ABOUT ARROW-ODD AND ME AS THE NEW leader with expressions of surprise, dismay, and confusion. That was about how I had experienced it, so I couldn't blame them. Hallfred Horsefly did the talking while I was busy fighting down nausea.

I did have to speak eventually, though. I told them all enough of Heidrek's story to show that Athils' information had proved useful after all. We would hold funeral rites for our dead, and then we would sail to Gotland, which was not far away. Tyrfing seemed almost within reach.

Within Styrgrim's reach, specifically. While he'd accepted my leadership of the army, he only did so on the condition that the sword was for him once we found it. With the choice between that and losing the crew of the *Long Claw*, it was an easy thing to agree to.

The sky went from overcast to dark before we left Adelso. Fog on the rivers delayed us as we sailed back to the East Sea. Before getting through all the islands and into open sea, rain and heavy winds whipped our sails and tossed us about.

Kraki agreed we had to land and take cover from the storm, and then it took us hours to find a shore to land on rather than a wall of solid rock, which most of those islands are. The tiniest sandy beach I'd ever seen only allowed us to land the ships two at a time and provided just enough space to pull them inland before hitting a thick canopy of trees.

One bit of good luck: I climbed a hill near our camp to get a better view of where we would go next and found a raven taking shelter from the storm just as we were. He was still so tired from fighting the crosswinds that he lay splayed out on a rock covered in pincushion moss. At first, I couldn't tell if he was dead or had just found a comfortable bed to lie on.

The raven's name was Impulse, and he'd been flying east for some time, looking for Uppsala. I suggested avoiding Uppsala and offered to take him to our camp on my shoulder. On the way there, I offered the story of the 'Steins. He started to offer a story in return, and I realized this raven was named particularly well.

"*Naglfar* sails south with an army!" Impulse screeched into my ear. "And the storm follows!"

"*Naglfar*?" I repeated. "The Nail-farer. The monstrous ship that carries the dead from Hel to attack the living at *Ragnarøk*. That *Naglfar*?"

"Well, I don't know about that . . ." The raven sighed, sounding disappointed at my lack of panic. "And I heard *Naglfar* carries *jotnar* to the final battle, not the dead. Now that you mention it, I did see dead men sailing! That was last year, though, and now they're gone."

I shook my head. "So, you are telling me you saw the mythical ship *Naglfar* or not?"

"It could be!" the raven flapped his wings and croaked. "Old stories coming true. Very exciting!"

"Well, what did the crew look like? Dead or *jotnar*, it should have been easy to see they were not normal people." In the second between asking that and Impulse's pause before answering, I held up my hand. "Wait, did the captain have a long black forelock falling across his ugly face?"

"Hardly! I would remember something like that. I don't think the crew was dead, just very ugly! The captain wasn't ugly or dead, though. She was quite pretty, her hair like strands of gold."

"The pretty one: Did she have a scar on her face here?" I traced a line down my cheek.

Impulse gasped. "How did you know?"

"I know her. Her name is Alfhild." I stopped a moment as a nasty inspiration struck me. "I can tell you more about her. She will seduce any man with even a drop of *Æsir* blood. If you doubt that I might know this, look for the birthmark under her left breast, and see if I lie."

"*This is very interesting.*"

I nodded. "She isn't very wise, though. Oh, she has some lore, but she doesn't use it well. She got her entire army killed when she attacked Lejre and ran away. I wonder what will happen to her new army, sailing on this ship with a scary name. Will she let them die while she runs away, too?"

"I think her people are not dying so much right now."

"Did you see them engage an army that could threaten them?"

"No . . . not yet."

"Maybe you should fly back west and warn her people not to be too loyal." I coughed, uncertain of the next part. Was it always wrong to spread lies? In some cases, no. Fighting honorably was reserved for fighting the honorable. "During sex, she likes to have her hair pulled and hear dirty talk." I winked.

Impulse's eyes were wide as shield-bosses.

Bringing a raven back with me turned out to be good for my credibility. And good for morale, too. The raven heard many more stories than he could repay, putting him deep in our debt. I told him that as long as he shared my good information about Alfhild with her army, I would consider us even.

That journey to Gotland, which should have taken a few days at most, took over a week. It felt like we had just crossed an ocean when we finally landed on that familiar southwestern shore near the monastery. It was a slog to pull the ships inland and secure them, and then a wet trudge up to see the monks.

The monks still had their three stone houses, simple and sturdy, just as we'd seen them when we'd come to kill Varg the Charmer. Tafi, Varg's old champion who had converted years ago, was still the abbot. And it turned out that Humor, the raven, had made his way back there.

I made some introductions. Tafi knew Orm by reputation from his Christian life. Apparently, a priest is higher than an abbot, a thing Orm made clear from the outset. Tafi knew Styrgrim by reputation from his not-Christian life and gave him a wide berth. Tafi also remembered some of us from the *Sea Squirrel* and asked after Haldor.

"Haldor fell fighting a monster," I said, uncertain of the best way to tell all of that story in brief.

"Did he take it with him?" He may have converted, but Tafi still had some of that old champion in him.

"He did. And he left his enemies with a verse that would have them watching their backs forever. He died laughing."

Tafi cupped his mouth as if to smooth his beard, but I was sure he covered a grin. He nodded and said we'd have whatever we needed, so I explained that what we needed most was information. Did he know of a woman named Hervor, probably from Gotland?

He did not. But there was a scribe who knew much of Gotland's history, especially its families. He might know.

*Please let it not be Efraim.*

"I will introduce you to Petrus," said Tafi, to my relief. "I think you did not meet the last time. He is often out exploring but has just returned."

The scriptorium that housed the parchments and codices was busy when Tafi brought me in. Four monks sat scratching away with their wooden pens. Silent. Serious. Not to be disturbed. That was three of them, at least. The fourth was, indeed, a bit different.

He had the same absurd haircut as the others, dressed in the same drab brown that might as well have been a rutabaga sack with a rope around the middle. There, the similarities ended. He grinned from ear to ear and nodded as he wrote. While the others remained silent, he hmmed and hmphed and chuckled to himself. I wondered what he was writing.

"Petrus," called Tafi. "Come here. And bring your work." Tafi's voice removed the man's grin immediately. Petrus looked up like a man caught stealing a goblet from a dragon's hoard. "Now."

"I have, um, I believe I was granted leave to work on—"

"Now." Tafi's tone changed in such a subtle way as to make the restraint itself sound dangerous.

Petrus set his pen down. He picked up the angled wooden slat holding his codex and shuffled out to greet us.

"This is Ansgar the Skald. He is a friend, and he brings many of his friends. They are setting up their camp near our grounds as we speak. We will aid them if we can. But first, let me see what you've been doing."

Slowly, Petrus turned around the wooden slat with the pages he'd been working on. The writing was in Latin, of course, still difficult for me to make out those loopy Roman letters. Though unable to read the words very well, I could make out the illustration. It showed two men, one of them bending down towards the other's . . . butt? It looked like he was inspecting the man's ass. The puff of air drawn from the inspection site made it unmistakable what was going on.

"You are working on the *Liber Absurdum* again," said Tafi. "You were to do this only after copying the *Liber Monstrorum*."

"It is finished!" blurted Petrus. One of the other monks in the writing room snorted. "Nearly! I had a sudden thought about this chapter, and I had to write it down before I forgot!"

"And this chapter is?"

Petrus hesitated. "*Bombulum*." Farts.

"Our guest has no need for fart jokes," said Tafi, despite this statement being objectively false. "You may work on this later. First, you will answer his questions, and then you will finish the *Liber Monstrorum*, as you were instructed."

"A book of monstrous busywork," said Petrus. "There is little detail or confusing description on many of those entries. Even if entries like the headless men who have their faces in their chests are to be believed. The other details often make no sense or can be interpreted one way or another as the reader likes. How do I preserve knowledge in writing down things I do not even understand?"

"You will preserve what was written before. You will add an addendum if you wish and explain what you believe to be the problems inherent in the text. The original text must remain unchanged. Perhaps we will find another text that clarifies some of its entries, but that, too, will be copied as it is."

Petrus sighed. "More work, then."

"You are copying a catalog of monsters?" I asked. "Perhaps you might prefer to add our accounts."

"That is true," said Tafi. "On your previous visit here, I remember your lot mentioning Heather-Back. Here, this is a good trade. Tell Petrus what details you recall of the monster, and he will add that to the addendum. And he will be sure to answer your question, about where to find this woman . . . who did you say again?"

"Hervor."

"Hervor," Tafi repeated. "Now, I must see to this new priest, Father Orm. I will leave you both to it."

Petrus waited until Tafi was out of earshot before speaking. "Ansgar the Skald, they call you? Ansgar Work-Doubler, I name you." Another snort came from inside the writing room. Petrus shook his head.

"You would rather be working on a book of farts?" I asked.

"A book of *jokes*. Farts are only one chapter. My brothers do not approve, but they believe only what they are told to believe, and do not understand their own sorcery."

"Are there sorcerous farts then?"

"Do not be daft. As a skald, you ought to know better." He shook his head as he beckoned me in. Putting away the *Liber Absurdum*, he pulled out the *Liber Monstrorum* and opened it somewhere in the middle.

Myriad ink colors stood out like rainbows on the pages. The precision of the handwriting was exquisite. Each letter was perfectly sized and spaced. I looked for different occurrences of the Roman letter "A" and found each one to be exactly identical. This was a thing of beauty. Comparatively, my rune carving looked like I'd done it with my toes.

"Here is a codex of knowledge," said Petrus. "But as you heard, there is no knowing if the knowledge it contains is true or not. What was known, what was inferred, and what was merely guessed at? What was mispronounced, misheard, or misunderstood? I think this is a copy of a copy rather than the original, so who knows what was already lost? And what is lost, I cannot transmit to the reader in my own copy."

"But in many cases, your copy must be accurate."

"Yes, in many cases. And therein lies a form of sorcery, to convey wisdom by traveling through time. Traveling beyond death. Roman sorcery, now ours."

"The Romans must have been powerful."

"Quite. Yet consider the value of this codex. The knowledge it conveys—what can it be used for? Perhaps a few heroes might know of the monsters before fighting them. There is little else might it change, though.

"Now consider *my* codex. To preserve good humor and to create, perhaps many generations later, a bit of laughter. Is that not also sorcery, and even more important to preserve? There are many more who need laughter than who need to read about the headless men with faces in their chests."

Another snort came from the writing room, but Petrus would not ignore this one. He called out loudly over his shoulder. "If your nose is having difficulties, Efraim, perhaps it is from that time yesterday when I saw you thumbing through these pages and giggling. You are *welcome*, my brother, as you are more in need of a bit of laughter than most."

There was no more snorting.

"I need no more convincing," I said. "This *Liber Absurdum* is powerful sorcery. I hope you complete it, and that many copies are made." And no wonder Humor had found his way here.

"Yes. Well!" Petrus straightened and flushed. Perhaps he was not expecting me to support his endeavor or was unused to compliments. "I must complete this other work first. What is it you can tell me of Heather-Back? How did you defeat the thing?"

I described how we'd mistaken the monster's back for an island full of heather. Huld had realized something was wrong, but not what, as she saw all that heather and yet could not smell it. I gave a blow-by-blow account of what happened next as the monster tried to swallow the *Sea Squirrel* but stuck the roof of its mouth on the mast after Ketill hardened the ship. The last part, about giving it wine and a gift always looking to be repaid, required a bit more explanation.

I didn't need to look around to know the other monks were listening. The sounds of scratching pens had stopped.

"So, it owed you a favor?" asked Petrus. "But it did not ask for wine."

"Wine was our most valuable commodity on board. A rare thing."

"What if it did not like the wine? Or . . ."

"The truth is that I don't know. I don't think the 'Steins knew, either, but thought it was a good guess. An even better guess was that such a creature had no wish to be under Ogmund's control. And in not wishing to do his bidding, Heather-Back may have found it more palatable to accept our wine, whether he had a taste for it or not, knowing it would indebt him to us and break Ogmund's control over him.

"Also, Haldor Skullsplitter had made it to the top of his head and was about to bring his axe down. So, it was two gifts, really: Wine, and no axe in the skull. Unfortunately, I lost my own Roman codex in the process. It fell into Heather-Back's mouth when he tipped our ship, but it was not given freely, and so it can't be counted."

"Tragic to lose a codex that way. But still—wine and safety. Does Heather-Back owe your crew two favors, then, and not just the one of not eating your ship?"

I considered this for a moment. "Perhaps it does."

Petrus said he would get as much of our story into his addendum as possible. Most of the entries consisted of brief physical descriptions only, so this one was quite interesting. "Now for your favor. This woman is from Gotland?"

"Maybe from here. Maybe she came here. I think she achieved some word-fame."

"I know of one Hervor in the northern part of the island, a fisherman's wife. I would not call her very famous, though."

I shook my head. "This woman would not be alive any longer. We are looking for her grave mound."

"Varg the Charmer kept a consort named Hervor at one time." Petrus paused to cross himself. "If she has a mound, it is likely somewhere on his old lands, but I doubt there is even a grave marker."

"No, neither of those," I said. "Let me be clearer: I suspect this Hervor was a viking of some renown. At least at one point, before she settled down. But this would have been many decades ago. Do you know of any such person?"

Petrus's jaw dropped to the ground. When he put it back, he shook his head and said, "No, no, no! That is not a good place for people."

"We have sailed to other such places and come back. I think we will go to this one as well."

"But *why?*"

"That will remain our business. I've given information to you as agreed. Where is this place, and why do you hesitate to tell me?"

"Oh, it is close by. And yet far away at the same time. Can I not dissuade you from going to this place?"

"You cannot."

Petrus looked at his feet and shuffled. "It seems I am bound to tell you. By Tafi, by the story you've given. I hope you will hear me and not go, however. And I might even be wrong about the location! She could have her mound somewhere else."

"What location is it, then? And why would we hesitate to go?"

"Because it is *cursed!*" When this statement did not make me go pale with fear, he continued. "One of the Karlso islands, southwest of here, a marshy place. You will know which one, as it looks like the worst island you would ever land on."

"I think we passed that island the last time we were here. So cursed that its ill effects bled across the water to this corner of Gotland?"

He nodded. "It does not affect us, by the grace of the Lord." He crossed himself again. "But I would not set foot on that island. We Gotlanders do not even tend to speak of it."

I thanked Petrus for that information and turned to go. He had his undesirable task, and I had mine. After I had gotten perhaps a dozen paces out of the scriptorium, the sound of fast, awkward footfalls got my attention.

Efraim chased after me, his face red, his breath short, a look of desperation on his face. It took him a moment to compose himself and ask his question, in Latin, of course. "*Where are the brothers?*"

I did not care for this little monk. He had denied me a request on our first visit, and I found his fragile nature unpleasant. Tafi told me Efraim's story about how he had been so mistreated by Varg the Charmer, which explained a lot. It did not make me like the man, though I also did not relish giving him sad news.

"Innstein and Utstein fell in battle, confounding our enemy. They chose to sacrifice themselves so that our crew and many prisoners might get away from an evil place. Their memory lives on, and that will become legend if I have anything to say about it."

Efraim bent over with his hands on his knees as if he might vomit. He'd been fond of those two. They had joked with him and drunk with him. Congratulated him when he translated the codex I'd found into plans for a weapon to use against Varg's battle-cow.

The 'Steins had been an easy pair to be around, and I missed them. I could see how much Efraim missed them even though he had only known them for a brief time. Petrus was right that Efraim was more in need of a little laughter than most. And I had just given him news that the sources of some of his fondest memories were dead.

The little monk mastered himself without vomiting, pushed off his knees, and stood back up. He switched to Norse, which surprised me.

"I did not record the brothers' lives. Now they are gone, and I cannot ask them to tell more of their story. They treated me well—I remember it perfectly. Will you tell me the other parts of their story so that I might write them down, preserve them? I will tell you anything you want. Anything from the codex."

"Hel's dragon, man! Did you not hear? I don't have it anymore. It disappeared down Heather Back's throat. So unless you copied it in secret, it is lost to us."

He shook his head. "I remember it all. I did not speak the entire translation for them, but I read it all myself. And I remember. Every page. Every word."

"That is some good memory—" I stopped at that word, which triggered a memory of my own. "You shared the ale with them. *My* ale, the memory ale Inga brewed!"

That memory ale was the last gift I got before we left Lejre. Inga, the brewmaster, knew her craft well. I never truly believed memory ale could be a thing, a drink that allowed for the precise recollection of everything heard and seen for a time. Who would believe that, given the usual memory-stealing properties of ale? And yet, that's how it had been.

I was still uncertain about the writing of stories. Ketill was right that passing knowledge on orally was the best way. But I saw the earnestness in Efraim's expression. He wished to preserve the memories of my Brothers with the sorcery he knew.

"Come by our camp tonight, and there will be stories of the 'Steins. And of Haldor and Ingolf. And of Hrafn, a warrior you never met. I warn you, though: Be careful if you ever repeat what you hear. If you change the paths their stories took, that will not just be one sin, but many."

Efraim brightened. "Must it be tonight? Not tomorrow?"

"It had better be tonight. Tomorrow we sail to a cursed island, and I won't pretend to know how that will go for us."

# CHAPTER 35

# THE WAKING OF HERVOR

KRAKI KNEW THE ISLAND PETRUS HAD SPOKEN OF. THERE ARE
two islands called Karlso, the Big Island and the Little Island. We were headed
for the Little Island. It was well-known as a place to avoid, just not for why to
avoid it. Petrus' words, "Not a good place for people," echoed in my mind as
the *Sea Squirrel* led the other ships in our approach. The sky darkened as
we did.

What looked like a sandy shore where we could easily beach our ships was
a ruse. We encountered too many rocks breaking the surface of the water to
take the ships in where we first intended. Most of the place was a low-lying
plateau, and we had to sail around to the other side of it to find a safe landing
spot at a low point.

We landed on a shallow beach encroached upon by marshes that suddenly
looked much longer and wider than they had from the sea. Farther in was the
plateau, and trying to see what was up there was like looking into shifting
shadows. The *landvættir* of that island gave me an ill feeling as we disembarked, as if the place drew only malicious spirits.

"You are confident about this?" asked Magnus.

"Confident that this is an ill place, confident that this place is where
Hervor's mound is, or confident that Hervor's mound is where the sword is?"

"All three."

"Yes, yes, and I have hope rather than confidence. I also don't have any better ideas. Do you?"

Magnus muttered something about drinking before voicing what was a good suggestion. "What about the wizard's bird?"

"I have no bird!" Ketill called from too far away for a normal person to have heard Magnus's comment. "But if you mean Humor, he is too enamored of that monk's book of jokes to follow us."

"Too bad," I said. "A scout in the sky would be most useful right now."

One little hut sat on a promontory connected to the larger part of the island at low tide. A small fishing boat was tied up there, while a cooking fire outside the hut roasted an emaciated fish. I left our beached ships and told Magnus I wanted to talk to the hut's residents first.

"Not without me," he said. "There could be more than one in that hut."

"Should we take a few others then?"

He laughed. "That hut can't house more than three, and I'm worth five or six standing on one foot."

An old man dressed in rags stepped out of the hut. "What fools have come to this island? Get out, get out now, before the sun sets!" He fell back into the hut, knocking aside the hanging animal skins that acted as a door.

I wanted to talk to this man. Not from inside his hut, though, so I stayed where I was and called out to him. "The sun will not set for a while, and we intend to explore this place."

"Unwise, insane!" he called back. "You've gone far astray to come here at all. To leave quickly is the best advice I can give you."

"You're here," said Magnus. "Apparently not doing very well for yourself. If it's so bad here, why stay?"

The man stuck his head through the hanging skins. "I am as cursed as the land of this place, unwelcome anywhere else!"

"At least you fit in, then."

"An outlaw?" I asked. "Never mind, that is your business. But how is it you survive here if it is no place for people?"

The man fell to his knees and turned toward the plateau. "I forage at midday. I fish. And I leave them alone. That is enough."

"See any mounds while you were foraging?" asked Magnus.

The man wrapped his face in his hands. "Do not seek it, or you will find it, and then *she* will speak!"

Magnus turned to me and whispered. "If it turns out we are in the wrong place after all, at least things will be interesting."

Maybe not the kind of interesting we were hoping for, but I had to agree as we left the man. He might be crazy and an outlaw, but he was sane enough to finish cooking his fish and take it inside as we took our leave.

We walked back along the edge of the shore to the ships. Styrgrim was waiting for us ahead of everyone else when we returned. Arms crossed, expression a normal amount of angry, it was no surprise. The surprise was that Svipul was standing beside him, almost as if she meant to speak to him. She just shook her head, though.

"What did you find out?" Styrgrim asked.

"We're in the right place," I said. "He's scared out of his wits, if he ever had any. Mostly about when the sun goes down."

Styrgrim nodded. "I am limiting the fires tonight. Don't want them visible to passing ships. Not Svart's, not anyone else. There is something wrong here on this island, and I will minimize our surprises."

"That seems wise," I replied without much thought.

Svipul spoke up at that. "He is not advising you. He is telling you what to do, asserting his dominance. Eventually, he will not need you to legitimize his leadership."

"Good," said Styrgrim.

"Is it?" I asked, meaning the question to both Styrgrim and Svipul.

"What do you mean?" he demanded.

"Why do you think Magnus' jaw is clenched so tight right now?" said Svipul. A quick look at Magnus confirmed she was right.

*Troll-cursed, stupid dominance plays! What am I even supposed to do?*

"It might be time for you to assert yourself," said Svipul.

I took a deep breath. One advantage of being part of a culture where people routinely infer too much meaning in simple statements is that one can make a simple statement, wait for it to be interpreted, and then affirm or deny that interpretation as is convenient.

"Have you ever fought a *draugr*? Because from this man's description, that is what makes the island such a terror."

"This is not the time for stories," he replied. Or in other words, *No, and don't call me stupid.*

"I have fought a *draugr* and won." I paused for effect, hands on my hips. "Which not many can claim."

"I have forgotten killing more things than you have killed in your lifetime or ever will," growled Styrgrim. "And I don't intend to stop now."

"Then on second thought, fires will be a necessity tonight. At least one big one."

"And signal our position to any passing ships?"

"Position our ships around it to screen the light, then."

A wordless growl said he didn't like it.

"We're going up on that plateau," I continued. "You and me, and I'll choose some others. Meanwhile, the army will be cold and concerned until we return. They can probably avoid this *draugr* since they are not going far inland. But in case it does attack them, they won't be able to sever its connection to Midgard, which is the most effective way to fight a monster like that. The only other option is to chop it into pieces and set those pieces on fire."

"I thought you had to cut off the head."

I shrugged. "I prefer to be thorough in such matters." I walked off without waiting for a response.

"Oooo," said Svipul, her tone strong with approval.

Magnus caught up with me. "Did you plan out that whole interaction?"

I shook my head. "When it comes to words, I am better as a free-fighter." I paused a moment, realizing I had taken a bit too much credit. "And my mother gives very good advice."

We rejoined the crew of the *Sea Squirrel*, and I told them to heed Styrgrim's commands about setting up defenses even though he wasn't staying in the camp. Then I called a brief council of the Brotherhood only. I had to go up that plateau, that much was certain. I let those who were most willing to come with me volunteer.

"Moose-boy says he will keep my ship safe enough," said Kraki, who had chosen himself before any choosing had been done.

Vilgrip was eager to go, arguing he was well-practiced at resisting strongly cursed dwarven objects already. "And you might need someone to make an off-hand joke."

Ketill, Nanthild, and Magnus also stepped forward. That was a good group to take. Maybe too many, in fact, but I wasn't willing to tell any of them to stay. I looked to Huld next, who appeared content with staying. "Have you got any advice for this sort of thing?"

"It is not some common mound dweller you face," she said, as if there was such a thing. "It is a legend-turned-mound dweller. Avoid a fight. You're unlikely to win, especially if she wields Tyrfing. Convince her to give you the sword, if you can."

Magnus shrugged. "How did Hervor get the sword when she confronted her father, Angantyr, at his grave mound?"

"Appealed to her birthright and demanded it as inheritance," I said. "And threatened him with curses."

Huld nodded. "Threatening with curses can work well. Praising her is also a consideration."

"Threaten and praise her at the same time?" I asked.

"No one told you this would be easy," she answered.

Ketill shook his head when I asked if he had any better ideas. It was plainly untrue, because he was already carving runes into one of his arrows.

Styrgrim seemed to want nobody else to come, but acceded to Josur's demand. He was a daring one, after all. As their skalds, Bjorn and Jorun also would come with us, and so ten of us readied to go as the first sign of twilight fell.

Caves dotted the plateau wall, all smooth limestone. These would certainly have provided better shelter than the open air, but no way would I have sent our people into them. We ignored the caves and found a slope gentle enough to walk up to the plateau. On that flat slab of moss-covered rock, nothing looked right. The less light we had, the more it looked as though the whole barren place was on fire.

"Any spells you have against fire?" Styrgrim asked the wizard.

"There is no fire," replied Ketill. "Illusions are best broken by disdain."

"We walk through it then?" asked Magnus. "That seems easy enough."

"The doing of it will not be. Boundaries between realms are thin here. The going will be more difficult before we reach our destination."

We advanced, and Ketill was soon proven right. The ground shuddered, and cracks a hand's length appeared before us. Once the rumbling of the earth was done, blue flames roared out of the fissures. I looked to Ketill, hoping for advice.

"Don't step into the cracks," was all the wizard said.

The fires raged as we approached. I tried to ignore them, but had to step back and question my sanity. The heat seemed real enough to me. The others paused and stepped back as well. Was Ketill right, or just guessing? I was in the lead, now that I'd asserted myself. And if I didn't trust the old wizard's wisdom, I didn't trust much of anything.

It still took a massive act of will to tamp down my fear. I stepped into the wall of flame, feeling the heat right up to the point I thought I was cooked. Then I was through it, as if it had been nothing but smoke, and I could not feel the heat anymore. It had been hot right up to the point of touching it, though. Denying the illusion didn't mean shaking my head. It meant embracing fear and vulnerability and moving forward anyway.

The others stepped through, and we walked on in near total darkness. This was truly a between-place, with all the disorientation that would suggest. Voices became too soft or too loud. Mist limited my vision, and I saw flashes of color when I closed my eyes. A mound glowed in the distance. No matter how far we walked, we didn't seem to get any closer to it.

After a while of walking, I got tired of the same mound being the same distance away from us. "I think the distance itself is an illusion."

Ketill looked at it and back to me, considering. "If that's true, we could be at the mound at this very moment and not know it."

"How do we deal with a thing we can't see?" asked Styrgrim.

If Ketill was right about how close we were, we were close enough to be heard. And I had already thought of a verse to get Hervor's attention:

> "Wake up, Hervor!
>     Ansgar awakens you.
> Noble lady,
>     take leave of your mound.
> Hardy folk
>     would hear you speak,
> the kind of heroes
>     you can't ignore."

The mist concentrated and swirled all around us. Soon, it was impossible to see more than ten feet beyond where I stood. Styrgrim's hand went to the hilt of his sword, but Ketill did not seem so disturbed.

The mist retreated, revealing the low mound in front of us. Shadows danced across its low, smooth top, briefly illuminating the skeletons splayed out across it. A door, or three-quarters of a door, sat at the base of the mound. A single step was dug out there, leading to a rotting, wooden lattice.

Something from inside the mound moved the lattice away, revealing a wall of green flames. A figure stepped through the doorway, the flames lighting her from behind. She climbed the single step, lithe for a corpse, and spoke a verse back:

> "The Hel-gate is lowered
>   the graves are unlocked.
> The island's surface
>   is seen all aflame.
> Hurry back to your ships
>   and shun this island.
> This is no place
>   for people like you."

Hervor had been sent off well, armed and armored. Her red cloak embroidered with gold must have been a queenly garment once, now eaten away at the edges with age. Her ring sword and chain shirt had lost less of their luster, but her face had lost quite a bit more. Dried skin was pulled taut along her skull. Hervor spoke well for that amount of desiccation.

Whatever power this woman had behind her was unclear and yet felt in the clearest possible way. She could not move from here, but here, she was all. It was indeed no place for people like us or otherwise. I looked to my Brothers, and all had readied weapons against this dark figure. Ketill kept an arrow nocked but was otherwise unperturbed. Not his first mound-dweller.

"Let us converse like civilized folk," I said, motioning for weapons to be sheathed.

"Do I make you quiver?" came the reply. "It is long since I made a man do so."

"Your skin looks smooth as tree bark," I replied, "and your countenance as sweet as a wounded boar."

Hervor's voice became smoother, sweeter. And all the more grotesque in contrast to her visage. "Who taught you to woo a woman? Come closer, and I will give good advice on that count. For a little manly attention, and I might even let you make off with a bit of the gold you came to steal." I think she meant to wink, but her eyelid was too dried out to move.

"I haven't heard it's advice you offer here," I said, "nor that you had gold.

"I haven't heard you had gold here, and if I seek advice about women, I will seek it elsewhere. Let's be plain, Hervor: We've come for the sword." The sword and her wisdom. This is the woman who wielded Tyrfing with impunity for years. The one wielder it did not slay. How did she do it? That's what I wanted to know, and we wouldn't learn that if we had to chop her into bits and burn them.

Hervor threw back her head and laughed, a terrible, screeching sound that echoed off the dark sky. "You are more specific in your grave robbing than others. But you'll likely be just as disappointed." She turned to wave at the bones atop the mound.

"I think you once wielded Tyrfing. For many years, in fact, until you gave it to your son, Heidrek. Do I speak rightly?"

At the mention of Heidrek's name, Hervor took a step forward and crossed her arms, the dry skin cracking as she did so. I knew how strong a *draugr* could be and didn't wish to get anywhere near her reach. It took all my will to keep my feet where they were planted. It helped a great deal to hear Ketill draw his heavy longbow behind me.

"Perhaps you speak rightly, but you don't speak the whole story. Tell me first what led you to Heidrek, and then to me. Why do you want the sword? Take your time. I have plenty."

I could hear the threat woven into the undertones of her voice. More subtle than 'Do I make you quiver?' What effect would time spent in this place have on us? I couldn't guess, but was sure we should be done as quickly as possible.

"We want the sword to destroy the Brisingamen. I took it from a powerful sorceress and would keep it from her permanently. As for Heidrek, we heard he had gone to Uppsala, where we found his testimony. The sword, and that he killed his brother with it, weighed on him. We guessed he'd brought Tyrfing here, to lay it with you and prevent others from finding it."

"My useless son," she spat. "Even with all that favor, he remained a failure. He was the second-born; he would never rise to the top unless he had an edge. He wanted Tyrfing as much as you do now. More, even, and with just as little knowing what it was. That's always the way with men: Grasping at hot things and then crying at burnt hands!"

I blinked in surprise. "You knew the sword would ruin him?"

"Ruin him?" she shook her head. "It could have given him fame that would never fade! But instead of wielding it with a strong hand, he used those hands to pull at his beard. My one chance for immortality in word-fame failed because of weakness." She spat the last word with such venom that I flinched.

"But . . . surely you passed on your wisdom to him when you gave him the sword? The wisdom that helped you wield it for many years without it destroying you, as it had with its other wielders?"

"Wisdom?" she laughed. "I did have that, yes. When I drew Tyrfing for the first time, I cut down a man who cheated me at *hnefatafl*. It was *good*. It was *right*. And as I could feel the sword's approval of me, I knew I must refuse it. Approval—fah! I am *Hervor!*" Her shout shook the ground, and I took half a step back to right myself. "I seek no approval! Not from my father, the weakling who warned me against it, and not from the sword itself!"

"So you didn't—"

"I kept that bloody weapon in its sheath!" She howled with mad laughter, nearly doubling over.

I looked over at my comrades to be certain they were hearing what I heard. Most winced in surprise. Kraki hefted his bone club, eyes on me, as if I might tell him to swing at any moment. Ketill relaxed, as if he had heard it all before.

Magnus shrugged. *So much for the wisdom!*

"I *did* use that sword, got the better of it right away! I used its reputation rather than letting it use me to do its bidding. I *won!* If only my son had not been such a failure, we could be spoken of as gods now!"

This was not the Hervor of legend, who had bravely taken up the sword from her father's grave mound. Who had wielded the sword but not fallen afoul of its nature. Who had finally put it away and settled down to have a family, spending all her time on her sons.

All her time on her sons. Hel's dragon, she had used them as puppets to further her own word-fame. She'd known that they were fodder years before they were born.

She was no different from Odin.

"So you used its reputation," Styrgrim began, "but you handed it to your son and expected him to do more than use its reputation. You wanted him to wield it and let it kill him before he might even get his own sons."

"If Heidrek had held strong, he could have made our names immortal."

Styrgrim said nothing more. He did not need to, his face curling into a thing I had never seen before. Anger, disappointment, and disapproval, I knew all of those well. But this was new, a thing that pained him. This was disgust. No doubt about it, Styrgrim would cheerfully chop this monster into pieces and burn them.

I did not want to find out the extent of Hervor's power here. "Let loose the sword once more, then. Give it to us, and Midgard will be reminded of you and yours. You may yet live again that way. Not as a half-remembered story, but as one who helped destroy the Brisingamen."

"Yes," Hervor wheezed, her breath heavy. "I would like that! Only my son, coward as he was, had some cursed wit to him. He did come here. He did bring the sword. He even told me all his wretched woes. And then he called down, down into the deeps, and gave it away!"

"Gave it away? To who?"

Hervor snarled, as if reliving the memory. When she spoke again, her voice was as gnarled as a bent tree, and her shout shook the ground again. "To the makers of the thing. To the *dwarves!*" The force of that last word rocked her back as well, and she stumbled, her chest heaving.

We had come all this way, solved so many mysteries. And this was after piecing together that there was a mystery in the first place! To find out that we were on a fool's errand was too much. Could she be lying?

No. The more bodies Tyrfing piled up, the better her story would be remembered. We were not her choice to give the sword to, but she had no one else. She would give us the sword, if only she had it.

"Is our journey ended then?" Magnus sounded as disbelieving as I felt.

Kraki stepped past me. "What dwarves?"

Hervor was still shaking her head, perhaps not even paying attention. She eventually looked up at the half-feral madman, appraising him. He was in swinging distance before I could stop him. Assuming I would try to stop him. Which I would not.

"Answer my question, dead thing, or I'll crush your mound and leave your severed head staring straight up your asshole! What dwarves?"

Hervor's low laughter sounded as though she would fight at first. This crazy old man challenging her, what could he do against the dead? But it was not that, and her laughter increased to pure ecstatic madness.

"You would find them?" she said through the laughter. "You would travel to the Down-Below and take it from them? Bring it back to Midgard?"

"What dwarves?" I knew Kraki and his tone, and this was the last time he would ask.

A great intake of breath into that dry throat, and then Hervor spoke through the broadest grin. "Two came for it. They gave their names to my son before he opened his arm. Dvalin was one, Durin the other."

Kraki turned back to me. "I know them."

"Can you call them as Heidrek did?" I asked.

The old man shook his head. "We are not offering something as Heidrek did. We must go to them. I know a place where they will come, if summoned."

"Use my runestone," said Hervor, her voice cracking with excitement. "Take the Stone Road after them. *Find it!*" Hervor stepped aside, and the flames engulfing the entrance to her mound disappeared.

Ketill's hand clasped my shoulder before I could step forward. "Wait a moment. We must send someone back to tell the others what is happening. They are waiting for us."

Much as I hated traveling the Stone Road, with its grinding sense of drowning in solid rock, I knew I could not stay behind. Nor could it be Kraki, who knew the Down-Below best and was our only chance of finding these dwarves. A great difficulty built in my chest as I wanted my other friends with me but also had a terrible feeling about this journey. Styrgrim would not be dissuaded, and Josur puffed out his chest to show he was no different. Having come this far, no one wanted to go back. I had to make a choice.

Magnus caught my attention with a quick movement of just his eyes toward Jorun. "Uh," he cleared his throat, "the wizard is also an archer, so he fills two roles in case we need them."

Jorun turned on Magnus with an angry stare. "Some of those staying with the ships can shoot."

"Can use a bow, but not nearly so well as you," he said.

Something was between the two, but I had no idea what. All I knew was that my closest advisor had an opinion while I struggled to find one. "Jorun, return to the army and tell them where we're going." I paused for a moment. "I want you with us no less than the others, but someone must go back. You add the most to the defense of the ships, should they come under attack."

Jorun clenched her jaw at that, but nodded. She hugged the wizard, as was her way, punched Magnus in the shoulder, and bounded back the way we'd come.

Kraki was the first one through the grave's door, and the remaining eight of us followed over the chilly threshold.

## CHAPTER 36

# THE KING BELOW

I STEPPED OVER THE THRESHOLD OF THAT GRAVE MOUND AND GOT a nose full of corpse-stink, worse than what I smelled as I passed by Hervor. The hollowed-out mound provided just a few inches of clearance above my head. Broad, soft mushrooms squished beneath my feet as I walked farther in.

The wall to my right curved away, revealing piles of wrought silver and gold inlaid with jewels, rune-carved goblets, and jewelry. These treasures all gleamed despite the lack of any light source I could see. The wall to my left curved in deeper to provide more room. A simple stone altar lay there, surrounded by racks of weapons and shields. All the grave's treasures were untouchable, unless we wanted to challenge the *draugr* directly, and there was no sense in that.

Hervor's runestone was set into an alcove on the far wall from the doorway. No treasures were piled there, but next to it, a man's corpse sat slumped against the wall.

He had been well-dressed in life. His body bore a golden brooch and necklace over his clothes. He'd walked with a fine set of boots, those in slightly better shape than his tunic or cloak, all of which were in far better shape than his rotting face. Here was Heidrek, then, who had found some wisdom, and finally found relief.

Whatever pictographs and runes had been carved into the runestone, whatever story it told, I could not tell. It was already shifting as we

281

approached, reverberating low as it began to open. Not *open* in any conventional Midgardian sense. We just had to step into what looked like shifting stone, and it would take us in. And deposit us . . . somewhere.

"Can we get back this way?" I asked, recalling the difficulty of our return the last time I'd gone into the Down-Below.

"If you have the sword," said Hervor, in her come-hither corpse voice, "I'll hinder you not at all."

"Hinder us one way or another," said Styrgrim, his right hand going to the hilt of his sword, "and I will cut your limbs away and burn them, tie your body upside-down in the earth, and plant an oak tree in your asshole."

Hervor laughed, her cheeks cracking as she grinned. "Would that you had been my husband so many years ago! What a family we—"

I don't know if being dead made it more difficult for Hervor to read social cues, or maybe she hadn't cared about Styrgrim's previous show of disgust. In any case, she had seriously underestimated the violence that man was holding back. Styrgrim grabbed her by the back of her head and drove her face-first into the ground.

"You *niðingr* kinslayer," he growled, grinding his knee into the back of her head. "You don't deserve to spit-shine my wife's shoes!"

Through the dirt, Hervor laughed again. Most of the rest of us, myself included, watched without knowing what to do when Styrgrim began to draw his sword. Nanthild put a gentle hand on his shoulder. He snapped his face up like a madman and froze, eyeing her.

"Nanthild is right," said Magnus. "We don't have time for this."

Styrgrim bared his teeth as he read Nanthild's expression. After a moment, he let his sword fall back into its sheath and let up on Hervor.

"Here is a real shieldmaiden, you wretch," he spat. "Look here, at your better." Difficult to tell in the low light of that tomb, but I have no doubt that Nanthild blushed.

"Look quickly," said Kraki, motioning for us to enter the narrow gap in the runestone. "Then, follow me."

Hervor's high-pitched chuckling continued, muffled less by the dirt as she drew her face up. I tried to ignore her as I stepped into the runestone after Kraki, but I was leaving one unsettling scene for another. Cold stone surrounded me, pushing me forward and down. I closed my eyes, hoping this would lessen the unnerving feeling that those deep *landvættir* could wind that rock in and crush me if they chose to.

The stink of rotting death lessened and was replaced with the familiar air of a limestone cave, full of dripping stalactites. I reached forward slowly and found the stone did not resist my movement. After some minutes, my hands felt open air, and I stepped out from a solid rock wall onto a plateau-like open area worn smooth by centuries (or more?) of foot traffic.

A few crystals glowed dimly from the high ceiling and bathed the area in soft light. Kraki was already there, waiting. The others came through the same wall I had, one or two at a time.

Magnus shook himself off. "The Stone Road seems to have improved. Does that mean it has put us close to these dwarves?"

"Closer than we would otherwise be, but first we must walk a crossroads," said Kraki. "That will bring us to Sindri's hall, and there we can summon Dvalin and Durin."

"Sindri is a lord here?" I asked.

"Sindri is king." Kraki's tone did not normally convey warmth, but in this case, it was even less so. I hoped this king would receive us well.

The plateau ended a stone's throw from where we'd come through. There began a great cavern with more possible paths than we had people to try. The pathways all shot out, going up and down, left and right. Some crossed over and under others, and ended up who knew where. Below the maze of paths, the canyon yawned as if it had no bottom. Given where we were, having no bottom seemed like a real possibility.

"And you know your way through all this?" I asked.

"It is not so difficult," said Kraki.

We followed him along those paths that wound and twisted around and over and under one another. Every time I thought we were headed one way, the paths seemed to change. It made me anxious, and being anxious, I began to ask questions. "It seems unexpected to me that Finnr would call anyone king. Will he be there?"

"That's not his name in this place," said Kraki. "Finnr is a name he took in Midgard. It means 'wanderer,' which he is. He will not stay in any one place long, especially as he intends to move the tribes against our enemies. Sindri will be sitting on his throne, a reliable spot."

I eyed the lightless bottom from our path. "We seem far from any throne."

"Crossroads are like your forests," he responded, which made it sound like *your* meant *humans*. "We are here to be seen as much as guided. It is a longer road than necessary, to show peaceful intent. But see there? Even now it comes to an end." I looked up to see that our pathway led down into another large, flat area. Ahead was a wide tunnel entrance. Had I failed to see it, or had it changed? "The next tunnel will take us to Undanborg."

I shook my head. "Undanborg? You can't be serious." The word literally meant *under-town*. But to dwarves, it wouldn't be under anything. It was also about the most boring name I could think of for such a place.

"It is not the name we use. That is the Midgard-name."

Dwarves sounded like an insular bunch, and that was saying something coming from any Northerner. To us, the next family over might as well have been a different race with tentacles instead of arms, given how narrow loyalty and consideration sometimes went.

I asked more questions as we walked through the tunnel. Kraki did not become annoyed with these, so I asked more. Whether it was my increased status or just that he preferred talking about dwarves to talking about people, I couldn't guess. Yes, I could. I think it was the latter.

Kraki described how it had been no easy thing for him to be accepted into dwarven society. I didn't fully understand him on that walk. I would need to reconsider my definitions of "accepted" and "society" just to begin to understand. And he didn't tell me his whole story at the time.

Finnr had offered passage from Midgard when Kraki was between boyhood and manhood. He didn't say what led to that, but gave plentiful details of what came after. When they arrived, the dwarves did not want him. He was a Midgarder, and most said he should go back to where he came from.

Finnr had argued that he had walked Midgard plenty, and that if a dwarf was able to stand in the sun, should he choose to, a man should be able to walk among the stone of Nidavellir. It was a hard argument, and the first indication Kraki had of Finnr's station.

"That dwarf wouldn't tell you," said the old cook, "but he is a famous one. I couldn't understand him at the time—he knew my language, somehow, or just enough of it. I did not know his language at the time, but that didn't matter. I could see how he spoke to that king. He said a lot, responded a lot. None of it was a request."

I would not have guessed Finnr's elevated status down here. As a wanderer, Finnr seemed like he belonged nowhere. It seemed, instead, that he belonged exactly where he was, wherever that was, and there was no one going to tell him otherwise.

"The dwarves have no laws," Kraki continued. "Only powerful customs. If they give us hospitality, there will be no breaking it. It was the same when I came to live with them. I worked hard at the forges to find my place, but my place was swinging weapons rather than making them."

"They were under attack?" I asked.

"They are always under attack. They have wealth unparalleled for their workings of metal and gems. Many a troll has coveted that. Some deep *jǫtnar*, even." He rubbed the head of his bone club as if stroking a memory.

"So, you fought for them and gained a measure of acceptance?" Kraki made a face, and I could tell something was wrong. I rephrased. "I mean, you fought *with* them. As one of them."

"Aye."

"That's not unlike Midgard," I said. "It's hard to be accepted as an outsider. But if you show sufficient value somehow, then people are more likely to respect the ways you don't conform than criticize them."

*Oh shit, did I just describe Odin in a way I could also describe myself?*

"Some accept more readily than others." The hoarseness in his voice made me stop asking questions after that.

We came to an archway carved into the stone. Four abreast could walk through it easily, and it was taller than needed even for humans from Midgard. White and purple crystals lit the area with their soft glow. In that glow, two guards stood sentinel. They wore no armor, only capes and cowls thrown back over loose shirts and pants, and held short spears. The dwarves dressed like we did, it seemed.

"Who's this, then?" one asked the other.

"Enemies if we're unlucky—which we always are," said the other dwarf.

"We are no enemies," said Kraki, in a less friendly tone than I expected. "Here is Fundinn Shinsplinter, if your eyes are so poor. I've brought friends in plenty, but patience not at all. Make way." He patted the weapon at his hip.

The dwarves exchanged wide-eyed looks and swallowed hard. They made way for us to pass immediately, and with apology.

"Please pardon us," said the first.

"I will run to the hall to announce your arrival!" said the other.

We passed through the archway and into a new cavernous area. Everything had to be cavernous underground, it seemed, otherwise it would be too closed-in, but this hardly describes the scene. We could see Undanborg from there, lit by crystals the size of buildings on either side. Smaller crystals dotted the landscape, revealing many paths to the center.

This was no cavern. It was a fertile valley underground.

The buildings I spied were from one to three stories—impossibly high, I thought. Then I realized nothing had been built in the sense I understood it. It had all been hewn into the existing stone. One "building" stood taller and broader than the others, and that is what we headed for.

As for the number of dwarves in the city, I couldn't guess. We saw a few dozen on our way to the hall. They were as varied as the humans of Midgard. Some were darker-skinned and haired or lighter. Few of the dwarves I would call tall, but most were not much shorter than Magnus. Their proportions, however, marked them as not human.

Some had scraggle-heads of hair and looked half feral. Others were plump and waddly, with well-fitting clothes. The contrast between thin arms and big bellies like Finnr's was a consistent feature.

As we neared the central building, it became clear it was the Down-Below equivalent of a mead hall. It was much longer than it was tall, with balconies running along the sides of the interior.

No one asked us to lay down our weapons when we approached the entrance to the great hall. Reliant on powerful customs? Perhaps. Or perhaps they knew how much better their weapons were than ours, should it come down to that. The dwarves had made weapons for the gods, after all.

A few of the hall's guests looked on, feigning only mild curiosity at us humans. Some of them nodded or even bowed as Kraki passed by. He returned those gestures with terse nods only, moving at a fast walk.

Firelight from torch sconces lit rich carvings up and down stone pillars along the walls, all painted or gilded. The hearth fire was along one side of the wall on our left rather than centralized, and I could smell barley toasting over it. Smoke holes ventilated the fire, which was high-ceilinged despite there being no need to keep out rain or snow.

The floor was uneven, inlaid with stones of many colors and hues, and had no discernible pattern. It looked as if many individuals had contributed their own singular pieces to the base of the hall. Though not uniform in height or color, they were all worn smooth.

A stone chair sat on a dais at the far end of the hall. The seat itself was plain and unadorned, and clearly too large for its occupant. A single dwarf sat in the middle of the chair. A forge hammer rested awkwardly in a loop hanging from his belt. The chair was too wide for him to lean an elbow on either armrest. He sat cross-armed, his legs not quite long enough to reach the step the chair sat on, and stared at the man boldly striding forward.

Kraki stopped about twenty paces from the king, all of us behind him. "Sindri."

"Fundinn," answered a low rumble from beneath inches of thick facial hair.

"I would speak with Dvalin and Durin."

Sindri nodded and gestured at one of the other dwarves. Would it be that easy? "It seems like only yesterday that you found your desire to rejoin the Up-Above."

"That was thirty years ago."

"As I said. Like yesterday."

I coughed out of nervousness. I was unsure how this was going, knowing what little I did about dwarf culture. They appeared in stories once in a while, usually as smiths, shape-changers, brewers, or all of those. As advanced as their smithing, magic, and brewing were, I had never heard any indication of a civilization. Even gods only happened upon them after searching at length, or by chance.

Yet here was their king in his hall. Sitting in a high seat that was far too big for him. Was it intended for a race more ancient? Did dwarves used to grow much bigger? Why was it unadorned when the rest of the structure spoke of artistry and meaningful composition? Questions I had no answers for, which meant I knew very little about how this might go.

After an awkward pause, Sindri continued. "Is it you or your guests who wish to speak to them?"

"Friends, not guests."

"Friends make for good guests."

"They are more than mere guests and won't be limited as such. And they came through a gate that was no easy thing."

"Oh?" Sindri turned his head to crack his neck. It sounded like a small rock shattering. He sat up, an interested expression blooming on his face. "I would hear more of this gate."

"I will let our skald do that, since it was opened by his influence."

"Hello," I said, immediately regretting it. This was not a culture with many niceties, even compared to my own. "I am Ansgar."

"What of the gate?" demanded Sindri. Little as I could tell about dwarven culture, I could tell the king was already annoyed.

"It was a runestone in the grave mound of Hervor the Shieldmaiden." The shuffling of feet all around us made me realize we had earned some more attention. I resisted the urge to look around and tried to hold Sindri's gaze.

"What of the mound dweller?" asked Sindri.

"She let us pass."

"Why?" he demanded, his voice hardening and drawing out the question.

Should I declare our purpose? Hold back as much as possible? *Should have asked on the way*, I thought. "Two dwarves received a thing from her grave mound, and she wishes us to bring it back to Midgard."

"And you do the bidding of dead things?"

"No!" Perhaps this was not like Athils' court, where we had to conceal our true intent. Or if it was, we were about to fail. Well, if I was supposed to keep our intent secret, someone should have told me. "Hervor would see the sword Tyrfing returned to Midgard. She believes it will bring her word-fame, though she is long dead. It is our intent to find Tyrfing, but not for her. We wish to use it to destroy the Brisingamen."

Sindri hopped off the high seat, his eyes wide. A difficult dwarf to surprise, but I'd named two dwarf-crafted items in two breaths, one we had, and one we needed. Shuffling toward us, he continued in a tone meant for everyone in the hall to hear. "That sword has returned to our realm. It is not a thing meant for Midgard. Never was, and never should have been, but for a thief long ago." The colors of the crystals lighting the walls changed as he spoke. Dimmer, redder. "It is arrogant enough to ask for the sword. Yet you also say you would destroy the Brisingamen, a thing of pride. Why?"

"I won't allow our enemy to have it again. Nor any sorcerer who might use it for similar purposes. I've felt its draw. It is more a user of the wearer than used by the wearer."

"Yet the thing you ask for, that is even more true for. Hmph!" He threw up his hands, now only a few feet from me. "What wisdom you younglings think to have! A score of years on you, and an object you've never felt the power of, let alone seen, and you are certain yours is the wisest counsel." He walked back to his high seat, shaking his head.

"Let my father speak his counsel," said Kraki, which turned a few heads, including mine.

Sindri took his time gathering his robes and plopping back down onto his seat. Kraki sneered at the king, who stared back with narrow eyes. "The last time I let Finnr speak so freely, there was a filthy human stinking up my hall for sixty years." *Some accept more readily than others*, Kraki had said. Here was one who was not so accepting, and he was the king.

And somehow, it is quite a bit easier to get under the skin of a king than of anyone else.

"So, two days." A few quizzical looks came my way, so I clarified. "You said thirty years was like yesterday, so sixty years with a filthy human must have been a mere two days to you. That seems like no great inconvenience." I paused for effect. "Unless the hospitality of your hall is puddle-deep."

Sindri ground his teeth. Plainly, he did not want us there, yet he could not deny us, given Kraki's presence and my challenge. I could feel his calculations, considering different measures of giving in and weighing them against the various amounts of time he would have to suffer our presence.

"It is late," he said after a long consideration. "Bring them ale. And then find them the best rocks to sleep on. We will host them for the night while we await Dvalin and Durin. And then our guests will accept my decision."

"Agreed," said Kraki.

"Agreed," echoed a familiar voice from behind us.

I turned but could not see at first. Many dwarves had entered behind us, and the throng blocked the entrance to the hall. Feet shuffled and that throng parted, and when it did, Finnr stood in the middle of them.

"Father," Kraki said with the barest nod.

"Welcome home, my son," Finnr said with the widest grin. "It is well you've brought such fine people!"

# CHAPTER 37

# DENIAL OF DESTINY

THE DWARVES KNEW HOW TO BREW, AND THE QUALITY OF THEIR ale has never been matched in Midgard. How did they get so much barley when they lived underground? One of the many questions I couldn't even guess at. Dwarves mostly look like humans, but they are closer to *landvættir*. They live on until killed or turned to stone, and it seemed to me that was a bigger mystery than "Where did they get the barley from?"

What they did with that barley was one secret they willingly shared: They roasted it just a bit until it turned in color and quality, and they knew the right amounts of roasted and not roasted to add to their brews. The result was a brown ale, rich with flavors I didn't even have words for.

We were shown to a table all to ourselves. Long and tall as the hall was, it was also much wider than normal and had room for many tables, all made of stone, laid perpendicular to the hall's length. The ale arrived soon after we sat, and other dwarves laid out smoked meats for us only minutes after that. Brown ale and smoked meats: The greatest combination of things the world has ever seen or is ever likely to. I may have overdone it on the consumption. And that was just in the first five minutes. It was only after I slowed down that I got involved in the conversation.

"You are different than I remember," Finnr told me. He'd taken a seat next to Nanthild after she'd made room for him. I belched loudly as I sat across the table from the two of them. I had to hold my chest, I'd eaten so fast. "Perhaps some things remain the same," he added.

"How am I different to you?"

Finnr fixed me with a look as if he wasn't sure he wanted to answer or how, and I noticed Styrgrim take interest in our conversation out of the corner of my eye. The dwarf thought for another few seconds and said simply, "Your beard is in." A better compliment would be hard to imagine, and I beamed. "Keep your head out of the quartz. This is no place to let your guard down."

"The hospitality is not genuine?" asked Styrgrim.

"It is more genuine than you can conceive. You'll be safe. You'll be fed. That does not mean you'll get what you want, or that Sindri will forget your manners here. Dwarves have long memories."

"But you can advise us!" said Magnus.

Finnr shook his head. "What I've heard so far raises only more questions. Even if I do decide to help you obtain Tyrfing, I wonder if it is the right thing."

"Of all the lore I know, I could not offer another idea how to destroy the necklace," said Ketill. "Do you know a different way?"

"Not at all."

The mood turned dour following Finnr's tone. As happy as we were to see him and he us, I think he knew this was a quest unlikely to get any good result. He wanted to know about our exploits that had led us to this point. I told him everything I could think of, with Magnus interrupting frequently to add dramatic details.

Finnr nodded grimly at the news of losing so much in that tower. Two betrayals and three deaths. And what we found there on our return.

"So now you know just about everything we could tell you," I said. "What have you been doing since you left us?"

Finnr sighed like a small mountain taking a breath. We'd brought some familiar people, but also people he didn't know. I hadn't considered the slow-moving nature of dwarves at the time and only based my question on what I knew of our friend. But looking back, Finnr must have seen these new people, Styrgrim, Bjorn, and Josur, and wondered how much he should say in front of them.

"Things and such."

He might've been a fast-moving dwarf, but he was still a dwarf. Kraki, at least, knew what was going on. "These are friends as good as any."

Finnr cocked his head as if to swallow something bitter, but at least he began to talk. "It was no easy thing to decide where to begin, even. Mind you, I know I don't have the whole of any story. I dropped in on a few old friends first, remembering my earlier mistake of moving too fast all by myself. My friends had heard a few things. Said there had been many an offer lately, made by a tall man with a shock of black hair covering his face. A wizard, no doubt. He called himself Grim Aegir."

"That is Ogmund's son, Svart," said Styrgrim. "What sort of offers?"

"I'm getting there. Offers varied, but all involved generous amounts of gold for weapons or armor. Not just good items, but the stuff of legend, like we used to make. Pfah! As if we need more gold."

"How many took the offers?" Styrgrim asked.

Finnr shook his head. "None I found. I even visited our old rivals, the sons of Ivaldi. They were no more impressed than I was. I slunk around a bit deeper after that. Even the greediest little shits, the ones who would've gladly traded some beautiful elf-maiden for their dancing daggers, did not like the feel of this Grim Aegir. So I got good hospitality and good aid when I asked for it. And I spent some time watching and listening.

"Just whispers at first. A mention of the man or his master, a promise of great power. Vague things. Then, more specific things. Things that goblins and ogres and the deep *jotnar* covet. The flesh of sacrifices in exchange for favors. Payments made in the blood of the unwilling. That's what Grim Aegir offered them.

"He did make his real name known, eventually. Had to speak with his father's voice, a voice they all knew. There was a great gathering last summer. Many tribes from the deep places sent someone to attend. I was there, too, hidden away, but I heard that voice. The promise of things to come later for their service now. Elevation of those things from the Down-Below in the Up-Above. Worship of them in place of gods or family spirits. A new way of things. If only they'd swear loyalty and fight for him."

"The way things are going with Ogmund," said Styrgrim, "it seems like he will make the whole of Midgard a bunch of trolls, or men subservient to them."

"That's the idea."

Long faces took long drinks and considered this bleak prospect. What was left of the crews had gone from seeking word-fame and rich rewards to just word-fame or revenge. This news sounded like our lowered expectations were now greatly optimistic; the best we might expect out of victory was that Midgard didn't burn.

"If it matters, he got only a little support," Finnr continued. "Most such trolls have little ambition for those sorts of changes. They were very much in favor, don't mistake that, but it's another matter for them to actually do anything."

"But some agreed?" asked Magnus.

"Some, I am certain. And more than that would happily do away with us dwarves. We are likely to be attacked at some point."

"We fought an army of monsters before," said Magnus as he stretched out. "We can do it again."

"If I recall that fight well, and I do, it was a rather close thing. If that fight comes to Midgard again, it will be harder still."

"Destroying the Brisingamen is more important than ever, then," I said. "We can't let Alfhild get it back."

Finnr shook his head. "And we can risk putting Tyrfing into play? The sword is more dangerous than the torc by far, and you'd have it out in the open! Perhaps you'd win a battle or two with it. What next after it turns on the one wielding it, and the enemy picks it up?"

"We need it for only one task."

"Two tasks," added Styrgrim. "I will kill Ogmund with it."

"Ha!" laughed the dwarf in my face. "You think to use the weapon instead of it using you? That has never been its way. Tell me about this first use, though—who is it to be sacrificed when you draw the blade from its sheath? You know it will require a life before it is resheathed, and that thing will not wait long before it compels a killing. Who will it be, then?"

"It is not practical to use it that way," said Styrgrim. "We will take the sword back to Midgard, where enemies are plentiful, and destroy the torc while the sword is still bloody. Then I will use it to kill Ogmund. It is folly to leave such a weapon in the Down-Below when I could use it against your own enemies."

"So true," said Finnr. "All you need to do is let it kill you and curse—"

"What would you know of our need?" interrupted Styrgrim. "Forge us something else to kill Ogmund, then. A half-giant broke every bone in that sorcerer's cursed body, and he still swam away. He has an army of Bjarmians at his back, more sorcerers behind him than we may even know of, and a winged dragon. Now it seems he commands monsters from the Down-Below, as well. I will have that sword to fight him with."

The dwarf and the Bear stared hard at each other without blinking. A foolish contest of no real consequence, yet neither would look away. I sat there not knowing what to say next. Finnr was right. Styrgrim was right. What way through did we have?

"What would I know of it?" asked Finnr after a long time. He stood with white knuckles grinding into the granite table. "I know more of it than I wish to recall."

Nanthild got everyone's attention when she slammed her own fists onto the table. There was no crunch of the rock beneath. Strong as she was, she was still flesh and bone and not a stone-child like a dwarf. It was the suddenness of it, the out-of-character-ness. She stood with her chest heaving, eyes wide, nostrils flaring. She pointed to her own sword and then pointed to herself.

"No." Styrgrim's voice was flat.

"She means to wield Tyrfing herself, it seems," said Finnr. "Perhaps you have competition. Assuming you can find it at all, which is unlikely."

"You will not speak for us?" said Kraki.

"I judge it wisest not to."

Kraki nodded grimly. "We sailed a long way to get here. Some of our Brothers fell to find this sword."

"My son, you do not know what you ask for."

Now it was Kraki's turn to stand. He rose slowly, having waited with utmost patience for his time to talk. "You fought alongside us, and so I think you ought to know better. These few," Kraki pointed at Styrgrim, Bjorn, and Josur, "they might not be our Brothers or our crew, but they are with us in this. And the others you know very well. We will see this thing to the end."

"To *your* ends? Because that is all but guaranteed."

"Bring a *vǫlva* to speak such a prophecy, and we will still continue on. There are no cowards here to run from fate. We will run toward it."

Finnr shook his shaggy head. "You've had all the counsel I have to offer. If you won't listen to that, then at least listen to others. My other sons are summoned and will be here tomorrow. Listen to them before you decide. Assuming Sindri is even moved by your offer, which is unlikely."

"Your other sons?" I asked.

"Dvalin and Durin, the ones you came to speak to. I told you I knew more of the sword than I wished to recall. You can hear the story from them, since they are the ones who forged Tyrfing in the first place."

C H A P T E R  3 8

# S Y M P A T H Y  F O R  T H E  E V I L  W O R K E R

I THOUGHT SINDRI HAD BEEN JOKING WHEN HE SAID WE WOULD get rocks to sleep on, but that's exactly what he offered. The sides of the hall were strewn with large stones sporting flat(ish) surfaces. When I indicated maybe the ground would be more comfortable, Finnr shook his head.

I lay on the cold rock wondering how much I would shiver through the night, but the feeling passed within minutes. The rock warmed up and emanated an oddly comforting feeling. I fell asleep feeling safe, the hospitality of the dwarves as ironclad as any oath.

Secure as that hospitality was, it could not keep me from dreaming of a most insecure host, one I wouldn't want to turn my back on.

I opened my eyes to a bright silver ceiling. I kept still, breathing silently, taking stock. Yes, I was dreaming, but it was the sort of dream that felt very real—like my *hugr* had left my body to visit another place. This was not Valholl, as that place was roofed with shields. But brightly polished silver for a roof? There was only one such place like it in the lore I knew.

I was in Valaskjalf, Odin's other hall in Asgard. Not as well known as Valholl, Odin would sit in his high seat here and look out on what was happening in Midgard. I sat up next to the central hearth. The hall was far smaller than the others I'd visit in Midgard. Turning around, I saw the only table in the whole place in front of the high seat.

The table's lone occupant looked at me with his one eye and took a deep

296

drink from his horn, sloshing inky-red wine down his long, silver beard. "'If you show sufficient value somehow, then people are more likely to respect the ways you don't conform than criticize them.'" Odin might be wise and cunning, but he did a poor job of imitating my voice.

"Not sitting in your high seat?" I asked.

He shook his head as he took another deep swallow of wine. "It is not the time for me to know things. I think it is time that *you* know things." He rose from his seat, grinning. And a bit drunk.

"I know you betrayed Styrgrim, who gave you nothing but worship. Not your first evil deed, either. What did you call us? Pieces on a *hnefatafl* board?"

"Your meaning isn't so far off the mark. Saying it as if you want weregild for an injury, though—that's not the sort of thing that makes a man's beard grow."

"You would prefer we all accept ill treatment from you without complaint." I stood up and shook myself off. I was fully dressed but unarmed. "In your position, that's not the sort of thing a *drengr* demands."

Odin gestured as he walked toward me. "I defy your idea of a *drengr*. Just as I defy all other norms, expectations, and mores." He leaned down to speak the next words directly into my face. "Isn't that very like you, after all?"

Ymir's bones, his breath stank. "We might be alike in that way, but not in other, more important, ways."

He stood up and threw his head back with a throaty laugh. "Know your own self, do you? Tell me then, do you want the sword or not?"

I was confused. "Of course I want the sword."

"Nooooo . . ." He poked at my chest with a single finger, and it felt like being stabbed each time. "You want the sword to do you a single good turn, and then you want to be rid of it." He took another sip and examined his drinking horn. "Which is something like wanting to drink a lot of wine but not wanting to be drunk. Don't think you can fool me—I saw your face as the dwarf argued against finding it. You are afraid of it."

"Should I be?"

"Yes." He turned away and walked toward the high seat. "But come along now, that's no reason to abandon your quest. Perhaps if you see a thing, you will rid yourself of that cursed ambivalence." He gestured toward the high seat. He did it casually, as if offering a weary friend a place to sit.

I knew better. Here is where Odin sat when he wanted to see and hear things happening in Midgard. And he wouldn't offer it to me, even temporarily, if he didn't intend me to see something that would benefit him. I stood my ground.

"Many a mortal would pay dearly to sit here, even briefly. A bold man would not hesitate."

"I don't trust you."

"Trust has nothing to do with it." His tone changed from light and friendly to low and gravelly. "The greater game is played on a board too big for you to see from your tiny perch. You either want to see more of it, or you want to look away. Pity if you've turned into one of the latter sort."

My jaw tightened. "What is it you intend to show me?"

"Some of the world you won't see otherwise. Now my patience wears thin. Sit or don't, but you will not get another chance." I had gotten myself into a lot of danger by taking such chances. I had also found my way out by doing the same. It was no time to hesitate.

So, I sat.

Stories told about how Odin could see and hear things from this high seat and instantly understand them. None of the stories described how that worked. Did he close his eyes and see visions? Did scenes from Midgard play out on the floor of the hall like phantoms?

I closed my eyes and nothing happened, opened them and saw only the hall. Then I looked up at that silver ceiling, polished bright. Only it wasn't silver anymore. On that ceiling, I saw a fleet of ships on wine-dark seas. Lightning flashing in the sky. White breakers rocking the ships. An army on the move. A big one.

At the rear of the fleet was one nasty-looking ship. Long even for a warship, I only saw its sail at first because the wood that had made it was black as night. Decay and shadow coated its strakes rather than tar or paint. A storm followed in its wake. Despite the seas tossing other craft about, this one floated undisturbed.

A figure sat in her own high seat at that ship's aft. I knew her before I could make out the claw marks on her cheek. This was Alfhild's ship, her army.

"Where are they going?" I asked, but I knew the answer before I'd finished speaking. Alfhild's army was headed for Hrolf Kraki on Sjaelland.

"It will be difficult to beat her this time," said Odin. "You need an edge."

"Hrolf Kraki has been mustering the Danes for some time."

"He has many on Sjaelland, of course, but not all. The Danes are on

Jutland. On Fjon. How many ships do you think would survive such a storm, sailing to Lejre?"

I shook my head, but I knew he was right. It was more than just sight and sound Valaskjalf conveyed, but understanding. Alfhild would attack Hrolf and prevent aid from reaching him. With him deposed, she would take the title of queen. She would demand loyalty from the Danish jarls, and those who did not swear it would be put down and replaced. Those who did swear it would be humored for a while. Then they would be found lacking in some way and replaced with god-children loyal to her. Or just destroyed, if their lands were not strategically important.

"We need to sail to his aid. We can land in the south of Sjaelland, away from the storm, and come to Lejre on foot."

Without a word, the image shifted to come down to sea level, flying across the water at an impossible speed. It approached the coast of Sjaelland. It went around the island, showing me ship after ship.

"They are surrounded. That army must outnumber us ten to one." I wasn't sure if I was saying it to Odin or just to myself.

"Is that hesitation I hear?"

I shook my head, trying to look for something I could use. An edge, as he'd said. Alfhild was bad at both strategy and tactics. I already knew that, though, so I looked deeper, focused my will on finding something unseen.

The vision on Valaskjalf's silver roof plunged into the water, and I knew I risked looking too deep. What I saw were flashes of scenes, all of them brief and confusing, until I heard a verse from Valborg's prophecy, the one I had followed her into the realm of the dead to hear.

*I see a winter,*
   *but not of snow,*
*when hospitality*
   *turns hostile*
*and ancient lore is*
   *likened as useless.*
*Inspired fables*
   *are fully forgotten.*

The images became more distinct. Limbs being cooked and consumed, Ulf awarded fine robes and ornate gold chains, the sun casting a ghastly pale light over Midgard. Sycophants replaced skalds as the gods became hollow memories of their old selves.

I had gone deeper than I'd intended, and the understanding came: This was possible future for Midgard, maybe a likely one. The burden of struggling against that future fell on Odin's shoulders. He would need to make terrible choices to avoid it.

Had his Spear of the Gods plan not been so capricious after all?

I pushed myself up from the seat, and the images on the ceiling faded. Fatigue and nausea ran through me, and I fought to catch my breath. Sitting in that seat was no easy thing. I ran my fingers through my hair as if that might wash some of the lingering effects away.

"Now you understand a little more. You should remember, though, the numbers were greatly against Angantyr, as well. The Third, I mean."

"Angantyr the Third is a fiction," I said, still panting. "I think you know that better than most."

"I know everything better than most. But the story tells a truth by telling a lie: That sword will cut down legions in the right hands. Whether it did so in the hands of someone named Angantyr, and whether those legions were Huns, whether it was in the past or the future," he shrugged, "what does any of that matter?"

"We don't need to cut down legions if we cut down Alfhild." My voice rasped, and I cleared my throat.

Odin handed me his drinking horn. "Getting near her will not be easy. She is strong with the sea, and likely to stay on her ship."

"How do we attack her, then?"

"Do you?"

I grasped the horn, but his answer gave me pause. "If we don't attack her, it will be very difficult to kill her."

"You have a thing already in your possession that would make her come to you." He paused to stroke his beard and grinned. "You have the power to choose the battlefield, set the trap. Will you use it?"

I drank the wine, just a single swallow. The unplaceable fruity aromas hit my parched throat with some relief. I tipped the horn further for more, and the flavor changed. As more of the drink hit my tongue, I realized it was not wine, but blood.

My eyes widened as I stared into the abyss of that horn, and I lost myself there.

## CHAPTER 39

# A WISE MAN'S HEART IS OFTEN STABBED

I WOKE FROM THAT DREAM TIRED IN BODY AND TIRED OF GODS and their machinations. The rock beneath me was still warm. Steady, reliable, comforting. So much for gods—I would rather have a good rock. That, and a friend I could confide in.

Magnus lay on his own rock nearby. He opened one eye at my approach. Not up early, just a very light sleeper, and the hall was still quiet but for the distant shuffling of a few dwarves going about their tasks. He nodded when I told him Odin had called me to Asgard the same way another man might nod at hearing "I had indigestion again last night."

We sat with our backs against Magnus' rock and spoke in whispers. "This felt like less of a dream and more of direct advice."

"Other than wine turning into blood, maybe. If Odin is giving you advice, though, that means he wants something from you. What is it?"

"To make sure we didn't turn away from the sword. I'm certain he wants to see it back in Midgard. He wants an epic battle for the ages, and it won't be very epic if we're easily overcome."

"He wants to help us just enough so that we give a good accounting of ourselves before we die?"

"I think so."

He shrugged. "That's not a bad fate at all!"

I shook my head, not in acceptance but in defiance. "He knows he won't

301

survive *Ragnarøk*, but he still gathers the *einherjar* to deny his enemies victory. And, I think, to be remembered and prevent certain ideas from passing out of the world. He means us to do that on a smaller scale, but how can he guarantee remembrance? Odin has taken for granted our fates will play out exactly as he interprets them, but he is not a Norn."

"So then . . . we might even survive!" Magnus brought up that prophesies were always short on details and could never cover everything. He suggested that next time I found myself in some hall in Asgard, I should piss into the nearest wine barrel like a *brunnmigi* and ask if that had been prophesied.

I wished I'd had that idea while I was still in Odin's hall.

By the end of our conversation, some of the tables had filled and the sounds of eating and low conversation had begun to warm the hall. We returned to the same table we'd sat at the night before and joined Kraki, Ketill, and Finnr there. Sindri nodded at us from his high seat as his only greeting. His was hardly the only complicated dynamic to navigate.

"The rock was more comfortable than I thought it would be," I said to Finnr, hoping to ease back into conversation.

"I will not support you getting the sword today any more than yesterday," replied the dwarf.

Kraki changed the subject, and I'd never heard the old man be so social. He was particularly interested in the sons of Ivaldi, who he knew of but had never met. They were another tribe of dwarves, like Swedes to Norsemen. I wondered if the sons of Ivaldi spoke with heavy accents.

Which led me to a more obvious question that I had glossed over completely. "Wait a moment—why are all the dwarves speaking Norse? What about the language of the Down-Below?"

"There is no such thing," replied Finnr. "If you mean the language you learned a bit of when you parleyed with Harbard and his little shits, that is just the old language before Norse. We know it, but we use the new language most of the time. Harbard and his ilk hate change, so they refuse to speak it, even if they understand it. Dwarves have too many dealings with humans to not speak it. Humans have forgotten it."

Ketill replied in the old language. It had been a while since I'd heard it, and I was slower to understand, but I think he said, "*Some humans.*"

The dwarf tapped the table, approving. "You'd need to be very old for a human to remember *that*." Ketill just nodded.

During our conversation, the dwarves brought out porridge, and the smell of the morning meal must have roused the rest of our little war party. Nanthild, Styrgrim, and Josur joined us first. Vilgrip followed with Bjorn, continuing to ask the skald about old adventures. Bjorn appeared to enjoy talking and to never tire of Vilgrip's hand-related jokes.

The hall filled with dwarves as we ate. Magnus noticed some seated nearby who had the sooty faces of smiths who'd worked all night. He announced, loud enough for the entire hall, that he wanted to buy or trade for new weapons. "Axe or seax. Or shorter swords. Non-cursed, preferably, but I will consider lightly cursed for a discount on price."

Dwarven laughter filled the hall. A few dwarves came by just to joke that he could not afford such things. One dwarf was an exception and was willing to negotiate. His price was not what Magnus expected, however.

"What do you mean, a night with my wife? I don't have a wife!"

The dwarf making the offer then made the mistake of pointing at Nanthild. Styrgrim barely got a hold of her before she leaped across the table.

"Why, Nanthild, I'm not so bad as all that! You could do far worse and still do well." Magnus turned to address the dwarf again. "But in all seriousness, we don't take such ideas about passing people around lightly. I could agree to such a thing as a trick, I suppose, but that's not our way, either. She would kill you with her bare hands."

Nanthild seethed, and the tension did not resolve. Jests about being passed around and used sexually were cause for duels or outlawry when directed at men. Nanthild was not about to concede any lesser treatment as a woman. And however stony that dwarf's body was, I had no doubt Magnus was right: She would kill him with her bare hands.

"Still might, in fact."

"Oh, I see it," said the dwarf, with what sounded like arousal.

"I've held her back because we are guests in this hall and have a needful thing we must acquire here," said Styrgrim. "But I won't deny a friend's continued demand. I'm letting her go in a moment, and I suggest you make amends if you want to keep your life."

A vigorous nod from Magnus confirmed for the dwarf: This was no joke.

The dwarf bent his knee and bowed low. Nanthild flew over the table. She stopped short of drawing her sword but circled the dwarf like an angry wolf. She settled for kicking him over sideways and turned her back on him. Which turned her toward Magnus. She fixed him with a look only slightly less furious.

"How is this my fault? I was merely trying to buy weapons, as any reasonable person in this place would do!"

She gave him a shove, came around to give Styrgrim a shove that knocked his spoonful of porridge from his mouth into his beard, and sat down. Then she banged the table twice and made a drinking motion with her hand. One of the dwarves seemed to understand and went to fetch her some ale.

"Can we consider trade of a different sort?" asked Magnus. The one who'd been pushed over got up and moved a few steps away from our table. Haggling resumed, but there was still no deal after several minutes.

"Ahem," interrupted Sindri. "Has potential barter ceased for the moment? Oh, good! It is well that the king of this hall might have a chance to speak. I trust our guests are well-treated and well-fed?"

"Very," answered Kraki.

"And I trust that our guests have had a chance to hear the wisdom of the Wanderer?"

"I have offered my advice," said Finnr. "They have yet to hear from my sons."

"Then by all means, they should speak," said Sindri. "Dvalin! Durin! Step forward and make yourselves known to our guests."

Two dwarves pushed their way through the throngs to approach the dais. The slightly taller one, with arms even longer than most other dwarves, took off his conical woolen cap. His long chin beard stayed tucked into the front of his belt so that it would not fall to the ground. He wore a pair of heavy gloves. Gloves of iron? It had to be a trick of the light. A pair of tongs, bright like polished silver, hung in his belt. That also had to be wrong—silver would melt in the heat of a good forge. "Dvalin," he declared, and bowed.

The slightly shorter and fatter one puffed out his chest beneath a forked beard, but his ample belly was the only thing thrusting forward. A forge hammer hung tucked into his belt, runes etched into the side of the head. He wore no gloves, and his hands were bigger than average. "Durin," he said, drawing a look of exasperation from Dvalin. Then he, too, removed his cap, revealing a bald pate as shiny as brightest gold.

"Father," both dwarves said in unison.

Finnr stood up. "My sons, you've been called here to tell a story. For the benefit of our guests, though it might be good for our folk to hear the entire tale straight from you as well."

"We know one of these guests," said Durin.

"Though we hardly recognize our little brother," continued Dvalin. Kraki nodded back at them.

"Yes, yes," said Sindri. "No need for long introductions, your audience is impatient. Tell us the origin of the sword, Tyrfing."

Durin rubbed the knuckles of one hand with the other while Dvalin pulled at his beard. Plainly uncomfortable and stalling, but time was up.

"We were young!" began Dvalin. "Still young in those days, though we had gained much skill as smiths. We wanted to forge a grand sword."

"A sword for who?" prodded Sindri. The chin on his fist made it clear he knew the story but would need to prompt these two to tell it fully to a new audience.

"For our father," said Durin. "Not that he required a sword, but to show him how far our skills had come. We were proud to show we had learned his teachings, proud of what we could make. We meant the sword as a gift, to hang in our hall, or have him do with it as he would."

"Perhaps he knew a hero he wished to give it to," shrugged Dvalin. "But it was a long time ago. Long before our younger brother joined us."

If this story was a means for Sindri to put us off our task, I saw no evidence of it. All I saw were two sons trying to impress their father, a thing I knew well enough.

"But you were the smiths only," continued Sindri. "Did you have other help?"

Dvalin wiped an eye with a cloth from his belt. Durin hung his head. Whatever Sindri alluded to in this next part of the story, it was not good.

"We had a different brother in those days," said Dvalin. "It's true we forged and honed the sword. But the two of us did not create the steel."

"That was Dain," said Durin. "We could have smelted the metal well enough. But Dain had a way with the crucible that no others had."

There was nothing about a third dwarf in the stories of Tyrfing I'd ever heard. It was always two. Where was Dain, then?

"We worked in Midgard," Durin continued. "In secret, or so we thought. Far from the forges below, where the gods are known to stalk our wares."

"But before we finished," Dvalin said, "we found our work had not been so secret. A man found us, a king, and caught us up. He saw the sword and demanded we finish it and give it to him."

I stood up. "This king, what was his name and where was he from? As we hear the story told, it was the king of Gardariki, but I wonder if there even was a Gardariki so long ago."

"Svafrlami was the name he offered, as I recall," said Dvalin. "But he spoke as if to conceal his name with sorcery."

"I remember the confusion, though I thought I heard it as Sigrlami," added Durin. "No mention of Gardariki, though."

"What did he look like?" I asked.

"Old for a Midgarder," said Durin. "We were surprised a king could live so long. You people kill your kings with great frequency."

"Old and canny," added Dvalin. "Long, silver beard. Piercing gaze. And a cruel smile."

"Any other details about him you can remember?"

They exchanged a look and then shook their heads. "It was long ago," said Dvalin. "He must be long dead, though we won't forget his voice."

Durin nodded. "Nor the certainty of his bearing. Told us it was not for him but for some 'greater game.' As if the thing he was doing was not theft at all, but some rare type of favor."

Blood thundered in my head. Had Odin just used that phrase, *the greater game*? Could it have been him in disguise under another name?

"Shall they move on with the story?" said Sindri, not really asking.

I suppressed a shudder and nodded.

"We resisted," said Dvalin. "But he overcame us with sorcery."

"Protested to our utmost!" added Durin. "But we could not break his hold. He refused our release until securing our oaths that we finish the sword and give it to him."

Having begun slowly, quietly, even feebly, the voices of the two dwarves rose above the growing din. Murmurs rumbled low along the stone beneath us, carrying the discontent from every dwarf in the hall.

Far-flung as their people might be, different as they might lead their lives, they knew the chains of coercion. Knew them and felt them with those brothers. Humans might steal from one another, but this was not the same thing. As Finnr had said so many times, the meanings of things were different in the Down-Below. *Vættir* were not humans, even if in these cases they were humanoid in appearance. Oaths carried more power here. The dwarves were angry, and the hall grew hot with their fury.

"All the passion we had poured into the thing turned to bitterness in kind, and more," said Durin. "The sword grew even stronger as we harvested that bitterness, though not as we had originally intended."

"We ruminated long into the nights, the three of us," said Dvalin. "Thought long about how to leave this thief with more than he bargained to steal. We worked our will into the sword and cursed it thoroughly. To have the barest cut be lethal. To require a life any time it is drawn, requiring fresh blood to be resheathed. To do ill deeds when least expected. And to turn on its wielders, eventually. The sword was cursed through and through, its bright blade a trap that hides its true nature."

"Thus, we sent this king off to die when we handed it over," said Durin.

The hall quieted before Sindri spoke again. "What happened then?"

The anger on those faces turned to utter misery, and the heat in that place increased.

"The thief questioned us about the making of the sword," said Durin.

"So we told him truly," said Dvalin. "That it was all of us, but we all three led in different parts of the making: Dain made the steel. Durin hammered the shape. And I finished the thing, polishing a blade that could cut through steel as easily as cloth."

Durin shook his head. "We failed to guess his reason for asking."

"And what was his reason for asking?" said Sindri.

"To decide . . ." Dvalin trailed off and turned his head.

"He thanked us for the information," growled Durin. "He was glad to know two good smiths, he said, but the essence of the sword should not be recreated for another. With the sword in hand, he stabbed our brother, Dain, through the heart."

The collective grief of the dwarves hung heavy in the cavernous hall. Despite the throngs gathered, none stirred, none spoke. Nanthild wiped away a tear. Raw emotion welled up in me at the wrongness of it all, and I hoped I would not need to wipe away a tear myself. A woman could cry in my world, but not a man.

"Dain fell into our arms, and the man stalked away, laughing," said Durin, almost a whisper. When he continued, his voice echoed through the hall, leaving no doubt as to the extent of dwarven magic. "But he did not get far before Dain spoke his last words. A final curse, fitting for the fiend: That the blade would cut down his line, and the line of whoever else used it! The sword will *never* be clean of our brother's blood, dealing death to its wielders and to their families, forevermore!"

I had told the story of Tyrfing many times. Often with humor, playing at the capriciousness of the dwarves. Never again. Those curses came from grief and hate. It would be a crime to characterize the story any other way.

Dvalin and Durin returned to the Down-Below and had no knowledge of what happened to the sword or the thief thereafter. Now I was convinced that the Rus connection had been made up in later tellings, but I couldn't tell anything more from the name of the thief. Odin had more names than I could remember, and he often went around Midgard with a different identity. If it had been him, why would he want the sword?

Or could he have stolen the sword, intending to place it in the hands of another as he now schemed to put it in our hands? Was this the connection to the Goths after all, that they'd had it, but long ago? I suspected the truth may have been cut away from Midgard forever.

"It was not long ago we heard a plea," said Dvalin. "A man's voice echoed into our forge. It had been many years since we'd thought of the sword. He called it Tyrfing, a name not familiar to us, but we knew what sword he meant."

"We found him in the grave mound of Midgard's foulest monster," Durin growled, clearly feeling about Hervor the same way Styrgrim did. "He kept the thing at bay with the sword and told us his intent, that we should take it back, keep it safe. I won't lie: I was afraid. The sword was unsheathed, and I feared it would now cut down either me or my brother."

"But that was not the man's intent," added Dvalin. "When we spoke of our fear, he grinned and drew the blade across his arm, resheathed it, and quickly handed it to us. The mound dweller could do nothing."

The dwarves nodded, their heads down. They fidgeted with their hands, a gesture I knew well. It's often what happens when a skald finishes a story, but in such a way that the audience doesn't realize it right away.

"Here is the story in its fullest," said Sindri. "It is a story about a thing that cannot be worked for good, and will work those who use it for ill. You won't find a weapon cursed more fully than Tyrfing. Now I want to ask our guests, knowing the sword's nature, would you still seek it out?"

I think he was asking the question out of form and expecting us to back away slowly from this foolish task we'd set ourselves. His tone certainly indicated that expectation. I had a hard time turning my mind away from getting the sword, though. How else would we destroy the torc? How else would we defeat Alfhild and her army?

And then I realized: That had been Odin's intent. How convenient that he would offer me the use of Valaskjalf to encourage seeking the sword the very night before Sindri would try to dissuade me. Maybe this was the predictability of fate, and why there was no getting away from it.

Styrgrim rose to speak. "Let me have it, then, and take it back after my death."

A hush fell over the dwarves and also the rest of us. This was not what I expected. Nor had anyone else, judging from their reactions. Finnr edged away from Styrgrim as if he were the angry bear of his byname. Nanthild stared at him with open hostility, glancing at me and then back to him.

"Styrgrim the Bear." Sindri's voice rolled over us, slow and disapproving. "A hero of Midgard. Odin's Man, they call you. Always seeking the next fight, the glory of battle. It is no surprise you grasp at this sword, even though it will be your death. What do you say about the ending of your line, though, as happened with Hervor and Heidrek? You still want the sword even though it will condemn Ansgar the Skald?"

I saw the problem as Sindri spoke. It was like watching a giant tree fall and having no means to get out of its way.

"I have no line." It was spoken matter-of-factly, an argument that he should wield the sword next, an assuaging of fears. "Nor can I get one. Ansgar the Skald is the son of another." The statement did not assuage fears so much as cause many looks going from Styrgrim to me and back. *What is going on?* and *What does he mean?* people must have asked themselves.

I, in turn, asked myself what to do now. How much would I need to explain? Did I have the right to hold anything back? My connection to Styrgrim had already been tenuous, and now it was clear I was not even kin to him. In such times, it is essential to have a reliable counselor who can see and explain things from another perspective.

Magnus leaned in to whisper some advice. I leaned in as well, hoping for wisdom or clarity. A mention of some minor detail only he had noticed that might aid me in deciding how to speak next. A unique perspective, with a suggestion of what to do next.

"Shit!" he said.

# Chapter 40

# Under Siege

"Let the murmurs continue as they will," Styrgrim's voice echoed through the hall. "My voice is not for low speech, cowardly and outside of hearing. Know this: I was wounded, and no children would issue forth after that. My wife was visited by someone wearing my skin. I know not who it was, but I am not the skald's real father. He cannot be part of the sword's curse as I take it up."

"This might change things," whispered Magnus.

"How so?" I demanded.

"No idea yet. But it might change things."

Which was as much help as a crutch for a man with no arms. At the same time, I read confusion and disapproval in the faces of the rest of our war party. Besides Magnus, only Ketill had known that I wasn't Stygrim's son, and the rest doubtless wondered why it was only coming out now.

"That is only one part of the curse you mention," said Sindri. "That sword will kill you."

"I am old! What do I care if the next battle is my last? To make it a good one is the thing, and we will need this weapon for it."

"You intend to die then?"

"I will die, intent or none!" Styrgrim roared back. "That's the fate of all men. I've heard your story, and I understand the sword's nature. I don't desire to avoid it or try to outsmart what is coming—I accept it as it is and won't try to pass it on. Take it back after I fall. Back to wherever you keep it safe."

Sindri shook his head. "The sword cuts more than intended, always."

Vilgrip had been quiet, but he stood up to speak. "If it will cut the Brisingamen, that will be a good start."

"Leave the Brisingamen here with us," said Sindri. "It is of dwarf-make, and that means it is part of us. We have handled more dangerous items by far. Then you will not need the sword."

I shook my head. "It is too dangerous. You think you would remain safe from its influence, but it pulls at anyone around it. Steel may be cold and cruel, but gold is a corrupter of minds."

"Corrupter of some minds," countered Sindri. "Beginning with Freya, and, if you describe it rightly, you humans are susceptible to it as well."

I was incredulous. "You think you are immune?" I heard the Brisingamen calling to me, tempting me to use it for influence. I pulled it out of my pouch, but not to use it. Instead, I held it high like a gutted fish to be gawked at. "You will see what it wishes you to see. Tell me, King Sindri, tell me truly as you look upon it: Does it not glow to entice another owner, the same as Tyrfing's blade? Is your offer of a trade not a whisper from the gleaming torc, a way to worm itself from my hands to around your neck? What do the whispers say— something like how much better you would do to protect your people, if only you used it just a little?"

"I do not . . ." Sindri trailed off, his eyes fixed on the thing.

The hall quieted, transfixed by the beauty of this one piece of jewelry. I waved it this way and that. Nearly all eyes in the hall followed the movement.

"Put it away," growled Ketill.

"I want them to see—"

"Away!" The wizard's voice shook the hall, and I obeyed.

Ketill rose and turned to address the king of the dwarves. "What this torc is, and what you think it to be, are two different things. You've no more hope of resisting such a lure than anyone else. That is how it made its way in Asgard, and then in Midgard. By being *desired*. That desire can make you believe anything, however untrue or unlikely. Can you say that in seeing the Brisingamen, you indeed felt no pull, no reaching out for it?"

Sindri pulled at his beard for a long moment before responding. "Troll-cursed gods. They ruin everything." He shook his head and pulled at his beard some more before continuing. "And how is it this skald has it in hand without difficulty?"

"It is not without difficulty. My bag quiets its voice. Even so, I have reached for it before. I've had help resisting it. Now I've had some experience carrying the thing, and it's become more obvious when it whispers to me, trying to make it seem as if its thoughts are mine.

"Right now, it whispers that only *it* can help convince you to give us the sword. Even though we want the sword to destroy it! It does not need logic, only to feel, to wrap its desire around you and squeeze until nothing matters but the feeling it feeds you."

The dwarf king rose and smoothed his long beard out. "That is a difficult thing to deal with, but not impossible. You are the best person to hold the Brisingamen for now. Until we can build a box suitable to hold the torc, you must carry it."

"If I have the sword, that's a fine idea," said Styrgrim. "Then I can destroy the torc at will, if our enemies come close to getting it back."

"No." It was simply spoken and powerful in its simplicity. "Tyrfing is the responsibility of dwarf-kind. We will keep it safe and unused. You will do the same with that necklace until we can take it as well. Letting one loose to end the other would invite chaos. My decision is made."

Kraki sighed. He was disappointed, but we had agreed to Sindri's decision. In the Down-Below, I knew there was no getting around that.

Finnr came to my side and clasped my shoulder. "I can make such a box. No one will get the torc. No one will even look for it."

"You think you're immune when Sindri isn't?" I thought of a conversation we'd had two years ago. "Finnr, this thing *is* dragon sickness."

The dwarf softened his tone. "No doubt, this is a hard thing to carry. But I can't be reminded of dragon sickness without remembering bitterness. You can trust me in this, and if that seems unlikely, test it."

"How would I do that?"

The dwarf pulled my head in close and whispered. "What does the torc say about giving it to me? Is it eager?"

The torc was screaming that I should hold onto it, get the sword, anything but give it to this nasty dwarf. That almost persuaded me to hand it over and be done with it, and at least deny it ever getting to our enemies. I wasn't sure, though, as conflicting feelings roiled inside me.

My chest heaving, I had to sit down. Not because I thought we'd failed, but because I did not know what to do next. As the leader on land, any idea was fine as long as it was clear. But to return to Midgard and tell the army, "I don't know what to do," might be tantamount to giving up command. Which might happen anyway, now that it was out that I was not kin to Styrgrim.

Kraki told everyone to finish up before we departed. Our people took final bites of food and downed the last from their cups. Styrgrim and Nanthild remained unmoving, a silent conversation playing out between their eyes. I couldn't eat anymore. With no sword and no word-fame from destroying the torc, what did we have? Not enough of an army to fight Alfhild, and not enough of a reputation to recruit a bigger army.

"We have wasted our time coming here," I muttered, my frustration boiling over.

"It was a long walk, but the meals were good," said Magnus. "Perhaps we can get some of their brewing secrets before we go."

I could not manage a laugh or even a grin. A void had opened up below me such that I had no idea where to go or what to do next, and it sucked the effect of the humor right away. I closed my eyes. It was as if Ginnungagap, the yawning void of the cosmos itself, had opened up. And out of that void I heard howls and screams, the sounds of snarling monsters, from the other side.

I opened my eyes to see looks of confusion and horror on the faces of the dwarves. The screams were not in my head. The sound of stone crashing onto stone rang through the hall, accompanied by shouts of command and cries of pain. In the distance, a hound bayed with an unnatural timbre.

A dwarf with a bloodied head and arms stumbled through the doors and collapsed to his knees, held up by Dvalin and Durin. "They come," he gasped.

Sindri was already on his feet. "Who comes?"

"All!"

"All what?" I asked, not certain who I was asking.

Finnr responded. "All our enemies. All those who took Svart's offer."

"Sound the alarms," Sindri shouted, with the kind of voice you could latch onto in the middle of chaos. "You all know where to go."

He followed that command with specific orders. Somewhere outside the hall, heavy gongs rang in a repeating pattern. I could feel as much as hear them—that would alert the entire city. Most of the dwarves in the hall gathered closer. Other dwarves were sent as runners.

The king pointed to Kraki. "You are guests, and I promised my protection. Now I cannot guarantee what I promised, as we ourselves are not protected. Finnr knows the secret ways and can guide you safely to the Up-Above. Go now, before we shut the hall doors."

Another crash outside, like a ten-foot wall breaking under an assault. High-pitched war cries followed.

"I have never failed to protect my people," Kraki growled.

"There have been many battles you've been absent for, Found One," countered Sindri. "One more will not matter."

"You seem quite confident for a king under attack," I said.

"As our enemies gathered, so did we gather allies," he replied. "We will hold fast in the crypts and wait for help."

Kraki palmed the head of his bone club, his jaw clenching. I couldn't hear his thoughts, but I understood them. And I knew he wouldn't speak them, because he did not lead on land.

We could have retreated to the Up-Above. Maybe should have. But I didn't know what we would do once we were Up-Above. Sometimes, leadership decisions come down to doing something as preferable to doing nothing.

"Our absence won't increase your safety," I said.

"As you wish." Sindri turned back to commanding his people.

"Is this a battle we need to fight?" asked Josur.

When I responded, it was to speak to everyone. "Our hosts are under attack. The attackers are those who took Svart's offer. Better to fight them now, and with allies, rather than show them our backs."

No one spoke, and no one needed to. I could tell what each person thought just by looking at them. Most agreed with my reasoning. Styrgrim didn't care about reasoning, he just wanted to fight. Magnus was a bit different. He grabbed that sooty dwarf by the beard and dragged him over, the one who'd wanted a night with Nanthild.

"All right, you!" said Magnus. "There's no more time for negotiating, unless you intend to sell your wares to your enemies, so how about it?"

It turned out the dwarf was eager to put two seaxes of his making into Magnus' hands for far less than originally asked.

# CHAPTER 41

# LET THE HAMMER FLY

THE STONES DECORATING THE FLOOR IN FRONT OF SINDRI'S HIGH
seat were layered with similar striations, unlike those throughout the rest of
the hall. The tiles of light and dark gray, interspersed with occasional streaks
of pink, must have come from the same place.

It was these stones that dropped, revealing a short staircase to a tunnel
beneath the high seat. I didn't see how Sindri made that change happen.
Another thing dwarves were not about to reveal to outsiders.

The dwarf king led all those still in the hall into the tunnel, and our war
party followed at the rear with Finnr. The dwarf somehow found a rope, and
he had us all take hold. It was dark as pitch down there. When my eyes finally
adjusted, I noticed there were new paths to choose every thirty paces or so.
Holding the rope kept us all together through the maze.

Dim light eventually appeared at the end of one tunnel, where raw stone
gave way to cleanly carved walls. I stepped onto a smooth, uniformly tiled
floor of dark gray with metallic spots. Deep as we had gone, we had come out
onto a balcony three stories up from the bottom of the cavernous room. Faces
carved in the stone looked out from the balcony. Dwarf faces, most with long
beards, all with serious expressions. Below each head lay a stone casket.

There could be no question that we had come to the crypts. But were
those caskets big enough for dwarf bodies? It seemed to me they were a bit
too small. If not bodies, what was in them?

We had come out in a rear corner of the crypts. The other rear corner was occupied by an ancient tree root. We were already Down-Below, and we had just gone even deeper. I started to wonder what tree root I was looking at.

Sindri must have seen me staring. "The skald sees what he thought was just a story. Go on, put your ear to it. Then you can tell me what it is, if you know your lore."

I did put my ear to it. I heard bubbling, like a cauldron at a simmer. More than that, I felt a pulsing, slow and soft. My eyes must have been wide when I turned back to the dwarf king. "But we can't be so deep as Niflheim."

He shook his head. "It goes much deeper than this realm."

"What's this?" demanded Styrgrim. "Stop speaking in riddles."

"It's, uh . . ." It seemed uncouth to say it, as if my voice wasn't sufficient. "A root of the world tree, Yggdrasil. The root that leads to Hvergelmir, the bubbling spring in Niflheim, from which many rivers flow. Even the Gjoll, the river that separates the living from the dead."

"The skald knows his lore," said Sindri. "I have my people to manage now. We should be safe here until our allies arrive. In the meantime, manage your own people." He poked me hard in the chest and then pointed the same finger down at the center of the first floor. "I would advise them not to approach that thing below."

We were in three stories of long walls with carved heads and caskets, stairs up and down, all carved into the sides of this great cavern, and all open to see from any vantage point. When I looked down where Sindri had pointed, I saw the source of light for the whole place.

In the middle of the crypts was a ring of blue flames. They popped up and down, more at ease when no one walked nearby, higher as anyone approached. The flames fell low for a moment and revealed a sword atop a short pedestal. Sheathed in thick but tattered leather, only hints of the blade's sun-brightness showed through the scabbard's worn spots. Its pommel and guard were of uniform width but thinner than most modern swords, marking its ancient origin. It stood tip-down on the stone pedestal, nothing holding it up that I could see.

Styrgrim stepped up next to me. "Here is Tyrfing, at last!" And we couldn't touch it. Or rather, most of us would probably not try to.

"I thought they would protect it better," said Magnus. "Locked away in a secret place, not out on display. A few buckets of water, and anyone could have that thing!"

"Hmph," said Finnr. "There is plenty to do here. Follow me if you can help with the wounded or with defense."

I nodded and motioned for my people to follow those directions. No point in wasting time when there were injuries to tend to.

Styrgrim pulled me aside and hissed into my ear. "We may have it yet. The dwarves are overwhelmed, however many more they think might come."

"The dwarves fight our enemies. Our alliance with them is inherent. You would make it contingent on a gift?"

"You would help them, but let them turn their backs on us after? Go back empty-handed, then. Or heed my advice, for once."

Oh, that last bit rankled me. "I can count on no hands the times you offered me advice, and I won't pretend otherwise."

We stood face to face for an awkward amount of time.

"Late is better than never," he said.

Which rankled me even more. My father or not, I had seen him as my father for so long that he might as well have been. Despite everything I'd learned, everything I'd been through, some things are left ingrained. One of those things was that Styrgrim could get under my skin like nobody else. And I knew how to do the same to him.

"You are certainly that. Late in returning to Svipul. Late in returning to Arrow-Odd's army. So late in mentioning how I was named, you still haven't done it." Based on his pale expression, I had him from early on, and I doubt he heard everything I said. In fact, he made that clear when he found his voice again.

"Svipul . . . how do you know that name?"

Whoops. "I am . . . stronger in lore than you think."

"That is no answer!" He grabbed my arm, the act of a desperate man rather than an angry one.

I wrenched my arm away. Well, I tried to. "What do you care what I know? You've had no shortage of opportunities to tell me my history, or at least prepare me for it. But you were content to be *late*."

He let go. "Oh, I will tell you that, then. Don't expect to thank me for it, though. Your mother died, and I held you in her stead. The *vǫlva* who birthed you said you were a gift from the gods and should be named as such. I said you were like a spear, and so the *vǫlva* called you Ansgar, thinking it a great compliment. I did not dissuade her, but I knew the real meaning: From the gods or not, you were a spear through my heart when you bled your mother out."

Bitter as it was, at least that story put to rest any idea that I was Odin's chosen one, named for his plan. "I think that was what I became known as, not my real name. What is the name you challenged me to earn?"

Punctuating my last word, a loud boom echoed through the crypts. At the far end was a set of giant-sized doors. A huge oaken drawbar held them shut.

The boom came a second time, reverberating through the crypts. Dust from the drawbar flew from the impact.

I ran to Sindri, who stood in the entryway. "You said we would be safe here."

He nodded, one eyebrow raised. "A subjective thing, being safe."

"Will the doors hold?"

"They have never failed." He turned to his people and ordered them all to be ready to fight. Which was not the answer I'd hoped for.

Our people were already organizing together at Styrgrim's command. I went to Ketill, hoping he could harden the doors against the attackers as he hardened the *Sea Squirrel* against Heather-Back. "The doors are iron," he said. Which sounded like *no* until he followed with "hmmm," which sounded more like *maybe* bordering on *yes.* "I will speak with the king."

The wizard did more than speak with Sindri. They went back and forth in low tones for a few minutes as the intermittent banging continued. Finally satisfied, Ketill approached the doors.

He sliced his thumb and drew runes on the drawbar with his blood. Then he held his palm to them and chanted the runes, one after another. As the pauses between different runes shortened, Ketill weaved those distinct sounds together until they created a new chant, like letters forming a word. As he chanted over and over, the dark wood of the drawbar took on the dull sheen of iron.

I joined him there, hoping to help my old teacher if I could. The terrible banging on the doors began to ring hollow. After a few more attempts, there was a pause so long I thought they had stopped. Sindri joined me, and the three of us stood there at the door. I tried to think of a verse, but wasn't sure what I should describe or what the point would be.

"Let him work," Sindri told me. "He knows a bit of our history now. It will aid him in his effort."

Out of the corner of my eye, I thought I saw a shadow poke beneath the doors. It was gone as soon as I looked directly where it had been. I ignored it, a trick of the light. I had a more substantive concern. "Why does he keep chanting? He cast a similar spell on our ship before and was done."

"I smell a counter-force at work, and I suspect it has something to do with that." Sindri sniffed again and moved away from the door, motioning for me to do the same. I shook my head, not wanting to leave Ketill by himself.

It took me a few more breaths to notice the hint of rotten eggs in the air. Not the sort that suggested actual rotten eggs. Instead, it carried with it that permeating sense that reached deeper than smell. The sense that this was the smell of *seiðr* being worked from the other side of those doors.

Alfhild's *seiðr* smelled of rotting blood and rusty iron, so it was not her. I'd encountered a friendly *vǫlva* some years ago, and hers smelled of morning dew and copper. This was a sorcerer unfamiliar to me. Could it be Ulf? Could I be standing mere feet away from avenging Haldor and the 'Steins?

I looked down at my left hand, scarred from swearing that blood oath. If I were really this close, would I take up Tyrfing to make sure I ended him, despite the curses laid on it? Assuming I could get through the ring of fire, I mean. And assuming Styrgrim didn't get it first. My mind said the answer should be no, but my heart countered with a yes too strong to ignore. In that long moment of reflection, I missed what was happening.

The dark tiles beneath the doors cracked and chipped. Slowly, a thing burrowed beneath the door and came to our side, like a nail driven too near the surface of wood. A dark tendril of smoke rose through the crack in the floor. It stopped its twisting and snaked along the tile, probing the wizard's near leg.

I drew Need and slashed at it, to no effect whatsoever. Ketill kept chanting and shook his head. I grabbed at the tendril but could not catch it up. It slipped through my hands with a slimy feeling like pond scum, but left no residue.

The tendril withdrew from Ketill's leg and worked its way upward on the doors, up to the drawbar, where it wound itself over and over.

Ketill kept his right hand pressed to the drawbar, his gaze fixed on the smoky tendril, his left hand waving me off as I reached for the drawbar myself. The smell of *seiðr* increased. Ketill's voice rose like I'd heard it few times before. The world around me wobbled and blurred as I felt him pour his will into that spell. I steadied myself with my back against the doors and recoiled from the bitter cold. If I could feel that through my tunic, what was happening to Ketill's bare hand?

"Stand aside!" Something about Sindri's shout made me not only move, but dive away. The dwarf king was still ten paces away when he threw his hammer. A dull thing, a forge hammer. This one looked no different than any other, and it flew end over end with no more grace than one might expect.

It was less expected to hear the crack of thunder and see the flash of lightning when the hammer struck those tendril coils.

I didn't hear or see much of anything for the next few moments. When I did regain some of my senses, Magnus was pulling me up and saying something I could barely hear.

"*What?*" I shouted back.

He shook his head and put one finger to his lips. Then, I think just mouthing the word, he told me to breathe and helped me to a sitting position. Turning around, I saw Ketill lying on his side, his cloak steaming.

Nanthild approached the wizard's unmoving form. She shoved him and got no response. Leaning in, she put a bare hand over his mouth as if to check for breath. Then she drew back and slapped him. Hard.

Ketill coughed and turned over onto his left arm. He examined the wreckage of his right hand, which was swollen to nearly twice its size. Massive blisters bubbled up all over his palm. Rivulets of blood ran down his arm. He did not move any of his fingers. I wondered if he ever would again. Despite the pain of that ice burn, he'd kept his hand on the drawbar rather than give in.

Sindri ordered his people to find honey and a clean bandage for Ketill's hand. Ketill allowed Nanthild to help him up. When some of the dwarves tried to approach the wizard and usher him back to a seat, he growled at them and turned back toward the doors. The drawbar was wood once again. "Skald," he said.

With Magnus' help, I shuffled toward him.

The wizard poked at the largest blister on his hand. "Whatever comes next, I suspect you will play a part."

"What happens next?" Magnus asked. "Surt's flaming ballsack, I'd like to know what just happened before we move on to the future."

"There's a sorcerer on the other side of the doors," I said. Turning to Sindri, I asked, "How did you know the hammer would counter it?"

The dwarf came to the doors and retrieved his hammer. "I knew nothing of the sort. I knew that your lucky blade was no use, but it has little history, especially with my people. An ancestral item, though, that is a powerful thing, especially here." He turned to Ketill. "There will be plenty of time for you to come back to the door and burn your other hand."

Ketill nodded and finally let Nanthild help him away from the doors, to where half a dozen dwarves waited to treat his injury.

I shook my head and hoped the other sorcerer was even worse off. I was a poor substitute for defending this entrance, whatever was on the other side. I hadn't even beaten King Athils in a straight battle of wits. "They went under the doors," I whispered to Sindri. "How is that possible?"

"I am not certain," he whispered back.

"How possible?" asked a voice, clear and sonorous.

The gentle echoes of that voice ran through the crypts. I had thought at first only I might hear it, but that was clearly not the case. Everyone stopped what they were doing to look for the source.

"You draw your power from the earth, Sindri, as do all dwarves. But mine runs from deeper than the earth, from unspoken places that have no names. Should this sort of closed-door hospitality continue, you can be confident you will see more of it.

"But why waste time and effort on such endeavors when they bring no profit? I can hear you well enough right now, and I suggest we parley! I'll even drop any pretense of false names. I am Svart Geirridarsson."

# CHAPTER 42

## CRYPTIC CHALLENGE

WE WERE FAR OUTNUMBERED. OUR WIZARD WAS DOWN. OUR defenses were nearly certain to fail. And it was down to me to outwit a sorcerer who had already outwitted me before. Or, at least, to stall for time.

Sindri kept a cool head despite our dire circumstances. "Hello?" He rapped his knuckles lightly on one of the doors. "Who else is there? A list of names is an important thing, as I'm sure you understand."

When there was no answer, I put my ear to the door. Sindri shook his head at me. Before I could ask "Why not?" a loud bang came from the other side, rattling my head a bit. Not a great start to a battle of wits.

Sindri grinned. "I'm afraid we don't open doors for rude knocking."

"How's that wizard?" Svein bellowed from the other side, a voice I hadn't heard in many months. "Not so good now, I bet!"

Magnus stepped forward to join us. "Oh, I am going to kill that *níðingr*. Kill him *slow*." Another bang on the door, which I took as Svein's fist, was his only answer.

A long silence followed before Svart spoke again. His voice didn't sound as if it were on the other side of foot-thick iron doors, but more like he was in the crypts, speaking softly, easily. "Must we move so quickly? I think things could get out of hand that way. You asked who was here, and here is one of your own! Familiarity is often a salve for inflamed tensions.

"And I think you all have something familiar to me, as well. I thought I heard the voice of the Brisingamen when you arrived at Uppsala! So unfortunate we could not speak about it openly there, but it was not in either of our interests for King Athils to hear about it. Now that we may speak freely, I say cheers to you, skald, for prying it from that witch's hands! I would have done so myself years ago, but my father thought it best she retain it at the time. But tell me, skald, is it still in your possession, or did you need to give it to the dwarves?"

"Is that why you came?" asked Sindri. "If so, I have to tell you it's poor manners to seek such a gift without bringing one yourself." A brilliant ploy by the dwarf king to find out what our enemy really wanted. Was Svart here for the Brisingamen as he said? Or had he somehow also worked out that we were after Tyrfing?

"Please forgive the lack of presents!" said Svart. "I was here on my own business, calling in a few banners as it were. I hardly expected to find such familiar acquaintances here, or I would have come better prepared. Is it you who holds the Brisingamen, King Sindri?"

"I have rarely favored jewelry. It clashes with my beard."

"Still in the possession of the . . . remnants, then. Oh yes, I heard some tales before going below. Arrow-Odd abandoned his army to go live in the woods as a hermit. Yet still, the remains of his army keep going like a body without a head!" Svein laughed in the background at that.

Styrgrim tapped me on the shoulder. We didn't have any set way to communicate with just hands, so it was down to theatrical ability. Which was not strong with this man, yet his message was plain enough: He wanted to lift that drawbar, charge the sorcerer, and cut his head off.

Sindri shook his head, and Styrgrim looked to me. How to theatrically say *He's probably not standing anywhere near the door* with just gestures? I couldn't think of a way, so I just put one finger up, hoping Styrgrim would wait. He waited, but not calmly. His mouth twitched and spittle collected at one corner of it, and he kept looking back at the blue flames that guarded Tyrfing.

"I wonder if those hangers-on will negotiate on their behalf alone or include you in a potential agreement," Svart continued. "I can offer favorable terms! But please, tell me what you would prefer. As long as I get the Brisingamen, which is to your benefit as well, I think there's a wide range of possibilities."

Svart bought loyalty in the Down-Below. He must have assumed we were doing the same thing with the torc. He obviously didn't understand dwarves very well. Perhaps not even his own allies. I had assumed all I could do was buy time before, but that gave me another idea. Whatever loyalty Svart had bought, it had to be tenuous. Vulnerable. Easily and entertainingly pricked, if I took my cue from Magnus as a heckler.

"How about you go hang yourself? If you do, people will forget the stories about you taking spirits up the ass to cast your spells."

"Is that the skald? You haven't done your reputation any favors with that retort. I had hoped for something wittier. Or at least alliterative." Which was really hurtful, because 'spirits' and 'spells' alliterate nicely.

"Why do you want the torc, Svart? It seems to me you have more pressing concerns, like having most of your fleet sunk. Did you come here to ask the dwarves to build you a few ships like they made for the gods?"

"That's better, but—"

"Because I don't think they're in the mood for that."

Svart laughed. "I looked for you out on the water, you know, but some gadfly dropped a cursed rune stick in my ship. Pity we did not meet. But I meant what I said: It is to your benefit to hand over the Brisingamen. Stealing it from Alfhild, that's understandable. Svein tells me she was no friend of yours even before your unfortunate association with Arrow-Odd."

"We had a frank exchange of views over a range of subjects in Lejre."

"A cheeky recounting!"

We went on like that for a few minutes. He didn't like Alfhild either, so why not give him the torc? With it, he could convince her people to join him. Then he would hand her over to us. We both win, and nobody foreswears vengeance. That was some smooth sorcerer. I'll admit, the idea that Svart didn't need to be our enemy began to sound reasonable.

I looked behind me to my crewmates and blinked my way past his spell. Sober, my eyes fixed on Vilgrip. He kept his expression plain, his breathing even. And he gripped his spear so tight, his fingers drove impressions into the ashen shaft.

When I turned back to the door, the sorcerous speech Svart had just used began to have the opposite effect on me. Everything he said smelled of aurochs shit. He was overdoing it, like a skald who thought he was telling a clever story but just sounded desperate to be considered clever.

"Alfhild is no friend to me," he continued. "And, I think, made my father far more enamored of her than was warranted."

It was time to put him back on his heels a bit. "I think you're jealous of your father's access in that case." I licked my lips as I loaded up on insults and insinuations, flavoring them all with vulgarity like a mad cook loading a stew with bitter herbs. Then I started cooking.

"Alfhild has a fine body to fawn over. When was the last time you enjoyed a woman's breasts, anyway? I saw some trollwives out there who would be more than willing to mother you, I'm certain. Or maybe you don't go as much for breasts. They say the way a man eats a chicken says a lot about him. Does he like the moist thighs most, or does he go for meat that's overdone? I wouldn't blame you for being resentful if Ogmund kept those moist thighs all for himself.

"Unless, of course, you like your thighs a bit on the dry side, Svart. It must be difficult to woo women with a face like yours. Perhaps you prefer the kind who don't fight back. You know, they do say 'never judge a wife until buried,' but if you're the type to dig them up prior to passing your . . . judgment . . . it would still be several degrees less strange than the practices of that pervert, Ulf.

"But you're a modern man, I think, not some traditionalist slinking around, trying to terrorize women so they're submissive. I know a *draugr* who would happily satisfy such an appetite. You two would make a fine pair!

"Or maybe you're not hungry for either sort of meal. Tell me, when your retinue passed into the Down-Below, was the hole just a bit too tight? The *landvættir* can sense that sort of preference, you know. In that case, maybe it's not the troll*wives* you need attention from.

"If that's so, then you definitely don't want the torc, Svart. It is a womanly thing, and you're already so far in that direction. Practicing *seiðr*, even! I mean, your captains must only imagine what you do with your distaff when nobody's looking. Think of your priorities, man, and go home! Get a good-looking girl from Gardariki as a wife—no prophecy needed to know that's preferred to what you'll find here."

I took a breath. Had any of that had an effect? I'd never performed for an audience I couldn't see.

"Oh, skald, how disappointing. I was really hoping for more! More battle, more wit. Did you take an injury on the way into those crypts, perhaps to the head? We can make it easier on you than it might otherwise be. I imagine you are fond of some of those with you. You can walk out with every one of them, if only you hand over the Brisingamen.

"Even if you win this fight—which you know you can't, or you wouldn't be cowering with the dead—will you challenge Alfhild's army? She'll do anything to get that torc back, you know. And Arrow-Odd's army, if I should still call it that, is no longer a thing to challenge her. What will you do when she comes for you? Put the torc in my hands, take my protection. Then Alfhild has no recourse. Who do you think my father will side with then?

"The power rising in Midgard is Ogmund Tussock and his allies. When you were with Arrow-Odd, an alliance would not have been possible. But he's gone! Left you all! Lost his mind! Here is a new ally, a more powerful ally to rely on. Vengeance for your past losses as well as a way out of certain defeat. Not many get such an offer."

I didn't believe Svart, but I knew that oaths sworn in the Down-Below had power. I could save my friends and allies with one decision. Maybe even cause a civil war between the two sorcerers by handing the necklace to Svart. That would stir up trouble, indeed. The Brisingamen pulsed in its pouch. That thing had no loyalty or preference—not to Alfhild or Svart or anyone else. But it wanted *out*. It wanted to be *used*.

The burden of leadership felt heavy. I had put myself in danger before. Out of curiosity, out of stupidity, maybe even sometimes out of bravery. But I had never made a decision I knew would cost my Brothers their lives.

"Oy!" Magnus whispered. "You're not done yet, are you?"

I grinned at my friend. As long as I was on this ribald rampage, I shouldn't limit it to one target. "Was that really Svein Helgisson with you? I never did let him know of the verse I composed for him. Some say, 'Better late than never,' though, so here it is:

> "Svart's fart-catcher
>     has heavy footsteps.
> They fade away
>     when fighting is hard.
> A warning to run
>     away, all sheep,
> When the tail-tickler
>     is trying his luck."

A bang on the door indicated Svein's meaty hand had hit it again. That gave me an idea, and I spoke another verse:

"How is the waddler
     so well-fed?
Those great bulges
     of blubber show
A diet most
     memorably obtained:
From a rock-maiden's
     moist outhole!"

Svein roared on the other side of the doors and slammed into them. First with his fists, and then, by the sound of it, with his ample belly.

"A fierce one you have over there!" I said. "Better get him under control, Svart, or else things could get out of hand."

Svart replied smoothly, to my great frustration. "You are stalling. If the parley is down to insults, I think—"

"Challenge!" shouted Vilgrip. I looked at the one-handed warrior for explanation. "Vilgrip Tyrsson calls you out, Svart, you cur." If there was one thing Vilgrip hated more than the Brisingamen, it was Svart. The casual way he'd toyed with the lives of his prisoners. The ease with which he watched them tortured. Not for information or even for punishment. Just for enjoyment.

"Who was that? Tyr Vilgripsson? I'm afraid I don't know him."

"What an inconvenience for you, then," said Vilgrip. "Because we are not in Midgard, where you can swear a thing and then forget about it. You accepted my challenge already, a fight only postponed until after we were outside Uppsala. Well, here we are, in a place where you can't ignore oaths so easily."

# CHAPTER 43

# ANOTHER THING COMING

I WASN'T SURE SVART HAD TO ACCEPT VILGRIP'S CHALLENGE. Things like sworn oaths and accepted challenges had more power in the Down-Below, but this one had been made in the Up-Above.

Svart 's failure to respond immediately suggested that yes, the acceptance was binding. A minute must have passed before he spoke again. "Will we duel through the doors? Understandable that you don't want to open them, given how outnumbered you are. I'll move my folk back a bit. Take your time coming out."

Ketill waved at me with his bandaged hand, beckoning for me to come farther back into the crypts with him. He explained that he thought the flaming barrier that protected Tyrfing might interfere with Svart hearing us. We stood behind the sword with Vilgrip and Magnus. Sindri joined us to discuss what would happen next.

That was when I addressed Vilgrip, wishing he had not put himself in such danger. "This was not part of the plan."

Vilgrip laughed. "What plan? Skald, if you had a plan, it has been chained to a boulder, shot with a hundred arrows, set on fire, and the ashes dumped into the deepest sea. My plan buys some time, maybe even revenge." It was difficult to be angry with the man when he was right. Those doors were unlikely to hold against another assault from Svart.

"Svart has his own plan," said Sindri. "Or he is creating one right now as he speaks with his allies. We have customs for dueling, and he will look for an advantage. Tell me—when you set this challenge Up-Above, did you specifically say it would be you against him, man to man?"

Vilgrip shook his head. "And I'm not about to refer to him as a man."

The dwarf king pulled at his beard. "He can choose a champion, then."

Magnus threw his hands up in frustration. "Surt's flaming ballsack! He's going to choose Svein. Can I fight in Vilgrip's stead?"

Vilgrip crossed his arms, as if slightly offended. "No."

"The challenger determines a few things," said Sindri. "The size of the fighting area, what happens to the possessions of the slain. But only the challenged can have someone fight in their stead."

Magnus offered his new seaxes before realizing Vilgrip could only hold one of them. He declined, saying he preferred his spear. I thought about offering Need, but the sword was heavy when wielded by anyone but me.

"Svart likely has something bigger than Svein, like one of the deep *jǫtnar*," Ketill cut in. "Which would make things difficult."

"I'll demand the arena be expanded to wherever I want, in that case," said Vilgrip. "Give myself plenty of room to run around and avoid him."

"Cut the tendons above one of his ankles," offered Sindri.

"Is that how the dwarves do it?" asked Vilgrip.

The dwarf king shook his head. "We use ropes and hooks to pull them down and stab them in the face with spears." Which was . . . something. "But you can't do that by yourself. So: The ankles. And make it go on for as long as you can. Try to not get killed."

"I intend to do the killing. The question will soon be: Do they honor a victory or do they shoot me full of arrows after I win?"

Finnr stepped into our little council. He cast a hard stare at Sindri. "I think there is a thing for that."

Sindri stared back, unblinking, his breath getting deeper and deeper as he considered whatever the implication had been. Then the dwarf king shuffled off, eyeing several caskets before he stopped at one. He shoved the heavy stone top aside and, to my surprise, dove inside. It didn't appear big enough for a dwarf, especially of Sindri's width. It was also no deeper than my knee, yet Sindri disappeared as if he had jumped into a large hole.

After a few moments, he emerged, seemingly without any difficulty getting up or down. He shook off a chain shirt, the dust making great clouds as the tiny rings clinked. "Wear this. Sleeves are long, though they won't protect your hands. What it does cover won't be pierced by any weapon. That would require something like Tyrfing itself," he half paused, slightly elevating the volume of his voice, "and that is safely in the ring of fire."

"What if the *jotunn* throws a rock at his chest?" asked Magnus.

"Then he should move!" hissed Finnr. "But as for arrows, spears, blades—this will turn them. It is no small thing the king offers."

Sindri nodded, looking like he had no intention of listening to fawning thanks. For him to disturb an ancestral item and offer it to a newcomer said volumes about what he thought, even if he did not say his thoughts out loud.

"How about the sword?" asked Magnus, as he jabbed a thumb behind him at Tyrfing.

Sindri hesitated this time but shook his head.

Vilgrip slipped into the armor. It conformed to his body as if it had sworn an oath to protect him. He hefted his short spear, ready as he might be for the coming fight. Dvalin and Durin lifted the heavy drawbar up and off the iron doors. They were slow in doing so, careful to avoid the blood Ketill had smeared onto it and the unidentifiable ooze where Svart's smoky tendril had gripped it.

We opened one door only. Kraki led the way, and we followed one at a time. Outside the crypts, the ceiling stretched much higher. Baby crystals held on high above like stars in the night sky, providing a low light to see by. The ground was not tiled or finished, but bare rock. We were virtually in an open field, but for a few columns already formed and a few more still forming. The area stretched back hundreds of feet until it met a misty gray crossroads beyond.

That left plenty of cavernous space for Svart's forces to spread out in. They shuffled and murmured at seeing Kraki and his bone club. Here were proper trolls: What you might call goblins and ogres were familiar from my last foray Down-Below, with other trolls of many shapes and sizes in between that neither had nor deserved their own names. At least there was only one *jotunn*, though he was even bigger than the giants of Risaland. He sat on a boulder behind the main host. A low growl rumbled from back there. I could tell it was not the *jotunn* but could not see its source.

A few dozen armored Rus flanked Svart on both sides. He stood tall and smug as ever with that greasy forelock falling in front of his face. Though his cloak had been bright yellow before, the dimness of the cavern made it look a distinctive shade of puke. The biggest difference, though, was that he now carried a distaff. The top of it was a web of carved wood, with just a hint of a green glow to it.

Svein stood ahead of a group of ogres. I had to hold Magnus back when he saw Svein carrying Silence. Haldor's old axe should've been sent off with him. But Haldor had not been given any proper funeral rites by those scum: He'd been eaten. Now, the same axe that had fought for many a Brother might be swung against us.

If only Svart decided to send Svein as his proxy. He'd never learned much more than that he was bigger and stronger, and that few could stand against him. Vilgrip had earned battle-lore the hard way, and he knew how to move, how to adapt. He would toy with Svein for a while and tire the man out before skewering him.

"You may mark the boundaries," said Svart.

"And will you do the fighting?" I asked. "Let's have no surprises about that."

"Ah! I've chosen my champion already, but I suppose it is time to announce him." He looked back at his lines where some particularly ugly trolls stood in front of the *jǫtunn*. "Release the hound!"

And so, the first of two unexpected things in that duel happened: The *jǫtunn* reached down and unhooked a long, thick chain. The crowd standing in front of him parted, all smirks and grins.

A howl filled the cavern as a hound the size of a pony padded forward. Red haze misted around a slick coat of black fur, eerily contrasting with the yellow eyes and bared teeth. Its claws dug into the rock beneath us. The wide muzzle's beard pointed down as the ears, neither dog-like nor wolf-like, pointed up and then flicked from one direction to another.

"How big did you want the fighting area?" whispered Magnus.

"Big," answered Vilgrip.

Sindri shot past all of us to point an accusing finger at the hound. "This is no legitimate champion!" His voice was pitched high, almost shrill with constriction. "That thing is on the wrong side of the Gjoll. Return it at once!"

My blood froze. The River Gjoll flowed from the spring beneath that root of the world tree in the crypts. It was only one of many rivers emanating from that spring, but the Gjoll was a river we all knew: It separated the living from the realms of the dead. Odin had crossed over and come back a few times, and the myths told of a hound howling at him there, guarding the entrance. This thing was no trollish dog. This was the hound of Hel itself.

Svart shrugged. "If the challenger wishes to rescind his challenge and pay a little weregild for the trouble, we can call off the duel."

"I've no fear of your dog's bark or his bite," said Vilgrip.

"Then we can make a wager!" cried Svart. "And here I thought this would be a waste of time. You don't fear a wager, do you, skald? Perhaps the Brisingamen? With a wager in place, we can make this the only fight necessary."

Sindri ground his teeth. He paced back and forth between some of the dwarves dressed for battle, muttering to himself and tugging at his beard. Finnr strode up to him and leaned in. Despite both dwarves whispering, their exchange was an intense one.

"You have nothing to offer in kind," I replied. "You don't even offer a legitimate challenger, as I see it. I will offer the Brisingamen as a betting piece only if you face Vilgrip yourself."

"What's done is done. The challenge is made, and my champion is chosen. But I think I can offer something much more valuable in kind—I can offer your lives!"

"It seems to me we already have those. Unlike the puppets of certain sorcerers I know. How does it feel to be an extension instead of your own person, Svart? Is it uncomfortable to have your father's hand up your ass?"

"Vulgarity is truly the refuge of the witless. And the leaderless, it seems. Where did Arrow-Odd land, I wonder? And will anyone ever care?"

"No one cares about your stupid questions, that is for certain," Sindri shouted. "The custom is clear: Duels cannot be taken advantage of by third parties. We will return to the crypts after the fight is over and need no wager to secure that."

Svart bowed. "Until your door closes, then."

One thing I had never seen before, despite some very harrowing circumstances, was a dwarf panicking. They have no shortage of certainty, and if uncertain, no shortage of patience. What I saw in Sindri was an absence of both patience and certainty. And a little bit of foaming at the mouth as he eyed that hound.

"The challenger needs one other thing," he announced, and disappeared back into the crypts. He returned minutes later with an old sword in an old scabbard wrapped in old, dusty cloth. "An heirloom appropriate for the occasion."

Even more generous than the mail, Sindri had raided another tomb for the weapon. It must be a great sword, I thought. He was chewing his lip and panting something furious, his eyes unfocused and darting. I had not realized King Sindri, or any dwarf, could become so agitated.

Those were the thoughts running through my head at first. The next thought was that this sword was old. So old, the handle and pommel were of a different style than anything I'd seen in modern use. The scabbard had seen better days for sure, though it looked like it would still protect the blade.

Sweat dripping into his beard, the dwarf whispered a single statement to Vilgrip as he pressed the weapon to the man's chest: "For shit's sake, don't cut yourself."

That was the second unexpected thing of that fight, the subtle reveal. The warning, by itself, would not have told me for certain, but Sindri's increasingly unhinged demeanor confirmed that the sword in the flames was a decoy. A big, ostentatious display to make any would-be thieves, should they ever succeed in raiding the crypt, focus on the wrong thing. That was not Tyrfing.

Sindri had just handed Tyrfing to Vilgrip Tyrsson.

# CHAPTER 44

# NO QUARTER

SINDRI TURNED FROM VILGRIP AND CAME TO THE FORE OF OUR group before turning to address Svart. "As your champion has nothing to offer when defeated, I think it's fitting that our champion's arms and armor are not in play."

I wanted to grab the dwarf king, shove him up against a rock wall, and demand an answer for what he was thinking. I did not. Any outward indication that something was not as it should be could tip off the enemy. Right now, they only knew Vilgrip had a dwarf-made sword for this fight. If they even suspected it was Tyrfing, there would be a scramble for the sword. That scramble would involve a lot of blood and guts before it was over, even if we survived it. Which, if Svart got hold of it, we would not.

Svart gave a backhanded wave and pursed his lips. "If that gets us to a resolution faster, it's as you say. You can collect the man's things after Garm kills him. Not his body, though. His body will be Garm's."

Sindri nodded and backed away from the front line, close to me.

"It's interesting how slow a dwarf's opinion might change at some times," I whispered, "and how fast at others."

Sindri's hands shook as he struggled to find a place to put them. His beard was so saturated with sweat, he'd soon need to wring it out. "Some things put other things in a new perspective. And some things cannot be tolerated."

"That's quite fast-moving for a dwarf."

"I can move fast when necessary."

"Better make sure the rest of your folk can move fast, too. I don't trust Svart's word, and now we are exposed. We need to fall back as soon as we can. This puts us not falling back right away, but going forward and collecting Vilgrip's things."

Sindri shook his head. "That monster . . . it should not be here. It is beyond me how it even *is* here. We need to send it back to Hel, whatever the cost. If that means we are exposed, so be it."

And exposed we were, against a much larger host. The crypts had emptied as every dwarf and human came out to watch the fight.

Garm entered the sectioned-off area snarling and slavering, and Vilgrip stepped forward and drew his sword. The blade shone like the sun, forcing the hound to squint. The contestants circled one another, looking for the best ground to fight off of.

I gathered my war party. Even Kraki, who was loath to take his burning eyes off of Svein. "Be ready for battle."

Ketill's jaw tightened as he examined the heavy bandages mittening his right hand. I could practically hear his thoughts accepting that he couldn't pull a bowstring, so he would need to find another weapon.

"More ready than normal?" asked Magnus

"Much more." I glanced behind me. "Given the stakes."

Vilgrip had no right hand, but he was naturally left-handed. The hound didn't know that yet, so he held the sword awkwardly, as if fighting from the wrong side. The deception worked and drew Garm to lunge at him, prompting a quick series of counterstrokes. My heart leaped at the possibility of a quick victory. But as fast as Vilgrip was, the Helhound was faster and retreated from the ploy before the sword could bite.

"If Vilgrip loses, why not just fall back to the crypt as the dwarf described?" demanded Styrgrim. "We want to fight a larger force from a defensible space. It's better for us inside, even with both doors open."

"It may play out that way, but we must be ready for the end of the fight. Win or lose, we can't abandon Vilgrip."

"We can if he falls," said Styrgrim. "And we may need to. There's more at stake than a few dwarven baubles important to the king."

"That is not—"

"No!" he interrupted, stepping closer and getting right in my face. "Listen to me! Listen to decades of battle speaking to you from one who survived them all. This is a hard choice, not a happy one, but lives ride on it! Loyalty to the memory of one often causes others to be killed needlessly. If you ever wanted wisdom from me, here it is!"

This was a moment I had dreaded for some time, coming to an argument with Styrgrim. It was a struggle for leadership against the man I least wanted to struggle against. He spoke honestly, and that made it even worse. I had no business making battle plans, no business contradicting him. Except that in this case, I did, I just could not tell him why. Unless I could speak in a way only he would understand. If Styrgrim and I shared knowledge of one thing, it was sayings from *Hávamál*.

"Confide in one, never in two," I said, glancing at Sindri. "Confide in three, and the whole world knows."

Styrgrim snarled, confusion blooming on his face. He understood I was trying to tell him something, but couldn't puzzle out what it was.

In the fighting area, Vilgrip attacked once, twice, three times. Garm hopped away from each slash. I knew Vilgrip: He could fight all day, fight in his sleep, and get up and fight some more. But the hound of Hel gave no indication of tiring. It had to get in closer to attack, however, and that was its disadvantage.

Unless it was biding its time. Not waiting for Vilgrip to tire, but studying his movements while it decided how to overcome him. I shivered at that thought. In the midst of my vulnerability, the Brisingamen pulled at my hand. In the echoes of that cavern, a subtle voice seemed to speak. *Use me*, it said. *I can convince him.*

My left hand moved toward my pouch and I snapped it back. It landed on Ketill's shoulder, to the surprise of both of us. The wizard grimaced, but I refused to move it. I would use it.

"Ketill, you know me as well as any here and better, in some ways, than most. You know my art more than you've ever let on, and how to say things in poetry, in stories, in every way. I say we must not leave Vilgrip out there, even if he falls. *Especially* if he falls. Give me no argument, only answer this one question: Do you trust me?"

The wizard nodded. He began to work his fingers free of the bandages.

"As do I," added Magnus.

Nanthild, Josur, and Bjorn nodded. "Kraki?" I asked.

"I trust this," he said, rubbing the head of his bone club. "As for you: You lead on land. Make it good."

I turned back to Styrgrim. "Some things can't be said out loud. You know that better than most. So hear me, and trust me now, if you have any trust for me: We must not leave Vilgrip if he falls, no matter the cost."

The old warrior looked behind him, back into the crypts. He stared at the sword he thought was Tyrfing. It made sense. We might have a fight too big for us, and the equalizer of that fight, the very thing we came for in the first place, looked close enough to grasp.

A yell and a howl brought my attention back to the fight. Garm leaped clear of Tyrfing once again, its howls mocking Vilgrip's attempts. Blood bloomed beneath the man's leg wrappings. It was not a bad wound, but it didn't have to be. Garm was getting his measure.

*If Vilgrip can cut that dog just one time . . .*

"Things that can't be said," Styrgrim repeated. "I have seen too much for trust, from people to gods. I trust in my own might and main, and nothing more. But I won't go against you as leader."

"I'll settle for that, then." I turned to the battle in progress.

Vilgrip favored his left leg. The bite to his right calf was deeper than I'd thought. Worse, it was too severe for him to conceal its extent. The Helhound paced about, forcing Vilgrip to take more steps. To bleed more. Only to disengage and make him do it again.

Shouts from our side cheered Vilgrip on and called the hound a coward. The more Garm avoided, the louder we became. The dwarves shook their weapons in defiance—spears and axes for most. Shields were in short supply. I worried that what came next might come faster than I could react.

Vilgrip stopped in the middle of the fighting area and let his leg rest. He called to the hound as if it were a cute puppy. I knew the man, and blood loss was hampering him. He was baiting the thing to charge.

The hound responded with a howl to overcome all our shouts together, taunting the man right back. It paced back and forth faster, attending to just about everything that was not Vilgrip. Then out of nowhere, it turned and shot at Vilgrip with all its speed and struck home.

Vilgrip's swing was too late to strike home. He must have realized that, because he moved his left arm across his face in time to block the great jaws from his throat. The hound's momentum hit, and Vilgrip found himself on his back. The mail protected him from Garm's teeth and claws, but not from the crushing power of those jaws. His arm crunched under the pressure, the blade pointing away from the hound's body.

Despite his broken arm, he held the weapon firm. Beneath the great bulk of the hound, he kicked at its balls as he locked eyes with it. With his right wrist, he pushed on the flat of the blade, and loosened his grip just enough to let the tip turn toward the hound.

Garm saw the cutting edge turn his way and tried to disengage. By then, though, Vilgrip held the hound with his legs, and Garm could not bound away. Tyrfing's edge singed the hound's fur as it edged its way closer. When he finally had enough of an angle, Vilgrip struck the back of the pommel with his right wrist, sending the sword's point into the hound's left flank. A shallow stabbing, but more than enough.

The movement gave the hound an opening, and it let go of Vilgrip's arm in order to tear at the side of his throat. With his weapon arm free, Vilgrip raked the blade into the hound's left foreleg.

Garm hopped away amidst a geyser of blood. The hound howled again, though this time there was no taunting involved. This was pain. The hound glanced at its left side, shook itself, and retreated farther back.

The fight was not over. Arm broken, leg and neck bleeding, Vilgrip kept hold of the sword and pushed himself up with his right arm. Despite the grievous wounds, he hobbled closer to the hound.

Garm's howls spoke of agony and confusion. The viciousness of Tyrfing's edge had gotten more than it needed to work its venom in, and the hound looked like it could feel every inch that venom advanced. The hound raised its left fore leg, then collapsed, whining and wincing, as its left side gave out completely.

Vilgrip stumbled forward, cradling his left arm as blood spewed from his throat. It took him nine steps to catch up with the hound before he could strike. Bracing the sword's grip between the hand of his broken arm and his right wrist, he brought the point down through Garm's body and into the earth, nailing the hound of Hel to the stone floor.

The hound cried out in what was unmistakably its last gasp.

Still holding the pommel for support, Vilgrip turned toward his Brothers, gurgling as much as breathing. "The hound," he managed, his grinning face ashen above a river of red, "is *hand*led."

He stood tall, holding up a phantom hand to punctuate the joke. A few long moments later, he fell. I have no doubt he died before he hit the ground.

# CHAPTER 45

# SKINS IN THE GAME

It seems appropriate, after witnessing a fight with a good friend meeting a grisly but glorious end, to remain silent for a moment. A long moment, maybe, as the next thing to be spoken will set the tone for honoring the dead.

"Vilgrip has put the hound to bed without its dinner," I said. Nods all around on our side indicated this was an appropriate response.

Sindri, by contrast, was already on his way to retrieve his "heirlooms." Still sweating buckets, he beckoned Finnr to come help him.

"That was well fought," said Svart. "Now, if only every one of your people is able to do the same, you will all die, and I will still have plenty of people left over. Sit in those crypts if you will, it will matter little to the outcome."

Sindri loosened the scabbard from Vilgrip's side. Finnr carried Vilgrip's body back to us, mail and all, while Sindri went to retrieve the sword.

Svart's host shuffled and hunched as if readying to attack but never getting quite organized enough to do so. The big *jǫtunn* sat erect but did not rise.

One of the dwarves stood at the rear of our host, his hands on the door. Sindri must have told him to be ready to close it as the last of us reentered the crypts. My people were ready for a fight rather than a retreat—all those I could account for, at least. Where was Styrgrim?

"Problem?" asked Svart.

I wheeled around to realize it was not me he was addressing. Sindri stood over Garm's corpse, hands on Tyrfing's hilt, pulling with all his might. The sword would not budge.

"It is fine steel," said Sindri, keeping his tone composed despite his vulnerable position. "Driven a bit deep for these old hands."

"It is a poor thing to leave the weapon in the body of my champion," Svart continued. "I will assist you."

"Dvalin! Durin!" Sindri called before turning back to Svart. "Only dwarf hands may touch this weapon."

"It was just wielded by a human."

"Yes, well!" Sindri was losing what little composure he had left, even as Dvalin and Durin came to his aid. "I pressed the weapon upon him, but that is all. Had he survived, he would have had just as much . . . trouble!"

I did not need to say anything to my people. They knew we were on the knife's edge of a hard battle. Where in Niflheim was Styrgrim?

Svart snapped his fingers. The *jǫtunn* rose to his full height. The crowd of ogres in front of him parted.

Dvalin and Durin ran to Sindri and tried to pull the sword. "We will have the sword removed and back in its grave right away," said Sindri. "Just a bit finicky, this one."

"As if it has a mind of its own," said Svart. His tone was casual, as if this were a thing on the periphery of his attention. "You need a bigger pair of hands, it seems to me."

"That is unnecessary and will only make things more difficult," snapped Sindri.

Dvalin locked the sword's hilt in the grip of his silver tongs. Sindri and Durin also grabbed the tongs, and all three pulled together. The sword did not move.

The *jǫtunn* took a tentative step forward, eyeing the dwarves and then Svart. He spoke in the old language, and I understood him well enough when he pointed and said, *"Bright blade."*

Still casual, Svart grinned. "What did you say that sword's name was?"

Sindri heaved and panted. "I did not! Neither is the armor named."

"A splendid weapon going unnamed? That is unlike your folk." Svart held a hand up to the *jǫtunn* and looked our way, as if scanning the crowd.

I expected Svart was calculating how fast we could retreat back into the crypts. The one dwarf stood ready to close that door, but the rest of us were ready to do anything but retreat. Even Styrgrim had returned. He patted his beard, part of which was smoldering.

I pulled him close and hissed through my teeth. "There is the issue of the sword."

"I know," he whispered. "The fire is impenetrable. I charged it, and it knocked me back."

"You oblivious blowhard!" It seemed impossible to convey to the man what I wanted without saying it outright. I wanted to punch him in the face for his inability to understand me, now and so many times in the past.

He stopped patting his smoking beard and snarled at me.

Svipul leaned in and cupped her hand over his ear. She whispered something in total silence. Styrgrim moved his eyes without moving his head and relaxed, letting out a single long breath. In a moment, he gave the slightest nod that's ever been given and stepped forward.

Nanthild, however, had been quicker to hear what I wasn't saying. She started forward slowly, avoiding attention. Styrgrim pushed past me and followed her.

Someone sneezed or held it in with a high-pitched sound. At the entrance to the crypts, the lone dwarf manning the open door trembled. His eyes darted as if seeing things I could not. With one hand still on the door, he took a tentative step back.

Svart *hmphed*. His tone was too smug to be by chance, and that's when I caught the hint of rotten eggs in the air. He hadn't been calculating the speed of our retreat. He had been working a subtle spell on the dwarf, trying to scare him.

The *jǫtunn* took another step forward. A dozen spear-wielding dwarves stepped forward in response. The dwarf at the door cowered at the rising tension. I headed for the ensorcelled dwarf, hoping to calm him.

"You dare desecrate my champion's body?" Svart's voice seemed to come from all directions at once and then echo for long seconds after he spoke.

The dwarf shrank from the sorcerous sounds. When his eyes finally met mine, I grinned and held my palms out. Whatever the dwarf saw made him yelp, hop back into the crypts, and pull the door closed behind him.

*Goat's breath and cat piss!*

"The doors are shut," Svart boomed. "There will be no r—"

"Forward!" shouted Sindri. He turned back toward us and pulled the hammer from his belt loop. "For our people, for our ancestors, do not let them touch this sword!"

The dwarves advanced. Svein waddle-charged at Sindri with a group of ogres behind him. Nanthild broke into a run, Styrgrim close behind her.

"That's the sword, that's Tyrfing," I shouted to our war party. "Don't let them get it!"

Magnus drew his seaxes and charged. Kraki's limping gait would get him there, though not as fast. The others were spread out. Some headed for Tyrfing, others I lost track of.

Tendrils matching the glow of Svart's distaff writhed out in all directions and wrapped him in shadow. The champions closest to him stepped back. The smell of rotten eggs went from subtle to overpowering.

"It is no use," said Dvalin.

"It will not budge for us!" echoed Durin.

Sindri told them to let go of the sword. His people's spears would not reach them before Svein did. Gripping his forge hammer in both hands, he stepped over Garm's carcass. "Meet your fates on your feet, boys." The brothers put their tools away and hefted their spears.

Svein went right at Sindri, leading with his shield. It's a good idea if you're bigger than the person you're attacking. Knock into them with the shield, then hack them down as they stagger. And Svein was quite a bit bigger than Sindri. He hadn't fought many dwarves, however.

Sindri brought his hammer down on Svein's shield boss, sending up a shower of sparks. It was nothing like the thunderous clap from before, but plenty to send Svein staggering back.

Dvalin and Durin leaped forward, forcing Svein farther back with their spears. He struck out with Silence once, twice, three times to bat their weapons away, but the brothers were quick on their feet and worked against him in tandem. It looked like it was going well, but the ogres not far behind would change everything.

Nanthild went for the sword. Sindri saw and winced as she reached for it.

Styrgrim came in from the side and blasted Nanthild away with his shield. Strong as Nanthild had become, the old warrior had more fighting experience by far and was a good deal heavier. Nanthild hit the floor in a roll, far out of the way.

A line of three ogres went wide of the dwarves and closed in on Styrgrim.

He raised his shield against an oncoming axe before he could even put a hand on Tyrfing.

I know a little about dwarf-made weapons. I can hear Need hum with intent and feel its meaning in my bones. And what I felt next was a sword, far more powerful than Need, giving its approval.

Tyrfing released its grip on the rock below. Stygrim, still holding his shield above his head, made a wide, horizontal slash. It cut the attacking ogre through the waist as if it had encountered no resistance at all. The top and bottom of the ogre's body fell in different directions.

The bright blade lit the cavern. The deep *jǫtunn* snarled with hate and covered his eyes. Ogres and Rus also paused, their faces ghastly pale, until they scattered ahead of the giant's advance. Heavy steps echoed through the cavern as they came on against Styrgrim.

That looked like too big of a fight for anyone to be near, so everyone stayed clear of it. Everyone but Kraki, who did not stop until he was shoulder to shoulder with Styrgrim the Bear and Tyrfing. The two elder warriors fanned out and charged the giant.

A primal roar unlike anything I'd yet heard rang through the cavern. Svart's people were moving, but mostly away from him. Svart did not appear to be a "him" anymore. Dull, green tendrils of smoke twisted and writhed, expanding with every breath, until a face poked through the smoke. A horned, reptilian face.

"A skin-changer!" Ketill shouted. "Svart is the dragon!"

And then, if there was anyone who could hear one thing above another in the chaos of that battle, it wasn't me.

Need changed to a spear as I ran to join a loose line of my friends and allies. Ogres and Rus joined in a loose line together, forming up with that big *jǫtunn* fighting behind them. That meant we couldn't get to Kraki and Styrgrim, but if that *jǫtunn* took too many steps and swung wild, he'd crash into the back of his own allies.

It also meant that Svart could crawl over that way undeterred. And then we might lose our two best warriors.

To my right, Josur held his shield up. It took him screaming into my ear to hear him over the roars of the dragon, the giant, and the shouting all around.

"*. . . kill the dragon . . .*" was all that was audible. Surely, he didn't mean for *me* to do that, did he? But it was me he said it to. Me, who led Arrow-Odd's army.

*Oh shit, it's just Josur and me.*

And that scared me one way, the losing-my-life way. What I saw next scared me a whole other way, and that was what brought me out of that brief torpor. Unable to use his bow, Ketill had taken up a spear. He was charging the dragon by himself.

Josur banged the shoulders of a few dwarves and gestured for them to join us. I shouted to Finnr, who stood behind the line, but to no avail. He held up a finger as if I should wait, for some reason, when waiting was the one thing I couldn't do. I shook my head and bolted toward Ketill.

The wizard was more than a Brother. He was my mentor, my teacher. A constant critic, but he demanded far more of himself than he'd ever asked of me. The wisdom he'd passed on made demands of me without making demands, the most powerful kind.

I caught up with the old wizard just as the dragon noticed us. It turned and snapped at Ketill's spear, finally getting a hold of it in its teeth. Ketill tried to shake it free of those jaws, but the dragon just pulled the wizard closer. I stepped to the side and jabbed at an eye. The attack came up short, but it forced the monster to let go.

I thought we were doing quite well until the dragon's tail came from the side and took my feet out from under me. Had it got me at a slightly different angle, I'm sure that would have been the end of my legs. Hitting the ground just knocked the wind out of me.

Ketill pulled me away from the monster's follow-up attack. "Shield!" he shouted into my face.

I'd learned to act first and ask why later, so I reached for Need and brought it up in front of us. It changed as soon as I had my grip, becoming an iron shield twice the size of a normal one. I realized why as the dragon drew its head back. It looked a bit like Nanthild preparing to spit a very long way, only what was coming was a lot worse.

The dragon's neck shot forward at us, jaws opening so wide they must have unhinged. An instant later, a blast of fire hit Need and spilled around the edges. We made ourselves as small as possible behind the shield, my foot bracing the bottom of it against the rumbling flame. For a moment, I thought I was about to sacrifice my own right hand as the iron grip went from cold to warm to hot.

I felt something through the ground that wasn't a blast of fire or the clash of arms. Something like a horse's gallop. I turned my head and saw that it wasn't a horse. That would make no sense. It was an aurochs.

A bull the size of a moose, its horns must have been nearly three feet long. Curving out and then back in, and always forward, that was a one-animal wall of spears coming our way, and fast. Head down, it bellowed what sounded like a warning. It took me almost an entire second to recognize the black and white stripes. The same coloration of Finnr's beard, same as when when he had changed into a badger. Now he was headed for that dragon's soft underbelly.

Svart's dragon neck unlimbered and the fire stopped, saving my hand. The tail came around at the new threat and struck at the charging aurochs low to trip it up.

I thought Finnr was going down right there, but the dwarf had more tricks than I would ever guess. Just before the tail hit his first foreleg, Finnr changed skins again. This time it was into an owl, still retaining the black-and-white stripe pattern. The dragon snapped where he had likely expected the downed aurochs to end up and got a mouth full of nothing when Finnr fanned out his wings and climbed.

The distraction gave Josur and four dwarves time enough to reach us. Ketill and I joined their line, and I added what I now knew of fighting a dragon. "His neck goes rigid when he breathes fire!"

Which I thought meant *so we need to dive away when that happens.*

Josur nodded, hefting his sword and crouching like a man about to pounce. "Then we wait for him to do it again."

"*What?*"

"Draw him into it! Then I will go in from the side and attack his underbelly!" We didn't call him The Daring for nothing.

The dwarves held the dragon's jaws at bay with their spears. Old hands at using long weapons to fight much larger enemies, they were more agile than expected. Svart snapped at the spearheads with talon-like teeth and batted others away with the side of his face. The dwarves knew how to work in concert, though, and whenever one spearhead was moved aside, at least two more were already there to threaten Svart's further advance.

Somewhere on the battlefield, that deep *jǫtunn* cried out, which sounded like a mountain dying. Hard to hear any more details over the clash of steel and shouts and grunts. Impossible to see through all the foemen, who still outnumbered us.

The dragon reared back again, and we could all see the fire coming. I brought Need up as a shield again, this time with the shields of the dwarves added to the sides. The dragon's neck shot forward. Josur left the shield wall to flank the monster but was a hair too early.

Svart had not fully opened those massive jaws. He must have still been able to see the movement, sense the threat. He pushed back on his short forelegs and gave himself just a bit more distance, brought his head down, and changed the angle. He caught Josur full on with that fiery breath.

The young lord kept his shield up and raised his sword, but it was no use. The linden shield burned away until nothing was left but the boss. Flames engulfed the man mid-stride, heating his armor, reaching into his helmet. Josur fell forward and did not move again.

The dragon stopped the flame and made a belching, laughing sound as it slithered forward.

We pressed our attack against the monster. I stabbed with Need, but none of us could get close enough to that underbelly to drive a point home. And I was so fixated on the dragon in front of me, I didn't see Svein coming from our flank.

He seemed to come out of nowhere when he brought Silence down on the hand of one of the dwarves. He followed up with Silence's spike through the dwarf's head. Before even freeing the axe for another stroke, Svein pivoted and brought a big, booted foot up to push-kick Ketill, who stumbled and fell backwards.

The other dwarves turned against Svein, but I'm certain Svart had been biding his time for that. His long neck snaked back and around the wobbling spears. Then it shot forward like a serpent to bite the head of the dwarf next to the one who had just fallen. Svart reared back, pulling the dwarf into the air and wrenching side to side as the rest of us fought Svein to a standstill. A headless body fell to the ground.

I called for a regrouping and retreated, keeping Svein at bay with my spear. I grabbed Ketill and helped him up with us, but our little group was not ready to fight on two fronts. If I could buy a little time, I could, I don't know . . . something.

The owl hovered behind the dragon and whistled. It got the dragon's attention, and ours.

Beyond the fighting, where even Tyrfing's light barely reached, a short figure stepped out from the darkness. He wore a black cloak that completely covered his body and carried a huge, yellow bag under one arm. In his other hand, he carried a small bow and quiver, but he put these down. He ran toward the enemy line, shaking the bag and forming a cloud of sparkling dust, and fled back into the darkness as quickly as he'd appeared. The cloud remained, and it floated into the midst of our enemies.

"Get away from that!" Svart's voice was part human, part reptilian.

Svein looked from the dust to the dragon to us and backed off. Slowly at first, as if this was no retreat but rather a canny means of regrouping. I knew better. Svart's tone said a lot about how bad that cloud of dust was.

Most of the goblins saw the dust cloud coming and ran. It reached some of the Rus, who clawed at their eyes. The ogres reformed their lines, trying to avoid the cloud. Then, arrows began to fly out of the darkness and into their ranks. Many more than could be shot by one dwarf.

The sons of Ivaldi had come, and that was the last straw before most of Svart's host broke and ran.

The dragon breathed fire at us again, but we saw it coming and distanced ourselves in time to avoid it. He could only move that rigid neck so much while breathing fire and could only do it for so long before someone threatened to stick a spear in his guts.

Soon, there was a lot more than our spears threatening the dragon. Kraki and Styrgrim stopped chasing those in retreat and came at the monster, Tyrfing's bright blade lighting a scene of carnage behind them. The *jǫtunn* had indeed fallen, along with many of our enemies. Kraki's body was painted red and black with gore, including a bleeding gash across one arm.

A few loyalists remained. Styrgrim cut through their weapons and shields and straight into their bodies. Kraki bashed a Rus champion in the temple, caving in the side of his helmet. He shouted for Svein, but Svein was already gone.

The dragon slithered back, putting more space between him and Styrgrim. Then he changed skins back into smooth-talking Svart with shocking speed and pointed at Styrgrim. "I see you've got more than just one dwarven artifact. Had I known you were so bent on self-destruction, I might have approached things differently. But for now, I judge it wisest to let you continue cutting yourselves!"

He sank straight down like a man dropping into a mountain of soft snow. Only there was no snow, there was only solid rock. The movement looked ridiculous, laughable, even. But the ground had opened up beneath him, and he disappeared into it.

I had just seen my first sorcerer take the Lower Passage. And I'd stood stock still while it happened. I did leap forward at that point, but he'd already gone. When I got there, it was as if the ground had never even been disturbed.

But if I had really been paying attention, I would have been focused on the task at hand. Our reason for being there was not slaying sorcerers, but destroying the Brisingamen. Fighting for your life will make you forget about other matters, and for good reason.

I remembered the task as soon as I saw Styrgrim sheathe the sword.

# CHAPTER 46

# THE CUT

THOSE OF US WHO WERE NOT BADLY WOUNDED SEARCHED THE battlefield. A dying enemy would give Styrgrim a chance to draw Tyrfing again and destroy the Brisingamen without delay. The cavern was dimmer without the sword's bright blade, lit now only by the crystals high above. It was enough light to look by, and soon we had our answer.

That torc's destruction would need to wait, as there was no remaining foeman, human or troll, still living.

I returned to the area just outside the crypt, where humans and dwarves helped with the injured.

Even with Tyrfing sheathed, Styrgrim was a frightening figure. His chest heaved and his beard dripped with gore. Red painted the bright steel of his mail and helm. Styrgrim lifted the sword in its sheath and examined it closely, as if in conversation. I thought I heard him mutter something under his breath.

Sindri approached him, Dvalin and Durin at his sides. Their clothes were torn and bodies beaten and slashed, but their faces were full of relief.

"If you think to ask for the sword's return," said Styrgrim, "you can have it after I'm dead."

"It's good for you to say so," said Sindri with sadness in his voice. "I did not mean to ask for it back just now. I meant to tell you to keep it."

Those of us who heard those words were silent in surprise for a long time. The dwarf king's tone expressed what his words did not: That the sword was a curse on Styrgrim, not a boon, even if he didn't acknowledge it.

As I thought about that, I noticed the black-cloaked figure with the ugly yellow bag approach. It was easier to see he was a dwarf now, but a bit different from the others I'd seen. A handsome face featured piercing eyes that felt like they looked into me as much as at me. He still had his bow and quiver as he marched right up to Sindri and started speaking without introduction or greeting.

"If I just heard correctly, you've handed over the one thing never supposed to be handed over, and now you say, 'Keep it.'" He shook his head.

"That's right," Sindri confirmed.

"Is that all you have to say about that?"

The dwarf king pointed in the direction of Garm's body. "See if you recognize that thing and where it came from."

The dwarf walked over to the hound's body and took a moment to examine it. "This thing is on the wrong side of the Gjoll!"

"Now you know why I don't ask for the sword's return."

The dwarf kicked the hound's body. "Unless you've developed the strangest propensity for butchering meat, I don't think you need to use the sword on this thing anymore."

Sindri shook his head. "The sorcerer responsible for it still lives."

"Lots of ways to kill a sorcerer." The dwarf left the carcass and shook his head as he walked back to us. "Depending on the sorcerer."

"I intend to kill Ogmund Tussock and his cowardly son, Svart," growled Styrgrim. "Who are you to second-guess such decisions?"

"Hmph! Some gratitude for coming to your aid. I'm called Mondul, though I think it's less important to know my name than the name of the fool swinging that sword."

Styrgrim grinned, showing his teeth. "Styrgrim Halsteinsson is the fool, though most call me the Bear. Some might call me 'Savior of Dwarves' if they were paying attention."

"I won't deny that you, personally, were doing well. Not well enough to survive a poisoned arrow or fire, however. And many of your people did not survive. It's good we arrived when we did."

"'We'?" I asked. "Who else is here?"

"The Sons of Ivaldi, of course!" Mondul put his fists on his hips with pride. "They're not especially social. I am more like a cousin. And, I think, they are rather surprised at the extent of this attack."

"Svart is the one who brought the hound," Sindri explained. "Don't think I handed the sword over lightly. And don't think I could take it back now, one way or another."

Mondul sighed. "I'll tell the others. They'll be no less interested in what you've done with the sword than in hunting down those who attacked."

"Come back after you do. The Sons of Ivaldi deserve rich rewards."

Ketill stopped Mondul before he left. It sounded like he asked some questions, but they were spoken too low for me to hear. Anyway, I was distracted from that conversation when Kraki called out for anyone in earshot.

"Where is that scum, Svein?"

"Pursue him, and you will lose time," said Finnr. The dwarf looked and sounded sadder than normal. "And there's little enough of that left."

I thought he was just speaking generally that we needed to get back to our crews and get on with it. He tapped Kraki's still-bleeding arm.

Kraki cut away a dead enemy's shirt and wiped away some of the gore he was splattered with. It was a clumsy rag to use, and it smeared almost as much as it cleaned. The slash on his arm was more than a scratch, however, and continued to bleed. With skin closer to stone, Kraki never wore armor. I'd seen him take small nicks, but bladed weapons never bit very deep. This wound was the exception.

A feeling welled up in me, that sort of suspicion that something is very wrong but you can't identify what. Sometimes it's the *landvættir* giving a warning. Sometimes it's just a thing too difficult to face. "Kraki, why are you bleeding like that?"

"Why do you think?" snapped Finnr.

"Ah, I forgot my own advice in the heat of battle," said Kraki, shaking his head. "'Give a man room to swing.' I got too close."

Understanding came to me with disbelief in equal measure. The fight had been utter chaos around them, the sort Kraki thrived on. He and Styrgrim had faced that big *jotunn* and then hordes of others, shoulder to shoulder.

Sindri's words came back to me with a shiver: *The sword cuts more than intended, always.*

"I thought I had moved aside well enough," said Styrgrim. "It is just a nick, though."

"Did you hear nothing!" shouted Sindri. "Or did you hear, but not listen?

There is no such thing as 'just a nick' with that sword. Every cut is fatal, and there is nothing for it."

Finnr reached up to put a hand on his son's shoulder. "Time," he repeated. "Maybe you have more than most. You were hardy before you came to live with us, and only got more so for growing up here. But it is a matter of time, now."

Dvalin and Durin looked more miserable than when they'd told the story of forging Tyrfing.

Kraki took a deep breath and put his bone club away. "However long this cut takes to bleed me dry, it can't shorten the life I've already had." He put his hand on Finnr's shoulder.

They didn't need to say anything else out loud. Some say expressions of love and gratitude need to be warm and tender, direct and explicit. I say that's not true for everyone.

"Our brother deserves a hero's interment," Dvalin said to Sindri.

Durin nodded. "He should have a place in the crypts. Among the best of us."

Sindri, who had described Kraki as a "human stinking up his hall," seemed unlikely to agree to that. But before an argument could begin, Kraki put the issue to rest. "That place is not for me. I will see the sky again. I was born to the Up-Above, and I will end there."

The dwarves did a great deal to heal the injured, which was just about everyone to one extent or another. There was nothing for the abyss that had opened in my stomach, however. I'd come to see Kraki as the rock upon which all our enemies broke. A fixture, a constant without whom there was . . . what was there?

We had lost Vilgrip and Josur, and Bjorn was badly injured. The skald had taken a spear to the shoulder, and the point had pierced his mail shirt. Styrgrim tried to help him rotate his right arm, but Bjorn, who could endure a lot of pain, shook his head after a single attempt. The dwarves put his arm in a sling and swore their poultice would be proof against infection. I wasn't sure Bjorn would be able to hold a weapon any time soon, though.

Nanthild stared at Styrgrim with her arms crossed, clearly angry that he had gotten the sword instead of her. I walked over and poked her. Hard. Like one of those times she poked us for saying what "men" did, forgetting about her. Her expression indicated she did not appreciate being poked.

"That was reckless and stupid. Do you know how much we would miss you if you were cursed by that sword?" Her expression tightened, resisting any show of emotion. "You're frustrated because you want to kill Alfhild, and your sword won't cut a sorcerer who is hard against steel." I tilted my head at Mondul, still speaking with Ketill. "Well, there's a dwarf who just said there were lots of ways to kill sorcerers. Go find out what other options there are."

Nanthild ran over to Mondul as fast as I'd ever seen her move. Meanwhile, Styrgrim made it clear he had overheard me speak. "But it's all right if I am cursed by the sword?" Styrgrim grinned. "Never mind, I was made for wielding this thing. We'll make a good end, together."

"You spoke of giving the sword back at your death," Sindri cut in. "Spoke of it Down-Below, where it cannot be taken back."

"I have neither design nor desire to go back on my word."

"The sword has a mind of its own and will try to put itself beyond our reach." The dwarf king shook his head. "I've never known a man to desire his own end as much as you do, Styrgrim. I only hope you finish it with less damage to your friends than you've already done."

Maybe I could have spoken up about the Helhound, about the *jǫtunn*, about Sindri's people who had survived because of that sword's 'damage.' My mind was not on arguing, though. It was on the logical extension of Kraki's death, which was defeat. Real, utter, permanent defeat, the result of my choices.

Magnus and I went to retrieve Josur's charred body and sword, and Kraki insisted on helping. Svipul stood next to him as the old man picked up Josur's top half, and Magnus, his legs. She watched, holding her spear on one shoulder with her other hand at her hip. She eyed the old cook up and down, a look of strong approval in her grin.

"Family dies for you, if necessary," she said, the same words she had spoken to me after Haldor's death. She had always meant that more than one way. She'd known my birth would kill her, and she had no regret. Just as Kraki showed no regret now, but gratitude for the life he'd had with Finnr as a father.

"I think," I said, clearing my throat as I picked up Josur's sword. "I think Josur had no regrets. He was not a Brother, sworn to our crew, but he deserved his name. He was Daring to the end. Vilgrip was our Brother, and he deserved his family name, even if he didn't care for it. He was Tyr's son, and braver than any god of Asgard."

"We'll honor them by following their examples," said Magnus.

Not much more was spoken as we prepared to leave. Dvalin and Durin argued a bit, the sort of arguing that is less about the argument and more about something else. They stopped after Kraki addressed them.

"Brothers, we have never spoken much. I can see your difficulty with what has happened, but this thing has not been your doing. Always, you honored your family, even when your family was a stinking human nobody asked for." The dwarves sucked back laughter at the joke and held their breath. "These are my Brothers in the Up-Above. I have neither time nor skill to tell their stories. But you know me, and I have never asked for much. Now I ask: Aid them if you can."

Dvalin held his arms behind him and sniffled. Durin kept his arms crossed and shuffled his feet. They both nodded.

Little as I wanted to walk back through Hervor's mound, we had to go back that way with our crews waiting. Finnr said he was coming with us and led us to a gate nearby. There were old stones there, and old spirits that didn't know us but for very briefly. They let us pass through without difficulty.

Hervor's grave mound stank even worse than before, if that was possible. We walked by her desiccated corpse lying motionless on that flat slab of stone. Was it the wrong time, as she would only walk and speak at night? Or had my verse awakened her for a limited time until another such poet spoke up to demand she rise? Of course there was a third explanation.

"She is wise to keep silent," said Magnus as we passed by. "Another giddy word from her, and I'll cut her tongue out!"

The walk across the island was uneventful. The sun was high, and none of the illusory fires appeared. The island was a barren place. We did pass the fisherman as he gathered moss to burn.

"Did you find what you sought?" he asked.

I did not stop as I answered. "What we found turned out differently from what we sought."

"That's always the way of things."

I knew of no one to put in command of the *Wave Climber* and was thankful when Styrgrim suggested Hjalti should be its captain. There was a great deal of demand to know how things had gone when we reached the ships. Styrgrim waved it off and told everyone to be patient.

"You will hear everything, but not on this island," Styrgrim said. "Suffice it to know that Vilgrip and Josur died well, fighting our enemies in the Down-

Below. Want to know more than that? Then get in and row us back to Gotland, fast!"

The crew of the *Sea Squirrel* required some explanation before we pushed off, though. "Who's this funny-looking fellow?" asked Moose-Frothi, pointing at Finnr.

"I'm your real father, which is why you're so ugly. Or at least, I had a lot of sex with your mother."

Frothi didn't take the joke well, but Thorir held him back, howling (literally) with laughter.

I explained that Finnr had been with us in Lejre. That only created more questions, the answers to which created more questions again. So, I ended up telling the crew of the *Sea Squirrel* just about everything on the way back to Gotland. It was an awkward thing when I came to the point of telling them about Kraki. From across the ship, he interrupted me, to my great relief.

"I got cut by the evil sword, and now I'm dying. Someone else will have to dole out rations. And you will need a new rudder man. But maybe not for some days, yet."

The rhythm of rowing ceased completely as crewmates looked up at Kraki or at one another. Oars came up and stopped or fell away and clanked on others. All of which angered Kraki, and he shouted at them to get their rowing back in time. That was the longest short sea trip I've ever taken.

Disbelief was the most common sentiment when we told the others that Kraki was dying. Even among those who'd never clasped arms with him, Kraki was known as a hero of the age, and in an age gone by. I could tell just by their faces that they felt much the same as I did. Shock. Loss. But they did not despair despite the loss, and I think that was down to one thing in particular.

Kraki was not as famous as Arrow-Odd, but Odd had left. And they knew this old man would sooner die than abandon them.

# Chapter 47

## Broken Blade

Kraki was a hard man to be around most of the time, but I found it impossible to imagine going on without him. Neither could the rest of the crew. They didn't say so, wouldn't say so, but I could see it in their faces that they now questioned the wisdom of finding Tyrfing. Good people had died to find that sword, and still the Brisingamen was still intact.

The army spread out near the monastery on Gotland again. I ordered people to keep their tents and fires at least half a bow shot away from the stone buildings so we wouldn't be right on top of the monks.

We would be there for at least another day, seeing to the funeral rites for Josur and Vilgrip. I also had no idea where to go next or what to do. Our quest had seemed like one long adventure to me, but Kraki's pending death made the whole thing seem like slouching toward certain defeat. It made me want to crawl into a barrel of ale and never come out, but there were too many demands on me to do that. I turned my attention to our most immediate needs.

We needed a pyre for Josur, but Vilgrip was more complicated. As a Christian, he'd liked the main idea behind one of their stories and taken baptism twice. But did that mean he wanted to be buried in one of their churchyards, apart from his Brothers? I had to consider questions like that and weigh the consequences of choosing wrong.

Magnus and I went to the monastery to speak to Orm. He did not want to allow any pagan presence at Vilgrip's funeral rites, claiming the man had been "one of the flock." Feeling very spent, I was slow with a response.

"Flocks are of sheep, and sheep are for shearing," said Magnus, drawing one seax. He looked up in thought and drew the other. "Or for butchering."

Tafi intervened in the conversation, suggesting we hold our rites for both Josur and Vilgrip that night and let the monks bury Vilgrip's body in the churchyard the following morning. I agreed to that, and we left to get preparations underway.

Twilight fell, and we lit Josur's pyre. I described his last moments to honor him, with nods all around. Then some called for the whole story to be told beginning to end, from the time we approached Hervor's mound. The skalds had already told everyone what happened, but it had been a summary. I started to tell the story in detail and stumbled early on when I mentioned how the sword cursed the line of anyone wielding it.

Angry looks turned to Styrgrim. I had to tell everyone no, I was not at risk, because Styrgrim was not my real father. I was a god-child, and I'd kept that a secret from my Brothers other than Magnus. If my credibility had been approaching a low ebb, it bottomed out at that moment.

It was a good night to get drunk, only not for me. I had the burden of leadership, even if people were displeased with me. And I was certain that sobriety would keep me plenty miserable enough to honor the dead that night.

I kept mostly to myself after speaking. Efraim came out to show me a thing he had written. He'd taken the time to write the stories we'd told him the night before leaving for Hervor's grave mound. "A true accounting! Just as you described!"

The little monk was excited at first but shied away and returned to his quarters when I told him I had another matter to attend to. Also, prolonged exposure to a bunch of drunk Norsemen is not for everyone.

It was a night to think about death, but I was thinking about life. I found Kraki sitting with Finnr around a campfire, each sitting on a log. Despite the circumstances, they were joking and laughing.

"Kraki," I said. I wasn't sure how to begin, so I just spoke the words as they came to me. "You're going to die, and I don't know your story. You knew the king of the dwarves, you had two dwarven brothers, Finnr is not your friend but your father, but you are still a Midgarder. Will you tell me about your past?"

"Why do you want to know?"

"Because . . ." I wasn't sure about that. Or I was, but it was so all-encompassing that I didn't have a short answer.

The old man shook his head and drank deep from a large cup. As he did this, Svipul appeared out of the corner of my eye. She strode out just enough to get my attention, turned to look at me, and then walked on and disappeared behind a tent. I blinked, and the thought came into focus.

"I've already known too many people whose stories went untold," I said. "Maybe their names are remembered, but who they were and why they did what they did—their stories—don't live on in memory the way they ought to. Sometimes I think that's what the *landvættir* are—memories still alive because people speak them and keep them in the world. Your Brothers don't want you to pass out of Midgard to be forgotten."

"Hmph," he said. "You speak like we can win, and you can go off skalding again to tell the world some exciting stories. My last day is likely to be yours, skald. The best we can do is spoil our enemy's victory a bit. Live to see it spoiled, though?" He shook his head.

It was a bleak outlook, and I wondered about the wisdom of disappearing into the forest like Arrow-Odd. I couldn't do that, though. Fate carved by the Norns or fate as my own refusal to choose differently, all I knew was that I wouldn't stop until Ulf was dead.

"My son," Finnr said, now less happy and more serious. "What did I teach you about your being different?"

"That I did not pass on opportunities as other dwarves would. I am too short-lived to be so hesitant to change."

Finnr nodded.

Kraki remained hesitant. "You know my story already."

"We have not spoken much about your life before I found you."

"Unpleasant business," Kraki muttered.

Finnr shrugged. "That's often the sort of business that molds people. But if you want to leave your Brothers Up-Above without telling them of it, that's your choice."

Kraki rubbed his forehead and stared into his cup. A thoughtful pose I had never seen from him. "I don't even know where I would start."

"Maybe start with your armring," I said. "Two wings. An eagle? A hawk?"

He stared into his cup for a while longer. Finnr did not prod him, so I didn't either. After a long time considering, he answered as well as I think he could. "They are just wings, not part of a bird. Part of a god half-remembered, a thing of the sky. I could not even recall all the parts of the symbol or what it was called, only that it had wings, and the wings had feathers in three parts."

"I'm not familiar with the symbol or anything similar to it. Where were your original people from?"

"Far away, in an unknown direction. I spent little of my life there. We lived in the hills and the mountains. Danger came, and we came down from the hills to the city, a safe place with thick walls. Khazars and the Christians besieged us. I remember their banners. And I remember how their kings danced. We held out for a long time, starving, retching from disease. And they danced, the kings. I thought the danger was over at one point. Then they killed most of us.

"The Khazars took me, and I was still very young. I doubt any of my family lived through the massacre. All I had of them was my father's old knife. A short blade, a working blade. Not the best blade, but mine, and they let me keep it since that is what they wanted from me: Work.

"It must have been years I worked for them. I was young, but strong for my age, and only became more so. Then I became a problem, always pushing tools too hard and breaking things. They set me to clearing forests or to fishing, and I often did the task too hard. It came to be a nuisance, even though I didn't intend it that way.

"But they fed me, and I had not enough memory to find my home again, if it even existed. So, I stayed and tried not to break things.

"One day, after we had been traveling a while, we ran into a group of traders on the Silk Road. Muslims, I think, as I remember the crescents. The Khazars said they meant to sell me, but that they would miss me. A strange sentiment, that. They baked me a boule of bread and offered that as a parting gift since I was going away.

"I never had much to eat and had less on days I broke things. Maybe I would have more with the Muslims? And at least I had good bread that day. So I cut into it and found their real gift.

"There was a rock at the heart of the boule. My knife found it and snapped as I stabbed into the bread. That was the last part of my family, the last part of my people. For all the whippings and cold nights and hunger, I had never known despair. Until that blade snapped and nothing was left.

"The Khazars and Muslims who had come together for business laughed. Laughed and went back to trading in their tents, while one strange fellow came out. Not a Khazar or a Muslim. Or a Christian." He nodded toward Finnr. "Here was a dwarf. He came out to see what was wrong. He listened, did not laugh. He did not speak my language, but somehow understood. He offered his own gift, and I took it and walked with him to the Down-Below, where he taught me the languages of that place. He called me son, and I called him father, and he showed me the ways of the dwarves."

Kraki looked up and locked eyes with me. "That was when the dwarves became my people. As much as dwarves might accept anyone, even each other. Fundinn, they called me, the Found One. Sindri never much liked me. None of them did at first, as I didn't even know their language. But some grew to like me after I fought for them. I was a terror of their enemies. Fundinn Third-Leg, Fundinn Shinsplinter.

"I stayed in the Down-Below for many decades. Time flows differently, to stay there a long time. Eventually, I knew I had to leave. Had to see the sky above me again.

"Where I came back to Midgard was far to the north, a fjord in Haloga-land. The mountains and the open sky and the sea! I met a man from a village nearby, and I did not wish to give my dwarf name. But I also could not remember my old name. The Khazars had called me 'little one' and then 'screwup.' I didn't wish to use those.

"The man said I was too skinny and offered me food. He kept calling me 'skinny' whenever I would eat. The name stuck, and I became Kraki. I worked, and they gave me food and shelter. I didn't even break things anymore.

"Until vikings came. But you already know how the *Sea Squirrel* got its name."

Kraki drained the last drop in his cup and rose. He took Finnr's cup and walked away. I suppose he meant to get more ale, though I'm not sure he was comfortable continuing. It sounded like the end of his story.

Sounded like. But Finnr had just a bit more to add. "Before you ask, I will clear something up about that 'gift.' What I offered him, a boy who'd just seen the last of his heritage destroyed, was my forge hammer."

"But he was not a smith, so—"

"It was not offered for forging," the dwarf interrupted. "I had already heard the boy was unnaturally strong. I couldn't see why he remained a thrall, other than he didn't know what else to do, where else to go. I found him in despair, but he only needed the slightest strand of hope to pull himself out of it. Freedom can't be given, only taken."

"He killed those who had tricked him?"

"The ones who sought to sell him and buy him, both. Smashed their bones to pieces."

"A powerful warrior to recruit for your people."

"Think that's why I took him Down-Below?" Finnr shook his head.

I was confused. "Was that not the reason? Or was it because you couldn't just leave him there atop a pile of ruined bodies?"

"Neither. It was shame." Finnr breathed deep at the memory. "Hearing an ancestral blade like that snap—it hit me like a clap of thunder, literally knocked me over. I knew something evil had happened, but all I heard was laughter and jokes. When I saw for myself, there was no more denying that I had been on a bad path for a long time. No excuse for selling good steel and taking no responsibility for what my steel became. I'd been trading on the Silk Road for too long, too happy pursuing profit to think about what my profits wrought. To think I would have traded it to the likes of those people!" Finnr shook his head and pulled at his beard.

"You had the dragon sickness. That's why you hit me. In Lejre, I mean, when I thought you would forge us so many things to sell. Why you reacted so fast when you saw it coming on me."

He nodded. "Mine is the way of steel, not of gold. I forgot that for a while. Didn't want you to forget it and have to do shameful things to learn your way back as I did. The only thing I could think of to undo some of my shame was to give that boy a chance at life, as his tragedy had given me my sense back.

"He saved me as much as I saved him."

# Chapter 48

## Meanwhile, on the Way to West Gotaland

THE 'STEINS TOLD THE IRISH IT WAS TIME TO LEAVE BEFORE spring had truly sprung. Utstein told them it was because his brother was so insane with the need for vengeance that he couldn't wait any longer. That was a plausible reason, and good diplomacy. But the real reason they announced an early departure from Ireland was that the stories were so boring.

Everything was about stealing cows. Or stealing cows back that had been stolen. Who wants to hear about that every night?

King Aed Roin mac Becce Bairrche may have had an off-putting name, but he had offered rich rewards to the 'Steins. When he offered gold, they asked for iron instead, and got it. Those brothers had worked hard over the winter smelting and hammering based on what Efraim had told them from the codex. They had even improved on the codex's general design idea.

Once they had heard "iron prow," nothing was going to stop them from making one. And as eager as they were to create it, the 'Steins were twice as eager to put it to use.

All that work had left little time for learning the local language. The brothers had relied on Skuli for that, and then on Fjornir. Skuli was a father now and had to swear he would never leave Ireland. Fjornir still said little but had learned enough Irish to tell dirty jokes. He was popular with the Irish, who called him White Hat. After Utstein announced their pending departure, Fjornir told the brothers about an unexpected reaction.

Some of the Irish in the king's hall, and even in outlying areas, wanted to join the crew. Freeholders with little more than spears to their name. Warriors with short swords and good armor. Many in between. And the king had given his blessing.

"A lot has gone on while we were busy," said Utstein.

"This is more than a liking for the jokes you tell," added Innstein.

"I think these Irish and recruits from Vagar might have similar motivations." Fjornir did not elaborate. The 'Steins didn't need him to.

The 'Steins made the rules clear that these new crewmen had to swear to. They reiterated, especially, that no fighting amongst the crew would be tolerated. The rule had held with Norse and Irish prisoners, but would it hold with Norse and Irish warriors side by side?

The Irish who wanted to join swore their oaths. They even clasped forearms with the Norse from Vagar. That satisfied the 'Steins, and the left the ship almost fully crewed.

The journey from Ireland back toward the North-Way was full of rough seas and freezing winds. It was also faster than normal. The *beitass* helped harness the wind. Olvor had overseen the weaving of a new sail to replace the one stained with Halfdan's sigil, and that helped, too.

When there was plenty of wind, the ship really moved. But what would happen when it hit another ship? It was a long trip for them to think about this, and a long time to wonder where they would even find Alfhild's people.

They reached the west coast of Rogaland but weren't sure where to go from there. The Irish were of one mind when they saw three crows circling to the south. The 'Steins decided this was as good a sign as any and and headed in that direction.

They found a Bjarmian shitboat there and sailed right into it. *Halfdan's Gift* hit their hull and gave them a good shock. Innstein said it still seemed a bit slow for a ramming ship, perhaps having hoped to break the enemy craft in two. Utstein replied that the ship would only ram as hard as there was wind to push them.

They pulled the ship in with grappling hooks. It was easy to close with the enemy, but difficult to hold the crew of *Halfdan's Gift* back. Fjornir led the way with his carpentry axes. Norse and Irish warriors followed together.

It happened so fast, the 'Steins didn't think to have them leave a man alive for questioning. So, they tried that on the next ship, but it turned out the crew was still too highly motivated to slow down once the fighting had started. Fjornir was so highly motivated, it left his hat dyed in enemy blood. White Hat became Red Hat.

The third ship they found was not full of Bjarmians. The brothers knew this was a good find when they saw Alfhild's winged *othala* symbol on some of the shields. It still took them shouting and swearing to hold everyone back before the last man was killed.

The survivor held up a shield painted with the winged *othala* rune like it would ward off the violence from those lower-born. That shield, and his chain shirt, indicated he must be important and likely to know some things the brothers wanted to know.

"What happened after the raid on Alfhild's shitty island?" Utstein demanded, being the more diplomatic brother.

The god-child spat at Utstein and proclaimed his superiority. Which they might have ignored. But he added a comment that was, for him, a big mistake. "I am a son of the sea god, Njord, and you are nothing!"

Innstein laughed out loud at that. He tied ropes to each of the Njordsson's legs and pitched him over the port side of the ship. He held one rope over the port side. The other rope, he tossed out in front of the ship and let the slack gather beneath the hull before pulling that rope across the starboard side. Soon, Innstein had both ropes taut, with the Njordsson caught beneath the ship. After a few long moments, Innstein pulled him to the surface on the starboard side.

Utstein reached over the gunwale and yanked the Njordsson back onto the deck by the hair. The man puked up a lot of seawater.

"What's wrong?" asked Innstein, in his sweetest possible voice.

"You are Njord's son," said Utstein. "Don't you like Njord's domain?" Utstein suggested they do this a few times, but the Njordsson was not in favor of that. He preferred to answer questions in a polite way, instead.

The man didn't have much information about the crew of the *Sea Squirrel*. They got away from the island, it seemed, and Alfhild took her people north and west around Finnmark. Alfhild had started in the far north and headed south. It turned out the 'Steins were fighting the ships she had left behind, a few scraggly fools left to keep hold of the halls and borgs of the defeated and capitulated. Alfhild's main force was moving along the coast of the peninsula. And it was Alfhild doing all the commanding while Ogmund lurked in the background somewhere.

The size of Alfhild's army was bad news. The 'Steins wouldn't get through so many enemies with a fast-but-not-that-fast ship. They would need more ships, more warriors, or a way to catch her unaware. Based on when Alfhild had left the Njordsson in charge of his newly acquired lands, the 'Steins estimated that Alfhild must be close to West Gotaland by that time.

The crew of *Halfdan's Gift* left Njord's son to Njord's domain and let him swim for it. Everyone laughed when one of the Irish said he saw fins in the water.

The 'Steins turned south. They rounded the peninsula and kept to the coast, creeping up back north and east. They passed Fretborg, where they wanted to stop just to see what had become of the place, but didn't have time for that.

West Gotaland was in Sirnir's lands, though they didn't intend to visit him. They found some locals who didn't flee at their approach, and suggested they sail a little farther south and up the River of the Geats, where Asmund Barrel-Beard had a mead hall.

"Maybe that's a place we can find some answers," said Utstein.

"You never know what you'll find in a barrel, so it's often a surprise," added Innstein.

Which it would be.

The 'Steins sailed up the River of the Geats, half expecting to find Alfhild's army there. There were very few ships, and no sign of battle as they approached the docks. The city had a lot of people staying in tents, or even less than tents, spilling outside the walls. The brothers asked around as they approached the gates and heard these people had fled their homes. Raids were happening all over the place.

Fjornir took the crew into the city surrounding the mead hall. That would give them a chance to spend some money they'd taken from those ships. The 'Steins needed information, though, the kind unlikely to be had by spending money.

The brothers entered the mead hall, which seemed a bit big for the likes of Asmund. Or maybe there were just fewer people about, given the trouble Alfhild was causing. A few shields hung on the walls, but there were no interesting carvings on the supports or doors. A few guests sat here and there, all appearing to be passers-by rather than big retinues. Asmund sat in the high seat, listening to reports of trade activity, or lack thereof. He appeared relieved to have a distraction when the 'Steins called for his attention.

Asmund recognized them as men of the *Sea Squirrel*, but he wasn't overly happy to see them. "We thought you two were dead!" Tone and expression made it sound more like *Why aren't you dead?* Which is not a warm way to receive guests.

"We thought you were with Arrow-Odd's army," said Utstein. His tone and expression remained warm as he practiced that diplomacy again.

The 'Steins seemed a little suspicious of Asmund, and Asmund seemed a little suspicious of them. But the brothers had a good story: Escaped the island, got picked up by the enemy by mistake, and decided to kill the enemy and take the ship. Having patiently assuaged Asmund's suspicions, the jarl told them what he knew.

Asmund's story wasn't as good as theirs. It involved a lot of explaining why certain things had not happened, most of which seemed to support Asmund's decision to leave Arrow-Odd's army with Sirnir. "I've mustered who I could from inland, and I still have barely enough warriors to defend myself against Ogmund's people."

"Pity there was no idea to attack them when you were all one big army," said Innstein.

Asmund frowned.

"What my brother means is that we intend to attack Alfhild. We need some provisions, which we'll pay fair prices for. But mostly we're looking for people of a similar mind to ours."

"I'll give you fair prices for certain, but I can't spare any men."

"How about women?" asked Innstein. Asmund seemed to think that was a joke. "One of the best warriors we fought alongside was a woman. Maybe you knew Nanthild the Silent? And some of our crew are women, Norse and Irish, both."

"Your business is your own," Asmund said in a disapproving tone. "I must keep what ships and warriors I have just to defend myself. Ogmund and Alfhild may have a large force right now, but large forces have ways of breaking up. I don't think they will be able to threaten us all at length, especially so far from home."

Which was one way of looking at it, though not a canny one.

Innstein looked a hair's breadth short of murderous at that point. He got frustrated sometimes and tried to force the frustration to stop. Only it can't stop because it's due to human stupidity. Utstein grunted in a way that told his brother *Calm down, let's go.* He was more of a frustration-avoider. If people were stupid in one place, he would suggest going to another place.

"We won't bother you at length then," said Utstein. "And we thank you for the fair prices on provisions."

Utstein knew they would take a bit more time there and see who they might recruit, but he didn't say so out loud. Asmund could find his own frustration later. The brothers left Asmund to his reports of no trade activity and took a closer look around the longhouse.

Not many happy faces looked up from cups of ale. The mead hall looked like it was as full of the displaced as the rest of the city, only these displaced people had more money: A few warriors for hire, a few merchants, some rich farmers who might not be rich for very much longer. One person got the brothers' attention.

"She look familiar to you?" asked Innstein. He pointed to a woman sitting in a corner of the mead hall. Red hair. Pretty despite some battle scars. Well-dressed, despite looking rather worn. Long seax at her belt. Long enough that it said *weapon* louder than *tool*.

"Maybe," replied Utstein. But he couldn't place her, either.

She sat next to one of the crazier looking stragglers. His posture was bolt upright while his expression conveyed extreme displeasure with everything in the world, including himself. Which is saying something, being that they were Norsemen. His clothes were difficult to see because he had covered himself in birch bark like it was armor. Even on his head, like some woodland helmet. Next to him sat a goat hide arrow bag and an unstrung longbow.

The woman picked up a lyre and said something to him. He sneered and turned his head. She started to play. It was clear from her first strummings that she was a skald, and a good one.

The 'Steins still didn't know who she was. The crazy-looking straggler, though—they knew exactly who that was, birch bark or not. The goatskin arrow bag and gold-fletched arrow were giveaways. It was hard to believe it was him, but it was, and the brothers exchanged a conspiratorial look.

They had to find out what Asmund knew of this man before anything else. They went back to him, again interrupting his trade reports.

"Is that one of your champions?" asked Innstein.

"That man over there, wearing the birch bark all over," clarified Utstein.

"Ah, *no*. I think he is simple. Gave his name as 'Barkman,' and that was all. He showed up with the woman, Steinvor. I was happy to take her in. But him?" Asmund shook his head.

"You don't think he looks familiar?" Utstein prodded.

"Not at all. And I'm not sure what to do with him. He asked for hospitality and said he would work for it. I asked him what skills he had, and he said, 'Absolutely none, and I fail at most tasks I attempt.' So I asked him if he would just do manual labor, and he said, 'Of course, but you should know I have the rottenest luck of any man here.' Who says things like that?"

The 'Steins thanked Asmund for the information and left him again. They found some cups of ale and sat quietly in the hall, drinking and listening to Steinvor's music. Eventually, the Barkman got up to leave.

The brothers followed him outside. A stone's throw from the longhouse, Utstein hailed him. "That's interesting armor you wear, Barkman."

The man shrugged without turning around. "As good as I deserve."

"Birch is good for many things," said Innstein, "but not armor. For armor, you probably want a chain shirt."

"That's often true, brother. But maybe not the *best* armor. The *best* armor would be more like . . ."

"Like a silk shirt woven by an Irish witch?"

Arrow-Odd turned like a cornered wolf. "What is it you want? I've left my army and my quest. I've nothing left. But if you've come here to taunt me, you will find more than words in response."

"I'm not sure what we would insult," replied Utstein. "We're not at all certain why you would be wearing all this ridiculous bark or go by the name Barkman."

"We heard your army survived, albeit in a smaller form, from Asmund," said Innstein. "But why aren't you with it? We'll pay for information if you want. News of our Brothers is of utmost importance."

Arrow-Odd refused to take money for information. He told the 'Steins everything that had happened up to his leaving of the army, including the prophecy by Huld that had made him abandon his quest. He'd taken a passage on a ship with some Swedes, Hemming and Steinvor following him. But the Swedes intended to go to Hrolf Kraki's court, and Odd had enough of kings, so he left the ship and headed west through the wilderness, where he became the Barkman.

"Where is Hemming?" asked Innstein, unable to keep The Tone out of his voice.

"Stayed in the forest," said Odd. "He helped me make this disguise. I wanted to live under a roof again but not go by my real name. I told

Hemming he'd served me well enough, and that I could tell he wanted to remain in the wilderness. I let him go."

"Pity," said Innstein.

"So, you've still got one loyal follower," said Utstein. "Are you in love?"

Arrow-Odd let out a bitter laugh. "That woman is the bane of my existence. I never asked her to follow me, but she trails me like a lost dog, reminding me of a past I'd rather forget. I've had little from her but noise and nuisance."

Utstein got the feeling that despite these complaints, the exact opposite of each statement was true. He also noticed that Odd had stared not at him or his brother as he spoke, but right in between them. When he turned to look, it was one angry-looking skald he saw.

"I set my purpose to glory and word-fame," said Steinvor. "Who knew the myth would turn into such a maggot?"

She had a familiar look. The kind of look one gets when one has been sleeping rough for a while and hasn't had the use of a good washbowl. And maybe that person can keep up appearances well enough, but it ends up getting difficult to keep bits of leaves and twigs out of your hair. Harder still to keep your clothes clean when you need to keep on wearing them. Red eyes to match her hair spoke of nights on watch with too little sleep.

But she had endured all that. And for the opposite of thanks, it turned out.

"If you were seeking to reinstall this man as a commander," Steinvor continued, her voice venomous, "you should rethink that idea. He's given up. Despaired. Made a virtue of invoking the prophecy he runs from. He is a man who decided to die, rather than one who had to be killed."

"Hmm," said Innstein. "I think it turns out, brother, that these two are not in love."

Utstein waved off the joking. "This prophecy, it said you could not pursue Ogmund?"

"It said if I pursued the sword any further, or led the army, I would only invite more calamity upon my friends. But I don't need her prophecy to remind me. I held a dying warrior after we fought Starts fleet. She was a woman, but she reminded me of my friend, Hjalmar. When I saw his face in hers for a brief moment, I knew something was afoot. And that was not the only sign in Uppsala warning me away from my quest. I've already caused my son's death. It's clear now that if I try to avenge him, it will tear apart my allies no less than my enemies."

Innstein furrowed his brow. "But the prophecy didn't warn you away from pursuing Ogmund, only that the sword was a bad path. And that you couldn't lead."

"There is no killing Ogmund without that sword! He has dodged every sorcerer-killing arrow I've shot at him. Vignir broke every bone in his body, and he still survived. Ogmund is as much spirit as man, and it will take Tyrfing to kill him. What else could do it?"

"Maybe drown him," said Utstein.

"Or burn him," offered Innstein.

"Chop him into small pieces and burn the pieces?"

"That works on *draugar*. Should work on Ogmund, too."

Suggestions like those carried on for a while until Arrow-Odd stopped them. "Don't believe that any such ideas will work. You should leave me be. I've spread my ill luck too far and wide already, none more so than to those who've kept the most faith. Keeping my ill luck contained to me alone is as much as I can hope for." He sounded so miserable, it was almost an apology to Steinvor.

"Luck has certainly made an interesting play for us to be here at the same time as you," said Utstein.

"It turns out you are exactly who we needed to find," said Innstein. "And a skald, too!"

Odd shook his head. "Needed for what?"

"We have a ship in need of a strong wind," said Utstein. His eyes got big as he took a step forward.

Odd stepped back, as if he'd seen something strange.

Innstein stepped forward as well. "You can still do that, can't you? You might be more full of hot air than ever!"

The Barkman hunched his shoulders. He'd found what might be a simple life, and here were two maniacs asking him to upend it. Tempting him with the hope of success, the thing that had always been within reach but had always slipped out of his hands.

"He can call the wind," rasped Steinvor.

But would he choose to? Much as Utstein wanted to drag the man to the ship right then and there, he knew it had to be a choice. "We need a good rudder man. And a skald. Because who doesn't?"

"You would need to be reliable when called upon," added Innstein, just looking at Odd.

"If you want those positions, join us at dawn." Utstein turned to leave with his brother.

A dozen paces away, Steinvor ran up to them. "Hey, you! I heard everything you said. Don't think I missed anything, and you said not one word about how you survived that fight or what you've done since. We had it from Ansgar himself that you died on that island. Explain yourselves."

The 'Steins exchanged one of those looks, and they both knew right away they would tell this one everything.

# Chapter 49

## So Much for Subtlety

Funerals for lords often stretched on for days of drunken honors and grieving, but we had a witch to kill and a dying captain. Most people tried to pack three days of inebriation into one night, so while I was up before dawn the next morning, I knew most of the army would be rising very late.

Sunlight reflected off a solid cloud cover, lighting the last cool mist of the morning. It would have been a lovely day to enjoy the scenery and scent of fresh air, except for the copious amounts of puke around the camp.

Ketill, still refusing alcohol, was also up early. I was grateful for that, because it meant someone to come with me and see Vilgrip's body off. Orm argued about it, but eventually let me and Ketill help carry Vilgrip's body from the war camp to the graveyard. The wizard managed despite his injured hand, still wrapped heavily in bandages.

Roughly-marked graves stood on the side of the monastery opposite the war camp. There was no fence or physical boundary, but I could still feel it as I crossed the graveyard's threshold. We carried Vilgrip to a hole that was already dug there. Tafi bowed and accepted the body, directing some of the monks with ropes and a wooden slat to lower Vilgrip in a more ceremonious way than Ketill and I could.

"It's very well you've brought the body," said Orm, "but I can't countenance your presence for the burial. You must leave the graveyard. For . . . for your own good."

Orm stuttered because, mid-sentence, a very old and very powerful *galdramaðr* stepped up and got nose to nose with him. Ketill said nothing at first, just stared the priest down. From the top of the monastery, a raven croaked.

"We will decide what is good for us," said Ketill.

Orm, now wide-eyed, tried to swallow and failed. "It is not my rule. It is a church rule!"

"That may be the rule, but it's a hardened heart that prevents close companions from seeing off a friend," said Tafi. "Is it more lawful to do good in the churchyard, or to lack compassion?"

Orm took the out and suggested we stay. Then he made up an excuse about Tafi needing to go out and gather food for later, dismissing him.

The priest spoke for a while, all in Latin. Ketill eyed me, and I ignored him. Eventually, Orm made the final gestures over the grave, and some of the monks began to fill it in as the raven croaked a second time. I didn't much like leaving Vilgrip in the churchyard, but I could only do as best I thought, given his most likely wishes.

"I don't trust that priest," Ketill told me as we departed.

The wizard's anxiety was beginning to wear on my patience. We had enough problems that might kill us, and Orm was not one of them.

"It all sounded fairly standard to me, as little of it was about Vilgrip himself. Now I need to look at the state of things in our camp. You can look with me if you like. Or . . ." *or if you are in a foul mood because your hand hurts, you'll do anything but admit it.* "I will need you soon. I would ask that you see Huld this morning and let her examine your hand again. It looks to me like it needs clean bandages."

"I am not in need—"

"Then you'll ask Huld when you should be able to carve again."

Ketill harrumphed, muttered something about puke all over the place, and went to find Huld. I walked the sleepy camp alone, careful where I put my feet. People were passed out in the most absurd positions, in the least likely locations. More people had fallen asleep with their pants down than I cared to count. Others hunched over logs with varying levels of drool. Magnus snored standing up, propped up under his arms by crossed spears stuck deep into the ground.

It would be one of those days.

I decided against waking anyone up just to talk to me and instead walked a ways to the beach. To my surprise, Kraki was already there, looking out across the sea to the west toward Hervor's island. The waves were dark, the sun not yet high enough to peek over the treetops to the east.

"We need a cart," Kraki said.

"You're looking at the sea, and thinking about a cart?"

He nodded.

"Why a cart?"

"For the *Sea Squirrel*. I had the dream again, only more of it. The ship was on fire, rolling across the ground on a cart."

"Are you sure we don't need buckets of water instead?" He looked at me with utter confusion. "To put the fire out, I mean."

"No!" As if *I* were the exasperating one. "I saw the end. I saw what we need to do!" He turned to face me. "We need wood to make a cart. We will mount the ship on it."

This would not be Kraki's first prophetic dream. I had dismissed the previous one because it sounded ridiculous, with that masturbating wolf. I would not be dismissive again.

"All right," I said. "Can we get the necessary materials from the monks?"

Frustrated, he shook his head again. "It would take too long. We need a place that has lumber cut already. Wheels already built."

If not on Gotland, I wasn't sure where we would go. Not that I was sure where we were going next anyway. For that, I had to take counsel with Styrgrim, so I left Kraki to his reverie and started back to the camp.

Halfway there, my thoughts were interrupted by a loud croaking. The raven glided low and landed in front of me. "Skald, I found you!"

"I did not know I was missed. Or who I was missed by."

"Honor." The raven bowed and splayed his wings. "You were busy with the wizard, so I was not able to repay your stories. I mean, I heard them from the monks, but they don't trade, and they were stories about your people. I overheard them early this morning, and in good faith, I must provide."

"That's very like *drengr* of you. But what was it you heard monks speaking of that we have not?"

"About your people who converted!"

I blinked so hard it kicked up a small breeze. "What men who converted?

No one has converted, man or woman, to my knowledge. Vilgrip was already a Christian."

"I mean earlier than that. The two who saved everyone at the island on the White Sea. They renounced Thor and invoked the Holy Spirit as they were fighting to their deaths. And the woman, Hrefna, asked for forgiveness with her last breath and was saved. But the man, Ingolf, drowned, and so could not be saved. And all that inspired Vilgrip to take baptism."

"You heard *what?*"

Honor hopped back a few steps. "I've only repeated what I heard!"

"Who did you hear this from?"

"The tall one in the dark robe, I recognized his voice. He was dictating to one of the others, it seemed to me. But I was on the roof, how do I know which one he spoke to?"

"We will see about this right away!"

"I can come back at a better time . . ."

"You come with me! What you've heard is false. You will hear the truth before you leave, or I'll have that wizard curse you so thoroughly, you become Dishonor!"

Birds chirped and ocean waves lapped in the background. The air was fresh with the scent of salt. It must have seemed a peaceful morning, other than my murderous outlook. I stomped my way back to the war camp and through it, heedless of disturbing the sleeping warriors.

As I crossed from the camp into the grassy area I had told our people to stay out of, Efraim ran out of the scriptorium. He sobbed and clutched a parchment to his chest. When he saw me, I was surprised that he turned my way. Orm shouted after him from inside the building.

I pointed at the little monk as I shouted. "Just last night I heard you speak of writing the truth, and now I hear fabrications instead!"

Tears streamed down the little monk's face. He could barely breathe, and I thought his heart might give out mid-stride. Angry as I clearly was, he continued on until he literally crashed into me. He looked back at Orm, looked to me, and shook his head, too upset to speak clearly.

Orm emerged from the stone building, baring his teeth and walking as fast as his long robe would allow. "Return that parchment immediately!" He held a short whip with knotted ends in one hand and a torch in the other.

Humor hopped off the roof of the building and poked his head inside. He flapped unhappily at whatever he saw and took off toward our camp.

"Help!" Efraim managed, now pressing his parchment into my chest.

"Help for what? What is written here?"

"Truth."

"What do you mean?" I demanded. "I heard you rewrote our stories, told of the 'Steins converting. You renamed Hrafn and condemned Ingolf as an unfortunate fool."

Humor screeched like I had never heard him do before. When the hungover army barely moved, he screeched again and again, a demand they all wake up. When some answered with annoyed groans, Humor got even closer and screeched into their ears.

Efraim shook his head. "I wrote the stories!"

"That is church property," Orm said, pointing at the parchment. Or maybe he was pointing at Efraim. Given that person at that time, he could have meant either one.

Efraim regained more of his voice and spoke so fast it was like he feared losing the ability. "I wrote them truly, as you told them to me! Father Orm read what I wrote and said it was crude and not godly. He said it must be written again, but that he would dictate it to be more correct. I started writing, but what he dictated was not true. I told him . . . I told him . . ."

"Slow down," I said.

The little monk held up his right hand, the back of which was bruised and swollen. "Father Orm said since my hand did not have faith, he would have another finish it. So he made Petrus take the dictation. I said nothing, because I knew Petrus would not write what he said."

"Efraim, turn from the heathens and give your love back to God," shouted Orm. Black smoke from his torch spiraled upward. "Look how wayward you have become, seeking their words over God's!"

I grabbed the monk by his shoulders and shook him. "Why do you have the parchment, then? And where is Petrus?"

Efraim pointed back toward the scriptorium where three monks had emerged. Two of them were in fine shape, each taking an arm of the third, who could barely keep his legs under him. That third man was Petrus. His back was bare and bleeding from whip marks.

Petrus, the scribe behind the *Liber Abdsurdum*, the book of jokes. No wonder Humor sounded so unhappy. The raven wasn't pestering the hungover. He was calling them to battle.

"Father Orm checked Petrus' work. He handed it to me before it could be burned, but Father Orm punished him for disobedience twice over."

"Efraim, return that parchment right now!"

I held that Roman magic in my hands, turning it over and considering its power. Here would be the story of the 'Steins, and others. The story, therefore, of all of us. Just in part, nothing complete, but more complete than might otherwise be known. And I could feel the knife-edge balance of the parchment. One side to be used to tell the truth behind our narrative as written. One side to corrupt our story by people who hated it, rewriting it thoroughly and destroying any trace of the original.

A spell to preserve or to abuse set into the sea of the future, when no speaker who truly knew the tales would be able to correct them. That was the danger Ketill had warned about.

I handed the parchment back to Efraim. "Keep this safe."

"That parchment must be rewritten," said Orm.

I started toward the priest.

"It is a better story to tell than some of those men deserve," he explained, "and thus it will better others by the telling. I will not glorify heathen men for their sins, but rather for their regret—"

I don't remember that moment leading up to his last word specifically. I don't remember Need coming out of the sheath. Only after I made the cut did my conscious mind take back over.

Orm's head hit the ground before the rest of his body did.

Some exclaimed. Monks gasped. The ravens croaked. Magnus ran up to me, panting, having roused from standing slumber at some point. "This is a lot to get involved in without me."

I looked at the corpse and considered the raven's earlier recounting.

*The two who saved everyone at the tower on the White Sea. They renounced Thor and invoked the Holy Spirit as they were fighting to their deaths. Then the woman, Hrefna, asked for forgiveness with her last breath and was saved. But the man, Ingolf, drowned, and so could not be saved. And all that inspired Vilgrip to take baptism.*

"Maybe it is not such a big issue as you think," I replied. "Orm has got no less for brains now than he had before."

# CHAPTER 50

# GRAVE THOUGHTS

THE MONKS LOOKED SCARED OF ME AFTER I CUT ORM'S HEAD OFF. That seemed ironic, since he had tortured one of them, and I had only killed the torturer. But they had their perspective, and I had mine. I thought I had once heard "the man who swings the sword digs the grave," but I couldn't think of where. Maybe I just made it up. It seemed like a good principle, though, and the monks, clearly frightened, left me to it.

The day grew hot as I shoveled, and I sweated in the bright sun without even a breeze to cool me off. I didn't feel right having anyone else help me with the consequences of my own choice, though. Besides, everyone else was busy preparing to leave Gotland.

The big question on my mind, other than 'How does a small army defeat a big one?' was about where we were going next. I sent for Styrgrim to council about that decision. Just Styrgrim, yet Huld had insisted on coming as well. We talked as I continued digging. I told them about Kraki's dream and his insistence on obtaining a cart for the *Sea Squirrel*.

The black-clad warrior wore a semi-disappointed look as he listened. "What sort of cart?"

"Four wheels, and it must hold the ship upright."

He paced a few steps back and forth, throwing his shadow across the edge of the grave every few steps. Huld sat on the edge and winced as the hot sunlight hit her every time Styrgrim moved a few steps.

"Stop pacing!" she demanded. "I'm trying to stay in the shade."

Styrgrim crossed his arms and stood still where his shadow fell on her. "A tragedy, should a face such as yours turn wrinkled from the sun." Turning his attention to me, he continued. "I've seen a thing like that before. It's not so difficult. We can get help for that on Borghund. Assuming it isn't overrun."

"I don't think it is," I said.

He laughed. "How would you know?"

I took a deep breath. "Because I have also had . . . dreams." I dug a few more shovelfuls of dirt before continuing. "Odin brought me to Hlidskjalf. Showed me the size of Alfhild's fleet, and that it was headed toward Lejre."

"Hmm." He growled like the Bear of his byname. *Why do you trust what Odin shows you?* He seemed to ask.

"That vision showed me the storm she has conjured behind her," I continued. "Perhaps that was Odin lying, but we already heard about that storm from the raven, Impulse."

Styrgrim raised an eyebrow. "The one who warned that Naglfar sailed?" He turned to Huld. "Can you wrest control of the weather from her?"

The *vǫlva* shook her head. "I can counter her, but not undo what she does entirely. And I will need high ground for that. Alfhild will stay on the water, where she is strongest."

"Here it is, then," said Styrgrim, his tone more confident. "It's fortunate we have not destroyed the torc yet. We will use it as bait. Lure Alfhild in, make her think she can win. Choose the right ground to fight on, and her numbers won't matter so much. Especially when her people see the sword at work."

"Choose the battlefield, set the trap?" I asked.

"Of course!"

"I have heard this strategy already. It's exactly what Odin suggested."

I looked up and saw Styrgrim's eyes locked on mine. After a moment, he realized I was not joking. "*Sons of Muspell!*" He stalked off a few paces.

Huld sighed at the lack of shade.

"Wherever we choose to fight, I assume it will be uphill from the enemy," I added. "Kraki sees the *Sea Squirrel* rolling downhill at our enemies."

"Of course we'll be uphill from the enemy!" Styrgrim returned, shaking his head. "But rolling a ship down at them? That sounds like a terrible idea."

"While it's on fire."

"And that is even worse!"

I dug a few more shovelfuls of dirt. The hole was getting deep enough that I would need to finish from inside it, so I jumped in. "We will go to Borghund. You're confident we can get what we need for building a big cart for a ship there?"

"If Gunnar the Marksman holds the island, we'll get any help we ask for. If he doesn't, then the battle begins. And we'll be the ones fighting uphill."

"It will be fine."

"You know this from another vision?"

"From a previous dream," I said, returning to my work. "Odin wants a big battle. A glorious one that people remember and tell stories about, probably adding details about how he intervened. He won't allow a smaller force like ours to be overwhelmed and defeated easily because that is not to his advantage."

The growl again. "So he wants us to die. Gloriously."

I shrugged, then realized he probably couldn't see me shrug. "Odin doesn't much care who wins or loses as long as it makes for new stories. So he might prevent us from losing easily, but not from losing after a hard fight. Kraki says the best we can do is spoil our enemies' victory."

"What do you say?" asked Huld.

I stopped digging and leaned on the shovel. "I think I am done calculating what any gods want. I think we need to kill Alfhild. I know I need to kill Ulf. Whatever the consequences might be, I can't stray from that course any more than I can breathe water."

"Hmph! Sounds like a long explanation for fate, which—"

"—none of us can escape," interrupted Huld. "Don't think for a moment that you can carve a different one. Your death was determined as soon as you were born, just as your name was, just as your parents were. How you handle those things beyond your control is what matters."

Styrgrim sucked his teeth but said nothing. I doubt he meant to disagree, and equally doubt he liked the idea of things chosen on his behalf.

It was during that break in conversation that Tafi returned. He handed a basket full of berries to Efraim at the edge of the graveyard and gestured for the little monk to go away. When Tafi headed toward us, it was the angriest I'd ever seen him. "I go off to forage for one morning, and you kill one of our people? God help the flock if I went out for an entire day to try for a deer!"

Efraim winced at the shouting but remained at the edge of the graveyard.

"If your God will help you find a deer, that's a strong argument in favor of going back out," said Styrgrim. "I'm hungry."

The abbot hardened his tone in the face of Styrgrim's flippancy. "It seems I am needed here. Bare your teeth to someone else if you think it will scare him off. This is a holy place, and I am telling you to leave."

I looked up. "I thought I would save you the trouble of digging—"

"*Out!*"

I tossed the shovel out of the pit and hauled myself up to find Tafi and Styrgrim in a staring contest. "You described this man as a protector of his people," said Styrgrim. "But here he stands accusing the one who did the protecting."

"You call killing an unarmed man on our holy grounds 'protecting'?"

"Styrgrim!" I shouted. "Is this the sort of prey the Bear looks for—a weaponless man past his prime, who has sworn an oath against violence? I figured you for harder challenges than that." That broke his stare. Styrgrim would take all comers, but he didn't seek out weaker opponents. It would be unlike a *drengr*. "Go and tell Kraki we're headed to Borghund next. And tell the others to hurry up. They're all hungover and moving like laggards."

Not many people could tell Styrgrim the Bear what to do. I wasn't exactly sure I could, either. But with no one he could honorably fight, he moved off and left me with Tafi and Huld.

"On holy grounds, I won't dispute," I told Tafi. "But if you say the man was unarmed again, we will have more than words. He had a torch and a whip."

"And where are your burns, your scars from whipping?" countered Tafi. "You could have stopped him without *chopping off his head!*"

I shrugged. "It's true he did not attack me." That seemed to calm the situation a bit. Efraim, still standing on the edge of the graveyard, let out a deep breath. Tafi nodded heavily, as if agreeing *Now we are getting somewhere.*

Like music, a good argument is not loud all throughout. It has crests and troughs. This was the trough. Time for a crest. "Orm didn't fight *anyone* who might pose a threat to him. Petrus was entirely under his power when he tortured the man. If Efraim hadn't run, Orm would have tortured him as well. The dead can't speak against his attempt to corrupt their history and burn their truth. I thought you did not allow such abuse. I suppose a man can always seek change."

Once a champion of that shitrag Varg Tiorfi, Tafi had fallen to drink when confronted with the shame of his own failures. A Christian had pulled him out of that spiral, though he never forgave himself for failing to protect

Varg's daughter, Valborg. Now Tafi fancied himself a protector of this community, and I was throwing in his face that he'd failed again.

Tafi's face went beet red with rage. "Father Orm was enforcing *our* rules on *our* grounds. This was not your business. To his mind, he protected our people from bad influence. Whether right or wrong was something I could have told him, but *you could not!* You are not part of this community, not part of this faith. You have no standing to make such a decision or kill a man who is no threat to your life!"

Which I supposed was all true, only I wasn't going to let anyone live who would steal the history of my Brothers. Huld was quicker with her response, though, and sharper, when she stood up.

"You are a lucky man, Gudmund." She drove Tafi backwards with a single bony finger to his chest. "Lucky" *jab* "that you found your way out" *jab* "from under an evil master" *jab* "not once," *jab* "but twice now!" *jab jab.*

Tafi bared his teeth at me. I was confused, though not as confused as he was. I put a hand on Huld's shoulder.

"Last time you tried that," the *vǫlva* growled, "you did not enjoy what followed."

"I'm not trying to wrestle you. I'm just reminding you that I lead on land."

She didn't like that reminder very much. And though I got a bad look from her, that was all. "Lead, then."

"Go and see to Petrus. Do everything you can for him."

"The crew does not want me to help him. They're angry the Christians tried to corrupt their Brothers' stories."

I shook my head. "That was one man, and his actions can't be attributed to an entire community. If the crew won't help someone willing to endure torture on their behalf and call him a *drengr*, you tell them I said they are troll-cursed fools."

She went, snarling and unhappy, and left me to speak with Tafi. If that was really his name.

"My story was not for sharing," he growled.

"I did not share it. Huld has ways of knowing things that I don't. I always thought 'Tafi' was a strange name, but you never told me a different one. She seems to think—"

"It is as good a name as I deserve, and that is that."

I nodded. "That is your choice, then, just as Hrafn's name was her choice and not to be dictated by anyone else."

He shook his head. "You don't know whether Father Orm had other knowledge regarding this woman."

"I conveyed her last request for a fighting death. I watched her lift her axe in agony. I heard her final war cry. And I *saw her die!*" Having begun quietly, my voice reached a shout by the end. "Orm tried to insert himself and was refused. If you were to set his version of her story down on parchment, that would be as bad as carving lies into her runestone. You would be telling unknown generations a falsehood. Come on, Tafi, I remember your instructions for Petrus! Twisting stories is not what you do here."

"What we do here is for us to decide," he shot back. "Not you, who has sworn nothing to us, made no commitment to the White Christ, who sacrificed himself for us."

"That was the story Vilgrip liked so much, the idea of sacrifice for us in Midgard. You honored his beliefs with a burial here. And you also honored his memory, the one we carry with us, by letting in pagans against your own rules."

"Do not presume to tell me my order's own rules!"

"Don't hide ill deeds behind fair beliefs, then!"

With great hesitation, Efraim approached us. Hard to imagine he wanted to be there, especially as the argument had turned into a shouting match. He wore his normal rutabaga-sack-with-a-hood looking garment, a rope tied around his waist. The little monk stopped, looked at me, and fidgeted with his rope of a belt. "I would . . . go with you . . ."

I bit my tongue to avoid showing my surprise. And confusion.

"You have responsibilities here," Tafi chided, unable to soften his tone as he usually did with the little monk.

"We are headed into the heart of an army of trolls. Against a powerful sorcerer. And, perhaps, a very angry dragon." I shook my head. "I don't wish to ferry you to your death."

"You will not! God spoke to me." Efraim crossed himself. "He told me to go. I was afraid at first, but he said he would watch over me."

"Why would he want you to go, protected or not?" I asked.

"His intent is mysterious. He spoke to me in a dream, through an angel."

"Maybe it was Odin playing a trick." I said that in jest and immediately realized: That sounded exactly like something Odin would do.

Efraim shook his head. "No, I could hear the ring of truth in his words. See the honor in his eyes!"

*See the honor in his eyes?* Something rang strange to me about that phrasing. It was unfamiliar, even from the followers of the White Christ.

"Efraim, do not be hasty," said Tafi. "I swore I would watch over you, but I cannot do that if you leave. I put away my sword. I cannot draw it again."

My mind was elsewhere as Efraim tried to assure Tafi. The thing about the eyes. Tafi's promise of watching. It put a particular image in my mind. "This White Christ, what did he look like when he came to you?"

"Angel!" Efraim corrected. "He was dressed as a warrior. A hardened leather cuirass with a ram's head emblazoned on his chest, an old sword at his hip, long hair bright as the sun. But his eyes! His eyes were the depths of glaciers, as if he could see—"

"As if he could see a hundred leagues at night as well as ten feet during the day?" I interrupted.

"Yes!"

*Goat's breath and cat piss!* What was Heimdall doing in some little monk's dream, playing like he was the White Christ's errand boy?

"I think you do this because of guilt," said Tafi. "But you will not bring those brothers back, Efraim. Going off and dying will not honor them."

"No, you are wrong!" Efraim's eyes twitched away from Tafi and toward me. It was quick, involuntary.

Perhaps Efraim did feel his memories of the 'Steins in his bones, and that was part of it. That look, though, told me his decision wasn't about the 'Steins. Efraim had been scared out of his mind, barely able to breathe, and he had run to me. I had protected him in a way not even Tafi had ever done. A friend will listen when you're in need, but not many people in this world will kill to keep you safe.

"I will record what happens." Efraim's tone was ironclad, daring Tafi to stop him. Then he turned fully to me. "I will write things so that even if you are killed, your stories can live."

"Assuming you aren't burned alive by a dragon with the rest of us," I said. "Or drowned. Or hacked to pieces until they take all the pieces and mount them on spears for display."

He made the sign of the cross and smiled. I didn't know what to say to that.

"Get out of the graveyard," Tafi said, shaking his head. "I will finish the digging and speak to you later, Efraim. As for you! Make preparations for your people to leave as soon as possible." He jumped into the hole and grabbed the shovel.

And that was Tafi's way. Never to coerce or threaten, and never to delegate the hard work. He was like Haldor in some ways, even as a Christian: Both men of completely different faiths; both men willing to lay down their lives for their people. We had argued, and though I had no regrets about killing Orm, I did not like that it had upset Tafi. Now I was potentially taking one of his people away, and for what? According to Kraki, we were all walking toward our graves.

But according to Haldor, we had been walking toward our graves our whole lives. The only thing that mattered was how we walked.

"We'll prepare to leave," I said. "But first, you'll hear me tell you that you were right."

That got the old champion's attention. He looked away from the half-dug grave back to me.

"After you told me your story about a year ago, you said, 'I think you'll fight for something more important than revenge before your story is finished.' I didn't understand then, and I thought you were wrong. But you were right. We're headed out for vengeance; there's no denying that. That's not the only thing, though.

"I know the face of the enemy. It is a wolf-face, a troll-face. A way of being opposed to ours. And yours, too, though not Orm's. I know that in your mind, I've done an evil thing, but there's a difference between a man living his beliefs and one who hides behind them. Orm tried to steal our people's history and call it virtue. And like Orm, the enemy says that torture was done for the benefit of the tortured, or that those they killed never even existed."

Tafi crossed himself and sighed. He was tired, I could see, both in body and mind. "You will be fighting the same battle forever, then. You can end your enemy, but you cannot end ill intent."

I shrugged. "That is no reason not to fight."

# CHAPTER 51

# WORDS UNSPOKEN

WITH OUR DESTINATION SET AS BORGHUND, THE ARMY READIED to sail. I had certain preparations to make myself, and they involved the ravens. After correcting every falsehood Honor had heard, the raven said he was obliged to me for many stories. Which was perfect, because I needed him to spread information, and fast.

"I've got Alfhild's torc," *and the means to destroy it.* I took the thing out of my pouch and showed it to the raven. "I think it could gain me my own following," *if I didn't know the cost.* "I'll be using it soon," *as bait.*

If Honor was suspicious of me, he didn't make it plain before flying off. Spreading word of our presence was part of the plan. Alfhild would not break away from attacking King Hrolf just to kill us, but I had no doubt she would break away in order to get her torc back. We just couldn't let her know where we were going. Yet.

I had to find Humor as well. He had been with Petrus ever since Orm had whipped him. I found monk and bird in the dormitory. Huld had already done her work cooling his angry wounds, but he still lay face down on a bed of straw to avoid aggravating the injuries.

"Skald!" said Humor when I walked in. "Have you heard the one about the beggar and the *vǫlva*? A man with only the clothes on his back ran into a wise woman on the road. She offered to give him advice so he could earn a living, but he asked her to change his fate instead. She thought about that and told him to sit down and hold his hands out with his eyes closed. He did that, and when he couldn't see, she hiked up her dress and peed into his hands.

"'Hey, what do you think you're doing?' the beggar demanded.

"'This is as close as I can come to changing your fate,' said the *vǫlva*. 'Now, you're no longer piss-poor!'"

Petrus shook his head, but still grinned. The raven flapped and croaked, absolutely drunk on jokes. It took me a few minutes to coax him out of the dormitory and tell him the plan I'd worked out with Styrgrim. Once it was clear I meant for him to play a joke on Alfhild, he gave me more of his attention.

"I want you to fly out and tell Alfhild we're regrouping on the island of Mon," I said. "But not right away. Wait a day or so after we leave. I won't say where on Mon. I want her to be delayed in finding us so we have some time to prepare."

"What?!" he gasped. "Few ravens can match my storytelling skill. When describing your last moments and how you were all bravely torn apart or melted by dragonfire, *do you really want to trust the telling to someone else?*"

Sadly, no. But the plan was to draw Alfhild away from Lejre, then weaken or kill her. That would buy King Hrolf some time, and we would just have to hope he used that time to his advantage. Humor agreed that it would ultimately be a very good joke. If it worked.

We sailed for Borghund later that day. Styrgrim even grinned when he talked about going there, which I found strange. Borghund was not just a big rock in the middle of the sea, but it wasn't too far from being a big rock in the middle of the sea, either. Much of its perimeter wasn't approachable by ship, unless you wanted to run into vertical bluffs. It was a good trading station, a great defensible place.

Horns from the coastguards announced our arrival as we approached the island. When we did, there were plenty of armed men to greet us. A man on horseback approached with a few dozen spearmen behind him. Those were backed by archers. I didn't like the look of things, but Styrgrim waved me off.

"Who is this who sails into my port?" Gunnar called out from his horse. "Declare yourself and your intentions."

"Styrgrim Halsteinsson sails into your port, if that's what you call it," said Styrgrim. "And I've three intentions: One is to show you what a fine man I've made of your nephew, Helgi. The second is to find a dragon and shove my sword straight up its ass. And the third is to drink so much of your ale that I drown our enemies in vomit while they mutter their incantations."

"Are those intentions stated in order of importance?"

"Not at all!"

It went on like that for some time, even as we followed our hosts to their fortress on the island. I had never seen Styrgrim be quite that way with anyone and wondered why.

The fortress was the most elaborate defensive structure I'd ever seen. Set atop a hill with multiple earthen ramparts, gateways north and south, the outer walls protected by a moat. Boulders so massive I didn't know how they'd been moved were placed and connected by earth and hard clay. The walled area was big enough to comprise multiple buildings, with plenty of outdoor space to muster. A pond at its center provided clean drinking water.

Inside, men and women worked and trained. The place had more energy than Arrow-Odd's war camp had upon our first arrival. I took that as another good sign as we entered the longhouse.

Gunnar brought us all ale and offered whatever supplies we needed. Kraki told him about the cart he wanted, and Gunnar replied that it would be done by the next day. He even offered that we should stay on Borghund with him in case of attack, which the ravens were all croaking about.

"I would send a ship to King Hrolf's aid," said Gunnar, "but he gave me strict orders to hold the island and not leave it lightly defended at any time. If you want Alfhild's fleet to come at you, let them come here! Sheer rocks, few landing spots, good defenses already built. And a few good fighting people."

That sounded good to me, but Styrgrim shook his head. "I've another place in mind," he said. "Borghund is too far to be threatening to the witch, and she might ignore us for the time being if we stay here. On Mon, we're close enough to Sjaelland to be a threat, close enough that she will abandon her assault to come at us. She'll think she can win a quick victory and be able to return before Hrolf can summon much support."

It would certainly make Alfhild think she could win. Because in all likelihood, she could. I had spoken to Styrgrim about our strategy at that point already, and he was quite confident. I wasn't so certain, but I thought it was wiser to defer to his judgment on such matters.

"Can she?" Gunnar sounded surprised. "From what I've seen, you've not even three hundred warriors on four ships. And at least one of them looks like he is not much of a warrior."

Gunnar turned toward Efraim, who had found a quiet corner of the hall.

"He knew the risks and decided to come anyway," I said. "He is not the strongest, that's true, but I won't question his spirit."

"You might be facing nearly three thousand," said Gunnar. "You will need more than spirit."

"We have more than Alfhild will expect." Styrgrim patted Tyrfing's pommel. The sword sat above his other sword, both hanging from leather straps held around his right shoulder.

Gunnar gave Styrgrim a long stare, seeming less warm and more wary now than he had been. "You must have your reasons, then. My orders are to hold this island."

"A friend understands when there's an oath to uphold," replied Styrgrim.

There was a long enough pause for me to notice that something wasn't being said before Gunnar responded.

"This island needs supplies from time to time. If I recall, we need some supplies right now. And the men are clamoring for more news about King Hrolf. I think I'll send a ship to Mon for supplies. I'll need to send some of my best men. And who knows? They might need to stay on Mon for a while to make room for supplies returning on the ship."

"It might turn out that anyone who stays on Mon, stays there a long time," said Styrgrim. "That would need to be taken into account."

"It might be that a troll does me in while I'm trying to take a shit," countered Gunnar, who shrugged. "But I'll mention the warning so that nobody stays who would rather leave."

I wasn't sure why Gunnar was willing to do so much for Styrgrim, why he clearly wanted to go with Styrgrim. I'd never heard Gunnar's name mentioned, so what was their connection?

I didn't put it together until Gunnar reached over for a cup of ale at one point. Barely peeking out from beneath his sleeve was Arrow-Odd's armring, the same one worn by Styrgrim and Gudbrand. A symbol of a war from twenty years ago, from which very few people had returned.

There was a lot unspoken but understood between Styrgrim and Gunnar. Even if I'd heard their stories, I was certain I wouldn't fully comprehend the friendship between them. Some experiences have to be lived to be understood.

# CHAPTER 52

---

# CORPSE SHORE

I TOSSED AND TURNED THAT NIGHT, LESS ABLE TO SLEEP THE more I willed myself to do so. I thought I'd at least gotten comfortable at one point, but my wool blanket seemed to ride up above my feet. Even more strange, it felt as if the blanket had wrapped itself around my ankle. Just as I meant to sit up and smooth it out, the blanket tightened around my ankle like a rope and pulled me down.

Down below the floor of the hall, below the rock in the middle of the sea that was Borghund, below the realm of Midgard. The earth made way for whatever malevolent essence carried me, and I fell through darkness and putrefying dirt before it was done.

A sandy hill vomited me up, and whatever had taken hold of my ankle let go. I stood up, panting from fear, and took a few deep breaths. The shoreline ran close by my side without the smell of salt spray. Only the scent of decay was present, as if a low tide had left life behind on a beach to let it rot forever rather than come to high tide again. A dark longhouse stood a bit inland, its walls made of some strange wood that seemed to shift more the more I stared at it.

Beyond the hall, what could have been half a mile or a hundred miles, a great root shot up from the land and into the sky. A faint glow emanated from it, casting the hall and the water in sickly yellow.

"Am I dead?" I asked aloud, then regretted not looking closer to be certain

I was alone first. Upon examination, I was. Nothing moved other than the shoreline and strange, undulating walls of the hall. No sound but for the lapping of those noxious waves. But I knew where I was.

I was standing on Nastrond, the corpse shore of Hel. Beyond the River Gjoll, well beyond any of my other travels. This was not a place for the living. And not for just any of the dead. Oathbreakers. Perjurers. Wife-seducers. Those who strike only unseen, those unwilling to commit to combat in the light of day. Every one a *níðingr*.

My hand went to grasp Need, but I found nothing at my belt. "Pants, but no weapons?" My voice rose as I spoke. "Who has called me here?"

The gently lapping waves dared me to test the waters. I wasn't about to go swimming in Hel. Then, a great crunching and rending sound, accompanied by screams, broke the air. Somewhere down the shore was Nidhogg, Hel's dragon, feasting on the corpses of the dead.

*And maybe on me, if he finds me here.*

I walked away from the shore over land full of moss and broken bits of wood. Farther in, the detritus became more recognizable. Broken pieces of weapons and shields, destroyed ships, tattered banners, and bloody flags all lay strewn amongst limbs hacked away and left to rot.

The door to the hall lay open. Looking in, I could only see that there was a great hearth fire in the center. I crossed that deathly threshold and took a good look around before taking my second step.

It was a large hall, built wider and longer than most others I'd been in, but as if the intent had been to convey a sense of envelopment rather than openness. The roof leaked. The walls on the inside writhed even more than they did outside. My eyes adjusted a bit more as I recognized the low hissing sounds. A better look showed me the walls were made of serpents, their heads facing inward, watching me.

"Perhaps I've overstepped my welcome," I said.

The door slammed shut.

I stepped away from the snakes along the walls. Some seemed disinterested while others bared their fangs with dripping venom. I chanced a glance up and then thought better of it. That was not the leaky roof in the same way I had thought it to be moments ago. The hearth fire glowed bright orange and lit the place, but no food had been set to cook on it. Benches nearby sat empty. This was a hall made for a huge number of guests, and it seemed I was the only one.

"Hello?"

The hearth fire extinguished as soon as I spoke the word, sending a chill through me. Beyond the hearth was a high seat and a single occupant. Dressed in the same rags I had seen it wear before, it was a familiar figure to me now. It held a gnarled iron staff inlaid with human teeth in one hand, the other showing long fingers ending in claws that dug into the arm of the chair. A great nose and chin protruded from under a tattered hood flanked by greasy black forelocks. From under that hair, hungry eyes stared out at me.

"I am no more dead than the last time I saw you. You cannot have me."

Two by two, glowing eyes opened behind him. Their owners came out and showed themselves. Dozens, hundreds maybe. They fanned out and pointed, laughing hoarsely through desiccated throats. The dishonored dead stood armed and armored. Their blades were dirt-stained and rusted. Their mail and helmets were rent. It would not matter much if they all attacked me.

Their voices came together to make an offer. "You are just a skald, though you could be much more. Join us. There is more power than you think. More power than you will find otherwise."

The troll rose from the high seat and started towards me. Its iron staff thudded after the sound of taloned feet shuffling forward. *Click-click-thud.* *Click-click-thud.* And it spoke a verse, stronger and more confident than the last time I'd heard it:

> "Troll, they call me,
> cradle of the moon's minions,
> scion of monsters,
> storm-sun's misfortune,
> witch's friendly companion,
> watcher of the dead's boundary,
> trampler of the sun.
> What is a troll, other than that?"

*Click-click-thud. Click-click-thud.*

It held out a clawed hand and closed it tight, and with the closing, I heard familiar voices. Fanya asking why I let her die. Kari saying he had wasted his life on me. Ulfberht saying he would have been better off without me. Haldor saying I had failed to honor my friends. Vilgrip moaning that I had used him up pointlessly.

Fear flooded my veins. My hand went to Need a second time, again finding nothing as I searched for the weapon. It was happening as it had the last time, only now I was fully in the troll's domain, not out at its boundary.

The stakes were higher here.

Nausea gripped my stomach hard, and I staggered back. There was little I could do to compose a counter-verse. In my previous nightmare, I had tried to respond but could not even get the first word out. I knew the first line, at least. If I could just speak it . . . but then what would come after?

*Click-click-thud. Click-click-thud.*

The voices of the dead whispered brutal truths. I thought I would double over and wretch. Haldor's voice repeated, calling me a coward, and in that moment, I heard a weakness. I set my jaw and listened for it again. And when it came, I knew I had found a crack in the troll's lore.

That was not Haldor. Haldor's voice was unmatchable, a thing that rumbled through your heart. It had grabbed me by the ear and broke down any walls I might put up to keep it out. Haldor was no wizard, but he had learned some of the deep lore with his burden of leadership. Out of that burden came a power through his voice, and this troll could not duplicate it.

*Click-click-thud. Click-click-thud.*

I met the troll's gaze and grinned. Seeing the crack, nausea turned to something else, something otherwise unfelt. I held it, pulled myself back up with it, let it smolder. I knew the troll for what it was, now. A leech. A hanger-on. A dead thing hoping to make itself more than that by the deeds of those living. A rotten thing, seeking to rot all around it in bitterness that it could never be hale again. Trying to use Haldor's voice, a voice it could never match.

So I spoke my counter-verse, and found Haldor's voice with it:

> "Skald, they call me!
>> Counselor of the highest,
> purloiner of wisdom,
>> poet most stalwart,
> Odin's ale-mate,
>> fury's architect,
> skilled smith of verse.
>> What is a skald, other than that?"

The force of the verse pushed back the horde of dishonored dead. The snakes' hissing silenced while my words echoed through the hall. The name-less troll stopped, holding a hand up to cover its face.

The power of my verse having peaked, the troll grunted and gestured at his army. More venom dripped from the ceiling. The hissing of the snakes redoubled. The dead all took a step forward.

*THUD.*

If I was surprised at the sudden sound that shook the walls, the troll was in shock. The dead looked to the troll, then to each other, uncertain.

*THUD.*

It was as if an angry giant was slamming a fist into the wall.

*THUD THUD THUD.*

Louder now, and quicker. Too quick to be a single giant. I heard the familiar grunt, the one that sounded like it was half demand and half insult. It had been years since I'd heard it, years since I'd even thought of the ram from my old dream.

More grunts. More thuds. They came every second, then more than every second, and from every angle. The door gave in, splintering under heavy horns. Another broke through the wall nearest to me. Soon, three sides of the hall had been breached.

The rams grunted as they knocked down their enemies. Snakes from the wall struck at them, but their fleece was too thick for the fangs. The rams ignored them. Having knocked enough of the dead down, the rams began to pummel them into the ground. Over and over, they struck like dwarven hammers, destroying the bodies, grinding their bones to dust.

One of the rams hopped onto the cooled hearth and stared down the troll. His fleece was so bright it bathed the hall in a faint silver glow.

"Burp," said the ram, and charged.

The troll made a gesture to the dead nearby. They formed a shield wall to meet the coming charge.

I put my hand to my belt. This time, Need's hilt was there. I drew the sword and charged alongside the ram. He lowered his head. I raised my sword.

As we met the army of the dead, I woke.

# CHAPTER 53

## HOLDOUTS ON THE HILL

I WAS UP AND WASHED WELL BEFORE DAWN, MORE REFRESHED than usual after that strange dream. Had the ram been Heimdall or a manifestation of my own will? Either way, I suspected I would not see that nightmare-troll again. Not after delivering that counter-verse.

Efraim was already awake and dogged my every step as soon as he noticed I'd woken. He looked like he had something to say, but kept quiet to avoid disturbing the hall full of sleeping warriors. I wanted to explore the fortress on Borghund a bit more anyway, so I led us outside. There was a thing I needed to tell Efraim, and he would not like hearing it.

We walked into the cold mist of the morning that carried the scent of the pines. I led the way up a ladder to the second level of the fort that ringed the hall's perimeter. Four guards paced the second level to keep watch from all four sides at all times. Efraim and I walked a short way and found a good view of the sunrise.

Impending death can make a person philosophical, and I didn't see a way out. The army could not divert its course, the *Sea Squirrel* least of all. Some wanted revenge on Alfhild more than anything. For me, it was Ulf, as the betrayal of a friend is worse than that of an enemy.

Efraim yawned.

"Not much sleep?" I asked.

"I stayed awake late into the night," he said. "Some of the people must have heard that I came to write their stories. They told me many! Too many to write down, but I listened to them all. I hope I can recount them accurately later." The little monk crossed himself. He had done this when he heard something he did not like or was in fear. This time was different. He did it and stood a bit straighter, raising his eyes a bit higher.

That seemed as good a time as any to deliver bad news. "I will send you away soon."

Confusion. "What?"

"Before the end. Before the end even begins, in fact. We will pin ourselves down on the island of Mon, our backs to solid rock, and we will fight until the end."

"But I will not know how your story ends!"

I shook my head. "Stay for that, and you'll likely be too dead to write our story."

He crossed himself again, this time with some of that old fear in his eyes.

The whole of Gunnar's ring fort was easier to see from the second level. Buildings stood at the center, and roads led to the north and south gates. A packed wall about ten feet high encircled the buildings, reinforced with wooden posts. Every layer of defense provided a wide area to work in, to duck behind, and to shoot arrows from under cover. I wouldn't want to be part of a force attacking the place.

Maybe Styrgrim was right that you have to make the enemy think they can win to draw them out. If they made enough mistakes, maybe we could win. I couldn't chance it for Efraim, though. Whatever he could write down before he had to leave would need to suffice.

What bothered me most was that even if we won, we lost. Any way you looked at it, it played right into Odin's plans. An epic battle, regardless of outcome, was good for him. I looked out over the sea toward the coming sunrise. The sky glowed red, as if the wolf, Skoll, had caught the sun and ripped it apart.

One of the guards making his rounds stopped behind us. "Are you the skald?"

He held a straightish spear. Not the best shaft, but it had a clean and sharpened tip. The rest of his kit was also basic and cheap, but in good repair. A leather cap would help with the cold, but wouldn't deflect much else. He wore simple leather shoes and a brown, woolen cloak. Not even a shield.

This man would be part of the front line of any campaign. He had next to nothing, but if he survived the worst place on a battlefield, he might be rewarded. Being on guard duty for a lord like Gunnar was a good deal for such a man.

"I'm one of the skalds. There are three others with us."

"You're quite well off then. We had a skald a while back, but he went with Arrow-Odd and died. Maybe you knew Olaf?"

I nodded. "We met once. I heard he died bravely."

"He was a good man. Jarl Gunnar is a great leader, but it was Olaf who got us through the cold nights when we thought the winter might never end. He is missed."

"Anyone might be a skald, you know. You don't need to play the lyre or flute, though it's good if you do. To practice verse and learn the old stories, that's not a thing you need leave to only a few."

He shook his head. "I wish I could. But I was a bit drunk most nights, not paying close attention. Just enjoying myself."

"Nothing wrong with that."

"Not at all! But it doesn't help me remember the stories. When I try, they come out all wrong. I don't suppose one of you skalds might stay with us, at least for a while?"

Now it was my turn to shake my head. "I intend to kill a man. The rest are like-minded."

He grinned. "Best be up early in the morning if you want to do that, that's what my grandfather always said!"

He nodded and continued on his rounds. I think he was quoting advice from the *Hávamál*, as I'd heard something like "Rise early if you intend to take a man's property or his life" in one version. Maybe he didn't even know what the *Hávamál* was, but his grandfather had.

I never did get that guard's name or give him mine. As he walked away, I could feel something strange about our conversation. A feeling similar to when the *landvættir* would give me signs to follow in the forest.

When I looked over at Efraim, I saw his expression had brightened quite a bit. "I have not told you the story! I must ask God to forgive such a grievous oversight."

"What story?"

He shook with excitement. "From the codex!"

"I thought the codex was full of designs and instructions."

"Those as well, but not at the beginning. The beginning tells about the first sack of Old Rome. Do you know it?"

I shook my head.

"A new story for you! Listen:

"In ancient times, Rome was still a kingdom and not yet a republic or empire. The Gauls came down and wreaked havoc. They slew the Roman cavalry and took the city, killing and stealing at will. A few soldiers held out on one of the city's hills. They sent birds, calling for aid. Much of the city burned.

"Brennus, the leader of the Gauls, called the last defenders down to parley. He offered to withdraw his men and leave if the last holdouts paid him a thousand pounds of gold.

"The last defenders looked to the horizon and saw no aid coming. They agreed to pay and met outside the city to measure the payment.

"When weighing the gold, the leader of those soldiers cried out. He accused Brennus of using false scales so that the Romans would be cheated even in their surrender.

"Brennus laughed at the man. '*Vae victis,*' he said, 'Woe to the conquered,' and threw down his sword on the weight of the scale, increasing the amount of gold needed.

"The Romans knew they could do nothing because they were indeed conquered.

"It was at that moment that another Roman appeared. A general exiled years ago, Marcus Furius Camillus had received the desperate messages and mustered his own army. He rode up to the scales and asked what was going on. He listened to what had happened and dismounted.

"General Camillus drew his sword and drove it straight through the scale on the Roman side. Then, he turned to Brennus and told him how he would free his city: '*Non auro, sed ferro.*' Not with gold, but rather with steel.

"And with steel, General Camillus drove the Gaulish army out of Rome. He rode down Brennus himself and slew him.

"That was the story in the beginning of the codex. I did not understand why it was there at first, but now I do! The author signed it as 'A Soldier of the Old Republic.' He must have been there for the civil war when Rome went from republic to empire. I think he wanted to preserve some of the old knowledge, but not for just anyone. He wanted it to go to people like those who held out on that hill.

"Only, how would he find them? He would have seen an empire interested only in amassing wealth. And he must have known he would not live long enough to speak this knowledge to the right people. So, he wrote what he knew in an old way, so that few could decipher it.

"And by God's will, the book came to you and the two brothers—you, who hold the golden torc and the sword to destroy it." He shook his head so hard I thought his lips would fly off. "You should not send me away—this is a sign that I must remain with you!"

"That is a good story. Especially for facing a hopeless fight. And that codex was a powerful weapon for us." I took a deep breath. I did like this 'Not with gold, but rather with steel' bit. It still did not address one antagonist.

"Yes!" Efraim believed his god was with him, but what I understood was outside his beliefs. I wasn't sure if I could make him understand the thing nagging at me.

"That is another story of battle. People slaughtered on both sides is part of what makes it memorable. Even if it is told in a completely wrong way, like the Battle of the Goths and Huns, there is still some vague memory of it to inspire stories. Here is my difficulty, Efraim: Odin cares not at all whether we win or lose, only that we are fodder for another story that he will doubtless appear in. Odin is our one enemy I can't overcome because he wins no matter what battle story is told."

The little monk's face fell a bit. Not into despair, but far from the elation he had just shown. "I know many stories not involving battle."

An even stranger sensation than before came over me as Efraim spoke. His lips moved slowly, and his words came out as if he were drunk. He stared into the sky at nothing in particular. Had time slowed down?

I heard Svipul's footsteps come up behind me. She walked around my side and over to Efraim. She passed behind him, speaking a few verses as she did. I knew them all. One verse spoke of being middle-wise as best for happiness. One verse spoke of trusting in one, but never in two, and that trusting in three meant the whole world knew. One verse spoke of rising early to take a man's life or his property.

She came around to my other side and walked by me. Like a gust of wind, she was gone again. But I had understood her meaning.

"Efraim!" I exclaimed, shocking the monk out of his reverie. "I know one story not of battle. Or rather, a poem of advice. That is what you must write down, the thing to counter Odin's ill intent. From my mouth to your hand."

"What is it you wish me to write?"

"The *Hávamál.* The Words of the High One. The Words of Odin. A poem of wisdom, to be passed on to others."

"Odin is one to avoid, you have said yourself. It is his wisdom you wish to preserve?"

I grinned. "Oh, not all wisdom as he would have it. Some of that poem is good—we'll preserve that. But for the rest, it will be advice for the betterment of Midgard rather than to further Odin's glory. We will use his voice and do something better with it than prepare people for war and misery. We will forward what wisdom I've learned with my Brothers.

"We are going to steal that poem, Efraim. Steal it from the grim god of death himself."

# CHAPTER 54

## ALLITERATING AND STEALING

Efraim sat bathed in candlelight at the farthest end of the farthest table in the hall. It was hard enough for him to know what to write, and Gunnar's longhouse was full of the table-bumping sort of revelry that might make his hand go astray or spill his ink. He hunched over his slanted writing board and blew on the parchment to dry the ink faster. "This is to be a poem of wisdom? It begins with 'Just look around so you aren't surprised.' That does not seem a profound statement to me."

I had prepared as well as I could during the day, thinking of all my experiences and all the wisdom I had heard from others. Especially from my Brothers, many of whom could not be there to repeat their previous words. That inspiration burned so hot in me, I thought I would burst.

I had not burst. Beyond a jumble of ideas, including a few fully-formed verses, I had to decide on a structure for the poem. Where to begin?

I stood a few steps away, pacing back and forth and frantically telling Efraim what to copy down while the noise of drinking and cheering distracted me. Far away from our little writing corner, Magnus led a new toast every few minutes. One might wonder why there was so much celebration when we had yet nothing to celebrate—it was because we were all likely to die soon, and then we would have no more celebrations after. Gunnar told us we'd all better drink the good mead now.

I had no room in my head for mead that night, though.

"It can be understood as a metaphor," I said.

"Will all verses be metaphors?"

"Most will not be. But maybe some, to varying degrees."

"It might be difficult to understand if they are mixed like that."

Every version of *Hávamál* I'd ever heard had a few commonalities, including this one: 'At every threshold, take a good look around before you cross it, because you never know what might be waiting on the other side.' Or doorway instead of threshold, and enemies might be waiting inside. Something like that. It is a good way to begin the poem, unless you are a troll-cursed monk.

"It is not entirely metaphorical!" I said, rounding on Efraim. "It is part practical and part to think about. Yes, it means literal doorways. But I remember when I joined the crew of the *Sea Squirrel*, I thought I knew what I was signing on for, but I had no idea. I hadn't paid the slightest attention to what should have been obvious—that it was far more dangerous than I imagined."

Efraim stopped his work to look up in shock. "You regret it then?"

"No! I—" This was turning out to be a lot more difficult than I had imagined. "I sought out safety over all else. I joined the crew to prove to my father —I mean to prove to Styrgrim, because I thought he was my father—something. That I was a man! That I was worthy of respect."

Bjorn came up behind and clapped me on the shoulder. When I turned, I saw his arm was still in a sling, and the bandages beneath his shirt were thick from holding a poultice on his shoulder. "You could have joined other crews before. Why that night?"

I realized I had divulged a lot of my own thinking. Maybe too much, and my face went red. That had been the first time I realized Styrgrim might be ashamed of me. I felt humiliated. Not just that he might be ashamed of me, but that I hadn't even known he was ashamed. So, I joined a monster-hunting viking crew—the worst decision of my life, and the best.

Was it wisdom to tell others to resist proving themselves, or folly? I couldn't tell. I knew other wisdom I could share, though.

"Too much mead, for one thing," I answered Bjorn. "And that was not the only night. Too much on too many nights. And then some of my wits would remain, but others would flee completely."

"Like a bird sticking its beak into a river, and plucking out a fish," said Bjorn, his tone pitched to both speak of experience and ask if it was like mine, "and the fish is one of your thoughts." When I nodded, he continued. "That bird often takes just one fish—one word—but it's always the most important one!"

"Exactly! Efraim, write that down! But my point about the beginning is that one would be well-advised to pay attention. Not just stumble around, waiting for things to be made too obvious to change course. Even a thing as simple as walking through a doorway."

"I cannot write two things at once!" The monk scribbled furiously. "I thought the point was you drank too much mead?"

"Both points are important, and they should have different verses," I said. "We will include more advice against drinking too much. Lots of it, so nobody forgets it."

"All the better to praise moderation, then," Bjorn added.

"Isn't Odin a drunkard?" asked Efraim as he wrote. "Consuming nothing but wine? I thought it would be mead, but Tafi told me it was wine."

I nodded. "Wine is harder to find and more expensive, and Odin is a lover of fine things. We will start with advising alcohol only in moderation, but moderation will be a theme throughout. Even for wisdom."

Efraim scribbled more on his parchment. "I thought this might involve more about some other things. Spiritual things. You have a Heaven, do you not? Called *Valholl*? And you avenge even the slightest of slights, and if that brings you to disaster, do you not call it fate, *fortuna*?"

"Fate and luck are different things, and Valholl is unlike your Heaven, if I understand it right. No, we'll have none of those things you've mentioned." A memory came to me about Huld speaking Arrow-Odd's prophecy. "Except to say that a person is happier not knowing their fate."

With no warning, the monk stood up and threw himself across the parchment he had been writing on as two drunken revelers wrestled their way toward us. I grabbed the two and had no chance of stopping them, but managed to divert them away from the table.

Hallfred joined the effort, and we separated the two men. He got their attention when he said, "That's a fine host you're insulting. Good luck with manners such as those!"

That paused the two long enough to take a quick look around. They saw Gunnar and Styrgrim staring at them from across the hall, arms crossed, expressions grim. The two men stopped their fighting.

"See!" Hallfred continued. "Manners! They are good because they help you not die, even in new and unfamiliar places. Ah, that should be in the poem!"

The Horsefly was into his cups but still had most of his wits. He sat on the bench next to Efraim, crowding the little monk and making him shift uncomfortably. He couldn't have known what to make of that, but looked to me for a hint. I cocked my head slightly away from Efraim, and Hallfred moved to give the monk a comfortable amount of space.

No one could accuse Hallfred Horsefly of failing to understand his own wisdom. He might push boundaries, but he pushed on them with good reasons, and not just to create difficulty.

"What else is good?" asked Efraim. "And what is bad?"

Horsefly pointed at the empty high seat. "A host has responsibilities to his guests, and the guests have their own responsibilities to the host. It is good to be a wise guest and have something to say worth listening to but not be boastful about it. Wisdom is worth more than gold, and lighter to carry."

"Too fast!" said Efraim. "Slower, so I can write it all down."

"Write what you can!" I said. "Many thoughts come to mind. Too many at once. Once we have things in order, I will dictate verses."

"And then it will be poetic?"

"Both poetic and easier to remember. The alliteration is for both. Then skalds across Midgard may remember the new poem even without reading it."

"So, you think we will win?" asked Bjorn.

No part of my mind said yes to that.

"More important," Horsefly cut in, "are you really going to dictate such thoughts without Jorun, and risk her wrath for being left out?"

"Some say a woman's advice . . ." Efraim began the sentence but did not finish, trailing off under the withering stares of three skalds.

"Many things have yet to be determined." My own words were an echo of a dream, wherein Heimdall had said that to Thor and Frey. It had not happened long ago, but it was still a lifetime of difference in the past. "One of those things is certain: Somebody go find Jorun."

Hallfred obliged me. In the meantime, Bjorn sat down with Efraim, giving him enough space to be comfortable. He pointed something out on the parchment and spoke a low comment. Efraim nodded and scribbled something. Monk and skald appeared to have an easy time with one another.

Hallfred returned with Jorun, who slapped me hard on the back and then hung onto my shoulders for support. "Be a friend to your friend, and also to her friend. But never be a friend to her enemy." She pointed at my nose with her other hand, which was a bit wobbly.

"It's good that Steinvor and I parted on pleasant terms," I said.

She nodded. "Otherwise, you would have had a *problem*."

"Having you as a friend saved my life."

She looked at me and started to say something, but burped instead. After a few awkward moments, she nodded and continued, her tone more sober. "There are plenty of people like that, and you shouldn't confine your wisdom to the ones good at saying it in verse."

And of course that should be the way of it: Finnr's hard-won wisdom about money. Kraki reminding me that there are only two reasons to rise at night. And a hundred other pieces of wisdom, tales of adventure, and brave deeds done.

People swarmed our little corner. Some came by and left; others stayed with rapt attention. All comers had their chance to speak. All of them had something worth adding, whether I had heard it before or not.

Even Nanthild got her chance. She did not speak; she just showed her sword and the etching along the fuller: ULFBERHT. Cattle die and kinsmen die, but her kinsman's name would live on that blade as long as it lasted.

It turned out the name ULFBERHT would live on a lot longer than that, though I didn't know it at the time.

Magnus was involved such that he stayed to hear what all the others shared. And with each one, he reminded me of something I had already noticed. They each spoke of something important to them, but no matter what they spoke of—wisdom, gift giving, patience—friendship was the most common theme.

"And no one should mock another for falling in love," said Magnus, a bit louder than necessary, drawing a snort from Jorun.

I thought he meant to speak to my experience with Fanya. She'd fallen in battle at Lejre, spending the last of her life on a spell for us while holding her own guts in. In the wake of her death, I had considered giving up on life. I repeated Magnus' words for Efraim but swallowed the emotion behind them.

Huld looked the parchment up and down over the shoulder of the shuddering monk. "You think this monk is up to the task of spreading such wisdom?"

"He showed courage when all it bought him was discomfort," I replied.

"That is more than I can say for the gods. Unless you can call Heimdall down and have him help us. Another good sword-arm would be most useful."

The *volva* shook her head. "He is better than most, but ultimately like the rest. They play for influence, and influence means they must watch the choices made without delivering outcomes."

"Odin delivered a fairly certain outcome when I first met him," I said. "I was on a delivery run for a sword, and I was lost in the woods. Or maybe not even in Midgard anymore. Anyway, he intervened against a witch, a real roof-rider who would have drained my blood and used it to dye her clothes."

One eyebrow shot up. "Tell me the details."

In that story, I had gotten directions about how to find my way through a foreboding forest from a raven named Judgment. It was before I met Magnus, but after I'd gotten some experience traveling. I described the story from when I met Judgment to the point at which I found Odin's hall sitting in the middle of a fog-shrouded forest.

Not that I knew it was Odin's hall at the time. He called himself Hrani and described himself as just a simple farmer.

"Ah," said Huld. "You had not entered the hall, but you had banged on the door and asked for hospitality. That would be enough, I think, for him to extend his hospitality to you."

"Must we be on their very doorstep, then?" I asked, more than a little frustrated with these gods. "We could use a bit of help right now, even if it is just influence."

The *volva* grinned. "It's never certain when you might have help unlooked-for." She had that *I know something you don't know* look. I suppose Huld had an ocean of lore to draw on versus my pool, but giving me that look was too much to stay quiet about.

I got close enough to whisper to her. "We have fair odds for foul outcomes here. I would have you speak plainly about things you know rather than in riddles."

She shrugged. "I guess at more than I know, and I won't give voice to guesses. Worse than telling a man his fate!"

I shook my head. "I don't speak of guesses. I think you still keep secrets even at this late hour. What is it you've done for Heimdall and not told us?"

"Done for him? Nothing. Done much with his advice, certainly, but that was for others. I did not help Finnr as a favor to the god, but because I had found a friend. He understood long life and regretful choices. I fought

Alfhild for me, for more reasons than I can count, not the least being she was a catty bitch who tried to run me out of town. I healed you because I did not like the idea of you dying. And I gave Nanthild strength—no, I gave her a choice—because I felt her anguish."

"What's this about Nanthild?" I stared at the *vǫlva* with wide eyes. Somehow, she could still surprise me. "What choice?"

"The heart of the lindworm you killed. Did you not wonder where it went?" She stared at me like I was stupid for having failed to make an inventory of dragon parts. "The girl fought her way forward, close to where you fell. She could not find Alfhild, and I could see in her face what was in her mind: That perhaps it was better to end her own life."

"And you saw, because you were the cat."

Huld nodded. "I was not a cat any longer by then. I saw her, and she spoke of being unable to avenge her brother. I told her there was a way to strength if she wanted, but it would come at a price. I offered the heart of the lindworm. She did not hesitate to devour it."

Finally, the mystery of Nanthild's oversized strength in an undersized frame was solved.

"Why did you never mention it?" I asked.

Huld was already walking away. "You never asked."

Styrgrim was among the last people to relate some wisdom. "Is this truly Odin's voice? It seems less like Odin and more like what you might wish Odin to be."

"I am done with gods telling us both who they are and what we should do for their word-fame," I said. "It is the greatest foolishness that we need them rather than the other way around. They need us, or they will wither and disappear like forgotten spirits. So, we will change Odin, even as he tries to change us, and change ourselves for the better in the process."

Styrgrim cupped his beard in a battle-scarred hand as he considered this. After a long time, he spoke, and those words I remember exact:

> "Only one
>   wide-traveled
> and wandering far
>   can fathom something
> about the minds of others.
>   Such a man is wise."

I didn't ask who he meant by that. Maybe he was giving me a long-awaited compliment. Just as likely, he was speaking about himself, with much unsaid about what "wandering far" meant. Or it could be that he was reminded of advice from my grandfather, Halstein the Smith.

But that was one of the aspects that pleased me most about this wisdom. It was our wisdom, and our wisdom was always a little ambiguous. That's part of why it had endured so long and would endure still longer. Times change, people change. Good poetry echoes down the corridors of time, inspiring people in far different circumstances from those who composed it.

*If* people heard this version of the *Hávamál. If,* by writing it down, that Roman sorcery was enough to change Odin. It was good. It would be poetic once turned fully to verse. But would it be repeated?

When quoted by a Christian? Not likely.

My face fell a bit as I realized what would need to be the last part of my plan. I let Efraim work, beckoning Styrgrim over to the side so just the two of us could speak. "The truth of that verse might be a hard one to face."

Styrgrim twitched just a hair. He didn't see what was coming, but he knew he wouldn't like it.

I stepped in and whispered. "Efraim's reading of this thing will convince no one. It needs a skald. A bold one."

Styrgrim refused to even breathe in response. That was some play at giving no reaction. I had to decide whether to make myself plainer, say the thing directly: That Bjorn would not survive the next battle. His shoulder would heal eventually, but not in time for our next fight. Was that message better conveyed without being spoken aloud?

Styrgrim's heavy hand fell onto my shoulder. Not a comforting gesture. His fingers dug into my muscles so hard that, for a brief moment, I thought things were going much worse than I had predicted.

With Styrgrim at my side, I saw Svipul appear through the crowd ahead of me. She wore he raven-blue hair loose, and it caught the flickering orange firelight. She slipped by all the revelry and came to my opposite side, whispering into my ear as Styrgrim spoke so that I heard both his words and her interpretation at the same time.

"Bjorn is loyal beyond loyal," he whispered back, fingers digging in even harder.

"*Bjorn is like a son to me,*" she said.

"No one would question that," I replied.

"Now is not the time for the breaking of close bonds."

"*I want to die with my family.*"

I swallowed hard. Any more pressure, and I would not be able to hide that I was in pain. "Family dies for you if necessary." No more pressure. Just a hard stare. I had little doubt he'd heard those words before, spoken by his dying wife.

"Where have you heard—"

"Some spirits are strong. I won't say more than that about where I hear things. Family does what it must, sometimes dying, sometimes living."

The stare did not soften, but I could feel the grinding in Styrgrim's mind. His grip relaxed. His voice was gravelly and worn when he spoke. "You must be Odin's son, to dare so greatly. To demand so much of me. A spear from the gods, right through my heart when you were born." He shook his head. "Well then, I suppose Bjorn is best kept with the monk, little spear. At least this will point your tip in the direction of the gods, for once."

# CHAPTER 55

# THE NAME OF THE SKALD

I STOOD OUT IN FRONT OF OUR FIRST LINE OF DEFENSES, LOOKING down the beach as the enemy landed. Styrgrim and Magnus stood with me, watching, appraising. I wasn't sure what we might see that might matter. The whole idea was to force Alfhild to attack us, and we had spent days preparing for that already.

I looked back at our "fortress" on the island of Mon. Styrgrim had chosen the location to suit our needs, a wide chasm between the cliffs accessible only through a narrow defile that faced the beach. The defile was crowded by two huge boulders, creating two extremely narrow passes and a wider pass in the middle. We'd taken two of Alfhild's ships on the way to Mon, one of which we'd torn apart for raw materials. That ship's strakes had been chopped up and nailed back together to create low fences for that middle entryway, but they weren't enough to keep anyone out, only enough to slow them down.

Our ships and the additional captured ship sat in strategic positions deeper in the chasm, not visible from where I stood. Most were overturned to provide emergency shelter from incoming arrows. Or dragon fire. Or who knew what. The *Sea Squirrel*, of course, sat upright on top of Kraki's cart at the back of the chasm.

Styrgrim had estimated the enemy would show up two days after we arrived on Mon, and he'd been on the nose. Their ships rolled over the waves like so many stiff lindworms floating toward us. I'm not sure how many warships Alfhild had down there, but I was confident she'd called them all in. They advanced ahead of her ship and to its sides, giving that monstrous craft a wide berth. Behind them all trailed a swirling storm.

"Guess they are worried about Hrolf Kraki following them and attacking from the rear," said Magnus. "No ship is getting through that maelstrom."

Styrgrim, standing to my other side, muttered something unintelligible. He'd been doing that for days, and we'd been ignoring it for just as long. "Unlikely Hrolf still has ships to follow her. If he meant to defend against a landing, he would have been ill-advised to do it at sea, where the witch is strongest. Likely, he sunk most of his ships to block the best inlets."

"He could have pulled them inland," I said. "Maybe used for defenses like ours, but maybe just to protect them."

Styrgrim had heartened our army, such as it was, with talk about how choke points conveyed greater advantages to smaller forces the more they were outnumbered. I wasn't sure how much of an advantage we could really get from controlling that narrow defile, but it was a lot better than being surrounded.

For two days, we'd considered every way our defensive advantage might turn against us. Our backs were up against sheer, chalky walls, which was good. And an enemy could go far around us, sit at the tops of those walls, and shoot us full of arrows. Unless you had a wizard capable of holding up a strong illusion, that is. Ketill was fully confident that nobody would be able to see into that space very well.

I didn't like the inability to retreat from there, but that was the rub: As Magnus had once described, an army moves to where it wants to fight, but if the other army doesn't like that spot, they just move to their own spot. The fight happens only when both armies like the ground. This spot was a disadvantage for Alfhild, so the bet was on: Did the disadvantage not matter given her numbers, or had she let desire for the Brisingamen lead her into a trap?

"You may be able to think up endless possibilities for what has happened with Hrolf's ships," growled Styrgrim. "But there is only one point worth considering, and that is how they are not going to come to our aid. Get your mind away from that and onto ideas about what we control."

I was out of those. My contribution had been to suggest the construction of a lot of staff slings and the accumulation of a lot of rocks before the enemy fleet arrived. Staff slings were simple to use and excellent against tight crowds, which I anticipated we would be seeing a lot of.

"We should have buried me in the sand down there," said Magnus. "Damn! Could've just waited for her and then cut her throat before any of those trolls got to me."

"Have you learned nothing from me?" demanded Styrgrim. He had been getting shorter and shorter with Magnus. "That beach will be lousy with ships, strake to strake. You would have been trampled for certain. Even if you hadn't, you would come up nowhere near her and be exposed, and they would mob you right away."

"I could wear an ugly mask to blend in."

"She won't even be on the beach!" shouted Styrgrim. "She will stay on that troll-cursed ship, on the water, or did you fail to hear your own *vǫlva* say so?"

Magnus grinned back at him. "Perhaps I'm just as keen on dying as you are!"

I looked from one man to the other and realized this was a joke that I had missed even though it had been in plain sight. Suddenly, a number of comments came to mind. What was it that Arrow-Odd had shouted to Styrgrim when we sailed to aid Thick Alrek?

*Now's your chance.*

Chance to die? Magnus seemed to think so, and he knew my not-father better than anyone who remained with us. Now I understood why Arrow-Odd had made the seemingly insane decision to leave the army under my command rather than Styrgrim's. Styrgrim wanted to die in battle more than kill Ogmund. But I didn't want to die, I wanted revenge. Like knew like when Odd had locked eyes with me.

If Bjorn were still with us, I could have looked to him to confirm, but we'd sent him and Efraim off with Gunnar's returning ship. In case we failed to kill Alfhild, and in case Borghund might fall later, Bjorn had suggested they drop him and Efraim at the southern tip of Scania, where he knew of a good mead hall.

Styrgrim shook his head and snorted. "I think you have misread the situation."

More likely, Magnus had read the situation before even Styrgrim had. Magnus ignored him and turned back to watch the approaching fleet. Most of the ships had already beached, the others drawing closer. That one demon ship, longer and wider than any of the others, black as night, held position just off the shore.

People and former people who were now trolls disembarked from the beached ships. Many bore the winged *othala* symbol of the god-children, and these were beached right ahead of Alfhild's ship. They numbered in the hundreds, but below us was an army of thousands. Viking hirelings. Lords who'd recently sworn allegiance. Some banners looked familiar. Others were different enough that I expected these were King Harek's Bjarmians.

Of the trolls, there was no telling their origins. Magnus had only been half joking when he suggested wearing an ugly mask to blend in. Most of these had grown in size to monstrous proportions.

"What do you think happened to Svein?" I asked.

"Is this another of your musings, most practical for the moment?" demanded Styrgrim.

These last few days, talking about nearly anything seemed to irk the man unless it was absolutely necessary. I would change the subject, and that would irk him even further. Sometimes, men just want to be angry.

Magnus had the wisdom of getting around this attitude. "I think he ran off and shit himself to death. Or at least, that's the story we should tell. About the troll, Svein Shitty-Pants! Found a back-alley of the Down-Below where he could let fly, but his shit was so hot and voluminous, it created a new volcano."

"Hmph." That was Styrgrim trying to stay angry.

"But I don't see any sign of a volcano to burn us," I continued. "Just a witch intending to make us all wet."

"Ha!"

"Enough joking," said Styrgrim. He cleared his throat. Anything to keep from laughing.

"I'm quite serious about Svein's fate," I said. "Svein was never far from that greatest of shitheels, Ulf."

"And?"

"And I see Ulf down there standing ahead of the rest. Can you not? He is holding up a shield painted all in white. He's holding up two fingers with his other hand."

"Are his fingers wet?" asked Magnus. "I can think of a good explanation for that. Two, actually. Three, even!"

Styrgrim cleared his throat, burying any potential chuckle. "He means to parley." He stepped forward and held up two fingers. "Two of them and two of us."

"Think they realize Ansgar is in charge?" asked Magnus.

"No," replied Styrgrim, gruffer than necessary. "And better it remains that way for now."

Magnus craned his head forward and squinted. "I think I see him! But I wouldn't have picked him out. Either way, I am going with you."

"He sees Styrgrim responding. I think the two who go need to be me and Styrgrim, though."

"It will be a cold day for Surt's ballsack before I let you go without me."

"Magnus will come." Styrgrim's clarification surprised me. Would I really not attend the parley? "I held up two fingers. What I meant was, 'Yes, I have two swords now.' If they misinterpreted the hand sign, that is on them. We will wait until they march forward, in any case, and then go down ourselves. You think their other might be Svein, the one so cowardly he chose to run rather than fight with a dragon on his side?"

"The other is bigger than Svein, and a troll." I took my time scanning the beach with so many there. "I don't see Svein anywhere. And that is good. I think we prefer that he never reported what he saw in the Down-Below, the name of that second sword on your hip."

Styrgrim nodded. "What the enemy does not know will hurt them. Now, let's see what these shitlings can tell us."

There was a conversation without words between me and Styrgrim as we made our way down to parley. Styrgrim cleared his throat to get my attention, directed my attention forward with his eyes, and grunted. I grunted back that I didn't understand. I understood, in general, that he didn't like what he saw. But I didn't know what he meant, specifically.

"It is best to show the enemy no reaction, no matter how deep their words cut," he said. "Deny that the enemy has had an effect on you, no matter what."

"Is that an attempt to make up for previous lessons untaught?"

Styrgrim breathed out and set his gaze forward, frustrated again.

"Good advice doesn't change its nature when it comes later than expected," Magnus whispered to me. He looked more serious than usual. Grinning, yes, but it was his wolfish grin, the one to hide his intent. I knew the man's tone well enough to hear what was behind it. Everyone seemed to understand what was happening but me.

*I could really use some advice from my fylgja right now!*

No advice, or even appearance, was forthcoming, so I tried to imagine what Svipul would tell me if she were here. Family dies for you if necessary? No, too specific. Something about family, though. Magnus was family, and he was telling me to listen to Styrgrim. Styrgrim was not technically family at all. But he was acting like it, and that was out of character. Why would he do that?

*Heimdall's teeth! He's protecting me. But from what?*

It was no good looking confused at a parley, so I put up a stony face as we got close to the middle ground. Ulf stood there smirking, arms crossed, in a fine mail shirt, and carried a sword rather than his long seax. Next to him was a big, trollish warrior, his beard thinned out to show his lower jaw jutting forward. He kept spear and shield at the ready, though he would have been quite dangerous unarmed.

Ulf looked quite cheery. "Welcome, friends. Though it's more of you than you indicated, I think it's a fine thing to include more ears when a good offer comes around."

Styrgrim grunted. A brutish and inarticulate thing in the face of Ulf's wordy welcome.

Or was it? He had said we would go down and see what they would tell us, not that we would have a war of words. Anything we said could give them information. Even the desire to speak gave them information. Saying nothing forced them to continue talking, which was exactly what we wanted.

This was not a war of words. This was just war, and Styrgrim was mountain-peaks higher in skill at war than I was. I crossed my arms and tried to look bored.

"A skilled heckler and a skald, both, and yet not a question between them!" Ulf continued. "I imagine there are many things unanswered in your minds. Here is an opportunity, if you wish to consider it as such."

Magnus turned to Styrgrim. "Sounds like a waste of time."

Though Styrgrim and Magnus meant to draw Ulf out, I saw a different vulnerability in that huge troll. I would insult his master, sow doubts and make them memorable. Ulf might be savvy enough not to repeat what he heard, but I suspected this troll would not be able to hold back on the gossip.

Ulf was quick to jump back in before Styrgrim could agree with Magnus. "A waste of lives not to listen, at least. Alfhild has come in force, but she need not use it. I am here to speak for her. Rather than be drawn into a protracted fight with such fine warriors as yourselves, she prefers to make a generous offer that will be mutually beneficial."

"Ha!" Magnus scratched his crotch as he laughed.

"I remember when Alfhild used trickery to have sex with me," I said. "Now she makes her offers explicit. That progress, I say." I let that hang there while the troll captain's eyes went wide. Apparently, Styrgrim's lesson about refusing to show a reaction had not penetrated to all corners of Midgard.

Meanwhile, Ulf was a bit slow in responding, so I continued. "Let me be clear, I only plowed that woman because she glamoured herself as Fanya. When I realized what was going on, the forge couldn't keep the iron hot any longer. I'd sooner look for warm hospitality inside an icy cave than inside that woman."

"I hear she likes having her hair pulled," added Magnus. "Was that true for you, Ulf?"

"I don't think he knows," I said. "Ulf enjoys a different sort of bush."

The troll was taking it all in, and we had just begun.

"You should consider the consequences of insults," said Ulf. A blink would have missed it, but I saw his smile turn to a snarl for the briefest moment. "But let's not be distracted by false stories: Alfhild wants one thing, and that is the return of the Brisingamen. That torc holds a great deal of value for her."

We were supposed to ask what was in it for us, but nobody did. To his credit, Ulf changed tone and tactic, given our stonewalling. He stepped forward with open palms.

"I see you're very resistant, even to consideration, and that's understandable. To you, I must seem the rankest traitor. There is no question you were brave and loyal followers of Haldor Skullsplitter. But truth is a hard thing sometimes, and here is one: Men like Haldor and Arrow-Odd are tragically selfish figures.

"Oh, they offer much by their mere presence. They promise much if you follow them. But ultimately, they care only about what you can do for them. They will use you up, grind you down in their petty wars. Every man must have no greater faith than in himself! That's a lesson from Odin, I think you know.

"Haldor had that rule against unwilling sacrifices. But what about all the sacrifices of his Brothers, the ones who didn't realize what was really going on? That rule was always going to turn in on itself. I knew it, and I helped it happen before he used me up. Any sane man finding himself in a cage will try to break free of it.

"Now, I want to be clear that everyone knows of your bravery and loyalty. There is no shortage of admiration among Alfhild's army. But you should consider that this has put your backs up against a wall of solid rock here. Alfhild doesn't make some sticky-sweet offer, full of warm feelings. She offers honesty in that she wants to rule the Danes and reward those who do right by her.

"You can number among those rewarded. Return the Brisingamen, and she will give you as many ships as you can sail away from here. Go where you will, do what you want. She will not bother you further if you do not provoke her.

"But join her, renounce your need for vengeance, and you will have those ships and privileged positions in her army. An army where you are already held in high esteem! All who join will be outfitted with the finest arms and armor and given a pound of hacksilver each. Ten pounds for captains, as she knows you're all good ring-slingers. You may keep your crews together as long as the captains answer to Alfhild. And those captains will soon receive land. There will soon be plenty of that to apportion once King Hrolf is defeated."

That was a long monologue, not too unlike the offer King Athils made. I thought it strange at the time that those two fork-tongued offerers would sound so similar. But if you have some years behind you, I think it's likely you've heard the same sort of thing yourself. Perhaps it is couched in a different tone or words, like "A new power is rising, so it is only reasonable to ally with it."

The names for these offerers change depending on the speaker. Opportunists. Collaborators. Traitors. People "just trying to get by" if they are particular cowards. Despite the different names, they are all the same. Which Magnus already knew.

"So, this offer of Alfhild's, to renounce revenge on her and take her rewards," he began, looking just about giddy. "It is not betrayal at all, but rather some rare species of honor?"

The troll captain, who had apparently lost his sense of ironic humor, nodded. Ulf gave a sad sigh, still grinning. He was about to say something, so I cut him off.

"Why does she want the Brisingamen so badly?"

He turned his attention to me and pursed his lips. "I think you know the answer to this already, as you are the one who stole it."

"I know what carrying the torc is like, that's true. I don't know what using it is like."

The troll looked confused at this. Something about what I had just said must have contradicted what he'd heard. Maybe from Honor, maybe from Alfhild. Either way, subverted expectations would result in yet more rumors.

"I want to be clear that I think I know the answer to my question, Ulf, but I don't know for certain. Why do you think she wants it? Is it because she would have trouble retaining loyalty without it?"

"Men are loyal to Alfhild because she is strong and honest in her aspirations. She does not need the torc to convince anyone to follow her."

"She doesn't need the thing," I said, looking at the sky in one direction, then changing to the other direction as I continued, "yet she is willing to pay dearly for it. Hmmmm." I scratched at my beard with a confused look.

"I have counseled her as such," Ulf responded. "We have fought and killed plenty already. Her offer is made out of respect for this . . . remainder of Arrow-Odd's army. Do you know where he went, by the way? Ravens that reached us said he abandoned you, but this story that he left Uppsala and disappeared into the forest made little sense." He shrugged. "It's only a matter of time before men claiming to be loyal to others finally show that they are most loyal to themselves, just like everyone else."

"What a twisted narrative you weave," I said, trying to hold back a snarl. "It does make me wonder where Ogmund has got to, however." Insults are most effective in verse, but I still had to maintain my veneer of aloofness. Delivered with a detached tone, I knew this would cut deep among their army:

> "Eythjof's killer is out
>    questing for a comb,
> with that monstrous face
>    even a mother couldn't love.
> Or is ugly Tussock's
>    tail tucked up
> against his big
>    brown eye?"

Ulf's grin disappeared. "I think you would not say such things if Ogmund were here."

I was getting to him. If he lost composure in front of the troll, that might create its own doubt to spread among their ranks. Even if he didn't, Ulf would be less effective as a leader the more this big troll heard him insulted.

"Yet he is not here." I readied a second verse as I spoke. "Nor is Haldor. I wonder who will save you now, Ulf?" Still detached, I held up a hand to Magnus as if I had, just by chance, thought of something:

> "How often
>     did hewing-Haldor
> pull this scared
>     puppy from peril?
> I stabbed Wet
>     Ulf once, but
> it was another penetration
>     he pined for."

The troll captain looked to Ulf with disbelief. Had I suggested that Ulf desired me sexually, or Haldor? The ambiguity added to the potency. I fought back a smirk.

Ulf shrugged. "I suppose I can only blame myself for making a generous offer to people too foolish to take it. You might consider how satisfied the rest of us will be in a month, whereas you will be dead and forgotten."

I shook my head. "Some might rather be dead than take to the manner of satisfaction you've grown accustomed to." Every comment he made was giving me new material, and this was no exception:

> "Lips sewn around
>     *seiðr* spewing from
> the witch's musty
>     windbreaker—
> How to remember someone
>     such as that?
> A *níðingr* with his
>     nether regions for sale!"

Ulf licked his lips. He was not just losing face, but standing idle for insults that would have otherwise made it legal for him to kill me. He was crafty, though, smarter than me in many ways. I crossed my arms, preparing myself to show no reaction to his counter, no matter what.

"Healthy Ansgar, I warned you about the danger of insults, but you have failed to heed wisdom at every turn. You emptied your guts every time we set sail, but your guts were not the ones you should have been watching. Did you never notice that witch's absence down the hill when we fought in Lejre? Never consider the nature of her wound?

"Fool, I bested you long ago when I gutted your girl, Fanya, in that burning hall, and still you called me Brother until I had to make it most obvious for you!"

The statement sent me reeling more than any insult could have. This was a revelation, one that had been right under my nose. It had even been in Valborg's prophecy:

> *One witch*
>    *went to her death,*
> *hewed down*
>    *by a Hero's hand.*
> *That history*
>    *is a hard one to face.*

Now that I understood the awful truth behind those lines, despair surged through me as if every ill-natured *landvaettr* hissed in my ears. My hands went numb. My legs went weak. Blood beat a thunderous rhythm in my head to drown out all other sound. I blinked, and the world tinted red and gray. I thought I might pass out.

I clenched my jaw. Going red in the face was an acceptable reaction, and I am confident I looked like an angry beet. Or maybe a pale one if the blood had drained from my face. It was difficult to tell which was happening. Unable to move my feet with any certainty, I kept my arms crossed, hoping I looked like I was standing my ground. I breathed, which was about all I could do to remain upright.

*It is best to show the enemy no reaction, no matter how deep their words cut.*

"Hmph," I said, grinning the hardest grin I have ever forced. "Maybe you need more time to put that in verse."

Ulf's snarling grin spasmed for just a moment, his face going in many directions at once. He regained himself quickly and started to speak, but Styrgrim cut him off.

"We have been patient in hearing your offer, but patience has run out." The old warrior's voice rolled over the parley like a wheel the size of a mountain. "Now you will hear our counteroffer.

"Go down to your witch and tell her I offer time to flee this place. She can take the night to consider and give her answer in the morning.

"She will first renounce her allegiance to Ogmund Tussock. She will explain that the Brisingamen caused her to make ill-advised choices, and that the torc has deceived both her, and those god-brats, about their sense of worth. She will admit to them that they were unlucky to chance upon a little wealth and power, and that they've grown in arrogance, but not good sense. She will tell them a withdrawal is in their best interest, so that I don't kill them all.

"Her people and her hired vikings may keep their armor, but they will leave their weapons on these shores. They will burn the shields with the painted runes. She will sail every Bjarmian back to the White Sea. She will tell King Harek to stop troubling the Karelians, or Styrgrim the Bear will come north, and not with praise poetry. She will continue on and sail every troll to the Ironwood. If these trolls remain there among their monstrous kin, they may keep their miserable lives.

"Whether she marries a troll and makes a new life or takes her chances in the rest of Midgard, that's up to her. I will hold back the crew of the *Sea Squirrel* for a day and a night after the shields burn. I suggest she move quickly after that, as the *Sea Squirrel* is likely to follow her right back to the White Sea. But their ship is not fast, so a day and a night should be plenty.

"As for you, Wet Ulf," he spat. "Kill yourself."

Then he turned, exposing his back to Ulf and the big troll. The painfully slow movement was a dare or even a suggestion that they should attack him.

The unnamed troll's nostrils flared. He was thinking about it. My right hand crawled down to Need's pommel. Not easy to do, as my hands were still numb. I hoped Styrgrim knew what he was doing.

Ulf turned away and tapped the troll's shoulder, indicating for him to follow.

Magnus and I turned back and headed for our makeshift fortress. I was thankful that I could walk without falling over. When we'd put enough space between us and our enemies, Styrgrim said, "They will attack sooner rather than later."

But that wasn't what was on my mind. "That advice saved me. Ulf had me. Outsmarted me. Out-positioned me. I might have broken the parley and attacked him, and that troll would have killed me. Even if I had just looked surprised, that would have been a victory for Ulf. How did you know to give me that advice before we even reached them?"

"Hmmmmm," Styrgrim growled. "I have survived so many cock-ups that I eventually learned from them. And one thing I learned: There are many sorts of clever people. Some use it for war or wealth. A few take heart in helping others. It wasn't until I saw Ulf's face that I placed him. He is the sort that needs to *feel* clever, to use it to get over on his fellows. I have seen that face a hundred times before, and I knew he was waiting to use it on *you*."

"Well done," added Magnus.

"Yes." Styrgrim held up a hand for us to stop and fiddled with a pouch at his belt. It was small and tightly bound. After untying the knot, he pinched an item out of it and cupped it in his right hand. "I've known a long time I was not your father. You are not Styrgrimsson, but you are Boddasson. And Ansgar was not the name your mother intended for you, only the byname you got by me and the *vǫlva* who helped birth you. I took Bodda's death badly, as if the gods had sent you as a spear into my heart. I let the byname stick rather than make it clear the name your mother had breathed.

"Well. Better late than never." He grabbed my right hand, those great, scarred meat hammers enfolding my palm. He placed a small, soft thing into my hand. "Your naming gift."

I opened my hand. In it was a lock of raven-blue hair.

"Your name is Bragi. Bragi Boddasson."

# CHAPTER 56

## SUFFICIENT PREAMBLE

"STILL USING THE OLD NAME, I NOTICED," STYRGRIM SAID.

We looked out over the enemy arrayed on the beach below. The sea was calm and quiet at the shore despite the dark storm that Alfhild held a few hundred feet behind her ship. I could almost hear the shuffling and grunting of her formed-up ranks. Not more than three thousand, but more than two thousand for certain. Bjarmians, god-children, trolls of many shapes and sizes, and viking crews from all over.

"It's the name everyone knows me by. I notice you're still wearing both your old sword and Tyrfing. Perhaps you should leave the latter behind our defenses in case—"

"No." Not loud, not angry, but not a response that would accept further argument. "Does anyone know about your name besides Magnus?"

I shook my head.

"I suppose it is a complicated thing."

"It did not seem the time to introduce complexity where it was not required." We had called the last War Council meeting before the battle started in earnest, and I had been keen to focus on anything but my name. Or more accurately, how I felt about knowing it.

"Nobody asked you about the bear thing during the War Council. And half the council was your people, who were with you when it happened." He turned slowly to give me an appraising look, as if I might start growing fur and claws at any moment.

"If you mean for me to change my skin into a bear's as I did in Lejre, I think you will be disappointed. In any case, I think it would not work out as well as the preparations we decided on."

I unlimbered my sling, running the loop over my middle finger and pinching the leather tab at the other end between thumb and forefinger. The braids were lamb's wool, with a diamond-shaped leather pouch at the center. A good sling.

Behind me, a few dozen other slingers readied their weapons.

Final plans had been decided in my makeshift circle in our makeshift camp. There were no rowan trees around, but a few beech trees had fallen from the cliff tops above us. I decided they would have to do and enlisted some help—meaning, enlisted Magnus—to help chop them up. I used the logs and branches to form a circle in the middle of our camp.

It made me feel better, like the Circle of Skalds. Only it was not just for skalds, but also for captains and other trusted advisors like Ketill and Huld. It was rather shitty, all in all. It was also much better than just standing around with no boundaries around us while we met.

"Did the bear thing happen?" Not a disdainful tone, just an inquisitive one.

I nodded as I rooted through my bag of sling ammunition.

"It was your mother, wasn't it?"

I was less bothered by his intuition than I thought I should be. "How did you know?"

"You know too many things you couldn't otherwise know. And she was with me once, in a similar way. Never imagined she could bring on a full skin change. But it's never been clear to me, the boundaries of can and can't, or how."

I shrugged. "I have spent most of my life stumbling through boundaries."

"Well, you aren't stumbling now."

*Was that pride?*

My first throw would be a long one, and it was important for morale that it connect with a target. I pulled a dark gray stone and turned it over in my hand. I had scratched the phrase *inherit this* into it. It was fine, but not for my first throw.

I'd had a few ideas about messages to leave on my stones during the previous night. *Catch* and *eat this* were easy. Other stones got symbols. I tried to carve a likeness of Mjollnir onto one, but it took a long time, so I switched to a bolt of lightning for a lot of them. Not that I thought this was of great use, but it had been a popular idea with the other slingers.

"A bear is all will, and that is what I needed at the time. But I don't think that's what I need anymore. I am . . ." *a skald?*

"More dangerous?" He gave a toothy half-grin. "That is how one goes from winning a fight to winning a war."

I palmed a stone shaped like a small egg and loaded it into my pouch. This was the one I had carved with the rune *nauthiz*. I nodded at Styrgrim, signaling I was ready. He strode forward a dozen paces and bellowed at Alfhild below.

"Where is Wet Ulf? He is wise if he took my advice to kill himself. If he did so before delivering my terms, though, I must take responsibility for that mistake! In that case, Alfhild, I want to be clear about your offer: Do you intend to leave here with your life, or would you rather waste it, and the lives of your followers, over a piece of jewelry?"

The witch sat on a high seat on her demon ship, the supposed *Naglfar*. The best-armored and most trollish god-children attended her there, some of them closer in size to the giants of Risaland than to humans. The biggest of these cuffed a prisoner held on a chain, knocking him down hard. He would be a sacrifice, no doubt, but that time wasn't yet upon us.

Alfhild did not rise from her high seat when she spoke, and she did not shout. Her voice washed over us as if she were so close by, from every direction at once. "If there ever was a man who didn't know how to woo a woman, it was you, Styrgrim the Bear. You invaded my home. You stole my treasure. You killed my followers, and you would deny the birthrights of those who survived. Now you think to impose unfavorable terms on me. But we know what it means when a bear growls. It means he wants you to go away, to leave him be. It means he is frightened!

"How low you've sunk, Styrgrim the Growler. I thought Arrow-Odd's betrayal would open your eyes, but you have shut them even harder instead. Now you'll lose your life, and what is that worth?"

"What a trollwife!" exclaimed Styrgrim, allowing a bit of surprise to creep into his voice. He strode back and forth now, an uncharacteristic restlessness about him. "I've heard 'dishonor' called many things, but 'open your eyes' is truly an idiot's idiom! Here is a difference between us then, our enmity the result of more than mere circumstance: I know that to lose boldly is better than to live by the dictates of fear. But Smooth-Cheek, you *worship* fear! You scurry at the first flick of its tongue, readying yet another appeasement. You've twisted yourself in every direction you can think of to avoid losing. When your people see how weak you are, they will scatter like dried pine needles in a strong wind."

Styrgrim had no sorcery of his own. He had to shout to be heard, unlike Alfhild. His voice was his own, but it reminded me of Haldor's. The voice of command, not to dictate, but to give back in courage to those who held fast.

"You've taught them well! Taught them cowardice as a virtue! Taught them they should do anything, *anything* but lose!"

I cut my right ring finger and smeared blood onto the rune. Not the sort of spell Ketill had taught, since there was no combination, but I thought it would help. I needed the stone to hit home, and it was a long throw, even for me. My first stone finding a gap in armor would set a tone for the other slingers. It set a tone for the enemy, too, reminding them they were vulnerable. I poured my will into the stone and focused my mind on the target: The big viking leading the biggest formation.

It was tempting to wind up for a long throw, but my grandfather had taught me long ago that windups don't help. Best to use the same technique I always used, with just a single rotation. I focused on my target, stepped into the throw, and released.

The stone flew high and fast, spinning into a gentle curve as it went. The distance was fine. I thought it had gone too far to the side, but it curved back in.

That viking wore a heavy chain shirt and a good steel helmet. Few people are outfitted such that every vulnerable area is covered, however. The stone struck him at the base of the throat, driving deep into flesh. He dropped his spear to clutch at the wound. It didn't help.

Someone below shouted, and the enemy surged forward. I motioned for the few dozen slingers behind me to move up and create a skirmish line on me and Styrgrim, and we rained stones onto Alfhild's army like deadly hail. It took two volleys before any of them went down, but I'd already set the tone I wanted. Not easy to charge uphill in soft sand. Especially not with your shield held up in an awkward position.

Styrgrim signaled to me, and I ordered the slingers to reposition behind our main line of defenses, in an orderly fashion, careful where we put our feet.

The first enemies to engage our people were a mix of decently armed and armored vikings. Shock troops, if you want to make them sound impressive. Expendable mercenaries, if you want to stop mincing words. Either way, they didn't know where to not put their feet. And putting their feet in the wrong spots, many a sole found many a nailed board we'd harvested and set into the sand as traps.

Those who didn't step on any nails closed in on the narrow spots we had left open, but could only fight two abreast in one and three abreast in the other. Both narrow passages were walled by high chalk cliffs on one side and huge boulders on the other. Those attackers found the ground beneath them was also quite uneven. They could surge, and a great group could try pushing through—only that was a lot more awkward when parts of the group stood two feet lower than anyone else.

We had blocked the middle opening that led farther into our camp with crude but sturdy fences reinforced with rocks. Rocks had quickly become a theme of our defenses, to the strong approval of Kraki and Finnr.

Some of the enemy braved coming up the slope of the earthworks to hop the improvised fences, others the boulders around it. Had we left those giant rocks as they were, they would have been as round and awkward for us as the enemy. Finnr, however, had chipped away at both of them so that they provided easy places for us to stand on. Spearmen bled anyone foolish enough to try going over. Most did not go over, and soon felt the change I ordered for my slingers.

Even less glorious than the sling was the staff sling. I had practiced with them, but never found much use for them. A regular sling is more flexible in use, easier to carry, and can let a bullet fly with much greater speed and accuracy. A staff sling is rather simple and crude, and more for flinging in a general direction. But it can take a much bigger pouch and can launch much bigger objects.

Like, say, fist-sized rocks. And bigger.

That's what started coming down on the heads of anyone trying to come up the middle against us. And also what started coming down on the heads of the backed-up force of vikings, most of whom were stuck waiting for someone to fight. Or busy looking at the sand to make sure they didn't step on any nails.

Those who did engage our front lines were stopped with shields and stabbed with spears, and more than a few were doubtless trampled by their own people. The back and forth went on for longer than maybe I am conveying. There was an initial flurry of attacks, as some men just can't hold themselves back. But others, more disciplined and experienced in warfare, were willing to conserve some energy and fight a grinding battle rather than a furious one.

High above but far back from the main fighting, Huld spoke something unintelligible, whispering on her inhalations and exhaling through her teeth. I was positioned on the ground near her. From that point, I could loose a stone at anyone coming over the top at our front line, hitting them with a more or less flat trajectory.

Arrows being more limited in number than stones, Jorun and a handful of other skilled archers were positioned deeper into the chasm on the tops of the upturned ships. It gave them a height advantage in case they had to shoot anyone getting too close to breaking our lines or, of course, getting too close to Huld.

I wondered what Huld was up to up there when I heard the first twang of a bow. The arrow passed far over me, far over any attackers who might even be close to breaking our defenses. Sure, there was a good chance of hitting someone by doing that, but why waste the arrow on a blind shot into a crowd?

Huld's reverse whisper became louder and harsher as I noticed a scent in the air. Silver birch sap and something else—the sort of sharpness you might encounter just after a thunderstorm if there had been a lightning strike.

More bows twanged. I looked back at Jorun and saw her eyes had gone cloudy white, the same as the other archers. They would nock and draw, holding for what felt like ages. And then they would loose.

I crawled up the wall of chalk as much as I could, getting about halfway up to Huld. The scent was even stronger there, and I realized this was the scent of Huld's *seiðr*. I looked up to see the *vǫlva* point her distaff at one of the vikings trying to regroup his people. She muttered something short and sharp. An arrow loosed and took that viking through the eye.

Only a few arrows flew, but each one found its target in an enemy commander. I didn't know if Huld granted Jorun and the other archers sight, or saw for them and guided their arrows. And I wasn't about to ask. I was just glad this *vǫlva* was on our side.

I climbed back down, realizing I should not have left my spot just to see what was happening.

Fewer attackers attempted to get in on us, and no arrows flew for several minutes. I could hear Styrgrim shouting from the front lines. It sounded like things were going badly despite all our preparations. I wasn't sure if I should hold my position or try to help elsewhere when the sand next to my left foot began to shake.

A black and white badger's head emerged from the ground soon after. The badger shook off the loose sand and wriggled out of the hole. By the time he emerged, Finnr had already changed his skin back to his more familiar dwarf form.

"Do we need to help Styrgrim at the front line?"

"Of course not," he said. "He's baiting them. Letting a few of them get in. Letting a few of them see a bit more than what they expected. Then pushing them out."

Seeing 'a bit more than what they expected' was courtesy of Ketill, the angriest wizard in Midgard. The enemy couldn't see very far into our defenses; that was one part. The next part was what they would see after crossing a certain point. Ketill had described the illusionary scene as "Like stepping into the primordial abyss and leaving your sanity behind" for anyone who hadn't been invited in.

I heard one of the attackers shout something about an abyss. Others warned their mates about giants throwing boulders, or trolls shooting arrow-sized spines, or werewolves, or demon moose spirits. The vikings called a retreat.

Little did they know that Moose-Frothi was *holding back*, under orders not to give chase. It might have gone much worse for them.

That was the first day of fighting. It didn't last long. We had plenty of time left to reset nails, recover arrows and stones, and look out on the army below to see what they were doing.

Much of what they were doing involved Alfhild executing people. She sent one of the ships out into the water with a lot of tied-up vikings on it. Then she had it set on fire, probably as punishment for being too afraid of losing their lives.

Which, to my way of seeing things, sort of made Styrgrim a prophet.

"That was good," I told him as twilight settled. "But what if they come at night?"

"Unlikely. Can't see well enough, so nobody fights at night. You're as likely to kill friends as enemies."

"Sounds like mainly a problem for the side with superior numbers if we were to attack."

"Especially if their commander is incompetent," he agreed. "But no. We could take advantage of that element, but it would put us out of position. We would be trading a strong advantage for a lesser one." He shook his head. "A lot can happen, especially now. Their armor shows gaps. Now is the time for patience and discipline, and to wait for the right vulnerability rather than the first one."

The next day didn't show us the killing gap, though. The next day brought the unexpected, and it nearly ended us.

# CHAPTER 57

# HEAVY INVESTMENT

HULD WOKE ME UP THE NEXT MORNING. STRANGE, THAT, SINCE I was almost always awake before anyone else. She didn't even wait for me to sit up after poking me with her distaff. "That bitch tried to ride me!"

Most of us had opted to find comfortable spots under the open air. Faster to muster that way, but vulnerable to a cranky *vǫlva*.

I craned my neck, still groggy. I may rise early, but only because I want to. Rising earlier than I want to is a thing I dislike in the extreme. So when I asked, "Did she succeed?" I was not entirely myself.

I got a kick in response, and was lucky for the second time in my life that witches are bad at kicking. Still, it was not ideal. And not very quiet.

"Does it *look like* she succeeded?"

Magnus yawned loudly, and for far too long for it to be a real yawn as much as a statement of disapproval. "It's still dark. Are they attacking early?"

"Yes," said Huld.

Magnus bolted upright, his eyes wide as he threw off his wool blanket. Then he stopped, all of a sudden. "Oh. You meant the riding."

Huld looked like she would crack that distaff right over his head.

"Not here, Huld," I said. "To the Circle. We will wake the others."

"Bah!" She left in a huff.

Magnus stood up with a groan. "You understand what she meant? Maybe from something Ketill taught you?"

I shook my head. There were plenty of stories about being "ridden" by a witch. Sometimes it seemed to be in the form of a nightmare that caused anything from discomfort to death. Others told of people ridden at night being found dirty and covered in scratches and bruises, as if someone had literally ridden them through a rough patch of forest.

Magnus and I split up to gather the other members of the War Council as quickly as possible. Tired warriors made tired sounds wherever I went, but we finished in a matter of minutes. One good thing about a small army is it's not difficult to find people.

My last stop was Kraki. Unlike everyone who appreciated a bit of soft sand to lie down on, Kraki had bedded down on the deck of the *Sea Squirrel* and showed no interest in coming down for anything but battle. The ship stood secure in its cart, the wheels blocked by wedges the size of my forearm. Remove those, though, and it would roll downhill. I climbed a short rope to get high enough to pull myself over the gunwale.

"There had better be . . . a fight . . ." Kraki wheezed as he propped himself up on one arm. He was so pale, he practically glowed. The cut from Tyrfing looked no worse than before, but it was clearly taking a toll.

"Alfhild tried to ride Huld during the night." The *vǫlva* had already advised us to expect something new from Alfhild. We'd all been concerned about her raising the dead again, but Huld had waved that fear off. Not the best idea for a spell in the face of strong counter-sorcery.

"Ha! Stupid." Neither was this one, apparently.

"I think Huld agrees with your assessment, but she is also concerned. She needs us to gather at the Circle right away."

The old man nodded and made a shooing gesture at me. Even in his weakened state, he leaped over the gunwale and down to the sand, ignoring the rope ladder. I shimmied down, hoping my knees never made the sounds I had just heard from his.

When we finally entered the Circle, Huld wasted no time in telling what had happened. "That bitch tried to ride me!"

"And . . ." Magnus put a placating hand up. "What does this 'riding' mean? She sent a spirit against you?"

"She sent her *hugr* at me in my sleep. I would ask, but I know your answers just by looking: She did not visit any of the rest of you."

"Are you certain it was Alfhild?" I asked. "Ulf may have learned enough *seiðr* from her at this point—"

"I am *certain*."

"Then Alfhild is wiser than she used to be," said Styrgrim. "She went for the biggest threat to her."

"I thought you and that sword were the biggest threat to her," said Hallfred.

"Not while I can't reach her. Though if I have the chance—"

"This is not why I warn you," Huld interrupted. All attention went back to her. "She will try again. Not me, not after the sendoff I gave her. She will try someone else, someone unpracticed at resisting such things."

It was deadly quiet for a moment. The next target could be any one of us, and what then? Death in the night, or a nightmare so real it blasted our minds? Could she turn one of us against the others?

"Ha!" Magnus' laugh broke the silence like a sheet of ice shattering. "She rode Ansgar once before, and he came away no worse off for it!"

Magnus looked surprised when no one laughed.

"Be wary," Huld said, eyeing each of us in turn. "Tonight, you must come and see me and have your people follow my instructions exactly to keep themselves protected."

"What are your instructions?" asked Styrgrim.

Huld stared at him, cupping her distaff like a club. "I will determine that later."

It was about that time when a horn sounded from our outermost defenses. One horn blast meant the enemy was preparing to advance.

"Early to rise, and before we could eat!" Magnus exclaimed. "Maybe they've gotten serious."

"Enough!" barked Styrgrim. "Ansgar goes to the front with me to see what's happening. The rest of you, get your people ready."

Though no early morning attack was expected, we had still kept a substantial group there to watch the enemy's movements. On shift at that time were mostly Gunnar's warriors who had volunteered to fight alongside us. They waved us on and pointed to the beach below as Styrgrim and I approached the front line. We headed through the narrow pass to our right to get a better look.

The enemy host was advancing on our position. All of it, as far as I could see. I turned and was about to yell for my slingers to form up, but Styrgrim grabbed my shoulder. "Don't use the staff slings unless they've breached the middle."

It seemed to me that more attackers, pressed in closer together, made perfect targets for blindly-chucked rocks. They certainly had the day before. The look on my face must have told him my thoughts.

"Orders now, explanations if we survive." Then he was off.

I suppose I could have ignored that command, as I still led the army. But I'd left my contrarianism behind some time ago, and you don't keep a veteran commander around in order to *not* take his advice.

I returned to behind our lines and called for my slingers to group up with me away from the front. Some of them were quite good. Few understood why we wouldn't use the staff slings once I described how much of Alfhild's army was marching up the beach. I told them, "Orders now, explanations if we survive."

Styrgrim gathered his crew and shouted at the front lines. Not orders, but what to expect. The low fences were coming down at some point; no stopping that. The enemy would hack at them, break through them, burn them, something. The defenders' job was to make that effort cost as much blood as possible and then keep the enemy encircled with a tight half-moon formation.

Alfhild could throw ten times our number at us, or a hundred, and the result would be the same: They would advance only far enough to be trapped between a shield wall four warriors deep and the crush of their own people, barely able to move. Control in battle was all, and we had it.

"Do you hear that?" I asked my slingers. "We have control of the battle!"

Then the first arrows came down behind our front line, and I wasn't so sure. Front-line defenders held their shields against the coming ground attack, relying on those behind them to raise their shields and cover them from above. Formations at the front tightened. Soon, the clash of steel on steel began.

I moved my slingers back, where they took cover under the overturned ship we'd captured. Wooden posts braced one side open toward our encampment, allowing easy access and shielding those under it from incoming arrows, should they fly that far.

Ketill and Finnr were taking cover there. The wizard was unlikely to move —he would just keep chanting over the runes he had drawn in the sand. How Finnr would play into this battle, I still wasn't sure.

Nor was I sure what to do with my slingers. I had general directions, but every decision seemed like it could result in disaster. Convert them to regular troops to help at the front? That meant taking most of our ranged ability out of the fight. Have them ready the staff slings incase the middle was breached? That would keep them idle when they might be needed.

Finnr seemed to read my mind. "Congratulations. You're knee-deep in a river of aurochs shit. Still excited to fight?"

"This must be armpit-deep at least," I countered.

"Not yet." He wasn't joking.

"Well, knee-deep, then. I don't know what to do with my people next."

"Why tell me?"

"You're a dwarf! Dwarves are wise! Say something wise!"

"Turn into a bear and eat them all!"

I shook my head. "That would help for a short while only. If I could have one spell from that battle, it would be the exploding bodies."

Finnr shrugged. "A good spell. Counter, though. Only worked on the ones who had already died and been raised."

"What's the counter for this, then? I can't even see what's happening, but I have to decide what to do."

"Yes."

I seriously considered punching him at that point.

"Oh, that is everyone's problem in battle. Nobody can see everything." He shrugged. "Except Huld, I suppose."

A seeress sitting on a high perch was exactly what I needed. I could run off to Huld and be back quickly. But as I turned to address my slingers, what I saw on their faces stopped me. These were hard, loyal people—the ones who had stayed with us despite bad times. There is no loyalty like that without expectation, and *I'll be right back* was counter to that expectation.

I turned to address Finnr instead. "You're not a fast runner, but I've seen you burrow. Can you make your way closer to Huld and ask her to describe the enemy's formation? When I know that, I'll decide how to redeploy."

The dwarf nodded, his skin changing into a badger's as he dove into the ground. A small hill of sand announced his path. Not as fast as I could run, but fast indeed.

The wait for him to return was probably no more than two minutes but seemed like forever under that ship. My mind split between trying to think of a spell to carve and what to say next to my slingers, who clearly needed something said to them. Every spell effect I could think of would drain me completely. Perhaps I could blunt the enemy's weapons? But against an army, that spell was far beyond my ability. Everything I could do seemed too subtle or too small in scale.

Ketill's chanting interrupted my thoughts. We already had two good sorcerers, and I would leave it to them. I had to focus on the warriors under my command. Which led to a most unpleasant thought.

"Unsling your shields, all of you." Which meant me, too. Gods, if there is one thing I never had a sense of, it is a shield. "It's slower reloading a sling while holding a shield, but no more difficult to throw. Keep those shields up until you're ready to loose!"

Some of them nodded, others shook their heads. As much as I hated shields, my grandfather had forced me to practice with one. Not much, just enough to know I could do it. Lucky for me, one of the better slingers spoke up.

"I've done that more than once," said Bui. "It's not so difficult. However, I always move my ammo bag to the side I throw from when I use a shield. That way, I don't have to reach across myself when reloading, and it's easier to hold the shield steady."

I nodded, the first to take that advice. I didn't need to make it an order before everyone else did, too. Then I divided them into two groups based on how fast they could reload and throw, and told them to only throw when I ordered a volley. I wanted groups of stones all coming down at once, hitting a wide area, rather than one or two at a time.

More nodding, shuffling, shifting. Bui had already given one piece of good advice, and I saw some of the others looking to him. "If I go down from an arrow or anything else," I said, "Bui takes command of this group."

I couldn't think of any further preparation to make. Soon, there was nothing left but to go out there and do it. And then be ready to do something completely different soon after.

Finnr tunneled back under the ship and leaped out of the sand like a fish out of water. He changed to his dwarven shape right away and shook some of the sand out of his beard. "Huld says they're in two main columns, sending attacks in waves and calling them back soon after, probably probing for a weakness. The archers are massed in one big group, about fifty yards back from the front line, straight up the middle. Does that tell you what you need to know?"

Very much so. "All of you, listen! Their archers are pressuring our front line, but they are within our range. Choose a heavy stone for your next throw."

I led the slingers close to the front lines. We passed a few arrows stuck in the sand. I looked up, and though I didn't see any incoming, I raised my shield above my head anyway. If the arrows around my feet weren't enough, the din of battle raging just ahead of us made the danger clear.

I stopped the slingers and had them form up into two groups, with the fast throwers in front. I made the first cast, modeling the angle and distance I thought we were aiming for. The first volley probably wouldn't get those archers, but that was fine. We would creep into range.

Arrows planted themselves in the shields of our front line, clanged off of steel, and some came within spitting distance of me. We would be creeping into range of their bows, too.

The first line threw, advanced with me, and reloaded. The second group threw, advanced, reloaded. We repeated that sequence, and I still didn't see another volley of arrows.

Helgi Piketooth saw what we were doing and gave me a shark-like grin.

I thought we had scared the archers off until another volley of arrows corrected me. The arrows came from a different angle this time. I saw it at the last moment and shouted, but not in time to warn everyone, and one of the slingers had lowered his shield to say something to the man next to him. He got an arrow in the shoulder. Another, holding his shield exactly as he should have, took an arrow in the leg. Shields stopped most of the other arrows, but the archers had guessed our distance correctly.

I pointed toward the source of the arrows to change our aim and continued ordering volleys from that position. I did my best to keep my voice steady while terror twisted my guts. I'd had this idea to counter their archers, but had no idea how to deal with our wounded. Pull them back and see if they could survive? Leave them be and make sure to execute the attack?

Another volley of arrows found more slingers in both groups. I told them to stand fast and throw higher, as the archers had moved closer. Which was the best guess I knew how to make.

Helgi pointed and shouted commands to his people in between my orders. "Pull back the wounded!" He remained at the front with his spear but sent a small group of reserves our way. Some people know what to do in war just by looking around.

Five warriors detached from Helgi's group, holding their shields behind them as they raced toward us. They did their best to cover themselves and the wounded as they pulled them back.

My fear lessened. The next volley of arrows came sooner than expected, and one clanged off my shield's boss, rattling my hand. There was the fear again. I called new volleys as fast as I thought the men could throw.

The smell of *seiðr* rose on the battlefield: Alfhild's rotten blood and iron against Huld's lightning-burnt air and silver birch.

Svipul appeared when I lowered the shield for my next throw. She had nothing to say at first, just stood there, her spear and shield readied as if she would take her place in the front line. Her helmet was down this time, the mail hanging from it protecting her neck and face. Still, I could see those steel gray eyes looking out from there, watching my slingers.

"We've got them scared now!" I shouted, hoping it was true. "Keep loosing those rocks!"

The clash of battle got louder. Our front lines bulged backwards from the swarming enemy. My pulse pounded in my ears. I told my slingers to change direction and hold against the archers. We were forcing them to move, slowing them down.

But my command had little effect. They were exposed, vulnerable, and didn't even know whether they were hurting the enemy. I didn't have Haldor's voice to hold them steady, or a spell to stop those arrows. I hoped the slingers would hold.

Styrgrim stood on the back of one of the boulders and shouted for us to continue. Then he pointed out and to the right with his sword—his old sword, forged by his father, Halstein. He gestured at Helgi, who nodded. Helgi turned to me and shouted. I could barely hear him, but I understood. The archers had moved back to the middle.

The next volley of arrows undershot us, which meant those arrows came down mostly on our front lines. Shields came together tight as dragon scales, but that made it harder to fight, harder to push back. The enemy host was concentrating pressure on our front, on breaking through and spilling into the defile.

With a quarter of my slingers wounded, I changed their direction, ordered them to throw as one group, and hoped the distance was right to hit those archers hard. Before the volley even launched, the enemy hit our front lines with the biggest sustained effort yet.

The clash of battle got louder. Our front lines devoured that first charge like it was a single, monstrous maw full of sharpened steel teeth. They kept coming, though.

My pulse thundered so that I could hardly hear my own voice when I ordered the switch to staff slings. I told my slingers to lob their heaviest rocks high, targeting the area just beyond our front lines.

Soon, the big, trollish warriors loomed over the other foemen, the powerful swipes of their axes knocking spearpoints away and threatening to open gaps in the shield wall. Hjalti's voice came from somewhere in that mess, shouting commands to have the shield wall bend back and then forward again to counter them.

Heavy volleys from the staff slings did not appear to lessen the pressure. Even very good warriors can only engage in swinging combat for so long before they tire, and this grinding fight was harder than the previous day's. Helgi rotated his people in. Nanthild scooted her way to the very front. Our lines still bulged backwards from the swarming enemy.

Styrgrim hacked down an enemy trying to come over the boulder. He looked out ahead, looked back at the throng before him, and whatever he saw made him pause for a moment. I didn't understand that pause until he sheathed his old sword, and that's when I knew: We were about to be overrun. It was time for him to leave the front line, draw Tyrfing, and destroy the Brisingamen to make certain the enemy did not get it.

I looked at Svipul standing next to me. She stared at Styrgrim. He looked my way, as if he could see her there, and drew Tyrfing. Then he leaped over the boulder, into the thick of the enemy host pouring into the defile.

I shouted a curse so profane, it would have made Magnus blush. Then I ordered the slingers to cease volleys to avoid hitting the idiot Styrgrim, who was supposed to be destroying the torc, but was instead striking out where that would be impossible.

A strong wind rose behind us. A volley of enemy arrows came up, black against the gray sky, and the wind pushed them back so they fell on Alfhild's host. The smell of birch sap was so strong I could taste it. Whatever the battle of sorcery was, Huld was winning, pushing Alfhild's influence back.

Kraki shouted something, and our shield wall in front of him parted. He waved on some of the others from the crew. Magnus, Frothi, and Thorir all surged forward into the melee. Kraki's bone club struck like thunder, and the biggest of the trolls went down. Our people moved forward toward Styrgrim, attacking the attackers. For now.

I couldn't tell where to throw or how much good it would do, but I knew our front lines had been hard-pressed. I ordered all slingers to find spears and relieve some of our people at the front.

We had to keep pushing. If we could keep pushing, the enemy would disengage. We couldn't rout them—or could we? That was where most of an army died, in a rout. With our numbers so small, though, I was unsure. I had to find Styrgrim and have him destroy the Brisingamen before we waited any longer. I took a few tentative steps forward, wondering how to find him in the thick of the fighting without getting myself killed.

"You might be going the wrong way," said Svipul.

A huge shape passed over the beach, silhouetted against the gray sky. A long, serpentine body with massive wings glided over the enemy host. I knew before I heard the dragon's voice that Svart Geirridarsson had arrived. "Fall back, you fools! Back to the beach and your master!"

The dragon banked toward the sea and circled back around. But instead of another pass over the enemy host, the monster headed straight for the chasm we were holed up in. "Skald! Hear me out, and profit!"

I turned to see Svipul still at my side. "Soft underbellies," she said.

"Do I bury myself in the sand and hope he slithers over my sword, then?"

"Sigurd the Dragon Slayer did that. It worked well for him."

Instead of landing on the sand forward of our lines, Svart pulled up before careening into the chalk cliff side. His legs were not long, but he had big, strong claws for a lindworm, and dug them deep into the soft stone. He crawled along the vertical cliff face, eyeing me as he advanced high above our front line and into the defile.

"But now he sees you." She shrugged. "So think of something else."

*Goat's breath and cat piss!*

# CHAPTER 58

## FLY LIKE AN OWL

WE HAD JOURNEYED ACROSS HALF THE WORLD, FOUND OUT secrets buried for decades, and fought multiple battles against long odds to destroy the Brisingamen. Now we had the means to destroy it, but between the torc and the sword, more or less, was a winged dragon. Who just wanted to talk, if you believe that. Which you should not.

I took off running and passed the ship the slingers and I had taken cover under. Just a bit farther were Jorun and the other archers. Giving them a clear shot at that soft underbelly was my only idea.

Svart clawed his way across the cliff face, then leaped and spread his wings. He glided down in front of me, throwing sand up in a great cloud I had to shield my face from.

Three men with spears charged the monster from the side, perhaps thinking they could surprise him. Svart threw his long tail out behind two of them, knocking them down. The third leaped over the tail and threw his spear, but it could not bite the dragon's armored flank. Svart turned away from me to grab the warrior's torso in his teeth and bite him clear through. The body dropped, and the dragon again turned my way.

"Skald!" he hissed in that horrid voice. "Call off your people. Parley. I'll let these two live if only you will speak with me."

"Hold!" I shouted to whoever was listening.

I looked around to make sure no one would attack the dragon for the

441

moment. From this angle, our archers only had a line on its armored back. I was also looking for some cover I might be able to dive behind. There wasn't much nearby, only the upturned ship. Ketill was still under it, an easy target if Svart did not hold to his claim of "parley." Which I expected him not to.

Three supports held the ship open to the side I was on. Ketill was in front of one. Could I get there in time to knock the other two away and give us cover from incoming dragon fire?

No.

But there was that tell-tale bump in the sand. Finnr was moving beneath the surface near Ketill, if slowly. If he could knock down the third support, that could buy us . . . seconds?

The wizard grinned and spoke low as he wiped away what he'd done in the sand in front of him. He was up to something. I hoped seconds would be enough time for it.

I couldn't hear any more fighting at the front. I expect Svart's arrival was quite the surprise for everyone involved. He didn't command Alfhild's people, so why did he tell them to retreat? To buy himself time, I supposed.

"Let those two go, and then we'll talk," I said.

Svart gave a last hiss at the warriors, who dutifully scrambled away. He snapped his head back toward me. He sort of slither-crawled along the sand with those short but thick lindworm legs. I suspected he could put on a burst of speed even if he couldn't maintain it very long.

I wondered how fast I could compose a verse that might help me out of this mess. On-the-spot poetry would never be as on-the-spot as that. No verse came to mind. I drew Need as a sword and pointed it at the dragon. "Stay where you are if you want to speak."

Svart stopped and bowed. "Let us aid one another rather than see our mutual destruction."

I judged that I was right at the edge of his range if he breathed fire. Remembering his limited range in turning as he breathed fire, I took two steps to the side, away from the ship. I thought I was being very clever, even though I had just made a big assumption about his range. That's the trouble with assumptions: You don't realize when you're making them.

"I once made an offer to you, and now I reiterate it." The snake-like hiss of his voice rang off the walls, hurting my ears. "But then you had only an idea of the offer, and now you see it before you: Alfhild's force will overwhelm yours. It is only a matter of time before they kill you and take the Brisingamen by force. Do you deny this?"

"Dying has only been a matter of time since the moment I was born. As for being killed, I have never yet experienced it despite many a man and troll trying their luck, so I think things are far from decided on that count."

"Hmmmm." An *I'm cleverer than you* sound rumbled from the back of Svart's throat. I think he was grinning. Hard to tell with dragons.

He rolled that lizard-like purr into his next attempt. "I can see your quality and the quality of your people. How many others might give the witch such a difficult time? Few, I think. She will come out ahead, though, victorious despite her inferior intellect, and this is an ill outcome for everyone. Alfhild commands even though she should be one of the commanded. She has a short-sighted view of things. An overly personal view of things."

I found myself caught between wanting Svart to continue on at length until Jorun could shoot him and wanting him to come to the point. I'm no slouch at praise poetry when I need to be, but he was going on too long, and with too obvious a goal, to be taken seriously. It was a mark of the sort of word-sorcery Ulf used to great success, but which I was never enamored of: Talking too much.

But it was clearly the best option not to interrupt. Above the dragon, about halfway between the ground and the cliff's top, a vaguely *vǫlva*-shaped thing moved. Its color matched the wall behind it, and its movements were so small they were hard to detect, even looking straight at it. I would not have even thought to look there if I hadn't already known Huld's position.

"Their loyalty to her is from the use of that torc," Svart continued. "Why should heroes fall at the hands of mere minions? Give it to me, and I will use it to good effect: Her people will abandon her and follow my orders. I will end her, and then what? You and yours will sail on, or even join me for rich rewards, unhindered either way."

"Sounds like we would be allies, in that case," I replied. "Which would ally us with Ogmund Tussock."

"Well, no." The dragon reared up, as if expecting me to act surprised. "I've spoken with my father about Tyrfing; pity I didn't realize what I was seeing right away. Ogmund insists on having the sword himself. Buying it, actually. Then you could ally with him, a reward twice over for a prudent decision."

"So, the torc for you and the sword for him?"

"Indeed. You've cast off the anchor of Arrow-Odd. What is there to do with no anchor holding you down, other than set sail once more? With gold-laden ships, I mean."

"Anchors are everywhere. Some to tie a person down. Others to keep you steady against ill influence. My armring anchors me." I paused, feeling for Haldor's silver armring beneath my mail.

"It makes demands of you."

"It does." Though his words and mine conveyed the same objective statement, the meanings could not have been more different. "And eating the flesh of the dead, trolling people—does this not then create demands on you?"

"I choose to increase my power rather than see it diminished."

"Power is power, then?"

The dragon nodded. "And a good deal is a good deal."

"You know, in addition to having issues with Alfhild, I have unfinished business with Ulf."

"The shitling with the silver tongue?" He laughed. "He fancies himself a man of *seiðr* now, but he is a fool. Do with him what you will."

I nodded. And I was running out of delays.

"The *Br—*"

"What about Svein?" I interrupted. "We couldn't find him."

"I know nothing of where he ran to, the coward." He huffed and flicked his tongue, his tone sharper than before. "The Brisingamen. Give it to me, and save your people who have fought so well."

Huld looked down at Svart. Slow as living stone, she pointed her distaff at him. The scent of silver birch sap and recently-struck lightning filled the air.

"Ah, well, that's a funny thing, you know? Because we retain a fairly strict hierarchy, requiring a majority of ship captains and skalds to be present for voting on decisions of major import, and—"

The dragon's head reared back. His nostrils flared and his eyes went wide as his neck shot forward. I ran toward the upturned ship.

Flames shot behind me by a spear's length, and I realized his range was greater than I'd judged. I could feel the heat on my back as the jet of fire followed me. The sand slowed me down, but Svart could not change direction quick enough to keep up while still breathing fire.

The fire stopped. The dragon roared. And with an unlimbered neck, he slither-crawled towards me. Very fast.

The first arrow hit Svart so hard, I thought it might have killed him. No such luck—the arrow rang off the bony frill on his skull. It did not shatter like an arrow hitting solid rock, though. Instead, it sounded like a javelin ringing off of inch-thick steel. The impact threw the dragon's head sideways, staggering him mid-stride.

That was enough of a delay for me to make it to the ship. I knocked the support at my end away while Ketill did the same. Finnr, now a dwarf, knocked away the third. The front collapsed, and we three were left in the dark hollow of an upside-down ship.

Outside, a storm of sand whirled against the hull of the ship. Minor gusts kicked up inside, but the openings for those were small. I tried to look out from one of them near the ship's aft, but the sand flying into my eyes was too much. The dwarf seemed to have no such difficulty as he peered out near the fore, closer to the cliff wall.

"Does Huld have him?" asked Ketill.

The dwarf's reply gave no details while conveying all we needed to know when he replied, "Shit!"

"It will be your idea, then," continued the wizard.

"I don't have any ideas!" I shouted. "Styrgrim was supposed to come back and destroy this thing. Or come back and kill this damn dragon! But he's not here, he's off fighting! *Again!*"

"Not you. Finnr's idea. And for that, you must give him the Brisingamen."

"*What?*"

"It's the wings," said the dwarf. "A few flaps and he can keep them blind in the sand. I'm not sure those arrows would pierce his belly, in any case."

"*What?*"

"Ansgar!" The wizard used his voice that turned the world topsy-turvy. It got my attention. "Give Finnr the Brisingamen, or that dragon will come here and take it."

"But—"

"I will explain, but *do it now!*"

The dwarf laughed. "How many children have you had? Did such commands convince them to change their minds?" He shook his head as he hurried over to me. "You want to destroy the torc, not send it back to the Down-Below, I know. It's your whole reason for seeking out Tyrfing in the first place. But listen: If you hold on so tight to what you wish had happened, you won't be able to grasp what remains as possible."

What the dwarf said seemed undeniable, but I had the feeling he was trying to trick me. I backed away a step, then fell on my ass and scooted as far away as I could get without leaving the cover of the ship. "You're not immune to the dragon sickness."

Finnr stopped and put his hands on his hips. "Who speaks now? The skald, or the torc?"

That's when I realized my left hand had made its way into the bag. I had nearly pulled the torc out without realizing it, had mistaken its intent for my own. I pushed it back down and pulled my hand away from the bag.

The dwarf stepped forward and knelt beside me. "I know you think you're the only one who can carry the thing, that it can't be contained. But you know my story. I'm a steel dwarf. Not a gold dwarf."

Efraim's story echoed in my memory at the dwarf's words. 'Not with gold, but rather with steel.' I swallowed hard. As I handed the torc over, I said, "I hope this isn't because we're all just pieces on a *hnefatafl* board."

The dwarf grinned. "I know one piece that's about to run into the table!" He crawled out of the small opening and leaped into the air.

I stuck my head out after him, shielding my eyes from the sand.

A snowy owl with a streak of black screeched as it flew, using a beat from one of the dragon's massive wings to gain lift. It screeched a second time, taunting the dragon, as it held the Brisingamen in its talons.

I wondered if a winged dragon could just take off from the ground, or if it had to find a high vantage point to leap off of. When Svart began climbing the nearby cliff wall, digging those talons deep into the chalk as he ascended, I had my answer.

"Come back quickly, and I will explain," Ketill called to me.

But I did not come back just then, because I saw something about to happen. On his climb up, Svart looked to his right. He growled low and angry, but was in an awkward position to breathe fire at Huld. Continuing to climb, he swatted her with his tail instead.

Huld put an arm up to protect herself at the last moment. The tail struck upward, crumbling much of the chalky wall before it hit her and threw her hard against the cliff face. She fell, hitting the narrow ledge she'd sat on before continuing on to the ground below.

I did not see her get up.

# CHAPTER 59

# BLACK BLADE

"Huld is down." I stated it as a matter of fact to determine what was next with Ketill's advice because there was no time for any other reaction. The world didn't slow down. There was no high-pitched ringing in my ears. My hands did not go numb.

Whatever the cost, I would have to pay it later.

There was pain on the wizard's face, but also a grim determination. "Find Jorun and the other archers. Gather as many spare spears as you can. If that lindworm has a soft underbelly, like every other lindworm I have ever seen, you must stick as much steel into it as you can."

The whooshing sound above us told me that Svart had taken flight. The flapping of those massive wings and the size of his body as he passed over kicked up the sand again.

"I think he might be outside our range."

The wizard shook his head. "Follow the owl. Finnr will lead him on a chase skyward. Then he will lead him down to the earth. Fast." He had traced some sort of bind rune deep into the sand. It was difficult to make it out, but easy to see the small bowl of blood he prepared to pour into it.

"I think this spell is something you did not teach me about. I don't understand it, or how leading Svart down to the earth will do us much good."

The wizard shook his head and poured the blood over the bind rune in the sand as he muttered something in what sounded like an old language. The blood pooled into the design, coloring the design in the sand. With one rune on top of another, I couldn't tell how many there were. Draw just about anything on top of *isaz*, which is just one vertical line, and it looks like a single rune instead of two.

The blood remained there, as if on a non-porous surface. Suddenly, it was sucked away, leaving only stained sand.

Beneath my feet—beneath even the sand, I think—something deep in the earth moved. A slow grinding, but not for some temporary trip to the Down-Below or the local *landvættir* giving a subtle sign. This was a shift on a scale I had not felt before.

"The earth moves willingly for dwarves," said the wizard. "Sorcerers and trolls know how to take the Lower Passage, move the earth by coercion." He looked at me like this told me all. "Finnr's blood. My incantation. Your return of the Brisingamen. I have marshaled every *vættir*, the very earth against such coercion for the time being."

I couldn't stop my eyes from going wide. "You affected all of Midgard with just—"

"Of course not, don't be a fool! Even I cannot go beyond natural boundaries." He shook his head. "I realize now that I've neglected some of the most basic lessons, but you will have to make do. This spell can't go any farther than water or horizon bind it. So if your witch dives into the sea, she will get away.

"But as for a dragon hurtling toward the ground at speed, expecting the hole an owl has flown through will expand for him as it normally would— such a dragon will find himself surprised. And quite vulnerable."

I stared at the wizard in awe.

"Archers!" he shouted.

I left the cover of the ship and ran to find Jorun. A crowd had gathered around Huld as I passed by. I couldn't see what was happening and didn't have time to find out. Hallfred Horsefly gave the orders there, and that heartened me. If anyone knew what to do for Huld, it would be him, the widest-traveled and wisest of us skalds.

Soaring high above, the dragon spouted fire. He could turn while he did this, but the stiffness of his neck limited that movement. The owl veered off and dove to avoid the flames, faster and far more agile in the sky. He hooted low at the dragon, as if egging him on. I hoped he could keep that up for a while.

I was so elated when I found Jorun that I launched into explanation before listening to her. Or looking at her. She finally held up a hand for me to wait.

"I cannot see."

Her eyes were clear, not even bloodshot. "Do you have sand in them?" I asked, desperately wanting it to be that simple.

She shook her head. "Svart hit us with more than sand. I thought I could fight through that, and I loosed another arrow, but the armor on his back was impenetrable. Then he went after Huld. I saw her fall through her eyes. Then the world went misty." She reached forward, uncertainly, to find my shoulder. "Ansgar, is Huld alive?"

I grasped her hand. "All I know is that we are alive. Ketill and Finnr have a plan to kill the dragon. I need as many of the other archers as can see."

She shook her head. I looked around. Everyone holding a bow had the same blank stare.

"Take my bow and quiver," said Jorun.

That stopped me for a moment. "I am not a great archer."

She let out a hard laugh. "Better than a blind woman!"

There was nothing left but to go and try. I ran toward our front line as fast as I could, calling for spears and shields. Most of those I passed asked what was happening, but there wasn't time to stop and explain. I reached the front line, frantic as I saw the number of our dead and wounded.

Thorir was covered in bleeding cuts. He examined an arrow in his brother, Frothi, who debated leaving it in or taking it out—a through-shot that had only pierced him an inch into his calf. Nanthild stared through a thumb-sized hole in the top of her helmet, her hair mottled with a mixture of wet and clotted blood. Magnus' face and hands were smeared red, his armor still dripping, a desperate look on his face. Kraki held himself steady on one knee as he breathed heavily, leaning on his bone club. Tyrfing's cut bled freely.

Helgi Pike-Tooth was in a better state than most. In the face of my near-panic, when I was saying too many words, too fast, without enough listeners, he put his left hand on my shoulder and held his right fist ready for a gut-punch.

"Slow down," said the sharp-toothed captain, which stopped me cold. "Don't forget to breathe." He looked over his shoulder and motioned for Hjalti. "Take three breaths. Then tell us: What is going on with the dragon?"

I took the three breaths, though Hjalti was there in two. I used the third breath to sling the quiver over my shoulder. "Finnr is the owl. He is using the torc as bait to lure the dragon to the ground."

"Why have you—" Hjalti started, but Pike-Tooth cut him off.

"Continue."

"Finnr will dive through the ground, as a dwarf can. But Ketill has cast a spell and hardened the earth against the dragon's passage. He will try to dive in, but he will hit the ground hard. When that happens, we attack the soft underbelly."

The owl screeched as it passed overhead, moving hard in one direction until the dragon committed, and then banking hard the other way. In a matter of seconds, Finnr doubled the space between pursuer and pursued.

"Better if Jorun did the shooting," said Pike-Tooth.

"She can't see. The archers are blind. For now."

"For how long?"

I shook my head. I hoped the answer was not "forever," but what did I know? Both commanders took this in and nodded. They wanted details, but they did not need details. They needed to act.

"You take a high position right here," Pike-Tooth said to me, slapping the boulder next to him. "Shoot what you can shoot. Wait, where is the dwarf coming down?"

"I . . . uh . . . don't know."

Helgi Pike-Tooth shook his head and pulled his beard. "Not behind our lines, and not too far ahead of them, I'm going to assume. But be ready to move if they come down somewhere unexpected, skald." He turned to Hjalti, "Take a group of six spears, fresh, fast movers. I will take another. As well as we can, we will attack at these angles."

Helgi drew a circle in the sand. "If this is the dragon, then this is your group." He drew a line angled down and to the left. "And this is mine." He drew another line angled down and to the right. "If we're lucky, the dragon comes down in bow range, leaving the skald with a clear shot." He drew a shallow line that went between our two lines and into the circle. "Understand?"

While I was still thinking about whether I understood, Hjalti was already calling for the six warriors he wanted to go with him.

"Badly as it has gone for the enemy, it was a hard fight," said Helgi. "This dragon does not need to fly again to break our defenses. We need to kill him quickly, or that will be the end of us."

I nodded. "Where is Styrgrim, and why is he not leading a group?"

"We don't know," said Hjalti.

"Broke their attack, went after one of the big trolls," added Pike-Tooth, his voice hard. "Lost in the melee."

Whatever cost I knew would be paid to hear about Huld dying became that much greater. "Well, at least if we die, we won't have time to feel grief."

Helgi Pike-Tooth grinned and slapped me on the shoulder. Then he chose six warriors for his group. He and Hjalti got into position.

High above, the owl whistled, now chased by an eagle rather than a dragon. Finnr dove and banked, the eagle's talons coming so close to flesh that they ripped tail feathers away.

The Brisingamen flashed in the overcast sky. Greater agility or not, holding onto that thing was slowing Finnr down. He dove for the ground.

"He's coming down!" I shouted.

Second later, Finnr flew straight into the ground at high speed, disappearing through a crack that opened for just an instant. The eagle was only a second behind him. It did not slip quietly into the earth, but thudded into the sand in a puff of feathers.

The spear groups took wide angles to stay apart as they advanced on the eagle's position. Soon, I saw the eagle flapping wildly. It had gone down in a trench among some of the fallen and was having trouble pulling itself up. Hopefully also having trouble moving. If Svart wasn't at least injured from that fall, this would be a hard fight.

The eagle shook its head side to side and appeared to prop itself forward as if its wings were hands. I loosed an arrow, but missed high. Jorun made it look easy, but Ymir's bones, that hornbow had a heavy draw.

Helgi was already leading his group at a full charge. "Once more!" he called back to me.

I focused on using my back more than my arms as I drew again, but still couldn't hold it for very long. I think my heart skipped a beat when the arrow flew true. But even before I loosed, the eagle's wings became arms as Svart changed his skin to human again. Hard to tell how vulnerable a sorcerer who changes shape is. In human form, though, they are very difficult to kill. So when Svart put a hand up against that arrow, it struck his palm and shattered as if striking an anvil.

Helgi's group locked shields and lowered their spears.

Even as Svart's hand descended, it was changing its shape again into the stubby claw of a lindworm. Svart's body stretched and lengthened, much faster than he had changed in the Down-Below. A sudden swipe of a mostly-formed wing threw Helgi's group backwards. The moments it took them to recover allowed Svart to fully become the dragon, his soft underbelly unexposed, hovering over the trench.

"There is little you've left me other than to be the hero of this battle," said Svart. "But that's a thing I can do, and in some ways better for my standing. So close, you were so close to victory! But you've thrown it a*waaaaaay!*"

I thought the skin-changing sorcerer was just being dramatic about our deaths at first. Maybe buying the mere minute or so he needed for a bit of backup from Alfhild's warriors, which would be more than enough to overrun us at that point.

But no, that tone spoke of pain.

The lindworm shuffled awkwardly to the side, its head bobbing up and down. It coughed up some sort of bile that burned the sand. Those short legs at its front worked furiously, moving it away from the trench, its head curling back in as if to see what had stung it.

On a brighter day, it would have been hard to see. But on a gray day like that, it was easy to see Tyrfing's glow, even before Styrgrim climbed his way up the trench.

"I have never called myself lucky," Styrgrim growled. "And so, Svart, what does that make you?"

The lindworm slithered away, but its body was long. Styrgrim drove the sword down, spitting its tail. For every new movement Svart pulled away, it cleaved more of him in half.

Roars of pain turned to human screams as Svart changed his skin back to that of a man. It freed him from being pinned in place somehow, but left him writhing on the ground in arm's reach of Styrgrim.

Styrgrim dragged the sorcerer up by his greasy forelock. He held the man there as if he'd caught the biggest fish of the season and bellowed at the army below. "Is this the best you could send? A sorcerer who cried for parley but bore arms with ill intent?" He cut off Svart's arms, the bright blade drinking in the blood before it hit the ground.

"A coward who ran the moment he faced a foe equal to the challenge?" With one stroke, he severed Svart's legs at the knees, still holding him upright by his forelock.

"*Where is his fire now?*"

I thought the next stroke would take the sorcerer's head off, but I was wrong. As he spoke, Styrgrim drove the sword through the back of Svart's skull. He did it slowly, and all the way down to the hilt so that the blade came through the dead man's mouth.

The body fell forward. As it slipped off the blade, the last light of Tyrfing went out. All the brightness, all the polish, the air of razor-sharpness dropped away from the sword. What was left was an aged weapon, notched and pitted. Worn well past its prime, if it ever had one, the blade turned black as night.

Waves of heat radiating off the weapon made it clear its power had not been spent. Only the glamour had slipped away, the thing it used to draw in new wielders, to make it seem a desirable thing.

I had never known Styrgrim the Bear to speak in verse, but he did so high on that beach, taunting our enemies. And in verse, he would forever be a man of terror to those below:

> "So! The denizens of Dafvik
>     in days gone by
> knew their heroes'
>     names well.
> No kings did we need
>     for courage and word-fame.
> Here stands Styrgrim!
>     Still alive
> despite every trial
>     of trolls and men.
> I got by on grit,
>     not gifts from gods,
> 'til another terror
>     of hall troops
> found its way into
>     these frenzied hands.
> Now the bright blade
>     burns black as night,
> its true glow
>     a gloom of shadow,
> no sorcerer it can't cleave!
>     This is some good sword."

As the sword's illusion dissolved, I saw Styrgrim more truly as well, saw the things Arrow-Odd and Magnus had seen for years. Saw what my grandfather Halstein had warned me about when he spoke of the fire that burned with heat but no light.

Tyrfing had finally found someone who wanted it not for some imagined rewards of glory or power, hoping to control its bloodlust. It had found a man who wanted it just as it was.

# CHAPTER 60

## GOOD WEATHER FOR SCARED PEOPLE

STYRGRIM THE BEAR EXECUTING ONE OF MIDGARD'S MOST powerful sorcerers and daring an army to come at him elicited cheers and the banging of many shields on our side. The enemy had failed twice in one day. Spirits were up, a high point for us in the battle.

But it wasn't a high point, and we weren't winning. Huld was down, and I didn't know if she would ever get back up to counter Alfhild. What few good archers we had were blind. Our best fighters were injured, fatigued, or both. It was not a good situation based on what I knew of our defenses. It was even worse when I saw what was on that beach.

More warships had arrived. Not many, only five or six. One of them was almost as ugly as the *Naglfar*, and just as long. I could tell they had only just arrived because their warriors were still disembarking. One man, in particular, caught my eye.

He was tall and wearing a coat that looked like it had been woven from human hair. The man stood well forward of the rest of Alfhild's army, staring out at Styrgrim by himself. It was hard to see his face for the big black shock of hair hanging over it.

When Svart said he had spoken to his father, I hadn't thought it meant that Ogmund himself had come to Mon. That's when I understood Styrgrim's verse. He hadn't been taunting Alfhild or her army. That verse had been meant for Ogmund Tussock, daring him to come and fight after seeing his son cut down by Tyrfing.

*No sorcerer it can't cleave!*

Ogmund raised one arm, his fingers splayed. He pointed them at Styrgrim.

"Shields up!" I shouted to Styrgrim and the two sorties. "Arrows incoming!"

Hjalti looked back at me, uncertain.

I didn't know that for sure, but I knew enough stories about trolls and evil sorcerers to expect it. It still wasn't clear to me whether Ogmund practiced *seiðr* or knew some other art. It was fair to call him a troll, though, and stories often described how trolls were dangerous at a distance.

"From his fingers!" I continued. "Watch out!"

The first arrow struck the sand where Styrgrim had been standing a moment before. He sheathed the sword but kept his eye on Ogmund as he started back toward the defile.

The scent of Huld's *seiðr* was gone, while the scent of Alfhild's *seiðr*, especially the rotting iron, was strong in the air. The wind blew at us, kicking up sand and throwing us all off balance.

Helgi and Hjalti sent their people back behind our lines while they themselves ran forward. They came up next to Styrgrim and put their shields up to protect him, high and low, and slowly all three men walked back.

Arrows thudded into the linden or clanged on the bosses. They were close to getting back when Helgi took one of those arrows in the leg. I heard him grunt, even over the wind whipping at us and the breakers rising below. He kept moving, though, and soon they were all back behind our lines.

Their army was not mustering. If anything, it looked like they intended to lick their wounds a bit. But we were under attack, as the storm behind Alfhild's ship parted around their fleet and rolled toward us. The sky above went from overcast to dark. The high cliffs shielded us from the worst of the wind but couldn't keep out the ice-cold rain.

Most took cover under the upturned ships, far back from our front line. Hjalti organized a few dozen of us to get as much done as quickly as possible. Those of us who were uninjured worked through the rain and wind to reinforce our front-most defenses. Our fences were destroyed. The trenches had been filled in. The bigger rocks thrown by staff slings had to be carried back. Sharpened stakes had been pulled up. Thankfully, most of those who had done the pulling hadn't thought to take those stakes with them.

The rain quickly turned into hail as the weather sent at us got colder. I looked back at Hjalti at one point, expecting him to call our work good enough. He did not.

"Keep a shield above your head for the hail, if you must. It will take longer to work one-handed, though."

Hjalti had us redigging earthworks that stretched farther out from our defenses, but allowed a slim, flat bridge of sand in the middle. North of the chasm entrance, the rain had poured down a cliff face and created a rivulet of water running down to the shoreline. I breathed a sigh of relief when he told us not to extend the earthworks nearly that far. But digging and reinstalling stakes in wet sand was cold, uncomfortable, awkward work. One-handed, it was impossible, so only my helmet protected my head from the hail.

When I could finally retreat to the cover of one of those ships, I was tired and shivering from the work, and for fear of what I might learn.

Huld was alive. She'd taken a hit from that dragon's tail, another when she hit the ledge, and a third when she hit the ground, so this "alive" state did not leave her very cheery or mobile. She could speak a bit. Hallfred thought she was unlikely to get up for a few more days. Sitting *seiðr* was no casual act to be done from a straw bed, and that was disheartening. As far as I could tell, Huld was out of the fight.

The fog in Jorun's eyes was lifting. She thought she would be able to see normally by morning. It was the same with the other archers. Healers had seen to Helgi's wound right away. He could still fight, but no doubt his leg would not bear him as well as it usually did. He was in the fight, for whatever was left of it. The arrow that had gone through Frothi's leg was gone, now referred to by the moose man as "a splinter." He was ready for the next fight and said as much. I checked in with the rest of my crew. They were tired and hurting, but not nearly done.

I wasn't sure if the next attack would come late in the day or the next day. Probably at the night, as Styrgrim had explained, but we would still watch.

The hailstones grew in size as the day wore on. I decided to call the War Council together under the cover of one of the ships to avoid the weather. Skalds, captains, and Ketill all gathered where Huld lay sitting upright.

"Before any of you ask," Ketill began, "no, I cannot counter this weather spell."

"The ships are all the protection needed from the weather," said Huld, sounding more tired than I had ever heard her. "Let her waste what energy she will. She has always been a fool when it comes to reserving strength."

"And if she tires herself out overnight," I said, "then what?"

The *vǫlva* eyed me with a saucy look. Despite sweating from being in obvious pain, she grinned. "Think I'm done, do you? It will take more than a slap and a fall."

I wanted to believe her, but her breath was labored. And I recalled the thrall in chains on the *Naglfar*. Sacrifice was part of Alfhild's vilest sorcery and was not yet in play. Even if Huld could sit *seiðr* by morning, I wasn't sure she would be strong enough to match Alfhild.

"You're all getting far ahead of things," said Styrgrim. "I want to know about a thing that's already happened: Why is the Brisingamen given away?"

"It would have been destroyed had you come back my way instead of charging forward." It was difficult to keep the venom out of my voice.

Styrgrim crossed his arms. "Trying to not lose precludes trying to win."

I took a deep breath. Then I described what had happened, from that point until hearing the dragon scream. "But how did you come to be in the perfect place at the perfect time?"

Styrgrim shook his head. "I got tangled up with a flock of retreating sheep and took a blow to the helmet, I think. Landed with some hapless dead man on top of me in a trench. I woke up in a position to shove my sword up a dragon's ass. Perhaps just luck, but I would guess that Finnr saw me in the trench and hoped for an outcome much like what transpired."

"If the torc is gone," said Magnus, "then—oh, they aren't leaving now, though."

"Not after witnessing Svart's execution," I said. Styrgrim sighed, and I realized what I had said could be taken as *Styrgrim damned us all when he did that*, which was not at all what I meant. "That was a good verse to seal his end. And one to make Ogmund afraid for his life."

Styrgrim nodded, a smirk poking through that stony face. "They could have regrouped and attacked again. Ogmund could have led the charge. But neither thing happened. Instead, Alfhild throws a storm our way to pin us down."

"They are afraid," said Ketill. "Ogmund has seen what the sword can do. The storm buys him time to think about how he'll avoid confronting Styrgrim directly."

"How will he do that?" I asked. "He's honor-bound to seek revenge, now."

The wizard shook his head. "Hence the storm. It looks like an attack, but it is really a delay. And he'll delay a direct confrontation even more by throwing every warrior he has at us tomorrow."

"They can throw scared warriors at us tomorrow." Stygrim's voice was cold iron. "Men looking for the first signs of certain death rather than ways to win through. And we still have Kraki's idea."

"Mmph?" Kraki was not looking well. He had gone from very pale to sallow. He looked up as if only now paying attention. "Death in fire," he wheezed. "From my dream."

Even between his hardiness, Huld's ministrations, and the shallowness of the cut, I counted eight days since that sword had sealed his fate. I doubted Tyrfing's bite had ever taken so long to claim a life. I swallowed hard and hoped the old man would live through the night. If I was going to die tomorrow, I wanted to die with my family.

"What is the plan involving 'death in fire'?" Jorun asked.

"Kraki has had prophetic dreams before, and may have had another," I cut in so that Kraki would not need to speak. "He saw our ship sailing, but on the ground rather than on the water. Hence the cart. It was also engulfed in flames."

"That sounds like a prophecy of doom," replied Jorun. "How is that an idea for us?"

"That ship is on wheels now, and it only has to roll so far," said Styrgrim. "The space between boulders at the front is wide enough for it to roll through. We could move it into that chokepoint and fire it there, and that would buy us time. Or we could fire it and send it downhill, right into their ships."

"Either way, once that fire is out," I said, "we're cooked."

Styrgrim must have seen how little hope that gave us. "There is never any telling what ill luck will turn out good or the other way around, only the willingness to seize the moment that appears."

*Easier to seize such moments with a vǫlva on your side.*

The state of things left me feeling deflated. I had gone from grim determination to thinking we could actually win at some point. Now it was clear that we could not even hold out much longer.

The hailstorm quieted and then stopped. No horns spoke of the enemy massing for an attack.

"Alfhild needs to rest like anyone else," said Huld.

"Will she sleep on that ship?" I asked.

"Likely," Huld replied. "Why do you ask?"

"I was thinking about seizing a moment in the night. Sending the *Sea Squirrel* down at them. Not to fire their ships, but to reach Alfhild quickly and kill her. Maybe Ogmund, too."

*Could I also find Ulf in that chaos?*

Styrgrim shook his head. "Without routing the enemy first, you might get to one that way, but not the other." He pulled at his beard and looked away as if visualizing such an attack, though.

"So, we're just waiting again?" asked Magnus.

"Not just waiting," said Styrgrim. "Ogmund thinks he can use up his people and Alfhild's for certain victory. But show them what Tyrfing can do, and pile the bodies high enough, and much of that army will flee. That's our moment to charge him, and then Alfhild." He turned to me. "I will call out Ogmund again, just as he's sending his people to die for them. I will need a verse to drive it home, break their morale."

I nodded, saying nothing about how my heart had just doubled in size.

"I was too occupied to be at the front today," said Ketill. "But no longer. And I have a trick from that dwarf we met Down-Below that will give them a hard time."

By the time we finished, night had fallen.

Hallfred Horsefly approached me after the Council. That warm and strong expression could buoy anyone's spirits. I expected he would say something encouraging, witty, or both. Maybe something I couldn't help but grin at. The value of a good skald can manifest in many ways.

"Can I have your crampons?"

I stared at him as if I had misheard.

"Just for tonight, I think."

"Because we'll both be dead after that?"

"Probably, yes! I am willing to buy them from you if need be, money not being much use to a dead man. I need to scale the walls here, get as high as I can."

"All right. They will cost you a thousand pounds of hacksilver, payable in increments of one hundred pounds per year for ten years, plus one additional year as a fee."

"I counter with an offer of this rock I found." He held a stone smoothed out by the sea. Oblong, with just enough heft to be an excellent bit of sling ammunition.

"I counter your counter—you must hand over the rock and also tell me why you are climbing."

"Sold!" He slapped the rock into my palm. Continuing, he pitched his voice lower. "In answer to your question: I intend to sit *seiðr*. Don't look so surprised! Huld had much to teach for one willing to learn."

Not a manly thing, *seiðr*. At least not by reputation. But in the brief time I had been out in the world, I had learned that most things people thought they knew were only things they repeated over and over and were not true whatsoever. If there was one skald I knew readier than anyone to challenge perceived truth, it was Hallfred.

I found my crampons and handed them over.

"Fear not, I will return," he said as he made his way off. "And who knows? Perhaps I will spy out an advantage for us to seize."

I doubted it. But I also knew that it was better to try something— anything—rather than worry over what would happen next.

So, I spoke with Styrgrim and prepared that verse. Short and to the point. I think he quite liked it.

With my work done as well as I knew how, I went to sleep early. I would need to keep as many of my wits as I could through the end.

But though I was done for the night, the enemy was not.

# CHAPTER 61

# NIGHT RIDER

SCREAMING WOKE ME IN THE MIDDLE OF THE NIGHT. NOT THE shouts of warning, though. This voice was full of pain and fear and confusion, and I couldn't believe what I was hearing at first. Not because there was pain, fear, and confusion, but because the person screaming was Styrgrim.

Magnus was up and running toward the commotion faster than I was, his dwarven blades flashing in the moonlight. I caught up quickly, heading toward one of the ships at the rear of the chasm.

Off to the side, where the *Sea Squirrel* sat on its cart, Kraki's pale figure popped up from the deck. "Are we under attack?"

"We've got horns for that," Magnus called back. "This is something else."

I couldn't imagine what it was, but the unexpected nature of those sounds made the hairs on the back of my neck stand up. Judging from Magnus' tone, he felt the same. Styrgrim's screaming rose in pitch and volume as we approached. Warriors spilled out from under the upturned *Long Claw* as Magnus and I ducked inside.

Styrgrim sat with his back braced against the other side of the ship, pushing himself back with his feet. He looked around, wild-eyed, breathing hard through his teeth and clutching the still-sheathed Tyrfing with both hands. Huld sat a few steps away. She spoke to him in soothing tones, assuring him he was awake now, that whatever he had seen had gone.

She turned to the two of us, the only ones left under the ship at that point. "Bring Helgi and Hjalti in. The others, keep out. No, skald, you stay. Say something to him."

Magnus was gone in an instant. I took a step closer to Styrgrim. "Have you been poisoned?" He turned his head while eyeing me from the side, clutching the sword even tighter. I took a step back, uncertain. "He looks delirious. Can he even understand me?"

"Not poison, just my own fool mistake. Wait a moment, so that I can explain once instead of three times."

Magnus returned with Helgi and Hjalti in just a few seconds. All three men asked some version of "What's happened?" at once.

Huld nodded. "Alfhild has ridden him. I was too focused on resting after the fall and forgot my own troll-cursed advice! Be grateful he has this much of his mind left."

Styrgrim muttered to himself and went from tense to hanging his head lazily, showing none of his characteristic discipline or steadiness. He kept rubbing his eyes and blowing his nose or snorting, uncomfortable in any position.

"Will he recover?" I asked

"Given enough rest and time, and my care, it is possible. His will is strong, but he did not know how to defend himself against a sleeping attack on his *hugr*. That is a nightmare like none of you has ever known. He is alive, but he will have a hard time."

"A hard time with what?" asked Hjalti.

"Anything! Now, listen, I don't have every tool I might use at the moment, and not nearly enough time. But better than herbs or grain for someone coming out of such a nightmare is the familiar."

"Familiar like shouting commands?" asked Hjalti. "Or familiar in a friendly way . . . which has not been quite so familiar for Styrgrim?"

"You can never tell with these things."

"Hey!" I shouted at Styrgrim, getting his attention. "Yes, you! You still owe me an explanation. 'Orders now, explanations if we survive' is what you said. Well, we survived, so I want the explanation: Why did you not want those staff slingers to throw—"

"Bigger rocks would've come back at us." For a moment, he straightened. "The longer you engage an enemy, the more likely they are to adapt to what you do. They saw what we did on the first day. They could have waited for us to do the same thing, then thrown those big rocks right back at our heads just ahead of a charge."

A few moments later, he went back to muttering.

"Good, that was good," said Huld.

Magnus snorted. "Nothing more familiar to Styrgrim than war, so I think he will be cured in short order."

"Let us hope so, because we will need him," I said. "Or we will need someone else to swing that sword."

Styrgrim held the sword tight to his chest and shook his head.

"You'll get nowhere with that sort of talk," said Huld. "Remind the man who he is. Tell him stories. All of you."

I started, though I had very little to share. I had more early memories of asking about Styrgrim than about the man himself. I understood now why he'd been gone so often, but reminding him of sad times didn't seem the right thing to do. Hjalti recalled times when Styrgrim had trained him to fight or steer the ship. Magnus shared the story of when Styrgrim found him, still rather feral, and how he used this feral warrior for some unconventional tactics. Helgi had tales about close calls on land and sea.

Feeling fairly useless, I thought I might rely on the memories I had run into rather than experienced. "Do you remember Gudbrand? I met him in Lejre, where is the king's staller. You knew him, but were you friends?"

"Gudbrand . . ." he said, grinning. "Always had a good quip to make." His face darkened a bit. "But never made light of any man's loss."

It sounded like he was describing the time Gudbrand had pulled that arrow out of his testicles. And Hel's dragon, I had made light of that injury when my feelings had been hurt. Now, facing the very real prospect of an arrow through my own balls or worse, I winced at my poor judgment.

"Gudbrand is a good man," I agreed. "And I wish Gunnar could have come with us from Borghund."

"Ha!" The grin was back. "The Marksman!" He laughed so hard, he slapped his own leg. Helgi folded his arms and grinned.

"Is he a poor archer, then?" asked Hjalti, no more in the know than I was.

Styrgrim shook his head between heaving laughs. "He younger was less certain than most. Wasn't even sure if he was allowed to piss at the same latrine we used, so he would go off to his own little spot. I asked him about it, and he said was just trying to hit the same rock every time, even though his real reason was obvious.

"Gudbrand called him 'the Marksman' one night, and we all had a laugh, but Gunnar was deadly serious and demanded an explanation. So we told him, and I thought a fight was going to break out at the worst possible time. But instead, Gunnar just said 'I appreciate the byname, but I've spent all my time learning to use an atgeir. Now I need to master the bow as well, or I'll never live this name down!'

"And you know what? He did!"

Now we were grinning and laughing with him. It lasted a few seconds before the look of confusion returned, and Styrgrim was muttering to himself again.

"Perhaps it's best for you to hand the sword over to Helgi," I said.

He clutched the sword tighter and shook his head. He turned away from me, as if I might try to take it from him. "No one else, no one else."

Magnus reminded the man about how he'd led us out of Alfhild's island fortress a year ago, and that seemed to help, but nothing we said brought the man back the way Gunnar's story had. Petrus was right about the importance of good humor.

Huld told us we'd done a fine job, but that Styrgrim needed to sleep to help wash away what plagued his mind. It seemed to me that he would need more than one night of sleep, but I let that thought go unspoken. We left him in her care.

While it was time for Styrgrim to sleep, it was time for us to reconsider our battle plan for the next day. There was no relying on Styrgrim calling out Ogmund anymore. Huld wasn't sure whether he would even be able to swing the sword by morning.

"This changes things," Helgi Pike-Tooth said.

I called the War Council together one more time to tell them the ill news and consider what to do. Making plans based on uncertainty was not easy, so we made our plans around what we were confident of: Trying to take Tyrfing from Styrgrim would go worse for us than not having the sword in play at all. Alfhild and Ogmund would throw everything they had at us a second time. And, I argued, Kraki's dreams were prophetic for a reason.

We were not likely to win. Too many things could go wrong, even if most things went right. And even winning had a narrow definition here. It meant killing Alfhild, but it did not mean us surviving. A bit like Haldor winning his last fight, even though it killed him.

With much of the night still ahead of us, we resolved to get as good a night's sleep as we could before we died laughing the next day. Personally, I could not sleep, or at least not right away. I walked up and down the camp along the cliff walls. Amazing how quickly one's outlook can change! Hours ago, I had joked with Hallfred Horsefly about dying in battle. I'd had a little hope, though. Now, I felt like a failure, having led the army down a slow path to defeat. We had denied the enemy the Brisingamen, that was something. But in making Tyrfing our goal, I'd set up a false expectation, even for myself. Now, I didn't even see a way to fulfill my blood oath and kill Ulf.

As I was alone, I decided to talk to myself, hoping a certain spirit would join me. "If I were a giant polar bear, I might just charge down there and tear Ulf apart."

"And then what?" asked Svipul. She appeared from somewhere to my side. "They would see you coming from a long way off and swarm you."

"I could swim to Alfhild's ship."

"Again, they would see you. And you wouldn't outswim the ship. With two oars to keep you at bay and a few archers, you would be done in."

I sighed. "We were waiting to take advantage of something in the chaos of battle. Now it seems we are just playing the best role we can before being over-whelmed."

"There is still time for decisions to be made, for the unexpected to happen. I think you will need to be yourself to take advantage of that."

"I think I need Styrgrim to be himself," I said bitterly. "He is not."

When Svipul said nothing in response, I glanced behind me. She was there, her steel gray eyes meeting mine with a deflated, disappointed look. "Are you truly Odin's son?" Now, even she was whispering. "Is that your value of people—determining what they can do for you?"

I shook my head immediately.

"Then act like it."

I blinked, and she was gone. Her last words stayed with me as I stood stock still.

I had gotten my name from Styrgrim, finally. And a lock of my mother's hair. That gift could not have been given lightly. Did that mean I was done with Styrgrim, other than how he might affect this battle for us?

Styrgrim and I were not close. There was still too much unfamiliarity, too much empty history. He had offered the lessons of a hard life to his would-be son because that was what he'd known. I had not received them well. He had suffered on behalf of his family, then bitten his tongue about it until I'd pressed him. What did he get other than a glorious death in battle?

Had he earned more than that?

Was I done with Svipul as well, now that she had aided me more times than I could count? What did she get other than a brief time to see her son?

I had let frustration run into despair. And here I had just been talking to a woman whose will was so strong, death had only slowed her down. The least I could do was march toward the end with my head held high, showing the enemy no reaction, even in the face of utter defeat.

Svipul didn't deserve my least, though. Neither did Styrgrim.

*What's familiar is most helpful in such cases.*

There was one thing most familiar to Styrgrim. I thought about Svipul, standing tall with equal sadness and intensity just a few moments ago. The image in my mind bloomed into a verse right away, and I knew what I had to do.

I would lose a great deal to speak that verse. That didn't matter. It was time to give thanks, to give my parents another moment together, even if it was only in the remainder of Styrgrim's dreams for the night. They had endured on my behalf in ways I didn't have the fortitude for: Bodda, living just long enough to see me born; Styrgrim, living long and being reminded by my mere presence that his wife had died for a child who wasn't even his.

I closed my eyes and whispered the verse. I don't recall it exactly, but it was about change and about letting Svipul change one more time. I poured my will into the poem with no idea what knowledge to channel for it. Loss and sadness? Excitement and gratitude? What I felt as I spoke the verse was difficult to describe, and I let the intensity of that moment itself be what I drew upon.

It was the best I could do in a difficult circumstance, much like the last verse I'd spoken for the 'Steins. Whether it had worked or not, the incantation left me feeling drained.

I went to sleep for what I expected would be the last time.

# CHAPTER 62

# SHOWDOWN

WE MOVED QUICKLY IN THE MORNING, BUT THE OTHER SIDE didn't seem to be in much of a hurry. Apparently, they hadn't heeded that advice from *Hávamál* about rising early if you intend to take someone's life or property. I'd been up early despite the events of the night. Even had time to make peace with wearing my armor and slinging a shield across my back.

The slow start gave me a chance to check on Styrgrim. He lay sitting up with his eyes open. Those dark brown eyes stared past me as I ducked under the ship and approached him. I whispered his name, got no response, then darted forward to check for breath.

He clutched the sword tighter and turned away as I did this. Alive, at least. I waved my hand over his face and got no reaction. It was as if he had gone from sleep to trance.

"You're not trying to wake him up, are you?" Hallfred Horsefly's voice was barely a whisper as he ducked down to look under the ship.

I shrugged as if to ask *Why not?*

He shook his head as if to reply *Trust me.*

Which I did, so I left Styrgrim as I'd found him and joined Horsefly outside the upturned ship. "I take it you heard what happened last night. I hope your . . . efforts went well."

He nodded, and we walked toward the front lines as we talked. "As far as reaching out to potential allies, my efforts went even better than expected. But then there is the matter of my amateurism in conveying a message, and it's impossible to tell if that went anywhere at all. It's hard to say what effect my efforts last night, or Alfhild's, might have. They don't call 'the unexpected' such because it's easily calculated. Huld has greatly improved, though."

"I noticed that." I eyed Horsefly to gauge his surprise at Huld's fast recovery.

He grinned and changed the subject. "Jorun told me about your new battle plan. A fine idea!" We approached the *Sea Squirrel*, now sitting close to the front lines, fully crewed, ready to roll down at our enemies. He patted the hull at the ship's aft.

"You don't think it's desperate?"

Styrgrim's plan had been to break the enemy's morale by killing them and calling out Ogmund for failing to fight. Without Styrgrim in play, Helgi Pike-Tooth had been right that things had changed for us, and we didn't have much choice but to try something risky.

If things went according to the new plan, the *Sea Squirrel* would roll down the beach, angled wide of the enemy formation. We would disengage the wheeled contraption and dump the ship at the water's edge, row to the *Naglfar*, and kill Alfhild. Hard against steel doesn't mean immune to being clubbed to death, and so we'd cut clubs for every crew member. We also had Midgard's foremost expert on clubbing people to death in Kraki Bentleg.

If our main host held out and our crew killed Alfhild, Huld would be sitting *seiðr* unopposed. How long would the enemy be willing to break on our main shield wall while Huld conjured miserable spells against them? Ogmund might be forced to choose between calling a retreat and seeing large parts of his army abandon him.

That plan had more potential points of failure than my entire adolescence. The ship could be stopped mid-way down the beach or collide with a beached ship instead of rolling into the surf. Kraki had waved those possibilities off because that's not what he'd seen in his dream. The giant size of Alfhild's many trollish bodyguards should have been a concern, but the old cook only saw it one way: Board that ship, and Alfhild was as good as dead.

We might then be swarmed and killed by half the enemy turning on us, but Kraki didn't see a way around that. Neither did I.

Luckily, Horsefly was most cheerful under the direst circumstances. "It's quite desperate! Using the enemy's confidence that they are certain to win has its downside: Namely, that they often *can* win. But the more desperate our situation, the more disheartening it will be for them if we make any progress at all. To gain even a foothold, at this point, well! They'll probably shit themselves."

"The wizard has a spell for that." When Horsefly raised an eyebrow, I realized I had to add context. "Well, if he can get you to drink out of his cursed horn. I'm not sure if he brought it with him, though."

"He has a more deliverable trick prepared, I think. As does the *vǫlva*."

To the side of the *Sea Squirrel*, Huld was already perched upon her hastily constructed high seat. The would-be chair was just a bit more than two barrels stacked vertically with a few spare boards nailing them together. A loose scaffolding provided a bit of stability and a way to get up and down.

"You look comfortable," I said.

"You are shit at lying," she responded. "And for all this effort, no one could find a pillow for an old woman's ass?"

"If we win, one of us will give your ass a good rubbing to aid your recovery."

"Oh!" said Huld, feigning surprise. "Which one? That young Hjalti boy—"

"We'll draw lots for that," I interrupted. Returning to more serious matters, I asked, "Are you certain you want to be set up this close to the front? You're within bowshot, you know."

Huld shook her head. "They still can't see in from outside. I can see them, though. Ogmund is on his way up the beach with a retinue, as if he intends to talk. Oh!" She patted the shield slung on her back. "Just in case."

I looked to Horsefly. "Ogmund wants to talk?"

He nodded. "Alfhild will have told him she rode Styrgrim the Bear last night, but she wouldn't be able to speak to his condition as of this morning. As long as we have the sword, Ogmund is in danger. He'll play for peace, trying to get that sword off the battlefield. Or, at least, get us to reveal Styrgrim's condition."

"He won't give us peace," I said. "Even if we gave him the sword and Styrgrim, both. We're all party to his son's slaying."

"I think that's right," replied Horsefly. "You're the leader of this army, and thus it should be you Ogmund negotiates with. However, I would offer my services on that count, as one who's spoken with Ogmund before."

I nodded. "Take a shield with you, and don't go far beyond our line to do that talking."

He bounded off wearing that unflappable grin, making his way through our battle groups arrayed near the front lines. No doubt, Horsefly was way ahead of me on anything involving Ogmund. I was grateful for his help, as I already had a mixed record involving those skilled in the sorcery of politics. Besides, I still wanted to talk to Huld.

"Still suspicious of me?" she asked.

I shook my head. "I understand you less the more I see of you, but a former valkyrie once told me to trust you. I wonder if she knew you from her mortal life, or from her days as a Chooser. Keep your secrets if you must, but tell me this: Why save my life, why fight for us, with no reward?"

"Ha!" Huld's laugh was amused rather than derisive. "The fight is the reward, same as for any of you. There's not enough time in the day to tell you why. Just know that age and regret often walk hand in hand, and that I finally got old enough to recognize how to face such regrets and sweep them aside."

The why is always more important than the what, and we'd run out of time for her to tell me why. "I'm not old, but I regret having expressed more suspicion than curiosity in the past."

"Oh, don't be so dour, Ansgar the Skald! Luck often finds a person whose courage holds." I started to respond, but she cut me off. "And if luck doesn't find you, at least you die with clean pants."

I thanked her for the encouragement, such as it was. Then I pushed my way forward to one of the big boulders at our front and hopped on top of it for a better view. Ogmund was stretching his lungs by then, and I caught the back and forth between him and Horsefly.

"Arrow-Odd's army is like an ember," said Ogmund. "So small, but it never seems to go out and might flare up at any time. Who knew it would burn so hot without Arrow-Odd to blow on it anymore? Give me the sword, though, and I won't have to drown that ember entirely."

If the back and forth had been a negotiation at its beginning, it no longer was. Ogmund's voice was pitched too loud, his words were too haughty and obvious. He was dressing us down, trying to hurt morale. Hallfred Horsefly was equal to the task in his response.

"You've always thought you knew more than you did, Ogmund. And your people have always thought more of you than you were, but I suppose those things go together. As for Odd, I think you're afraid he'll find you in the end. I see the storm protecting your backside is just a fog now, to hide you just in case Odd comes back around. As for the sword, I think you're afraid it will get you in the front. Some leader, having his people take it in both the front and the rear while he remains protected."

"I won't deny a fly a few bold words before it's swatted," replied Ogmund. "After all, you'll die just the same whether you've spoken insults at me or not. I thought you might be glad to be out from under Odd's yoke, but I guess what's learned early becomes habit."

"It's true that I'll die, just like anyone else. But I'll die content, and not in fear, when that day comes. You've run from Odd twice now rather than face him. Now you've witnessed the end of your hapless son, and instead of asking for a duel, you come forward to fight with nothing but words."

"I've no need to abandon my advantages just to give you a chance. And I would need to abandon my advantages, as Odd abandoned all of you, for any of you to see another sunrise."

"Your advantages?" asked Hallfred. "You count incompetent leadership, mercenaries who will run at the first sign of defeat, and slavering idiots as advantages?"

"We all have our uses," replied Ogmund. "You talk a lot, and always have. You won't talk your way out of this, though." Ogmund walked away, his retinue fanning out behind him as if we might try a few chance arrows. Hallfred returned inside our lines to shoulder slaps and cheers.

I thought it had been well spoken, but I didn't have it in me to cheer. The fight was about to begin. My limbs were cold, my hands almost numb. I tried to show nothing on my face.

Ogmund faded back into the lines of his army, and I lost track of him. His people were organized into one big mass, with only general placements of different troop types. By Surt's flaming ballsack, even I could see some more effective possibilities than lack of formation, and I was far from an expert in the field of war.

Soon, the smell of Alfhild's *seiðr* worked its way up to me. The middle of their horde began twitching and jerking, turning into big, lip-chewing warriors. They bore shields with Alfhild's winged *othala* painted on them, but some looked like they wanted to toss the shields away and just have at it with axes. Or bare hands.

I recognized the look from when she sent them at us last time. What else might she throw at us? Raising her dead warriors? Ketill thought that unlikely in the face of an opposing sorcerer. Torpor that came from below to pull us down and make it hard to move? Ketill's bind rune might be proof against that.

Or not. You could never tell with these things.

"On-the-spot *berserkir* incoming," I called out to the wizard. "Main host not far behind. Ketill, is this you or Huld?"

"Both," replied the wizard. He shoved his way forward, past our shield wall, carrying a spear in one hand and cradling a small bag in his injured palm.

A hailstone half the size of a sling bullet came down nearby as the smell of rotting blood and iron increased. More hailstones rained down on us. Most covered their heads with their shields, including me.

Behind me, Huld let out a loud "harrumph!" that might have been disappointment or excitement, I couldn't tell. "Has she really miscalculated so badly?"

The wizard waded past our formations and stood a full bowshot ahead of our forward-most position. He drove the butt of his spear into the ground and then fiddled with the little bag. Leather, maybe? It was a sickly yellow color, just like the one had by Mondul, the dwarf in the Down-Below. Ketill uncinched the bag and walked parallel to our line, slowly pouring out its contents as he did so.

The silver birch smell of Huld's *seiðr* mingled with Alfhild's. A light wind blew at our backs. I hoped Huld was just starting slow.

The wind was enough to kick up the dust that Ketill had spread. Clouds of yellow formed and swirled ten feet into the air, all out of proportion to the wind, and floated toward the advancing enemy host.

Some of the *berserkir* paid no heed to the dust and ran right through. Some even continued charging when they cleared it, heedless of its effects. But most, in their ecstatic states or not, slowed or stopped and rubbed at their eyes as if they couldn't see.

Ketill took up his spear and pointed it at the enemy. The wizard's voice rumbled low with the storm gathering in the sky. He spoke a spell in *galdralag* and laughed out loud as the straggling *berserkir* began to lash out at whoever was closest or charge blindly in random directions. Some lost their way so badly that they went back against their own army and were cut down. Part of the main host slowed or stopped, looking for ways around the remaining eddies of dust coming their way. Not all of them avoided it.

The enemy advance shifted to our right, allowing a clear line of sight between where the *Sea Squirrel* would start and where it needed to go.

Ketill ignored some would-be *berserkir* racing blindly around him as he walked back to our lines. Cheers greeted him as he returned behind our shield wall.

Alfhild redoubled her efforts, blasting us with wind and sand. What remained of the dust dissipated into nothing. Some turned their heads or had to take off their helmets to get sand out of their eyes. I angled my shield down for protection, felt the massive hailstones hammer my helmet, and brought the shield back above my head. Meanwhile, the enemy host spread back out and advanced.

Huld did not appear to push back at the wind spell at first. The *vǫlva* muttered something low and guttural as she clutched her distaff. I couldn't be sure if my mind was playing a trick on me, but I thought I saw a spark inside the distaff's carven head. The *vǫlva* yawned, her neck going slack behind her as her mouth opened wider than it should have been able to, accompanied by a long, dry inhalation.

The sweet scent of birch sap rose as Huld's *seiðr* competed with Alfhild's. Huld's head came back to face forward. She spoke a verse in the old language, the one I'd known as the language of the Down-Below. I didn't speak it fluently, but I know a verse when I hear it.

Clouds above darkened and roiled. The hail kept coming, but now there was more than hail. Thunder boomed above us. The wind turned. It didn't blow against or behind us, but swirled so hard that it nearly ripped the shield from my hand.

Huld's voice turned into something more than her voice, muttering a few phrases over and over. As she pointed her distaff at the enemy host, the bitter storm scent overwhelmed all others.

Lightning hit the front rank of the enemy host with a deafening boom. Shards of the bolt spread out and away from the warrior it had struck, downing others nearby. Again, the host slowed, avoiding the area that had been struck and creating the path we would need.

Huld spun her distaff slowly, as if she directed an invisible thread from it with her left hand. She continued speaking in that doubled voice, saying nearly the same things over and over but always changing them just a bit. I did not follow anymore, as it was no verse form I was familiar with. It was more like a free-flowing variation of the final lines of *galdralag*.

Alfhild's shrill voice below spoke in the same pattern as Huld's, and the wind shifted. Huld redoubled her guttural incantation.

The wind screamed like a horse being whipped by two riders at odds with the direction. I thought I would be blown off my perch one way, then had to steady my footing when a gust took me the other way. Holding the shield made it hard to balance, but I needed it as protection against hail that had started big and only grown in size.

The sky darkened even more as Huld and Alfhild fought for control over the weather. Thunder boomed as lightning flashed from cloud to cloud. The hail lightened but did not stop. Huld pointed her distaff and spoke in multiple voices once again. Lightning struck, sending some to the ground and others running.

On came the enemy host. Captains kept their banners up and ordered shield walls to form three deep, clearly expecting to be hit with slings. Ulf emerged from the middle of the pack to near their front, shouting and directing the banners.

Need hummed at my hip, and I had to fight the urge to direct an attack his way. We had a plan, and I had to play my part. I signaled to the dozen or so warriors managing the *Sea Squirrel*. Two of them prepared to knock the wedges away while the others got ready to give the cart a good shove. The crew on board lit torches in case we really did need to set the ship on fire. I shouted for our front-line defenders to move out of its way.

Alfhild's vulpine screech hit us and just about blasted my brain, causing me to cover my ears and bend sideways to keep the shield between me and the hail.

Sitting at the base of Huld's high seat, Hallfred Horsefly closed his eyes and started a low hum. As his voice rose, Alfhild's became more bearable.

The widest-traveled of us skalds, Hallfred had crossed more boundaries than anyone I knew. Now it seemed he would support Huld as she sat *seiðr*. Humming soon turned into chanting runic sounds. Chanting turned into singing that vibrated the air. Each repetition of the rhythm changed a bit from one to the next, always moving a bit faster.

Just like I might improvise on the lyre. Just like Huld, who roared back against Alfhild's shrill voice. I recognized a rhythm to the sorcery at hand now, felt it in my bones. It was part of all my verse forms, all my music. Part of the way stories weaved in and out, changing a bit, the good versions preserving the spirit of the thing even as the details changed.

The enemy host crossed the invisible threshold I had in mind, and I waved to the warriors managing the *Sea Squirrel*. They pushed, and soon the ship's prow passed me by. I stepped up to the highest part of the boulder and leaped onto the ship. I nearly lost my footing as I did, given the distraction I saw at that last moment.

Styrgrim fell to one knee as he staggered toward the front lines. His helmet flapped at his side. He held his shield with the raven symbol loosely, as if his hands were numb or unfamiliar. At least his facial tics had gone from over-vigilant to the more familiar snarls. He rose with a stumbling, uncertain gait as if he were drunk. I couldn't tell if this was the Styrgrim we needed, or one we feared.

That would be something for Helgi Pike-Tooth to decide, though. In the meantime, those of us on the *Sea Squirrel* had a witch to kill.

# Chapter 63

# Final Voyage

WE RAISED THE SAIL TO HARNESS THE WIND HULD SENT US. THE *Sea Squirrel* picked up speed as it rolled down the beach. It was even headed in the direction we wanted. Mostly.

We had intended it to go wide of the enemy host, but we would not quite clear them and had no way to steer the cart. Some quick-thinking commander must have had a sense it was important to stop us, sending warriors on the flank right into our path. Not easy to aim from the fore deck, but I argued against their movements with a few stones from my sling. Jorun, who had joined our desperate attack, made an even better argument with a few arrows.

However fast I thought the ship would roll, the wind at our backs pushed us faster. I ordered shields up as we came near the enemy. It was a good idea, stopping a ship of about two dozen warriors headed straight for their witch. But to no surprise, the enemy wasn't quite sure what to do against a ship on a cart rolling down at them.

The result was some ineffectual banging on the hull, a few spears flying overhead or into our shields, and a lot of shouting. One of the rear wheels hit a large bump. Judging by Magnus' laugh, I assumed it was one of those warriors being run over.

"Why have we never done this before?" Magnus asked.

"This sort of plan happens once in a lifetime," replied Jorun.

As we passed by the enemy host, I caught sight of Ogmund. He kept to the middle, surrounded by what I took to be his best people. It looked like he was sending commands to Ulf farther forward. The unorganized mass was not as unorganized as I'd thought, but they were exactly as over-committed as we needed them to be.

With no one left between us and the water's edge, all we had to do was not run afoul of chance dips in the sand or crash into one of the enemy ships.

Alfhild took a deep breath between chanting. Huld used that breath as an opening to call down another bolt of lightning somewhere on the battlefield. Power between the two women pushed back and forth, as if two spiritual shield walls were having at it. Huld pushed when Alfhild breathed, but it must have taken something out of her. When Alfhild pushed back, it was like a gust of wind hitting us.

The *Sea Squirrel* continued rolling forward, but the sail went slack when Alfhild's screeching gained in volume and confidence. In the battle of sorcery, Huld was back on her heels. Hallfred's song rose to support her. Despite Ketill adding his voice to the song, the scent of rotting blood pushed out all others.

Turning my attention to the *Naglfar*, it's port side facing us, I could see why. The chained thrall on that ship was now lashed to the mast, the insides of his thighs sliced open. Alfhild's sacrifice had bled out at that point, or nearly so. Her huge, trollish bodyguards kept a safe distance from the witch, leaving her alone at the aft.

Water just off the side of the *Naglfar* began to bubble. Then the bubbles started moving toward the shore. The bubbles reached the shallows, and the summoned creature broke the surface.

The sea serpent's neck was long like an eel's, but its face was like a wolf with a severe underbite. Tusks jutted up from the long lower jaw around a snout and whiskers. The monster's pale body was both scaly and veiny at the same time. Two powerful legs that looked equally at home in the sea and on land propelled it forward while a long, finned tail trailed behind.

As the monster crawled up the sand, its eyes went from the battle ahead of it to sideways. Toward us.

Not only had Alfhild been content with a frontal assault, she had also lined up defenses directly in front of her. Maybe a dozen warships were all lashed together and anchored like a sea wall between the shore and the *Naglfar*, as if to protect against a breakout attack of, I don't know, a hundred swimming *berserkir*. Nearly at the water's edge, we were lucky to be headed for a narrow gap between two of their unlashed ships to one side, the last obstacle before hitting the water.

Kraki thumped me on the back of the shoulder. "The steering oar."

"That's no one's but yours," I replied.

"No, fool! Pull it up, or it will catch on the rocks as soon as we hit the water!"

He shook his head as if I should have known this. I had assumed he would do it, taking his natural position on the ship. Not this time, though. He sweated like he had a fever, clearly weakened by Tyrfing's cut, but pushed past me to stand at the fore. Weak or not, Kraki meant to be the first to board the *Naglfar*.

I ran to the aft and pushed down on the rudder, lifting the steering oar into the air. A bit heavier than I expected, I had to put all my weight on it so that I was practically lying down on top of the thing. The wheels rattled as they went from soft sand to rough rocks at the tide's edge, then slowed as they encountered the surf.

Kraki pulled the lever that disengaged the cart from the ship. The *Sea Squirrel* slid into the water with some momentum, kept up as Frothi and Thorir led the rowing. I dropped the steering oar once the water was deep enough and pulled it to port to send the ship more to starboard, angled at the *Naglfar*.

We passed the line of lashed ships, and nothing was slowing us down. Halfway between the water's edge and our target, I made the mistake of developing a real hope we would get there. That was when I heard the sea serpent roar. I looked back to see it disappear into the surf, moving much faster in the water than it had on land.

A moment later, the wind changed from neutral to go against us, luffing the sail. Magnus was up immediately, directing much of the crew to take the sail in, while others continued rowing. The ship moved backwards and to its side. I leaned into the rudder hard to right our course, but the effort amounted to little.

I caught a glimpse of Alfhild, grinning on her perch. She had let us get just close enough before stopping us. Styrgrim would have approved. Whether Nanthild read Alfhild's expression the same way or just saw me lose hope for a moment, I couldn't say. The Frank threw off her helmet, ran forward, and dove into the water ahead of us.

Kraki scrambled back across the ship with a newfound energy. "Get to rowing or get to swimming! Skald, put your back into that steering oar!"

Hard work, working the steering oar in a circular motion rather than just turning it to the side. I had seen Kraki do it, but had never tried. Harder work for the rowers, though, as they tried to keep time with Kraki's heavy strokes. Not the way to row a ship and keep your arms from falling off, but it was row hard or die.

"It's coming!" Jorun's shout needed no explanation.

"Shoot Alfhild!" I shouted.

Jorun hesitated but ran to the fore with her bow. Even with the ship unsteady beneath her, I knew Jorun could make that shot.

Seconds passed. I managed to look behind us, with no sea serpent in sight. Perhaps it was lost among the lashed ships. Or maybe it got tired of taking commands and left.

Alfhild's grin got even wider as she chanted. Jorun loosed an arrow headed right for her face. Alfhild held a hand up, and the arrow shattered on her palm.

Hard against steel. Well, you have to try. Or, in my case, sometimes you just forget in the desperation of battle.

Before I could even think *now what?* something big hit the underside of the *Sea Squirrel*. Big enough to knock anyone standing off balance. The ship started to move away from the *Naglfar*. I froze for a moment, staring at Kraki.

The old man grimaced. Not from pain, I don't think, but at the idea that we had gotten as close as we were going to. "Oars in! Grab spears! Skald, lower the steering oar and give the thing a hard time!"

I wasn't sure what he meant until the sea serpent really started pulling us back. I turned the rudder hard one way, swinging the ship out. The crew looked out over both sides as we turned, spearpoints hunting for a glimpse of the monster below. Two of the crew on the port side must have seen it. One thrust his spear with a single hand; the other used both hands to drive his spear downward.

One or both must have struck home, because the sea serpent roared under the water. The *Sea Squirrel* dipped and then rose suddenly, as if it had dug those claws farther into the hull and then released them. A second later, that finned tail lashed up from beneath the surface and struck the spearmen, cutting through both of them.

The sea serpent clawed its way up from beneath the ship, snaking its head over the port side. The ship rocked, and I lost my balance and twisted my ankle before falling hard on the deck. I feared we were all going over for a moment, but that passed quickly. For one, a wide-decked ship like the *Sea Squirrel* is extremely hard to capsize. For another, the monster curled its tail up onto the starboard side from beneath the ship. At least we wouldn't have to swim while we fought this thing.

My crewmates had locked shields on the starboard side, forcing the serpent to attack one way around the mast and then the other. Kraki shouted something about trapping it like a rat, which I'm sure made sense to him, and I think meant "envelope it within a wedge." Easier said than done, and they would need every hand to do it. I abandoned the rudder and joined the shield wall.

The sea serpent snapped at Thorir as it drew itself over the gunwale. Frothi overlapped his shield with his brother's, blocking the monster's jaws. The thing drew back quick as an adder to avoid the counterthrusts aimed at its eyes. For a brief moment, the monster held back and hissed, which was the moment Jorun shot it in the back of the neck. The arrow stuck, but couldn't penetrate very far through that scaly armor.

Enough of that thing's body had come up the side of the ship that its taloned legs gripped the edge. More than half in the ship at that point, it was like dealing with a white shark set loose in a rowboat. I stuck the thing with Need as a spear, but instead of coming back to guard, I pressed the point forward. The serpent's tail flicked my way and found the opening I'd created under my shield. Razor-sharp bone or horn—or whatever made this creature —tore open the links on the left side of my chain shirt. I fell backwards, breathless and bruised, but not bleeding.

Turning its attention to the ship's fore, the monster saw Jorun standing there alone.

The wedge couldn't move fast enough to support her, but one man could. Despite his limping gait, Kraki seemed to have the agility of a mountain goat while on a ship. He charged the thing alone and struck a glancing blow off the monster's face with his bone club. That was enough to stagger the monster, but not stop it. The thing struck Kraki in the leg before he could land another blow. Wrenching its head back and forth, it bit through completely, taking his leg off just below the knee.

Jorun shot the monster in the face with another arrow. Again, it stuck, but not far in. The serpent winced from that and from Thorir's spear hitting home on its lower body. Frothi bellowed as he went for the serpent's throat with his seax, but the monster rolled and slithered over the side. Magnus pulled the old man back to the safety of the huddled crew.

Vaguely aware the monster might attack us from the other side, I glanced at the water. But I couldn't keep my eyes off of Kraki and what remained of his leg. With too many voices shouting to make out any one of them clearly and my heart thundering in my ears, it was like being caught in the maelstrom of my nightmare from months ago, only I was the one panicking this time.

Unlike my nightmare, we weren't in the middle of a storm, or even far out to sea. We'd floated all the way back to the line of ships lashed together. Gentle breakers knocked the *Sea Squirrel's* aft into the prow of one dragon ship, turning us and bumping our starboard side against other prows next to it. It left our port side facing the *Naglfar*. The ship wasn't far off, but now it sat beyond an uncrossable divide.

Kraki ordered the crew to board the enemy warships. Most of them went, quickly driving off or killing the skeleton crews left on those vessels. Magnus would normally be the first into such a fight, but he was busy bringing the old man a length of rope. Thorir and Frothi tried to help him stand, but he just shook his head.

Three times, Kraki called me over, and only on the third time did I hear him and heed the command. I approached the old man, thinking I would need to help him, but that was not the case. He moved slowly, his right arm reddened below Tyrfing's cut, his skin white as bone, but he had no trouble tying the rope Magnus brought him around his bone club.

"Take the torches," he wheezed. "Then get off my ship." The old man was going for the whale oil.

"Fire won't get us to Alfhild," I said.

"That witch's fate is already delivered." Rising on one leg while the other bled his life out, he shattered the top of the barrel and started spilling its contents onto the deck.

I shook my head in disbelief. Then I hopped out of the way of the oil and dutifully grabbed a torch from one of the sconces.

"The rest of you off, now!" No one still aboard moved.

"We don't abandon our Brothers," said Thorir.

"This is no time for disobeying orders on my ship, dog boy!"

I didn't want to obey but knew I had to. Sometimes, family dies for you. "You all heard him!" I shouted.

Magnus grabbed a torch and hopped onto one of the enemy warships. Thorir and Frothi followed. I acted like I had dropped something important, whatever that might be, playing for a moment of time to think of something to say. Kraki pointed to where the sea serpent's veiny white back broke the water's surface.

"That thing is coming." The old man wheezed as he tied the other end of the rope to the mast. "I am spent. I will die holding my club, not a torch. The torches are your responsibility." He turned to glare at me. "Don't screw it up!"

I stood a moment longer, a skald in search of suitable parting words and finding none. Then I, too, left the *Sea Squirrel*.

Kraki leaned against the mast for support, his bone club secure in his belt. I wasn't sure when we should throw the torches until I traced the rope that was tied to both the mast and his club. The old man wheezed as he gripped the barrel with both hands.

"Kraki!" I swallowed hard. "No matter what happens in the rest of this battle, nothing can take away our time as your crew."

The old warrior eyed me, then seemed to remember how my words echoed his gratitude to Finnr. He grinned and gave me a subtle nod. "A final story for you, nearly as good as the first. Once, the squirrel oppressed the eagle. Now, the bait will cook the fish!"

The sea serpent climbed aboard at the aft, probably thinking it was a big advantage to climb fully into the ship without facing any resistance. That much weight on one side tilted the ship in that direction, and that was when Kraki dumped most of the rest of the oil. The monster used its legs a bit, but still had to slither forward, right through the old man's greasy trap.

Using the mast as a barrier and the barrel as a shield, he forced it to continue moving around, covering itself in yet more oil for those few crucial seconds. He even blocked a bite with the open end of the barrel. The monster's tusks dug deep as he pushed the barrel up and sloshed the remaining oil into its face.

But those were powerful jaws, and they wrenched the barrel out of his hands. With its head back and a clear line of attack, the serpent struck.

Kraki had time to draw his bone club, but only held it with one hand. With the other, he steadied himself on the mast. And instead of bringing the club down against the monster's face, he held the weapon at its midpoint, thrusting his arm straight forward.

The serpent took the bait, its jaws engulfing club, hand, and arm up to the shoulder. And then it was hooked when the sharpened butt end of that club embedded itself in the monster's mouth. Kraki drew the sea serpent in, his left arm still wrapped around the mast.

Magnus and I threw our torches, lighting the oil concentrated in the center of the ship, on the serpent's belly, in its mouth, in its eyes. It screamed, allowing Kraki to free his arm. With his freed arm, he grabbed the monster's neck and pinned it to the mast in a massive bear hug. And there he held it, laughing through the fire, while the monster writhed and bucked.

The captain of the *Sea Squirrel* held his grip until life finally left him. The monster slithered away from the mast, only to find itself on a short tether attached to the bone club still stuck in its mouth. Whale oil burns hot, and eventually burned through the rope enough for the sea serpent to get away. It managed to get partway over the side of the ship before it stopped moving forever.

"Even after dying, Kraki made good on his word," said Magnus. "That fish is fully cooked.

I nodded and stepped back. The light of that much whale oil burning lit the sea. It would also catch some of those warships on fire. I thought that might be the best we could do. We made our way across the ships lashed together and looked out at the *Naglfar* again. Magnus suggested Jorun try another arrow, even though it was a long shot. She said she wanted to save her arrows for people they could pierce.

A raven flapped overhead and perched atop the mast of the ship we were on. An old bird, but not a doddering one. Its croak was low and hoarse, like it was Odin's proxy sent to laugh at us. More ravens flew in and perched nearby, as if waiting for our eyeballs to be ready to eat.

Rage burned in my limbs. But all my rage, however hot it burned, was just as irrelevant to Alfhild, to Ulf, as the fire on the *Sea Squirrel*. Vaguely aware that I had to make a decision, I had trouble tearing my eyes away from Alfhild's smug expression. Even more smug, apparently, as another ship beyond the *Naglfar* sailed straight for the fight. As if Alfhild hadn't had enough reinforcements already.

Then I noticed three things in quick succession, and the sequence was such that each one defied belief even more than the previous.

The first was the ship's speed. It cut the water so fast, it was kicking up a wake.

The second was that Nanthild pulled herself up and onto the *Naglfar* by the rudder. With all attention on *Sea Squirrel*, neither Alfhild nor her body-guard noticed.

The third was so wildly unbelievable that I blinked as if to clear my sight of a hallucination. But Magnus saw it too. He slapped my shoulder, mad with laughter.

In a great mythological irony, the *Naglfar* was under attack by dead men.

# Chapter 64

# Meanwhile, Close By

"Are we still in line with the lightning strikes?" asked Utstein.

Innstein shrugged. "I think we have not changed direction, or not much."

"It's very little we're basing this on," Utstein reminded his brother.

"You don't need to remind me," snapped Innstein. "I'm the one who found the talking horsefly. How do you think I felt? I thought I had eaten the mushrooms with the long stems again."

Ustein laughed at the memory. He had eaten maybe one mushroom, which often makes one drowsy and happy. Innstein had been hungry and eaten a whole handful, which made him see faces in the trees for a few hours. That had happened years ago, though.

It had only been the previous evening when a horsefly the size of Innstein's thumb spoke to him. He'd been sitting in Hrolf Kraki's longhouse, drinking ale and brooding over how they had missed Alfhild by mere days. He thought maybe he'd wolfed down his stew too quickly to notice long-stemmed mushrooms in it. That, or he was bewitched. You can never tell with these things.

"You heard the horsefly speak, too," said Innstein. "So, it wasn't just me. And what it said made sense."

"Do you hear yourself? *What the horsefly said made sense.*"

"He said his name was Hallfred. As in Hallfred Horsefly. Remember him from that meeting with Odd?"

"Not really. I was focused on whale stew at the time, and don't tell me you were any different. Anyway, how—"

"He said Alfhild was sitting just off the southeast coast of Mon," growled Innstein. "Now, do you want to turn this ship around and sail back to Hrolf Kraki's hall to wait for some other message? No?"

"No."

"No! He's out of ships, and even if Gorm Tin-Whisker was already on his way and then sailed through the night, they are at best still hours behind us. Now we have lightning strikes, just as the horsefly said we were likely to see."

"How are you the patient one right now?"

"I am not patient right now," Innstein clarified with some volume. Calmer, he continued, "I just don't want to overthink the situation and steer to the wrong spot on Mon, where there is no one to kill."

"The right spot—I can't see a troll-cursed thing through this fog." Utstein peered out from the side of the ship. "How can there be this much fog on the water with this much wind pushing us at the same time?"

Steinvor stood in the fore with the 'Steins despite the argument. Most people didn't want to be anywhere near the brothers when they raised their voices. Steinvor seemed unperturbed by them. Amused, even.

With keen eyesight and a steady demeanor, the 'Steins had made her next in command after them. Arrow-Odd would have been a better choice if he had been himself, and if there hadn't been a prophecy warning about him commanding. In any case, he was only enough of himself to call the wind. Fjornir, now Red Hat, could lead a charge, but he reminded the brothers too much of Kraki to have him decide on strategy or tactics. He was the wedge that splits the log, but not the voice that commands the other axes.

There had been that big Swede with one eye in Lejre who expressed so much interest in the 'Steins. He would have been a reasonable choice if he had joined, but he had already sworn himself to Hrolf Kraki as a champion. Just as well. He had looked rather suspicious of Barkman. And hardly anyone could understand him through that thick accent.

"Arro– I mean, Barkman," Steinvor began, "none of his abilities have ever been very clear. Be glad he still has this one."

Innstein looked at the crew to see if any of them suspected who was really steering the ship. Arrow-Odd had what you might call a "complicated" relationship with the Irish. And everyone else in the world, too, but especially the Irish.

"Praise the day once it's night, the ice once it's crossed," said Utstein.

"And the ship once it's smashed its iron prow into some other ship and drowned all the sailors?" added Steinvor. The skald knew the poetic reference Utstein was making, and she was being salty about it.

"Hey!" barked Innstein. "This ship has already proven itself. Now it's just a matter of pushing it fast enough, and in the right direction."

Innstein patted the cold iron of the ship's prow. Some would have fashioned a dragon head for the prow, but the 'Steins had agreed: A ram's head was far better.

"So his talent is to call wind that can fill a sail, but not push fog?" Utstein continued.

Innstein sniffed the air. "Now the fog has a familiar scent."

Utstein sniffed the air in turn. "I know that rot. We're close."

"How is that smell on the sea?" asked Steinvor.

Innstein shrugged. Like they knew all about how sorcery worked? "Barkman!" he called out to the tiller. "What lies ahead?"

Disgust with the world was writ heavy across the man's face as he shouted from the stern. "Broken promises and grave disappointments. Lessened in their awfulness only with lowered expectations and the anticipation of ill luck at every turn."

Utstein turned to his brother and nodded. "He's cheerier than usual."

"He's getting chatty," Innstein agreed. "That's a good sign."

Thunder rumbled above, but the storm they expected to pass through seemed confined to the sky, with only moderate breakers on the water. Moderate for the 'Steins' tolerance, at least.

The ship's speed was excellent. But direction? Hard to tell. Something glowed through the fog. Not lighting. This was fire, burning hot and bright.

"Speaking of signs," said Utstein.

Innstein leaped onto the gunwale and held the forestay as he leaned out over the water. He peered out, squinted, opened his eyes wide. Anything to see something through the fog. Soon, he was cursing the water spirits that kept him from seeing.

"That never helps," chided Steinvor.

"There, we differ," he growled back.

At the edge of Innstein's vision, the fog seemed to clear. In that clearing, the light bent in strange directions and flashed in eerie yellow. It was faint, so faint, he wondered if his mind made it up at first. But no—there was a dark warship, a massive silhouette against the fire beyond. He could make out a figure sitting in a tall seat on the deck.

"There!" Innstein shouted, pointing his axe. "That has to be the witch."

"Barkman," Utstein shouted, "a hand's span to port, and call every wind spirit you know!"

"If that's what you want," he replied. "I suppose it is best to get disappointment over with sooner rather than later."

"Hmmph," said Red Hat, finally chiming in. "You know, you could just drown yourself any time. Or die in battle, as we're about to have one."

"And deny myself the tiny pleasure I get from making you listen to me complain?" Barkman let out a mirthless laugh. "Not likely. I think I will continue living, and make certain you do as well, just to spite you."

If Red Hat knew who "Barkman" was, the old man was canny enough to not say so. Red Hat translated the conversation for the Irish. Or, more probably, he said something that was very loosely related to a translation.

The Irish laughed. Barkman scowled even harder than before.

The wind rose and pushed *Halfdan's Gift* like the hand of Njord. Innstein kept his eye on the outline of that huge warship, guiding them toward its center.

Utstein readied the crew. The Irish whooped. The Norse made a few low comments. The few former thralls who had stayed on bared their teeth like wolves.

Red Hat stood up slowly, grumbling the entire way, as if standing up was the greatest pain in the world, and oh—how would he ever bend his knees again? The 'Steins were not fooled. They had seen what that old man could do with his axes. After the two of them, he was the nastiest one on board.

"They're ready," Utstein said.

The 'Steins had the enemy's smell, and now had them in sight. And now that they were in sight, something else was going on. A warrior was climbing up the steering oar of that big warship. Was that Nanthild? And what was happening beyond Alfhild's ship?

"There's quite the battle happening up the shore," said Utstein.

Blood thundered in Innstein's ears. "Steinvor! Land the ship after we hit, and then do as you think best."

The ship swayed in the low breakers, its unnatural speed making for a rough ride.

"Don't want to share in fighting the witch?" Utstein asked under his breath. He was calm before and during a fight.

"No." Innstein was calm while sleeping. Sometimes.

Utstein patted his brother's shoulder and grinned. "Just as well. They can't help us with this fight, and it looks like our friends need whatever help they can get."

*Halfdan's Gift* continued picking up speed, as if the sea was under Barkman's command as much as the wind. The elements seemed to cry out in those last moments. The 'Steins could see as well as hear that the codex had truly given them the right weapon, and they had sailed it right to where it needed to be.

That was one foul-looking ship they were headed for, a fitting vessel for that witch. The iron prow of *Halfdan's Gift* struck it with a thunderous crash. And though the enemy ship survived that initial blow, the sound could be heard for many miles.

It was the sound of everything changing.

# CHAPTER 65

## FURY

With a crack echoing across the battlefield, Alfhild fell from her high seat on the *Naglfar*.

The struggle between *vǫlur* had felt like two shield walls pressed tight together, one never giving ground without taking some of it back the moment after. After the collision, it felt like one side had taken two steps back, and that this stymied side was now fighting an uphill battle.

The *Naglfar* turned after the collision, bringing the fores of both ships close together. Some of its crew grabbed oars to push the attacking ship away, but too late to prevent a boarding. The 'Steins leaped over the remaining gap, grabbed the gunwale of the *Naglfar*, and pulled themselves the rest of the way.

With Alfhild at the other end of the ship, they would have to fight through her biggest trolls to get to her. That would be a long distance for those two to cross. I assumed the rest of their crew would board behind them, but no, the ship's tiller aimed it for shore. He was a strange one—looked like he had tree bark all over him instead of armor. And was that a woman at the fore, directing the ship by pointing her spear?

*Ymir's bones*—was that Steinvor?

Nanthild had disappeared after the collision. I thought she must have fallen off, but no, she must have just slipped down the steering oar. Her head soon reappeared over the gunwale, her eyes fixed on Alflhild.

491

The raven that had first set down croaked, louder this time. I asked the raven its name, but it didn't respond. "You're not here by chance, I think," I continued. "What is happening?"

"Many things," replied the raven with a voice unlike any other. "The ram arrives. The bear awakes. But which way will the arrow fly?"

I shook my head and turned to see the fight playing out on the *Naglfar*. Fights, plural.

The 'Steins, both bigger than I remembered them being, wielded long axes without shields. They were still at the enemy ship's fore, facing a tight shield wall held by trolls even bigger than they were. Step by step, the brothers pushed them back.

Utstein charged with a roar and brought his axe down with a big overhead swing against the narrow enemy shield wall. It looked like a big, clumsy attack, despite staggering the two trolls holding their shields against it. That didn't matter—those two worked in concert.

The shields raised high, Innstein snuck in fast and low, hooking the leg of one of the god-children-turned-trolls, and pulled him in feet-first. Innstein dragged the hapless god-child back, stepped on the back of his elbow, and broke his arm backwards. Then it was even more ill luck for that particular warrior, as Innstein flung his helmet off, shoved his mouth atop the gunwale, and brought a forearm down on the back of his head.

These were Alfhild's champions, though. Her picked warriors, her most devout. And the biggest, most thoroughly trolled. Probably the ones she used the Brisingamen on the most. They held their ground, protecting the witch and slowing the progress of the 'Steins.

The other fight was at the stern. Nanthild slashed at Alfhild, but the Frank's characteristic agility was less than usual. A swim in cold water and a subsequent fight in soaked clothing and dripping armor will do that to the best of warriors.

I saw a brief exchange before Alfhild took the upper hand: Nanthild scored what would have been a killing blow against the sorcerer, but the blade stopped cold. That sword was Nanthild's make, and though it was forged under Finnr's tutelage, it was no dwarf-sword.

Alfhild struck a hard blow to the side of Nanthild's head with her distaff. Iron rang on steel, and Nanthild's helmet went flying. Nanthild staggered back, barely keeping her feet. She avoided the next blow but took a kick that tripped her up, and she fell to the deck. Alfhild moved like she was stomping on my friend's hand.

The 'Steins waded in, hacking, shoving, kicking. God-children fell to horrific axe blows around the mast as they reached the ship's middle. The group counterattacked and tried to flank the brothers. They failed, but the tactic forced the 'Steins to retreat a few steps.

Utstein said something I couldn't hear. Innstein replied louder. Their sense of urgency to reach Alfhild was palpable. I did not think the trolls would ultimately win. But they would slow those two down long enough for the witch to finish off Nanthild and retake her high seat.

And then?

That witch was stronger on the water than anywhere else. I wasn't sure what would happen then.

Utstein was in a shoving match against half the warriors on the ship, and Innstein was fighting himself free from netting and rope. It was as if I could hear their thoughts about not getting there in time.

Nanthild picked up a sea chest and flung it at Alfhild. The witch dodged, moving unnaturally fast. The Frank rolled and came back up with her sword. She slashed with her left hand, her right curled into an injured fist.

Battle rage can narrow a warrior's judgment as much as vision. Maybe Nanthild thought a harder stroke would hurt the witch, if not break her skin. But these things with sorcerers aren't so logical as that.

Alfhild extended her arm and blocked the blade again. The force of this blow was so great that the sword itself could not take it. Nanthild's blade, the one etched with her brother's name, ULBERHT, broke with a high-pitched clang.

Alfhild grabbed the disbelieving Frank's throat and lifted her into the air like she weighed no more than a rabbit. With her distaff in her other hand, she mouthed something I could not hear. The head of the distaff produced a dull glow. The water just off the stern began to roil and bubble.

Utstein was pinned to the gunwale by five big trolls trying to shove him over the side. He pushed them all back, but slowly. Near the mast, Innstein charged those surrounding him, but was repulsed as defenders filled in with layers of spears and shields. He read the battlefield on that ship and must have known he could not get there in time. The brothers looked at one another, and in the next instant, they shouted one word that echoed over the sea:

"*Barkman!*"

The tiller of the 'Steins' ship turned his head to the *Naglfar*. He had already nocked a gold-fletched arrow and drawn his longbow. He had aimed it far inland in Ogmund's direction, where the main fight was taking place.

That distance would be an impossible shot for almost anyone, and against a sorcerer who would easily shrug it off. Unless . . .

The tiller's head was covered in bark. He snarled as he turned his gaze back to Ogmund, where his longbow was still pointed. He paused, holding his aim on the sorcerer.

In a flash, he pivoted and loosed in the other direction.

Alfhild dropped her distaff and put up her hand, palm out, to block the arrow, just as she had done against Jorun's. The gold-fletched arrow pierced her hand and stuck halfway through her palm. She shrieked, dropping Nanthild, and pulled the arrow out. Muttering some curse, she snapped it and threw it overboard.

The Frank coughed, but was up before the witch turned back to her. She took a grip on Alfhild from behind, that short stature helping her get in under her adversary. With one hand on Alfhild's shoulder and the other at her belt, Nanthild lifted the witch over her head and slammed her back onto the gunwale.

I heard Alfhild's back break even that far away. As unambiguously dead as the witch had to be, Nanthild hefted her again to give her a second crack across the gunwale. She let the limp body flop onto the deck.

The strange raven took off with a satisfied croak to parts unknown. The distraction turned my head, and I saw that the fire raging on the *Sea Squirrel* had started to catch some of the warships.

Across the battlefield, not everyone knew at once that the tide had turned. But enough of them had seen Alfhild's end, lit bright by the burning *Sea Squirrel*. I could see pockets of warriors—Bjarmians and viking hirelings, mostly—turn and point, shouting to their mates.

The witch and her sea serpent were both dead. An enemy ship pulled up to the shore. And many of their ships had started to burn. Something was very wrong. Did the main host need to turn to face a new front now?

Yes, in short order, they would. But many of them had a more immediate problem.

Near the very top of the slope was Styrgrim. The ebb and flow of the fight offered brief glimpses, flashes of that black blade coming up and down.

Glimpses too brief to make it clear what I was seeing, but long enough to suggest a ghostly figure fighting with him.

I led our little group down the beach to where Steinvor and her crew were disembarking and ran right up to her despite my ankle still not being quite right. Her reappearance was surprise enough. Then there was the tiller, who was clearly Arrow-Odd. A man in a would-be comical hat with a large, fuzzy ball at the top shouted commands. Or, it would have been comical, had it not been stained and crusty with blood. He started in Norse and then switched to a language I couldn't even guess at.

"Is that really Arrow-Odd?" I asked Steinvor. "And who are—"

"Norse and Irish, and there isn't time for more questions," she interrupted.

The rowdy crew had little uniformity. Most of those who were identifiably Norse just had spears, axes, and shields. The Irish were even more mixed. A few of them wore scaly armor and had short swords. Others kept to light weapons—spears, javelins, and shields. Some weren't even wearing pants.

"I need to know how best to deploy this lot," snapped Steinvor. "Is that a thing you know, or must I guess?"

"Goat's breath and cat piss!" I said. "If Arrow-Odd has any more sorcerer-piercing arrows, then—"

"No." The absurd bark armor had fallen away by then, showing Odd's golden headband and scarlet cloak. Alongside the sword hanging at his side was a huge, wooden club.

"We have Tyrfing," I told them. "Styrgrim swings it now, so don't get too close to him. We need to get Styrgrim closer to Ogmund."

I hadn't even finished talking before Odd loosed arrows on two very long shots that found their marks. "Styrgrim is far off," Odd said after a third shot. "Probably can't even hear you over the din of battle."

I looked at him and at Steinvor. She was in command of his crew. Her crew? The 'Steins' crew? It would take a week just to ask all my questions.

"What about pushing Ogmund closer to Styrgrim?" asked Magnus.

"That's more likely with the two brothers," said Steinvor, looking back out to the water. "They've cleared the deck of that ship, but now they need to take it in to shore."

"There's no time to wait for that," I said.

Growls from Thorir and Frothi sounded in agreement. Ogmund's army still pressed our people hard. They could still break through and roll up our lines, slay Huld, and win.

Steinvor shook her head, clearly not liking any of her choices. "A shield wall with this number will be overwhelmed and flanked."

Odd, who had continued to shoot, put his longbow down. "I'm going up there with my club." He pointed up and left of the main host. "If you attack their rear, Ogmund will turn his attention toward you. Then I'll come in at their flank and call him out. He'll have to fight me or take the Lower Passage, and either way, his army loses its leader."

I shook my head. "He can't take the Lower Passage. Ketill has hardened the ground here, marshaled the *vættir* against it."

Odd's eyes flashed wide for a fraction of a second. "Then it can finally end." He didn't wait to confirm this plan with Steinvor, just took off running up the slope and wide to the left of the fighting.

Steinvor ordered a swine array to form up, two lines deep. Those with armor lined up on her, carrying longer, heavier spears. Behind them were those with long spears but no armor, ready to fill the gaps, and the skirmishers, ready to throw their javelins, behind them.

"I don't have many shield-wall fighters," I said.

She looked to Fuzzy Ball Hat, who held a heavy carpentry axe in each hand. He twirled one of them with his fingers like it was a quarter of its weight. "I should stay in the middle. For the Irish."

"We both know why you want to stay in the middle, Fjornir," said Steinvor.

Fuzzy Ball Hat, apparently Fjornir, shrugged.

Steinvor sent Frothi and Thorir to protect our left flank. Magnus and I would protect the right flank. Jorun stayed close behind, still with plenty of arrows to back up whoever needed it.

We started forward, slow at first and gradually picking up speed. We passed single warriors and those taking the wounded out of the fight, and ignored them. They ignored us, too, looking like they were more interested in putting out fires on ships than in fighting.

We covered much of the distance at a light jog. It would move us fast enough but not tire us out before the fighting started—Steinvor knew what she was doing. Then, we were running fast, a full-on charge headed uphill. A disadvantage, yes. But from the enemy's perspective: Who were these maniacs who had bypassed the witch and now attacked from the rear?

Momentum is as much a concept as a physical thing, and is closely related to fear. Some fear had already been spreading from the end of Alfhild's aid, from some shouting about her death, from the panic of seeing their ships aflame.

Enough of the enemy turned around to form a shield wall. Steinvor and some of the heavily armored Irish broke their wall at the head of our formation right away. We continued driving forward, surrounded by disorganized foemen. It soon became clear that fear was doing work for us far in excess of their uphill advantage.

I had Need as a spear and came up against some god-child holding a shield with the winged *othala* rune. The nose guard and eye sockets of his helmet were visible above the shield. Poking his shield seemed pointless, and his face was a small, armored target, so I lowered the tip at the last moment, stabbing him in the thigh.

Score one for the skald! Only I didn't keep on driving forward, but instead stopped, withdrew the spear, and looked for a more lethal opening.

He didn't give me one.

Quicker than I expected he might react, especially with a thigh wound, he leaped forward and used his shield to bat away my spear. He was closing fast with a long seax, already inside my range.

*Shit! This is what Magnus does to people!*

But I am a lucky skald, and Magnus was there on my right side. He rolled forward and took off the warrior's leg with one slice. The man fell forward just short of killing range. I nodded my thanks to Magnus, and then we were back to driving forward, the swine array still intact as it rolled through the mob.

The smell of silver birch and fresh lightning was stronger than ever. I didn't know what Huld was doing, but I was confident it had something to do with fear and indecision.

Huld's *seiðr* gave us an edge, but it was not an easy fight by any means. Jorun used her last arrows and picked up that downed warrior's seax and shield. She slipped into our lines when one of our Norsemen took a spear to the throat.

On our other flank, Moose-Frothi charged the side of the opposing shield wall such that he knocked four or five men down. Thorir was on them immediately, breaking the counterattack.

The enemy was so numerous, but almost entirely disorganized. More of them broke away toward the ships below. Others stood back and looked this way and that, having lost any sense of command or direction.

Running into some of Ogmund's followers was like hitting a snowbank and realizing the back of it was solid ice. All tall, cloaked, and ugly, they had the look of ill-natured sorcerers rather than battlefield lieutenants. But they commanded lines of god-children to form up, stopping our advance. We had to spread out against them, and the fighting turned far harder. I locked my shield with the man next to me and tried to keep the enemy at bay, while Magnus watched my flank and rear.

Not far from where I stood, but a long way given the number of warriors between us, was Ulf. He was gesturing and shouting, gathering commanders. One was the big troll from the parley, who led the effort against the lines held by Helgi and Hjalti. I couldn't see a way to get at Ulf to fulfill my oath. We had killed Alfhild, but that was little consolation to me. I wanted to rid Midgard of this foul man's influence. I *had* to avenge Fanya, no matter the cost. And there he was, as far away as ever despite being so close.

Closer, but no easier to get to, was Ogmund. He kept some of his followers protecting his rear against us, but most faced the other direction, on the threat that was far greater.

The Bear had truly awakened. Styrgrim was constantly surrounded, but the enemy gave him a wide berth so that the open space near him shifted as he did. His movements were the same combination of lazy until they became as brutal as any other fight. His raven shield had taken a few hard hits, and his armor was stained red. Tyrfing hummed as it cut the air, trailing waves of heat off that black, beaten blade. Notched and dull as it looked, it had lost nothing of its mythic sharpness.

A big, heavily armored Bjarmian charged him with a two-handed axe. Styrgrim took a blow on his shield boss and turned the axe away, then brought Tyrfing down in an effortless cut that sheared through mail and took the man's arm off. He shoved the flailing warrior into the next man coming at him. They collided, stopped, and were both cut in half at the waist when Styrgrim lunged with a low, horizontal slash.

Svipul's form floated just off his body like vapor, guiding his movements. She would raise her ghostly shield against arrows and spear thrusts threatening to sneak in on him, and Styrgrim would follow the movement a fraction of a second later. She would strike with her spear, Styrgrim would cut down the enemy indicated.

Their faces were pale fury as his guttural roars mingled with her gleeful shrieking. Here was the valkyrie I had never known, the lover of bloodshed, the weaver of intestines. Finally loosed of both their tethers, my parents would end just as they had met.

Further to our left was Ogmund, moving into a position where he might have a clear shot at Styrgrim. Arrows flew from Ogmund's fingertips. They nearly found Styrgrim, but for his shield and a gust of wind that followed Svipul's spear to move them aside.

Ogmund's voice rolled over all of us, smooth as silk, thick as honey, cutting through the din as only a sorcerer could do. "Listen, my legions! Give no leeway to these lady-killers. They'd have you be less than you are right now and ignore your noble birthrights! This is a fight to the finish—at the end, there will be a boot on your neck, or not. But I won't expect you to succeed against such trickery without some assistance."

Something deep beneath us rumbled and then subsided, accompanied by the odor of rotting fish. Ogmund paused, but it sounded unnatural for such a practiced orator. It was breaking his own tempo, as if he had tried to summon something up from below but failed. He drew his sword and led a group of big champions in Styrgrim's direction.

"Now, take your freedom!" he continued, as if hoping nobody noticed the failure. "Fight for your dominion in this world, or fall to theirs!"

Ketill's voice rang out from behind our lines.

"Feed your army human flesh and frighten them with fables, is that the best you can do, Ogmund Tussock? I can feel you reaching downward. Keep reaching around, you wretch! It's not just men of Midgard who hate you!"

The wizard's voice boomed with a fury dormant for generations. He had fought but eventually been worn down and had given up. As for Huld, now was his chance to sweep those old regrets away. But there was one other bit of wisdom in Ketill's speech—the phrasing of that last sentence was no accident.

It was not just Midgard. He had marshaled the *vættir* of the Down-Below, the dwarves who forged beneath, the unseen spirits that breathed memory of the land. Ogmund could not pull some ill-natured thing up from below to bind our legs now any more than Svart had been able to part the earth.

Ulf shouted for Ogmund and gestured in the wizard's general direction, and Ogmund pointed his fingers at the chasm opening. Arrows shot from his fingertips one by one, over the heads of the front lines. If any of them did find Ketill, he kept his shield up. Ogmund must have known his biggest threats—

Styrgrim, Huld, Ketill—but he had failed to focus enough effort on any one of them.

It was late in the game to do so now, but Ogmund turned toward Styrgrim and let more arrows fly. Svipul laughed as Styrgrim dodged some and blocked others. Ogmund slowed to let his champions go forward to fight the man with the demon sword.

Styrgrim responded to the new challenge with the verse I'd given him:

> "As much spirit as man
>> is Spineless Ogmund.
> A quivering twig
>> cowering in the rear.
> He hasn't a hope
>> when I hack him down.
> At this massacre on Mon,
>> no mercy from the Bear!"

Ogmund's champions exchanged looks, a bad sign in the heat of battle. Warriors focused on winning need to have their attention ripped away from their enemy. Those having second thoughts look to their comrades rather than to the next engagement. Styrgrim was wearing down their morale, just as he had planned.

The champions tried encircling him, throwing spears before rushing in, feinting a rush from one side while the other side attacked. Their attacks remained tentative, mere delaying tactics to wear the man down while keeping him away from Ogmund. One of the champions called for more javelins.

Huld held her chanting on a single syllable while Hallfred sang an octave lower for support. Wisps of the *volva*'s white hair rose eerily, without the aid of any wind.

The tone was not so loud to my ears, but some of the enemy covered theirs. While we still faced a solid shield wall, still had to watch our backs, the opposing attacks became more tentative, less committed. More and more, vikings on the periphery of the fight disengaged and headed toward the ships.

Somewhere to my left, Steinvor created a gap in the enemy ranks with a few bold spear thrusts, and Fjornir charged past our line at the opening. He hewed down a foeman as he burst through the enemy line, ball hat flopping, heavy carpentry axes reddened. He missed a swipe at Ogmund's nearest follower, and ignored him as he advanced.

Steinvor ordered a heavy push, but it was of no use after the enemy line was reinforced.

The white-bearded man headed straight for Ogmund, who didn't do much to defend himself. I shouted for Fjornir to back off, but he was a man possessed. He blocked one swipe of Ogmund's sword with his axes and followed up with a heavy swing. Ogmund dodged so fast, a blink would have missed it.

Fjornir followed up with his other axe as if he'd anticipated just that, and this one connected with Ogmund's neck.

The sorcerer grunted from the force of the blow, but the axe couldn't bite his skin. He pulled his sword back and stabbed Fjornir, pulling on his back until he'd run his sword all the way down to the guard.

Ogmund said something to the old man, but it was too low for me to hear. I think Fjornir replied. I suspect his last words were good ones, because what he did next said everything. He held Ogmund's arm with one hand, preventing him from pulling the sword out. He snaked his other hand through the sorcerer's belt. He finished entangling himself by wrapping his legs around one of Ogmund's.

Ogmund laughed at first. It was awkward, but not a threat at all. Until he realized the threat was coming from another direction.

To our left, Arrow-Odd crashed through the enemy lines, screaming for Ogmund's blood. That stilled a lot of spears, made more than a few heads turn. Trails of blood followed the arcs of Odd's sword as he cut down one after another of the enemy. When suddenly faced by one of Ogmund's new followers, he dropped the sword, pulled his wooden club out, and struck the man so hard that he fell with his chest up but his face down.

Ogmund scrambled to get Fjornir off him, abandoning his sword in the man's body. As the sorcerer looked over one shoulder, he must have seen that Styrgrim had cut down half the champions he'd just sent. Now he had to face Arrow-Odd's fury, out of absolutely nowhere.

He was more spirit than man, maybe. But even Ogmund Tussock didn't want another beating that broke every bone in his body, especially not with Tyrfing waiting in the wings to finish him off. He ran.

Seeing this "rising power" take to his heels, Ulf broke away from his commanders and ran after him. I broke away from the shield wall, trying to track Ulf's movements without losing him.

Magnus seemed to understand implicitly and stayed by my side. "Where do they think they're going? Even if they get clear of the battle, they still need to get down to the ships."

"They don't need the ships, just the water." I quickened my pace. "They want to take the Lower Passage, but they can't on land! So, they will run as far as they can near the cliffs, and then down to the sea."

Magnus didn't seem so sure of this. "It doesn't look like they're tracking a clear path to the shoreline."

"Ha! Us lucky or them incompetent—" I realized what they were headed for. Not the sea. Just a bit north of us, the cliffs above sloped downward. The downward slope dropped water draining from above to form a rivulet down the beach and into the sea. And just like the sea itself, that little rivulet was a boundary.

*This spell can't go any farther than water binds it.*

I dropped my shield and broke into a full run. "They're headed for that rivulet. We need to stop them before they get beyond it!"

"Or what?"

"Or they take the Lower Passage and get away!"

<h1 style="text-align:center">Chapter 66</h1>

<h1 style="text-align:center">No Mercy from the Poet</h1>

Running on sand is worse than running on anything other than snow or ice. My twisted ankle threatened to delay me even further. Need, at least, made itself a small knife, much easier to run with than a spear.

Breaking away on our own was dangerous, but there was no time to explain or wait for backup when seconds counted. Some who'd seen Ogmund run were now running themselves, with many others having broken away already.

Arrow-Odd ran like the wind and bashed some god-child's head in without breaking stride. The wood of the club not being nearly as hard as steel, the blow probably left the helmet it struck in usable condition. The head inside that helmet, not so much.

Three of us pursuing two of them, with one big, trollish god-child behind us. Ulf was faster than Ogmund and overtook him. Both remained in a tight race close to the cliffs. Magnus was already falling behind, as he was not much of a runner. Odd was fast, but well behind. I was the fastest as long as I ignored the pain in my ankle. And the god-child who might spear me seconds after I closed in on Ulf.

"I have the troll, just get Ulf!" shouted Magnus.

It still looked like even I might not get there in time.

Odd's eyes narrowed. He must have seen the same thing I did—that he

503

could not close the distance in time. All his wrath poured into this last effort, all his suffering directed toward Ogmund, and it would all mean nothing if the sorcerer crossed that boundary.

"I hope the dwarf who made these was a special one." I had no idea what Magnus meant until, in a long stride, he used all his momentum to throw one of his seaxes.

Did that dwarf-made weapon have any properties that would lend it to throwing? Probably not. But Magnus had skills allowing him to succeed where others failed. The throw took everything out of him, off-balancing him and making him stumble as he veered off to intercept the troll.

Awkward as throwing a long seax was, it was still two pounds of razor-sharp steel spinning at Ulf's head. He ducked but couldn't duck low enough, so he stumbled and fell.

The threat of the thrown blade only slowed Ogmund by about half a step. After it was clear the blade was headed for Ulf, he got back to his full pace, that greasy black tussock of hair flapping behind him, and made to hop over Ulf rather than go around him. But Ulf got up just a hair earlier than Ogmund must have expected and got in the way when Ogmund hopped. Then it was Ogmund's turn to stumble, but he didn't quite fall down.

They were just short of crossing the rivulet, and a lot happened in the next few seconds.

Odd launched his club at Ogmund. Ulf had to duck and roll to avoid it. The club smacked Ogmund in the back of the head and took him down. Clearly dazed, the sorcerer continued on all fours. I was closer to Ogmund, but it was Ulf I wanted. I stepped on Ogmund's back and used it as a platform to leap at Ulf.

I thought I had the coward with a big, angry, downward stab. The thing about big, angry movements is they are easy to spot and counter, and all of a sudden, my arm was blocked, I was turned with my back against solid rock, and the wind was knocked out of me from a gut punch. All I could do was give him an awkward, desperate hug to stop him from crossing.

Ogmund crawled over the rivulet and grinned as the earth parted for him. Arrow-Odd dove, one arm outstretched, and grabbed his beard as the sorcerer was already partway down. He yanked, set his feet, and bellowed as he yanked again. Ogmund screamed as he disappeared into the earth. Odd fell backwards, holding a handful of thick black beard and torn skin.

Though Ulf was a coward, he was a highly competent fighter and far better at wrestling than I was. I pivoted one way and thought to roll us both away from the water. What I thought was a sure win, he countered by adding to our momentum until we were back where we started. He broke my grip and crossed the rivulet. I lumbered after him, gasping for breath. Only two things stopped him from getting away completely.

One was that Svart had been right that Ulf was a poor sorcerer. His ability to take the Lower Passage was slower than Ogmund's. He was only down to his chest when I reached him.

The other was that I had seen what happened with Odd grabbing Ogmund's beard. That was not the grip I wanted. I had just enough time and space to reach into that hole and grab the top of Ulf's chain shirt.

I pulled. I gave everything I had. I thought I might yank him out of there. Then, a surge of pain shot through my ankle as it twisted in the sand. I lost my stance and pitched down head-first. The earth swallowed us both as I held fast to Ulf's armor.

Being an unwanted passenger taking the Lower Passage had some similarity to traveling the Stone Road in that we were surrounded by solid earth but still able to move. Move a little, at least. Ulf squirmed and tried to break my grip. I pulled myself down and wrapped my legs around his chest.

The smell of salt and sand gave way to earthier aromas and softer confines around us. Fertile dirt, worms, dry fungus. My back and shoulders bumped against jagged granite wall as we sank deeper.

And then the trip got weird.

Things can come unhinged in the spaces between realms. I had thought I understood that to mean foreboding forests and dark cave tunnels where you're never sure what you'll run into or in which direction you're headed. But in this case, we were falling through a deep, narrow cavern. Falling, but not like we had fallen off a cliff. More like floating uncomfortably fast.

My knee hit the edge of the granite with enough force to rock my whole body. It shocked my leg grip enough for Ulf to free himself. I kept a tight hold on his mail shirt with my hands, though.

He drew me down further and kicked off one side of the narrow space we were falling through. We floated or flew or fell to the other side of the tunnel, where he thumped my head against the stone.

I saw stars. I held on.

Soon it seemed as though we had changed direction. If Ulf was directing us somewhere, I couldn't guess where that would be. It felt far, though, much farther than I had ever traveled below Midgard before.

We fought for grips and to pummel one another as we fell-floated through deep, dark places unfamiliar to humanity. I kneed him in the chest with my good leg, but his armor blunted much of that. He twisted my fingers with two hands, and I countered with a thumb to his eye. Neither of us succeeded in injuring the other much. We continued on like that for some time as the tunnel seemed to turn us sideways.

Trollish hands reached out from the rock and struck me, and that nearly broke my grip. I reached for Need and realized I had lost it. I turned in the air and kicked back at the hands, throwing us to the other side of the tunnel as we continued falling.

I wanted to draw my carving knife, uncertain why I hadn't thought of it before, but I couldn't. I gripped Ulf's armor with one hand while my other hand was busy holding his weapon arm down. He kneed me in the balls. I grimaced but was undeterred. I would feel that one later rather than right away.

How long we grappled and traded blows, I couldn't guess. Time seemed to flow differently there. We shuffled and fought for position. I bit his wrist and drew blood, but I was on the losing end of the fight overall. Soon, I knew, he would have his sword free.

I shouted a wordless cry into his grinning face with desperate effort. The momentum took us to the other side of the tunnel to a narrow shelf where we both found our footing. Ulf's back bumped against solid rock, which bumped me in turn and created just enough space. He drew his sword, and I barely had time to hold his wrist back before he struck.

Whether the dwarves had heard my shout or had simply bided their time, I don't know, but I recognized their tools. Dvalin's silver tongs reached out from the solid rock. They grabbed a hold of Ulf's sword and twisted, locking the blade in place. Durin's hammer reached out to strike the blade on the fuller, breaking it a third of the way up from its guard.

Now it was my turn to grin, and I headbutted Ulf once, twice, three times in the nose.

But I had to change my grip to do that, and Ulf's sword came unpinned. Free to move the broken blade, he stabbed me in the side with what remained of his sword. Right in the gap where that sea serpent had torn through my armor.

I pushed his wrist away and stepped backwards and off the shelf. My foot came down on nothing as Ulf came at me again. Then we were spinning through the tunnel again. Only it seemed like we were falling up rather than down, faster and faster.

The speed of ascent was like the earth was vomiting us back up. We tumbled out of the Down-Below and back into Midgard through solid, cold stone. A cloudy sky lit the landscape of light greens to light browns.

None of which cushioned our exit. We slid down a near-vertical rock face and landed on stone. I banged my head in the fall, and that is what finally made me lose my grip on Ulf and allowed him roll away.

I got to all fours, only slightly stable. I reached for my carving knife but could not find it.

"All that effort for such a paltry fight now," said Ulf. "You should have sent someone else. Anyone else!"

My head rang, a constant, throbbing sound. I grabbed a rock the size of a rutabaga and fought the dizziness to get to my feet. My side was warm and sticky. Warmth would not last long, I knew, and neither would my strength.

Ulf stood up, steadier than I was. Blood oozed from his nose and onto his beard, but he grinned at me and picked up his sword. It was very much shortened, but still provided a solid grip with part of the blade.

Most fights begin with skill and end with brutality: A broken sword against a rutabaga rock, in this case. I had a few good strikes left in me, but then I would fade fast. Not that it would matter. Ulf was a better fighter than I was.

The ringing became louder, angrier. My hands shook with rage. I had to end this man, not just for vengeance, but for duty, as if this was the fight I had been conceived for from the start. But I was failing.

"You never were any good. Not at fighting, and not even with words. A hollow skald." Ulf circled me, biding his time like a wolf watching his prey.

"*No,*" I whispered, from the very depths of my being.

Nothing changed other than my perception. There was no ringing in my head. It was a hum rather than a ring, only it was more full of fury than I had ever heard it. That is why I hadn't recognized the pitch of *nauthiz* at first. It was the rock, humming the tone only I could hear, the one that told me it was no rock.

I did not grin, but remembered Styrgrim's wisdom, the wisdom that had laid an army low.

*They have to think they can win.*

"I remember."

I didn't watch his hands or his blade as he closed on me. I wasn't trying to avoid losing anymore. I watched his weapon arm, just beyond where the sleeve of his chain shirt ended. And I made an overhand strike with my rock, because I would end it here, no matter the cost.

At the last moment, Need changed back to its true form. The blade reached out, hungry for that traitor's blood, and severed his arm at the elbow.

The attack carried me forward and past him. Pain surged through my abdomen, but I turned back toward Ulf. He looked at the bleeding stump of in disbelief.

"I remember the wisdom of the dead."

I brought my blade down on his other arm.

"I carve their memories into verse."

I kicked him in the chest, throwing him backwards against a boulder. I cut off his legs below the knees with a single slash and dragged his body atop the boulder by his nose.

I hammered his mouth with the pommel. "Use your words as weapons when you meet the gods, if you think it can save you. See if they want your glib wit, your false charm." I struck his face again. And again. And again.

"See if they recognize you!"

It was a long time before I was done grinding Ulf's face into that rock. My hands went numb. My side had gone from warm to burning. My head pounded. My insides felt like they'd come undone. I stumbled toward a rock face, but had to turn around and have a last look.

I had already lost a lot of blood. I knew what was coming without my *fylgja* telling me, but I looked for her anyway. Then I remembered I had loosed her to fight alongside Styrgrim one more time. I missed her, wished she could see me, but I had no regrets about what I'd done.

A raven croaked somewhere above me. It glided down and settled on Ulf's corpse. It looked at his face, but did not start on his eyeballs as I expected. Instead, it looked at me and cocked its head.

"Tell Fanya I avenged her."

The raven croaked as if in answer, but was interrupted by the rapid chatter of a kingfisher. The copper-breasted, blue-backed bird flew in from the side like an arrow, straight at the raven, which flapped to steady itself. The kingfisher doubled back and perched next to the bigger bird and poked at it with its sword-like beak.

I didn't know what to make of that. I sat back against the stone, clutching Need and fading. I had nothing left to even hold myself up anymore. Or that's how it felt as I leaned back. And back, and back.

Not against the solid rock, but into it.

# Chapter 67

# Odin, Outsmarted Again

"It seems to me you've gotten everything you wanted," said Heimdall.

"Is that why we're discussing what you want?" countered Odin.

I blinked back some of my senses and found myself in a small cave. I lay on my unstabbed side, which was good. Even better, a small campfire separating me from the two gods kept the place quite warm. For a few moments, I felt like I might not bleed to death, so I tried to sit up.

Shifting my legs reminded me how badly my balls and side ached. Lifting my head shot pain up through my neck like lightning. Sitting up was out of the question. Breathing was quite uncomfortable enough. So, I breathed, and listened to two gods engaged in a verbal sparring session.

"We are discussing the future," said Heimdall, his tone icy. "If you are not interested in the future, you can be off right now without concern."

Odin chuckled. "Out-scheme me, will you? I doubt that very much."

"Do you?"

"I do."

"Then why do Thor's sons sail the seas while Alfhild's body feeds the fish?"

Odin shrugged. "That is the way it turned out. Do you claim to have guaranteed the events would transpire in such a way? Or that you had one over on me in a game where I won regardless of outcome?"

"I think you self-congratulate overmuch. Over deaths and destruction, as if *you* had set such things in motion. Those things will happen no matter what we do. But to have a hand in heroes who come to be, that is by no means guaranteed. That is something to take pride in."

Odin snorted. "Take pride in the doings of someone else? That is exactly what this one and his ilk have warned against. Even to the point of minimizing *us*. And now you would prop up a bastard half-breed? He is no better than any of those god-children, and where are they now?"

"You equate heritage to quality, but you know it to be a false thing. Who was it beaming most bright when Styrgrim swung that Hel-sword? Don't expect me to believe you had no preference either way. You were never as proud as when they called Styrgrim *Odin's man*."

"Believe what you will, you'll get no intervention from me. Now, will you sail the entire Encircling Sea before coming to your point?"

"It is you who must come to the point."

"I need not justify myself to the likes of you, *Watchman*." Odin leaned in, his tone sharper, nastier.

Heimdall leaned in, an iron wall against the sharpness of that tone. "Then *begone*, Hooded One. You can't conceal your intent in this cave. Your presence speaks your thoughts aloud."

"Can you hear those even with the noise of all that grass growing?"

"You may think yourself wise and sorcerous beyond the rest of us, but you forget who you're talking to. I can hear your asshole clench when you lie." Wow, Heimdall really did have good hearing.

There was a silent pause.

"Haha, there it goes again!" laughed Heimdall. "Master of fury and forbidden wisdom, and the one lesson you refuse to learn is that you *cannot control everything, nor should you*."

Odin shook his head. "I counted you among the wiser of us. Yet you sit there waiting for the end, like the rest. Control? Ha! We will *fade*, and fading will serve none, least of all the children of Midgard Thor thinks he protects so well."

"Serve them yourself, then."

Odin picked up a horn from somewhere unseen and took a long drink. My lips and throat as dry as they were, a sip of wine seemed like a good thing. I tried to ask for one, but a croaking sound was all I managed.

"You be quiet," Odin continued between drinks. "You've done enough talking for one lifetime and more."

"There it goes again!" Heimdall laughed. "Lore-learner, wisdom-diver: You claim a unique courage in confronting the hard truths, so let's have one out right now. You are angry about his *Hávamál*."

"Hmph." Odin drank even deeper than before, draining his horn.

"You were willingly spear-stabbed and hung for nine nights. I would not have guessed a sharpened bird feather could wound you so deeply."

"Those were not the words of the Lord of Fury." Odin did not hold back in tone, and the cave reverberated with his wrath.

"You left the son of Odin's man to find his way alone. Only a journey like his could result in hard-won wisdom worth being remembered. Do you find real fury in pretend *berserkir*, or from those who've wandered far and seen much, won and lost, and dared boldly?"

"I cannot hear it," replied Odin, "but I think your asshole clenches now. This is no Battle-Chooser's son, wherever he might wander. You mean to flatter a flatterer, and you're failing."

"He seized on old lore from the first stories he ever heard. Some of which echoed memories of the Goths."

I couldn't see where Odin got the wine from, but he drank again.

"Ah, ever the touchy subject," Heimdall continued. "It all goes back to the Goths and unintended consequences. To providing the sword that earned them victory at first, but sowed their doom."

"It was not I who fouled that sword."

"You cannot blame Loki for everything."

Odin rounded and snapped at the Watchman. "I will not forget you said that."

"I will not forget you held up this illusion." Heimdall gestured in my direction, but past me. "Those men, mere feet away, would see the wounded skald and help him if not for your trickery. A petty behavior for anyone with real power."

Despite throbbing aches and shooting pains throughout my body, I turned just enough to look behind me. There was the mouth of the cave, Ulf's mangled body decorating a boulder not far beyond. Now that I had time to look rather than fight, I saw we were on a large hill or a small mountain, high enough to see the grasses and trees extend for miles over mostly flat land.

Two riders on moose slowed and stopped. The one I didn't recognize hefted his spear, keeping vigilant for threats all around. He looked straight at me for a brief moment and then looked away to something else. The other dismounted and crept forward to examine Ulf's body, and him, I knew.

That was Joni, the man who'd led us from Varg Tiorfi's rotten compound to Arrow-Odd's camp. That trip through the Lower Passage had taken me all the way to Karelia, then. Again, I tried to speak, but even less of a croak came out this time.

"And have the skald do what?" asked Odin. "Use more of that cursed Roman sorcery to hold my wisdom captive?"

"All your work since the prophecy was to guarantee your own lasting word-fame. The skald has preserved it in a new way. That Roman sorcery does not replace the oral tellings, but will add to them. It may even survive war and winter, unlike the old stories. You remember those, don't you? Before the long winter, after which everything changed."

"Changed for the better, in many ways."

Heimdall came up to me as I reached toward Joni with a feeble arm and rolled me back onto my unstabbed side. Two quick pats told me to remain still and quiet, and then he went back to the other side of the cave. Apparently, I would just have to wait for their argument to play out.

"Better for your Goths?" asked the Watchman. Odin's lack of a flippant answer told me the question had cut him deep, and Heimdall did not stop there. "Perhaps you changed without realizing it, and Styrgrim was not Odin's man after all. Perhaps you've become more modern with the times, needing a modern man. Like Ulf! Whatever words were necessary to get what he wanted, those were the words he spoke, just as you have many times. Oh, but wait—Ulf was no seeker of deep lore, nor stoic in the face of difficult wisdom. His charm and deception weren't there to conceal a fury, but rather to hide how fragile he was."

Odin's face was red with rage.

"Or, perhaps this skald has elevated your voice. Made it more memorable and prevented the fading you warned of. He hasn't made you any less the Battle-Chooser, but has made you more the wisdom-speaker, more of what Midgard needs now. He is the Spear of the Gods, after all, if not in the way we intended."

"'We?' When last I heard, it was Odin who got the prophecy, Odin who formed the plan."

"And it's Odin who will fail to see what's right in front of him. Those men," Heimdall pointed past me again, "they have something we don't. Foremost in their stories is a skald—the eternal skald, Vainamoinen. These folk have fewer mead halls, fewer trading centers, and more dangerous borders. Yet they persist through the toughest times, a hardy bunch. We have no skald among us in Asgard, and look what a position that has put us in. Twice."

Odin stroked his long beard. "You say *we*, but it is *my* decision you're after. And I think two ill-born children given those apples are two too many."

"Thor made a choice. He knew he could not control those two. He set them loose, let them choose their path."

"Foolish."

"Unafraid to dare boldly, more like."

"And if they misrepresent him, what then? Now they reflect on Thor rather than Thor guiding them to act as they should."

"Thor chose them, and that was his guidance. Whether his choice was good or ill, that should reflect back upon him. Now you have a choice that will reflect back upon you. One choice sends the skald back into the world to act as he will. An unafraid choice. The other way means you are hiding. And no one will ever forget that story."

Odin's laughter echoed through the cave, a low and furious thing.

"He's a wise one in some ways," said Odin. "But he has a long journey in Midgard before I'll ever consider a place for him in Asgard."

"I think that's wise."

Odin snapped right back at him. "Don't think to congratulate yourself too quickly. You may have gotten what you wanted here, but will he thank you for it? The life he knew is behind him. Think he wants the same loneliness Arrow-Odd gets from seeing his friends slaughtered over and over? Think he wants Ogmund Tussock chasing him forever? He will, you know. He knows Ansgar's name."

"Ogmund does not know his real name. And I'll leave my son's life to my son, a thing I'm proud to call him, whether he's really mine or not. I wouldn't have him wander any less than he has already."

Those last words came through barely intelligible as they faded. The cave shifted, making the world around me wobble. In a few moments, the two gods had disappeared, leaving me alone.

The illusion faded with the gods, and Joni stepped into the cave. He asked what happened, but gave me water without delay. I just pointed to my side at first. Joni spoke quickly to his companion to fetch medicine. After a few sips of water, I could speak again.

"*You found a moose after all,*" I croaked in broken Karelian.

"*Steady, now, stranger,*" replied Joni. "*We will see to your wounds. You are not from here, not Bjarmian, not Rus. Who are you?*"

I suppose my beard had really come in for my friend to not recognize me. Just as well. I had a different name, anyway.

"Bragi," I said, my breathing labored but steady. "Bragi Boddasson."

# CHAPTER 68

# LITTLE BEAR

WHEN I LAST SAW MAGNUS THE RED, HIS HANDS WERE SO FULL from wrangling children that I had to pour the ale for both of us.

I hadn't seen him for years, had never even met his two youngest children. As an itinerant skald traveling Midgard with stories to inspire people, I was always on the move. Sometimes to huts made of little more than mud, sometimes to grand mead halls. Even compared to the grandest halls, it was these trips to see my old friend and his family that I most enjoyed, at their small house on their small farm.

It's an easy road to a good friend, however long that road is. Especially when that friend makes very good ale.

Magnus' boy, thirteen winters old, was splitting knotted wood when I came upon him. He was always big for his age, and now he wielded a heavy maul against the most stubborn firewood with ease. A younger boy hefted a new piece to split with both hands while a younger girl pranced from flower to flower nearby. Those two were new additions to the household since my last visit. The older boy recognized me, though.

"Go tell father the skald is here."

"The skald" was how most people knew me. I liked it that way.

The little ones ran squealing toward the house while the older boy and I took a leisurely pace. He offered the hospitality of his house with some overly formal words and gestures. I grinned and nodded, remembering that need to feel important.

Magnus came around the other side of the house carrying heavy pails of water. He put those down, and the smaller children attached themselves to a leg each. Slowed due to his new leg weights, he strode out to meet me.

Magnus and I clasped hands. He told me I looked the same as ever, just with a longer beard. I couldn't say the same, as lines had started across his face and some of the red in his beard had gone white.

"You look happy," I said, and meant it.

He grinned and picked up the little ones in one arm each. The older boy held the door and ushered me inside.

Benches ran along the walls, piled high with odds and ends: Wooden swords, straw dolls dressed with stray bits of wool, balls, carved animal figures. Also, child-size blankets, half-filled baskets, and a half-filled milking bowl. A cookpot steamed over the central fire pit as a girl stirred it. She had the appraising look in her eye of someone much older than her eleven winters. I couldn't tell if she remembered me.

"You two," Magnus gestured with his head at the older boy and girl. "What sort of hospitality is this for the storyteller you like so much? Clear off those benches! Make some room!"

The children under Magnus' arms squealed with delight. The more he held them, the more they resisted. Not in defiance—I could see and hear that they thought it was the best game in the world. Magnus had speed and strength, but I don't think he ever had a test of balance that involved squirming, laughing adversaries.

"Overmatched?" I asked. "You know, you could just put them down. We've handled worse."

He shifted his weight, hopped, and changed his grips. "They will tear the place up when they're this excited." He shook his head. "I thought Jorun would be back by now."

"Hunting?"

He nodded. "Hares have gotten too many vegetables this year."

The older boy stared at me instead of clearing the benches. He didn't talk much, but in the sort of way that hinted he had a great deal of thoughts behind his silence. Maybe too many.

I knew that feeling well enough.

Magnus raised his voice. "Are those benches going to clear themselves?"

The boy gave his father a defiant look while the girl went over to him. She pulled gently on her brother's shirt to get his attention, then handed me two empty cups from the shelves nearby.

I poured the ale while they cleared the benches, and Magnus held onto the agents of chaos. When that was done, the girl went back to tending the cookpot while the boy sat on one of the benches along the wall.

I was about to sit next to him when Jorun came into the house carrying three hare carcasses. I went to greet her and made the mistake of setting both cups down on the side toward the boy.

He grabbed a cup and downed the contents before Magnus could react. "That is a man's drink," he snapped. "You must be prepared to do a man's chores, then."

"I can fight like a man!"

Jorun raised an eyebrow. "Who knew our finest brew was only for men? Especially given it was a woman who brewed it!" She put the hares down, and we clasped hands. She also looked older, also looked happy.

"All that time with Nanthild," I said, turning to Magnus, "and you're still making that mistake?"

"I only meant to say . . ." Magnus trailed off, probably unsure what he might say now to get him out of trouble. "He is still a child."

"Man," snapped the boy.

Magnus growled and leaned in toward the one so eager to drink. "I have no need of fighting. I have a need of splitting wood and milking goats and shearing sheep and tilling a field."

The boy sneered at his father. "That's boring."

"Would that I had such a boring childhood," replied Magnus, his voice rising. "Do you know how hard—"

Jorun's gentle hand grasped Magnus' shoulder, and he calmed. I'd seen the man face twelve *berserkir*, one after another, with a calm demeanor. Children, on the other hand, had his blood boiling and carved aging lines into his face.

"You know they called me lucky," I said, nodding at Jorun. "But I think you are the lucky one, Magnus."

He turned to his wife, handed her the two squirming children, and kissed her. "I am," he said with a deep breath.

Jorun chided the little ones softly and spoke to them in verse. A familiar one, it seemed, because they both ceased their playing and nodded. When she put them down, they went to the other side of the house and sat quietly.

The older girl poked at the hearth fire. Quiet, but not shy. "Who is Nanthild?"

I grinned as I thought about how long that answer had to be to do Nanthild any justice. "That's a long story. But for one thing, she was the strongest of us, after Haldor Skullsplitter."

"She was that big?" exclaimed the boy.

"Not at all," I replied. "A little bigger than your sister is now. Nanthild the Silent we called her, because she never spoke after her brother died."

"She never talked again?" asked the girl.

"I don't think so. That was the cost of her strength. But I heard some time later, when she was among her friends, she managed to laugh."

"Few deserved it more," said Magnus. "It seems like a long time since you were last here, though! Any new stories we might like to know?"

"Actually, two that came together! I finally found Steinvor after she left Arrow-Odd's service."

"Find a different legend to latch onto?"

Jorun looked up from skinning one of the hares and gave Magnus a look.

"Not at all," I said. "She settled down in a quiet spot. By the time I found her, she was the leader of her little township, and doing very well."

"Did she marry someone we knew?" asked Magnus, suspicious.

The little girl looked up.

"Not quite. She killed Svein. He, uh . . ." I trailed off, suddenly realizing the disgusting nature of the story was perhaps not quite right for my young audience. "He did some bad things, and she ended him. They ended up calling him Fancypants the Troll."

All true.

More true: Svein had found his way to a churchyard and tried to cast Ketill's prank spell, the Dead Man's Pants. The townspeople screamed in horror at the sight of this giant who had dug up a dead man, skinned him from the waist down, sewed a coin into the scrotum, and tried to wear the skin as pants.

Steinvor had been there by pure chance, looking for a quieter life after becoming disillusioned with word-fame. Slaying Fancypants the Troll might have earned her some inadvertent word-fame, so she'd been ready to leave at the time. But the townspeople were so grateful that they offered to build her a house if she stayed.

"Why did they call him Fancypants?" asked the girl.

"He wore . . . peculiar clothing. Thought it would make him rich."

"Hmph," said Magnus, hearing exactly what I wasn't saying. "When you said you had a new story, I thought it might be that you'd caught up with Huld. Horsefly never did give a satisfying answer about what happened after the battle. Huld disappeared, and he just shook his head when I asked about it."

"Shook his head while grinning is how I remember you describing him."

"Yes, well . . . sometimes a *vǫlva* would be most helpful, here."

Magnus sat down heavily, and I noted but didn't mention his changed expression.

The boy stood up, his arms crossed. I knew that look. He was still angry about all the things boys can get angry about and didn't know what to do with himself. The pause in conversation must have unnerved him even more. "Don't you drink ale?" he asked me.

"I drink with my Brother, Magnus," I said, picking up his empty cup. "But he appears to be at a disadvantage at the moment."

The boy's face turned red. He snatched the empty cup in an instant and went to fill it.

I leaned over and whispered to Magnus. "Tell him to pour for himself and his sister."

"But—"

"Have him cut those with water."

The girl continued poking at the fire. Her eyes flickered up and back to it. "Huld was the *vǫlva*?"

"A wise and powerful one," said Jorun. "I've told you about Huld before, remember?"

The girl nodded. "It seemed as though there was more to tell."

"I might never run out of questions for Huld if I have the opportunity to ask them again," I said.

"Big assumption she'd answer them with anything but riddles!" said Magnus.

"That's possible," I said. "But I thought the same about Ketill, once, and he was far more forthcoming after a certain point."

"Like after he made you shit your brains out?"

I grinned. "Right around that time. If anyone wants to—"

"Save that story for the mead halls, if you please," Jorun interrupted, to the great disappointment of her children.

The boy brought Magnus a cup of ale. Magnus told the boy to fill two more cups partway for him and his sister. I could practically hear the boy think as he considered the proportions. Too much ale, and he was being rebellious. Too much water, and he risked thinking himself unmanly, cowed, lorded over by his father.

Oh, the unending joys of adolescence.

He settled on a bit more than half full of ale. Then he offered a cup to his sister before taking a drink himself. I could tell the boy had his struggles at home, as we all struggle during such an age. But he treated his little sister with respect, and that was a good sign.

Magnus and I drank together. "Frothi disappeared too," he said. "Sort of."

"I thought he was given some land in Scania with his brother."

"He was! But he got bored and went off to live in the woods somewhere. Left Thorir in charge of everything. I imagine you can still find him if you want, especially if you ask his brother about it. Why you'd want to, though— ha! That's a different question."

"Sounds like he got more feral over the years," I said. "Hrolf must have seen that coming, as he tends to do."

Magnus was quick to ask about the king's court. "Is Svipdag still among his champions?"

"Is that the big man with the axe?" asked the boy. He was so excited, his drink dribbled out of his mouth as he spoke. "I want to hear more about him!"

"He's still one of Hrolf's champions," I said. "Is Svipdag your favorite among the heroes your parents know?"

"Of course! He beat those *berserkir* all by himself!"

I swallowed some ale down the wrong pipe. Once I'd recovered, I had to ask Magnus what he'd left out among his travels.

Jorun brought the cleaned hares to the cookpot simmering over the fire. The two young ones left their bench and attached themselves to a leg each. They peeked out at me and ducked back behind. Jorun ignored them, and they remained quiet.

Magnus shrugged. "Can't tell my own stories. They get bored and think I'm exaggerating."

It's the way of children to misunderstand their parents, and these were no exception. Nor had I been any exception. I thought I'd known Styrgrim's mind despite his absence. When Kari Swifthand let on that I'd been wrong, I traveled halfway across Midgard to see for myself. Then I still didn't understand him. Not until those last few days.

"Not so believing of your father's stories?" I asked. "I suppose I was no wiser about my father at your age."

"About Styrgrim the Bear?" all the children asked at once.

I wasn't about to tell the world I was the son of a god. Too many people in Midgard still placed a high value on godly heritage. I had long since seen straight through to the rotten entitlement it created, and wanted none of it.

And besides, I felt I owed Styrgrim something. It would still be my mother's name I used to mark my family, but I wouldn't deny Styrgrim some credit. A good father? Not really, but he'd been thrown into the role in the worst sort of way, and without the one person he needed to help him learn to be a good father. He'd suffered in silence a great deal with nothing but insult as thanks. Despite all that, he had protected me when he was able to.

"He wielded the demon sword, Tyrfing," I said, switching from conversation to theatrics. "Great swipes felled five and six warriors at a time! None could stand in his way, and eventually, even the sorcerer Ogmund had to run for his life, tail between his legs!"

The children *oohed* and *aahed* at that and asked for more, just as expected. Then I sprung my trap.

"And do you know what happened with Ogmund?" I asked, meeting each pair of eyes before I continued. "He started to take the Lower Passage, to sink down into the earth and disappear. But Magnus the Red," I said, pointing at their father, "he and Arrow-Odd grabbed Ogmund by the beard and gave it a mighty yank! I thought they would pull Ogmund back up out of the ground. Instead, Ogmund's face came right off! The rest of the sorcerer disappeared down into the earth, leaving him even uglier than he was before."

"Whoa!"

"Really?"

"What?"

"I thought Styrgrim did that," said the boy.

"What's this now?" I asked. "Styrgrim did quite a bit that day, but he never got his hands on Ogmund."

"I heard Styrgrim farted lightning!"

"I heard Styrgrim threw the sword, and it cut Ogmund's butt cheeks off!"

"I heard someone cut off Styrgrim's head, and he kept fighting for ten minutes after!"

"I heard Styrgrim died like a hero," said the older boy, a bit quieter than the others. It seemed at least one thing Magnus said had been heard.

"That's what I heard, too," I said, turning to the boy. "I was after the traitor, Ulf, and that took me far from the battle as we fought, twisting through the Lower Passage. The earth spat us out on a mountain in Karelia, where I finally took his life. Mount Vottovaara, they call it. That was a long way from home. It was years before I returned and heard about what happened in the rest of that battle.

"There was lightning, but that was a thing called down by Huld. I don't think Styrgrim threw his sword, as that would be unlike him. And if it had cut Ogmund even a little bit, it would've killed him. And I don't think anyone cut off Styrgrim's head, because nobody could get so close to him.

"No, what I heard was that much of Ogmund's army fled when he ran, but those who remained still outnumbered our friends by a lot. And though our friends were a hardy bunch, they had been pressed hard for a long time and were tiring out. That was his decision point, when Ogmund ran from Arrow-Odd. Styrgrim could have chased Ogmund and made himself famous forever by killing him. But he didn't give chase.

"I heard that Styrgrim set himself against the entire army to take the pressure off our friends, taking such blows from weapons that they rent his chain shirt and broke his shield. That many arrows found his chest and back, but he fought on. That he kept fighting as spears stuck him over and over. And that once he was dead, he was so full of spear shafts from every angle that his body couldn't fall over. The enemy was afraid to go near him in case he was just playing dead. When Hrolf Kraki arrived with his army, the sword finally fell from his hand. And then the enemy had a bigger concern."

"Did Hrolf Kraki kill all the trolls?" asked the boy.

I shook my head. "Some had already fled in their ships. Most of the enemy host that remained were not trolls at all, but were Bjarmians or Rus. Hrolf Kraki offered them mercy if they surrendered and returned to their lands."

"But they could just come ba—"

"King Hrolf has always been the most magnanimous of kings," I continued through the interruption. "But he has never been magnanimous out of weakness. He knew very well that Ogmund and Alfhild had told these people a lot of stories that weren't true. So, he asked those Bjarmians and Rus "Do gods flee from battle? Or is Ogmund not a god at all, but a man very good at putting others in front of him to draw the blows?"

"There was no more Brisingamen or sorcerous voice to confuse these people: They were far from home, abandoned by the supposed god king. They could see pretty plainly this king didn't need to let them keep their lives. Sometimes you can win a friend with half a loaf of bread and a tilted cup. I imagine they took some stories back to Bjarmaland and Gardariki that would make it difficult for Ogmund to gain influence again."

"That's how I remember it," said Magnus, quieter than usual. "You lot! Help your mother with the rest of the cooking. I need to take our guest out to see the farm before sundown."

I knew something was up as soon as he'd spoken. Magnus was never one to sound sad, no matter how he was feeling. There was a tinge of it in his voice, though. See the farm? That meant he needed to speak privately, so I drained my cup and laid it down, and followed him out of the house.

"Wait!" cried the boy. "What about the sword?"

"Oh, Tyrfing?" I asked. "Well, after it dropped from Styrgrim's hand, the dwarves took it down into Nidavellir, and there they keep it locked away forever."

It is not a good thing to lie, especially to a child. But that particular lie— well, I judged it more of a big guess since I wasn't there. Better that sword should fade from the memory of Midgard.

Magnus nodded, affirming the lie. Harder for him, I knew, since it was his child and since he'd been there. He knew as well as I did that it had been time to end the lore of that sword.

We got up and took our leave together. We were a good five-minute walk from the house before he said anything.

"Still nothing from your *fylgja*?" he asked.

A strange question. "Not since the battle. Why?"

Magnus shook his head. "She was reassuring to you, appearing as a woman. I could never understand these things. Guardian spirits. Luck spirits. Death portents."

*Oh, no.*

"I think I have seen my *fylgja*. It was not like yours."

I swallowed hard. Spirits were strange things, but to catch a glance of one was not usually a sign of good luck. Svipul had been doubly strange, appearing to me often and wanting to converse. More likely, a person's *fylgja* would remain unseen, bringing some luck or protection without a person's knowledge. To catch a glimpse of one, though, especially in animal form, likely meant the thread of that person's life was coming to its end.

"You saw what, exactly?"

"Well, first I should say, it was not always Magnus the Red that Styrgrim called me. When he took me on, I was still half-feral. He said if he was a bear, I was a wolverine. That name didn't stick because people liked calling me 'the Red.' I haven't even thought about it in years. But I had a dream last month that reminded me. I was walking through a dark wood, and I came upon a longhouse. There was a wolverine knocking on the door like a person. No one answered. I went up to the door, and the wolverine turned to look at me with these big, human eyes."

"That is . . ." *a terrible sign* "not something I have heard before."

"Then last week, I was chopping wood. I saw a wolverine pop its head up from behind the wood pile, but I was awake."

"There are wolverines around. Even if they don't usually come by the wood piles."

Magnus shook his head. "He stared at me, and I looked into his eyes. Human eyes. And I just knew. You know?"

I did.

"So," he said. "I am glad you've come."

Best skald in Midgard, and I had no words.

"My son is a difficult one, and he's been holding back since you arrived. The defiance was cute when he was little. Maybe you remember, I called him my little bear. Now he makes everything difficult—unless there are guests to show better behavior to, he either sits sullenly or rages when I speak. There's too much of me in him. I don't know what to do with him, but it cannot be the same way I learned, by losing my family. He thinks he is angry at me for not letting him go on adventures, but he will be even angrier when I'm gone, for reasons he can't understand yet. I may not know much parenting lore, but I know he will take it out on Jorun. She will have too much on her shoulders already."

"Parenting lore is the most esoteric lore of all. Take heart that you've done a fine job."

"My job is about to end," he said, stopping and turning toward me. "I need no such reassurances on that count."

This was really happening. "What do you need?"

"Take him. Teach him."

My brain went in many directions at once, and it took me a moment to make a coherent response. "You think I can make an angry boy study poetry or runes or languages? Learning is a choice. If I know one bit of parenting lore from my own foolish self, it's that no one can make a child choose to learn."

He waved me off as if I'd misunderstood. "Not like that. I mean, teach him what it means to be a Brother. What loyalty and courage mean. He knows them from stories. He doesn't know what it means to go hungry so your Brother can eat, or to take on pain for another's relief."

"The *Sea Squirrel* is long gone. And our friends sailing *Halfdan's Gift*, I don't think they could take a child, even if I looked after him. It would be a harsh life on their ship anyway, and that's assuming I could find them in a reasonable time. The boy will need a home."

"This home will not do it for him!" This was the first time I had heard Magnus sound frustrated. "Listen to me, skald: He is half mine and yet almost all me. He won't accept a farm life, but he has no tools for anything else yet. Will you help your Brother solve this problem?"

He didn't really have to ask. I would have done anything for my Brothers, especially Magnus.

We walked again, and I pulled at my beard in thought. It was a long time before I responded. Not because I was afraid of the responsibility, but only because I didn't know what to do. "I wish Halstein and Taika were still around. This is tricky, but they would know what to do. They always did with me."

"All you have to figure out is what they would do, then!"

I turned this over in my mind, about how I had gone from boy to man. Taika had offered much wisdom and love, even though I took it all for granted. Halstein had refused to accept laziness, but otherwise allowed me to make my own choices, even stupid ones.

I kept coming back to the most difficult part: Magnus' son was not like me. He wanted to be a warrior, wanted to be Styrgrim the Bear. Which nobody should want, but he was too young to understand why. I could be a good example for many things, but not the kind he would take after.

"I have it! I will bring him to Hrolf Kraki's court."

Magnus' eyebrows shot up. "He will get into the business of every champion there."

"Exactly. He idolizes those heroes, and they are more than just warriors. They will be good models for him and tolerate no bad behavior. He will not get away with raging at them as if they were his parents. I will stay a while, but then I will leave him to them and return a year later. If he still wants to stay, he can stay. But he may learn what a good place this home is. If that's the case, then I will bring him back here."

Magnus nodded. He seemed to turn it over in his mind a while and then nodded with even more vigor. "Yes, that is the best plan."

"Then that's what I'll do." I clapped my Brother on the back in joy at his presence, in sadness that this might be our last visit together. "Now I have to tell you, I didn't mention a few things back at the house. I did find Huld, and she finally told me some of her story. I think she would want you to know."

We walked a while longer as I told him. He reacted with astonishment and laughter. By the time we returned to the house, he was Magnus the Cheery again. And would be until the end.

Everyone thinks they have a plan until the first arrow flies, the first foothold proves false, the first unexpected weather hits. My plan to take the Little Bear to meet Hrolf Kraki marked the end of one story. The end of high adventure and deadly intrigue, grand heroism and terrible tragedy. The end of my going from boy to man in ways more important than growing older.

And the beginning of many others.

# EPILOGUE

I'VE LIVED A LONG TIME AT THIS POINT. APPLES OF IMMORTALITY will do that. First, I was a skald among the people of Midgard, and then I was *the* skald among the people of Midgard. Bragi the Old, they called me, after a while.

Eventually, I became the skald of Asgard, just Bragi.

Not many stories of me survive. Even fewer good stories. At least you still have the battle of verse against that troll, even if the scribe who wrote it thought it was just a poetry lesson.

Not that there were never stories about me, but they were told many centuries ago, and the one constant about stories is that they change over time and from place to place. It wasn't my place to tell my own stories, but to preserve the stories of others.

Maybe you've heard some different versions of these stories already. Stories about Hrolf Kraki and his champions, for one. About how they all fell to foul sorcery because there was no Christian god to swoop in and save them. That's how it was told in the written version of that saga. Therefore, that's how it's remembered: Hrolf Kraki and his champions needed a foreign religion to overcome the monsters of their world.

What a chauvinistic load of aurochs shit.

Stories always change over time. That's how gods and myths are born—by absorbing the stories of real people, real events, and becoming big ideas to believe in. Different people heard different parts of stories and stitched together a patchwork of new narratives. That's why nobody can agree who Beowulf was or when he lived, or if he lived. Without the stories of Haldor Skullsplitter and Styrgrim the Bear weaving together, there is no Beowulf.

Echoes of truth still survive in that poem. Something of the monsters they fought and tragedies they faced. Something of the way they acted and what they cared about. Even the way they were called. Beowulf, or *bee-wolf*, captures both at once. Bee-wolf, a kenning for bear, like Styrgrim was called. And a wolf of bees, as Humor called Haldor one chilly morning when the huge warrior heaped honey all over his porridge.

That Roman magic of writing things down has more power to preserve stories than speaking them. Stories change over time, but what if the story is corrupted rather than changed, and that corruption is what's preserved? The writer may hear a story and convey it honestly, but still fail at good preservation if they don't understand the critical themes and subtle nods that give it meaning. Worse, they may assume their way of thinking is the same as, or superior to, people from the past, and end up placing their present-day values over people they don't, and can't, understand.

I think that's what happened when Hrolf Kraki's Saga was written. The writer just couldn't see things any other way, and confused certainty of belief with truth. Any modern reader looking at that saga should be taken aback upon reading that line. Not just because of the line itself, but that it calls into question the rest of the story, which still retains a lot of truth.

But there one other type of poor storyteller, the type that knowingly warps narrative away from real people and true events. For gain, for convenience, calculating the outcome for them, but never for others, never about how those lies might change the future. Ulf wasn't just a man. He was a living philosophy to oppose—the opposite of what we called a *drengr*. And while Ulf's ruined body was never coming back, times change, and his rotten philosophy has rarely been better received than in recent times.

Seeing that way of being rise, hearing many versions of aurochs shit about my time, I despaired for a while. My way of direct telling couldn't compete with the Roman magic of writing, and for all my skills, I could not write.

Finally, a new idea came to me: I had to whisper the story to a modern. My saga, but as a means to tell the stories of many others. Those whispers took decades to become books, but here they are.

It was a lesson I was too long in learning. I was right to have Efraim write down what I dictated as the first written *Hávamál*. And I was right to send him away with a good skald. But even after that first writing, time and location change things. And that first written *Hávamál*? It fell into the sea soon after completion.

Good thing Bjorn could remember most of it to tell, and Efraim was able to remember much of what he wrote. There were other attempts to preserve it, but other writers copied what they could remember, or wanted to remember, all based on what they had been told. What they were told was based on what someone else was told, and so on. Yet most of the meaning survived.

It would be unlike *Hávamál* to suggest that doing well in one life might earn a big reward in a life after, and even now, the poem gives no advice about getting to Valholl. There is nothing in the text to justify constant vigilance about every possible injury or about avenging perceived slights. There is no glorification of *berserkir*, the value of one tribe being more than another, or anything about the need to die in battle. Nothing about fate, other than you're better off not knowing it.

Common as some of that was, and common as it was to take thralls and sell them for profit in my time, you won't find any of that in *Hávamál*, either. Some things from the past are better left in the past. Kraki may not have intended word-fame, but he had been a thrall, and he knew thralldom was one of those things to leave behind long before it was a common sentiment.

In the retellings and rewritings, others asserted their voices. Odin, I think, came to value his role as Asgard's wise sage over his obsession with death, and it did elevate him. That wariness bleeding into cynicism in some verses—I think that was the old fury god coming out again, never entirely comfortable. As much as Odin tried, though, he was never able to eliminate the verses about socializing well, about seeing the world and sharing knowledge, about moderation and sobriety.

As much as Bjorn and Efraim did to preserve that version of *Hávamál* and as much as I had put into it myself, I think it was Ketill who did the most to fend off foul influences. The wizard walked away from that battle and wandered again, donning a broad-brimmed hat and an eyepatch. He traveled Midgard speaking the verses of our *Hávamál*, as if this advice about sobriety was straight from Odin's mouth.

Ketill had lost nothing of his characteristic intensity. He channeled all his fury and disappointment at the gods into becoming the thing he wanted the gods to be. That was the most powerful wizard I ever knew—one whose influence can still be felt.

All those different variants of *Hávamál* survived long enough until the version read today was written in the 13th century. As if there was nothing that came before it!

So why begin and end my saga with Magnus the Red? He was not big like Haldor or fierce like Styrgrim, not a sorcerer or a wise man. The best of warriors, the difference maker at the beginning and the end, happened to be the shortest, and was left out of sagas. Left out even in my tellings. I knew Ogmund might come after such a man, and I didn't want that, especially once he had decided to make a new family.

Maybe it wasn't all *exactly* as I told it. Maybe Kraki didn't bash that man's head so hard it literally came out his ass. Maybe some of these characters had more foibles and flaws than I mentioned. They were my friends, after all, and I want to put them in a good light. My liberties are not the changes of corrupting a person's history as Orm tried to do, however. And it's the characters and deeds I hope the reader can take some value from, rather than picking at their corpses to find imperfections.

I often think about Kraki and my old Brothers. That includes Nanthild, of course. Without her, there would be no Vidar the Silent. They made Vidar a man and gave Thor a daughter named Thrud (strength), but I had no control over those changes. The sword with Ulfberht's name gained its own reputation, one with many imitators. The Magni and Modi of myth would not exist if not for the 'Steins, however their origin stories changed.

So it goes with all the myths and legends of the North. Even the stories I knew very well, I didn't know their origins or how many different versions had unfolded before I heard the variants of my time. I can only speculate about how most myths and legends began. Don't approach those stories without a lot of tolerance for ambiguity. Even mine.

But if you listen closely to the past, you might get a sense of who those heroes were and what they meant. There's always an idea there, some thread of truth that holds fast in stories even as they change. Not so if the changes come the way Orm and Ulf used them. The threads are severed in those cases. Memories of friends and ancestors, experiences inspiring and traumatic, are lost.

I started this epilogue by criticizing a monk who did a poor job. But let me tell you, there's one monk I wish I could have shared a horn of ale with!

He (probably a he? who knows?) wrote down *Gongu-Hrolf's Saga*. As a story, it's all over the place. Some of it borrows from my saga. Some of it mixes in historical politics with legends. I don't criticize this monk—I think he wrote it exactly as well as he could figure, noting the contradictions, mentioning the many questions he had himself. He accepted that his version was imperfect but didn't cram his present into the past. He cared about what he was preserving.

That monk had some attitude. He ended the saga with the following line:

"I'd like to thank those who've listened and enjoyed the story, and since those who don't like it won't ever be satisfied, let them enjoy their own misery."

If that isn't a good way to end a legendary saga, nothing is.

# About the Author

Gregory Amato made a career of selling his quill as a mercenary writer for many years. He wrote true and important things for newspapers, magazines, academia, and, for over a decade, intelligence analysis for the FBI.

Now, he writes fantasy stories based on the myths and sagas of the vikings. His fiction is often influenced by tales lost to time, usually full of high adventure, and always the sort that makes readers late to dinner.

Outside his time spent spinning yarns about vikings and wizards, he teaches Judo, brews beer, and plays DnD when he gets the chance.

Gregory lives happily with his family in the Pacific Northwest.

# Acknowledgments

Like the skald in my story, I did not get where I was going by myself. I owe thanks to many people, including but not limited to the following.

My wonderful wife CJ. Without your love and encouragement, this series would not be finishing in 2025. "This is good" means more coming from you than from anyone else.

Author Michael J. Sullivan and marketing genius/seeress Robin Sullivan for your friendship and mentoring, especially around our little group of writers. Little but mighty!

Angela Howe and Michael Klaas, for beta reading. And for not balking when I told you how long the manuscript was this time!

Rowdy Geirsson, for your continued friendship and support, and for helping me stay sane. Here's to many more beers together in one Portland or the other and to keeping the asshole ratio of "That Northern Thing" as low as possible.

Dr. Tom Shippey, whose books on Tolkien, vikings, and Beowulf have been great sources of inspiration as well as knowledge, and whose correspondence has been humbling. I eagerly await your next book.

Dr. Jackson Crawford, for patiently answering my questions and giving me the reading list that took my studies to a new level.

Joseph Hopkins and Lauren Fountain at Hyldyr for your excellent books on myth and folklore featuring academics and artists, and for all your events in the Pacific Northwest.

Liam Hall, for getting all the little references I throw in. "He knows what he's talking about!" Well, I hope you didn't see the end coming from too far off!

So many wonderful people who interviewed me, including Terri Barnes and CJ Adrien of Vikingology, Josh of Already Overbooked, and Kimberly Grymes of From Ideas to Pages to Publishing.

Dr. Daniel McMahon, the first person to put a book of Norse mythology in my hands.

All those who supported the *Fallen to Fury* Kickstarter campaign, my most successful campaign yet: You are awesome. That includes, but is not limited to: The love of my life, Dussssssstttyyyyyyy, Robert Amato, Bernhard Conz, J. W. Devlin, Sylvia L. Foil, Chris Brooks, Kevin F. Killigrew, James J Lew USN Ret, Thad Brenum, Bryce Vollmer, Kelsey Stenberg, Tygran, Julie Drucker, Joshua Milstead, Robert Kotowich, Gordon Sturgeon, A. Chan, Royce Hays, Chandler Jensen-Cody, Astrowolf, Quentin Foster, Athanasios Baroudos, H.I.M. Jimenez, Cole Barrett, Angela Miles, Rowdy Geirsson, Sarah Rogers, Kevin Scott, Marc J. Waters, GhostCat, Ted Mattos, L. Yap, Chris Twedell, Bethany Cobb, Neil Houston, Douglas A. Rist, Lyan Lopez Hung, Marcos Castro, Sarah Rollins, Brock Beisel, Kerry C, Keisha Havermale, Ben Flygare, Samantha Ghormley, Zack Fissel, Jenny Lowe, Joshua Johansen, Michael F Johnson, Bruce F., Cory Padilla, N.M. Friese, Dan Martinez, Brittany H., Shaun Homrich, MrGrome44, Andrew "Big Ugly" Hale, Cathy McLoughlin, John Adams, Tommy Maguire, Ryan Uhlig, Brian Willis, Brittany Williams, Wayne Lidbeck, S Busby, Cheryl Ruckel, Steve Reckelhoff, Anora Rayne, Ian, Nicolas C, Manuel De La Cruz Jr, Joshua Williams, Brian Cross, Stephen Hill, Anastasiya, Chris Mahers, Seamus & Gilberto Sands, Christy.S, The Grinch, Sarah L. Stevenson, Gerald P. McDaniel, Miles Sledd, Tracy Popey, Duncan Wilcox, Stu Brown, Ballisantirax, Marvin Langenberg, Susan Lair, Rae Steward, Steve Bodow, David Holzborn, Christian + Greg, Mary Jones, Justise Briones, Robert Brown, Erick Madrid, Josie Straka, Stephen Linden, J.T. Emmons, Ian, Russell J Handelman, Kylee Doyle, Michael Johnson, Blaine Moore, Annarose Willhite, Nicholas Paynter, Jennifer Katsch, Dr. Charles E. Norton III, Eric Vilbert, Mason Rensch, Quinn Giguiere, Phil Wallace, Matthew Rosengren, SnapDragon Esq, Ralph Iannone, Alex Taylor, Bradley Bolt, Jason and Nisa Martinko, Patricia Oleson, Justin Wearing, Karen M, Speedtrip, Billye Herndon, Franchesca Caram, Mark Geier, Sarah Birchard, Cortney Babcock, Adriana Loughridge, Irinel Finco, Stephanie Fischer, Steven Mitchell, John P., Lauren aviles, Lilith Mist, Jenny O, Matt Guzman, Scott Frederick, Jessie Kwak, Ernest Ridley, Benjamin Trejo, Amy Meskill, Jennifer Hilmoe, Greg Blaney, Cody L. Allen, Angela Marie Howe, Tate Hausman, Joshua B., author Michael J. Sulivan, SarLitten, M Pepe, C.K. Sorens, John Muir, Phillip H, Charles J Keller, Nolalisse Han, Bret Vandevender, Bjørn Tore

Pettersen, Kelvin Neely, Jose Javier Soriano Sempere, Rosie Vincent, Jens Bejer Pedersen, Robson, Haley Sembaluk, Per M. Jensen, Matthew Varley, Erick Garcia, Zackary Cassada-Ward, Zilla, Jenni D Strand, R.S. Johansen, David Bellia, Jeffrey de Lange, Håvard J. Reigstad, Thomas Poon, Frank J. Wilder, Michael Knopp, Robin Hill, Sarah Peachey, Brandyn Hobbs, André Laude, A. Clemens, Christine L Smith, Kristel Alger, Richard Khoury, Jacob and Monica, John Leonard, Mary-Lynn McGregor, Samu K., Allison Rohrer, Valkyrie, Katherine Leslie, Samuel Ludford, Ryan H, Jacob Magnusson, Lea Padgett, Kasia "Ket" Taczala, MajikJack, Björn Henke, Jim Reilly, Rhonda Parrish, K Raine, Creative Branches, ELIZABETH Marlene DAVIS, Ryan Burns, C.H. Brown, Jason Gollhofer, Bradley Gill, Rebecca Reed, Miggel, Hiram G Wells, Jennay Campbell, Naomi Hovey, M.C. Abajian, Christian Emden, Blaine Alderks, Drew Jenson, Eric Ludwig, Lesley Anderson-Pomeroy, Heiko Koenig, Broddrskegg, Leslie Claire Walker, Gianna Christopher, Regina D., Stacy Shuda, John Idlor, J Goode, J Mills, René Schultze, CMT, Elizabeth K, Ian Brown, Ty Rowdon, Dominika, Amanda Balter, Ivaylo Lyubenov, Kurt Boulianne, Lahman Marcel, Justin Greer, Andy99000, Laura Nelson, Aaron Granofsky, Nathan Turner, and Nikki Auberkett.

This book was written during a particularly insane time. Thank you to GWAR for insane music as a soundtrack to insane news. Almost every writing session began with Madness at the Core of Time. And thank you to Wardruna for being fantastic musicians and positive influences in the field of That Northern Thing. Einar Selvik's comments at the Portland show in 2025 really resonated with me. History has a lot of wisdom to be preserved, and that's important work to do, but some ideas are better left in the past.

Finally, the biggest thanks of all goes to you, the reader. Without you, there would be no Ansgar, no skalds, no stories. Thank you for reading!

# Major Characters

**x next to name:** This character died in book one.

**xx next to name:** This character died in book two.

**xxx next to name:** It's complicated.


**Aldis** — Alfhild's former handmaiden and witch, recruited by Huld. Grudgingly employed by Hrolf Kraki.

**Alfhild Smooth-Cheek** — Powerful sorceress allied with Ogmund Tussock. Alfhild attacked the city of Lejre and was barely defeated in *Burden to Bear*. In *Rune to Ruin*, Alfhild was busy kidnapping as many god-children as she could find, using the Brisingamen to obtain their loyalty.

**Ansgar Styrgrimsson** — The narrator and protagonist of the saga. A skald by trade, he joined Haldor and crew to prove himself to his father, Styrgrim the Bear, in *Burden to Bear*. In *Rune to Ruin*, he found out that Styrgrim is not his father. He is the son of an unknown god.

**Arrow-Odd** — The legendary saga hero and seemingly ageless enemy of Ogmund Tussock.

**Athils** — King of the Swedes. Reputed to be a sorcerer, or at least a cunning lord.

**Bec** — Irish thrall taken by Halfdan the Toothless. Lost her child while at sea. Later given Alfhild's child, Sigurd, to nurse.

**Beigadh the Bold** — One of two Danish champions loyal to Ragnvald and Hrolf during Alfhild's attack on Lejre.

**Birki the Obstinate** — One of the jarls loyal to Arrow-Odd. A bit dour in mood. Captain of the *Sea Goat*.

**Bjorn the Skald** — Styrgrim the Bear's skald and advisor. A particularly strong and tough skald with more battle experience than most.

**Borisu (Youdog)** — A warrior from Gardariki and true believer in their king, Valdar. Captured by Arrow-Odd's army in the fighting at the end of *Rune to Ruin*.

**Dvalin** — One of the dwarves who forged Tyrfing.

**Durin** — One of the dwarves who forged Tyrfing.

**Efraim** — A monk on Gotland who knows many languages.

**xFanya** — Ansgar's love interest in *Burden to Bear*. Formerly a handmaiden to Alfhild, Fanya chose to help save the city of Lejre. Her final spell, as she was dying from a belly wound, lit the sky to show Ansgar where Alfhild was hiding.

**Finnr** — A dwarf, master weaponsmith, close friend of Kraki and Huld. In *Rune to Ruin*, Finnr was sneaking around the Down-Below to find out more about Alfhild when he was wounded and nearly died. Gave Ansgar the shapeshifting sword, Need. Left the crew shortly thereafter to do more work Down-Below.

**Fjornir** — An old man from Vagar who wears a badly-made conical hat with a poof ball on top.

**Gardar** — Danish jarl pursuing Ogmund with Arrow-Odd.

**xxGrimhild** — Ogmund's troll of a mother. Slain by Haldor before he was killed.

**Gudbrand Shirtless** — The Danish king's staller. Ostensibly the keeper of the king's horses, he is more like the king's general problem-solver. Said to wear a chain shirt even when he's bathing. Prefers to fight from horseback, unlike most others, and uses an atgeir (heavy hewing spear). Fought alongside Styrgrim for Arrow-Odd twenty years ago.

**Gunnar the Marksman** – One of Hrolf Kraki's jarls, he holds the island of Borghund. Has some shared history with Styrgrim.

**xxHaldor Skullsplitter** – Former leader of the Brotherhood. He led the crew of the *Sea Squirrel* on land until his death in *Rune to Ruin*. He lost an arm slaying Ogmund's mother, Grimhild, and then was swarmed by the traitor, Svein, and many of Alfhild's other warriors.

**Halfdan the Toothless** – Tried to invite the crew of the *Sea Squirrel* into his hall to betray and kill them in *Burden to Bear*, but was foiled by Huld's *seiðr*. Jarl of Fretborg, but answered the call to sail north, hearing that Ogmund was paying well.

**Hallfred Horsefly** – Arrow-Odd's skald, and the organizer of the Circle of Skalds.

**Halstein the Smith** – Ansgar's grandfather and foster father. A smith of great renown in Midgard.

**Harek** – King of Bjarmaland. Ally of Ogmund.

**Heimdall** – The watchman of the gods. Incredible vision and hearing. Has appeared in Ansgar's dreams before. Possibly his father.

**Helgi Pike-Tooth** – Styrgrim the Bear's second in command. He filed his teeth to be sharp and savage-looking, hence "Pike-Tooth."

**xxxHemming** – The Brotherhood's former tracker, trapper, and forward scout, until joining Ulf in betraying them. Stabbed by Ulf and left to die in *Rune to Ruin*.

**Hervor** – Shieldmaiden who supposedly wielded Tyrfing for a long time before settling down.

**Hildigunn** – Daughter of King Hildir of Risaland. Lover of Arrow-Odd, mother of Vignir.

**Hildir** – King of Risaland and friend of Arrow-Odd.

**Hjalti** – One of Styrgrim's favorite crew members.

**Hrafn** – Female warrior in Arrow-Odd's army who goes by the male form of her name. Brave and bold in fighting. Extremely high threshold for pain.

**Hrolf Kraki** – Danish king after the death of his uncle, Ragnvald. Strong friend and ally of the *Sea Squirrel* and sworn enemy of Alfhild. A magnanimous king with a reputation for treating his highest lords the same as his lowliest subjects.

**Hromund the Hard** – One of two Danish champions loyal to Ragnvald and Hrolf during Alfhild's attack on Lejre.

**Huld** – A mysterious and powerful *vǫlva* who has been helping Ansgar and his Brothers for some time. In *Rune to Ruin*, Huld revealed she was the white cat that saved Ansgar on multiple occasions.

**Humor** – A raven who frequents Ketill's company.

**Idunn** – Keeper of the apples of immortality in Asgard.

**Inga** – Lejre's main brewer after her husband, Lambi, was killed by Lejre's troll. Brewed memory-ale for Ansgar in *Rune to Ruin*, which was consumed by the 'Steins and Efraim.

**Ingolf** – Joined the *Sea Squirrel* crew with his sworn brother, Leif. Serious, stoic, dependable.

**xxxInnstein** – One of the two shipwrights who keep the *Sea Squirrel* seaworthy. Brother of Utstein. The inside 'Stein. A bit shorter than his brother, but faster. Sacrificed his life so the crew and Alfhild's prisoners could get away. Might not be quite as dead as previously thought.

**Jorun** – A very pretty skald with Arrow-Odd's army. Prefers a hornbow as her weapon.

**Joni** – Karelian who guided the *Sea Squirrel* to the White Sea and Arrow-Odd's army. Last seen when the crew dropped him off somewhere south of the White Sea, where he hoped to find one of the Karelian king's moose riders.

**Josur the Daring** – A young jarl loyal to Arrow-Odd who is particularly prone to taking chances. Captain of the *Wave Climber*.

**xKari Swifthand** – Haldor's closest advisor in *Burden to Bear*. Tall and agile, always tense before battle. Saved Ansgar once by catching a spear thrown at him, a second time by shielding him from a goblin javelin, and a third time by distracting the lindworm that was crushing him. Killed in the Battle of Lejre.

**Ketill** – A *galdramaðr* (wizard) known for his knowledge of runic magic and intensity. Expert archer. Former alcoholic. Ansgar's mentor.

**Kraki (Bentleg/Sinsplinter)** – Elderly captain of the *Sea Squirrel*. Carries a bone club. Never wears armor and usually doesn't even wear a shirt. Despite his advanced age, he is still strong and is hard against steel. Known as "Fundinn Shinsplinter" Down-Below.

**xLeif** – Joined the *Sea Squirrel* crew with his sworn brother, Ingolf, shortly after Ansgar. Silly, awkward, fun. Sacrificed by Alfhild.

**Lyngbakr/Heather-Back** – Sea monster. His back looks like an island full of heather, and he uses this to lure sailors close and eat them. Almost swallowed the *Sea Squirrel* in *Rune to Ruin* before swallowing a barrel of wine, and then left the crew alone.

**Magnus the Red** – Ansgar's first heckler and closest friend. Short with bright red hair and arms like iron. Not a great fighter in a shield wall, but almost without a peer in a melee.

**Moose-Frothi** – Moose from the waist down (but with two legs), man from the waist up. Strong like a moose and sometimes sounds like one when he's angry, which is almost always. Brother of Thorir Houndsfoot.

**Nanthild the Silent** – Young Frankish woman who was kept as a thrall at the Danish court with her brother, Ulfberht. Avoided ritual sacrifice by Alfhild when the crew of the *Sea Squirrel* intervened. Fought bravely in the Battle of Lejre but stopped speaking when her brother was killed in the same battle. Uncannily strong, especially for her size.

**Njord** – God of the sea. Supposedly has very pretty feet. Husband to Skadi.

**Odin** – A god strongly associated with war, sorcery, death, and wisdom. Hung on a tree as a sacrifice to himself in order to gain knowledge. Capricious and fickle, yet charming and wise. Originator of the Spear of the Gods plan. Possibly Ansgar's father.

**Ogmund (Eythjof's Killer/Tussock)** – The son of Grimhild and a sorcerous king, Ogmund was birthed and raised to be a weapon for the Bjarmians to use against Arrow-Odd. A powerful sorcerer himself, Ogmund has feuded with Odd for generations.

**xOlgram** – Lejre's troll in *Burden to Bear*. Actually Alfhild's secret god-child she planned to put on the Danish throne as her puppet. Killed by Ansgar as a mercy after having his arm ripped off by Haldor. Called Ansgar "cousin" at the last moment. In *Rune to Ruin*, Ansgar realized this must have been because Olgram could see Ansgar's divine heritage.

**Olvor** – A very old witch, and Ireland's behind-the-scenes ruler. The creator of Arrow-Odd's silk shirt that protects him from weapons, hunger, and fatigue.

**Orm** – A priest who hid from an attack by trolled vikings.

**Petrus** – A scribe on Gotland. Much more adventurous than his friend, Efraim.

**Redbeard** – Previously a mysterious but charismatic advisor who introduced Arrow-Odd to Gardar and Sirnir and encouraged them all to become sworn brothers. Disappeared when Odd's army was attacked and is now understood to have been Odin in disguise.

**Sigurd the Screamer** – Alfhild's child, given to Halfdan the Toothless' crew to watch over since they have a thrall who can nurse (Bec). Fathered by Ansgar, though neither he nor anyone else knows that. Hates sailing and screams very loud about it.

**Sindri** – King of the dwarves.

**Sirnir** – Geatish jarl pursuing Ogmund with Arrow-Odd. Haldor's brother.

**Skuli** – Norseman who helped raid Halfdan the Toothless for thralls, who then became a thrall himself. More recently, a babysitter for Sigurd the Screamer.

**Steinvor (the Skald/the Slim One)** – One of two female skalds in Arrow-Odd's camp. Has been in many fights and has the scars to prove it. Took Ansgar back to her tent once, but ultimately might be more interested in earning word-fame than in finding a man to marry.

**Styrgrim the Bear** – Ostensibly Ansgar's father, but not really. A man with a reputation for fighting. Previously Odin's man, now bitter that he had placed any faith in Odin.

**Svart Geirridarsson** – Ogmund's son. Sorcerer, torturer.

**Svein Helgisson** – Joined Ulf in betraying the Brotherhood in *Rune to Ruin*. Bigger than Haldor and younger, but also fatter and slower. Good fighter. Dumb as a rock.

**Svipdag** – King Athils' foremost champion, who has a personal vendetta against the king's former *berserkir*.

**Svipul** – Ansgar's *fylgja* (follower). A spirit only Ansgar can see or hear. Also, his mother. Svipul is her name from when she was a valkyrie, while Bodda was her mortal name. Hair so black it has a blueish sheen like raven feathers in the right light.

**Tafi** – An old champion, now a Christian who has sworn off his sword. Took over responsibility for a monastery on Gotland when his teacher, Candidus, died.

**Taika** – Ansgar's Sami foster mother and grandmother. Wife of Halstein the Smith. Taught gave Ansgar a lot of good advice he wishes he'd paid more attention to.

**Thick Alrek** – Second in command of Athil's Swedish fleet. A stubborn man, called "thick" before he ever got fat, but is now rather fat anyway.

**Thorir Houndsfoot** – Mostly man, unlike his brother, Moose-Frothi, only with a dog's feet. Less temperamental than his brother. Can run very fast.

**Tyrfing** – The cursed sword of saga legend that cuts through steel like butter. Any cut is lethal, making every fool in the North want it. Has a history of turning on its wielders.

**Ulf the Wet** – The *Sea Squirrel*'s former *þulr*. Creepy voyeur in *Burden to Bear*. Betrayed his brothers in *Rune to Ruin*, resulting in Haldor's death.

**xUlfberht** – Young Frankish man who was kept as a thrall at the Danish court with his sister, Nanthild. Avoided ritual sacrifice by Alfhild when the crew of the *Sea Squirrel* intervened. Fought bravely in the Battle of Lejre and was killed while protecting Ketill.

**xxxUtstein** – One of the two shipwrights who keep the *Sea Squirrel* seaworthy. Brother of Innstein. The outside 'Stein. A bit bigger and stronger than his brother, but not quite as fast. Sacrificed his life so the crew and Alfhild's prisoners could get away. Might not be quite as dead as previously thought.

**xxValborg** – Alfhild's former handmaiden and witch. Crushed to death in *Burden to Bear*, her head was reanimated by Harbard the goblin. She helped and was helped by Ansgar, ultimately asking him to end her life as just a head.

**xxVarg (Tiorvi / the Charmer)** – A powerful jarl on Gotland, whose magic battle cow made armies turn on themselves, until he was killed by Haldor's Heroes in *Rune to Ruin*. Valborg's abusive father. Died very, very painfully.

**xxVignir** – Arrow-Odd's half-giant son. Though very young, he was much bigger than his father and wanted to make a name for himself. Easier going and more popular with the army than his father. Died fighting Ogmund.

**Vilgrip Tyrsson** – Son of Tyr, whose right hand was cut off by Svart in an attempt to see if that gave him any "abilities." Saved by Ansgar, he helped the Brotherhood fight their way out of Alfhild's fortress in *Rune to Ruin*.

# Glossary of Old Norse Words

**Æsir** – Group of gods living in Asgard, including but not limited to Odin and Thor.

**beitass** – Stretching pole used to hold a ship's sail taut.

**berserkr** – Literally 'bear-shirt' or 'bare-shirt.' Usually, a bully who is overrated in martial ability but howls a lot and wears too many animal skins. Occasionally, a dangerous warrior who is hard against steel. Plural: **berserkir**

**brunnmigi** – A troll that pees into drinking water.

**draugr** – A dead person who returns to harass the living. Usually, this person was not well-liked in life. A ghost, but not in the sense of being a spirit, as they are fully corporeal; more like a ghost/zombie/vampire. Plural: **draugar**

**drengr** – A person of integrity and honor; a stalwart, courageous/brave person; a badass.

**einherjar** – Odin's army of slain warriors, chosen to reside with him in Valholl and eventually fight alongside the gods during *Ragnarǫk*.

**fornyrðislag** – The meter of stories. A simple but effective poetic format consisting of eight half lines, each with two stresses, where one of the even-numbered half lines contains a stress alliterating with the above half line. Example of two half lines (stresses underlined):
This writer's blood
   blackens the page.

**fylgja** – A female guardian spirit. Not subject to worship like *dísir*, this kind of spirit usually follows families. Plural: **fylgjur**

**galdr** – Sorcerous incantation, spell, sorcery, magic, song (with magical connotation), charm.

**galdralag** – The meter of magic. Poetic format with the intent of casting or describing spells. Structure is *ljóðaháttr* with one to two additional long (three stresses, sometimes just two) lines. Example:
This writer's blood
   blackens the page;
Summoning the ink elves.
Crushing the keyboard warriors.
Whispering the unheard words.

**galdramaðr** – Sorcerer whose chief magical practice involves *galdr* and *galdralag*, focusing on linguistic aspects to cast spells. A wizard.

**hamr** – Shape, form, or skin.

**hákarl** – Fermented Greenland shark, the worst food in the world.

**Hávamál** – 'Words of the High One.' Practical wisdom delivered in verse, supposedly from Odin himself.

**hnefatafl** – Board game pre-dating chess, where one player tries to move his king from the center of the board to one of the edges, while the other player tries to capture the king.

**hugr** – Mind. Related to Odin's raven, Huginn.

**jǫtunn** – Member of a tribe equivalent to the *Æsir*, but antagonistic to them. Frequently translated as 'giant' despite *jǫtnar* being of the same size as *Æsir* most of the time. Some are giant in size, but not all. Plural: **jǫtnar**

**landvættir** – Land-spirits.

**ljóðaháttr** – The meter of wisdom. Poetic format consisting of a full line of *fornyrðislag* followed by a third line, where the third line has three stresses (two of which alliterate). Example:

This <u>wr</u>iter's <u>b</u>lood
　　<u>b</u>lackens the <u>p</u>age;
　I <u>h</u>ope it <u>h</u>ad an e<u>ffect</u>.

**níð** – Scorn or libel so strong, it could lead to the speaker's outlawry.

**níðingr** – Villain, traitor, truce-breaker; a person worthy of scorn.

**Ragnarǫk** – Series of events involving the doom of the gods and the end of the world.

**risi** – A giant. Historically, this word had significant overlap with *jǫtunn*. In this book, however, a *risi* is a giant from Risaland, which is only one kingdom in the realms of the *jǫtnar*. Plural: **risar**

**seiðr** – Sorcery involving spirits used to work spells or for divination. Generally performed by women. Considered 'unmanly' despite Odin being its foremost practitioner. Possibly a victim of post-viking age sources' dislike for such magic.

**útiseta** – Sitting out in the open air for the sake of sorcery or prophecy, especially at night.

**vættir** – Spirits or supernatural beings, including but not limited to land-spirits, *dísir*, dwarves, and *jǫtnar*. Singular: **vættr**

**vǫlva** – A female practitioner of *seiðr*. Prophetess, wise woman, or witch, depending on the intent of the speaker. Plural: **vǫlur**

**þurs (thurs)** – Giant, ogre, monster. Carries connotation of malevolence, but not necessarily large size.